The Fox & the Flag

and

The Fox & the Fortune

Dan Parkinson lives in Texas, where he is writing his next novel.

The Fox & the Flag

and

The Fox & the Fortune

Dan Parkinson

Pan Books

The Fox & the Flag first published 1990 by Pinnacle Books
The Fox & the Fortune first published 1992 by Kensington Publishing Corporation

This omnibus edition published 2001 by Pan Books
an imprint of Pan Macmillan Ltd
Pan Macmillan, 20 New Wharf Road, London N1 9RR
Basingstoke and Oxford
Associated companies throughout the world
www.panmacmillan.com

ISBN 0 330 39881 4

1 3 5 7 9 8 6 4 2

A CIP catalogue record for this book is available from
the British Library.

Printed and bound in Great Britain by
Mackays of Chatham plc, Chatham, Kent

The Fox & the Flag

Special thanks to Fred H. Lake,
Ministry of Defence, Whitehall Library,
Naval M3;
and to J. C. Andrews, Chief Librarian
ON HER MAJESTY'S SERVICE

Part One
To Harry The Fox

I

On a night so clear that stars crisped aloft and
Polaris shone bright above the bowsprit's diamond
shadows, a line of ships stood off Nags Head, north-
bound on a steady onshore wind with ice in its
breath. Six vessels there were — four sugar barks with
stacked sails hauled hard alee to take the wind in tack,
a broad-beamed old galley cutting beat-and-tack
wakes to hold abreast of them, and a trim snow standing out from the rest, lean and agile under racer's
sails, guiding and guarding the merchantmen as a
graceful collie works its sheep.

At times the snow veered in upon the fleet and
hooded lanterns spoke of course and placement, often
holding the sailing barks in check while the old galley
beat for better wind to stay in convoy with them.

Great silent shadows against the lower stars, they
slid due north and thanked the moonless night that
hid them from their enemies, the bright stars that
gave them a true course. And those on watch and
those on rudders and sheets blessed the wind that
drove them and dreaded the morning that would discover them once these hours of free run came to their
end. For there were predators in these waters. Men-
of-war held blockade off the American coast, and

among them were frigates and cruisers out for the taking of prize.

Four barks and a galley, the merchantmen were heavy-laden and ponderous, ill-equipped to fight and even less equipped to run. Twice since leaving Savannah's sheltered waters they had stood challenge, though no rounds had been fired. Swift and deadly with its massive sails and its eighteen guns, the little snow had each time swept in and stood off the challenger—one a brig of the Union Jack and one a Tory cutter—and each time the predator had retreated to await easier game. In these days and in these waters, few ships smaller than a frigate would willingly enter single combat with an armed snow.

Though dwarfed by the barks it escorted, and even smaller than the galley, the snow was a warship—foot-for-foot and ton-for-ton the deadliest vessel of its time.

Like a swift, dark carnivore it herded its convoy, dancing here and there on the winds that caused the barks to lumber and the galley sometimes to balk. Massed agile sails aloft on two stepped masts and a jackmast, the little warship was a dashing, circling shield for its charges and they had learned to respond to its signals. That lesson had come only hours a'sea, when the lead bark's master had decided to judge his own course. The snow, its young captain somber on his quarterdeck, had leaped down upon the errant merchantman and put a shot across his bow that made his stays sing.

Then when he had their attention, the snow's captain had run up buntings that left no doubt of his intentions. They would follow his directions, each and severally, without hesitation. If any one of them failed in this, the snow would sink him itself rather than leaving him for some predator's prize. Masters aboard the five cargo ships had fussed and grumbled, had cast dire eyes upon the audacious escort, and had made note of the charges they would file against the

10

upstart once they were safely delivered. But for now they followed orders and held their convoy.

They had met the young mariner at Savannah, introduced one by one to him at a place on Front Street where they had gathered to receive their orders from their factor, the Virginian Ian McCall, delivered by his clerk.

"Gentlemen," the clerk had said, "may I present your escort, Captain Patrick Dalton of the snow *Fury.* Commander Dalton, I present to you Captain Isaiah Poole of the bark *Indies Lane,* Captain Harkin Webster, the galley *Hispania,* Captain Porter Hennesey, the bark *Fair Winds* . . ." The introductions had gone on, each man shaking the firm hand of the tall, somber young man upon whose fighting skills they were staking their voyages and possibly their lives. Young, they noted. Not over thirty years by appearance, yet in his eyes lurked a cool, reserved wisdom possibly beyond his years. Black Irish, one or two of them read him — thick black hair, a complexion ruddied by sun and wind and yet hinting at the pale, dark-smudged visage of Celtic ancestry. They noted these things and they noted the boots he wore — not buckle shoes, as was the common practice, but grenadier's boots reaching almost to the knees of his white britches. And on his blue coat were no ornaments of any sort, though the coat itself, with its white lapels and turned cuffs, might have been Royal Navy style. His hair was drawn back to a simple queue at the nape of his neck and he neither wore nor carried a hat. But the buckler at his hip held a curved longsword and he wore it with the ease of one who knows the use of such things.

"One escort?" Captain Poole rumbled. "One ship to convoy five freighters? What manner of ship is it, sir? And what colors do you fly?"

"My ship is *Fury,*" the young man told them solemnly. "She is a snow, and the colors I raise are my own business and not yours."

11

"May one ask how many guns you mount, then?" Captain Webster snapped, offended at the younger man's brusk answer.

"Enough to see your galley safely to Chesapeake," Dalton told him, "and to see these other gentlemen to Portsmouth in good time, providing each of you follows my directions under sail. I tell you now, gentlemen, I have neither the patience nor the inclination to tolerate anything less."

It was a statement each could take as he chose—as an affront or simply as a statement of fact. Something in the manner of the young Irishman suggested they take it in the latter fashion.

Still, Poole was rankled. "For myself, I should like to have a look aboard this snow before we depart," he said.

Dalton shook his head. "The snow is mine, sir. It is not open to visit." He turned then, tipped his head at Ian McCall's clerk and said, "I understand all cargo is aboard and all craft are ready to sail. Please have these gentlemen put out at my signal with the tide at first light. Good afternoon, gentlemen." He left them there to wonder what sort of escort they had acquired against the warships and the prize-takers waiting to the north.

But they had learned soon enough, and as they stood off Nags Head in the star-dark hours of a crisp night, the little convoy held a steady five knots with Chesapeake ahead.

At the sounding of seven bells of the midwatch—thirty minutes past three in the morning hours—Patrick Dalton awoke in the tiny starboard cabin of *Fury*. Closing the shutters of the little gallery above his cot, he lighted a candle by means of a striker, then used the candle to light a wick lamp. Carrying this, he opened the low hatch and stooped to peer out into the companionway—a cramped, head-high space separating the galley and stores from the two stern cabins

12

and the helmbox housing between them. Dalton lifted his lamp. "Mister Caster?"

At the sill of the port cabin a quilt-wrapped figure stirred, then sat up, a boarding pistol coming level as he did. Then he lowered it. "Aye, sir," the boy said, rubbing sleep from his eyes.

"Seven bells, Mister Caster. Is cook in his galley?"

Before the ship's clerk could answer, the galley's hatch swung open and one of the brothers O'Riley— Dalton rarely knew which was which—looked out. "Aye, sir. Just laid my breakfast fire in th' cook tub, sir."

"Very well, Mister O'Riley. I'd like a basin for shaving and tea when it's ready."

"Aye, sir." The O'Riley disappeared into his galley. Billy Caster was on his feet and folding his quilt, the boarding pistol thrust into the back of his waistband.

"All quiet, Mister Caster?"

"Aye, sir. Quiet enough." The boy draped his folded quilt on a bulkhead rail. "As usual, a couple of the new men managed to steal down here, sir . . . just to see if I was still guarding the ladies, I suppose. They just looked and went away."

"Very well, Mister Caster. Please go on deck and advise Mister Duncan that I shall take the deck at eight bells for morning watch. You can come along then and help me fair the morning . . . but first, have your breakfast."

"Aye, sir."

Dalton started to turn away, then turned back. "Also, Mister Caster, I believe you can begin sleeping in a proper bunk again shortly. I have decided to put the ladies ashore when we reach the Chesapeake."

"Aye, sir. Ah . . . does Miss Constance know that, sir?"

"I haven't discussed it with her yet, Mister Caster."

When his basin of water came, Dalton shaved, combed back his hair and tied a queue at the nape of

13

his neck, then folded away his quilts and put on his coat—a coat that had once, recently, borne the braid of a lieutenant in His Majesty's Navy and the buttons of first officer of a king's ship. Now it was only a blue coat with white trim. Accused of treason by reason of a one-time acquaintance with the Fitzgerald, fierce old chieftain of a troublesome clan, Patrick Dalton had passed his twenty-eighth birthday as a fugitive in war-darkened waters. Unable, because of his Irish ancestry, to return to England to face the charges against him, and unwilling to cast his lot—as some had done—with a growing throng of rebellious Colonials in the American colonies, Dalton wore the coat now for its warmth alone, a barrier against the chill of late autumn. It was only a coat, and he was a fugitive and nothing more. The proud cruiser at his command—the snow *Fury*—was a stolen ship. Spanish pirates had taken her from the master of an American merchant trader, and Dalton and his men had taken her from the pirates. He had no intention of returning her to Ian McCall, the merchant who had fitted her out as a privateer. And yet, he felt an obligation to the man who had lost such a vessel, and thus was repaying him in kind by serving escort on the convoy of merchantmen now in his charge. It was not a thing he was obliged to do, but it eased his conscience to do it.

The O'Riley in the galley produced tea and he sipped at it, reviewing the day's business ahead, then, with coat buttoned and his sword in its buckler, he went on deck, a shadow among shadows in the dark of starry night. Only a hooded lantern at the quarter-rail gave light, but his ears and the song of sea and ship told him of the morning. On jib and jigger and a single square sail slanted hard about on the main, *Fury* crept through the dark hours, herding her flock.

For a moment he stood at ease beside the ladder, just listening while his eyes adjusted to the starlight. Just aft the mainmast with its hard-hauled lower

14

course, the ship's great driving spanker thrummed quietly between its high gaff and its boom, gathering the steady wind across the starboard rail and driving the ship along at sixty degrees off the wind, the main course hauled alee just beyond it so that the span between canvas and canvas over the portside was a scant six feet.

Forward, well up on the gentle sweep of gundeck, stood the foremast rising sheer, its sails clewed high like dark festoons on their yards, and beyond rose the triple batwings of foretop staysail, jibsail and flying jib, their silhouetted shadows soaring aloft like cathedral spires. *Fury* crept along her course on only these sails—only five of the eleven standard and fourteen extension cloths she was built to fly—and still she seemed to strain at the plodding pace. The necessity of pacing her escorted vessels in the dark hours, not to lose them or be too far from them at morning, was a harsh burden upon the lithe snow. Like a racehorse harnessed to a plow, he thought . . . bred to run, almost to fly, yet circumstance dictated she must crawl.

He sighed and turned his collar up against the chill of autumn winds. At the quarterrail a shadow moved, a hand flicked a single slat on the hooded lantern there to illuminate the sandglass on its pedestal, then a hand appeared in the dim light to turn the glass. That done, the lamp was shielded again and the seaman on bellwatch rang the ship's bell . . . once, twice, again.

As the eighth toll sounded Dalton stepped aft where Charley Duncan waited by the helm. They exchanged crisp salutes and Dalton said, "Eight bells, Mister Duncan. End of midwatch."

"Aye, sir." Duncan stepped aside, a shadow against the horizon's mist. "The watch is yours, sir. Our course is north by west a point, wind steady at twenty to twenty-two by the gauge, log and line reads short

15

five knots, convoy is broad a'port, responding each half-bell, though the galley was lagging a bit at seven bells, sir."

"Have you logged the watch, Mister Duncan?"

"Aye, sir. Mister Jackson writes a fair hand, so I've had him tend to it."

"Very well. Mister Caster will be up directly. Ask Mister Jackson to tender the log to him, and you can take your lads below for their breakfast. But keep them clear of the ladies' cabin. Some of the new ones are still being a bit forward in their curiosity."

"Aye, sir." Duncan turned away, then turned back. "Ah, Cap'n, there's been a bit of grumbling about that, sir. The ladies, I mean."

"I know about the grumbling, Mister Duncan. It is uncommon to them—the new ones, at any rate—to have ladies aboard a warship. Some think it's bad luck, I imagine."

"More than that, sir. Discomfort, as well. We're short of hammock-space in the forecastle and the lads are concerned about not having access to the companionway rails for bedding those off watch. It's growing colder, and they fear they may catch the vapors."

"We'll have bunk space soon enough, Mister Duncan. I intend to put the ladies ashore at Chesapeake when we deliver Captain Webster and his galley. I hope also that we can pick up a few more hands to bring our crew up to six-watch. We have been lucky so far, but I wouldn't want to have to fight *Fury* shorthanded."

"Aye, it would be a comfort to man all stations," Duncan agreed. Then he paused and even in the gloom Dalton could see the lift of his brow. "Ah . . . about putting the ladies ashore . . . does Miss Constance know you mean to do that, sir?"

"She will know when I decide to tell her, Mister Duncan."

"Aye, sir." Duncan sounded relieved. "It will be

16

yourself that discusses it with her, then."

"It will."

"Aye, sir. I am grateful."

"Grateful, Mister Duncan?"

"That it will be you and not me, Cap'n."

When his first officer was gone, Dalton set the morning watch to its tasks, John Tidy as bosun relaying his orders with voice and whistle. Thirty-eight officers and men formed the complement of *Fury*—hardly a full roster for a ship that might make twenty-five sails if occasion demanded, and that mounted eighteen cannons as beam batteries and chasers. He would have preferred ninety had the choice been his—fifteen at station for each of six watches. Six deck officers, six bosuns, at least thirty able seamen to man the tops and tend the sheets, a dozen capable gunners and another dozen gunner's mates, carpenters and sailmakers and enough ordinaries to fill the roster. . . . In the gloom his cheeks tautened in a grim smile. Royal Navy training, he reminded himself. I would man a ship precisely as a king's ship is assumed to be manned, and never mind that not one in fifty of His Majesty's men of war can boast such a perfect roster. Thank the present hostilities that I have a crew at all, and thank the same hostilities that I have a ship under my soles.

But then, were it not for the revolt in the colonies, Dalton told himself, I should never have been a fugitive to begin with. The charge of treason might have been lodged, whatever the circumstances, but I might not have lacked the means to get myself home and face down the charges before an Admiralty court.

The shadows of the midwatch topmen swarmed down from aloft, and Dalton brought himself back to the business at hand. "Tops aloft," he called. "Fore and main."

"Tops aloft," the bosun's voice echoed him from the shadowed midships. His whistle bleated its call and fresh lookouts swung out on the shrouds to scramble upward, clinging to ratlines as dark spiders might cling to tall webs.

"Signal the convoy," he called. "Come a point a'port and trim. And tell that galley to stop lagging and come abreast."

"Aye, sir." In the forecastle a hooded lantern blinked its messages, and Dalton watched as the signals were returned from the west. By these he placed the locations of all the merchantmen in his charge. The barks were in good order, all directly off his port beam and all within easy sight. The galley, an obsolete and cumbersome vessel, lay a half-mile back, directly astern of *Fury*. Even as its signal was completed he saw it begin to bear a'port, taking advantage of the slight course change to begin a long quartering run that would bring it once again abreast of the steadier barks. He judged wind and course, and frowned. It would come abreast, all right, but it would be miles to the east of the convoy when it completed its fair tack. Then by the time it beat back into position, fighting the wind, it would once again be lagging astern.

Trying to hold back sailing barks to accommodate a galley had begun to wear on his nerves . . . almost as much as trying to hold back a dancing snow to the pace of barks. Dalton looked back at the galley again, now full into its tack, and squinted. He rubbed his eyes, strode to the port rail and leaned there, trying to pierce the morning darkness. He turned and raised his face. "In the tops!"

"Aye, sir," the voices floated down from above.

"Aft the port beam, far out! What can you see?"

Silence from aloft as fresh eyes in the tops peered across dark distances. Then, "Maintop, sir. I don't see anything."

"Well, keep looking!"

Billy Caster had come on deck and stood beside his captain, his adolescent voice touched with concern. "Is

18

something amiss, sir?"

"Something is very much amiss, Mister Caster. I believe I saw riding lights off there, just where that galley will be going."

II

A half-bell passed—a turn of the glass—before Dalton's suspicions were confirmed. The voice from aloft floated down from starlit heights, "On deck!"

Dalton looked up, placing the source at the maintop. At his side, Billy Caster said, "That's Mister Geary, sir. Mister Unser is in the fore."

Dalton cupped his hands. "Report, Mister Geary!"

"I make lights, sir. Hard down off the port beam, holding our same course. One an' two, just in sight."

One and two. Forecastle and stern lanterns of a cruiser. No merchantman, then, but a man-of-war holding northward off their west flank. A frigate, possibly, making upcoast to join Admiral Howe's blockade on the Delaware. Had she seen his convoy? Not likely, not yet. But she would. Harkin Webster's eastward tack would put the old *Hispania* far westward with first light, a duck in the water ready to be brought under great guns and claimed as a prize.

He made his decision. "Signals, Mister Tidy, if you please. Tell the four barks to hold line abreast and come due north, with foretops manned. They are to hold course and await our return, unless they spy vessels ahead, in which case the discretion is theirs. But only in that case. Make that very clear, signals, if you please."

"Aye, sir."

"Hands a'deck, man sheets for coming about a'port. Mister Mallory, attend the helm. Stand by to steer full and by at west by north, with the wind."

"Aye, sir."

"Laggers a'deck, Mister Tidy. Reefers to the yards to set sail, courses and tops, then stand by on the topgallants."

"Aye, sir." The whistle bleated its calls and the shadows of men came up from the forward holds to take station. Only the watch just relieved would remain below, with a brief opportunity for rest before they were called upon again.

Topmen swarmed the shrouds, deck hands took station by their rails and fifes and *Fury* clattered with abrupt activity. Dim-slatted lanterns cast tiny pools of muted light on dark decks and pinrails, the men there only shadows in their glow. Dalton's eyes roved the bustling dark deck ahead and told him which sheets were ready to be hauled trim, to bring sails into alignment with the wind. His ears heard the rattle of foot-ropes aloft as topmen spread along the high yards, ready to drop great sails from their furling. Even in the darkness he knew his ship, and he felt the quiver of its rolling deck beneath his soles, for all the world as though the snow had just come awake and now flexed its sinews awaiting his call. "Up spencer," he said. In the gloom ahead a tall triangle of dark sail grew from its riding boom and fluttered in the wind. Its sheet-lines drew taut and it billowed, adding its thrust to the force of the spanker and maincourse behind it.

Fury surged ahead, picking up speed, and Dalton's trained ears judged the hum of cloven waters along her beam. Six knots now, and rising slightly.

"On deck!"

He raised his eyes aloft. "Aye Mister Geary?"

21

"I make the tops on the near bark, sir. "We are beginning to overtake."

"Bring us about, helm. Hard a'port."

"Aye, sir."

Fury leaned with the wind and her high jib veered across the northern sky . . . a point, two points, three . . . "Hold with the wind, helm," Dalton said. "Trim fore-and-afts a'deck, Mister Tidy. Full and by the wind."

Sheet lines were released and re-trimmed, and *Fury* steadied on course, the pitch of rushing water again rising along her beams.

"Signals, have all four barks give us a bearing light, please."

The lantern's slats chattered and one by one, little sparks of light appeared ahead, one muted lantern astern on each of the convoy merchantmen. Dalton judged placement and distances. Already, *Fury* was gaining speed and closing on the nearest bark, Captain Poole's *Indies Lane*. One miscalculation, Dalton thought with grim irony, and the man's misgivings about his escort would be violently confirmed by ramming.

He hesitated, letting the gap between the snow and the bark close further, seeing how the bark at its placid five knots slid slowly ahead. Its single light moved from left of *Fury's* bowsprit to dead ahead, then to the right.

"Make sail," he called. "Fore course, fore tops'l, main tops'l."

Tidy's whistle shrilled and yards boomed aloft as clewing was released and blocks took the weight of great sails, lowering them into the wind. *Indies Lane* was a cable's length ahead now, but its tall stern had cleared the shadows of *Fury's* stem. "Sheet home," Dalton ordered. "Trim full and by." Tackle sang, sails boomed and *Fury* leapt ahead, her growing wake splashing the sternpost of the sailing bark as she passed.

"Something else for Captain ⟨...⟩ about," Billy Caster commented. "⟨...⟩ log for rebuttal, sir?"

Dalton stood at ease, his gaze fixed ⟨...⟩ lights of the other three barks clearing ⟨...⟩ it by all means, Mister Caster. It might ⟨...⟩ McCall to have a full cruise report from u⟨...⟩ ⟨...⟩ from our charges."

Amidships Cadman Wise, the off-duty bosun, had a lead overside and was reading speed by log and line — a fair trick in the dark hours, but something Dalton had seen him do before. After a moment he reeled in his line and called, "Twelve knots and steadying, sir."

"Thank you, Mister Wise." Dalton peered ahead and to the left. Somewhere just out there was his clumsy galley, plodding along on its inshore tack, unaware of predators in its path. In this wind, and at its angle, the old ship might make nine knots, and he assumed that it would. Its captain was a fair sailor, despite the vessel under his feet.

"Hands to topgallants fore and main," Dalton ordered. "Ready to make sail when we've cleared the fourth bark."

"Aye, sir." The whistle shrilled. One by one, the snow passed astern of the high-tailed barks — great stepped shadows against the northern sky. When she had cleared them she added sail. Taking the fair wind on her starboard quarter, she lifted her nose, took the spray in her teeth and ran as her builders had intended. Dalton took a deep breath and willed the tension from his shoulders, enjoying the illusion of freedom in the song of a fine vessel on a fair wind.

Freedom. Would he have it one day in fact as well as in feeling? Could a man without flag or country know freedom? Or honor?

In front of the quarterrail the companionway hatch

nt lamplight silhouetted a small figure
the open deck. Dalton suppressed a smile
sight of her. How tiny she seemed sometimes, this
Constance Ramsey . . . how soft and vulnerable in a
harsh world of turmoil where tall ships with great
guns faced each other on stormy seas . . . and how it
would offend her ever to think that she might seem so.

She was the daughter of a respected American merchant who dabbled in smuggling — as did most of his
ilk. Dalton had found her aboard a dainty schooner,
the *Faith*. In darkness like this now, they had
boarded — he with a crew of stockade escapees and she
with a band of Colonial adventurers — each determined to take the ship, but for different reasons. For
Patrick Dalton, *Faith* had been a means of escape
from the Long Island yards, where hunters sought
him. For Constance Ramsey, *Faith* had been her father's prized vessel, stolen away by a warrant ship of
the king, and a prize that she intended to recover at
any cost.

Pixie-pretty and fiery-tempered she was, this slip of
a girl from the central colonies, and Dalton admitted
readily that never in his career had he seen a better
hand with a cannon.

She reached the deck and peered around her in the
darkness, then recognized him and climbed the four
steps to the quarterdeck.

Billy Caster tipped his hat. "Good morning, Miss
Constance. Did you sleep well?"

"Quite well, thank you." She peered around in the
darkness. "What is happening? Are we under attack?"

"Captain thinks the *Hispania* may be heading into a
trap, Miss. We're going to have a look."

"On deck!"

Dalton had been turning toward Constance, now he
turned back and looked upward. "Aye, Mister
Geary?"

"*Hispania* sighted, sir. Off the port bow and bearing

24

north of west. She's showing riding lights, sir."

Dalton pulled out his glass from a tail pocket and scanned the dark horizon. In a moment he saw it, visible even from the deck. The triple beams of the old galley's working lanterns—fore, aft and amidships—winked merrily across the distance. Dalton snapped his glass closed and swore. "That idiot! What is he trying to do?" He stepped to the quarterrail and squinted upward. "Tops ahoy! Do you make the unidentified lights?"

"Aye, sir. Still in sight, hard down, still bearing north."

"So he hasn't seen *Hispania* yet," Dalton muttered. "But if he hasn't by now, he will soon enough."

John Tidy came to the cockpit deck below the rail. "Shall I have him signaled, sir? Something on the order of 'put out your frigging . . . oh.'" He lowered his head and his voice. "Beg pardon, sir. I didn't see the lady come on deck."

"No signals," Dalton said. "Yonder is a cruiser, and he would see our signal and understand our situation."

"But he'll see the galley's lights, sir."

"On deck!"

"Aye, Mister Geary?"

"The far ship has altered course, sir. It's beating into the wind, making to intercept."

"Thank you, Mister Geary. He has seen the galley, Mister Tidy."

"On deck!"

"Aye, Mister Geary?"

"I make the vessel, sir. High forelamps a pair, and a bit of color. It's a king's frigate, sir."

Dalton lowered his head. "Blessed Mary," he growled. It was the sort of nightmare that had troubled him—had troubled all who had set out those long months back on a stolen schooner, who now, by the grace of God, still ran free aboard a retaken snow—to be faced with a choice between death and dishonor.

To turn tail and run—leaving behind the slow convoy for which he was responsible—that would be dishonor. To open fire on a king's vessel would be dishonor. Dalton had fired on king's vessels in his time as a fugitive, but he had never opened fire. And yet—a frigate! Twice the size of the snow and twice the guns. To face off against such a cruiser and *not* take the first shot might very well mean death.

He turned to Constance Ramsey, who still stood awaiting his notice. "Good morning, Miss Constance. You've come on deck at a bad time. We have a bit of trouble."

"I can see that," she said, coolly. "Do you suppose the time has come when you must choose sides, Patrick?"

He lowered his head and turned away, stung by her words. The understandings between them often were strained. His situation made it so. Yet he counted on there being those understandings. After a moment she stepped to his side and laid a hand on his arm. Her voice no longer held its cutting edge.

"I am sorry," she said. "That was thoughtless. But Patrick, if that *is* a king's frigate out there, and it comes for us, what will you do?"

"What I must," he said quietly.

"What you must."

"Of course. But only if I must. Sometimes there are other ways." He peered upward through the rigging. Vaguely, he could see the dark spars, stays and sundry tackle against the sky. Between the main course spar and the bulging luff of the main topsail just above it, he could distinguish the shape of Ethan Geary crouched on the maintop trestletrees. The morning was clear and there would be light soon. "I expect you should go below now, Constance. . . ."

"I won't be sent below," she stated. "I am much more comfortable up here, and I want to see what is happening."

26

"Go below and have your breakfast," he finished. "It will be a time yet before there is anything to see. Mister Duncan!"

"Aye, sir?" Charley Duncan had appeared at the companionway hatch.

"Are all of your lads fed and a'fore?"

"Aye, sir. I've sent them to have a bit of sleep. Do you need them?"

"Not at the moment, thank you. But if the galley is cleared, you may escort Miss Constance and her maid to breakfast."

"Aye, Cap'n. Be my right honor."

Constance shrugged and started away, then turned back. "I overheard what you told Mister Caster," she said. "About putting me off at Chesapeake . . . if we get there. I must tell you, Patrick, I have no intention of being put off this ship. If nothing else, I have an obligation to Mister McCall. . . ."

"This is not Ian McCall's ship, *Miss* Constance. It is mine."

"He rather considers it his," she said. "It was taken from him by those awful pirates."

"And I in turn took it, if you will recall. From pirates. Ian McCall lost his ship. I gained a ship of my own, by right of recovery. It is a procedure that I think men like Ian McCall — aye, and John Singleton Ramsey as well — should thoroughly understand."

"At any rate, *Captain* Dalton, whether and when I leave this ship shall remain my decision and mine alone. Now let's hear no more about that."

With a stubborn swish of her skirts, she was gone, to be escorted to breakfast by Charley Duncan. Duncan waited, hat in hand, while she preceded him down the companion ladder, then he turned toward the quarterdeck and Dalton saw the glint of his teeth as he grinned. Dalton sighed. There had been times, he knew, when his life had been less complicated. He simply couldn't remember when.

By two bells of the morning watch there was faint light in the sky, and the galley *Hispania* could be seen from the deck, her shadowy sails a double hump on the horizon as she made her best speed westward on a favoring wind.

She was due south of *Fury* now, a scant three miles away and off the snow's port quarter. Ahead, low morning mist had arisen to hide the frigate, but Dalton knew where it was . . . five miles off, six at most, beating toward them on tack-and-tack, making to intercept.

And not very many miles beyond it, was the Atlantic coast of North America where armies contended for control of England's crown colonies.

Life had been simpler then, Dalton thought. Far simpler, the first time he had seen those shores. An officer of the king he had been, second in command aboard His Majesty's brig-of-war *Herret*, sailing with the White Fleet under Admiral Lord Richard Howe. It had been "Black Dick's" intention to put a quick and quiet end to the festering insurgence in the colonies. In that, he had failed. What had been scattered rebellion was now all-out war.

For Dalton, though, things had been simple. He had done his duty and served his flag . . . and been ill-used by that flag in the end. As an Irishman, accused of treason in wartime, he had no chance of facing a court martial and clearing his name. If he were apprehended, he would simply rot in a prison hulk.

How things could change . . . and how fast.

"On deck!"

He looked up. "Aye, Mister Geary?"

"I make the ship again, sir. It is a frigate and it flies Crown colors."

"Colors? It is showing its colors at this hour?"

"No, sir, not its color. I mean . . . its pennantry is White Fleet."

28

"Whereaway, Mister Geary?"

"Almost dead ahead, sir. Maybe five miles an' a bit."

"Very well, Mister Geary. Keep a sharp eye on it. 'Hoy the foretop!"

"Foretop, sir."

"Foretop, can you see our barks?"

"Aye, sir. But just a glimpse of tops, hard down an' holding course."

Dalton nodded, chewing his lip in thought. It was unlikely that the frigate had seen the barks, or could see them now. So his problem narrowed itself a bit. How to get a slow old galley—and himself—out of harm's way without doing standup battle with a frigate . . . a frigate that flew his own flag.

"Have you decided yet what you will do, Patrick?"

Dalton turned in surprise. He hadn't heard Constance return from the ship's mess, but now she stood beside him, small and lovely in the early light, great dark eyes shadowed by the bonnet from which her auburn hair strayed. She held a quilt wrapped about her against the morning's chill.

"There is a thing I might try," he said, slowly, musing on the idea as he stated it. "Yon galley captain will have fresh charges to level against me, but there is just a chance we might amuse that frigate enough to change its mind this morning."

"What do you plan to do, then?"

"I am thinking that we might just go head off that galley and attack it. Mister Caster!"

"Aye, sir?" Billy was right behind him.

"Go to the flag locker, Mster Caster, and break out the Union Jack. As soon as that frigate is in good sight, *Fury* is going to become a king's blockader out for a bit of sport. We shall see if that frigate's captain is gentleman enough to honor another's prize."

29

III

Of the mismatched twenty-odd fugitives who had made sail long months past at Long Island Yards in a stolen schooner—British tars escaped from the stockade and a long handful of Colonial saboteurs led by a young woman—only nine remained now . . . ten, counting Constance Ramsey. Many were dead, some put ashore when conditions warranted as *Faith* had fled, then finally turned and fought. *Faith* was gone, too, though Constance had said that her father had commissioned another schooner to be built to her pattern.

Nine *Faiths*, Dalton thought, and felt the bleak weight of his responsibility to those who had placed their trust in him.

Then in a cove in Chesapeake they had discovered an abandoned ketch. When she was repaired and equipped, they had christened her *Mystery*, and other refugees from the war-torn lands had been found to help with the manning of her. Seven of those now remained, veterans, with the rest, of a nightmarish cruise down the coast, *Mystery* carrying a cargo of shore batteries in exchange for her outfitting.

Of *Faiths* and *Mysteries* now aboard the snow *Fury*—taken from pirates off the coast of the Carolinas—

sixteen. Sixteen motley souls and a woman hardly more than a girl. The rest aboard were the scourings of taverns and back streets from Charleston to Savannah. A mix of British and Colonial, they were an oddly assorted lot but had a thing in common with all the rest. Each for reasons of his own would not — or could not — take honest employment aboard any craft of either British or Colonial registry.

As he watched the light of morning grow and strained his eyes westward for first clear sight of the approaching frigate, Patrick Dalton's cheeks twitched in grim humor. Where there is war there are fugitives, he thought. Like smuggling, the art of escape provides employment for many a soul these days.

Fury's decks were crowded now, as were the footropes aloft. Here in first dawn sailed a fighting snow, taking good wind in its canvas and crooning the song of the sea while huddled figures waited at every station, waiting for the orders that would determine whether they might live another day.

With Dalton on the snow's little quarterdeck now were Charley Duncan, accomplished able seaman and accomplished thief, late of His Majesty's stockade on Long Island and now first officer of *Fury;* Claude Mallory, another former *Faith,* at helm; Billy Caster, clerk; Mister Hoop — if he had a first name, no one had ascertained it — a huge, glowering man whose Royal Navy career had ended somewhere on the Chesapeake and who now was Dalton's master at arms; and Constance Ramsey, present by right of insistence.

Like Dalton, they all strained to see through the lingering low mist that obscured the sea to the west.

"On deck!" The call came muted from the foretop lookout and Cadman Wise received the report in the forecastle and relayed it back. Before the quarterrail John Tidy turned. "Mister Unser says our sugar barks are hard down and still keeping course, sir.

31

They'll be out of sight directly."

"Thank you, Mister Tidy. Let us hope they don't decide to come back and have a look."

Again, for long minutes, *Fury* sailed in silence, the only sound the song of her sails and rigging, the hum of her sleek hull cutting a long wake across the swelling dark waters that were her home.

Then, from the maintop, "On deck!"

Dalton raised his eyes. "Aye, Mister Geary?"

"That frigate is closing to a mile, sir. Her tops are clear and she's seen us. She's running up an inquiry."

"Then we shall respond," Dalton nodded. "Mister Caster, have you our Union Jack?"

"Right here, sir." The boy drew a folded flag from his coat and Dalton nodded his approval. Billy had chosen carefully from among the many colors in the flag locker. The flag was not the familiar white ensign of fleet duty, but the Grand Union, emblazoned with its bright cross-bars. A fleet ensign might have aroused suspicion in a king's officer who saw it flying on a ship so obviously American-designed as a snow. The Grand Union said nothing except that this was a Crown vessel.

"Very well," Dalton said. "Run it up, please." He looked around at the others with him, and irony tugged at his cheeks. "Welcome to the Royal Navy," he said. "Miss Constance, will you go below now?"

"I will not," she said flatly.

He shrugged. "Then pray stay out of range of that frigate's glasses. No British captain would tolerate a woman on his quarterdeck." Nor any other captain in his right mind, he thought, but there was nothing to be gained by saying it.

Astern and a quarter a'port, less than a mile away, the old galley *Hispania* trundled along its inshore tack, blissfully unaware of what was happening ahead of it . . . or what was about to.

"Condition, Mister Tidy?" Dalton could see for

himself now where each man above decks was stationed, but the question was more than ritual. A captain had to depend upon more eyes than his own, and those sailing with him had to know they were depended upon.

"Standing by to come about a'port, sir."

"On deck!"

"Aye, Mister Geary?"

"The frigate is clearing the mist, sir. You'll see her hull in a moment."

The Union Jack rose over *Fury's* stern, snapping in the wind as it unfurled, its gaudy red, blue and white emblem bright even in the dim dawn light. Somewhere ahead, even now, lookouts high in the frigate's shrouds would be reporting to their deck.

"Will you wait for him to respond, Captain?" Charley Duncan's eyes glinted as brightly as his red hair. His lips were drawn back in a feral grin, and Dalton sighed. Despite everything, Duncan was anticipating the roar of cannon, the clash of headlong combat. As usual, he was spoiling for a fight.

"We need no response, Mister Duncan. We have declared ourselves, and now we must rely upon his believing us. Ah!" Dead ahead, a tall shadow had materialized in the flattening mist. A frigate.

"Come about, Mister Tidy."

"Aye, sir." The whistle shrilled and all along the working deck men scrambled to loose and recleat sheet lines, to haul great yards around for a new wind.

"Bring us about, helm."

"Aye, sir." Mallory spun his spoked wheel and *Fury* responded nimbly, her rudder biting the flow in concert with the booming of new-set sails. She seemed to almost leap into the turn, leaning sharply to the right as broad spans of sail took the fresh wind on her port beam, and Dalton felt the old thrill of an agile ship on a working sea. Racehorse she was, this snow *Fury* . . .

racehorse and warhorse, and she did love to stretch her legs and test her teeth.

"Miss Constance, off the quarterdeck now, if you please."

"I told you, I . . ."

"You may watch from the cockpit if you insist, but for heaven's sake, stay out of sight!"

For once, she did not argue. When he looked around, she was gone. Yet he felt her presence, just below the rail, and it tugged at him. Among all his concerns, her presence here stood out. Now *Fury* would play a delicate game, and if it did not work she would have the choice to run or to stand and fight. Such was the life of a fighting ship and the men who manned her, yet each decision came hard with Constance aboard. Despite all they had shared, Dalton could not readily put the girl in harm's way.

She mattered to him . . . far more than he could allow himself to admit.

With a final glance at the frigate materializing from the mists now broad a'starboard, Dalton turned his attention to the galley plodding along on what was now an intercept course. The old ship had its best wind now and was making a likely eight knots, heading north of west. Dalton took out his glass and peered through it. He saw white faces turned toward him and could almost see the stunned surprise in them, at the colors their familiar escort now flew.

He raised his glass. In the galley's stubby tops, her lookout leaned from an old-fashioned crow's nest. Pointing ahead, he looked down and cupped a hand to shout.

I have judged Harkin Webster a fair seaman, Dalton thought. Now we shall see what sort of actor he is. He sees two hostile flags. Does he know why? "What gunners are at the bow chasers, Mister Tidy?" he asked.

"Misters Crosby and Pugh, sir."

Dalton turned to Duncan. "Would you care to do the honors on the gun deck, Mister Duncan?"

"Aye, sir!" Duncan grinned and snapped a salute.

"Please contain your enthusiasm, Mister Duncan. Remember, the galley is not our enemy. I only wish it to seem that way."

"Sir, I wouldn't . . ."

"I'm sure you wouldn't, Mister Duncan. I should hate to have to explain why we sank a ship of our own convoy."

A somewhat more serious Charley Duncan hurried forward to command the guns, and his voice echoed back, "All guns, run in! Off vent aprons and see to your prime! Run out and stand by! Misters Pugh and Crosby, a word with you, please!"

"Signals,"—Dalton turned away—"hail that galley yonder and tell him to show his colors."

"Aye, sir." Buntings were run up and a moment later the *Hispania* ran up her merchant's ensign and her factor's flag. Dalton glanced around at the now thoroughly visible frigate, hoping that the man on her quarterdeck was seeing the show.

"Signals," he said, "tell the galley to come about into the wind and strike her colors. Tell her to prepare to be boarded."

"Aye, sir."

Play your part now, Webster, Dalton willed. His shoulders had tensed again, almost as though the frigate on the sidelines was bringing its guns to bear. He glanced aside quickly. A half-mile away the frigate had altered course, turning its stem a point or so northward. Laying by, to see what comes next, he thought. He isn't ready to believe a thing at first glance. A careful man.

"The galley isn't striking, sir," Billy Caster said. "See, he's laying a'port, to evade."

"Topgallants fore and aft," Dalton ordered. "Sheet home and trim."

35

Tidy's whistle shrilled. High overhead clewing lines were loosed and the topgallant sails fell from their yards. Sheets drew taut and *Fury's* pitch rose as the additional sails took the wind. She leaned harder a'port and took spray across her bow as her sleek prow sliced through rolling sea. At the midships rail a sailor called, "Fourteen knots and makin'!"

"Helm, ease just a bit a'port," Dalton ordered. "Cross his course and make about to turn him."

"Aye, sir."

Like a hound to the kill, *Fury* closed on the lumbering galley. At three cables they could see the frenzy of activity on *Hispania's* deck. "Either he understands very well," Dalton muttered, "or he doesn't understand at all."

Sudden smoke billowed from the galley's starboard beam, and the thumping roar of twin cannons rode across on the wind. A second later iron balls sheeted water, one falling short, the second directly under the snow's bowsprit.

"A foot higher and he'd have clipped our dolphin striker," someone breathed.

"Mister Tidy, relay to Mister Duncan that he may fire at will," Dalton rasped.

The order went forward and gunners knelt to their quoins in the bow. Paired chasers there thundered. A ball sang over the bow of the galley, and a hole opened in the center of its stubby steering sail, directly above its sterncastle. Dalton grinned. "Repeat signals to the galley," he said.

Pennants ran down and up again, a demand that the old ship strike her colors. "Now, Mister Webster," Dalton muttered.

As though in answer to his words, the galley put over smartly into the wind, its sails going dead. Its merchant flag crept down its halyard, and it lay defeated, in irons and ready for boarding. Dalton glanced around. The frigate still stood a short half-mile off, just watching.

Dalton waved a curt hand at Victory Locke, standing near the port davits. "Mister Locke, assemble a likely boarding party, if you please."

"Aye, sir. Ah, what shall we do after we have boarded her, sir?"

"Just board as though taking a prize at sea, Mister Locke. Make it look as though we are serious."

"Aye, sir. Ah . . . aren't we serious, sir?"

Dalton sighed. "Mister Caster, please go amidships and explain to Mister Locke what we are trying to achieve here. Better yet, I believe you should go over with him. My respects to Captain Webster, and please ask him to attend me here. I should like a word with him when all this is done."

"Aye, sir. But it doesn't look done yet, sir. That frigate is still sitting over there, watching every move we make."

"Then let's invite him to make himself useful," Dalton snorted. "Signals, to the frigate there. My respects, and I request that he stand by to assist in escort of a prize vessel for Crown registry."

"Aye, sir."

A bonnet appeared below the quarterrail and Constance Ramsey stepped out of the cockpit and started toward the port bulwarks to watch the outfitting of their boarding party. Dalton swore under his breath. "Miss Constance! Get back out of sight!"

She turned, put a hand to her mouth, said "Oh," and scurried back into hiding.

"Mister Tidy, please tell Mister Duncan that I need him aft."

"Aye, sir. Mister Duncan! Cap'n needs you aft!"

"Thank you, Mister Tidy."

"Not at all, sir."

When Duncan came aft, Dalton gave him instructions that made the tar's eyes widen. Then he sent him on his way and called to the maintop, "Mister

37

Geary!"

"Aye, sir?"

"Is there any chance that the frigate might have seen our sugar barks?"

"I don't think so, sir. They're out of sight now, at any rate."

"Signal from the frigate, sir," a sailor hurried across from the starboard shrouds. "He says compliments to you, sir, but you can damned well escort your own prize because he has better things to do."

Dalton glanced back at the man-of-war. Even now, it was turning northward again to resume its original course.

"Thank you, Mister . . . ah . . ."

"Abbott, sir. Noel Abbott. You hired me aboard at . . ."

"I remember, Mister Abbott. But about your report on the frigate's signal . . ."

"Yes, sir?"

"The manual of signals does not contain such phrases as 'damned well,' and 'better things to do.'"

"I imagine it doesn't, sir." The youngster grinned. "But it's officers that read th' manual, sir, an' it's common sailors that sends th' signals. Things get added, sometimes."

Wouldn't the Admiralty benefit from a discussion of that possibility, Dalton thought. "Thank you, Mister Abbott," he said.

By the time the launch had carried the boarding party to *Hispania* and brought back her captain, the frigate was a dwindling bright speck on the horizon, its high sails catching the morning sun.

Dalton went forward to meet Captain Webster at the rail. "Thank you for supporting my ploy," he said. "Things could have become very complicated otherwise."

"At first I thought you had turned your coat." The older man frowned. "Then I thought you had lost your sanity. But when that Britisher hove into view . . ."

"Yes," Dalton nodded. "Well, at any rate it worked. Though you very nearly wrecked my stem in the process."

"And you holed my best sail," Webster pointed out. "Do you intend to leave your crew of barbarians aboard my vessel, sir? They are a far rowdier lot than my lads are used to associating with."

"I dare say. But no, they will return to *Fury* when you are back on your deck. I do, though, have a change of plans to discuss with you."

"I don't wish to change plans at this juncture," Webster snorted. "We are within a day of my destination."

"I realize that. Therefore, instead of waiting for that scow of yours to creep back to convoy . . ."

"*Hispania* may be old, but I'll thank you to watch what you call the damned old tub, sir."

"My apology, Captain."

"Accepted, Captain."

"I think it best to escort you directly into Chesapeake from here, sir. As I understand your destination, you have a safe port just beyond the hook?"

"That is correct."

"Very well. We shall proceed directly there; then I can resume escort of the sugar barks with fewer ships to worry about. But I shall require you to provide space for two passengers for the remainder of your journey."

"Oh?"

"And your guarantee—your absolute guarantee—to see them safely home once they are ashore."

"Who are they?"

"Two ladies, sir. Miss Constance Ramsey and . . ."

"What?" Constance's voice from below the quarter-rail was a howl of outrage. "Mister Dalton, you will do no such . . ."

Dalton ignored her. ". . . and her maid, Dora. Miss

39

Ramsey is the daughter of John Singleton Ramsey, whom I believe you know."

"I do. Fine gentleman."

"That's as may be, but my concern is for his daughter. Do I have your guarantee, sir?"

"You do, and with pleasure. I've hauled cargo for Squire Ramsey many's the time."

Dalton was tempted to inquire as to whether any of that cargo had been legal, but he held his tongue. Constance had reached them and planted her small self directly between them, hands on her hips, her bright eyes blazing up at Dalton.

Dalton took her arm, said, "You will excuse me, Captain Webster?" and hauled her away toward the relative privacy of the cockpit.

"I certainly will," Webster said to no one in particular.

In the shadowed cockpit, Dalton pulled her close and hushed her protests. "Listen to me now," he said. "You have told me that I must choose sides. Maybe there is a choice to be made, here in this land. I see others choosing."

"Then choose, Patrick," she urged. "You owe nothing to the English Crown. Declare yourself and . . "

"It isn't the Crown, Constance. I have sworn service to a flag—the flag of England."

"Many now fighting for the colonies once held the same oath. Most of them were Englishmen. Most still are, in their minds. It's the Crown they fight—King George and his party's arrogances where these colonies are concerned."

"Constance, today I faced the flag I am sworn to, and only subterfuge saved me from having to open fire on it. I don't know what might happen next time. I'm a fugitive, Constance—neither fish nor fowl in a world that demands we be one or the other, and until I find a way to clear my name . . . to face the charges against me with honor . . . I have nothing to offer.

Not to any man who matters, and certainly not to you. I know your feelings, my dear little friend. I share them. But until my honor is restored I have nothing to give you. Don't you understand?"

"Your honor! Your pride, you mean. Your damned black Irish pride. Patrick, I . . ."

"Pride, then. Does Constance Ramsey want a man without honor and without pride? I don't think so, Constance."

She pressed close against him, and there were tears in her eyes. "Is it impossible, then, Patrick? You can't go back to England. You said so, yourself. So what can we do?"

"I don't know," he said sadly. "I must discharge the obligation I have for the holding of this ship; then I will try to find a way. But not with you always in my sight as well as my mind. Too many times I have seen you at hazard, Constance. It clouds my judgment. I must see you safely attended; then maybe I can come to terms with such things as honor and pride."

"I don't require them of you, Patrick."

"They *are* me, Constance."

"Yes." She withdrew from his arms, her voice now quiet and matter-of-fact. "Yes, I know. Tell me, then, Patrick—if you do find a way to clear the charges against you, then can you choose between flags?"

"A man of honor can always choose, honorably."

"And which will you choose then?"

"I can only choose then, not now."

"Patrick Dalton, you are insufferable!"

"Aye. A cold and irritating man, you once told me." His smile was wistful. "I shall put you aboard *Hispania*, Constance, and see you safely to a secure port. Then perhaps I can find a way."

"They say there is a king's officer who has tracked you like a hound on the scent."

"Yes. Felix Croney, an officer of His Majesty's Guards. I should like to meet that gentleman one day.

41

He seems to know more about my problems than I do."

"If you ask me, he is your problem."

"Possibly so." He looked out at *Fury*'s open deck. "I had Mister Duncan go below and persuade Dora to pack your things. They are coming up now, and the launch is waiting. I trust Captain Webster with your care."

Her dark eyes held on him, almost taking the breath from him. "Then what will you do, Patrick? I mean, once I am safely ashore?"

"First I shall go and find those sugar barks and take them to Portsmouth as I agreed. I do not owe Ian McCall a ship, but I do owe him a debt."

Part Two
A Turning of
The Winds

IV

Now winter's winds swept down upon embattled
lands, and with them came a time of quiet which
none mistook for peace. It was a binding of wounds, a
laying of new plans, a drawing of lines for what must
come next. Already, in two years of growing war in
and around the American colonies, thousands had
died, but it was far from being over. In England and
the colonies they counted casualties, planned new
strategies and strengthened their resolves—the ministers of the king to put an end to insurrection, the
Continental Congress to gain, once and for all, independence from Crown rule.

Burgoyne's and St. Leger's campaigns had ended in
disaster with Burgoyne's surrender at Saratoga and
the laying down of arms by 5,700 British regulars and
Loyalists. But to the south, the Howes and Cornwallis
held the Delaware ports and Washington was repulsed
at Germantown. Now General Sir William Howe held
Philadelphia, Admiral Lord Richard Howe held the
seaways and Cornwallis looked to the south, while
Washington at Valley Forge worked to consolidate a
continental army from militiamen and volunteers.

It was a time for the taking of stock and the assessment of tactic. In London, Lord North was preparing

a new offer of conciliation while Lord George Germain laid plans for General James Clinton to mount new assaults out of New York. In Baltimore the fugitive Continental Congress had adopted the Articles of Confederation. In Paris, Deane and Franklin learned—as did the British agent Paul Wentworth—that the council of the French king had decided to recognize the independence of the "Thirteen U.S." What had begun in civil protest at Machias, at Lexington and at Concord had, in the seasons since, become full-scale revolution. And now with the drawing of alliances, the ratification of accords, the fielding of troop units and the gathering of fleets of warships, it was all-out war.

For two years, the British Crown had tried to mount a crushing offensive on the soil of America—a single, decisive blow to put an end to the rebellion there. In two years it had been tried four times, yet each final, knock-out blow had fallen short of its goal, and with each failure the determination of the American patriots had grown. Lord North's peace commission would find no attentive ears. The colonists were resolved now to accept nothing less than independence. The failure of Great Britain's best efforts to quash them was the stuff of that resolve.

Now winter's winds brought a brief and nervous quiet to the land, but all knew it would not last. And where men gathered to speak of such matters there was concern. In truth, the colonies yet stood, but there were those who realized that no conflict can be won until it is carried to the enemy. Independence would not be won by battling the forces of the king even to a standstill on American soil. The fight must be taken to the home islands.

A little squadron of armed ships stood now, flying the new colors, "thirteen stripes alternate red and white . . . the union thirteen stars white in a blue field." But it was a tiny and outmatched fleet, too small by far for fleet actions, suited only for individual actions and defense escort. Far more vexing to the British were American privateers. Of 733 prizes taken on the seas by the Royal Navy since Machias, only seventy-three had been taken in the past year, and some said there were more than a hundred privateers at work, escorting merchant vessels and harassing the British men-of-war at their leisure. Some said there were twice that many, and no one could count them and be sure. Of commissioned privateers of record in this year of 1777, there were 115. But how many more were there that carried no true warrant . . . and how many men-of-war sailed American waters that were logged in no registry? How many private raiders, looking for a prize? And how many fugitive ships outside the stream of war?

None knew the answers, but all knew that there were some such.

In winter docks at Portsmouth now, the three-masted sloop of war *Ranger* was being fitted out under the supervision of a querulous little captain whose name had been John Paul and now was John Paul Jones. Not two hundred yards away, just off the breaker jetty, a proud and battle-scarred snow stood at anchor awaiting stores and chandlery. And though few enough of those who looked at the two ships thought much about them — they were only two of many — and though few knew the man who would command the naval vessel with its proud new flag, and none knew the man commanding the privateer beyond, still there were those who thought they saw there a thing worthy of note. "These are our best hope now," they told one another. "Here a warrior of the Continental Navy, there a warrior of private warrant, yet each has the teeth to rake at a blockade, and mayhap one or the other will find the legs to carry her fury to call on the king."

"It is a fine selection of word," others said. "For see

47

there, the escutcheon on the privateer. It is her very name. *Fury*."

And though the men of *Ranger*, outfitting with requisitions from Congress, and those of *Fury*, outfitting in more private ways with coin earned with her guns, did not cross paths there at Portsmouth, there was another thing of note about the two who were in command. A thing in common. For both of them had been sailors of the king and both had been fugitives. One of them still was a fugitive.

To those whose curiosity had lingered at the tall lines of the silent snow resting in the anchorage, it seemed a dark and forbidding ship, and few had come ashore in the two days of its presence. The curious had noted them, and had tried to place their origins, but they were a motley crew. Two Virginians, two Carolinians as alike as peas in a pod, a mariner from Massachusetts and a boy barely on his way to becoming a man, his words carrying the clip of Connecticut. One of the Virginians placed the orders, saw to the manner of payment for their supplies and seemed to be in charge of the shore party though he bore little of the manner of command. The other Virginian was a carpenter, and the Massachusetts man a capable-seeming young sailor who knew the ways of Portsmouth.

The Carolinians were of red Irish stock, obviously brothers, and obviously deck hands. Ordinaries, then, the curious decided. The boy was in all ways a captain's clerk, and he tagged about after the rest, seeing everything, noting everything, jotting items and columns of figures as they went.

"They're from the snow yonder," a chandler's helper shrugged. "Mister Romart, he's the one in charge, though he don't say who his master be. Th' ship's th' *Fury*, private register out of th' lower five. She's up

48

from Savannah, sailed as escort for four sugar barks on contract to a Virginia merchant named Ian McCall."

For the downright curious, who ferreted tidbits from the harbormaster's clerk, there was little to be added. The vessel was the *Fury*, a full-rigged snow of New England pattern but fitted out on Chesapeake, maybe seventy feet of gun deck and maybe eighteen guns not counting the two punt guns mounted on her oversized launch. She was private registry, commanded by one P. Dalton, and she was at anchor now to make some repairs and stock her larder.

They had to settle for that, the curious among them, because there was no more to be learned. Even in the comfort of the Cock and Penny, where the two Virginians stopped off for a tot of good rum while the rest were loading their launch, the two didn't open their mouths except to exchange civilities. They had their rum, paid their fare and left, and if anyone had learned anything it was the two of them, not those who had gathered to listen.

Some said that others might have come ashore as well, maybe two or three in a jollyboat, but if they did no one knew where they had gone, and when they glassed the snow the jollyboat was at its davits.

So with the limited patience of the habitually inquisitive, the curious looked elsewhere for entertainment. Most did, but in a rebel port in wartime there were those whose scrutiny was more than idle curiosity, and some of these watched the snow very closely indeed.

Through this day the weather had held clear. A cold offshore wind swept the tops of waves with frost and made mare's tails of the high clouds. Those standing anchor watch in *Fury*'s tops had seen sail offshore, hull-down with distance, but no traffic had come to Portsmouth since *Fury*'s arrival there, and only a few coasters had been outbound. The bunting on the harbormaster's standard said that a king's squadron was patrolling offshore. Taking advantage of good winds, all knew, to harry the lanes off this shelter of patriot ships.

It's what I'd be doing were I they and given the choice, Patrick Dalton told himself, standing at the snow's afterrail, dark, moody eyes looking out to sea. I'd lay off there and hope for a prize. They know the prizes that are here. He glanced aside, looking down the line of ships at anchor and beyond to where three men-of-war lay at the fitting docks. The nearest of those was the sloop-rigged three-master, *Ranger*. But the two beyond also flew the colors of the Continental Congress—the frigates *Washington* and *Montgomery*. One eighth of the navy of the Continental confederation, he noted. What a strike it would be for the Crown, to take or sink those three. But they would not try to come in. Portsmouth's shore batteries were limited, but well-placed and backed by the firepower of the floating arsenals in port. Just on the ships he could see and identify—the three Continental Navy craft and a half-dozen armed privateers among the dozen or more barks, schooners and ketches of the Colonial merchant fleet—were at least a hundred great guns, all loaded and ready—as were the eighteen at his command.

Off there flies the Union Jack, he thought, and here lie prizes waiting. And were they to come, I would be one of those prizes.

The bleak humor of it tugged at his cold cheeks. Patrick Dalton, officer of the king, at anchor now among the king's enemies and flying false colors to avoid notice, while the flag to which he had pledged his service waited offshore to kill him as surely as it would try to kill any who broke from this port on this day.

Bad luck and stubborn pride, he thought. I have my share of both.

"On deck!" The call came from above and he turned, peering upward into the snow's high rigging, identifying the man at the mainmast's buttressed top platform. "Aye, Mister Fisk!" he responded.

"Sir, the launch is putting out from chandler's dock. They'll be alongside in half a bell."

"Can you see who is aboard, Mister Fisk?"

There was a pause, then, "I make it four, sir. The O'Rileys are there, and . . . ah, Mister Tower and Mister Caster, sir. The launch is loaded high an' floatin' low."

"Very well, Mister Fisk." Dalton got out his glass and scanned the distant chandler's docks. There were few enough people out and about in this brittle weather, but the ones he saw there were none of his. He saw no sign of Michael Romart or Sam Sidney, and he put away his glass with a frown. Possibly there was no room for them on the laden boat and they had found a warm place to await its return, but he didn't like it. Nor did he like the continued absence of Charley Duncan, though he himself had permitted Duncan to go ashore, "just for a bit of quick scout," as Duncan had put it. It had not been his understanding that Duncan would send the jollyboat back without him, and the two who had served at the oars had no idea where he had gone.

Charley Duncan was a resourceful man, he reminded himself. Still, it set his nerves on edge to be here, a sitting duck among hostiles, and not know where his people were.

Bad luck and stubborn pride, he thought again. The bad luck had come long months before, when he brought in the wreckage of the brig *Herret* to the fleet base at New York, only to find himself branded as a traitor because of a long-ago association. He had known the Fitzgerald, back in Ireland. All who knew the Fitzgerald now were under king's warrant. And for an Irish officer in the British Navy, accused of treason in wartime and abroad, there was not a chance in creation of finding passage home to clear his name.

The stubborn pride was of his own making. He would, he knew, have been accepted with open arms by the Colonials now making war against the king. He was an experienced mariner, a fighter of warships, and there were many such who had turned their backs upon the Union Jack and now stood at American helms.

But to join the rebels would seal forever the charge of treason clouding his name. The treason of choice would forever prevent his exoneration of the treasons he had not committed.

Thus he stood now on the deck of a fugitive ship, in a cordoned port, at risk both from those around him and from those waiting offshore. No king's ship this, despite the nationality of its master and most of its crew, nor of the Continental persuasion despite its colors. *Fury* was a fugitive, and every man of her complement shared that condition.

Forward of the small quarterdeck the companion-way hatch swung open and Victory Locke appeared, carrying a wooden tray. "Cap'n's permission, sir," he said, "Mister Mallory has a fire in the cook-tub and thought you might like tea. It's a brisk day."

"Indeed it is." Dalton nodded. "Hot tea's the very thing, and please thank Mister Mallory for me." As Locke brought up the tea, Dalton turned to his watch bosun, John Tidy, a grizzled and monkeylike man of middle years, huddled in a heavy coat beside the fife rails. "Come and have tea, Mister Tidy. It fends against the vapors, I'm told."

"Aye, sir. Thank you."

With the tea served, Victory Locke went to the quarterrail, stood by the glass for a moment and then turned it. "Bells, Mister Tidy," he said.

"Captain's permission?" Tidy's breath misted with

the warmth of fresh-swallowed tea.

"Sound the bells, Mister Tidy. We are, after all, a good American ship in a secure American port. No reason for stealth."

"Aye, sir. Bells, Mister Locke."

Locke reached to the little ship's bell suspended above the quarterrail and rang it three times. Here and there about the harbor, other bells were sounding. It was 5:30 of a winter's evening, four bells of the dogwatch.

"On deck!"

"Aye, Mister Fisk?"

"Launch approaching, sir. Permission to board?"

"Permission to board," Dalton told Tidy. "Bring up some of the hands, please, and have them drop a hoist from the lower foreyard. We'll deposit our goods in the forehold for now, and sort it out later when Mister Caster is here to inventory. Mister Locke, please greet them at the starboard rail and see if you can determine where Misters Romart and Sidney are."

Tidy called below and others appeared on deck. Dalton let his eyes rove the nearby ships, the docks and the buildings beyond, hoping that no one had more than a casual glass on *Fury*. Despite their heavy coats and winter wraps, some of those he had kept aboard looked just like what they were—British tars. Claude Mallory, Victory Locke, Ishmael Bean . . . No one would mistake them for Americans at more than a casual glance.

In moments a sling was hoist from tackle on the lower foreyard and swung out to take the cargo of the launch, just coming alongside. John Tidy met it at the rail, called a query, then stepped aside as young Billy Caster scrambled over the rail and saluted himself aboard. He hurried aft, his eyes wide in a pale face, and almost skidded to a halt facing his officer. "Captain's clerk reporting, sir." He started another salute and Dalton waved a quick hand.

53

"Yes, Mister Caster. Where are Misters Romart and Sidney?"

"They're in the town yonder, sir," Billy pointed. "Mister Duncan came and found us. Ah . . . sir, I wonder . . . did you tell Mister Duncan that the securing of cargo is a responsibility of the first officer, sir?"

Dalton blinked. "I likely did tell him that. He asked about such duties, and I recall I recited them for him. Why?"

"Mr. Duncan was discussing the securing of cargo, sir . . . while he was talking with Mister Romart."

"Cargo? I don't believe I understand, Mister Caster. *Fury* is a man-of-war. We have no cargo, only ship's stores."

"I . . . ah . . . I don't believe Mister Duncan understood the word, 'secure,' sir."

"Didn't understand?" Dalton squinted, peering toward the town behind the harbor. "To secure is to make fast. To batten and lash, to so ship and stow that objects will not break loose or shift in heavy seas. How else could that be understood?"

"I'm afraid Mister Duncan misapprehended that, sir. I believe he feels that as first officer, if *Fury* has no cargo, then it is up to him to go and secure some."

"Mister Caster, where are Misters Romart and Sidney?"

"Yonder on the quay, sir. Mister Duncan asked them to go and rig a loading sling and tow-raft at the draypath."

An ominous feeling crept over Dalton. Loading slings and tow-rafts? What was Charley Duncan preparing to put aboard his ship?

"Mr. Duncan asked me to present his respects to the captain, sir, and to request that the launch be waiting at the draypath at six bells, with line and rowers for tow."

"It will be nearly dark by six bells, Mister Caster,

and near high tide. I don't suppose Mister Duncan let slip just what this 'cargo' might be, that it must be shipped at such a place and in such conditions?"

"No, sir. He only said that it would be paying cargo, and he mentioned to Mister Romart that he hoped *Fury* would be ready to set sail on short notice. Then he put on a wig and went up to the town, sir."

Dalton's brow was thunderous in the sun's final soft light. He had no intention of taking on cargo. He had only made port here because *Fury*'s larders were depleted after her run upcoast from Savannah, escorting two brace of sugar barks for Ian McCall, and he had felt it best not to start back without adequate supplies. He took a deep breath, sighed, and turned to the rail. "My fondest hope is that Mister Duncan has selected something discreet," he muttered.

Billy scuffed a foot on the deck. "I doubt whether Mister Duncan understands the word 'discreet' exactly as the captain does, sir."

"A wig?" Dalton glanced around at him. "Why did he put on a wig? Where was he going?"

"I believe he was going to the opera, sir."

V

In the foresheets tackle rattled and lines sang as bales
and barrels were hoisted from the launch to *Fury*'s slim
deck, then into the forehold aft of the catheads and
chainlocker. Dalton ignored the proceeding, scanning
the sea beyond the quay. One of the king's vessels yonder had run in again, tacking to the wind in a display of
presence. He noticed that it was the same vessel again,
a sleek-ported brig of perhaps twenty guns. He could
not fault the tactic. Ensigns aloft at the port said there
was a squadron out there, yet all of them held away, far
out, letting one work its way in again and again to
harry those in port.

There was a twofold purpose for the maneuver, and
he understood it well. As long as the light held, the
commanders out there wanted the rebels to know of
their superior presence, but at the same time they tried
a baiting game. The brig was attempting to entice
someone to come out and fight, offering what seemed a
chance of a quick kill. But the brig probably was the
fastest of those ships available to the squadron leader,
and would stand only long enough to bring a foe out
into open water, then would turn tail and run on the
wind. Any captain foolhardy enough to give chase
stood the chance of facing a frigate in an offshore wind,

with no chance of retreating back to the battered harbor.

"On deck!"

Dalton turned and squinted upward. "Yes, Mister Fisk?"

"Cap'n, that mailboat that came in at midday—one of its passengers is up in that church tower now, looking out at us."

"Looking at us, Mister Fisk?"

"Aye, sir. He's been there an hour now or more, looking at us."

Dalton turned his glass toward the town, sighting on the belltower of a church just beyond the port buildings. He could see the man in the tower, his face hidden by a woolen scarf, a hat shadowing his eyes. Dalton cupped his hand, looking upward again. "Why do you report that, Mister Fisk?"

"Sir, I think I recognize the man there. His face was clear for a bit, and I believe he's Commander Croney, sir."

For a second the name didn't register; then it did. "Are you certain, Mister Fisk?"

"Fair sure, sir. Any man that's laid over at the Long Island stockade likely would recognize that face."

Croney. Felix Croney. Guard Commander Croney, crown warrant officer, chief of military police and security for fleet headquarters at Long Island. Dalton peered through his glass again. He still could not make out the muffled face, but he trusted the eyes of Purdy Fisk. If Fisk said he saw Felix Croney, likely he did see Felix Croney. But what was the man doing up here, in a rebel-dominated port town in New Hampshire? And what was his interest in *Fury* . . . unless he knew what ship she really was?

If he knew about *Fury*, then he knew where Patrick Dalton was. A chill not of the cold wind crept up Dalton's spine. Did the man never give up? He had been told—though it was hard enough to believe—that

57

Croney had followed him all the way from New York to Virginia, broadcasting warrants against him. And now at Portsmouth — the implacable quest, the unswerving dedication of the guard officer to running him to ground — made Dalton shiver. He turned away, thinking, then looked upward again. "Maintop ahoy!"

"Sir?" the response floated down from sixty feet above.

"Mister Fisk, do you see the other passengers who came on the mail launch? There were two more, I believe."

"Moment, sir."

A minute passed, and then another, while Purdy Fisk aloft scanned with his glass. Then, "Not certain, sir, but there are two gentlemen yonder near the end of the quay, fishing."

Shore fishing? At this hour, in this weather? "Waiting to relay signals, more likely," he muttered.

"Sir?" Billy Caster was at his elbow, as usual, and had heard the comment.

"I'm thinking there might be more than one reason why that brig out there keeps beating inshore, Mister Caster." He turned to the helm. "The deck and the watch are yours, Mister Locke. I shall be ashore for a time."

"Aye, sir."

"Mister Caster, please go and find Mister Hoop. Have him provide himself with club and cutlass and attend me in the foresheets."

"Aye, sir." The boy hurried away.

"Mister Tidy!"

"Aye, sir?" The bosun came around the mainmast, distracted from the shipping of stores.

"Mister Tidy, can you arrange to have the jollyboat run down to the fore, so that a person watching might not be overly interested in the placement of it?"

Tidy pushed up the rear brim of his hat and scratched his head. "Aye, sir. I could have a lad or two swing around there with line, like they was splicing spreader stays, sir."

"Very good, Mister Tidy. Then have four rowers swarm down from the cathead there and stand by oars."

As Dalton strode forward, his hand rested on the hilt of the curved sword at his hip and his boots thudded on the deck. The stormy mood that had been upon him of late — a mood combined from the absence of Constance Ramsey since he had put her ashore above Cape Henry, and months of dismal reflection on his own predicament as a fugitive from king's justice and a flier of false colors — still clung to him but now was muted by an opportunity to take a hand in his own destinies — and the decision to do so. Felix Croney. Well did he recall the gray little man who had hounded him — almost trapped him — at Long Island, then apparently had followed him all the way to Chesapeake. He had heard from none other than Captain Peter Selkirk — old Hawser himself — that Croney was obsessed with bringing him down.

Well, if indeed that was Felix Croney in the church tower ashore — and he had little doubt of it — then the least he could do was to confront the gentleman face-to-face.

Dalton paused at the foreshrouds for a moment to watch the shipping of supplies being completed. Just ahead, Mister Hoop came from a cable tier, followed by Billy Caster. A huge man, taller by inches than even the slim Dalton, Hoop had a club at his waist and carried a cutlass that in his hand looked like a breadknife. As with every man of *Fury*'s crew, Hoop was a fugitive. At one time he had served as master-at-arms aboard a proper man-of-war, the crown frigate *Prowler*. But after a gang of his shipmates threw him overboard off Albermarle Sound, he had decided not to return to His Majesty's service. Dalton, transporting a hand of shore batteries to Charleston aboard the salvaged ketch *Mystery*, had signed Hoop on and made him master-at-

59

arms, and the position had transferred to *Fury* when Dalton and his fugitives took the snow from pirates.

On deck, Hoop paused to grin at his somber captain. "Bit of mayhem needin' to be done, Captain? I'm your man, if so."

"We shall be going ashore in the jollyboat, Mister Hoop," Dalton told him. "I'll have need of an escort to that church yonder."

"Aye, sir." Hoop grinned again, fingering his cutlass.

"Shall I go along, sir?" Billy Caster asked, anxiously.

"You are to remain here, Mister Caster. When Mister Duncan shows up presently with whatever cargo he has found, you are to inventory and register it, but do not commit it to log without my approval."

"Shall we ship it aboard, sir?"

Dalton hesitated. *Fury* was a warship, not a merchantman, and he was more than a little irked that Charley Duncan would even consider placing cargo aboard. On the other hand, he had no doubt that Duncan at least *thought* he was doing the proper thing . . . whatever it was . . . and he would withhold judgment until he had the entire story. Also, knowing Duncan, he suspected that whatever his cargo, it might be best to get it aboard and stowed as quickly as possible. "If Mister Duncan feels the cargo needs to be inspected aboard, then ship it aboard. But I would like to have a look at it before it is consigned either to the hold or to the log."

Billy nodded, keeping his face straight. Captain Dalton had been stung once with blind cargo. The shipment that the merchant John Singleton Ramsey had consigned to the poor old ketch *Mystery* had turned out to be five battery guns weighing four tons apiece. Four of them had been delivered at Charleston, at high risk to everyone aboard. The fifth had gone overboard when Charley Duncan sank a cutter with it. "Aye, sir," the youth said.

Little wind-blown wavelets tattooed against the bow

of the jollyboat as it made its way to the foot of the chandler's pier, out of sight of the church tower that rose behind the waterfront structures. Wind caught the curling tops and made spray of them, and the twilight sky was a pale violet to the west and gave no warmth. Dalton felt thoroughly chilled by the time he stepped ashore at Portsmouth's abandoned serryway, and pulled his coat tighter about him. "Wait here and stand by your oars," he told his rowers. "Mister Hoop, come along and try to be inconspicuous."

"Aye, sir."

Past the lamplit fronts of a pair of seamen's inns he led, then through a dismal alley, and paused in shadows to look across at the stone church. In this second street above the docks there was little traffic at this hour, and the church looked dark and empty. From where they were, they could see the face of the tower but not the man within. "There was a man up in that window," Dalton told the hulking Hoop. "I think he is still there, in the tower. I would like to have a talk with him, uninterrupted."

"Aye, sir."

"Be very quiet, then, and come with me."

"Aye, sir."

They scurried across to the church door and found it unlocked. Inside, it was dark and empty. Dalton paused to listen, creeping to the foot of the curving stairs that led upward to the tower. For a moment he heard nothing, then a tiny clink as though a telescoping glass had touched stone. Very well, the man was still there. He turned to motion for Hoop to wait where he was, but the big man was already moving, starting up the stairs, silent as a panther despite his great size. Dalton had no choice but to follow.

The winding column was in almost total darkness, a rock-walled shaft rising at least twenty feet, with the outline of an open trap above. When Hoop raised himself through the trap into the bell chamber, his bulk blocked out all the light and Dalton paused, fearful of making a sound to alert the man above. Then Hoop was through, and suddenly Dalton heard abrupt scuffling sounds overhead—feet on planking, a muffled voice, the beginning peal of a large bell abruptly silenced, then a thud and another series of scuffles. He sprang up the last few steps and through the trap. In the bell loft Mister Hoop squatted over the sprawled form of a fallen man, his club in one hand and the rim of the church bell in the other.

"Beg pardon, sir," the big man said. "Slippery one, he is. Skinned past me and tried to ring the bell, so I knocked him in the head."

Dalton stooped to peer at the man, rolling him over. Even in the dim light, it was a face he had seen . . . a long time ago, it seemed, in the village of New Utrecht above the Royal Navy yards on Long Island. It was the man who had led guards to Clarence Kilreagh's inn to capture him—the man he had evaded by clinging to a roof brace while his guards searched the inn from roof to cellar. Commander Felix Croney, Officer of the Guards, On His Majesty's Service. "You are a long way from Long Island Yards, Commander Croney," he muttered. Then he looked up. "How hard did you hit him, Mister Hoop?"

"Oh, hardly at all, sir. Just enough to keep him quiet for a bit."

"Well"—Dalton stood—"we can't very well wait around here while he completes his rest. I suppose we must just take him along with us, so that we can have our chat when he feels more up to it."

"Aye, sir." Hoop squatted by the inert guard officer and lifted him as one would lift a small child, then draped him over a huge shoulder. "There's a bit of baggage there, sir. Do you want it, too?"

"You take him along, Mister Hoop. I can bring the rest."

"Aye, sir." Hoop lowered his bulk through the trap,

62

and Dalton winced as Felix Croney's unconscious self acquired some fresh bruises in the process.

Dalton gathered up the officer's things—a fine telescoping glass, a duffel sack and a valise—then paused to look out the tower opening. Below, the harbor spread, with its lanterns and lamps, its ships at dock and at anchor, its arms opening toward the quay and the open sea.

Fury was fully visible from here, open to scrutiny by glass. Far out, beyond the harbor, the British brig had beat inshore again, and was just making about to head out. Dimly, near the end of the quay, he saw flickers of lantern light. Signals. Elaborate, he realized. Church bell to alert the watchers, their lanterns to signal the brig, the brig to carry the message to other ships waiting offshore. Felix Croney had prepared a gauntlet for *Fury* to run, when she made for the sea. Dalton picked up the guard officer's things and followed Hoop down to the entryway.

"Let's get back to the boat, Mister Hoop," he said. "This man is an officer of the king, and we wouldn't want the colonials hereabout to get their hands on him. They might well be unkind."

"Aye, sir."

"If there are unkindnesses to be done to Mister Croney, I shall attend to them myself."

In deepening dusk they made their way to the chandler's dock, and Hoop handed his burden down to the men waiting with the boat. Dalton stepped aboard, Hoop followed, and Dalton said, "Cast off and lay to the oars, lads. With a will." I hope all of our wandering mates have returned to the ship, he thought, because, with or without them, we are about to take our leave of Portsmouth.

They didn't skirt the shallows this time, but made straight for *Fury,* and in the gloom Dalton could see a cargo raft lashed alongside, a sling just hoisting the last of whatever it had held on board *Fury's* deck. Aft of it was the launch, ready to be run up to its davits, and there was bustling activity on deck.

Felix Croney still lay limp in the jollyboat's scuppers as they snugged alongside *Fury.* He had begun to snore. "Take him aboard, Mister Hoop," he said. "Stow him in the portside cabin for the time being, and put a guard on the hatch. Have his belongings placed in my cabin, please. Rowers, ship and secure, and rig the boat for tow."

He scrambled over the near rail and returned the salute of a shadowy deckwatch. Nearby, John Tidy's whistle piped "Captain aboard," and Charley Duncan appeared from the foredeck, followed by Billy Caster.

"I've secured us a cargo, Captain," Duncan said proudly. "Assembled on the forecastle for inspection."

"Then secure it according to the original meaning of the word, Mister Duncan, and let's get this vessel rigged for running. There are people just beyond the breakwater who will lay a trap for us if they can."

"Aye, sir!" Duncan turned. "Foredeck, get lines on anything that might shift, then stand to station! Tops aloft to make sail, hands to sheets. Sir, the launch has just been hoisted. Shall I lower it to tow us out?"

"We have no time for towing, Mister Duncan. Prepare to make sail."

He headed for the stern, Billy Caster half running to keep up with him. "Make sail, sir?" The boy sounded stunned.

"Yes, Mister Caster. I shall take us out under sail. Mister Tidy, get a man out on the spreaders, please, and stand by to relay aft. We shall have close quarters for a bit. Up anchor! Courses and tops, make sail. Trim full and by the wind. Mister Mallory?" He cleared the quarterdeck ladder at a stride and stepped to the helm.

"Aye, sir?"

"I'll take the helm, Mister Mallory. Please stand by for relays from the fore."

"Aye, sir."

Even as the capstan began to squeal, *Fury* trembling in response to the tug on her stream anchor as it broke loose from its hold on the bottom, sails were snapping into place and the high jibboom—a hundred and fifty feet forward of the helm—began to sweep across the panorama of the harbor. With the wind in her nose, rising staysails pulling her, she swung in stately grace, one hundred and eighty degrees to settle her prow upon the distant harbor entrance where bell and oilwick marked the farewell buoy.

"Small boat in tow?"

"In tow and secure, sir."

"Launch in its davits?"

"Secure, sir."

"Mister Caster, did all the stores and tack come aboard?"

"All boarded, sir. Nothing is inventoried, but it's secured in the forward hold."

"Foredeck secured?"

"They seem to be working on it, sir."

Dalton squinted. There seemed to be a lot of people milling about on the foredeck, and several of them were strangely dressed.

Sheetlines snugged at the pinrails and *Fury* surged forward, the hum of cloven water sounding up through her trim hull. They were under way and accelerating, aiming for the tiny-looking slot of water that was the harbor's mouth. "Stand by topgallant sheets!" Dalton ordered.

Beside him he heard the hiss of Claude Mallory's indrawn breath, and he felt the tension in his own shoulders. It was nearly a mile to the harbor's funnel, and *Fury* would be making at least fourteen knots when she hit it. If they steered true, she would clear Portsmouth harbor like a cork shooting out of a bottle. If they didn't . . . Dimly, in the distance, he saw the Royal Navy brig entering the chop that marked the dropoff to deep water. Somewhere out there, much fiercer predators waited for the message it carried. Dalton gritted his teeth. "Unfurl topgallants main and fore," he said. "Sheet home full and by."

With the offshore wind on her tail and tall sails drumming to its beat, *Fury* lifted her nose, took the spray in her teeth and crested her bow wake. To port and starboard, tall shapes flitted past, vessels at anchor just off the fairway, and the snow sent a slapping wake out from her stern to tell them of her passing.

On the far foredeck, men milled about, struggling to secure something that seemed determined to move about on its own. Dalton squinted ahead. "Mister Caster, what is that they are trying to lash down yonder? And who are all those people?"

"That is a harpsichord, sir. I started to tell you about that. We have a harpsichord, a kettledrum, and several lesser things. Those people are musicians, sir. Our cargo is an orchestra."

VI

There were few secrets in the realm of naval operations in this the third year of insurrection in the American colonies. Colonial traders, privateers, mail packets, coasters, fishing boats and even skiff-handlers up and down the coast provided the Continental forces with an extensive intelligence network regarding movements of the White Fleet and its squadrons of support vessels. Rare was the American mariner who didn't know — reliably — where this or that crown vessel might be found at any given time. The warrant vessels — privately-owned warships at limited service to the Crown — were less exactly tracked. They came and went at the pleasure of their masters, as often on privateer business of their own as on fleet assignment. But even there, it was generally known where they had been, if not where they were at the moment.

By the same token, the Admiralty's forces — from Admiral Lord Richard Howe right down to the least seaman with his bare feet and tar hat — kept a working knowledge of what colonial and independent fighting ships were in their waters, where they could be found and who might be planning to use them. Privateers commissioned by each separate colony, privateers holding letters of marque from the Continental Congress, merchant men-of-war assigned to escort convoys past British blockades — all of these were the opposition, and His Majesty's officers kept close inventory through their own network of colonial royalists and Tories, turncoats among the revolutionaries, and carefully placed spies.

Thus it was no accident that the seventy-four-gun ship of the line *Royal Lineage* prowled the frigid waters between Maine and Nova Scotia, a great, dark presence flanked by two heavy frigates, a light cruiser, a signal schooner and a pair of brigs, in these darkening days. For here, in the rebel ports north of Cape Cod, ships were being outfitted to fly the new stars and stripes ensign of the Continental confederacy. No privateers these — though their combined strength was marginal. These were the beginnings of a navy. "Five ships of 32 guns, five of 28 guns, three of 24 guns," the orders from the Naval Committee read. At Portsmouth and elsewhere these were being fitted out, and their purpose would be to carry the war to the Crown fleets and even to the home islands. The Admiralty frowned on such a possibility. It would be most embarrassing — particularly with Wickes's audacious sorties still fresh in mind — to be confronted at home by an American navy.

Thus Isaac Watson, commanding HMS *Royal Lineage,* maneuvered off the coast of Maine and kept lookouts and spotting vessels busy perusing and harassing the various battered ports there. It was not his choice of duty, but a penance of sorts for suffering large-scale desertions months earlier at Point of Elk during General Sir William Howe's landing of troops. On a Thursday following punishments, forty-one hands had gone over the side and disappeared into the wilderness, including two of his most capable gunners.

During the day, *Royal Lineage* and one frigate had beat up the offshore wind to within sight of Portsmouth's batteries. Beyond, in the safe harbor, a ship at dock had run up one of the new flags. A gesture of contempt, it seemed. A very taunt to the might of his guns, from the relative safety of the colonial port. "The mouse lies in its hole," he had muttered, "snarling at the cat outside."

"Sir?"

"Nothing, Mister Cord. I was thinking aloud."

"Aye, sir."

"Mister Cord, signals to *Bethune* if you please. Have the brig make abeam of us for hailing."

"Aye, sir."

When the brig was just abeam, Watson took up his horn and stepped to his port rail. "Ahoy *Bethune*," he shouted. "A word with your captain."

"Aye, sir." The voice was replaced by another voice, clear across the single chain's distance between vessels, "Blake here, Captain. At your service."

Watson looked down at the smaller vessel, dwarfed by the massive size of the seventy-four. Next to the line ship, the brig looked like an elaborate small boat. "Captain Blake, did you put the guard officer ashore safely?" Almost, he had said "that idiot guard officer," irritated at the blatant interruption of his mission by the gray man with his miserable fugitive warrants. But he restrained himself. It was best never to let juniors see one's anger — only one's wrath upon occasion.

"He's ashore, sir. He is set to signal from end of quay if the fugitive attempts to leave port."

"Very well. Stand in at intervals and watch for his signal. Let us get this business done as soon as we can."

"Aye, sir."

The brig hove off, making across the wind to beat toward the harbor mouth. "Bring us about, Mister Cord," Watson ordered.

"Aye, sir."

"Resume maneuvers north to south."

"Aye, sir."

Watson resumed his pacing of the high deck. Typical of the guard service, he thought. We are attempting to conduct a war here, yet all must give precedence to some peerage-appointed zealot with a warrant in his coat and a grudge in his heart because some fugitive has eluded him.

In the ten days that Felix Croney had been aboard *Royal Lineage* as passenger and guest, Isaac Watson had developed a strong distaste for the little man. The fugitive Dalton must be caught, of course. His exploits had become a source of frustration in some circles. There were even those who claimed that the Irishman had hunted down and destroyed a forty-four-gun warrant frigate with nothing but a modified trade schooner at his command. But Watson felt inwardly that he might almost applaud the man who had aroused such enmity from such a one as Felix Croney.

He was still incredulous at the nature of the charges against Patrick Dalton. There were two warrants — a Crown warrant and an Admiralty warrant — and it appeared that the issuance of the first had led to the acts set out in the second. The Crown warrant . . . Watson shook his head . . . What had come over the Court of St. James? High treason, it said. The particulars? Simply that the accused seemed once to have been acquainted with a fiery old Irish chieftain who had somehow displeased the king. Nothing more.

But that second warrant listed particulars, starting at the point when Dalton had fled from arrest on the first warrant. Mayhem, sabotage, giving comfort to the enemy, release of prisoners from a stockade, the destruction of a fish dock, destruction of a wind-wall, damage to two men-of-war which had fired upon each other when the fugitive sailed between them, the sinking of a gunboat and destruction of two others . . . The charges went on and on. Incredible, Watson thought. Simply incredible. He could well understand how the man had become an embarrassment. And yet — he had pondered upon this during his enforced association with Croney — as far as he could tell, Patrick Dalton had never once initiated an attack on a ship of the king, or in any manner dishonored the flag of the Royal Navy. Even if,

70

as some whispered, the man had somehow hunted down and destroyed a frigate, the frigate was not under the flag of Great Britain. It was a vessel already dishonored, its captain himself subject to charges of piracy.

Nonetheless, Watson reminded himself, it was the duty of every officer to assist in the capture of Dalton if opportunity should offer. He himself would not hesitate, in that circumstance. It was duty.

He was glad to be rid of Croney, though, and wished the man no good. *Royal Lineage* was here to discourage the deployment of a colonial navy, not to help some hot-eyed zealot apprehend felons.

Intelligence said that in the port over there, and two others along this stretch of shoreline, were at least ten of the thirteen ready vessels threatening to carry the revolution to the home islands. He himself had seen the ensign rise on one of them — a vessel designated *Ranger*.

Royal Lineage and her escorts had a simple blockade strategy. A watch northward, then make about for a watch, plus or minus differences in wind and bearing, to the south. For as long as he needed to, Isaac Watson would sail the seventy-four-gunner in a long oval course off the rebel shores, ready to run down upon any ship making outbound and take it or sink it.

Cold dusk was settling on land and sea when the brig *Bethune* completed her latest approach to the mouth of Portsmouth harbor and began to make about for the windward run back out to sea. Thomas Blake was about to go below for a warming spot of tea when the maintop sang out, "On deck!"

Blake raised his head. "Report, tops."

"Signal fire at quay's end, sir. It is that guard officer's signal that his fugitive is preparing to leave port."

"Thank you, tops," he called, wondering why he had not also heard the pealing of the church bell that signaled the bonfire. *Bethune* was close enough, with the wind coming from the church tower, that it should have been quite audible. Yet if there had been any bell, it had been only one stroke, cut short as though someone had muffled the bell's ring. Still, the signal fire was there, and he had seen the readying aboard that trim snow anchored in the harbor. Something was afoot, certainly.

His second came aft at the call, and raised a glass toward the diminishing harbor. "It must be that snow, sir. I believe she is making sail . . . No, they wouldn't do that. He must be setting a luff course to assist his tow. But she is readying to make way, sir."

Blake tugged at his chin. The brig had good wind behind it now, and was cresting the swells toward the dark water. "Let us shorten sail a bit," he said, "but maintain course. Possibly we can have a look at the snow before it clears; then we can decide upon the action to take. Far easier to herd it to the seventy-four than to bring the seventy-four back here at this point, don't you think?"

"Aye, sir."

"Shorten sail, then. Bring us down to eight knots, by the wind, and we shall wait. Yonder is no fast channel. It might take him three bells to make the breakwater."

Out on *Fury*'s bowsprit, just at the base of the prodding jib, Purdy Fisk sat astride the spritcap with the forestay at his back and his knees wrapped around the brace spreaders. Twenty feet forward of the ship's bowstem and twenty feet above the harbor's darkening waves, he rode his bucking perch and watched the keg buoys that marked the narrow passage channel beneath. The harbor was deceptive, its channel hidden below the shallow waters of the natural cut within which it was set, and only the kegs told a vessel of deep draft, where it was safe to go, and where it would run aground. Though surface waters here extended a mile either way from the channel, the cut itself was barely a hundred feet wide. *Fury*'s keel must navigate this ditch now at the racing speed of fifteen knots, and the only eyes guiding it were his.

The kegs seemed to race past, and Fisk held his breath each time he aligned from one to the next. The channel was not a straight line. It curved slightly, first to starboard and then back to port, a lazy S-shaped ditch dredged into the bottom of a bay, and a heavy vessel that ran afoul of its walls even at five knots might well destroy itself. At fifteen knots, he had no idea what might happen.

He aligned on the kegs ahead and spread his arms, raising his right arm as a semaphore to signal a veer a'port. Somewhere behind him, amidships, he knew that Cadman Wise and John Tidy were relaying his signals to the helm. *Fury* responded, easing left just a bit, and again the kegs ahead were in line. He breathed again and squinted for a new sighting. The farewell buoy was less than a mile ahead, with clear water beyond, but it seemed a hundred miles. Somewhere aft, in the receding distance, he heard the boom of a single cannon-shot. He wondered whether someone back there was saluting the audacity of a captain who would dare take a warship out of harbor under full sail in a thirty knot wind—or more likely someone expressing his outrage that anyone would take such chances of blocking the only good exit channel with a wrecked ship. Again the kegs edged out of alignment, and again Purdy Fisk held his breath and semaphored, praying for a prompt response. From the fore topgallant stay at the point of her jib to the heel of her spanker boom, *Fury* was at least a hundred and fifty feet in length. And eighty feet of that length was sheathed hull now slicing through deep water, with disaster bare yards away to either side. Fisk had seen a stoven hull, just once, and he never wanted to see one again.

Before the helm, Patrick Dalton leaned over the quarterrail and frowned as John Tidy, just below, waved his arms in exasperation. ". . . hard to relay signals, sir," the

73

bosun was saying, "with those people a'fore raising such a ruckus."

Dalton nodded and turned away. "Sharp eye, helm. Mister Hoop, please go forward and lend a hand to Mister Duncan. Whoever those people are, put them into the forward hold and make them stay there. They are interfering with navigation."

"Aye, sir." The big man grinned and hurried forward in the gloom.

"An orchestra?" Dalton muttered, in disbelief.

"Aye, Captain." Bill Caster was beside him. "Fifteen members, thirteen instruments, Mister Duncan said. I believe they are trying to secure the harpsichord right now."

"An orchestra." Dalton sighed.

Somewhere near the milling shadows a'fore, Cadman Wise signaled frantically, and Dalton turned to his helmsman. "Bit a'port, if you please; then I shall take the wheel again."

"Aye, sir." Claude Mallory's voice was tight with tension.

Fury careened past a keg buoy, nearly swamping it with her beam wave, and Dalton took the helm again. Far ahead he could see the great silhouette of Mister Hoop moving among the crowd on the foredeck, and the crowd diminished as — by twos and threes — people vanished into the forehold. Some seemed to go willingly, but at least a few went head first or head over heels. Mister Hoop enjoyed his work.

Another correction was relayed back, and Dalton eased the plunging snow to starboard. Just ahead now was the farewell buoy, and beyond that the chop of channel waves gave way to the dark swells of open water. *Fury* trembled violently as her starboard beam grazed a channel wall, then righted herself. Out there, not a half mile away, stood the brig, riding on shortened sails, seeming barely to move as *Fury* began to overtake her. "Gunners to guns," Dalton called. "Fore chasers and port

74

side, please."

"Are we going to fire on the brig?" Billy Caster wondered.

"I hope we aren't going to fire the bow chasers just yet," Claude Mallory told the boy. "Purdy . . . ah, Mister Fisk is still out there on the spreaders, and I expect he wouldn't fancy an adventure of that sort."

Like a projectile from a gun, *Fury* cleared the harbor and dipped her striker — and Purdy Fisk's feet — into the wide waters of the Atlantic. Fresh wind astern caught her booming sails and she surged to new speed, cold spray sheeting over both bow rails. "Hands to sheets, Mister Tidy," Dalton called. "Set for starboard quarter winds. Look lively!"

Tidy's whistle was almost drowned out by the thud of feet on deck planking as hands raced to the pinrails to retrim for a new course. At nearly eighteen knots, *Fury* closed on the stunned brig and put hard over to starboard, crossing the other warship's wake a chain length behind its fantail. White faces there stared out at the nimble snow, and hands clung to rails to ride her surging wake as it bounced them. Hands at *Fury's* bow and port guns knelt to their pieces, ready to respond to fire, but it was so abrupt that not a shot came from the brig until *Fury* was beyond effective range. Smoke billowed then along the brig's starboard beam, and thunders echoed across the water, but the iron balls were too late. They skipped and sank in *Fury's* wake as the snow took new wind on her flank and headed east of south.

At the stern rail of the brig *Bethune,* Thomas Blake stood open-mouthed while men cursed, and stared all around him. "Did ye see that?" "Lordy, like threadin' a needle!" "That man is crazy! A madman, right enough." "Are we going to give chase, Captain?"

Blake came out of his stupor. "Give chase? Chase that? How many sails does this brig carry, Mister Clay?"

"Eleven, sir. Six square, five fore-and-aft. But not all at once, of course."

"Precisely, Mister Clay. Ten at best. Did you peruse the rigging of that vessel that just blew past us? That madman can put up studdingsails if he cares to, and a skysail on the main. He can run out a ringtail aft and drop a spritsail if it pleases him. Twenty-eight sails, Mister Clay! Though how he'd keep from capsizing if he used half of them God only knows. That snow might go twice its hull speed if he felt the need of it, and there's no question he knows how to handle a ship. Make all standard sail, Mister Clay. The only thing we can do at this point is to go and try to explain this to Captain Watson. Maybe a seventy-four could run that snow to ground, but no brig is going to."

Spotters on the quay watched the brig head north to rendezvous, and in the two days following, vessels of war would slip one by one from Portsmouth, vessels that carried the new ensign with its circle of thirteen white stars on a blue field and its bold red-and-white bars. Some faced battle in these waters; others would take station to the south of Cape Cod while strategies were developed. One, the *Ranger*, made eastward to begin raiding the home islands of King George III.

VII

"The gentleman still sleeps, sir," Billy Caster told Patrick Dalton as the captain came below for his supper. "Mister Hoop said he only swatted him a gentle tap, but I wonder if Mister Hoop knows his own strength."

"Has someone checked to make sure Commander Croney hasn't died?"

"Yes, sir. Mister O'Riley looked in on him."

"Which Mister O'Riley?"

"The cook, sir. Gerald. He has tended stock, so he is well versed in medicine. He pried open the gentleman's eyes, and ran his thumb down his throat and suggested a purgative. He says the gentleman will have a headache, but nothing worse."

"Very well, Mister Caster. Please advise me when Commander Croney comes to his senses."

"Aye, sir. Will you want supper in your cabin, sir?"

"On this occasion, yes. I need to have a chat with Mister Duncan regarding the cargo. He'll be along when he has told off his watch. What is for supper?"

"Boiled oats, sir . . . as usual, though this time Mister O'Riley has added boiled cabbage and some meat that the lads found when they were ashore. He swears it is beef, though he does call it racing beef. He boiled it, sir."

Dalton sighed. One of the drawbacks of a fugitive

77

crew was that he had not found a real cook. Seamen who could prepare palatable dishes were so rare — in any service — that no one ever maintained charges against them no matter what sort of felonies they had committed. He knew of a man who had run amok with a chopping axe and murdered six people in Heathrow, who was now serving parole as senior cook aboard a Blue Fleet first-rate because he could serve up fine plum pudding and a passable kidney pie.

Mister O'Riley's best accomplishment so far was boiled oats.

Wearily, in the relative quiet of his tiny starboard cabin, Dalton took off his coat, stock and weskit and brushed them out for hanging. He pulled off his boots and set them by the hatch for blacking, then he secured his stern gallery, lighted a second lamp and spread out Felix Croney's belongings for inspection. It was the weathered and worn assemblage of a man who has traveled far, by various means. Uniform coat with commander's insignia and the belting of the Royal Guard, a relatively clean shirt and stock, a proper uniform weskit, britches and stockings rolled in with it, and a second set of traveling clothes much like those he wore — gray and dun civilian attire that would go unnoticed in any port either side of the Atlantic: these Dalton perused and put away, feeling the almost automatic distaste of any career military man in the presence of that cloudy and sinister world where the courts of kings and the strange posturings of political appointees were the order of each day.

The valise was far more interesting. In it were sheaves of carefully scribed paper, held in bindings of leather and tortoiseshell. He thumbed through one, and his eyes became speculative. It seemed to be a manual for the conduct of courts martial under Admiralty regulation. He set it aside and opened another, thinner one, and for the first time saw with his own eyes the nature of the charges against him, issued in London as part of a general warrant and transcribed in detail — specifically detailing the charges against Lieutenant Patrick X. Dalton, HMS: treason against the Crown, conspiracy to commit sedition, aiding and abetting by way of association . . .

He closed the file and set it aside, anger smoldering within him. Association with the Fitzgerald, it said. Treason by way of acquaintance. The idiots. The bloody, hot-headed idiots. Had it never occurred to them that the only way any unlanded Dubliner might have been associated with the old firebrand chieftain was through attempts to attract the notice of his pretty daughter? Couldn't they have at least inquired as to whether the Fitzgerald knew *him?* Dalton doubted that the old man did, really. He was just another unwelcome suitor that Molly Fitzgerald's father had set the churls on.

Molly Fitzgerald. Pretty Molly. Dalton tried now to bring her face to mind — her dark-bright eyes, her impish laugh — and found that he could not exactly recall her. Instead, each time he tried, another image came to mind and lingered there. Constance Ramsey.

Molly Fitzgerald had faded from his mind so that he could no longer quite imagine her, but the vision of Constance Ramsey that lived there was far more vivid than that other had ever been.

He wondered where the old chieftain was now. Sean Quinlan O'Day, Lord Fitzgerald, head of clan Fitzgerald of Dunreagh — fiery, arrogant old rebel — probably he rested now in one of Gay Georgie's famous gaols, if he was not already dead. And what, exactly, had *his* crimes been, that spread their taint of guilt to even chance acquaintances? Probably he had owned something that someone of the British peerage — someone not Irish — coveted. It might have been nothing more than that.

Full dark of chill night lay upon the sea now, and *Fury* rocked rhythmically as six-foot seas drummed her starboard quarter, pushed by a steady offshore wind that held at twenty-two knots and carried the scent of winter on its frosty breath. With the Halibut Point light hard-down abeam, the snow ran on courses and tops, holding a comfortable twelve knots with fresh eyes in her trestle-trees and fresh hands on helm and sheets. It had been a bit of luck that they had cleared the blockaded waters off Portsmouth without a fight, although Dalton had expected no exchange. The brig standing off the break-waters could not have guessed that a deep-draft vessel might come out under sail, and rare was the British officer who could judge the speed of a snow. They were used to brigs, and many among them might mistake a snow for a brig—until they saw it in action.

The empire has become complacent, Dalton told himself. Our shipbuilders repeat their designs and patterns, and our mariners repeat their mistakes. We underestimate the determination of those who oppose us, and we underestimate the craft of our subjects.

It was American shipbuilders who had seen the limitations of the brig design and recognized what could be done to modify it. They deepened the keel to give it balance under formidable weight of sail, then set a jack-mast behind the main and proceeded to pile on canvas as though the modest little craft were a heavy frigate. The result was *Fury* and others of her breed, and Dalton felt a savage exhilaration in the handling of her. Fast and sure, lithe and quick to respond, she had the legs to outpace anything of her hull class and the teeth to stand and fight if necessary.

Still, there had been luck in the latest escape—favorable wind, favoring tide, a vessel of exceptional design and the luck of the Irishman at her helm. How many more times would such luck stand by him?

With the action past, the dour mood that had haunted him of late returned. How long can one trust to chance? he wondered. At what point does the fox in chase turn and confront the hounds? How long can a fugitive blow blindly with the winds before he must confront the issue of being a fugitive?

Billy Caster brought his supper from the galley, and he stared at the unappetizing mess that was Mister O'Riley's best effort. "What of the cargo, Mister Caster?"

"I've begun inventory, sir. We have a harpsichord, a kettledrum . . ."

"I mean the human parts of it, Mister Caster. I presume those people have been fed and attended?"

"For the moment, sir. They are all in the fore hold, and some extra hammocks have been slung."

"Thank you, Mister Caster. I shall need a register — both people and implements — of what is to be considered cargo. Also a factor's warrant, if such can be had. Have the ship's stores been inventoried yet, so that Mister O'Riley can. . . ?" He paused, noticing suddenly that the boy was on the verge of exhaustion. "Mister Caster, belay all that for now. Get some rest."

"Sir, I don't mind . . ."

"I said belay that." Dalton stood, stepped to the hatch and looked out. Just across, at the port cabin's hatch, Michael Romart squatted with a rifle across his knees. Dalton's appearance brought the colonial to his feet. "Mister Romart, is our prisoner still unconscious?"

"Was a moment ago, sir. I checked."

"Very well, Mister Romart. Please step inside and bring out Mister Caster's personal effects . . . and also a hammock."

"Aye, sir." Romart ducked through the portside hatch. A moment later Dalton heard a distinct thump from beyond; then Romart reappeared with an armload of items. "This seems to be the lot, sir. Where should I put it?"

"In my cabin, please, for the time being."

"Aye, sir."

"What was that sound in the cabin, Mister Romart? It sounded like someone falling."

"Well, it *was* someone falling, sir, you might say.

There was only one bunk in the cabin, and the prisoner was on it. So I rolled him off, sir. He's sleeping on the deck now, and didn't complain at all."

Dalton stood in the companionway while Romart placed Billy Caster's logs, rosters, writing tools and personal items in the starboard cabin and suspended the hammock in a corner by the gallery. Charley Duncan came down the ladder from the deck as Romart resumed his place at guard. The redhead ducked under a deckbrace, flipped a salute and said, "You wanted to see me, Cap'n?"

"Aye, Mister Duncan, I certainly did. Please step inside. Thank you, Mister Romart."

"Aye, sir."

Dalton followed Duncan into the cabin and closed the hatch. His "first officer" removed his hat and glanced at him sheepishly.

"I expect it's about our cargo, Cap'n? Some of the lads told me that yerself had seemed a bit taken aback at what I'd managed to secure. . . ."

"Who told you that, Mister Duncan?"

"Well, sir, there was Mister Romart, and Mister Locke, and Mister Mallory—he was the first one that suggested that I might be in for a bit of weather, beggin' your pardon, sir—and Misters Fisk and Bean told me. . . . Then of course Misters Crosby and Pugh expressed some doubts about lashing a harpsichord onto a gundeck, though when Mister Wise asked them where they thought I might put it, they enjoyed some unkind remarks at my expense. . . . Then when we changed watch and you called for me, sir, Mister Tidy suggested that I should batten down for a blow."

"Very well, Mister Duncan. You appear to have received the message that I was displeased to have an orchestra aboard."

"Aye, sir. Are you, sir?"

"You might say so, Mister Duncan. What in God's name are we supposed to do with a fifteen-member orchestra?"

"Deliver them to Baltimore, sir. Or Philadelphia, if they have finished fighting there. And there is some question, sir, as to whether it is a fifteen-member orchestra. One of the gentlemen seemed a trifle reluctant to come along. . . ."

"That's Mister Miller, sir," Billy Caster's voice came from the shadows beneath the gallery, where he was sorting his lists and jot-notes. "He is the harpsichordist. He says he has been kidnapped."

"We didn't kidnap anybody, Captain," Duncan assured him. "I made a deal fair and square for the delivery of one orchestra to a Chesapeake port, an' since we are going that way anyway, as you said . . ."

"An orchestra is hardly cargo, Mister Duncan, even if this vessel—which is intended to be a fighting ship, though presently unemployed as such—were to carry cargo, those people are *people,* and therefore passengers. I can understand—barely—how one might have misunderstood the securing of cargo. But did you feel you had leave to place *passengers* aboard this ship?"

"No, sir." Duncan assured him. "I know better than that, sir. That's why I only took that lot on as cargo."

"Cargo." Dalton slumped onto a gallery stool, shaking his head. "Paid cargo, I believe you said?"

"Aye, sir." Duncan withdrew a sheaf of papers from his shirt. "Mister Hickman—ah, Alfred Hickman, sir. He is their manager, and a fine sort he is—somewhere here I have his promissory note, that passage will be paid at Baltimore or Philadelphia, whichever one the war isn't at when we get there." He extended the papers to Dalton, but Billy Caster came and took them. He carried them to the hanging lamp to read through them.

"This is a promissory note, right enough, sir," the clerk said. "And here is a list of the members and their instruments, though I don't see a harpsichord here, or anyone named Miller."

"Well, we got 'em both," Duncan said, proudly. "Worst

part of the transfer, too. That harpsichord is clumsy as the very devil, and that Miller . . . you wouldn't believe the ruckus he raised, the whole way. I had to offer to knock him in the head before he'd quiet down."

"Mister Hickman describes the ensemble as being all indentures, sir," Billy said, still reading the papers that Duncan had brought. "They were indentured to a Newport gentleman who had them perform at social gatherings. But the Newport gentleman took a ball through his sitting-room gallery, and his widow's brother doesn't care for chamber music, so they have decided to earn their own way as a touring orchestra to pay off their indentures."

"Remarkable," Dalton muttered.

"They have a string quartet, a woodwind ensemble, and they have been performing the works of Mozart as well as some of the better-known composers." Billy's eyes widened. "One of them claims to be Zoltan Ferrestrekov, sir!"

Dalton blinked. "Who is Zoltan Ferrestrekov?"

"Why, he is a bassoon, sir. I mean, he plays the bassoon. He is very famous . . . or so I've heard."

"An orchestra," Dalton said to himself.

"Aye, sir." Duncan beamed. "I heard them play, myself. They have all kinds of fiddles and some thumpy drums, and horns and things."

"Cello and viola," Billy recited from the manifest, "first and second violins, bassoon . . . Do you suppose the man really is Zoltan Ferrestrekov, sir? And oboe, clarinet, flute, another flute, a French horn, trumpet, kettledrum . . ."

"Mister Caster . . ."

"I certainly don't see a harpsichord, though."

"Billy!"

"Aye, sir?"

"That is enough about the orchestra. Go to your hammock and go to sleep. We shall sort this all out in the morning."

84

"Aye, sir." Billy put the papers with his ship's log and other materials. "Their conductor's name is Galante Pico, sir."

"And I suppose he is famous, as well?"

"I don't know, sir. I never heard of him." Billy headed for his night's rest, his head swimming with the idea of having a famous bassoonist just fifty or sixty feet away, in the forward hold.

"You surely don't intend to turn back, do you, Cap'n?" Duncan looked worried.

"Of course not."

The redhead brightened. "Then does that mean we can keep them, sir? The orchestra, I mean?"

"Short of putting the whole lot over the side, I don't see what other choice we have." Dalton shook his head, bleakly. On top of everything else—a harpsichord on his gundeck. "Please resume your watch, Mister Duncan. We will discuss this further by day's light."

"Aye, sir. Have a pleasant night's rest, sir."

When Duncan was gone, Dalton paced the tiny cabin for a time, then settled himself at the galley table under the hanging lamp and opened again the leather-and-tortoiseshell wallet that he had found among Felix Croney's possessions. For a time he stared at the fixed volume whose title was imprinted in scroll lettering on its cover page: *His Majesty in Council—Articles of Procedure—Governing the Conduct of Courts Martial Extraordinary—Regulations for the Exercise of Magistracy for and by the Lord High Admiral.*

The document was dated at several different years, the earliest being 1731 and the most recent 1773. Some annotations and explanations had been appended over the years, but what Dalton was looking at, he knew, was the rules and procedures for the conduct of courts martial at sea. He knew there were such procedures, but had never actually seen them. Such matters were generally not the province of junior officers.

He rubbed tired eyes with impatient knuckles, opened the document and began reading . . . And somewhere deep in his mind, something said that just possibly he might count on the luck of the Irish just one more time.

VIII

Shifting winds brought high clouds by morning, and *Fury* cruised southward in a world without horizons. Rolling gray seas broke at the snow's bow and faded into milky distance all around—gray above and gray below with nothing to give perception of distance. "Sailing in a bottle," old salts called such weather, and kept wary eyes on the luff of their canvas. Times of dead calm sometimes followed.

"Wind is eighteen knots by the gauge, sir," Cadman Wise reported as Patrick Dalton sent fresh lookouts aloft. He would change spotters each two hours while this weather held. Even the best of eyes tired quickly when there was nothing—not even a horizon—to see. "Log and line reads steady ten."

"Thank you, Mister Wise." Dalton arose from his deck chair just abaft the helm—an odd-seeming chair constructed of shingles and roof timber, a chair constructed in the hold of a long-lost schooner so that a lady might have a comfortable place to sit. It was practically the only item of furnishing that remained of the schooner *Faith*, and he kept it as a memento—of a beautiful ship and a beautiful woman. A nostalgic whim, he admonished himself. *Faith* is gone and Constance only a dream. The bleak mood that had haunted him of late drifted in again, as gray as the day, and he fought it off, stepping to the quarterrail to have a look at *Fury*'s decks. Ahead of him stretched the slim lines of the sleek ship, working decks at pinrail and fiferail stations, interspersed with gundecks, a sloping platform for the bases of the great masts stepped into the snow's keelson to rise high into the gray sky aloft — masts that were the smoothed boles of northern pines, pond-cured and shackled, great towers of timber standing between their webbed shrouds — and beyond it all the jaunty bowsprit with its jutting snout rising above the sea ahead.

Along the rails men came and went, doing the business of manning a ship, some pausing to cast suspicious glances at the cluster of oddly dressed men amidships, others sternly ignoring them.

Dalton shook his head, looking there. Sixteen souls in all, yonder. One was Billy Caster. The rest were cargo. Most of them wore the fusty garb of court musicians — elaborately-emblazoned greatcoats with wide, flared skirts over black velvet knee britches and white stockings. Several wore elaborate curled wigs, though some had divested themselves of these. Several held instruments, and now and then the steady sounds of sea and ship were pierced by eerie wailings as one or another tuned his strings.

Nearby stood the bulky block shape of the tarp-covered harpsichord, belaying lines running from it to gunports at each side, and to the foremast stage.

The companionway hatch opened, and one of the O'Rileys raised his head above the coaming — Donald O'Riley, Dalton decided, noticing the floppy hat he wore. Not the cook, but his mirror-image brother.

At sight of him, the O'Riley blinked, then raised a hand. "Cap'n, sir?"

"Yes, Mister O'Riley?"

"Th' prisoner is awake, sir. He's raisin' quite a ruckus below, demandin' audience with yerself, sir."

"See that he is fed, Mister O'Riley, and look to his comforts. I will see him directly."

"Aye, sir."

The O'Riley disappeared below, and Dalton signaled the bosun. "Mister Wise, please have Mister Duncan report on deck. Tell him I am ready to inspect his cargo."

"Aye, sir."

As Wise started forward, seeking Charley Duncan at the main hold, one of the court-suited figures on the foredeck squinted aft, then broke from the group and strode toward the quarterdeck. Billy Caster hurried after him, protesting.

Dalton watched the man approach. Short, square-shouldered and bowlegged, he looked like a fighting cock in his dandified attire. If he owned a wig, he had discarded it. Brown hair was pulled severely back from a blocky face where wide-set blue eyes burned with indignation.

As he neared, the man frowned up at Dalton. "Are you the captain?"

A pair of deck hands stepped in front of him. "You can't go up there, sir," one said. "That's the quarterdeck."

"I don't give a hang what it is," the man snapped. "Is that your captain there?"

Dalton stepped to the head of the short ladder. "I am the captain," he said. "And who might you be?"

"Joseph Miller," the man said. "Will you tell me why I have been pressed aboard this ship? I am not a sailor; I am a musician."

"Ah." Dalton nodded. "You must belong to that harpsichord. As to why you are aboard *Fury*, sir, I hope to get to the bottom of that very soon."

"I demand that you turn this boat right around and take me back to Portsmouth," Miller rasped. "Squire Landess is going to have a deal to say about all this."

"Oh? And who, pray tell, is Squire Landess?"

"He owns that harpsichord your villains stole."

"It isn't yours?"

"Of course not. I only play it for him."

"Mister Miller says he isn't a member of Mister Pico's orchestra, sir," Billy Caster interrupted. "He says there has been a mistake."

"I can attest to that, your honor!" Another of the court-dressed crew had come aft. "Permit me, sir. Hickman is my name. Alfred Hickman. I have contracted with Señor Pico to manage the business affairs of his ensemble, and I assure you, *Mister* Miller is certainly no part of it. He is nothing more than Squire Landess's house servant, sir."

"Valet!" Miller shouted. "I am personal valet to the squire, not a house servant."

"Well, whatever you are, you are not a member of Galante Pico's ensemble. Mister Pico would never have a harpsichordist who scrambles études as you . . ."

"Insult!" Miller raged. "That fumbling clown doesn't know how to conduct so much as a three-quarter trill, much less a . . ."

Charley Duncan stepped among them, looking up at his captain. "You sent for me, sir?"

"That's the villain who took me!" Miller pointed and stepped back. "That is the very one. Captain, I demand you arrest this man and turn this boat around, immediately!"

"I am ready to inspect cargo, Mister Duncan." Dalton ignored the outburst. "Please assemble all parts and parties aft."

"Aye, sir. Ah . . . could we leave the harpsichord where it's at, sir? Hate to let that thing loose on a rolling deck."

"By all means, Mister Duncan. I can see it very well from here."

"Aye, sir. Mister Hickman, please ask your gentlemen to assemble here—just here will do, beside this jackmast."

90

"Certainly." Hickman turned away, then cast a glare back at Miller. "Lout!" he added.

On the foredeck, people popped in and out of the hold, bringing up various things, and an erratic procession began to move aft.

"I understood you to say that there were only a few instruments, Mister Caster," Dalton said. "It seems to me I see a great many."

"Manner of speaking, sir," Billy said. "For instance, when I said first and second violin, I referred to two positions in the orchestra, not to how many actual fiddles they own. The fact is, they have several. I can make a list if you like."

"I would like that." Dalton frowned as parcels and things kept sprouting from the hold. "A proper cargo manifest should itemize implements, I believe . . . that is the third kettledrum I have seen come up. How many do they have?"

"I believe three is the lot, though of course there is only one timpanist."

"Of course." Dalton shrugged. "I don't expect there are spare harpsichords down there, as well?"

"Oh, no, sir. Only one harpsichord."

"It is Squire Landess's harpsichord," Joseph Miller blurted. "This lot of indentured poltroons couldn't afford a harpsichord if they sold their bumbling souls for it."

A pale Irishman with a bag of flutes glowered at him. "If we had one, we certainly would find a better player for it."

"Quiet in the ranks," Cadman Wise hissed.

"Cargo," Dalton pointed out. "Not ranks, Mister Wise. Cargo."

"Right, sir. Quiet in the cargo. Form up here for Captain's inspection."

Duncan came aft, herding the last of them ahead of him, two of them carrying a drum apiece and one struggling with an armload of fifes and a French horn.

91

Duncan got them arranged in a semblance of presentation order and turned to Dalton. "Sir, may I present our cargo . . . Señor Galante Pico and his continental chamber ensemble."

Alfred Hickman whispered something, and most of the assembled musicians—those not occupied with preserving instruments against the roll of the ship's deck, executed sweeping bows.

Beside Dalton, Billy Caster pointed and whispered, "That one is Zoltan Ferrestrekov, sir. The one with the double mustache and the two bassoons. He's famous, sir."

Hickman stepped forward. "Captain . . . ah . . ."

"Dalton," someone hissed. "His name is Dalton."

"Captain Dalton, allow me to present Galante Pico"—a wiry man with a goatee bowed again—"leader and conductor of this extraordinary group. Señor Pico is"—again the goatee bobbed—"widely acclaimed throughout Europe—at least the civilized portions of it—for his interpretations of the works of Handel and Vivaldi, as well as for having rendered étudinal themes from the more massive compositions of Johann Sebastian Bach. It is said of Señor Pico . . ."

Once again the conductor bowed, and Dalton tipped his head at Hickman. "Does he speak English, sir?"

"Not a word of it, sir."

"Then I suggest you stop saying his name before he becomes seasick. I do not care to have my decks fouled."

"Very well." Hickman looked pained, but continued, "Also we have Herr Sigmund Jodl, cellist of reknown, and Franz Himmelmann, our virtuoso of the viola . . . Tempore DiGaetano and Ansel Cleride, first and second violinists . . ." Cleride bowed. DiGaetano, who had a bruised lip and a black eye, merely glared. "Our timpanist, Vicente Auf . . . and Claude Auber, who plays oboe as well as saxophone. Then here is Gunther Lindholm, clarinetist extraordinaire, and our flute player Sean Callinder . . ." Lindholm nodded curtly and Callinder waved and grinned. ". . . Romeo Napoli, who doubles at trumpet and the keyed cornet . . . Franco Anastasio, our other flute player, and Zoltan Ferrestrekov . . ."

"I told you," Billy chirped.

". . . bassoonist, and Johann Sebastian Nunn of the French horn."

With a gratuitous wave of his hand, Hickman completed his introductions and stood at attention, beaming.

"You left out the harpsichordist," Dalton noted.

"As I said, sir, he isn't one of us. He was only filling in to provide the continuo for certain selections by Herr Wolfgang Amadeus Mozart, where a bit of tonal color is required. He is a servant in the household of . . ."

"Valet!" Miller exploded. "Damn your arrogance, Hickman; you know the difference!"

"Quiet in the cargo," Cadman Wise urged, brandishing a belaying pin.

"An orchestra," Dalton muttered. "How did these people come to be at Portsmouth, Mister Duncan?"

"Well, sir," — the redhead scratched his chin — "all the fiddlers and the like . . . the musicians . . . were indentures brought over by the late Lord Wilsey. He had them to entertain his guests, like. But then when Lord Wilsey's house was bombarded by Whigs — with Lord Wilsey in it at the time — then this Squire Landess bid at auction for their indentures and shipped them all up to New Hampshire, an' he's been having concerts . . ."

"And charging admission," Hickman interrupted. "You see, sir, that is why these accomplished artists decided to strike out on their own. Being put on public display for profit is no part of their conditions of indenture. When he did that, the squire invalidated the contract."

"Squire Landess has good money invested in these people," Joseph Miller snapped. "There is no reason he should not recover his investment."

93

Cadman Wise edged toward Miller, menacingly. "Quiet in cargo, ye popinjay! I won't tell ye again."

"There was some question about whether that squire would relinquish these gentlemen." Duncan nodded. "It was for that reason that we sort of spirited them away, you see."

"I see." Dalton frowned. "And where did you agree to take this . . . orchestra?"

"Like I told you, sir, to Baltimore or Philadelphia, whichever one is doin' business at the moment."

"I plan to schedule a season of engagements for them," Hickman said. "With advance guarantees, of course."

"And how much is *Fury* to realize . . . for the delivery of this cargo?"

"Ten pounds sterling a head, sir," Duncan said. "And another sixty-and-five for all the fiddles and things . . . though I wasn't expecting there would be so many of them. Then again, if the harpsichord doesn't count . . ."

"That instrument is the property of Squire Landess," Miller pointed out, edging away from Cadman Wise.

Dalton closed his eyes for a long breath. "Mister Duncan, in what manner did you obtain this cargo from the squire's house?"

"Well, sir, they was performing an opera there . . ."

"Concert," Hickman corrected. "Señor Pico does not do operas."

"A concert." Duncan nodded. "We went and sort of gathered them all up and spirited them out through an upstairs window while all the guests were otherwise occupied in the drawing room."

"Otherwise occupied, how?"

"Catching pigs, sir. It seems like there was a stam--pede of pigs just about then, an' quite a lot of the porkers came in through these open doors on the garden side, and sort of mingled with the crowd."

Dalton shook his head. "How very timely of them,"

he muttered. "Very well, Mister Caster, since we have no alternative short of putting the lot over the side, please draw up a proper cargo manifest . . . and you men!" He raised his voice and pinned the musicians one by one with cold eyes. "You are to understand that this vessel is a warship, not designed for either passengers or musical instruments. You may make shift in the fore hold, and you will be fed and attended as the crew is fed and attended. I shall expect — in fact I will insist firmly if such is required — that you keep yourselves and your instruments out of the way and off the working decks. You are aware, I trust, that there is a war going on, and we are right in the middle of it."

There was a buzzing among them as some translated his words for others, and Galante Pico spoke rapidly to Alfred Hickman, who turned to Dalton. "They understand all that, sir. But Señor Pico respectfully inquires which side we are on."

"Of what?"

"Of the war, sir. Are we . . . moment, sir. He wants to be very careful in how this is asked, so as not to offend . . ." He listened to Pico again, argued with him for a moment, then shrugged in resignation. "He asks . . . his words, sir . . . are we thieving English tyrants, or barbarian Colonial usurpers?"

The mouths of Charley Duncan and Cadman Wise dropped open. Billy Caster choked and Victory Locke momentarily lost his grip on the helm. *Fury* shivered. Dalton gritted his teeth, keeping his face straight. After a long moment he regained his composure. "Yes," he said, "you might say we are."

"On deck!"

Dalton raised his eyes, seeking the maintop. "Report, tops!"

"Sail, sir!"

"Whereabouts, Mister Fisk?"

"Hard down, sir! Ahead, starboard bow, port a'beam . . . port quarter . . . two there, I make it . . . one

95

astern . . . another on the starboard quarter . . . seven . . . eight . . . maybe more, sir!"

"How do they bear, Mister Fisk?"

"All seem bound westward, sir. Beating and tacking. Lord, sir, we've come right up in the middle of a squadron!"

As Dalton strained his eyes, trying to see from the deck what his spotters could see from the trestletrees, *Fury* seemed to sigh. Her sails drummed, then fluttered and slacked.

"Wind's dying, sir!" John Tidy called from amidships. "She's shifting again, and slacking to calm."

IX

With the shifting of winds and gray mists, what had
been unseen in the milky distances without horizons
now could be seen plainly. While hands went to station
on the decks and in the rigging . . . while musicians
and instruments were whisked unceremoniously into
the slight shelter of the fore hold . . . Dalton turned the
deck to Charley Duncan and went aloft to see for himself.

A squadron indeed. All around *Fury*, at distances
ranging from two or three out to a dozen or more miles,
the sea was alive with ships. Most of them, even from
the maintop, were vague, misty shapes hard down
on the uncertain horizon. But nearer at hand some now
stood clear, and he scanned them with his glass. "Nine,"
he counted. Then, "Ten . . . eleven . . ." There could
be still more out there somewhere, shrouded by distance and the milky fine mists. One by one, he glassed
the nearer ones. Four-masters, mostly. There and there
were tall barks, beyond a trio of ship-rigged broad-bel-
lies that might have been converted galleons. Another
pair were lesser three-mast cargo vessels, and one
barely visible in the distance might have been a refitted
ketch. He read the colors on a bark and knew them for
what they were — troopships and supply packets, mak-

ing for His Majesty's fleet headquarters at New York. Fresh troops for Clinton's garrison there, or possibly to strengthen Howe or Cornwallis to the south. His glass roved further, seeking what he knew must accompany a troop convoy. After a moment he found one of the escorts, and whistled in awe. A ship of the line. A seventy-four, hard down and just visible in the tricky atmosphere. There would be others as well — a second seventy-four, he guessed, and maybe two or three frigates. Such a convoy would be well guarded.

He sighted again on the distant seventy-four, wondering what ship it was. Probably one that had been doing service in these waters — a ship of the White Fleet, gone out on signal to contact and escort the convoy. Unlikely, considering the tensions between England and France — and between England and Spain — that the Admiralty would have drawn warships from the Blue Fleet to do transatlantic escort. More likely that some Blues had escorted part of the way — possibly as far as the "turnabouts" east of Nova Scotia where the season's winds could assure them of a quick dash back to service off Gibraltar — and vessels of the White Fleet had run up to meet them there and bring them to American harbor. Admirals would stand to certain courtesies among themselves, but the admiral of the Blue would balk for certain at diminishing his fleet for a season, just to escort troops to Lord Richard Howe, admiral of the White. Woolsey had his own fish to fry.

The big warship lay hull down, miles away, yet something of its high rigging seemed familiar to Dalton. He was sure it was a vessel he had seen before.

Michael Romart had come aloft with a glass of his own, and perched on the trestletree with Dalton and the lookout, also squinting at the distant warship. "He's seen us, too," the American said. "He probably wonders who we are. Should we fly some color, Cap'n?"

"Not just yet," Dalton decided. "He can hardly overtake us from where he is, beating into the wind. Possibly we can just fail to see him, and slip quietly away."

"If the wind holds," Romart said, glancing up at the flying gauge. It hung lethargic, its flutter slow. "Not more than twelve knots, and slacking."

Dalton glanced around. "Do you wager it will come to calm, Mister Romart? Or will it hold a breeze for a time?"

Romart blinked, wondering why the captain should ask him such a thing. Most aboard were able seamen, and could fare the weather passably well, but few had the wizard's touch that Dalton had when it came to predicting what would happen next. "I don't know, sir, but we've been sailing in a bottle since first light, and I've seen calms come of this."

"I have, as well," Dalton said. "But mind how it has shifted in the past hour. We were on broad reach all morning, but now we have it aft our starboard quarter. There is no clear signal what it might do."

"That near troopship ahead is watching us closely, sir," the fore lookout called.

Dalton turned his glass. The nearest of the sailing barks, barely two miles away and on a tight converging course, had spotters in its tops now and was keeping an eye on the snow. Dalton watched the spread of ships ahead and to port, estimated their speed and calculated wind-course. On tight tack for square-riggers, almost sixty degrees off the wind, they were beating westward with bare steerageway, their forward speed hardly a quarter of *Fury*'s even with the sluggish winds in the snow's sails. The nearest one balked slightly at a gust, waggled its masts, then settled back to its creeping pace. Should the wind hold just as it was now, and no sail be changed, *Fury* would pass within a few cables of that bark's stem, then sometime later pass astern of the next one out — it was at least six miles distant, ghostly in the milky atmosphere. Beyond that one, he saw nothing more. There might be another escort vessel out

99

there on windward flank, but if so it was not in sight, and he felt a slight relief. The convoy had spread itself over half an ocean, it seemed, in its sluggish process against unfriendly winds. They might have had these conditions for days, and would surely have been fighting the Atlantic Stream as well, and each captain had done his maneuvers with an eye to keeping way. As a result, they were a scattered flock, miles of ocean between one ship and another.

If the wind held, *Fury* would simply stroll through the flock and be on her way, with no need to confront anyone.

If the wind held.

And if there wasn't another heavy warship somewhere upwind that might grow curious about an unidentified snow in the midst of the convoy, and come to have a look.

As if reading his mind, Michael Romart had his glass turned aft, sweeping the indistinct horizon from west to north. "I don't see any more," he said. "Doesn't mean they're not out there . . . in this murk who can say?. . . but there's nothing nearby at any rate."

"The bark is only curious, nothing more," Dalton noted. "No surprise, really. If these transports have been relayed from Blue to White in midocean, there's a good chance they'll think we're just another escort vessel."

"That seventy-four out there isn't going to think that."

"He might think we're a messenger, though—or a king's ship just passing through, if we are civil about it. Let's go back on deck, Mister Romart. We have eyes enough up here for the moment."

Romart hesitated. "I'm fresh, sir. Let me relieve Mister Abbott here at maintop. I'll keep a good eye on things."

"Very well, Mister Romart." Dalton suppressed a grin. The Colonial was covering his bets. Here they

100

were surrounded by English shipping, with English eyes in their tops, and the American would naturally favor having an American point of view involved. Dalton had no argument with that. Michael Romart was one of the original *Faiths*, as was Ishmael Bean at fore lookout. He could ask for no more loyal and capable seamen than either of them, whatever their politics.

He put his glass away in a tail pocket and swarmed down the port shroud as nimbly as any topman might, with Noel Abbott pacing him down the starboard. They stepped to the rails, swung inboard and Dalton waved a bosun over. "Mister Romart has replaced Mister Abbott at maintop. Mister Abbott can go to the foresheets."

"Aye, sir. What have we got ourselves into, sir?"

"A troop convoy, Mister Wise. Mostly mercenaries, I'd wager, on their way to harass General Washington."

"Aye, sir. One might wish they would get it done smartly. This ocean is getting right crowded."

"It is that, Mister Wise." He peered ahead. Though the shifting wind had given *Fury* a better bearing for her sails, its velocity had dropped again and the snow crept along at only seven or eight knots, closing steadily on the nearest transport, which was beating westward at two or three. No more than a mile separated the two vessels now, and the transport bark stood like a stumbling giant off *Fury*'s port bow. In sheer size, any of the transports would dwarf the snow, but such comparisons at sea meant little. The bark was designed for carrying things from place to place. *Fury* was designed to fight. Were they to confront, even though the transport carried guns, there would be little contest.

The same could not be said of the convoy's escorts. They too were warships, and Dalton very much doubted whether there was anything among them less than a frigate. He had seen the great seventy-four in the distance, a fine big fighting ship twice the size of any frigate—meaning at least four times the size of the snow—and where there was one seventy-four there might be others, and frigates as well.

That seventy-four . . . Why did it seem familiar to him? He reflected on the dim, distant silhouette. It was nothing specific, maybe nothing more than the manner in which its masters chose to trim to the wind . . . Still, he felt he should recognize it.

He returned to the quarterdeck and resumed command from Duncan. "We have blundered into a troop convoy, Mister Duncan," he said. "With any degree of luck, though, we should clear those two freighters yonder and pass on by without particular notice."

"If the wind holds," Duncan said, frowning as he gazed aloft.

"Aye, if the wind holds. Take the maindeck, Mister Duncan, and have an eye to our appearance as before. It was important at Portsmouth that we seem a Colonial privateer, but that certainly is the last thing I'd want to be taken for just now."

"Aye, sir. That could be uncomfortable, couldn't it?"

"Distinctly." He frowned. "Please drop a cloth over that fore hold, to assure that none of our cargo takes the notion to wander about on deck, and have Misters Tower, O'Riley and O'Riley remain below for the time being. They don't pass well for British."

"Aye." Duncan cocked a brow, looking along the deck. "There is that harpsichord yonder. I wonder what it can pass for?"

"Just keep it covered, Mister Duncan, and hope that no one comes to ask."

"On deck!"

"Aye, Mister Romart?"

"Sir, that seventy-four to the east, it's putting on more sail and making about to match our course!"

"Whereaway, Mister Romart?"

"Due a'beam, sir. Hull and courses down. Maybe ten miles or so; it's hard to tell."

"Something has made him curious, then." Dalton ran

102

practiced eyes over *Fury*'s masts and spars. "Let us have more sail, Mister Wise. Tops and royals, and run out the studdingsails. Helm, two points a'port, please. Signals, advise the bark that we will pass astern. Also ask him if he has any sightings to report."

"Aye, sir. Sightings, sir?"

"Something to amuse him." Dalton nodded. "While we are about it, please ask him to identify the ships of his escort, and run up the white jack." He cupped his hands and shouted aloft, "Mister Romart!"

"Aye, sir?"

"Would you judge that the seventy-four yonder can see our signal hoists?"

"Not unless he has a glass at his t'gallant spar, sir. He is well down as yet."

If I were he, Dalton told himself, I would indeed have a glass in the high yards right now. Still, he had no better plan.

With new sails and a tailwind course before the faltering breeze, *Fury* revived a bit and added a pair of knots to her way. Signals rose on their hoists, and the white-fielded fleet flag on its halyard, and the approaching bark responded, bright buntings running up its various lines in signal sequence.

"He says pass astern if you please, sir, but don't cut close and block his wind. He hasn't any to spare." Again buntings rose and the message was read and relayed. "He says there are four escorts, sir. A ship of the line and three frigates."

Dalton made a guess. "Ask him why there aren't more, signals. Tell him I expected at least two line-of-battle ships."

He waited, while elaborate signals ran up and were answered. Then the relay came, "He says there should have been more, sir, but one battler and some cruisers were told off to blockade a rebel coast. His signalman adds that in his captain's opinion, things have gotten thoroughly mucked up of late."

103

"Who is the line ship escorting him? And ask him where it is, as though we had not seen it."

Again the buntings flew. Less than a half-mile separated the two vessels now, with *Fury* on her new course cutting toward the long wake of the bark.

"He says the battler is standing back to harry stragglers. He hasn't seen it just lately. The frigates are two at flank and one at point."

We're squarely in the middle of this matter, Dalton noted, feeling the tension return to his shoulders. We wander among transports here, with frigates blind to the north, east and south, and a seventy-four east that has seen us and wants a better look.

"The battler yonder is the *Cornwall*, sir. A seventy-four. He says his tops have it nine miles astern and angling southward on a broad reach. He offers to relay our message, if you would like."

"Thank him, signals, but say our message is fleet communication for another seventy-four."

They could clearly see the faces of crew and passengers lining the starboard rail of the transport now. Hundreds of them, all except the dozen or so sailors wearing the gray and crimson of Hessian mercenaries. Some of those on *Fury*'s fore waved, and the waves were returned.

Hesse Castle must be a lonely place for the women there, Dalton thought. They are selling their young men to King George by the tens of thousands. Closer still, now, he could see other uniforms among the young Hessians—red tunics of Royal Marines, and the gaudy uniforms of Prussian officers and sergeants. If all the transports were loaded as this one was, the convoy must be bringing an entire regiment of Germans to throw at the beleaguered colonists.

"He signals that the other battler that was supposed to come for them was HMS *Royal Lineage*, sir. But she went north under separate orders . . . Moment, sir, something else . . . He asks what sort of brig this is,

104

that it carries a jackmast and studdingsails."

The big bark was dead ahead now and passing, struggling with uncertain winds that boomed and fluttered its hard-hauled sails.

"On deck!"

"Aye, Mister Romart?"

"New sails, sir, aft and a quarter a'starboard, just down. It's a frigate, sir, ranging back this way on the wind, flying an advisory."

"Signals, read that signal, if you can, please."

"Aye, sir." A long moment passed, as the bark's stern cleared *Fury*'s course at a distance of three cables. "It's the land ho, sir. The frigate is telling the convoy that they are sixty miles from port. He asks all ships to relay, and form up in proper convoy."

"Thank you, signals." Dalton grinned, then suppressed it. There was no room for laxity aboard a proper ship. "Let us give them a hand, then. Please relay that signal, and add 'immediately' to the message."

The signals flew, and the four or five transports within sight responded. For several miles around *Fury*, big ships hauled sail for fresh tacks, homing toward the still-distant frigate.

Charley Duncan came from the bow and joined Dalton on the quarterdeck. "That should amuse them, sure enough." The redhead grinned. "If that frigate yonder doesn't amend the signal, it is going to be up to its scuppers in troop transports very soon."

"Give him something to hold his attention." Dalton shrugged. "I don't fancy a footrace with a frigate in these waters."

At a luffing eight knots, *Fury* passed well astern of the first bark, and pointed her stem at the next one out, just now making about for a new tack in response to his appended signal. It was a half-mile ahead, a ship that was the twin of the one they had just passed.

"On deck!"

"Aye, Mister Romart?"

"Sir, that seventy-four is still on course with us, and angling a bit. I make her eight miles out now."

Dalton wasn't surprised. With the seventy-four identified, he knew her and knew why her attitude had seemed familiar with him. The man commanding her was an old acquaintance, a figure from his days amidships, the nemesis of his classroom years: Senior Captain Peter Selkirk. "Old Hawser," he had been called, and he would not be one to be distracted by the ploys and amusements of a fugitive vessel trying to escape. If Hawser set himself to bring *Fury* to ground, then sooner or later, Dalton knew, he would find himself under the guns of the seventy-four. Captains of transports might be confused by false signals. Captains of brigs might misjudge a snow's ability to exit a harbor under sail. Even a frigate's master might be distracted by erratic behavior of convoyed vessels. But not Captain Peter Selkirk.

Dalton prayed for luck now, prayed that Selkirk might find the game not worth the playing. Once before, Dalton had been at the man's mercy—had in fact been on the deck of the *Cornwall,* with his salvaged ketch *Mystery* helpless under its guns. For his own reasons, whatever they were, Selkirk had let him go—a decision involving honor, circumstance and the old man's unyielding personal ethic of conduct.

Could he count on such again? Probably not. Hawser's message had been clear enough. Stay out of this conflict, Patrick, and stay out of my way from here on.

Long minutes eased by, and *Fury* closed toward the second troopship. With its change of course, he angled to pass ahead of it, beam to stem, and signaled his intention. The ship responded, as the other had, with the indifference of a captain whose task it is to deliver troops to foreign shores and who does not concern himself with the vagaries of fleet maneuvers.

Fury drifted along at six or seven knots, her sails spread high and wide to catch as much of the faltering wind as she could, and angled ahead of the bark at two chains' length—then faltered, trembled and settled into the swells.

"Losing way on the helm, sir!"

"The wind has failed, Captain!"

"We're adrift, sir."

Even before he could respond, the last breath of the prodigal wind huffed out, and sails fell slack on their yards to hang dead-calm. The snow drifted on a few tens of yards, then lay still, and barely fifty yards away the great bark stood lifeless, towering over the little warship, its hands staring up at their own lifeless sails.

Needlessly, Billy Caster said, "We've lost the wind, sir."

Ahead of the quarterrail, the companion hatch thudded open and John Tidy's head appeared, his eyes wide. "Cap'n, your prisoner has got loose. He put a knot on Mister Unser's head and we can't find him."

X

The calm held, and a dozen hands began a systematic search belowdecks for the escaped Felix Croney while deck crew and topmen secured hatches and galleries to seal the ship, and odd sounds wafted from the forward hold where Galante Pico's orchestra had taken advantage of the motionless condition to begin a rehearsal.

Dalton was about to send Cadman Wise to belay the music, when Billy Caster, staring across forty yards of water at the great hull of the transport bark, said, "Sir, we seem to be amusing them."

Dalton hesitated, looking at the nearby ship, then changed his mind. By the hundreds, men lined the rails and hung out of chutes and gunports, curious faces scrutinizing the odd little warship off their bow. Dozens of them, crew and fighting troops alike, had swarmed up to the lower yards and sat there now elbow-to-elbow like so many birds on a rafter beam. It was probably, Dalton realized, the first entertainment they had encountered since putting out from Land's End.

A ship's officer, a young man in the groggin coat of merchant marine, pressed to the bow rail and raised a speaking horn. "Captain's compliments," he called, "and are you having difficulties aboard that we might help with?"

Dalton waved while Billy Caster disappeared down the companion hatch and returned with a speaking horn. Dalton took it and responded, "We are well under control, thank you."

"Aye, but you seem to be practicing a seal-and-search, so the captain wondered."

"We've a prisoner aboard," Dalton told him. "He's out of his quarters just now, so we are securing until we locate him. Wouldn't want him to make deck and fall overboard, at least until he's been properly questioned."

The officer relayed the information back to the stern of the big transport, then raised his horn again. "Captain wants to know what sort of prisoner you have. Rebel officer, or spy, or saboteur or what?"

"Compliments to your captain," Dalton called, "and tell him we aren't sure just what the man is. We plucked him out of a rebel port at New Hampshire. Word is, he tries to pass himself off as a king's officer."

"Spy, then." The transport officer nodded sagely while the message was passed along. "Jolly well hope you get him secured before he blows up your ship or something. We're a bit close for comfort here."

"We have sealed the magazines and blocked off the stores. There's precious little damage he can do, unless it's to himself."

The bark officer leaned his elbows on his bow rail, conversationally. "We had a deserter two trips back, that tried to hide in the chain locker. Can you imagine anybody doing that? Of course, we found him when we dropped anchor . . . You know what happens in the chain locker when the hobs are dropped."

Dalton suppressed a shiver, imagining it.

"A few bits of him popped out through the port chute," the man went on. "Most of him was still in there, though, but he was splattered all over the place. Not hardly a piece left that was still connected to any other piece. Brought him out in buckets, we did. Bloody mess."

"I can well imagine," Dalton called back, then turned to Cadman Wise. "Have some of the lads search the chain locker, Mister Wise. Our friend might just be barmy enough to have gone there."

"Can't help noticing," the bark officer said, "what lyrical strains and groans seem to come from your direction. How do you manage that?"

"We have an orchestra aboard." Dalton shrugged.

The speaker's eyes went wide, along with the eyes of several around him. "An orchestra? You blokes carry an orchestra on your vessels? When did that start?" He turned, pointing the horn aft. "The brig has an orchestra. That's where all the racket is coming from."

The coaming sprouted a tar-hatted head. "Found him, Cap'n. He was in the bleedin' chain locker. You want him brought up?"

"Absolutely not! Get him back to the port cabin and sit on him if you have to. I'll be down directly."

"Aye, sir."

Dalton turned his horn toward the bark again. "Thank you for your suggestion, sir. We have recovered our prisoner. He was in the chain locker."

"The chain locker!" The man shook his head in wonder. "Doesn't that just beat all."

The sounds in the fore grew in volume, then erupted in discord and ceased, then started again. Dalton stared aloft, frowning. The weather was unreadable. It might come around to blow again, or the calm might hold for an indefinite period. He put away his speaking horn and hooked a thumb at Charley Duncan. "Take the deck, Mister Duncan, while I go below and interview Commander Croney. Keep Misters Crosby and Pugh at idle near those portside guns, just in case anyone becomes hostile, but let's have no linstock showing. Wouldn't do to have several hundred subjects of the Crown suspect we aren't who we seem to be."

"Aye, sir. Shall we reef for tow, in case it doesn't begin blowing again?"

110

"Not just yet. Hold all sail for now. Should we get a wind, there is a seventy-four yonder and a frigate back there who'll have it, too."

As Dalton started for the ladder there was a commotion in the bow and a sailor came hurrying aft. "Sir . . ." He looked from Dalton to Duncan, unsure who was presently in charge of the deck. "Ah, sirs, the musicians seem to be having a conflict in the fore hold, and that Mister Hickman wonders whether it would be all right for him to send that Mister Miller on deck so he can play the . . . that thing yonder. He says without it they don't have a proper . . . ah . . . they aren't satisfied with how they sound."

"Mister Miller claims he isn't a member of that group," Duncan pointed out.

Before the rail, Cadman Wise cocked a brow toward them. "If the captain wants him to come up and play, sir, I expect we can persuade him to do that."

Dalton glanced aside at the big transport drifting just off *Fury's* beam. Everywhere from rails to ratlines to coursetops to the butt of the jib, men had made themselves comfortable and were watching the little warship, simply being entertained.

"I think that might be a fair notion," Dalton decided. "Bring them all up and let them assemble forward of the foremast. Have them play some tunes. The more we can amuse those people over there, the less likely they are to notice that we aren't exactly Royal Navy."

"Aye, sir." Duncan grinned. "See to that, please, Mister Wise. Some music might be just the thing." Cupping his hands he shouted at the bark, "Settle yourselves, gentlemen. We are about to have a concert." That attended to, he went below.

At the hatch of the portside cabin, Paul Unser crouched with a club in his hand and a bandage on his head. He looked as bleak as the coastline of his native Maine. At sight of Dalton he got to his feet. "Sorry about the prisoner, sir. He got behind me and bounced a

111

candlestick off my head. I'll see he's watched better after this."

"Never mind, Mister Unser," Dalton reassured the man. "No harm done, so far as we know. What is that sound he's making in there?"

"I'd call it groaning, sir. Mister Hoop is sitting on the bugger."

Dalton opened the hatch and ducked through, then stopped, letting his eyes adjust. With its stern gallery sealed, the only light in the little cabin came from prisms set into the tiller deck overhead. That deck, in turn, was shadowed by the quarterdeck at the stern, so very little light came through. It was a minor oversight on the part of those who had designed and built *Fury*. While many brigs and most snows now had wheel helms, not all of them sported quarterdecks. The skylight prisms in the stern cabins had been carefully installed in the tiller deck, according to custom, though hardly any light ever came through them. No two ships of the time were ever exactly alike, and *Fury* had her foibles, just as any other might.

For a moment it was hard to make out the shadows in the cabin; then his eyes adjusted. Felix Croney lay face-down on the cabindeck, writhing and groaning, with Mister Hoop sitting on his back.

"You said take the scutter below an' sit on him, Cap'n." The big man beamed. "So that's just what I'm doing."

"I expect you can get off him now, Mister Hoop. I need to talk with him, and this is hardly a proper situation for discourse."

"Aye, sir." The big man got to his feet, stooped in the short confines of the cabin, and lifted Felix Croney with a massive hand to set him on his feet. "Cap'n will have a word with you," he rumbled. "Mind yer manners."

"You can wait outside, Mister Hoop."

"Aye, sir." Hoop crunched himself through the hatch and closed it behind him.

112

Dalton waved a hand at the gallery bench. "Please sit down, Commander. You look somewhat the worse for wear."

The man glared at him in the dim light. "Who are you, sir, and what do you want of me?" Then he stepped closer, peering up, and his breath hissed. "By the good God," he said. "You're Dalton."

"That's right, we haven't met, have we?" Dalton snapped a quick, correct salute. "Patrick Dalton, sir. Lieutenant senior, His Majesty's White Fleet . . . presently, ah, detached and in command of this vessel which is my own by right of seizure, the snow *Fury*."

"Traitor!" Croney pointed a shaky finger at him. "Turncoat fugitive! I vowed I'd run you down. I arrest you, sir, by order of His Majesty's general warrant . . ."

"I know about the warrant, Commander. I read it, along with other documents in your possession. I have a great many questions for you, sir, and I shall expect answers. But first, what did you have in mind, that would require a special warrant on me, a schedule of charges and incidents, all those affidavits and a . . . what was that other? Ah, yes . . . an *Order in Council for the appointment at sea or elsewhere of a Judge Advocate under provision of Section 65 of the Naval Discipline Act?* I am intrigued, Commander. Tell me, what was it you intended to do when you captured me?"

Croney's eyes glinted. "Exactly what should be done with traitors and saboteurs. I intend to take you before the nearest qualified officer and have you tried before court martial, convicted and punished." He paused, scowling up at the tall young man. "Well?"

"Well, what?" Dalton's face was expressionless.

"Do you submit to arrest?"

"I can't think why I should. At least not at the moment. Oh, do sit down and relax, Commander Croney. I am not planning to attack you."

Croney eased back toward the bench. "I have already been attacked."

"Yes, that was my man Hoop. He's a good lad, and as loyal as they come. And you know, we could hardly allow you to complete your signal from that bell tower. As it was, we barely got away."

"Along with your other felonies, Dalton, you have interfered with a king's officer in the performance of his duty."

"Oh, nonsense, Commander." Dalton drew up a stool and sat himself on it. "We probably saved your hide by intervening when we did. I don't expect those New Hampshire Colonials would have taken kindly to a king's officer using their bell tower to send intelligence to ships of the king, do you?"

Croney backed to the far end of the bench and perched on it, warily.

"I find it hard to understand," Dalton said, "why you have pursued me so zealously, all the way from New York to the southern colonies, then up to New England. When I first heard of it, I assumed you to be some sort of zealot . . . a man obsessed, possibly because I had escaped your guards. But since reading some of your correspondence, I believe I understand."

"You are a traitor and a renegade, Dalton."

"*Captain* Dalton, please, Commander. Or *Lieutenant* Dalton, if you prefer, but I must insist you do me the honor of protocols, either for my position aboard this ship or for my rank in His Majesty's service."

"You have forfeited . . ."

"I have not been convicted, Commander. Only accused. Tell me, then . . . If I should submit myself to arrest, what witnesses would you require to present your case?"

Croney peered at him, wondering what he was devising. "Only myself," he snapped. "I'd have no need of any others . . . unless you have destroyed the affidavits of testimony which are in my possession."

"They are quite secure. Who would stand as accuser?"

"I would! By right of the king's warrant and my duty

as an officer of the expeditionary guard."

"You could be both accuser and witness?"

"Could and will. I shall see you hang, D . . . *Captain* Dalton. Or see you rot aboard a prison hulk . . . unless you intend to have me murdered to save yourself."

"I don't think that will be necessary," Dalton said softly. "I found your manual for the conduct of courts martial very instructive, Commander. I had never actually realized the precision of the military justice process . . . or, for that matter, its simplicity."

"Are you toying with me, *Captain* Dalton?"

"Oh, not at all, Commander Croney. I shouldn't be too surprised to see a determined officer like you achieve what he has set out to do, in the end. You have expended a considerable amount of effort toward it. I really only have one further question at the moment."

"And that is?"

"How much of the holdings of Clan Fitzgerald do you expect to receive from Lord Sotheby in return for providing him with my conviction . . . which I understand would complete his case against the Fitzgerald?"

Croney fumed. "I shan't dignify that with an answer. You have no right to accuse me of . . ."

"Let's not compare accusations, shall we? But, my, isn't it British of us that we must abide by the rules of procedure, even when we set out to cheat and steal."

"I don't know what you are talking about."

"Of course you do, Commander. I perceive that the king's case against the Fitzgerald has not been proven, and that Lord Sotheby is very anxious for an accomplice conviction, *outside of the British Isles, where it is not likely ever to be thoroughly researched.* Such would be worth possibly a fifth of Ireland to His Lordship, and he would pay handsomely for it. Oh, don't bother denying it, Commander. I know what your correspondence has told me."

Croney's voice in the dimness was almost a snarl. "I don't care a fig what you believe, Irishman. I still intend to see you brought before a judge advocate."

Dalton stood. "In that case, Commander, please behave yourself while you are aboard my ship. And by all means, stop trying to hide in chain lockers. A man could get himself killed doing that."

Dalton left the guard officer there and went back on deck, his eyes alight and musing. Music dimly heard from the confines below smote him as he came up the companionway. On the foredeck of *Fury,* Galante Pico's ensemble was striking into the second movement of some composition of the *Concerto Grosso* manner — possibly a Bach arrangement — with alternate violin and flute solos providing the tone color and Joseph Miller's harpsichord weaving a tinkling continuo through it. Forty yards or so away, hundreds of men — German mercenaries, British redcoats and merchant marine sailors — crowded the rails of the transport and balanced on its shrouds and yardarms, being grandly entertained.

For the first time in months, it seemed to Dalton, the bleak mood of despair did not hang over him. Instead, there was an excitement that lurked just behind conscious thought — a hope where there had been hopelessness.

All through these long months he had run, fled, hidden — concentrated all his energies on simply staying away from the combatants in this war-stricken part of the world — on simply trying to stay alive. But now there was something more. For the first time, a plan presented itself, and he mused over it point by point as he took up the work of manning his ship.

There just might be, he thought, a way to clear himself, to free his honor and his name, to be free to make the choices that a man must have his honor intact to make.

It was not quite hopeless after all.

But first, he must deal with a troop convoy, various hostile great warships and a sea that could shift in this weather from dead calm to black squalls at a moment's notice.

XI

During the calm, Charley Duncan had doubled the topwatch. It wouldn't do, he felt, for reports to be shouted to the deck with a transport-load of potential hostiles as likely to hear them as were those at *Fury*'s helm. Now Pliny Quarterstone swarmed down the starboard main shroud, his movements keeping involuntary time with the rattle of the kettledrum as the power of Johann Sebastian Bach rang out over the water. Whatever else Galante Pico's escaped indentures might be, they were musicians, and the very structure of the ship seemed to respond to the soaring scope of Bach's design.

As were many of the recent additions to Dalton's crew, Pliny Quarterstone was a fugitive tar. He had escaped the stockade at Point Barrow along with James Stork and Andrew Wilshire, then had fallen in with a half-dozen other unfortunate tars beached by a minor mutiny aboard the frigate *Carlson*. A Canadian named Alexander Jackson—a deserter from the brig *Sorrel*, had joined the ranks outside of Savannah, and a pair of Colonials, Chilton Sand from New York and Grover Colegreave from New Hampshire—both fugitives from assorted allegations—had fallen in with them on Water Street where the band, now a dozen strong, had liberated provisions from a merchant's shed and put themselves out for hire.

It was there that Patrick Dalton had signed them on to serve *Fury*, and read them their articles along with another seven or eight newfound crew.

Pliny Quarterstone was not at all sure whose side of the present hostilities his captain and his ship were on, if any. He was not at all sure what the hostilities were about, or who was whose enemy. Like most English sailors of his time, hardly anybody ever told him anything beyond what sails to make and whose draft it was to holystone the deck. But one thing Pliny Quarterstone was, along with the rest of his dozen mates and most others aboard *Fury*. He was an able seaman, and he respected the dangers of his profession.

So he moved with a will when Mister Romart sent him down to report to the deck, and his urgent whisper to Captain Dalton might have carried across to the looming troopship had it not been for the interference of Johann Sebastian Bach.

"Mister Romart said there's mist a'makin' northward, sir. He says the seventy-four is no longer in sight, but there's swirls risin' off there an' he allows there may be a squall line makin' up."

"Thank you, Mister Quarterstone," the captain said, and Pliny beamed at the calling of his name. It was an unusual captain, in his estimation, who would know the names of his ables and ordinaries. Most commanding officers of his experience took pains never to know the men who served them.

"What of the other sightings?" the captain asked him quietly. "The frigate and the other transports?"

"Aye, sir. The frigate made about when its signal was relayed. It turned westward again, though right now it's just settin' off there on calm water, like almost everybody else, waitin' for some wind."

"*Almost* everybody, Mister Quarterstone?"

118

"That first bark we passed, sir, it's got launches out for tow and it's comin' over here. Mister Romart says this here bark"—he waved a hand at the big transport almost beam-to-beam with *Fury*—"waggled to that other bark that there was an entertainment here to pass the time."

"Thank you, Mister Quarterstone. Please return to the maintop, and keep a sharp eye."

"Aye, sir."

Behind him, Dalton turned to Charley Duncan. "That doesn't sound at all encouraging, does it?"

"They probably mean no harm, sir. When it's calm like this, what else is there to do except listen to good music?"

"But we have a transport abeam, and another coming to slide in alongside on the other beam. I don't fancy sitting becalmed among a thousand or so armed mercenaries while a seventy-four positions itself to head us off when there's wind. I believe we shall turn *Fury* part about, Mister Duncan, and bring the orchestra up to the quarterdeck. That should encourage our audience to line up astern of us, rather than crowding in. Please go forward and tell Mister Hickman that we are rearranging the stage a bit; then cast off the launch with rowers to haul as a quarter about to starboard."

"Aye, sir."

"Mister Caster . . ." He looked around. Usually at his heel, the clerk now was leaning on the quarter-rail, engrossed with the orchestra and its music. "Mister Caster!"

Billy turned abruptly. "Aye, sir?"

"Mister Caster, we need to rearrange the music a bit."

"We certainly should, sir. Bach is unfair to bassoons. Mister Ferrestrekov just stands there most of the time, not even playing, and he hasn't had a single solo."

119

"I mean, we are going to remove them to the quarterdeck, and come about so that they can amuse those people from the fantail."

"Oh. What about the harpsichord, sir? It might be difficult to move."

"I'll have Mister Wise get a line on it from the mainshroud blocks, and we can swing it about and reset it. I would rather have it here than forward, at any rate. It interferes with the gundecks."

Within moments the little warship was a welter of activity, and the music faltered and failed. Dalton retrieved his speaking horn and directed his voice at the troopship. "Intermission, gentlemen. We intend to reassemble and play you from our fantail."

There was a moment of silence while the message was relayed along the big ship in various languages; then thunderous applause broke out and the crowd there shifted as crowds do—some going to the off rails to relieve themselves, others taking the opportunity to get better seats.

"Maybe we could impose on them to play some Mozart selections," Billy Caster muttered, watching the musicians being herded astern by enthusiastic sailors while the harpsichord rose above the deck and swung out over the water. "Mozart is much kinder to bassoons than Bach."

As the launch took the tow, *Fury*'s nose swung slowly to the right, bringing her stern about to face the transport. Beyond, slack sails of the second transport hove into view, with a dozen tows working from its bow and beams.

"Signal that second bark to come into line with the first," Dalton said. "Jib to jib would be best, so everyone can hear."

"And be in no position to chase us when we run," Duncan muttered, grinning.

"Tell Mister Hickman to douse his tobacco pipe," someone suggested. "If he should set off our stern

120

chasers at those ships, we'll have the entire navy out looking for us."

Far to the north, on cold seas off the coast of Maine, the trough of low pressure was drawing winds from landward to give good speed to the scouting brig *Bethune*. The brig had run the coast for two long days, fighting shifting winds and braving privateers to gather messages from ashore, then had stood in once again at Portsmouth, this time to take passengers aboard from a furtive coaster that lay waiting among shoals until *Bethune* was near. With the gathered messages from spy points, and the information from the pair of Crown guardsmen from Portsmouth, *Bethune* went in search of *Royal Lineage*. Late in the day Blake's topmen sighted the big warship and they homed on it while signals told the story.

Felix Croney's signalmen had been retrieved, but Croney himself had disappeared. There was no sign of him at Portsmouth, and it was assumed he had fallen into the hands of Colonial militia. Further, both the snow he had ordered a watch upon and several of the Continental Navy commissions were gone from the harbor. Short of privateers, there was no longer anything there to watch or harass. In the evening, *Bethune* hove alongside *Royal Lineage* on rolling seas, and Blake went aboard the seventy-four to personally deliver his intelligences to Captain Isaac Watson. Watson questioned him carefully, his heavy brows thunderous. Weeks of cruising, patrolling up here, weeks of tedious ship-handling and endless drills, and it had come to nothing. He would have some words for Admiral Lord Howe at the earliest opportunity, he decided. Words about inefficiency of deployment, about last-minute changes of tactic that produced wasted time and no results.

But what could Howe do? Black Dick's hands were

tied, Watson knew, in such matters. Howe could send messages of complaint to the Admiralty—to Lord North himself, for that matter. But what would it come to? Many among Great Britain's old-line military had worried when the so-called "King's party" gained power in Parliament, and had worried when that power began entrenching itself in the ministries. Even the War Ministry in recent years had begun to reflect the personal politics of George III.

Our worries were well founded, Watson reflected now. Politics takes precedence over proper procedure. Even our efforts to put down the insurrection in the American colonies is hampered by it.

"Our mission up here is completed," Watson told the brig commander. "You may return to your ship, Captain, and carry word to the remainder of the squadron to reform and make for Long Island."

"Will you accompany, sir?" Blake asked.

"I think not. I've wasted far too much time here now. Had it not been for the expeditionary guard's interference, *Royal Lineage* might at least have served as escort to General Clinton's latest troop convoy. I shall go ahead, work southward and possibly jump a prize or two along the way."

"Aye, sir. We will rejoin you at Long Island, then."

As Blake was lightered back to his brig, Watson went to the poopdeck of his ship and studied the sky. Clouds had formed to westward, and a lively wind came down from the upper coast of Maine. Even in the past hour, it had shifted a point more northerly.

"Course south by east," he told his first. "There may be squalls behind this, so let us have adequate sail to run ahead of them, and topmen aloft to spy for prizes as we go."

"Aye, sir." The junior saluted him and stepped down to take charge of the quarterdeck below. Orders were called, bosuns' whistles shrilled and *Royal Lineage* came alive. Massive timbers thrummed as great sails came taut. Like a lethargic giant awakening, the seventy-four stretched itself, swung its great stem southward and surged forward, rolling aside the protesting waters at its bow as though they were not there. Most dreaded of the warships of its time, huge and lithe under its massive weight of sail, the seventy-four went hunting, and Isaac Watson stood high above the sternpost of his domain and was relieved that for now — at least until he reached Long Island and the Royal Navy yards — he need have no further discourse with politicians.

He had cordially disliked his earlier passenger, and saw the gray little man as an example of all that was wrong with the realm.

"Probably fell out of that bell tower," he muttered to himself, feeling the vital song of the great ship soothing at the soles of his shoes. "Probably lost his balance and fell, then was found and carted away by rebels. Hope the buggers enjoyed their sport with him. No great loss to England, certainly."

It probably was too late now to join escort on Clinton's convoy. But no matter. *Cornwall* was there, with several lesser ships, and as far as he knew there was nothing the colonists could put under sail that would be more than an annoyance for a seventy-four. *Cornwall* and *Royal Lineage* were sister ships, in a way, launched the same year by the same shipyards, and both had seen service under the admiral of the Blue in the Mediterranean and off Gibraltar before being transferred to the White Fleet, at which time Watson had become captain of *Royal Lineage*. Selkirk had already had *Cornwall*, having come from semi-retirement to bring her over to America.

"Hawser will have sport with me," Watson told himself. "Sitting off up here while he takes his ship and brings in the troops. I shall hear about that in due time."

A prize or two brought back enroute might even

the score, he thought. At least, if *Royal Lineage* could bring in a Colonial privateer or two, or maybe a flotilla of smuggling packets, Hawser might not crow quite so loudly when they met again.

"Sharp eye for sail," he called down to his first. "We've been inactive long enough."

The American schooner *Glorietta,* a private sniper operating under letter of marque, had prowled the lanes off Newport since the turning of seasons and had done well for her investors. Three fine prizes— an armed Crown sloop and a pair of provision shuttles—lay now to her credit, and scarcely a mark marred her sleek hull and bright fore-and-aft sails. A dozen times she had been confronted. She had sent a pair of gunboats to the bottom, exchanged shots with a Crown brig on two occasions, and had been chased a number of times by cruisers. But luck and skill had paid off each time, and again and again *Glorietta* returned to the upper sound and the breakwater region, to annoy the British there.

It was Nathan Smith's boast that nothing short of a heavy frigate on a favoring wind would ever see *Glorietta's* colors fall, and many who had seen the dancing schooner in maneuvers tended to agree. As captain, Smith was a canny man—daring at the right times, a good judge of wind and water, and a man who knew his ship and what it would do. With long nines doubled at stem and stern and stubby sixes at her beams, *Glorietta* could speak with authority when not outclassed, and it was a test of her captain's skill that, to date, she had never been forced to stand against anything larger than a brig.

Yet on this day, the luck of Nathan Smith ran out. Word had come from up the coast of a Union Jack brig harassing the lanes at Portsmouth, and annoyed port officials had put a bounty on the brig.

Smith decided to go and have a look.

Offshore winds that threatened to bluster but yet held steady made the run upcoast a pleasure for the jaunty schooner. Spanker and spencer laid hard out and her staysails drumming high, *Glorietta* held due east on a broad reach past Vineyard Island, then put a point to starboard to clear the funnel and aimed her stem at Cape Cod and the Atlantic waters beyond. As winds shifted to northerly she came a'port on an easy tack and rounded off the cape, her lookouts for the moment on deck to lend hands to the hauling of sheets. The wind was rising, and it would take all hands to bring the headstrong fore-and-after smoothly into an upwind beat to pass the cape, then bring her nose through the wind and reset for travel, forty-five degrees into the wind.

The first turn was made and the second begun when a man in the fore shouted and pointed ahead. Black squalls were moving down from the north, their tumbling forms shrouding the far waters. And ahead of them, nose high and a good wind on its tail, came a vessel that was no brig. The huge ship loomed suddenly ahead, altered course a scant point and came for them, and for once *Glorietta* had nowhere to run or hide.

With a sinking heart, Smith watched his career ending. At a half-mile, indistinct against the squalls beyond, the great warship still could not be mistaken for anything other than what it was. Twice the size of a frigate, four times the size of a brig and maybe five times that of the schooner, its booming hull carried down on the wind with the voice of doom.

A seventy-four.

Smith tried—and his crew tried—to bring *Glorietta* about for a cross-wind dash, but it was far too late. Even as the schooner took fresh wind in its staysails and edged about, great ranging guns at the warship's bow spat flame and smoke, and iron balls the size of

125

a man's head screamed down upon *Glorietta*. One passed through her mainsail ten feet above the deck, then carried on to splash, skip and splash a hundred yards beyond. The second sheeted water under her bow.

Smith's face went ashen, his eyes staring at the Union Jack flapping at the warship's stern. "Ease sheets," he said through clenched teeth. "Reverse and come into the wind. Mister Larkin, run up our colors one last time, then strike them."

Had it been a Crown brig or the like, he would have fought it. Had it been a frigate, he would at least had exchanged shots and tried to escape. But for all his daring, Nathan Smith was a realist. For a lesser vessel under the guns of a seventy-four, there are no options. One must simply surrender.

Isaac Watson put a prize crew aboard *Glorietta* and escorted her past the skirting shoals, then watched her on her way to Long Island Yards with his prize flag at her halyard. "That's one," he told his first. "The squalls yonder have given us good cover. Let us go and see if we can find another prize or two."

XII

Peter Selkirk, Captain and Commander HMRN, had not seen the small warship that seemed to have appeared amidst his escorted convoy. First sighted at a distance of a dozen miles, it was visible only from the high crosstrees of *Cornwall* — a precarious perch almost a hundred and thirty feet above the battleship's highest deck. In his sixth decade of life, his mane of iron-gray hair tight-bound beneath his tricorn hat and his shoulders adorned with the twin epaulets of senior captaincy, "Hawser" Selkirk had long since outgrown any desire to swarm the high shrouds and dance aloft on footrope or masttop platform. He was content to trust the sightings of younger, sharper eyes.

And when his lookouts reported unidentified sail southbound through the wide-scattered convoy — sail with the silhouette and rig of a warship, though small — he decided to have a look for himself.

Likely a messenger, he thought, though his topmen had seen no colors or signals from such a distance. Still, it was time to tighten the flock a bit, and a flanking sweep to the south could begin that and give him a look at the stranger at the same time.

"Have the officer of the deck bring us a quarter to

port," he instructed. "And while we are about it, have the master see to tightening those sheets a bit. We have luff on the main and mizzen courses."

"Aye, sir." The midshipman attending him hurried to comply, stifling a grin as he turned away. The captain was a warrior and a sailor, but he seemed always to be first a teacher. Talk amidships—most of the young men chartered at such duty aboard *Cornwall* were of naval families—was that Old Hawser had taken a hand in the training of fully a fourth of the presently active senior officers of the Royal Navy, and counted among his students at least one peer of the august group, the Right Honorable the Lords Commissioners of the Admiralty. A good half of the present complement amidships were sons of men who had sailed under Peter Selkirk.

Cornwall came to her new heading gracefully, and Selkirk pointed aloft. "How do you fare the weather, mister?"

The youngster paused for a moment, reading wind gauge and pondering the featureless gray above and below. "We are sailing in a bottle, sir. Wind is eight to maybe ten, but faltering, visibility is intermittent . . ." He shrugged. "It could hold like this, sir. Or if the wind shifts northerly we could see squalls."

"And the third possibility?"

"It could come a calm, sir."

"Very good, mister. Now, which, in fact, will it do?"

The youngster frowned, straining for the answer, knowing because the captain asked the question that he should know the answer.

Selkirk waited, then said, "You mentioned something about visibility?"

"Aye, sir. Intermittent . . . ah! It likely will come to calm, sir."

"Very good, mister. More than likely, it shall. Have you spent your off-watches studying the mariner's

128

manual?"

"Aye, sir! . . . Well, that is, most of them, sir."

"Be assiduous, mister. Remember, somewhere in that material is the fact—or the skill—that one day will save your ship and possibly your very life."

"Aye, sir."

Signals from main crosstrees to maintop to deck were relayed back. "Lookout has had another view of the stranger, sir. Still southbound, closing course on a pair of our transports. Our distance possibly ten miles."

"Can he read the rigging, Mister Mull?"

"Vague, sir. Weight of sail as a frigate, but it is a smaller vessel, like a brig."

"Colors, Mister Mull?"

"Still spotting, sir."

Cornwall ran on, angling east of south. If the wind held, Selkirk judged he would have a decent view of the stranger in two hours. If not, then he would look when he could. A suspicion had crossed his mind. The vessel could be a snow. Weight of sail and size indicated that. If so, it was not a fleet vessel. Several of the fast American-built cruisers—like a reinforced and rebalanced brig, yet capable of far greater speed than a brig—had been taken as prize in recent years, but he knew of none that had been commissioned to the admiral of the White. It suggested that the intruder could be a privateer . . . or a fugitive.

Well, if such were the case, he would know soon enough. And if so, then likely another snow would be added to the Crown's prize list. An armed snow might stand against—or possibly escape from—a frigate, but not from a seventy-four. The thought held no particular pleasure for Peter Selkirk. In this campaign against the rebel colonies, many a fine ship was being wasted that could be turned to better service. *Cornwall*, her sister *Royal Lineage*, the doughty *Earl of Kent*, the *Essex* . . . Such ships were built for

129

war at sea, the standing of bow to bow against vessels of their own weight for exchange of fire until one or the other struck or sank. This escorting of convoys against an enemy with nothing larger than frigates to field, this tedious threatening and taking of brigs and snows and schooners, was an inefficiency that grated on him.

Cornwall slowed, seemed to settle her massive bulk more comfortably into the sea, and sails gone luff smacked and fluttered.

"Wind's dropping off, sir. Going to calm."

"You see, mister," Selkirk told his attendant, "keep a weather eye to the elements and you'll know what shall occur." Yet have no more power over the occurrence than if you had not reckoned it, he thought to himself. To his first he said, "I'd like the latest on that stranger, Mister Mull."

"Aye, sir."

Within minutes the calls ran down and aft. "Nine miles at most, sir. He is becalmed alongside a transport yonder, and he flies the white union."

So, Selkirk nodded bleakly. False colors and fair game. "Keep an eye on that one, Mister Mull. When this calm breaks, make sail to intercept him. He is not what he claims to be."

On *Fury*'s quarterdeck the ungainly harpsichord had been swung inboard, lowered and lashed, and Galante Pico's orchestra was rendering select segments of Wolfgang Amadeus Mozart's Symphony in D Major for the awed diversion of some eight hundred soldiers and sailors crowding the rails of two tall sailing barks. Billy Caster was overjoyed, as Mozart's mastery of woodwinds as divertimenti gave full rein to the bassoon skills of Zoltan Ferrestrekov. Patrick Dalton, for his part, was pleased that the masters of the two transports had accepted his suggestion that they lash the bowsprits of their ships to each other's bows, this creating a pair of huge balconies over and around the concert stage that was *Fury*.

It was not so much an interest in their enjoyment of the pastime, though, that had moved him to suggest it. Rather, it was a careful scrutiny of the darkening line on the north horizon that said the calm would break soon.

They will have a very devil of a time getting these ships untangled and under way, he noted to himself. They should be far too busy to concern themselves with what we are doing in the meantime.

He waited patiently while the noted Ferrestrekov completed a rising bassoon aggrandemiento, then put his hand on his clerk's shoulder. "If you can tear yourself away, Mister Caster, please go forward and have a look to the north; then tell me how you fare the weather."

"Now, sir?"

"Now, Mister Caster."

"Aye, sir." With a sigh, Billy hurried off toward the bow, puzzled as always at his captain's constant prodding of him on matters of winds, weather and navigation. It was not part of a clerk's task to do such things, but Dalton insisted on it. It was as though the captain, no matter what else he might be doing, took time at regular intervals to instruct his clerk in matters maritime — as though the captain had taken it on himself to be a teacher, and Billy was his midshipman performing the drills.

He was gone for several minutes, then returned to the quarterdeck.

"Well, Mister Caster, how do you fare the weather?"

"Darkening northward, sir. I think there may be squall lines coming down."

"Very good, Mister Caster. How long will the calm hold?"

Billy thought, then made a guess. "Two bells, sir?"

"Or a bit more. What do you expect we should do then, Mister Caster?"

"Go on our way, I suppose, sir. We certainly should have good winds the rest of the day."

"On our way, Mister Caster?" Dalton's eyes held a trace of humor, as of one preparing a surprise.

"Southward, sir? That's where we are supposed to be going."

"Precisely. And there is a bloody big seventy-four sitting off there to the east, expecting us to do that so that he can intercept us. No, Mister Caster, when the wind returns it will be time for us to stop amusing these people and see to the amusement of others far more dangerous. Mister Duncan!"

"Sir?"

"In two bells I'd like fresh spotters in the tops and all hands to station. Maintop on general watch, foretop keep a sharp eye on that frigate yonder, and I want to know its every move, including the set of its sails."

"Aye, sir." Duncan's grin curved around white teeth and his eyes glistened. "Thinking of bashing us another frigate, are we, sir?"

"Not unless we absolutely have to, Mister Duncan. You are spoiling for a fight again, I take it?"

"Oh, no, sir. Not me. It's just that things have got a bit dull of late, you know, an' . . ."

"Carry on, Mister Duncan."

"Aye, sir."

"Mister Wise!"

The bosun hurried to the rail. "Sir?"

"We shall allow these gentlemen to frolic a'deck for another hour; then I want them put below smartly, and all hands a'deck to sheets. Mister Locke!"

"Aye, sir?"

"Stay close at hand here, Mister Locke. I shall want you to take the helm when we have wind."

"Aye, sir."

At the stern rail, the orchestra had done all that fifteen pieces could do with selections from the D Major work, and had launched into a set of Vivaldi obligatos, heavy on harpsichord and strings. John Tidy scampered across from the port to the starboard main fiferails to check the setting of sheetlines. "I hope those lads will finish tuning up soon and play us a song," he told Claude Mallory.

"Aye." Mallory heaved a lashing and secured a hitch to the rail with a belaying pin. "It's seemed for an hour now like they might just break out and play a tune most any minute; then off they go testing their harmonies again. I'd fancy a bit of the pudding dance, or maybe *Ode to Life's Dismal Shores* . . . heard that last time I was in London. It's a real rouser."

"Well, there's some who like what they're hearing even now," Tidy allowed. "I saw Mister O'Riley doin' a hornpipe jig just a bit ago."

"Which Mister O'Riley?"

"The one that isn't the cook. The other one."

"Well"—Mallory shrugged—"He *is* Irish. Some of the Irish has been known to dance to the squealin' of pigs, or even the gurgling of a Dublin sewer."

"Mister Tidy!"

The watch bosun turned at the sound of the captain's voice. "Aye, sir?"

"See to the securing of our launch, if you please. Snug a'deck, and the small boat as well."

"Aye, sir."

The fresh wind, when it came, was only tentative cold gusts at first, but steadying nicely. And with the first breath of it, *Fury* came alive. Musicians and their paraphernalia—all except the harpsichord—were whisked forward and below, out of the way, and yards came about fore and aft for a new setting of sail.

"The frigate is making sail for a starboard reach,"

topmen called. "She's already moving westward, sir."

"Any sign of the seventy-four?"

"No, sir. It's east, and these transports' sails have blocked the view."

"Then he can't see us, either," Dalton mused. "Very well. Mister Locke, take the helm please. Rudder amidships for a beam reach."

"Aye, sir."

"Set for beam reach a'starboard, Mister Wise. Mister Tidy, a hand at signals, if you please. Mister Duncan will take the gundeck for now." Sails aloft felt the first touches of steady wind and rounded themselves out on yards hauled hard back to port. "Sheet home and trim," Dalton called. *Fury* heeled to port and slid out of the vee between the transports, picking up way as she cleared the lee of their tall sails. Dalton picked up his speaking horn and turned to wish them a pleasant journey, but decided not to.

Lashed nose to nose for the concert, the two ships now had their jibstays fouled and were drifting sideways in the freshening wind. Those aboard had their hands full and would for some time.

"Are we going after the frigate, sir?" Billy Caster asked, seeing their heading. A few miles away the tall frigate headed west, and *Fury*'s course exactly flanked it.

"Only for a time," Dalton told him. "The day will clear for a time before those squalls come down, and we shall lose our screen directly from those transports. I'd like some distance before that seventy-four finds out where we are again."

Running point for a widely scattered convoy, the frigate was in no hurry. With good wind now, it idled on reefed sails, just cruising ahead of the pack and waiting for them to reform. From its fantail, the little warship coming on was clearly visible, and some aboard wondered about it—but only about why it had dallied with a pair of troop transports instead of

134

seeking out its own kind, and what its message might have been. Nothing about it had indicated hostility or anything out of the ordinary. It had even relayed the frigate's signals—though somewhat clumsily.

Beyond it, two transports seemed to have fouled their stems, and there were grins and whispers as Royal Navy subjects—officers and seamen alike—mused on the prodigal capabilities of merchant sailors.

The wind continued to freshen and the frigate again reduced sail to stay with its pack. Within minutes the smaller ship had come directly astern and was signaling for upwind passage—a courtesy expected by and usually extended to the smaller of vessels in passing. The frigate's buntings went aloft, with a routine inquiry for identification. The small ship hoisted the white union again, and edged right to come alongside the frigate, overtaking with remarkable speed.

They paid closer attention to it then, noticing the huge press of sail its rigging could carry, the sleek, racing hull, the trim stern and high, jaunty stem . . . and the presence of a small third mast immediately aft from its main. The stubby mast carried a spanker twice the size that a brig might have managed, with extender yards at hounds for the adding of even more canvas in a "bobtail" sail beyond.

"What in God's name is that?" some asked.

And some more current in the building of modern ships in the Americas gazed at it admiringly as it slid by. "It's a snow," they said. "American design. All teeth and legs, and the very devil to hit when it's dancing."

"I wonder where we got it," a master seaman mused.

"Some prize-taker had a lucky day," a bosun suggested.

At three cables' length the snow passed, and men

on both vessels waved and watched.

When the snow was a furlong ahead of the frig-ate—just beyond fair gun range—it furled its high sails and reefed some lower ones.

"He's reducing speed, sir," a watcher told the frig-ate's deck officer.

"A sport." The man frowned. "He had himself a lark in passing us by, but now he has the lead he is content."

With fresh wind in its big sails, *Cornwall* took the seas under her bow and continued course west of south while her lookouts scanned the clearing waters westward. Seven miles away, two transports had be-come fouled and were just righting themselves. A bit beyond, hull down from the tops, the point frigate was leading toward base port, and all around there were transports beginning to reform upon it.

But nowhere in sight was there any unknown ship. The small warship they had seen from the crosstrees before the calm had simply disappeared.

Peter Selkirk paced his deck, deep in thought. It did not make sense that the ship could be gone. Visi-bility was good now, the straining mists cleared in advance of the squalls growing on the north horizon. From his tops, his spotters had unobstructed view in all directions. A ship's sails should be visible any-where within twenty miles, and there had been no way for the little vessel to go two miles during the calm, much less twenty. Still, it was gone.

"The man is a fox," Selkirk told himself. "Somehow, he has gone to ground, but how could he have done it? A very fox . . ." A face came to his mind, and with it a name. There was a man who could have done such things . . . a young man who had once trained as midshipman on Selkirk's own command . . . who was now a fugitive, hounded and harried by some charge that seemed to make very little sense but was, nonetheless, a charge against him.

"Mister Mull, bring us about," he ordered. "Make for those two transports that have been untangling themselves. I'd like to have a word with them, if you please."

XIII

Screened now by the frigate as she had been screened before by the transports, *Fury* plodded westward on a starboard beam wind, only gradually lengthening its distance from the frigate while sharp eyes at mast-tops peered through the follower's sails for glimpses of what lay astern.

"The seventy-four is in sight, sir," the maintop called. "Hull down by a bit, maybe nine miles back. It's changed course, sir. Now it is making for those lads we entertained back there."

"Tops and helm, keep that frigate between us and the seventy-four, please."

"Aye, sir." Victory Locke peered upward, to take his directions from the maintop. Along the deck, late additions to the crew glanced at one another, eyebrows raised. Some had seen the tactic of frigates screening behind ships of the line, to dart out and harass a wounded foe. Some had seen smokes used as cover in battles at sea. Few enough, though, had ever considered escaping one foe by hiding behind another.

Fury eased aport as the maintop guided the helm, then eased aport again, slowly. Miles behind, the battleship was making slow work of it, beating sixty degrees on the wind to home on the sluggish transports, and Dalton clenched his teeth, reciting to himself from the manual of arms and lectures he recalled from his days as a midshipman. It was likely in this wind that the seventy-four would come up behind the transports. No seasoned warship commander would refuse himself the advantage of an upwind position, even when approaching a friend. Once in position, he would make inquiry about the vessel they had been consorting with. Would he let signals suffice, or would he summon the transports to send launches to give him intelligence on the situation? And what would a seasoned captain do with the apparent disappearance of a vessel he had already seen, on open sea?

I know what I would do, he told himself. I would signal all vessels to search and report.

Yet, when would I do that? The day still has hours to go, and he might want to reckon who he is seeking before he sets a search. Nor would a seventy-four's captain be overly concerned about a vessel as small as a snow escaping him. Despite the ponderous size of the ship of the line, there are few enough ships that can outrun one in an open chase. A fore-and-after in favoring winds, possibly. But *Fury* is square-rigged for all the sail she carries, and cannot dodge by tacking.

"Give us a bit more sail, Mister Tidy," he called. "We are about to run out of hiding places."

A quarter-hour passed, and *Fury* led the frigate by more than half a mile.

From the maintop came, "Sir, the seventy-four is out of sight now. It is beyond those two transports."

Dalton nodded. It was the best chance he would have to break and run. Soon there would be signals; then he would have a frigate hard on his tail, as well as the distant seventy-four. "Stand by to come to starboard, Mister Tidy! All fore-and-afts full out and

139

trim, courses and tops full hauled for wind on the
starboard bow. Hands aloft to run out the bobtail,
please."

Tidy's whistle shrilled and *Fury* heeled as new sail
in new position took the eastering north wind.

"Bring us over, helm. Full three points to starboard
and hold us there."

"Aye, sir."

Beating toward the wind, *Fury* gained no speed
with the turn, but neither did she lose any, and when
the bobtail drummed open above and beyond her
stern, she surged with the power it gave her. Fifty
feet of canvas, twelve feet wide, had just been added
to her driving spanker.

As the snow veered away from the frigate's course,
Dalton looked back. Miles away he could see the tall
sails of the pair of transports, and beyond them just a
hint of warship's canvas — not as tall as the skymasts
of the big barks, but far more complex in its blend-
ing of courses, square upper rigging and graceful
fore-and-aft maneuvering sails at every boom and
stay. Despite the urgency of his situation, Dalton felt
the thrill of admiration that always came with sight
of a worthy ship. The seventy-four was distant and
almost totally hidden from him, but even the bit of
silhouette he could see was totally formidable. Because he felt like it, he squared his shoulders and
raised a hand in salute

Nearer at hand, the frigate still plodded along on
reefed and tight-hauled sails, ignoring the snow that
had so abruptly headed off on its own erratic course.
Dalton was not surprised. The frigate's commander
had his task to do, and certainly the tracing of other
armed vessels bearing his own colors was no part of
it. His was not the flagship of the squadron, and
until ordered otherwise he would continue to lead the
convoy toward New York Bay. Having enjoyed his
salute, he repeated it for the frigate, then turned

back to his own deck. "How do you fare the weather now, Mister Caster?"

Billy paused, looking off to the north and then at the gauge overhead. "The wind is coming up to twenty knots, sir. I expect it will increase, with those squalls approaching yonder. We may see a steady thirty before we see rough weather."

"Aye." Dalton nodded. "And the warships yonder . . . when they decide what to do, what might it be?"

Billy studied on it, aware that the captain probably knew exactly what they would do, but wanted to hear his answer. He glanced astern. The frigate was a mile away now, maybe more, its deckline low upon the swell of the sea and sometimes not in sight at all. Much farther away, the high sails of the seventy-four were just now coming clear of the intervening transports.

"The frigate might give chase, sir, but not very far. He has seen our sails and he knows he can't catch us in rough seas. If I were guessing, sir . . ."

"I wish you would, Mister Caster."

"Well, sir, my guess would be that the seventy-four will have the frigate continue on, and he himself might try to have a better look at us, but the wind is not to his advantage now, and maybe he will turn back."

"When?"

"Well before dark, sir. I believe you said he is the only ship of the line escorting these transports, so that will be his first duty."

"Very good, Mister Caster!" Dalton's dark eyes lit with approval, and Billy blushed with pleasure. "Think as the man must think, if you'd know what the man might do."

"Yes, sir."

"Hold us steady for a bell, helm, then put over for port tack. We don't want to come too close to the shores yonder. There might be unwelcome surprises."

141

"Aye, sir."

"And let's get a cloth over that harpsichord, please. Lash it well. We shall see some weather soon. Mister Duncan . . ."

"Aye, Cap'n?"

"My compliments to the musicians in the foreway. Please tell them that I am grateful for the turn they did us back there, keeping those transports entertained. Then see to their security belowdeck and explain to them that we expect rough passage within the next few hours. And have Mister Tower break out the necessary timbers and batten that hatch securely with grating and a drip ledge."

"Aye, sir. Some of them have noticed that we are going north, sir, and they wonder why, since the direction to Chesapeake is south. What should I tell them?"

"Tell them we are going north because it seems the safest way to reach Chesapeake. I am sure they noticed that these ships coursing about here are British ships."

"Aye, sir. They noticed that. But most of them sort of reckon that we are British as well."

"I thought it had been explained to them that there is a war going on, and we are trying very hard not to be on either side."

"Aye, sir. But you know how musicians are." Duncan shrugged, spreading his hands. "They have no ear for politics, at all."

"Get them properly thanked and safely secured, Mister Duncan, and we shall discuss politics at another time."

"Aye, sir."

Though *Fury*'s tops could not make out the signals from the line ship, they did read the frigate's response. It would lay back, closer to the reforming convoy, then carry on toward New York. And even as the frigate reduced sail even further, the big warship's sails grew on the east horizon, a leviathan in chase.

"He will make a game of it." Dalton nodded. "The man yonder is the man I knew, right enough. He will do no less than I expect of him, just as I can do no less than what he expects. Matter of honor all around, I suppose."

"He can't catch us, can he?"

"Oh, if he had nothing better to do, he could make life unpleasant enough for us. A seventy-four can pile on sail as much as it needs, Billy, and have little worry about capsizing itself or breaking up in squalls. *Fury* has no such luxury. Sturdy as she might be, she still is a small hull and there are limits to the stresses she will stand. But no, I expect your guess was right. He has better things to do than to chase us all over this part of the Atlantic for the next day or two. But he *will* see us out of his part of the ocean, and see that we are quick about it."

"You've never sailed a ship of the line, have you, sir?"

Dalton's eyes went distant — almost melancholy. "Served on one, yes, as a midshipman . . . student of that very man who is harassing us now. But never sailed one, never done regular service on such a ship . . . nor ever likely to. Though such would be a marvelous thing, for a man who wants to sail."

"You admire him, don't you, sir?"

He wasn't sure whether his clerk meant the ship, or the man who commanded her. But . . . "Yes, I do. One of the finest fighting ships afloat now or ever, and one of the finest fighting men I've known, in command."

"The seventy-four is gaining on us, sir," came from aloft.

And of course it was. Angling toward *Fury*, the seventy-four sailed just off a beam reach, using its close-hauled great sails to good advantage in the

143

freshening wind, while *Fury* held to tight tack, as near the wind as she could beat and still maintain a running speed. Dalton estimated times and distances. "He'll come closer still, before he gives up the chase. He knows I will come about to the northeast rather than make for land here, and he will do us the honor of making it as difficult as he can."

"Downright uncomfortable, as I see it," Charley Duncan observed. "That line ship has a third more wind than we, and he's using it."

At the starboard pinrail Claude Mallory leaned outboard, clutching a shroudstay, and pointed. "Just look at the troop transports, Mister Romart. Forming up, they are, to parade the bay for your Colonials to marvel at. It strikes me the Ministers has had about enough of yer American foolery and are out to put a stop to it."

Beside him, Michael Romart stifled a growl. "A bit of simple justice would have stopped it before it started. But it will take more than what you see there to stop it now. We're a bit tired of outmoded British ways over here, and plain done with being subjects of the king."

Purdy Fisk, coiling lines beside the mast, peered around for a look. "I don't see what difference the king makes, Mister Romart. Me, I've been an Englishman all me life, an' never yet laid eyes on him."

"Nor have I." Chilton Sand crossed to join them at the rail. "But I saw his troops burn New York, and I saw what the redcoats did at Chesterton. I was there."

"Bunch of seditionists," Mallory snorted. "Served 'em right, was how I heard it."

"Seditionists, is it?" Sand balled his fists, glowering at the grinning tar. "I might show you a bit of sedition, Georgie."

But Romart pushed between them, restraining the New Yorker. "Now hold on, Mister Sand. Claude is

only proddin' you. He's nobbut a sailor, and probably doesn't even know what sedition means."

"If you feel so about the war,"—Mallory glared—
"why are you here and not yonder fightin' for your
Colonial mates?"

Sand subsided, staring at the deck between his
feet. "I can't go back there. I'm wanted . . . on
charges."

"A penny if you find a man on this ship that isn't,"
Mallory reminded him. "Yet I apologize for what I
said . . . though if you've a mind to, Yankee Doodle,
you an' me can have us a lovely tussle sometime
when we've nothing better to do."

"I accept your apology," Sand decided. "But I still
believe your king is a buffoon."

"Cap'n says the king is German," Fisk pointed out.

"I mean the king of England!"

"The very one." Fisk spread his hands and
shrugged, overwhelmed by it all.

On the quarterdeck, Dalton had noticed the commotion and beckoned John Tidy. "Mister Tidy, what
are those men doing there?"

Tidy cocked a brow. "I believe they're discussing
politics, sir. Would you like for them to stop?"

"I'd like them to pay attention to what we are
about."

"Aye, sir. I'll tell them. Ah, sir . . . is that right?
About the king being a German gentleman, I mean?"

"That is correct, Mister Tidy."

"Then how does he come to be our king, sir?"

"It is very complicated, Mister Tidy."

"Aye, sir."

By four bells of the dogwatch, *Cornwall* had gained
to within five miles of the fleeing *Fury*, and the seventy-four's gundecks were visible from the tops. Also
visible was the eastern shore of Long Island, and
Patrick Dalton could wait no longer. "Hands to
sheets," he ordered. "Haul about for a hard port tack.

145

Helm, bring us about to starboard, through the wind, please, and jibe spanker and spencer by the whistle."

"Aye, sir." Whistles shrilled and *Fury* came dead in the water as her nose traced the closing squall line from northwest to northeast. Yards were hauled over, sheet-lines belayed and trimmed, and she took the spanking wind on her port bow and in tight-hauled canvas aloft. For a moment she bobbed on the rolling sea, while eyes turned toward the seventy-four behind them, coming about for its own reverse tack to intercept.

"Playing it a bit close to suit me," Charley Duncan muttered, then grinned at his own words. Far from being troubled by the closeness of course, he found it exciting.

Fury took the new wind in her high sails and began to move, gathering way.

"Wind is shifting a bit more easterly, sir," Billy Caster noted. "Did you expect it to do that, sir?"

"I rather hoped it might. Mister Tidy, hands to the sheets, please. Stand by to come about again. Helm, stand down. I'll take the wheel now."

"Aye, sir." Victory Locke's retort ended in a sigh of relief. The snow's lithe hull and responsive rudder were a delight to guide in a lesser wind, but this tacking close-hauled into winds of nearly gale force had put knots in his shoulders and an ache in his head.

Dalton took the helm, thrilling as always at the feel of a nimble ship in his hands. No more plotting of courses now, he knew. From here it would be sailing by guess and by luck, and he willed the wind to do what the squall-dark north said it might — swing around to the east . . . rapidly, if God willed it. A slow shift, on this tack, would drive *Fury* right back down upon the *Cornwall* with no recourse. Already she was angling more and more toward the big ship's closing path. They were four miles apart now . . . then three, both beating hard into a shifting wind. In the distance to the north, not more than ten miles away now, the horizon was a close dark wall of walking storm.

Handling the wheel as a skilled craftsman might handle his tools, Dalton held *Fury* at the very edge of her wind, her stem more than sixty degrees into it. A degree more, and she would be in irons, sails dead and no way to move. A degree less, and she would fall right into the lap of the seventy-four less than three miles away and closing relentlessly.

"Now," he breathed, reading wind gauge, horizon and the increasing coldness of the wind on his cheek. "Now . . . or never. Mister Tidy! Hands to all sheets! Haul full about and trim for a broad reach with wind on the starboard! Smartly, now!"

Wide-eyed sailors complied, and Dalton put the helm over smoothly. *Fury* swung her nose through the wind, faltered and stood, helpless and motionless in a wind that did nothing for her sails.

"Now," Dalton whispered, lowering his head.

As though obeying his command, the wind shifted. For an instant it stilled, then gusted, and a new wind came out of the east to take waiting sails and fill them. *Fury* heeled sharply to port, raised her nose and began to crawl, then to stride, then to sing.

Billy Caster let out a long-held breath. "Whooee," he said.

Two miles back, *Cornwall* had been taken off guard. The great ship sat, still on tight tack with no proper wind to hold it. Rather than *Fury* being in irons, now it was the seventy-four that had the wind on its nose and nowhere to go.

A moment passed, then white clouds erupted at four points along *Cornwall*'s port battery, and the maintop called, "Sir, he has fired!"

"What is he shooting at?" Duncan gawked.

147

Dalton trimmed the rudder and didn't look back. Odd, he thought. I saluted him. Now he has returned my salute.

Within minutes the dwindling ship behind them had come about and had the new wind on its tail, racing away to return to its duty.

With good wind on her starboard beam, *Fury* cruised northward, jaunty and dancing on rising swells as the darkness ahead grew. "We shall hold this course for a bit," Dalton told Victory Locke as he returned the helm to him. "I think the convoy will be well past when we come about and resume our journey."

Cloud-deck running ahead of the advancing squalls reached outward to blot the northern sky, and below it was seething darkness. They ran on, relaxing a bit after the tension of escape, and Dalton sent Billy Caster below to copy some selected portions of the documents they had taken from Felix Croney. Charley Duncan went forward to see to the comfort of his orchestra, and pans clattered faintly in the galley below the companion hatch where one of the Misters O'Riley was preparing supper.

"We will come about once more, Mister Tidy," Dalton told his aft bosun. "Then when we are secured you may tell off watches and shifts. Send those aloft below first. They have had a trying . . ."

"On deck! On deck! On deck! Holy mother of . . ."

Dalton turned, craning to see aloft. "Tops report!"

"It's a line of battle ship, sir! Another one, an' the bleedin' thing is . . ."

"Whereaway?"

"Starboard bow, sir. Came right out of the friggin' weather. It's runnin' right for us, sir!"

148

XIV

With north wind square behind her, Isaac Watson's HMS *Royal Lineage* had rounded off the cape at fifteen knots and ranged far out to sea, scouting and hunting, hoping for a second prize to match her first. From quarterdeck to forecastle, hands worked with a will as Watson paced his high deck and sharp-eyed lookouts aloft scanned for sail.

As a commissioned ship of the line, *Royal Lineage* adhered to Admiralty regulations in the dividing of prizes, each man-jack from officers to the lowest cabin boy receiving a prescribed share of what the auction block produced. So, despite their captain's annoyance at having been pulled from fleet duty to harry the north coasts, it was a gleeful crew that set about the task of seeking prizes of war. Life at sea was hard at best. An able seaman's pay was barely two pounds per month, and for that he must work two watches each day on a fair cruise, double that in hard weather and watch-on-watch in combat. He must subsist on a regular diet of salt-something-and-onions (the onions were reliably onions, but the salt-something might be anything), oatmeal, tack and occasional juice of limes. He was on call at all times to perform the most arduous, bone-crushing tasks at a moment's notice, often in extreme hazard, and life expectancy for a man who served before the mast was approximately three years. Each watch brought with it the chance of being impaled upon a boathook, crushed by a runaway cannon, broken at the capstan, swept over by a rogue line, thrown from the tops by a gust or torn apart by chain or cannister from an enemy's guns. His comforts were four hours of uninterrupted rest when he could find it and the occasional ration of watered rum. The ships of the king were killing machines, and their own crews were not immune.

Balanced against that, though, was the chance of riches. A captured merchantman or privateer might make anywhere from ten thousand to eighty thousand pounds at the auction block, and each man of the victor's crew — captain to cabin boy — shared in the remainder after the Crown took its share.

A man could grow wealthy on His Majesty's service, if he lived long enough.

At an easy seventeen knots, *Royal Lineage* cruised east of south, keeping the forming squall line behind her, sweeping broad in an outbound arc looking for prey. It was a rare opportunity, this change in the weather. The big ship could use the wind to her best advantage, and still be hard to see by anyone ahead. Still, the chance of spotting a prize off this coast — it would be well known by now that a convoy with escorts was inbound — was slight, and when the wind shifted easterly, Isaac Watson had the seventy-four brought over on the wind while his sailing master reckoned a proper course to bring them home to the Long Island anchorage.

With the change in wind, the squall line began to break up. Separate little storms skittered off, rolling away from the dark cloudwall to sweep away on the wind, forming and reforming in a widening band southward. Skirling winds whipped *Royal Lineage*'s pennants and sang skirling tunes in her rigging, and rains swept down upon her to flood and spray from her sails and drive at the embellishments of her stern. Hands a'deck, their oil skins whipping about them, waded barefoot in torrents that sometimes swept ankle-deep toward the scuppers, and clung to rails and hand-lines as they went about their work. Then, as quickly as it had come, the squall would pass, making way for another which must follow.

In the sheltered quarterdeck recess, Watson stood at ease, enjoying the weather. Fine sailing, for a big ship. No day for lesser craft, he told himself, but a bit of blow now and then is but a dancing tune to this big lady—a chance to sway and roll a bit, to get her timbers resettled and her blood flowing.

Rising seas bounded to meet her, and her great bow split them and coursed through them, hull strakes of hardwood four inches thick booming like a great drum. Another squall swept over her and she rode in its murk for the turn of a glass while Watson noted how the spray of wavetops blended more and more with the spray of blown rain, waters of two elements mingling as wind gusts increased. Black squalls, turning to white squalls. "We shall find no more game this day, Mister Race," he told his deck officer. "No small craft will be out in this, if it has a haven to go to."

Blind walls of rain stood around the ship, pelting astern and hissing along her bows. Even with sails reefed now, *Royal Lineage* still thundered on at a strong ten knots. The wind gusted, shifted and the gray wall ahead brightened.

"We are clearing," Watson told his officer. "Lookouts aloft, please, Mister Race."

"Aye, sir."

Like a great, dark beast coming into morning, *Royal Lineage* broke through the curtains of rain and raised her nose on rolling swells to sniff the clearing air. A topman halfway up the port shrouds pointed and

151

shouted, and others turned to see. There, just ahead off the port bow, sailed a ship close-hauled, beating up the wind's front and on collision course. Hardly a mile separated them, and Watson and Race got out their glasses.

"A brig, sir," Race said. "One of ours, do you think? A messenger?"

"Possibly. Run up our colors, please, for a response." Watson stepped to the quarterrail and braced himself, steadying his glass. A brig—but yet not a brig, somehow. Even close-hauled and on short canvas, the smaller vessel had a trim and rapacious look to it—more predator, somehow, than messenger. The Union Jack whipped and snapped as it rose on its halyard to flare out alongside the seventy-four's mizzen shrouds, but Isaac Watson snapped his glass closed and strolled back to the recess, not watching for a response. "He won't answer, Mister Race," he said, not looking around.

"No, sir, he is not responding to colors."

"He will put about and run," Watson said.

For a long moment there was silence, then Race said, "He is making to put about, sir. As you said."

"Let us have a bit more sail, Mister Race. We have a prize in sight."

"Aye, sir." Race called the order, then, "How did you know, sir?"

"Because I know the vessel, Mister Race. Yonder is not a brig, but a snow. Quite a different breed of fox, though they look a bit alike. And I wager it is that same snow that our recent passenger, Commander Croney, was out to find. The fugitive ship, if you recall."

"Yes, sir. I certainly do."

"A nice snow," Watson said. "I'm told that another, very like her, brought forty thousand pounds at the London block. The *Fair American*, it was. The buyers probably have hired her on warrant, and I wager she sails with the Blue Fleet now." He glanced at his watch officer, saw the narrowing of his eyes, the hint of a smile at his cheeks. "Aye, Mister Race. Your personal share of forty thousand pounds would be a thousand. Not bad for a brief evening's work, eh?"

He turned to look ahead again. The snow was running now, dead with the wind, and had gained a quarter mile while the larger, more massive sails of *Royal Lineage* were being sheeted home for the chase. "A good start," Watson said. "The man is a sailor. I've seen men come near to capsizing a small vessel by wringing it around so."

"Aye, sir," Race nodded, appreciating the sleek, jaunty ship in the distance. "He may give us a bit of sport before we bring him under our guns, don't you suppose?"

"A bit, possibly. But only a bit." He looked upward at the great ship's canvas, snapping into place. "Very well, Mister Race. Let's go and get him."

Alfred Hickman, as manager of the Continental Chamber Ensemble of Maestro Galante Pico—and one of the few among the group who could speak English—was unhappy. Stowed away in a fore hold that actually was not a hold at all so much as a stubby and dark little cloister between the capstan housing and the shot locker, tossed and tumbled about in this vile space with a bunch of spitting and fretting musicians while various things seemed to be occurring above that no one saw fit to tell him about, and thoroughly tired of the sulking glares of the harpsichordist Joseph Miller, Hickman made the decision to go somewhere else.

Since there seemed no way through the grate that several brawny sailors had secured atop the hatch, Hickman explored until he found a crawlway leading aft. On hands and knees he eased himself into the little space—nothing more than a skeleton frame consisting of hull members below, deck braces on the sides, and a roof which was actually the underside of the stores locker—and worked his way along in near darkness, aiming toward a glow of lamplight beyond.

The little tunnel seemed to go on and on, a cold, vertiginous chute that rolled him first one way and then another as the ship braced growing waves and walked across them. Within five feet, he bumped his head soundly against a deckbrace, acquired torn breeches and several bruises, and came within a hair of falling through a spill chute into the gurgling bilges just below. All around him, timbers whined and grunted, things slipped and sloshed in the murk, and noisome odors of tar, hemp, wet wood and cooking onions wafted about. He might have turned around and given up the adventure, but clinging as he was to a monkey puzzle of dark timbers and slats in the bowels of an enthusiastically rocking ship, he couldn't fathom how to turn around. He went on.

The hole widened slightly where beams made way for an upright, cylindrical shadow with barely space to crawl past it on either side. Pushing forward, he rested his head against it for a moment, then shifted to press his ear to its wooden surface. The thing sounded as though it were alive. A symphony of sounds seemed to live within it—muted cracklings, deep-pitched moans, distant rattles and creaks . . . He listened, fascinated, until something nudged him from behind. He tried to turn, but had no room to move. "Who is that back there?" he hissed.

The voice behind him was muted. "Pardon, M'sieu le manager. It is I, Ansel Cleride. Where are we going?"

"I'm trying to find my way to the . . ."

The dim light faded, a shadow loomed ahead and a voice said, " 'Ere now! Who's this dallyin' amongst the keelin'?" A lantern hove into view just beyond, spilling

154

light past a squatting sailor, and the shadow said, "Why, it's some of the music gentlemen! What are you doin' here?"

"Trying to crawl through," Hickman said. "I want to talk to the captain."

"Oh, he's busy right now," the shadow said. "Why don't you just turn around and go back where you're supposed to be?"

"I can't turn around! What is this place, anyway? And this thing here?"

"This is th' struts, sir. What else? An' that there is the foremast." The shadow shrugged. "Down here it's like any foremast. Can you back up?"

"I don't know." Hickman partially turned his head. "M'sieur Cleride, can you back up?"

"I regret I cannot," the second violinist said, behind him. "I am stuck here."

"We can't back up," Hickman told the silhouetted sailor.

"Aye, well, I expect you'd better come on through, then." The sailor scampered back, out of the way, agile as a monkey among the incomprehensible structures. "Have a care, here. We're bucking just a bit."

With an effort, Hickman half crawled and was half pulled from the crawlspace. The tiny area in which he found himself was almost filled with great coils of dark rope, some of it a foot thick, it seemed. The sailor helped him get his feet under him and Hickman tried to stand upright, bumping his head against a deckbeam. The sailor, crouched comfortably in the short space, steadied him, then gripped his hand in a callused palm and shook it enthusiastically. "Abel Ball, sir. Able seaman. Yonder with the lantern is Mister Tower. He's the ship's carpenter. We greatly enjoyed the music today, sir. We certainly did. Do you play one of the fiddles, or something?"

"I am Alfred Hickman," he said, rubbing his head. "I am the manager." Bending carefully, he pointed back into the dark maze of timbers. "That is Ansel Cleride. He plays one of the . . . fiddles."

"How do you do," Cleride said from the hole.

The sailor stooped to look into the crawlway, while Joseph Tower thrust his lamp closer. "It's a great pleasure, Mister Fiddle . . ."

"Cleride," Cleride corrected. "Ansel Cleride."

"Aye, sir. Though I didn't care for the Mozart as much as some. A bit modern for my taste, y'see."

"Vivaldi is more traditional," the carpenter agreed. "Times must change, though, for all that. Mister Ball, I believe the fiddle gentleman is involved with that stanchion brace there, where the gundeck strut angles it."

"Aye, I believe that's his trouble. Mister Fiddle, sir . . ."

"Cleride," Cleride said.

"Aye, that's the spirit. Sir, if you could remove your head from that scupper notch and sort of straddle the keelson there . . . Aye, the big timber just beneath you . . . No, that's just made it worse, hasn't it?"

"Now he is involved with the futtock scarph," Tower pointed out.

A second lamp appeared beyond the carpenter and a red-haired face peered around him. "Make way, lads. I need dried peas." The new arrival squeezed past the carpenter and squatted to peer into the footings. "Who is that?"

"One of the fiddlers, Mister O'Riley. He's got himself bound up between the scupperbrace and the futtock scarph. What's the word above? Are we still on a north heading?"

"That's what I wanted to talk to the captain about," Hickman said.

"Oh, that's all right, sir," Abel Ball assured him. "The captain generally knows which way we're going." He peered into the crawlway again. "Mister Fiddle, would you like us to see if we can pry you loose with a boathook?"

"Have him pass the dried peas first," the cook urged. "One of those bales yonder, just a'starboard of his knee. Aye, that's them. One of those, please, Mister Fiddle."

Hickman edged past the growing crowd in the cable tiers and stooped to duck through a hatch. Beyond, a pair of stripe-shirted sailors worked to renew lashings on stacked bales, crates, kegs and barrels. One of them squinted at him and he asked, "Can you give me directions to the deck?"

"Through there." The sailor pointed at another dark monkey-puzzle crawlway very much like the one he had just escaped. "Past the footings is the main stores. Beyond that's the galley; that opens on the companionway, and that goes up to the deck."

Pale, shaken and disoriented, Hickman entered the main crawlway and continued his journey.

At sight of the huge ship driving down upon them, Dalton knew no choices remained. "Hands a'deck!" he shouted. "Topmen aloft to make sail! Courses full, tops and to'gallants! Gunners aft to the stern chasers, please! Mister Wise, haul a'right for full and by the wind! Helm, hard a'port, Mister Locke. Mister Tidy, to the fore! Ask Mister Duncan to come aft, please! Mister Caster, please go below and have us secured for chase. Then help cook secure his galley. Mister Bean, please tell those musicians to take hold of something solid and hang on. Then secure that hatch."

In the driving wind, *Fury* responded to her rudder as quickly as a boat, swinging to the left with a force that chattered her stays and shook her timbers.

The companion hatch, just rising, snapped full open and a black-coated figure with torn breeches popped through and tumbled on the deck alongside the coaming. Sailors hurrying to station leapt over him and went on their way.

High yards swung out square with the deck, and sheeted sails drummed like musketfire as they took the full weight of the wind. Beside the coaming, Alfred Hickman clambered to his feet, clinging to a spar pulley. *Fury* surged, plowed a wave with her bow, bunched her haunches and sprang forward, nose high and rising, to thunder into the next roller. Hickman lost his grip on the pulley and tumbled, disappearing into steerage beneath the quarterdeck. John Tidy stooped, looked into the space, then straightened. "One of the musicians is in steerage, sir. He's trussed up in hammocks there."

"Tell him to stay where he is, Mister Tidy. We're a bit busy right now."

Through the open companion hatch came ringing, crashing sounds followed by the voice of an O'Riley: "There goes the friggin' porridge! Mind where you step, mister. . . !"

Billy Caster threw himself into the companionway and pulled the hatch closed behind him. A moment later his head reappeared. "One of the musicians is tangled in the foremast struts, sir!" The hatch closed again.

As *Fury* took the spray in her teeth and high staysails billowed above her nose, Dalton turned, braced himself and raised his glass. Even at the distance, the ship back there—putting on sail now to pursue—seemed huge. Dark and massive, a floating fortress beneath a mountain of sail, it positioned itself serenely and began its chase.

At *Fury*'s helm, Victory Locke glanced astern, his face pale under its windburn. "Can we outrun him, sir?"

"That is a full seventy-four back there, Mister Locke," Dalton said. "Her hull speed is more than twice ours, and she has the weather gauge. No, we cannot outrun him . . . not in this wind or any other."

XV

Still, he had to try. All the months of running and
hiding, all the frustrations, the dishonor done his
name—and only now had he glimpsed the dimmest
hope that there might be a way to set those matters to
rights. All the trust that had been put in his hands, by
so many young men made fugitive by circumstances
of time and place—and the trust put in him by an
auburn-haired girl who somehow could look at him
and see beyond what he saw of himself—all these
hung now upon a single fact: no matter how futile the
hope that a vessel less than a hundred feet in hull
length could escape a vessel of two hundred and
twenty feet, still he must try.

All these factors weighted upon Patrick Dalton as
Fury's wide sails took the biting wind and her bow
boomed and skimmed the winter waves. Yet, oddly,
only one such thought came clearly: I have not yet
settled accounts with Ian McCall as to whose ship this
rightly is. To lose a ship I have not proved is
mine . . .

As though mocking him, a formula came to
mind—a thing that every midshipman learned by
rote, just as he learned the use of sextant and the
proportion of beam to length of a proper craft.

The square root of waterline multiplied by one-point-four.

Hull speed.

Long legs wide-spread to ride the pitching deck, Dalton looked forward, his eyes musing upon the slim gundeck of *Fury*, the trim, rising prow beyond the high, stepped masts, the elegant strength of her long bowsprit, the span of spreader says there, the lean, challenging thrust of her jaunty jib. Sleek, he thought. Trim and deep-keeled. Lively and vital as a fine lady, she is. Such craft was never meant to be curtailed by formulas. Formulas were for brigs. *Fury* was a snow!

His eyes roved upward, to the drum-tight great sails on their spars. Courses full out and snapping, topsails alive with the driving wind, topgallants high above, straining at their tapered yards . . . And above that still more mast, and other tackle.

What brig was ever built for skysails, he reminded himself. Or for studdingsails and a ringtail?

Why did the Americans call it a bobtail? He put the thought aside.

And aft the mainmast a second main — a jackmast for press of canvas beyond all else she carried.

"Belay that, Mister Locke," he muttered.

"What, sir?"

"What? Oh . . . what I said about hull speeds, Mister Locke. It was a foolish comment. Outrun him or not, certainly we are going to try."

"Aye, sir. But the hull speeds?"

"By formula, Mister Locke, we have a best speed of not more than fourteen knots. That seventy-four rates twenty-one knots or thereabout. It is an English shipbuilder's formula, Mister Locke. *Fury* is American-designed." He stepped to the quarterrail. "Mister Tidy!"

"Aye, sir?"

"Cruise reports, Mister Tidy?"

160

"Wind steady and near thirty, sir. Hard to read, but near gale force at the moment. We are at twelve knots and gaining, maybe thirteen now."

"Very well, Mister Tidy. Hands to courses, tops and t'gallants to clew in studdingsails, please."

The bosun's eyes widened, his cheeks going pale. But he nodded, "Aye, sir," and lay to his whistle.

Charley Duncan had come from the fore, and his eyes also were wide with wonder. "Studdingsails, sir? In this wind?"

"Studdingsails, Mister Duncan. And smartly. Run out and sheet home wing and wing, and you can give Mister Tidy his next instructions. Give us a two-knot gain, then have the skysails run up, fore and main. Not main and fore, Mister Duncan. Fore and main, by the drill."

"Sir, we will break up . . ."

"Possibly, Mister Duncan. Or possibly this ship's designer did their mathematics properly. I know of only one way to find out."

"Aye, sir."

"And have four hands stand by the main. Mister Hoop, I believe—he is the strongest we have—and three other sturdy lads. The weather is pacing us, have you noticed? We might want to do some things with our spanker directly."

Along both sides of *Fury*'s banks of sail, extender yards ran out and new sails snapped to full, almost doubling the width of her great lower courses, tapered topsails and high topgallants. The howl of stressed timbers rang hollow through the hull. Aloft, spars bowed visibly and stays sang shrill as they took the pressure of the bound masts. Everywhere along the deck, men clung for support as *Fury* sprinted ahead, bounding from the crest of a broad wave, thundering with shock as she hit the next bow-on. High sheets of bright water grew along her forerails, towered over the deck and streamed off in the wind. Rushing water foamed ankle-deep through the fore scuppers and streamed back along the rising deck. She faltered for an instant, fighting the mass of water at her keel, the mass of wind-force aloft . . . then rose above the trough she had made and settled into her new stride.

"Sixteen knots, sir! Coming to seventeen . . ."

"Now, Mister Duncan!"

His voice thin, white-knuckled hands clutching the rail, Duncan called, "Skysails, please, Mister Tidy. Look alive, please. Haul afore!"

"Aye, sir." The whistle shrilled, and a patch of canvas rode a spar aloft to shudder into its braces a hundred and twenty feet above the deck. *Fury* shuddered and sang.

"Main skysail, Mister Tidy! Haul a'main!"

Again the whistle, and another sail rose atop the main royal, ten feet higher than its forward twin.

Victory Locke found himself in a struggle with his helm. "She's trying to heel, sir!" he called.

Dalton leapt to the helm and gripped a pair of wheel-hobs, adding his strength to Locke's to hold it from turning. "Mister Duncan! Two hands to steerage to assist on the tiller! Rudder amidships and steady!"

"Aye, sir!"

A pair of sailors scurried out of sight, beneath the quarterdeck, and in a moment the fighting wheel subsided as their brawn was thrown against the coupled tiller below.

"Can you hold it now, Mister Locke?"

"Aye, sir. Thank you, sir."

Dalton took a deep breath and looked astern. In her swift dash, *Fury* had gained distance. The huge warship looked smaller now, with distance. A good two miles back, its high hull was visible only when it climbed the swells.

"At the very least," Dalton muttered, "we have given the gentleman a bit of a surprise."

"Sir?"

"I'd wager he was expecting to put us under his guns within an hour, Mister Locke. Now he is recalculating, wondering whether he can close in time for supper."

"Can he, sir?"

"I don't know, Mister Locke. It depends upon what kind of seaman he is."

In the bowels of a bounding snow, pounding its way through ten-foot seas while every square sail it can set is battered by a thirty-knot wind, things scream and writhe and resettle. Timbers shift to take new stresses, mast footings moan the lament of lost souls. Lashings twist and shift. Lockers chatter and besieged hull timbers are rolling thunder. Great forces play the vessel, tension against tension, and even the treenails in their driven sheaths join in the song. Things twang, things shrill, things crash and things go boom.

Surrounded by this, Ansel Cleride shrieked, contorted himself in ways he would never have thought possible, and abruptly ceased his involvement with *Fury's* underpinnings. Abel Ball and Joseph Tower pulled the second violinist dripping and reeking from the bilges and deposited him in the cold nest of a coil of mooring line.

"If I was you, sir," Ball suggested, "I believe I would just stay there until we have smoother sailing."

The comment was unnecessary. Cleride wasn't about to go anyplace.

"We're needed topside," Tower told him. "We'll have to take the lamp—wouldn't want it running afoul of the powder magazine, you see—but someone will be back to retrieve you directly. If we're still afloat."

"That is a madman yonder, sir." Calvin Race rubbed his eyes, then peered again at the fleeing snow.

"In this weather, with all sails set. A point a'shift and he'll capsize. Or more likely, break that brig's back. There won't be enough flotsam left to be worth coming about for."

"Snow," Captain Isaac Watson said.

"Sir?"

"I said, it is a snow, Mister Race. Not a brig. They are a bit different."

"Aye, sir, I've seen the trysail mast behind the main. But that won't keep it from tearing itself apart."

"No, it won't," Watson admitted. "I wonder, though. Would a marine architect devise the means for extra sails and not modify the hull accordingly? Have you inspected a snow, Mister Race?"

"No, sir. I haven't had the opportunity."

"Nor have I. But Jamie Feldon spoke of one his *Duke of York* took off Bermuda last year. Privateer belaboring the Cape trade. Quite an extraordinary vessel, he said. Extended keel or something. Very stable, for a small cruiser. And strong, by his reckoning. I suppose our shipwrights have had a look at a few of them by now . . . and I suppose we are witnessing what they can do. What is our speed, Mister Race?"

"We're full on, sir. I estimate twenty-four, twenty-five knots. The wind has come up to about thirty-three."

"And still he runs ahead of us."

"Oh, we are closing, sir. But slowly. Master Chaplin reckons his speed at more than eighteen."

"Extraordinary." Watson raised his telescoping glass again, for a better look. The little ship was still more than a mile ahead, racing down the wind with every sail full on. Broad courses on the lower yards, topsails above, topgallants stacked above those, and six studdingsails spread wide at each mast—and above it all, skysails billowed at the very tops of the triplex masts. Let one stayline part, one shroudpin give way, one brace at its keel slip the least bit, and the snow would

164

tear itself apart in an explosion of shattered timber and scatter itself across a half-mile of ocean.

"Extraordinary," he muttered again.

"I could have a spritsail run out, sir," Race suggested. "It might give us another knot—though we are overrunning our hull now by three or four."

"And have him respond the same, Mister Race? I think not. Just steady on. He can't outrun us, even at that speed, and I'd rather not press him to panic. How he is holding that ship together now is a mystery."

"Aye, sir." Race was a bit relieved. He had visions of the snow breaking up . . . and of his share of a pretty prize flying away as wreckage on the wind. Still, as officer of the watch, it was his duty to suggest. "The squalls are pacing us, sir. He may yet be forced to take in sail. A squall would certainly wreck him."

"Yes, no doubt. Well, in any case, that gentleman will be either ours or God's within two bells."

Fury raced. Half past her hull speed—or very near that, for it was no longer possible from the low rails to test by log and line—she clove the waves and thundered in the troughs while strong hands on two plank decks struggled to keep her tail precisely square to the wind. A degree off could skew her about in this weather. A compass point off true could capsize her.

Dark squalls danced out from the hanging clouds to parade the darkening sea—lashing, swirling little storms that joined running seas to low skies in patches of oblivion—sometimes so near at hand that their deadly gusts rattled the sprockets of the little ship's widespread studdingsails.

She ran and she danced and she strained. Backstays on both tortured masts keened in torment, and her sails strained at the limits of their clews. The three staysails at her thrusting stem belled upward, almost level with the whitecaps ranked ahead.

Dalton himself manned the helm now. Victory Locke stood below the quarterrail to signal those in steerage. In the murky space there, Claude Mallory and Michael Romart struggled with the long tiller-bar coupled below the helm, adding their strength to Dalton's above. Charley Duncan clung to a handline on the pitching quarterdeck, drenched with spray, to relay signals to the working deck beyond.

For a time it had seemed that they might outdistance the big warship trundling along behind. Distances were hard to estimate on rough seas. But it was obvious now that the seventy-four was steadily, relentlessly overtaking the snow. In an hour's time, the distance between had closed from two miles to one, and *Fury* had nothing more to give. Nothing of her size— no matter how cleverly built—could outmatch the great mass of sail stacked above a ship of the line.

And when the big ship closed, it would be over. The seventy-four carried big ranging guns that could reach out a third of a mile, and keep reaching until they found their mark. Even should the snow turn and fight, there was no gun among its eighteen that could do more than bounce ironshot from the warship's hull at the range where its larger guns could beat the snow to death.

Spray dripped from Patrick Dalton's lashes and from his bound queue, and the eyes that blazed from beneath his furrowed brow were bleak. Another hour of time—time to run and dodge in fading light—another three knots of speed . . . would have given him a chance. But the seventy-four closed steadily, looming dark against the squalls beyond, and there was far too much daylight remaining for the distance that remained. He glanced aside, where four burly sailors awaited his orders. Mister Hoop, huge and wet, seemed half again the size of any of the others, but Purdy Fisk was all whipcord and shoulders, and the two Colonials—Abel Ball and Paul Unser—also were exceptionally strong men.

They would need their strength soon. *He* would need their strength. It was clear that the final gambit—the thing he had prayed would not be necessary—must be played soon. It was only a matter of time, now.

Of time, and of precise opportunity . . . and of hope that the man commanding *Royal Lineage*—now so near he could almost hear the drumming of its hull—would hesitate to damage or destroy a vessel that could be a valuable prize.

He won't chance sinking us if he can help it, Dalton told himself. If he must fire, he will fire to impede or cripple, not to destroy. He'll want *Fury* as a prize.

I hope.

Within a bell . . . less than that—within half a bell—we shall know.

Another squall had formed nearby. Wide and dark, maybe a mile across, it walked aflank the port beam, pacing them, and *Fury's* studdingsails rattled as its perimeter winds harried them. A quarter mile away, dark and angry, the storm strode—death awaiting a ship oversuited to its wind. Death aport . . . and defeat astern. And nowhere to go.

"Hands to all sheets, Mister Duncan," he called, and heard it relayed to the bosun on the deck. "Stand by to make about . . . on call and by the drill."

Moments passed, and now he could in fact hear the warship in his wake. The rolling thunder of its great hull came clearly on the wind, deep-pitched and relentless. At a thousand yards he could also hear the pitch of its mighty sails. He tensed, waiting, half expecting its bow chasers to speak. But the guns were silent while the hull-thunder grew. He glanced around and drew a hard breath.

Royal Lineage stood tall and dark behind *Fury* now—so near that he could read her proud name on her

167

escutcheons. As dark and deadly as the black squall pacing him to his left, the big ship closed — methodical, merciless, a predator preparing to take its prey.

Charley Duncan stared up at it, his warrior's face alive with fierce excitement. "We could salute him, sir. We have the stern chasers . . . We could at least give him some scars."

"He has not fired at us, Mister Duncan."

"No, sir, but he's about to."

In easy gun range now, the big ship was edging to starboard — coming on, closing and angling to bring its main battery to bear.

XVI

In steerage, Alfred Hickman lay bruised and battered, trussed among slung hammocks like a rabbit in a snare. He wasn't at all sure where he was or how he came to be here—in a murky, low place too short for an ordinary man to stand upright, while near at hand two straining sailors braced bare feet on planking and strained against a writhing pole that jutted from the dark rear wall and was bound with rope and pulleys. The room had no wall in front, just an overhang beyond which stood another sailor, clinging to ropes and watching intently something above, that Hickman could not see.

He had determined that the things binding him were hammocks. They were twisted and looped around his waist and arms, and around his knees so that he was suspended between floor and ceiling with only his head free to look around. On the other side, beyond the place where the men struggled with the pole, were other hammocks—narrow rope nests suspended from hooks, ranked in rows less than two feet apart and less than two feet from those above and below.

He did know, though, that he was in a dire situation, and so was everyone else aboard. The ship was

169

being pursued by something big, formidable and hostile . . . something the sailors called a "seventy-four." And the ship was moving much faster—from what he had overheard—than it was really intended to go. Glum comments had been passed around, within his hearing. Ominous comments, having to do with the certainty of death and destruction momentarily. The only question seemed to be whether they would all die by act of war or by act of God. The two men straining at the long pole seemed to be involved in their defense against God. Someone else, he gathered, was conducting their defense against enemies.

He struggled, trying to free himself from the restraining hammocks, realizing that the bucking pole the two were gripping was so near that, should it get loose, it would surely brain him while he hung helpless. He twisted again and got one arm free from his restraints. The sailor nearest him, the one he had seen below in the awful crawlway, gritted, "Just hold still, sir. We don't have time to attend to you just now."

Beyond, on the deck, someone said, "Lord help us, that seventy-four is right on our tail. If he lets go with those bow chasers now, we'll never know what hit us."

"Can you swim, Mister Romart?" Abel Ball panted, fighting as the tiller bar tried to break free.

"Aye," the other said. "Though I wish sometimes I'd never learned the art."

"Blessed right," the first said. "It's better not to swim. Such only prolongs a man's drowning."

Out on the deck whistles shrilled, and men scurried about the rails and masts to take stations beside various bundles of cables that soared upward from pinrails. The sailor standing just beyond the ledge said, "Captain's called for coming about."

Abel Ball's face blanched in the dusk. "Do you mean, 'reef sail and come about,' Mister Locke?"

"No. Just . . . come about."

"I've heard that there are things in the sea that pick

a man's bones clean on the way to the bottom, so that all that ever stands to greet Davy Jones is a bleedin' skeleton."

"Mister Ball . . ."

"Aye, Mister Romart?"

"Shut your raving mouth and mind this tiller."

"Aye, I believe that's best." Ball grunted and sagged as his foot slipped on the wet planks beneath. "I've lost it! Hold . . ."

In sudden blind panic, Alfred Hickman saw the tiller inch aside, starting a swing toward his head. He braced his feet against the framing behind him, stretched out his free arm and caught it.

Ball secured his footing, got his shoulder into the tiller again and gasped, "Aye, but that was a sweet piece of work, sir. We are obliged." He glanced around. "Sir? Ah . . . you can turn loose now, sir. I believe we have it under control."

Hickman hung suspended, straight as an arrow from his braced feet to the hand gripping the bar, and seemed not to hear.

"You can turn the bleedin' thing loose now, sir," Ball encouraged.

"I don't believe he can," Romart said. "I think he has had a fit or something."

"Ah, the poor soul," Ball said. "I suppose I had better prize him loose, though. Coming about will be difficult enough, without a musician attached to the tiller."

"Try not to break his fingers," Romart suggested.

"Stand by to come about a'port," Victory Locke relayed.

"He's doing it," Michael Romart muttered. "All sail set and he is going to take a tack. God help us all."

Now it was by rote and by drill, and Dalton breathed a prayer that his two bosuns had instructed their men precisely. Tacking any square rigger was difficult. Coming about for tack in a strong following wind had been the final act of many an incautious seaman. But *Royal Lineage* was veering to bring him under her portside battery, and his time and options had run out. Had he had a hand free he would have crossed himself as he had seen his grandmother do so many times.

"Loose the course sheets, fore and main," he ordered, and Charley Duncan relayed the signal forward. Abruptly, *Fury's* two largest sails, the courses at her lower yards, flew free, snapping from their spars like huge horizontal banners. Their freed sheetlines popped in the wind, lashing outward like drovers' whips. *Fury* lost the edge of her racing speed, settling by several knots as the wave she rode tugged at her hull.

"He's lost his courses," Calvin Race pointed. "Is he breaking up, sir?"

"I don't think so." Isaac Watson peered through his glass. "No, they aren't lost. He's released his sheets."

"But why? What is he trying to do?"

"Who's to say, Mister Race? How long before we have him under our battery?"

"Only a moment, sir. He is losing way, it seems."

"Spencer a'starboard," Dalton called. "Sheet home, sheet home!"

The high fore-and-aft sail on *Fury's* foremast snapped taut, bucking at its gaff, its forward edge rippling and rattling. *Fury* plowed the crest of the wave she rode and slipped down the far side, her deck disappearing for a moment from the seventy-four's view.

"Release and haul in studdingsails!" Dalton called. "Loose the sheets."

At three banks of spar, studdingsails flew limply outward, snapping like pennants. Again *Fury* seemed to hesitate as her speed slacked again. She rode a trough that was a wide valley between the slopes of waves. Dalton clenched his teeth, counting seconds and estimating distances. Then he glanced to his right. "You men! Run out the ringtail! Lively now!"

Thunders came down on the wind, and the lofty towers of the battleship's great sails thrust high off *Fury's* starboard quarter. The proud stem of *Royal Lineage* thrust above the top of the following roller and grew as the warship's bow climbed the water. Just behind the starboard mainshrouds, *Fury's* driving spanker seemed to grow as the ringtail extension was run out on its gaff and boom, increasing its size by half. "Rig for starboard tack on the fore-and-afts!" Dalton called. "Maindeck, all yards hard a'lee!"

The bucking helm fought him as *Fury* tried to skew her tail to the right. Dalton fought the wheel as he knew those below were fighting the tiller. At the rail, Victory Locke watched him, waiting for his signal.

"He may have lost a shroud, sir," Calvin Race said. "See? His yards are askew. He will capsize."

Captain Watson scowled, rubbing his whiskers, trying to recall . . . something the guard officer, Croney, had told him . . . something about what this fugitive almost under his guns had done . . . about another vessel that he had stolen, so the charges said . . .

Now the great shoulders and massive weight of Mister Hoop and the strength of his three mates was put to the test. Even with blocks at tail and tow, setting and trimming a ringtailed driver in a thirty-knot wind was something few men could have done. Dalton held his breath as they struggled with the

173

lines; then the big sail over his head ceased its flutter and boomed in the wind.

"Spanker set, sir," Hoop panted.

Fury leaned to the right, trying to regain a bit of the speed she had lost. Her bow rose slightly as her masts tilted farther and farther to the right and spray washed across her starboard rails. She began to climb the slope of the wave ahead.

"There he goes, sir." Race sighed. "He has capsized the ship. There goes our prize."

For a moment Watson did not respond. What was it that chattering, prancing Croney had said?

Then he had it. A schooner. Patrick Dalton had escaped New York aboard a schooner, and had played the winds all the way up Long Island Sound, outrunning and outmaneuvering everything they could throw against him. A schooner! A vessel with fore-and-aft sails.

Hard intuition hit the senior captain and he cursed. "Come a'port, Mister Race."

"But sir, our port battery is nearly . . ."

"Come a'port, Mister Race! Now!"

"Ease the tiller by my call!" Dalton shouted. Victory Locke's shout was an echo of his own, and the feel of the helm changed as hard hands on the tiller below responded. Spoke by spoke, Dalton turned the wheel to his right, feeling the shudder and cant of the deck as *Fury*'s rudder turned to answer the demands of her sails. He braced his feet for balance. The snow's starboard gunwales dipped toward the slope of the wave ahead, and threw water in broad, bright sheets as her bow hit the sea aslant. He turned another point, then another. Skewing, slipping, *Fury* lurched and leaned as her nose swung to the left. The starboard gunwale dipped below the water, sending torrents racing along a strip of deck there. The high masts seemed almost to lay themselves upon the cheek of the fronting wave. He held his turn and watched nothing except the luff of the big sail above his head. It rolled and crackled, billows running along its surface. Then it fluttered and was still, a great drumhead of canvas tight-trimmed to the wind.

"Steady now!" Dalton shouted, reversing his turn of the wheel. In steerage below, muscles knotted in two sets of shoulders as the tiller was forced to respond. "Rudder amidships!" Dalton called. "Set and lash!"

With a thirty-knot wind on her port beam, tilted masts laying over at a frightening angle, *Fury* caught the flow with her deep keel and surged. Again the starboard gunwales went under and sailors clung to lines and rails everywhere.

"He's misjudged it," someone whispered.

"Mother Mary, pray for my soul," another responded.

For a long moment, *Fury* seemed to hang in precarious balance, deep-cutting keel against wind-battered sails. Then she surged again and long-held breaths were let out in whistles. She was gaining way, raising her nose. Seventy degrees from the gale and thirty degrees aslant, the snow rode her trough and scurried southward, while the turning bow of the great warship crested behind her.

"He has tacked," Calvin Race breathed. "By the great Lord Harry . . . he has changed sail and tacked. In this!"

"A snow," Isaac Watson muttered. "He plays it like a schooner."

"A snow." Race shook his head. "A brig that thinks it is a schooner." He glanced about at his captain. "Sorry, sir. I was thinking aloud. Sailing master!

Bring us two points to port! We still have the range, sir. I can bring him under our bow chasers."

"Possibly," Watson took a deep breath.

"Sir?"

"Look beyond him, Mister Race. He has sealed his own fate."

Race turned again, peering. Just ahead of the fleeing snow, a black squall paced the heaving seas, and the little ship bore down upon its deadly skirts as a moth to a flame.

At a pounding fifteen knots, *Fury* raced for swirling darkness that became a wall of water as she approached. There was no time now for another resetting of sail, no time for more than just to free the foot of the ringtail, lash down the helm and dive for cover. A few near the main made the companionway hatch and tumbled through before the first swirling cross-winds took the snow's stem and skewed her about, a toy boat in a millrace. Dalton was the last to leave the quarterdeck. Thrown off his feet, he skidded under and past the lashed harpsichord and crashed against the quarterrail. He tried to pull himself up, and pain shot through his left arm. Beyond the little rail he saw a massive wave wash across *Fury*'s deck amidship, waist-high to the men scrambling for cover there . . . and when it passed it seemed there were fewer of them than there had been. A whitecap slammed the ship's port quarter and drenched him with salt water. Levering with his right hand, he dragged himself half upright at the rail, and something collided with the back of his skull.

Charley Duncan and Victory Locke grabbed their captain by his boots and dragged him into the crowded steerage. They tried to rouse him, then tried to secure his limp form into a wildly swinging hammock, but something hit *Fury* like a great fist and they fell with him, rolling helpless about the deck.

Within, the black squall became a white squall and lashed at them, a rage of blindness. Torrents whipped past the open steerageway, first one way and then another, and they could barely see the throbbing jackmast just a few feet away. Distantly, somewhere ahead, something shrilled and splintered, and *Fury* writhed like a thing in pain. There were thudding, splashing sounds that blended themselves with thunders. *Fury* skewed this way and that, her timbers howling belowdeck, her stays wailing. Then she steadied, and somehow seemed to run, going with the storm like a craft in tow.

Darkness came, a blackness that was more than the murk of the storm, and those crowded into the steerageway, those below astern and those packed into the forward keep clung to whatever they could find to hold to . . . and prayed.

Royal Lineage achieved a sweeping broad tack, and penetrated the edge of the squall, her massive rigging protesting as she went. Beyond was blindness, and they brought her over to veer aside. They reefed sails, battened down and waited.

When the squall had passed, most of their daylight was gone. But still there was cloudlight, and still the winds held. Like a hunting hound, *Royal Lineage* worked this way and that across several miles of sea, looking for flotsam. A few things they found — several casks, a gunner's tub, a bit of sail aloft on a wavetop . . . a dead man tangled in the broken lashings of a water cask. But little more. No floating wreckage, no spreads of shattered hull or bits of framing timber.

The snow was gone. They searched until the light was gone, and found no further trace of it.

Part Three
In The Name
of Honor

XVII

Against a backdrop of glare and thunder, on a shifting stage where sometimes musicians performed Mozart between arguments about libretto, vibrato, allegro and destination, scenes were unfolding. An auburn-haired woman with her skirts tied up between her ankles touched fuse to the vent of a cannon and it sputtered there. She turned and her eyes were pleading. "You must decide, Patrick," she said. "I cannot do this alone." She faded — a shadow always there but backing off to wait. Smokes rolled across hazed waters where ships stood and fought and among them strode a gray man with ferret eyes and his hands filled with foolscap sheets. He turned abruptly, pointed an impaling finger and said, "If you are a traitor you must be tried. I shall see you tried . . . and I shall see you hanged." Lights shifted and there was another man there, broad-waisted and graying with his tied mane beneath a tricorn hat. Twin epaulettes caught sunlight to reflect on ruddy cheeks. He stood, studious, then shook his head. "I see no traitor here," he said. "He who stands accused does not necessarily stand convicted." He turned slightly away, and some of the years seemed to fall from him. "Mister Dalton," he snapped. "Please recite for me, Mister Dalton, the

181

formula for weight and placement of guns aboard a proper three-decker."

Darkness swirled close about, heavy with the reek of powder smoke, and mighty guns flared and thundered within it. By the light of their discharges, a flag waved in the breeze—a flag that kept changing—Union Jack with a field of blue, Union Jack with a field of white, red and white bars of the privateer, then the same with a corner device: blue field with a circle of white stars. It shifted, one flag and then another, and became the driving mainsail of a flying schooner coursing silent through sunlit mist . . . flying to find and destroy a renegade frigate with an emblazoned fore topgallant—a frigate with the blood of decent men streaming down its hull strakes.

A clumsy, trundling ketch, hard-helmed and slow. A ketch with a cargo of giant guns, trying to go unobserved and wearing colored feathers on its sails . . . Its deck swirled and shifted and was another deck, and an old seaman stood there, a man with a leg and a peg. "You'll find a way," he said cheerfully. "I've not known you to fail when it most counts." He smiled—a warm smile on a war-ravaged face—then turned away and died.

A snow. A jaunty, ferocious, beautiful new snow, its suit bright as the morning sun, its gundecks cleared for action. It took the wind in its sails and the spray in its teeth and could take a man anywhere he chose to go—if he were free to go, unburdened by promises unkept and debts unpaid. If he had his honor. Fair winds sang in its high sails and it spoke to him, and its voice was a woman's voice. "You must decide, Patrick," it told him. "I would decide for you if I could, but it cannot be that way."

Thunders and roars. Storm and turmoil. Agony . . .

. . . and the rocking of a ship at rest, little repetitive creaks of timber and gurglings of bilges, and the constant thump-whoosh-thump-whoosh of bilge pumps being manned. Someone groaned, and it seemed the voice might be his own.

"He's coming around," someone said. "Go fetch Mister Duncan, please. Tell him the captain is waking."

Whose voice? A young voice, breaking with the unreliable tones of adolescence. Billy . . .

"Billy?"

"Aye, sir. It's me." Hands were on his face and a thumb pried open his eyes, one after the other. Billy Caster leaned close, peering at him in concern. Then he turned away. "I expect he'll be all right, Mister Romart. He's still in there."

He was in his own cabin, aboard *Fury*, and cloudy daylight came in through the slatted gallery. His head ached abominably and there was a deep pain in his left arm that seemed to go from shoulder to fingertips. He considered it all and decided he was, indeed, alive. Footsteps thudded on the companion ladder and a moment later Charley Duncan was there, with a number of others, looking down at him. "You've rejoined us, Captain?"

"So it seems," he rasped.

"There is tea here, sir," Billy Caster said. "Would you like to sit up and have some?"

"Very much." He sat. His head swam dizzily for a moment, then cleared, and his parched throat welcomed the sipping of the tea. "Where are we?"

"That's a bit hard to say, sir." Duncan perched himself on the gallery bench. "Mister Caster and me, we had a look at the charts; then Mister Romart looked at them, but we don't know quite where to look. We are in the lee of a little island that doesn't seem to have anybody on it, and there's a spit of land to the south that might be Sandy Hook."

"Might be Montauk Point, too," Romart pointed out.

183

"So we think we're in either Long Island or Virginia, sir," Billy Caster finished. "None of us was quite sure where we started from."

Dalton suppressed a grin, and noticed that he needed to shave. He raised his good hand to touch his cheek. Not more than two days' growth, he decided. "If it could be Montauk, then it probably is. We are still a long way from Virginia. Are we secure here?"

"Best we can tell, sir." Duncan shrugged. "And I surely hope we are, because I don't think we'll go anywhere else right away."

Dalton put down his cup. "Report, please, Mister Duncan."

"Aye, sir. *Fury* is afloat, sir, but we're taking a bit of water through the portside wales. Bilge pumps are handling it for the time. But that isn't the only problem, sir. We're less a bowsprit at the moment, we have some damage at the forerails, and some of our sails have been blown clear out of their bolt ropes. That, and some other things as well . . . sir."

Dalton looked from one to another of them, seeing the grief in their eyes for the first time. "Who did we lose?"

"Three, sir. One was Mister Tidy."

"I see." Damn the captain who comes to know his men, he thought. It would be better not to. He thought about the monkey-like old bosun, and his eyes misted slightly. "How?"

"Rogue gun, sir," Romart said. "Second on the starboard side. It broke loose and Mister Tidy stopped it from going into steerage. But it crushed him against the pinrail, sir."

"And the other two?"

"Two of the new lads, sir. Mister Stork and Mister Colgreave. They must have washed over the side. They are gone."

Stork, he thought. Bucktoothed and mischievous, barely twenty years old, if even that. An escapee from the stockade at Point Barrow. And Colgreave. Lanky, dour . . . and wanted for arson in his native New Hampshire. Felons both, fugitives both, and as fine a pair of able seamen as a man might want to meet.

"We thought we had lost one of the cargo members, as well, sir," Billy Caster said. "But we found him."

"One of the fiddlers," Duncan explained. "He wasn't afore where he was supposed to be, but we found him under a pile of spilled lanyardstock in the cable tiers. He's all right, except he jumps at sight of his own shadow."

"The galley is sort of a shambles, sir," Romart added. "But we have both O'Rileys there for the time, setting it to right. That tea came from their efforts, and there is oat porridge."

"The tiller is fouled, as well," Duncan continued. "We have a split spar on the main, and a fair rat's nest of a tangle on the fore. Two of our escutcheons are gone, and about half the lashings a'deck are either gone or damaged. All of our shrouds need some cinching, and the main backstay has stretched so it sags . . ."

Dalton sighed, gazing at the splints on his left arm. He didn't need a report to tell him the arm was broken, or to tell him who had set and bound it. Joseph Tower. Only a ship's carpenter would devise splints with turnbuckles.

"Is there anything that *isn't* damaged, then?"

"Oh, aye, sir." Duncan nodded. "As far as we can tell, that bleedin' harpsichord came through it all just fine."

On a bright, cold day, *Fury* lay at anchor in the lee of Shelter Island, snugged in close in a deep cove where the shoreline's trees masked her sheered spars aloft. Brisk northerly breezes—onshore winds to the shores of Montauk not far away—had been in the fugitives' favor, as any fishermen who might be out were south of the point, working their trawls and netlines in the Atlantic waters. For the time being, *Fury* had the cove and its surroundings all to herself.

They had careened her on a tidal flat to expose the leak in her hull, and patched it soundly with strake timbers, copper plate and tar. Then they had floated her again with the new tide and towed her to this place of temporary shelter, where she had lain now for several days as repairs were done for her more serious wounds. Wind and storm had battered the snow relentlessly, but her timbers were still sound, her footings secure and her rigging repairable.

The sundered stem had been Dalton's primary concern, but inspection showed the bowsprit to be secure. The damage had been done at the cap—the heavy iron frame which capped the end of the sprit and through which the jib extended. The cap itself was intact, though shaken free from the sprit and dangling now from its martingale stays. The jibboom was broken in two. Its stump still clung in bindings atop the bowsprit, but the rest hung from slack stays, severed from the stump by the pressure of a gust on the jibsail and flying jib.

For two days a timbering crew of English and American tars had explored ashore, finding and cutting the proper timbers, and now Joseph Tower and several others worked at the stem, fitting in a new jibboom shaped from a sturdy and straight young ash tree. Spreaders and stays had yet to be refit, though this would proceed from the setting of the new jib.

Cable tiers had been ransacked for line to replace or splice broken sheets and lifts on several spars, and a new-shaped spar lay ready to be lifted on the main, to replace one damaged there. Working in teams, the *Furies* had converted the near shore of the cove into a sail loft for repair of canvas and lines, and the calm water around *Fury* bustled with activity. The jollyboat and a pair of rafts lightered materials back and forth and served as lift stages, while the launch with its pair of punt guns—a boat that by whim was called *Something* because Charley Duncan had once suggested it be called something—stood guard on the site. The entire operation resembled nothing less than a miniature shipyard complete with floating drydock.

And above it all, safely ensconced on *Fury*'s quarterdeck, Guard Officer Felix Croney looked on cynically. "So much effort to no avail," he drawled. "You cannot possibly escape your punishment unless it is by dying first." He squinted toward the shore, then pointed. "Those men yonder, sewing sails. Why do they dress like that?"

Patrick Dalton lounged in his shingle chair, only half listening to the intermittent tirades of his prisoner. Now he turned to look where Croney pointed. "They are musicians. I suppose that is how musicians dress."

"Musicians." Croney snorted. "Those are your runaway indentures, then. Yes, I heard something of that, in my cell."

"Your 'cell,' Commander, is the best cabin this vessel has to offer. Were it not reserved for your . . . ah . . . confinement for your own good, it would house two officers and my clerk."

"Officers!" Croney waved a scornful arm. "There isn't an officer in this lot. Runaways, deserters, scalawags and felons. Renegades, every last one. Miserable fugitives. What a fool you are, Dalton."

"*Captain* Dalton," Dalton reminded him. "Or *Lieutenant* Dalton, as you prefer. I do not permit laxity, Commander. Especially from people I don't like."

"Well, you are a fool for all that. What is to keep these wretches from simply jumping ship here and stealing away to fend for themselves?"

Dalton smiled coldly. "Yes, I heard that you had suggested that to some of them. Nine of them, by my

187

count."

"Nine? How do you know the number?"

"All nine of them told me about it. One or two would gladly have notched your ears for suggesting such a thing, had I allowed it."

"Then what keeps them here? Do they fear you that much?"

"You really are a nuisance at times, Commander. Tell me, why do you pursue me?"

"It is my duty!"

"As you see it." Dalton nodded. "I don't know why all of these men are loyal to this ship, but I rather think it is for the same reason."

Croney turned to glare at the Irishman. "Duty? Absurd. What do rabble know of duty? The lash . . . that's what men like these understand. I daresay most of these you have here have felt the lash more than once on proper ships."

"Several have," Dalton agreed. "In fact, most of them have, either on shipboard or in one of your stockades, and maybe that has contributed to their understanding of duty, Commander. The lash does more than score a man's back, you know. It also scores his pride."

"First it is duty; now you talk of pride. What do these rabble know of either?"

"Possibly more than the masters they have had, Commander."

Croney was in a ranting mood, and he continued to do so, but Dalton was no longer listening. Instead he was thinking of the procedures of courts martial—the rules for justice according to the Lords of the Admiralty. He had memorized every detail of the procedures in the books he had taken from Croney, and now he turned them over in his mind, studying them.

What does any man know of pride, he asked himself. A man knows what he finds in himself, and in the end it may be that pride and honor are of more

188

value to each of us than anything else we might have.

On the foredeck, men worked to bring up line from the cable tiers and canvas from the sail locker. Mister Hoop hoisted a prodigious bundle to the deck, set it in place, then turned to throw a scowl astern. "Blest if I know why Cap'n keeps that bugger aboard," he said. "Be far easier just to knock him in the head and feed him to the fishes."

"Not his way, Mister Hoop," Charley Duncan said. "The captain is as fierce a fighting man as ever I've seen, given the need. But I've not known him to kill for convenience."

"Still doesn't explain why he keeps him," Hoop reasoned. "Why not just beach the bugger somewhere, if he doesn't want to kill him?"

"I can't rightly say." Duncan shrugged. "Maybe he has a use for him, though I can't see what such would be."

Michael Romart, working alongside them, paused for a moment and glanced around at the red-haired seaman, his eyes narrowing. In the time since the two had joined Dalton—Duncan escaping from the Long Island stockade and Romart part of a group of Colonial saboteurs firing Crown ships in New York Bay— the Englishman and the Colonial had worked side by side and had shared adventures. As with such circumstances, they had become close friends, though neither would ever have admitted it to the other. Still, neither had learned more about their dour, black-Irish captain than he had chosen to let either know. Now Romart realized that there were times when the captain might discuss a thing with one man and not with another.

It had not occurred to him until that moment that Charley Duncan didn't know what the captain had in mind for Guard Officer Croney. But then, he reminded himself, the only reason *he* knew a bit about it was because he would be a part of it when the time came.

On a rocky beach in the sheltered cove, musicians sat cross-legged on spread canvas, muttering and fussing among themselves as they worked. Each wore a sailmaker's "palm," a leather handstrap with a thumbwidth thimble secured to the palm section, and each had a needle, twine and beeswax. Some were repairing wind-torn seams between the cloths of various sails. Some were adding in new canvas to fill holes where pieces of sails had been torn away, and some were repairing grommets and reef cringles damaged by the storm. Most, though, were sewing sails back into their boltrope frames. All worked under the careful eye of Cadman Wise, and most took the occasion to grumble each time he turned his back.

"Humiliation," grunted Johann Sebastian Nunn, whose chosen occupation was the French horn. "Stish, stish, stish. Crow-stish und crow-sower, Mein fingeren . . . to make mit die niddle, ach!"

"Not cross-stitch," Sean Callinder whispered. "An' ye heard wha' th' man sayed, same as me. Bind-stitch and loop, not cross-stitch."

"Cross-stitch is for quilts, he said," Gunther Lindholm of the clarinet agreed. "He said for sails it must be bind-stitch and loop."

"Bine-stish, crow-stish . . . ach du lieber! Stishen mit fingeren . . ."

"Shut up and sew," Cadman Wise suggested. "Think of it as a fingering exercise."

XVIII

A few inches of bright snow lay on the land beyond the cove as they completed the setting of stays and shrouds. With all cables spliced and replaced, lanyard line was riven through the triple eyes in the big hardwood spools called deadeyes — one secured to the base of each shroud line and a matching one below on the hull channel. Then each coupling was set taut with a purchase, and the lanyard hitched around the shroudline and seized. Cable stays and backstays, top stays and preventer stays, bobstays and mainstays, forestays, spreader stays and martingale stays were set, tightened and trimmed, each thrumming line tensed against all the others until the masts and spars rode among a frame of cable that was the vital structure of the ship.

Braces and lifts were placed and tested, blocks and tackle dressed, and the repaired sails were hauled aloft for bending onto their spars and stays.

From helm to tiller blocks to rudder to sternpost hoops, each piece and devise was reinforced, tested and dressed. And when Michael Romart led a shore party across to Montauk for forage and brought back five goats along with the bits of timber and hardware that a village warehouse had offered up, they mixed the blood of goats with lamp oil and put a bright coat of paint on the gunwales and the new jibboom.

Some of the meat went below to the galley, where one or more O'Rileys managed to render it as greasy, gray and unpalatable as what they had been dipping from the salt-something kegs. The rest went ashore, where four of the Colonials took charge and smoked it over a drying fire to make jerky.

Kegs were a problem. Several had been lost in the storm, and water would be in short supply for a cruise from Montauk to Chesapeake. But the enterprising Charley Duncan took the launch out again and returned in a day with stave-wood, hoop strap and a Colonial named Jordy Good.

"He's a cooper," Duncan told Dalton, while Good waited in the launch for permission to come aboard. "He says if we'll take him as far as Morgan's Cove, he will supply us with barrels enough to take on all the water we need there. He says there will be no problem, for he has kin at Morgan's Cove, and he swears there are no partisan folk there."

"Partisan which way?" Dalton asked.

Duncan went to the rail and called the question to Good, who stood and saluted awkwardly before answering. Dalton found his appearance startling. A middle-aged man, Good was at least as tall as he . . . maybe taller. But the man seemed all bones — sundark, wizened skin stretched over a skeletal face, and a frame that for all its lofty height seemed to weigh almost nothing. Duncan returned. "Either way, sir. He says the folks at Morgan's Cove don't hold with the king, and they don't hold with the rebels, either."

"Who do they hold with, then?"

"Nobody, sir. He says the lot of 'em moved down here from Maine because it had got overcrowded."

"Is he a good cooper?"

"Swears he is, sir. And he has his own tools."

"Very well, Mister Duncan. Bring him aboard and have Mister Caster take his mark. See that he's read his articles. Did he say why he wants to go to Morgan's Cove?"

"Aye, sir. It's because his wife is a pious woman, sir."

"Well, that might be a blessing. But why does he want to go to Morgan's Cove?"

"Well, sir, that good woman said if she had to spend another winter in a cabin with him, she would surely take the Lord's name in vain. So he wants to spend the winter at Morgan's Cove, sir."

Dalton shrugged and dismissed the matter. There were more brands of adversity in this world than he was prepared to cope with.

Jordy Good was hoisted aboard, with his tools and materials, and assigned a space to work just aft the foremast. Soon his drawknife was hewing there, and his cooper's mallet rang as he fashioned hoops. Still, his eyes turned often aft, and within the hour—when everyone seemed busy at other enterprises—he went to the quarterdeck and walked several times around the covered harpsichord there, trying to seem as though he hadn't noticed it.

When it seemed that no one was noticing him, he stooped and looked underneath the lashed tarp, and a grin spread across his homely face. "My, my, my," he said to himself. "Will 'e look at this here."

A few minutes later the strains of lively harpsichord music soared aloft from *Fury*'s quarterdeck, and all within earshot turned and peered in that direction. Several aboard swore under their breaths and headed that way.

Cadman Wise was first to arrive on the scene. He bounded up the ladder, rounded on the errant cooper and skidded to a halt. "Here now!" he bellowed. "What do you think you're doin' here?"

Without interrupting his playing, Good glanced up

193

and grinned. *"Orpheus and Euridice,"* he explained. "Part of it, anyway."

"You can't play that," Wise told him.

"I don't know." Good cocked a brow, still playing. "Thought I was doin' passable. What's wrong wi' it?"

"You don't belong where you are!"

"Oh, that. Well, y'see, I only heard the whole thing once, so I prob'ly tend to start in th' middle. Do the same thing with th' *Messiah* chorus, too, but that's because I don't care for some parts of it. Just th' lively parts." He shifted notes, shifted cords, and a rousing, fast version of Handel's *Hallelujah Chorus* lofted on the cold, bright air. The music grew, swirled, built upon itself and stopped, and Good launched into something entirely different. "This is Spanish gypsy music," he confided to Wise. "I don't generally do any of it, because folks around here don't hold with it. They say it leads to ungodly notions. Lively, though. Puts me in mind of some rousin' Irish tune I've heard."

There were thudding feet a'deck, shouts and splashes from the near shore. Dalton had taken a turn in the launch with four rowers, and Charley Duncan was in the foretop shrouds. They both headed for the source of the commotion. The companionway hatch popped open and Billy Caster came up, his face smudged with ink. There seemed to be a ruckus on the quarterdeck, and someone was playing Irish jigs on the harpsichord. He scampered to the portside ladder, took it in two jumps and pushed past several tars. Cadman Wise had found a belaying pin and was advancing purposefully toward the man making the music. Billy stopped him. "What is happening here, Mister Wise?"

Wise pointed. "Stranger has got aboard and begun banging on that thing, Mister Caster. I'm about to reason with him."

"That's no stranger, Mister Wise. That is Mister Good. He's our cooper. Captain just signed him on.

But what is he doing on the quarterdeck?"

Good glanced around, recognizing the serious boy who had taken his mark in the log. " 'Hoist me down to th' Blarney Stone,' lad. It's a jiggers' tune. Do you like it?"

"I don't know why he's here, Mister Caster. He won't tell me who invited him." He advanced on the player. "Cooper, eh? Well, cooper, I'll have ye get away from that instrument this minute."

Good looked up, his long fingers hovering over the keys. "Is it yours?"

"By God, no, it's not mine . . ." Wise began.

"Then wait your turn. I got here first." Good went back to his playing.

Victory Locke came from below, carrying a rifle and followed by a pair of O'Rileys. Charley Duncan rushed past them at the rail and stopped, staring in amazement. The cooper sat on a stool in front of the lashed-down harpsichord, and was playing the thing. Cadman Wise looked fit to be tied, and others had crowded around. Duncan laid a hand on the distraught bosun's shoulder. "Mister Wise, why is the cooper playing the harpsichord?"

"That's what I've been trying to find out, Mister Duncan. But I swear I can't get a straight answer from him."

Duncan turned to the musical cooper. "Mister Good, what do you think you're doing?"

"I think it's one of those new things," Good said. "They call them walds or some such. Sort of a cross of a minuet an' a *schoddische,* but everything's by threes. This is a real nice boxed harp. Where'd ye lads get it?"

The jollyboat bumped the snow's starboard strakes, and several musicians swarmed over the rails. In the lead was Joseph Miller, shouting and blustering. "Get that man away from the squire's harpsichord! He can't play that!"

Good hesitated, sighed and looked around. "If all ye lads would take a vote on just what it is ye'd like to hear, I'll try my hand at it. I know some of the Gluck opera tunes, an' a bit of Haydn . . . generally anything a body'd use to tune a Flight an' Kelly barrel organ, I can likely pick it out."

Restraining the blustering Miller, some of the other musicians glanced at one another. " 'La Pescatrice,' " Tempore DiGaetano suggested.

"Don't care for it, myself," Good said. "Name somethin' else."

"Artaxerxes? Il momiente basse?"

"Aye, that's lively in parts." Again Good began playing the harpsichord. Vicente Auf borrowed Cadman Wise's belaying pin and tapped an accompanying staccato on the ship's bell. Zoltan Ferrestrekov, who hadn't the slightest idea what was going on but was always ready to perform, came running along the deck with his bassoon and joined in. Romeo Napoli provided the bridging adagios on his trumpet. Within a minute a violin, a flute and a French horn added their voices.

Galante Pico listened for a bit, tapping at his lower lip with a judicious finger, then sought out Alfred Hickman and belabored him at length.

Clinging at the doubling of the main topsail mast where he had been securing a lift block, Claude Mallory listened in wonder to the sounds rising from eighty feet below, then raised his eyes, idly scanning the forested ridge above the cove, and almost fell from his perch. "On deck!" he shouted. When there was no response below, he wrapped his legs around a crosstree brace, cupped his hands and tried it again. "On deck! Ahoy the deck!" Still, no one looked up. Mallory sighed, righted himself and started down the topmast shrouds, scampering down the ratlines like a spider on a narrow web. At the maintop he swung around the deadeyes, cupped a hand and bellowed, "On deck!"

This time several faces turned upward, though the selection from *Artaxerxes* continued. Charley Duncan squinted. "Aye, Mister Mallory?"

"Sail, Mister Duncan!"

"Sail? Whereaway?"

"Right there!" Mallory pointed. "Just past that point, an' comin' along. You'll see it yourself in a moment."

"Can you make it?"

"Not certain. A small craft of some notion. Sloop or maybe a coaster. All I saw was its hounds."

Duncan swung around. "Where's the captain?"

"Out in the launch, Mister Duncan." Billy Caster pointed. "You can just see him, see?"

At the harpsichord, Alfred Hickman squatted beside Jordy Good. "Maestro Pico asks . . ."

"Who?"

"Maestro Galante Pico. This gentleman. He asks whether you have performed on the stage, sir."

Good's finger faltered on the keys, and he chuckled. "On th' stage? Mercy, no. I be no player."

"But you play!"

"Oh, aye, I play a bit. Th' pattern of keys is very like to th' pianoforte, an' that's like a barrel organ's board."

"Well, Maestro Pico wonders whether you would consider joining his orchestra."

"What?" Joseph Miller roared. "Why him? Why not me?"

"You said you didn't want to join the orchestra, Mister Miller."

"I don't! But I was invited first."

"Besides, this gentleman plays better than you do."

"He does not! The man's a lout!"

At the starboard rail, Charley Duncan waved at Ishmael Bean to get his attention. "Mister Bean! Signals, please. Run up 'sail sighted,' so the captain will return to the ship."

"I think he is already returning," Billy Caster noted,

shading his eyes.

"Well, maybe he can return faster. Where would you say the wind lies, beyond that end of the island yonder?"

"Northerly," Billy judged, wishing the wind-gauge had been remounted.

At the maintop Claude Mallory shouted, "On deck! The vessel is a coaster, Mister Duncan. It's off the point now and making to come to starboard. It's coming this way!"

Duncan leaned over the rail, shading his eyes. In the distance, *Fury's* launch was raising sail, but the captain was too far away to arrive in time to make the critical decisions. Therefore, the first officer must act.

"Mister Wise!" he shouted. "Please get all these people off the quarterdeck. Mister Locke, stow that rifle and take the helm. Misters Crosby and Pugh, please stand by the starboard guns. Hands a'fore, to the capstan and get a messenger seized to the anchor line. Mister Hoop, please go below and stand guard on our prisoner. Mister Fisk, if you please, take the jollyboat ashore for lightering of the rest of our people and gear."

"The coaster is coming about," Mallory called. "He's in sight and he's seen us, but he has the wind. He'll be here directly whether he wants to visit with us or not."

Duncan glanced around. The vessel clearing the point of the cove was small, sleek-hulled like a cutter, but sloop-rigged. It showed no colors, but it was close enough that he could see the surprised scurrying of people on its deck and the muzzles of a pair of bow guns athwart its stem. It was obvious that whoever was over there had not expected to encounter a ship in this cove.

From the starboard rail, Purdy Fisk shouted, "Where in God's name is the jollyboat?"

The last of the crowd was just leaving the quarterdeck, herded along by Cadman Wise, and several looked around in confusion. Then Billy Caster pointed. "There's our jollyboat, Mister Duncan. Out there."

The small boat was just clearing the cove, climbing the chop of the main channel, heading for Montauk across the way. Two men were at its oars, and both were rowing desperately.

The large head of Mister Hoop appeared at the companionway. "The prisoner isn't here, Mister Duncan. Port cabin is empty an' it looks like Captain's quarters has been ransacked."

Duncan didn't need his glass to make out the men in the fleeing jollyboat. He knew them both, and a bitter taste arose in his mouth. The one in the bow, at the short oars, was the prisoner, Felix Croney. The one with him was Michael Romart.

Mister Hoop came to the ladder and peered past the rail. "Was it me," he suggested, "I'd let the gunners have a bit of sport with that bugger."

A cannon barked, its thump echoing from the land beyond the little beach, and a ball sang high over *Fury*'s bow. In the forest beyond the beach, a tree exploded.

"Are they firing on us?" Billy Caster asked, astonished.

"I think that was an inquiry," Duncan decided. "We had better hoist colors. Hold fire, gunners! But if he fires again, sink him!"

"Aye, sir."

"What colors, Mister Duncan? We have all sort."

"I don't care. Just whatever is handy. What is that they are raising?"

On the coaster's halyard an ensign rose, a simple device of green cross on a white field. "He says he is a mail packet," Billy Caster said.

"Do we have one of those flags?"

"Aye, I believe so. We have quite a collection of colors."

"Then run it up. That should amuse him for a time."

Out on the bay, the jollyboat veered toward the coaster at sight of its ensign. But after a few pulls at the oars they turned again toward the far shore.

"I don't think that coaster is a mail packet, Mister Duncan," Billy Caster said. "But I don't think it is friends of Mister Croney, either. What I don't understand is, why is Mister Romart out there with that man?"

XIX

The launch named *Something* had been part of the boat complement of HMS *Doughty*, but that was in a time now past. At present, *Something* sported punt guns fore and aft, a step-in mast and a pair of stubby sails, and was the ship's launch of the snow *Fury*. Patrick Dalton had never seen fit to inquire of Mister Duncan as to how the sandy-haired young man had appropriated a launch from the deck of a Royal Navy vessel . . . just as he had not inquired deeply into how *Something* came to have her own armaments now. Some of the abilities of Charley Duncan, he felt, were better left unexplained.

On this day, though, *Something* had provided a nice diversion for Dalton. The mending of *Fury* was well along, and there was little he could do to help at this point, especially with the burden of a fractured arm bound in turnbuckle splints. So he had taken *Something* and four rowers, and gone for a scout of the bay beyond the west point of *Fury*'s cove.

The past three nights had been cold and clear, and on all three nights his lookouts had seen lights somewhere to the west. It was reason enough to have a look, and Dalton sent himself. For days he had been close about the snow, usually aboard and often below in the privacy of his little cabin, poring over the documents liberated from Felix Croney. The provision under Admiralty regulation for courts martial extraordinary fascinated him. There were, of course, provisions for trial aboard ship for certain sorts of charges, but he had never known that capital charges also could be brought and tried—in unusual circumstances—at sea or on occupied soil.

The procedures and requirements were complex, of course. For nearly a century the Lords of the Admiralty had compiled bodies of regulations aimed at satisfying the laws of Parliament and decrees of the sovereign, while still managing to retain control of naval justice within the navy. It was a webwork of procedure that covered every circumstance that had been encountered or imagined, and its anchor lines were snugly ensconced in those quarters beyond the forecourt and antrim of the Admiralty headquarters off Whitehall Street in London. Reading the material so carefully assembled by Felix Croney, one could almost picture the intricate pattern of steps, down through the years, that the Lords of the Admiralty had taken—regulations so obscure that each was no more than a protocol, yet severally they limited the interference that the Ministers of Parliament, even the House of Lords, could impose upon Admiralty justice. Even appeals to the Crown were carefully spliced into the web in such a way that—short of overturning countless judgments long since rendered and of record—the king himself would be hard put to intervene where Admiralty law held sway.

Remarkable, Dalton found it all. Really quite remarkable, how the Royal Navy had insulated itself from the very government that wielded it as a tool of state.

He had nothing in mind that might properly be called a plan, but sharp intuition told him that the answer to his own dilemma—how to clear his good name and regain his tarnished honor—rested just here.

Sometimes, his thoughts told him with Irish irony, the fox in the trap might be caught by nothing more than his ignorance of how the trap operated.

The studies and the thoughts took the edge off that

bleak moodiness that had so haunted him in recent times, and on this day the bright sun and chill air called him on deck, and he climbed down to the launch and went out to scout.

The waters here were broken by islands and peninsulas, a spare maze of lands and channels that condensed to the south and west into the mainland of upper Long Island, that thinned and opened eastward toward Block Island and the open sea. Lights in the night in these ways, and in this season when each rise of land was bright with first snowfall, probably meant smugglers or scavengers in the vicinity. His only real concern was to assure himself that they were only that, and not a threat to *Fury*.

Beyond the small island where the snow lay in repair, the launch worked westward half a league until he could make out features on the peninsula beyond with his glass. What he saw was reassuring. There had been people there. Even from a distance, the tracks of carts were clear in the pristine snow, coming down to a shore where a thin pier lay almost hidden. A transfer dock, it seemed. A place where smuggled or salvaged goods might be put ashore by boats. Screened from the wide sound beyond by forests, a small sloop or cutter could rest hidden there while boats plied back and forth to the dock. Nothing large could hide there without fear of being seen from the sound, but a small craft could . . . and obviously had. He studied it carefully. Whatever craft had been there was gone now. But there had been activity.

Sad land, he thought . . . where men must work by lanternlight in the dead of winter night to pursue their commerce. In a way, it reminded him of Ireland.

"I've seen enough," he told his oarsmen. "Make about and we will return to our ship."

Halfway back, strange sounds drifted on the winds and they listened, then looked toward *Fury*'s cove. Thin and distant, music came from there. "Lay to, gentlemen," Dalton said. "I had best go and see what they are doing." It was another half-mile before *Something* cleared the lee of the spit of land to the north, and the cold, brisk wind slapped wavelets against her port beam. *Fury* was in sight, and he raised his glass. There seemed a crowd on her quarterdeck, and the jollyboat was just hauling up under her channels, filled with musicians.

"Rest your oars," he told his rowers. "Let's step in the masts and use the wind from here."

"Aye, sir." Finian Nelson tipped up his oar and turned. "Lend a hand, you Colonials, and I'll show you how masts are stepped."

"Lend a hand yourself, English," Chilton Sand chided him. "I'll wager I've twice the time in small boats of any bloody tar." The New Yorker glanced back at Dalton. "Beg pardon, sir, but these British need occasional taking aback. Otherwise they often become arrogant. I believe that's what the present hostilities may be all about."

"Step the masts," Dalton said. "We can save the politics for another time."

"Aye, sir." Sand took one stubby mast and Nelson the other, showing the other two — a pair of ordinaries, one from the Connecticut uplands and one from New Jersey — how to set and secure them for sail.

Dalton resettled himself in the stern, resting his splinted arm on the punt gun there. A "slight fracture," the carpenter Joseph Tower had judged it. "One of the strut bones just abaft the elbow — the inner one it seems — not cloven so much as a split with the grain. The turnbuckles will keep it from sliding about in there while it heals."

Probably as precise a diagnosis as any ship's surgeon might have made. Though it did ache abominably, no matter how "slight" the damage. Turning his mind from it, Dalton let Chilton Sand's comment run through his mind, while he watched the sailors rigging the launch. The English need occasional taking aback . . . otherwise they often become arrogant. True enough . . . a thing any Irishman knew. Yet here before him, in the persons of Nelson and Sand, were the representations of the two

204

sides of the present conflict in the colonies. English and American. Sailors both — boisterous, capable young men, long of will and short of fuse — and there was no hostility between them, only the strutting give-and-take of young men anywhere who share an occupation.

There is war here, Dalton thought. But the hostility is between governments. The role of men such as these is simply to provide the sweat and the blood to sustain it to its conclusion.

"Sir!" Nelson had glanced ahead. Now he straightened and pointed. "Look yonder!"

Beyond the still-distant *Fury*, beyond the ridged spit that sheltered her from the east, another vessel had appeared — close by and making about to approach. Abruptly, a single smoke blossomed at the stranger's bow and a ball arced over *Fury*'s nose. On the slope across the cove, a tree seemed to explode.

"Why, th' bloody wee rotter!" Nelson gaped. "That's no way to behave."

"That ship is hardly more than a bay sloop," Phillip Ives said. "Why did it fire?"

"Surely didn't do any damage, though," Hob Smith noted. "Look, it has colors. What is that?"

Chilton Sand was shading his eyes, squinting at the little vessel that had so abruptly made its presence known. "Cap'n, I believe I . . . Why, of course! I know who that is. That's Pembroke, by damn. That's his *Christine*. Land, I wondered what had become of him. Cap'n, can you tell our lot not to shoot at him? That's just old Pembroke, is all that is."

"And what does this Pembroke do, Mister Sand? Besides putting iron shots across the bow of my ship, that is?" Dalton had his glass out, studying the stranger beyond *Fury*. Very small, hardly more than a sloop-rigged boat. Less than a cutter in length, though carrying at least two guns and possibly four. A coaster.

"His name is Alf Pembroke, sir. He's a scavenger, mostly. Does a bit of whatever's handy, I suppose. Can

205

you make the colors he's flying?"

"Aye, he says he is a mail packet."

Sand chuckled. "Aye, he's a mail packet. And I'm a Spanish Don in disguise. See, *Fury* is responding to his colors."

It was Dalton's turn to chuckle. "So she is. Mister Duncan is telling your Mister Pembroke that we are a mail packet, too. Possibly it is the stylish thing to be, these days." His chuckle grew and the others laughed with him. The notion of an armed snow pretending to be a mail packet was ludicrous . . . on the order of a ship of the line trying to pass itself off as a schooner. Still, it was as appropriate a response as any. He raised his glass again, then swerved it to the right. Out there, just hitting the open water south of the cove, was *Fury*'s little jollyboat. The chuckle died to silence. His eyes narrowed. A man in the boat was Felix Croney at the fore. Just aft of him at the main oars was Michael Romart.

"Hands to those sails," he ordered. "Our prisoner is escaping."

Felix Croney had felt that fate might turn his way, the instant Patrick Dalton told him that nine of his crewmen had reported Croney's attempts to subvert their loyalties. For a time he was unsure, but he was almost sure that he had approached ten in all. Therefore, there might be one willing to help him escape — in return for some payment or favor, of course.

Still, it wasn't until the man actually came to his cabin and told him what he wanted that Croney knew which it was, and then he was astounded. Not one of the Royal Navy deserters at all, but an American Colonial. Michael Romart, a Virginian. When Romart made it clear what he wanted, though, it was no longer surprising to the guard officer. The sailor obviously had decided that the uprising wasn't going well for the Colonies. He was interested in jumping sides before the reparations began.

"Papers and transport, sir," Romart told him, eyeing him warily. "Papers that makes me a loyal subject of the king, and transport to England . . . and of course a purse to help me get established there."

"And you offer me. . . ?"

"Escape, sir. I'll get you across to Montauk, then see you safe to the Admiralty yards downcoast."

"I think that, once ashore, I can make my own way . . ."

"Aye, sir, but leaving you early, how would I know where and when to collect my fare?"

"I see." Croney nodded. "When, then?"

"Do you agree, sir?"

"Yes. Yes, I agree."

"I have your word of honor, sir?"

Croney scowled, then subsided. The lout might be his only chance. "My word, on my honor."

"Then come along, sir. Just follow me and be quick about it. The captain's off the ship and there's a ruckus topside. We'll not likely have a better chance than right now."

Thus it was that Croney found himself now at the short oars of a jollyboat hauling through the chop of Montauk Bay with a cold following wind throwing spray into his face. There was another vessel there, just off the point, and a shot was fired. He hauled hard on his left oar, veering the boat, but Romart turned hard eyes on him.

"What are you doing?" the Colonial demanded. "That's no Crown vessel. Even if it was, it'd be no match for the snow. Now hard on those oars . . . *sir*. Make for that land across the bay, as I told you."

The coaster was barely four cables from *Fury* by the time it got its sails trimmed and its tiller hauled over to veer away, and by that time it was in the lee of the island. The two vessels stood there, beam to stern, so close that their occupants could stare across at one another.

207

"Christine," Charley Duncan recited, reading the coaster's escutcheon. "Do you suppose that truly is a mail packet, Mister Wise?"

"About as likely as us being one," the bosun allowed. "But I don't think he's fleet, either. Those are Colonials aboard, by their dress."

Out on the bay beyond, the jollyboat was making its way southward, and Duncan stared at its distant silhouette sadly, wondering what had persuaded Michael Romart to strike out on his own . . . and thus betray the trust of Patrick Dalton. He noticed that Billy Caster also was gazing southward, his young face troubled. "I suppose he found an opportunity for himself, Billy," he said. "You know, he was the only Colonial left of the ones that was *Faiths.* All the rest of us are English . . . excepting yourself, of course, but you're Captain's clerk."

Billy didn't respond, and Duncan turned his attention back to the problem at hand. No further shots had been fired, after the one high ball the coaster had sent over in challenge or salute, and now the coaster, *Christine,* drifted a'lee, sails luffing in the slight breeze. She would drift farther away for a bit, then find the wind out there where the waves were choppy . . . and probably just go on her way, relieved that the chance encounter had been nothing more serious.

"Captain Dalton is going after the jollyboat." Cadman Wise pointed. A mile or more to the west, the launch had wind in its stubs of sail and was veering southward. "I'd say he's leaving it to us to deal with the little sloop and keep it from interfering."

"It could, at that, couldn't it?" Duncan rubbed his jaw thoughtfully. "Not much it can do to us, but it could go after the launch if it had a mind to. Signals, Mister Wise. Send to the coaster, 'Stand about and take in sail.' "

"Aye, Mister Duncan."

Signals climbed the halyard, and they watched the coaster. It seemed slow in responding, and as moments passed the tops of its sails began to tauten with found wind.

"He's thinking he'll just slip away," Duncan decided. "I'm thinking the captain would want to decide whether to let him do that or not. Mister Pugh, have you the chasers trained?"

"Aye, sir. Just tell me where you'd like a ball delivered and I'll send it off."

"His spanker makes a nice target, doesn't it?"

"Aye, it does."

"Then put a shot through it, please. About midway, if you can."

Pugh grinned and stooped to the quoins of *Fury*'s starboard stern chaser—one of a pair of neat long-twelves that had the range, if not the muscle, of the eighteens at the snow's bow. He sighted, adjusted and touched his fused linstock to the vent. The gun thundered, smoke billowed and a hole appeared precisely in the center of the coaster's mainsail.

Duncan nodded his appreciation and turned to the portside gunner. "Mister Crosby, please line your piece on his mast."

"Aye, sir."

"Signals, run down and repeat the last signal. Let him know that we insist."

Again the flags climbed, and now the coaster responded. Even as its sails were taken in and its spanker gaff crawled deckward, responding flags climbed above its stern.

Cadman Wise chuckled. "He says if he'd known we felt that way about it, he'd have dropped anchor the minute he set eyes on us. At least, that's the general drift."

"Please tell him that if he'd like to come across in a boat, we can serve tea."

XX

Tacking on stub sails, even with four oars to assist, *Something* closed only slowly on the fleeing jollyboat, and when the rocky strip of beach that was Montauk's north shore was in clear sight it was obvious that the launch had started too late. They were still a quarter-mile apart when the jollyboat grounded and the two aboard waded ashore to climb the steep bank and disappear into the winter brush beyond.

Angling on the freshening wind, the launch hove to when its keel touched gravel. "Put the jollyboat in tow," Dalton told his men. He climbed the first cutbank, then the second, and squatted to look at the footprints there. They told him nothing more than he knew . . . the cut-heel boots of Commander Felix Croney of the Expeditionary Guard overlapping the sturdy shoes of the Colonial, Michael Romart.

Dalton stood, gazing into the gray wilderness beyond, then turned away and went back to the beach. His rowers had a line on the jollyboat and anxious expressions on their faces. Finian Nelson cocked his head, looking beyond at the forest. "If the cap'n wants, I could go after them, sir."

Dalton didn't look back. "You won't find Mister Romart ashore. He was a woodsman before he was a sailor."

"I could find him," Chilton Sand said. "I know this

210

country. It's where I was born."

"We've done enough here," Dalton said. "Let's return to *Fury* and see how Mister Duncan is treating Captain Pembroke."

He waded to the launch and stepped over its high gunwales and the others followed, exchanging puzzled glances. The captain's manner struck them as odd . . . almost as if he didn't *want* to recapture his escaped prisoner and his runaway crewman.

Across the narrow bay, *Fury* still stood at anchor and men still worked aloft, bending on repaired sail while Charley Duncan and his guest watched from the midships rail. Alf Pembroke was stocky and wide-shouldered, a man of middle years with gray whiskers from temple to chin and an Indian tobacco pipe which he seemed to be constantly puffing or tapping. Further, his wizened features were set in a deep scowl of indignation. He considered it an outrage that the sandy-haired young man who seemed to be in charge here had first invited him to visit the snow, then had promptly commandeered his boat to shunt work parties back and forth between the ship and the shore. Worse yet, it was Pembroke's own rowers who were hauling at the oars.

"First you shoot a hole in my best sail," the scavenger complained. "My best sail! Why, I've only had it for . . ."

"You shouldn't worry too much about that, sir," Duncan told him cheerfully. "It was the second shot you needed to worry about."

"What second shot?"

"Oh, well, if you hadn't responded nicely to our signals — which, of course, you did, once you noticed them — then Mister Crosby yonder was going to take down your mast with a twelve-pounder. Seems to me you should be grateful, sir."

"Grateful! You hole my sail . . ."

"You did fire first, sir."

". . . then you invite me to tea and take my boat . . ."

"We're short of boats right now, sir. We only have two,

211

and they're out chasing each other, and there is a dreadful lot to be done here, as you can see. I'm sure Captain Dalton will tell you how much he appreciates your assistance."

"But this is outrageous behavior, Mister . . ."

"Duncan, sir. Charley Duncan. I'm sort of first officer when the captain's away. Would you care for more tea?"

"Where exactly is your captain, Mister Duncan?"

"He's out with the launch, sir. He's . . ."

"On deck!"

Duncan looked aloft. "Aye, Mister Fisk?"

"Launch is coming across, with the jollyboat in tow, but there isn't anybody in it. The jollyboat, I mean. The launch has the same ones it started out with."

"Thank you, Mister Fisk." Duncan turned his attention back to his guest. "You see? Captain will be here shortly. He'll decide what to do about you and your sloop."

"Coaster," Pembroke corrected. "It is sloop-rigged, but it isn't a sloop. Are you English, then?"

"As ever was," Charley Duncan admitted. "London born an' bred, though I haven't seen the place since the White Fleet put its tails to Spithead."

"Is this a British vessel?"

"Not just exactly," Duncan started to explain, then decided he had said enough. "I expect you can take all that up with the captain, sir. See yonder? That's him coming around the stem of your sl . . . your coaster. Ah, I do hope your lads over there know to behave themselves. We wouldn't want to sink your vessel unless the captain says to."

"Decent of you," Pembroke muttered. He turned back to the rail. "You certainly have the most oddly garbed sailmakers I have seen."

"They're musicians," Duncan explained. "Maestro Galante Pico and his orchestra."

Billy Caster had come from below, carrying ledgers and books. He paused beside Pembroke and pointed.

212

"That one there with the powdered wig is Zoltan Ferres-trekov."

"Who?"

The youth glanced reproachfully at him, then went about his business.

"One of the musicians," Duncan explained. "Mister Caster is taken with him because he's famous. He plays the bassoon."

"This obviously is a warship," Pembroke said, slowly. "Why do you have an orchestra?"

"Cargo," Duncan said. Again he decided he had said enough, because the scavenger captain was looking at him shrewdly, as though suspicions were being confirmed behind his shaggy brows. Duncan changed the subject. "What cargo might you have, sir? Captain'll surely want to know that before he decides what to do with you."

Cadman Wise called from across the deck, "Captain's launch is alongside, Mister Duncan!"

"Come along, sir," Duncan told Pembroke. "I'll introduce you."

"Blankets," Pembroke said.

"Sir?"

"My cargo. Blankets." As they started across the deck, Pembroke was looking aft, his eyes speculative. "Part of your cargo is on the quarterdeck, I take it?"

"Sir?"

"That large, flat-topped object covered with canvas, there. I am wondering, Mister Duncan. Could that be a harpsichord?"

"Panic and bad judgment," Alf Pembroke told Patrick Dalton. "Nothing more nor less. The last thing we expected to find in the cove on Shelter Island was an armed snow, and by the time we realized you were here, it was too late to veer off cleanly."

"So you fired on *Fury*."

213

"Captain, my gunners may be nothing more than jet-sam from the wharves of Canvastown, but I assure you: at that range, had I intended to hit your ship, I would have hit it."

"Then what did you intend with that salute?"

"I don't know, exactly," Pembroke admitted. "A threat, perhaps. A demand that we be allowed to pass without interference."

Dalton shook his head. "Bad judgment, indeed. It is the nature of fighting ships—and their complements, Captain Pembroke—to return fire rather promptly when threatened. A person sailing these waters would do well to know that."

"Well, my lads and I haven't encountered hidden war-ships before. Generally we just stay out of everyone's way and go about our business."

"Smuggling, I take it."

"I move odds and ends here and there. It is a living, and most of the vessels about the Sound are used to the sight of *Christine*. A coaster is no great prize, and every-one knows I carry only a bit of scavenge."

"So you come and go—in the midst of a war—and no one bothers you?"

"Life and commerce." The scavenger shrugged. "Both go on, war or no. It has always been so. *Christine* serves a purpose, you see. All this banging around of ships and armies, it upsets things. The normal commerces become all tangled up, but people go right on having things they don't need and needing things they don't have." He shrugged again. "That's where I come in . . . aye, and others like me."

"Tell me about the blankets," Dalton said, fascinated despite his weightier concerns. There is far more to war, he realized abruptly, than warriors know.

"The blankets are a fine example." Pembroke helped himself to tea. "There is a village not far inland from here where the people raise their flocks and card their wool and bring it in to sell. The townspeople had quite a thriving weaving industry before all this began, you see. Well, now the blankets they make must be distributed in . . . well, in other ways. But they still make blankets, and there are still those who need them."

"Who in particular needs these?"

"General Clinton's regiments downcoast. A large troop convoy has just arrived, and there aren't enough blankets."

"So they will condone smuggling?"

"Or do without blankets."

"Remarkable."

Pembroke sipped at his tea. "I believe I know you, Captain," he said quietly. "I think I know this ship. There's talk . . . you know how talk can spread . . . Some of the sailors who came with the convoy, they tell the strangest tale. Of a brig that wasn't quite a brig, that entertained them through a calm with Viennese music. Can't say I believed any of it, but stories do get around. And then there's the talk of a snow that tacked into a squall and disappeared. I've a cousin who provides cheeses for the marshaling yards, who swears that's what happened. Oh, there were traces. Talk is, the snow broke up and sank." He looked around, smiling slightly. "Quite extensive repairs your lads have been doing here, Captain Dalton. And a harpsichord on the quarterdeck! Ah, some things do come clear when one puts all the pieces together."

Dalton frowned at the older man. "Captain Pembroke, I believe your boat is at my wales."

"Am I free to leave, then?"

"To go back to your ship, of course." The Irishman paused, drumming his fingers on the helmbox. "Captain Pembroke, do you have a cook?"

"Cook?"

"Aboard *Christine*. Do you have a man who can cook a palatable meal?"

"Well . . . yes, I'd say so. Given the materials to work with."

215

"I think I would like to be invited to dinner this evening."

Pembroke stared at him.

"Have you ever eaten anything prepared by anyone named O'Riley?" Dalton asked blandly.

"I can't say that I have."

"Then invite me to dinner, aboard *Christine*. Myself, my first officer and my clerk, and take it on my honor that you'll be doing a kindness."

"I don't see that I have much choice in the matter. But if you insist . . ."

"I'd be delighted," Dalton said. "Have your cook send over a list of what he'll need, for the materials to work with."

Pembroke blinked, suddenly confused. "I don't really understand."

"You will, eventually. Suffice it to say, I believe we may have business to discuss. But first I have things to attend to, and I'm sure you do, as well. This evening then, Captain? Shall we say at four bells? Tell the cook to set an extra helping and I believe I can provide a fiddler for the occasion."

When Pembroke was gone, Dalton asked Charley Duncan and Billy Caster to join him below. In his little cabin he lit a lamp and looked around. Cupboards and chests had been opened, and someone in a hurry had flung things about. He raised the seat of the gallery bench, looked in the stowage beneath, then let it down, nodding. When he turned, Duncan and the clerk were waiting at the hatch. He ushered them in and closed the oaken door, then sat in his shingle chair, resting his splinted arm on the writing desk beside it. "How did it happen?" he asked.

Duncan sighed, his ruddy face a study in shame. "All my responsibility, sir. Things got a bit hectic and . . . well, I just never would have suspected that Mister Romart might turn his coat. Not after all the lot of us has gone through."

"Nobody saw them leave, sir," Billy Caster added. "Mister Duncan's not to blame, either. First there was the cooper playing the harpsichord, then the musicians became agitated, then that coaster came on us . . ."

Dalton waved his good arm. "No apologies are in order, or called for. I simply want to know the manner of Commander Croney's escape."

"Well." Charley Duncan shrugged. "Obviously, Mister Romart helped him. He couldn't have got off the ship by himself. I just can't imagine what could have persuaded Mister Romart to . . ."

"The manner of the escape," Dalton urged.

Billy Caster said, "It looks as though Mister Romart stood himself as guard; then when the commotion began he let the prisoner free. They came here to your cabin then, and searched it . . . Did they take anything, sir? From your effects, I mean?"

"Yes, they did. Please go on."

"Well, the jollyboat had been brought alongside, and I suppose Mister Romart simply spirited Commander Croney to the gundeck and over the wales while nobody was watching. We didn't see them until they were some distance away."

"Mister Duncan?"

"That's how I see it, too, sir. Except I wonder if the prisoner somehow forced Mister Romart to help him. I mean, I've come to know Mister Romart, sir. Bleedin' Colonial that he is, and aggravating in many a way, still I can't believe he would betray you, sir, no more than I would or any of the rest of us that's sailed with you."

"Sit down," Dalton said. "Both of you, and stop looking so glum. It isn't what you think about it that matters, you see. It's what Commander Croney thinks. That is a dangerous man. He is a zealot, and quite ambitious. If he were to suspect even for a moment that Michael Romart was acting at my direction . . ."

Duncan's eyes went wide. "You mean he didn't turn his coat, sir?"

217

"Of course not. I asked him to help Commander Croney escape, and to get him safely to fleet headquarters."

"Why? I mean, ah . . . why, sir?"

"Because the likelihood of Commander Croney engineering his own escape from this ship is next to nothing, and even if he could have done it, I don't want him running loose without someone to keep an eye on him. So when Mister Romart told me that Commander Croney had tried to bribe him to help him — as he had several others also — I asked Mister Romart to take the offer and proceed at his first opportunity."

It was Billy's turn to ask, "But why, sir?"

"Because the man was a nuisance to keep as a prisoner, and of absolutely no value. But at fleet headquarters — with a bit of guidance — he could do us all a great service . . . so long as he doesn't realize that's what he is doing. Every man-jack aboard *Fury* faces charges of one kind or another. We are fugitives, and Commander Croney has set himself to bring us to justice — especially me, because he believes he might be richly rewarded by certain ministers of the king, if he does. The problem is that, left to his own devices, Commander Croney is well on his way to muddling the entire business. Those charges he has against me . . . they address everything except the real issue, which is whether or not I am guilty of treason against the Crown."

"You intend to stand trial, sir?"

"More than intend to, Mister Duncan. I shall demand it."

"But . . . well, why?"

"Honor, Mister Duncan." Dalton gritted his teeth and resettled his splinted arm on the desk. It ached no matter how he positioned it. "Dalton is an honorable name. Not a grand name, as most Englishmen would see it — it is only an Irish name — but it carries honor and I intend to see it cleared of scandal. I intend to stand court martial specifically on that charge, and before a judge advocate who can't be biased or bluffed by Felix Croney or the

Home Ministry or by the king himself."

"But, where? Are we going back to England, sir?"

"*Procedures for the Conduct of Courts Martial Extraordinary,*" Dalton recited. "In its wisdom and for its own reasons, the Right Honorable Discipline Committee of the Lords of the Admiralty has provided for trial at sea."

They sat in silence for long moments, simply staring at him. Then Billy said, "But, sir, the charges. I don't think the accused in a trial is given the opportunity to decide what he will be tried for."

"No, the accuser makes that decision. What I am hoping is that Commander Croney will serve as my accuser. He has the correct charges in his possession at this moment."

Billy's eyes went wider still. "The copies! The copies you had me make . . . with changes in them!"

"Aye, Mister Caster. And my compliments to you, by the way. Service aboard a sailing vessel does tend to bring out the best of talents in a person. Among other aptitudes, Mister Caster, you have developed excellent skills in the art of forgery."

XXI

Supper aboard *Christine*, though oddly appointed because of the diminutive size of the coaster, was a meal to be remembered, all the same. Alf Pembroke's cook, a runaway Arcadian from Nova Scotia, served up platters of roast pigeon basted with Madeira and maple sugar, steaming orange tubers rich with goat cheese, a pudding of barley flavored with honey and rum, and thick Spanish coffee. They feasted on deck by lamplight, at a galley table placed within a canvas pavilion for the occasion, and Tempore DiGaetano played Italian music on the violin between covert gorgings at the side table.

"I never realized that scavengers live so well," Dalton admitted. "I am tempted to abscond with your cook, Captain Pembroke."

The older man finished a huge mouthful of squab and washed it down with two-water grog. "Damned difficult to deny liberties to one whose bloody warship holds my poor little boat at ransom, Captain Dalton. But I swear if you try to take Henri, I shall make a fight of it."

"Well, there is enough fighting to be had these days, so I won't press the claim. But I've more serious business to propose. First, so that you may relax, I assure you that my men and I are neither hostiles nor mercenaries, and despite what you may have heard or assumed, *Fury* poses no threat to you and your vessel . . . provided you can refrain from firing any further shot over my bow. Rather, I should like to strike a bargain with you, since you are bound for fleet headquarters. Are you familiar with a ship named *Cornwall?*"

"Aye, I've seen her. A great, bloody seventy-four."

"*Cornwall* is commanded by Captain Peter Selkirk, and I'd like you to deliver a post to him when you arrive there."

"I don't see how I could do that. Just because the Royal Navy chooses not to notice *Christine* when she's about, doesn't mean I'm free to come and go about the yards."

"You'll have to contact someone there, to deliver your blankets."

"Aye, a supply sergeant at the quartermaster's depot."

"Then tell the supply sergeant that you carry a private dispatch for Captain Selkirk. Tell him whom it comes from, and emphasize that it is *private*. I trust you will have the opportunity to deliver it, then."

"I could simply post it by fleet messenger . . ."

"No, I shall be asking for a reply from him. I want you to bring the reply to me."

"Where?"

"We will arrange a rendezvous. Will you do it?"

"What do I get out of all this?"

"Not much in advance," Dalton admitted. "I can manage seven or eight pounds sterling. I have no American dollars, but I'm certain you can deal in either."

"Not very much for a cruise the length of Long Island," Pembroke pointed out.

"You are going there anyway," Dalton reminded him. "But there is a chance of you earning far more, if my plans come to pass."

"How so?"

"You might, one day soon, have a chance to collect retrieval on delivery of a fugitive. There could be a fair amount of value involved there."

Pembroke sipped at his grog again, squinting at Dalton in the lamplight. "I must say I am hard put to

221

riddle out what you are trying to do, Captain. In fact, I haven't the foggiest notion."

"Me, too," Charley Duncan put in. "Beg pardon, sir, but I can't for the life of me follow what you're about."

"The best for us all," Dalton said. "But only if a great many things work out."

"What would you have done if I hadn't happened along?" Pembroke wondered.

"Oh, I would have gone and found you, Captain. I knew you were somewhere about. I saw the signs where you shipped aboard your blankets. We would have met directly, one way or another."

"My word," Pembroke breathed. "You are audacious, Captain Dalton."

"Merely tired." Dalton shrugged. "I have business to settle, and some accounts to set in order, but I am fair tired out from being a fugitive from my own flag and I intend to settle that problem once and for all."

"What's the problem? Change flags. Many have done so, you know."

"They've done so or not by choice, Captain Pembroke . . . choice made cleanly on the basis of merit. There is no honor in flying from one flag to another to hide or to escape. Do we have a bargain, Captain Pembroke? Will you serve as messenger for me?"

"We have a bargain, I suppose. I'll carry your mail, and I'll bring your response when you tell me where and when. I only hope you know what you are doing."

"So do I, Captain."

At six bells, Dalton and his party returned to *Fury*. by lanternlight he inspected his ship, hearing reports from each repair crew. There was still some minor work to do—a bit of studding below the midships deck, and some lines that must be worked with the marlinspike, but the work ashore was finished and all of the snow's sails were bent on and ready. "I'll want the launch at first light, Mister Wise," he said. "I shall be going across to the coaster once more. But please be ready to sail upon my return."

"Aye, sir."

In his little cabin, Dalton took out paper, pen and ink and began drafting a letter. It was a long, detailed missive, couched in the progressive logic of Admiralty form. He was still at it when Billy Caster came in and draped a wrap around his shoulders against the evening chill. At first he paid little attention; then he paused, frowning as he lifted a corner of the wrap. "What is this?"

"It's a blanket, sir." Billy scuffed his feet. "Mister Duncan says the coaster yonder has a hold full of these, and he thought they would hardly miss just a few of them. So he . . . ah . . . he sort of helped himself. You know how Mister Duncan is, sir."

"Just a few? How many?"

"Fifty-two, sir. I counted them."

Dalton sighed, wondering how Charley Duncan had done it this time. "That will be all, Mister Caster," he said. "Go and get your rest."

Fifty-two blankets. They would all sleep well tonight, despite the cold. Enough blankets for every crewman and every musician in cargo, and some to spare.

Dalton returned to his writing.

Pale dawn hung in the eastern sky, and a brisk northwest wind blew cold across Shelter Island when Dalton returned from delivering his post to Alf Pembroke aboard *Christine*. He climbed the snow's side, stepped over the gunwales and strode aft to the quarterdeck while hands rushed to hoist and secure the launch. The jollyboat was already up, and men stood at station, waiting for their orders.

For better or worse, Dalton told himself, the game is in play now. Felix Croney is on his way south, with Michael Romart to help him along and keep his mind off the papers he has "recovered." Soon my letter to Hawser will be on its way as well. Far easier to predict what Croney will do than to estimate how Hawser will react. Once again, I am trusting to the luck of the Irish, because I know of nothing else to do.

"Tops aloft," he called. "Hands to the capstan; secure messenger to the anchor line. Hands afore to cat and fish the anchor." His good hand behind his back, legs wide in firm stance, he drew a deep breath of the snow-cold morning air. "We shall come about to port and take the wind on our starboard quarter, Mister Wise. Once we've rounded off that point yonder, we shall set for due south. Mister Duncan, tell our cooper to have our barrels ready before we reach Morgan's Cove, if he wants to be put ashore there and not simply overside."

"Aye, sir."

Fury shuddered slightly as her anchor came up, and began to drift astern. "Make sail, Mister Wise," Dalton said. "By the drill."

"Aye, sir."

"On deck!"

"Aye the tops!"

"All is clear, sir. Open sea and nothing in sight."

Billy Caster came from below, bearing tea. Dalton took a mug absently and breathed on it, watching the steam drift off on the cold wind. "How far is 'all is clear' today, Mister Caster?"

"Sir?"

"Our maintop reports that all is clear. How far is it clear?"

Billy squinched up his face and scratched himself behind the ear. "Is it another formula, sir? I don't remember."

"Aye, it's a formula, and one a sailor should not forget. Make note of it, Mister Caster. Memorize it. It could save your ship, one day."

"Yes, sir. I'll try."

"The formula is: eight-sevenths of the square root of feet of height of the observer above the waterline equals the distance to the horizon in miles. It was Mister Mallory who called the report, from the maintop. How many feet would you say it is from sea level to Mister Mallory's eyes?"

Billy looked at the mainmast towering above them, and tried to estimate the height of the deck above the waterline. "Maybe a hundred feet, sir?"

"Not quite," Dalton said. "But a bit over ninety feet as he stands on the trestletrees. So if the square root of that is nine and a half, then eight-sevenths of that will be ten and eighty-five hundredths. Therefore the horizon that Mister Mallory sees is just short of eleven miles away, and on a clear day he should be able to see the maintop of another ship of our size at twice that, or nearly twenty-two miles."

"Yes, sir."

"Remember it, Mister Caster."

"Aye, sir." Billy went away, his head spinning. At least the captain hadn't asked him to fare the morning, as he often did.

As *Fury* came about, sliding past the still-anchored *Christine* to take fresh wind in her sails, Dalton was remembering his own lessons in such formulas . . . more than a decade ago. Few such formulas would he ever forget, because his teacher had been Captain Peter Selkirk. Old Hawser, now commanding His Majesty's Ship of the Line *Cornwall*. Senior Captain Selkirk, whose rank and years in rank qualified him to serve as Judge Advocate Extraordinary in certain circumstances, by the provisions of Admiralty law dealing with courts martial at sea.

Felix Croney was footsore, weary and totally out-of-sorts by the time Michael Romart led him down a snow-crusted lane and into a tiny settlement that Romart approved of. It was not the first settlement they had seen, but the third. The first two, though, they had gone around. "Whigs," Romart had said, by way of

225

explanation.

Now, though, Romart scouted the place and approved. "Tories," he decided. "We might hire a coach here, sir. Or at least a cart, though you'll have to pay the fare. I could hardly collect my wages back there, and my purse is in a poor way."

At the outskirts they met a man leading a cow, and Romart asked, "What place is this?"

"Tuckahoe," the man admitted. "What of it?"

"We've come a long way," Romart explained. "We need a place to rest."

"Then you should have stopped at East Hampton. There's an inn there."

"We hadn't come that far when we passed East Hampton. Isn't there an inn at Tuckahoe?"

"Aye, there might be."

"Well, where is it?"

"What do you want it for?"

Felix Croney's patience was at an end. "Food and rest!" he barked. "What does anyone want an inn for?"

The man studied him solemnly. "You'd have to pay your fare."

"I'll have you know I am the . . ." Croney's ranting was cut short when Michael Romart's hand rested companionably on his shoulder, slipped behind his neck and twisted itself into his stock, cutting off his wind like a garotte. He struggled, gasped, and began to strangle. Romart held him thus for a moment, then loosed his hold and slapped him on the back as though he had choked on a morsel.

"The gentleman is subject to fits," Romart explained to the man with the cow. "That's why he needs his rest. 'Twould be a kindness if you'd show us the way to the inn. The gentleman is willing to pay, right enough."

"It's extra if he has a fit and wets the bed," the man decided. "Come along and I'll show you. It's my inn."

Behind the man, Romart whispered to Croney, "Beg pardon, sir, but you seemed about to tell the man who

226

you are. That would be unwise; take my word."

Croney was still catching his breath and rubbing at his throat. "I thought you said the people here are Royalists," he rasped.

"Aye, sir. They're Tories, by an' large. But favorin' a king doesn't mean they like the one we have at the moment, or any of his representatives. Especially guard officers, if you take my meaning."

The "inn" at Tuckahoe was a mean place, nothing more than a shed tacked onto a cabin, with a barn behind. A pot of greasy stew hung over the fire, and the two guest beds were straw mattresses on rope frames. Each bed was barely large enough to sleep three men, and the inn had five guests at the moment.

"Let the gentleman have the bedspace," Romart said expansively. "He needs the rest. Just give me a quilt and I'll sleep yonder in the hayloft."

Croney was too tired to argue. But when he opened his valise to pay, Romart hauled him aside quickly. "Don't show your coin just yet, sir. There's folks that would knock a man in the head that pays in advance."

"I'm not paying coin," Croney said., "I don't have it. I was about to write the innkeep a voucher."

"A king's ticket?" Romart paled. "Ah, sir. It's well I'm with you, for you'd not last a day on your own."

"My voucher is acceptable. They *have* to accept it. It is the law."

"Ah, sir." Romart sighed and took the valise from his hand. "At least wait a bit. I'd like to be ready to leave in a hurry when these gentlefolk learn they've a bloody king's man as their guest."

Croney subsided, making another mental note to get even with Michael Romart when the proper time arrived. His belly sated with evil-tasting stew, he went off to share a bed with a tinker and a gunsmith.

Romart explored a bit, chatted with a few locals, and finally made his way to the inn's barn for a peaceful night's sleep. Rarely, he had found, was the straw in a

227

hayloft infested with anything worse than the occasional mouse. It was the beds in public inns that teemed with tiny life.

Felix Croney had in mind to spend a few moments by a lamp, reviewing the papers and documents he had recovered from Patrick Dalton's cabin. He had counted them quickly on the ship, to make sure they were all there, but he had not had a chance to look at them closely. He discovered, though, that his valise had gone off with Michael Romart . . . for safe keeping.

Irritated but too exhausted to pursue the matter further, Commander Felix Croney put himself to bed.

XXII

Once separated from the harpsichord — by being forbidden to set foot on the quarterdeck — Jordy Good proved himself a gifted cooper. By the time *Fury* made inshore to sight Morgan's Cove, he had repaired most of the snow's damaged casks and fashioned four new ones capable of holding sixty gallons of water apiece.

"They'll seep a bit at first filling," he told Cadman Wise. "Ash wood is slow to meld. But they'll serve your purposes. Now do you suppose a man might be permitted just a bit of relaxation with that boxed harp yonder?"

"Not under any circumstances," Wise told him. "Our fore hold has become a battleground since Montauk, and Captain says there is no clear precedent in maritime law for the discipline of cargo."

"What kind of precedent is there for mounting a harpsichord on the quarterdeck of a warship, then?"

"We can use a pair of kegs, Mister Good. Please return to your craft."

On a broad and easy tack, *Fury* stood off the little cove while Dalton glassed the place and his tops studied it from aloft. Hardly more than a fishing village, Morgan's Cove still carried the scars of being shelled briefly two years before. Refugees from Manhattan Island had gathered there during the first push of Crown troops from the yards at Long Island, and had raised a militia flag—a serpent on a linen field. Some said they had expected support from General Arnold, some that they had hoped for a general uprising of farmers in the region. Neither came, though, and a pair of frigates detached from the squadron of Vice Admiral Sir Walter Jennings sailed upcoast with bombards and brought down the rebel flag.

The surviving rebels had moved on, and the frigates had gone their way. Patrols from the lower island had come and gone, and Dalton understood, as he perused the settlement, how those who remained there might be a bit testy about the whole incident. It was their settlement that had been half destroyed.

Beyond and on both sides of the village, low hills arose—hills where little fields and meadows formed a mosaic with patches of winter forest, the entire landscape now bright beneath several inches of snow. In the cove itself, several vessels rested: fishing boats, a wintering merchant packet, some masted barges and an old ship that might once have been a whaler. Slim rigging rose beyond it, mostly hidden, but Dalton identified it even as his foretop lookout called the sighting. A revenue cutter. Dalton stalked to the quarterrail and called, "Mister Wise! Bring the cooper here, please."

When Jordy Good came aft, Dalton pointed at the distant shore. "Mister Good, there is a revenue cutter in harbor there, with its mast sheered for wintering. Did you know about that?"

Good blinked. "Aye, sir. It always lays over there in the winter. It has been stationed there since seventy-five or so."

"You didn't mention it to us, Mister Good."

"Sorry, Captain. I didn't think about it. It's just there. Sort of an object lesson to the townsfolk, since they have to quarter and feed the crew. But it doesn't do anything. It's just a nuisance."

"Does it have guns, Mister Good?"

"Well, yes, sir, I guess it has some because it volleys

sometimes just about when the cows are ready to milk. Upsets the folk no end when it does that, but the crew seems to think it's great sport."

"I am tempted to put you over the side, Mister Good, and let you swim ashore."

"Aye, sir. I'm truly sorry I forgot to tell you about that."

"Can you swim, Mister Good?"

"No, sir. Not a stroke."

"I was afraid of that. What does Mister Wise have you doing just now?"

"Making a pair of kegs, sir."

"Then get back to your kegs, Mister Good. And make them tight. I may yet decide to let you float yourself ashore with them."

"Aye, sir."

When the abashed cooper was gone, Dalton raised his head. "Tops ahoy!"

"Aye, sir?"

"Have we been sighted from the shore?"

"Not likely, sir. No lookouts anywhere that we can see."

"Very well. Mister Duncan!"

"Aye, sir?" Charley Duncan came hurrying from amidships.

"There is an armed cutter in that harbor, Mister Duncan."

"A cutter, sir? Mister Good never said anything about . . ."

"I have already belabored the cooper on that point, Mister Duncan. But the problem remains. I do not care for an exchange of fire with a cutter, just for the taking on of water. Do you have a suggestion?"

"Aye, sir. Sail right in and sink the cutter before it has a chance to shoot."

Dalton clenched his teeth, waiting. Faced with any problem, it was always Charley Duncan's impulse to attack head-on and open fire. It was simply second nature to the sandy-haired seaman. But it was his afterthoughts that sometimes proved interesting.

231

"Then again," Duncan added, more thoughtfully, "we might just keep them amused until we've finished our business there. They aren't likely to follow after us. That would be very foolish of them . . . a cutter against a snow."

"I seem to recall a schooner one time, that set out to find and destroy a frigate."

"Aye, sir." Duncan's grin faded. "But that was a personal matter. Matter of honor, you might say . . . for all of us."

"Yes. Yes, it was. Mister Duncan, would you care to exercise our launch this evening?"

Duncan brightened immediately. "Aye, sir. I believe that might be entertaining."

"Then come up and we shall discuss it. Helm, bring us to port. Two points, I think, for now. Mister Wise!"

"Aye, sir?"

"Trim for course correction, Mister Wise. Two points to port, and reduce sail. We shall bypass that harbor yonder, then come about and stand for a bit."

"Aye, sir."

In chill twilight *Fury* beat inshore just south of the channel at Morgan's Cove, put her nose to the wind and furled sails on all spars. A kedge was laid out, the launch lowered from its davits and Charley Duncan assembled his shore party on deck — eight men in all, including the cooper, Jordy Good. As the only one familiar with Morgan's Cove, he would serve as scout. Six of them carried cutlasses.

"Behave as gentlemen, gentlemen," Dalton told them. "We are not here to fight. You are simply to make your way aboard the cutter if you can, and see that it is secured long enough for us to take on water."

"I've told the lads that, sir," Duncan assured him. "Just as you told me. We'll have a look, then do just as much as necessary to make the harbor safe."

"And no more," Dalton repeated.

"Not a bit more," Duncan said.

"You can expect two men aboard. The rest will be snug ashore somewhere."

"Aye, sir. We know that."

"And no ruckus of any sort if it can be avoided," Dalton said.

"Don't worry, sir. We'll handle the situation."

"Very well, Mister Duncan. Be off, then, and bring back the launch for towing when you have the harbor secure."

"Aye, sir."

The shore party boarded the launch and cast off, a dark many-headed shadow on the twilight water. *Something's* stubby canvas rose and the boat began the first of two long tacks that would carry it into the harbor's entrance.

Dalton stood at the midships rail and watched them go, the fingers of his right hand pressed through his turnbuckle splints to rub his aching arm.

"Does it bother you, sir?" Billy Caster was in shadows beside him.

"What? Oh, the arm. It aches a bit, and it itches. But it is only a distraction. How do you fare the wind, Mister Carter?"

"East of north, sir, about ten knots. Steady and clear . . . and cold as a pirate's heart. Beg pardon, sir. It's an expression I've heard."

"Apt enough." Dalton nodded, distractedly. "What will it do, then?"

"The wind will shift by morning, I imagine. It will come from the west or north of west, and strengthen during the day."

"Very good, Mister Caster. Why do you believe that?"

"Well, sir, there were clouds on the west horizon at last light, that made the sun go blood-red. When I've seen that before, in winter, it means there will be such a change."

233

"And the tide?"

"Past ebb, sir."

"Very good, Mister Caster."

"You are worried about them, aren't you, sir?"

Dalton glanced around, wondering if the boy had learned to read his mind. "Not worried, Mister Caster. Mister Duncan is a resourceful man. I just have the feeling that there may have been some eventuality I did not cover in my instructions . . . that I should have considered."

"Are you doubtful that they can secure the harbor, sir?"

"Oh, no. Not at all. It's just that I don't really know *how* they will do it. Why do you suppose such intuitions occur, Mister Caster?"

"Probably comes of knowing Mister Duncan, sir."

The longshore wind pushed rolling waves ahead of it, long troughs and rounded peaks luminous in the pale glow of a three-quarter moon. *Something* had gone far enough out to come down on the mouth of the cove with good wind, and now the launch crested the last of the light breakers and slid silently into the shelter of Morgan's Cove. Charley Duncan manned the tiller, with Jordy Good beside him. The rest were spread forward, with Mister Hoop in the bow.

There had been no alarm, and the harbor lay dark and quiet under the winter sky. Duncan eased *Something* past a row of fishing boats, and had the sails taken down. Then, on oars, they eased toward the old whaler, beyond which lay the king's cutter.

"It's called *Purity*," Jordy Good whispered.

"What?"

"The cutter's name. It's *Purity*."

"I know that," Duncan reminded him. "You already told us."

"Has a crew of about a dozen," the cooper said.

"You told us that, too. Be quiet."

"It's usually tied fore and aft at the fishhouse dock. Only decent dock in this place, and the cutter takes it over."

"Hush."

"What?"

"I said, be quiet."

"Oh. Right. The dock'll be on the other side of it. Did I tell you that?"

"Quiet!"

Faces forward in the launch glanced back, glowering at Duncan. Good drew his long face into a pious and aggrieved expression. "It isn't me that's liken to wake the dead."

As *Something's* nose slid astern of the old whaler, Mister Hoop motioned and grabbed a dangling line. As one, the rowers unslung their oars and brought them inboard as quietly as possible. Hoop hauled at the line, tugging the launch tight under the old ship's tail, then began pulling it forward, leaning out for a view of what was on the other side. *Something's* stem cleared the port quarter of the towering, dark ship, and stopped. Hoop whispered to the man nearest him, and the report came aft. "He sees the cutter, sir. Just a chain away. Two men on deck. He thinks they have a tubfire there to keep them warm."

"Can we approach unseen?" Duncan whispered. The whisper went forward, and its response returned: "Not bloody likely. Both of them are facing this way."

"Back us off, Mister Hoop."

Silently, *Something* slid back under the whaler's tail.

"Too much moon tonight," Duncan muttered. "We'll need a diversion."

"How about a distraction?" Jordy Good whispered.

"That's what I said."

"No, you said diversion. That's different. But if a distraction would serve, I know how to do that."

"How?"

235

"Well, you see how near the cutter is to this old slab-side here. They had it hauled over to give them on watch a windbreak. But there's water casks topside on this tub, best I remember, and there's hoist lines on its lower yards. I'd need that wide lad yonder to help me, but I could . . ."

He outlined his idea in whispers and Duncan grinned.

"I wish I'd come up with that, myself," he admitted.

A few minutes later, with *Something* snugged to the whaler's sternpost, Jordy Good and Mister Hoop grasped wale channels on the old ship and climbed away, up the dark hull.

"Settle in, lads," Duncan told the rest. "If this works, we can give the captain all the harbor he wants for as long as he wants it, without a cutter to worry about."

On the dark, littered deck of the derelict, Jordy Good poked around until he found a span of heavy net, then had Hoop lift a huge cask of water and set it onto the webbing. The ends he folded upward. Three corners he secured together with tied line, the fourth with a slip-hitch in a separate line; then he found a sheet line a'dangle from the portside course spar and fixed it to the netted cask. "That should do it," he decided. "See if you can prize the lid from the cask without raising a ruckus."

Hoop's removal of the lid was almost soundless. Inside the barrel, foul-smelling water reeked and chilled. "Lovely," Good said.

With a quick prayer that the tackle above still bore its grease, Good set Hoop to the line. "Hoist away with a will," he said. "I'll handle the slip."

The netted barrel made scuffing sounds on the deck when Hoop began to hoist it. Good peered over the wales at the cutter below. Neither of the men there had looked up. They sat huddled at a wood fire burning in a sand tub, wrapped in blankets against the cold. Both had scarves tied over their hats and under their chins, muffling their ears.

Hoop hauled on the hoist line and the barrel slid up the wale, then swung free, a bulky pendulum swinging in the moonlight directly over the cutter's deck. Good raised a hand and Hoop tied off his line. The swings diminished, and finally the water cask hung motionless in its web. Good judged position, grinned and jerked the slipline free.

Slowly, the freed corner of the net fell away. The barrel canted, hesitated, then turned over in its sling. A cascade of icy water descended upon the cutter below, drenching the two men there, dousing their fire. They scuttled aside, soaked and freezing, and looked for the source of their disaster. There was nothing to be seen, except a slung cask dangling above them.

For long minutes they paced back and forth on the slippery, frigid deck, their teeth chattering uncontrollably. Then one said, "It was the wind. Must have been the w-wind. Nobody around. I'm for a stove and some dry clothes."

"The old inn." The other shivered. "Not far. We'll come back for a better look."

Trembling and light-headed from cold immersion, the two stumbled to the longside dock and hurried away. They were gone for the better part of an hour, then returned . . . to nothing. The little fishhouse dock extended out from the draypath, and beyond it the old whaler sat dark and forlorn. But *Purity* was nowhere in sight. The cutter was gone.

XXIII

Off the south point of Morgan's Cove *Fury* waited,
dark and silent under a riding moon, her stem like a slow
windvane easing gradually a'port, telling the wind and
the tide. As many aboard as could be spared wrapped
themselves in quilts and blankets and took to the hammocks for what rest they could get. But in the tops sharp
eyes were posted, and men were on deck at station
points, waiting for the return of the launch.

There would yet be work to do before they could enter
the little port and take on water. *Fury* would have to be
towed in. A schooner or a sloop — any fore-and-aft sailed
vessel — might have tacked seaward and back, using a
beam wind to enter the harbor under sail. But despite all
her staysails and her powerful spanker, *Fury* was yet a
square-rigger, and close tack to the wind was not her best
skill. So when the shore party had made the harbor secure — or at least free of the threat of cannon-shot from
the armed cutter bedded there — the next task would be
to rig the launch for towing and put muscle to its oars.
Though easy of helm, the snow would yet be slow to start
against a wind, and balky in the channel. It would be
shift-and-shift at the oars until *Fury* was in and sheltered.

They watched, though there was little enough to see.
They listened — musketry or cannon might carry down
on the wind — but heard nothing. The moon climbed

higher and the wind began to ease about, as Billy had guessed and Dalton had known it would. The hours passed, and all who could, slept. Dalton fidgeted. Whatever had occurred in the sheltered harbor, it should have been done long since. Yet there was no sign of the shore party. He was toying with taking the jollyboat and going for a look when the call came: "On deck!"

Dalton raised his eyes aloft. "Tops aye!"

"A mast sir, I think. Beyond the spit and moving outward."

"A mast, tops?"

"Aye, sir. No sail, just what looks to be a mast . . . Aye, it is a mast. I see its stays."

"What of the launch? Could it be a step mast?"

"No, sir. It's taller . . . like the mast of a sloop, though doubled a bit lower . . . mainmast, topmast and topgallant, right enough . . . no spars. I believe it is the mast of a cutter, sir."

The cutter. Dalton clenched his teeth. Had something gone wrong? Was the cutter trying to stalk them? Sweeps might move a cutter, but only slowly . . .

"On deck! I see the launch, sir. It's our lads, just clearing the spit. They're bringing the cutter out, sir. They have it in tow."

All along *Fury*'s deck, men were awake now and peering ahead, trying to see detail in the moonlight. Billy Caster came up from below, rubbing sleep from his eyes, and came to the quarterdeck. "Are they returning, sir?"

"It appears they are. Mister Caster, you were present when I discussed the shore mission with them. Did I use the word 'secure' with reference to the revenue cutter?"

"No, sir. I'm sure you didn't."

"I didn't think so."

"You might have said something about removing the threat . . ."

"Never mind, Mister Caster. I only wondered."

"Yes, sir."

Once clear of the spit, the launch made good time in

towing the battened-down cutter with its sheered mast. The wind drifted it along daintily. But once it was alongside *Fury* and a chain length away, there was the problem of stopping it. It was obvious that there was no one aboard, and the launch had the entire weight of it to turn and head into the wind. Even then, they had to keep rowing to hold it in place, and Dalton saw the perplexity on Charley Duncan's face even as the sandy-haired sailor realized his problem. He strode to the starboard rail and leaned his good arm there, casually. "What have you there, Mister Duncan?"

"The revenue cutter, sir," Duncan called back.

"Marvelous. Why did you bring it out of the harbor, Mister Duncan?"

"I don't know, sir. It just seemed . . . ah . . . tidier than leaving it there, you see."

"Have you committed an act of piracy, Mister Duncan?"

The sailor's face, now only thirty yards away, was a pale study in innocence. "Oh, no, sir. We just sort of relocated it to out here, sir. We didn't steal it or anything. Perish the thought . . ."

"What of its crew, then? What of its duty watch?"

"Well, sir, that was the thing about it. There wasn't anybody aboard when we decided to relocate it. Nobody at all. It was just sitting there unattended."

"Commissioned vessels—especially armed ones—are rarely left unattended, Mister Duncan."

"There wasn't anybody on this one, sir. I think the lads on watch had gone up to the town, you see." Duncan scratched his head. "Would you like for us to put it back, sir?"

"Would you like to put it back, Mister Duncan?"

"No, sir, I wouldn't. What I'd like to do is cut the bloody thing loose and let it drift to Bermuda if it wants to. We're about rowed out, sir."

Dalton turned, shaking his head. It never failed to amaze him, the feats of thievery that Charley Duncan could manage. Still, he was right — if they neither took nor damaged the cutter and therefore stopped possibly short of the commission of piracy. It *was* tidier to have the cutter out here than to share a small harbor with a little fighting craft that might open fire at the first opportunity. "Mister Wise!"

"Aye, sir?"

"Lay out the jollyboat, please. Crew of six. Take one of our lesser anchors over there, and secure that cutter. Do not use its equipment, and do not set foot on it. Just secure an anchor line to its stem and drop the anchor to windward. Lively, please. Those lads look to be fair worn out."

First light of morning was in the sky when *Fury* cast off tow within the confines of Morgan's Cove and crept across the harbor on spanker, spencer and jibs. The launch went ahead, its forward punt gun trained on the knot of scowling sailors of the king who waited at the stub of the fish dock. The punt gun, with its hardwood mount and blunderbuss bore, was the very essence of authority — a nasty contrivance which could spray a pound of shot on the lightest load and which offset the friendly grin of the sailor behind it. As the launch closed on the little dock, Charley Duncan waved and called, " 'Hoy the dock. We've brought a passenger and we want to take on water."

The one in charge, a ruddy young man with the tricorn and buttons of a lieutenant commander, stepped forward and pointed. "What ship is that?"

"*Fury*, sir." Duncan smiled again. "A peaceful trader going about her business."

"Trader, nothing!" the man asserted. "That is a warship. Did you take my cutter?"

"Take what, sir?"

"My cutter! The *Purity*, a king's revenue vessel duly chartered. Did you take it?"

241

"On my honor, sir, there isn't a man-jack of us that's set foot aboard a cutter anytime lately. Where did you last see it?"

"Right here! It was right here last night."

"Did you inquire of whoever was aboard? They might know where it went."

"There was no one aboard . . ."

"Then it must be somewhere near." Duncan made a show of gazing about the harbor, then shrugged. "A cutter wouldn't have gone very far by itself in a little cove like this. I wouldn't worry about it. It's bound to show up. Who's in charge here?"

"I am," the lieutenant commander said.

"I am." A burly man with a heavy coat stalked down the draypath to the dock. "I'm the mayor. What is it you want?"

"Passenger for Morgan's Cove, sir. And to take on water. Can we lighter from this dock?"

"For a fee," the mayor said.

"Absolutely not," the lieutenant commander said. "This dock is requisitioned for the king's cutter *Purity*."

"Then where is your bedamned cutter?" The mayor scowled at him. "I don't see it, and it is still my frigging dock!"

Something had nosed up to the dock, and Mister Hoop stood by with a mooring line at the wale. Jordy Good didn't wait for formalities. Hoisting his packs, he balanced on the wale and stepped across to the dock. "Hello, Nathan," he called. "I'm back."

The mayor turned, scowling. "Oh, it's you, is it?"

"None other. I told these lads they could take on water here. Made some new casks for 'em, as well." He glanced around, taking in the village above the bank. "Doesn't look like much has changed here in a season."

The mayor shot a hard look at the lieutenant commander. "Not what needs to change, at least."

The lieutenant commander was still frowning at Charley Duncan. "You haven't identified yourself."

242

"Duncan's the name." Duncan grinned. "Charley Duncan."

"I mean your vessel. Who are you? What are your colors?"

"*Fury,* sir. I already told you that. And the captain doesn't choose to raise his colors. Now who is going to give me permission to moor this launch?"

"I am," the mayor snorted. "It's my friggin' dock."

"Thank you." Duncan nodded. "Tie us off, Mister Hoop." He glanced around. *Fury* had come to mid-cove and furled her short sails. From where the snow sat, her guns commanded the entire cove. "Pair of you lads come with me, we'll see about water. The rest of you stay with *Something.* We wouldn't want her punts to discharge accidentally or anything of that sort. Lead on, Mister Good."

"Aye, Mister Duncan. Nathan, if you could scare up some hot rum for some cold bellies, we'll talk about water."

The mayor and the cooper started up the draypath, and Duncan tagged after them, followed by a pair of *Fury*'s sailors. As they came abreast, the lieutenant commander snapped, "I shall see you in hell if you have my cutter."

Duncan turned innocent eyes on him. "Do you suppose that's where you left it?"

Within the hour, flatboats were hauling between the dock and the snow, bringing casks ashore and returning full casks to the ship. They were not the same casks, for those that had been kept filled in the mayor's shed were frozen solid. So they simply traded containers and *Fury* took on barreled ice.

Townspeople grouped on the ways of Morgan's Cove and watched in fascination, their eyes turning again and again to the little harbor. It was not so much the sight of a trim, deadly cruiser sitting there that interested them. Ships of any sort were not rare sights along the east shore of Long Island. This one, though, had music coming from it. That was something that none among them had encountered in the past.

With Charley Duncan running the lightering of water from ashore, and a deck guard manning guns and glassing the harbor while topmen kept an eye on the sea beyond the spit, Patrick Dalton found opportunity to spend a bit of time below, studying charts, sailing times, and — again — the procedures for courts martial extraordinary. Billy Caster had been thorough in his work, while Guard Officer Felix Croney had been their "guest" aboard. In addition to the slightly altered charge papers that Croney now carried on his way to fleet headquarters, the young clerk had copied all the rest of his papers and Dalton now had the copies.

He was at his gallery bench, lost in his thoughts and his studies, when Billy knocked at the portal and then entered. "Some of the cargo wishes to go ashore, sir. Is that all right?"

"Eh?" Dalton glanced up. "What cargo?"

"Misters Hickman and DiGaetano, sir. And Maestro Pico."

"Why do they want to go ashore?"

"I don't know, sir. Mister Hickman said it is orchestra business."

"Which of them speak English?"

"Only Mister Hickman, sir . . . Oh, and Mister Miller, of course. They said they want to take him, too."

"How goes the lightering?"

"A bit longer, sir. They might catch a flatboat and return with the launch."

"Very well, Mister Caster. What cargo does is up to cargo, so long as the ship is not endangered or compromised. Make sure they have the same instructions as our shore party . . . about not talking to anyone about who we are or where we are going."

"Aye, sir. Ah, sir, I'm not sure Mister Miller knows yet that they intend to take him ashore."

Dalton waved him away and returned to his papers. "Tell them that anyone not aboard when we set sail will be left behind."

"Aye, sir. They were saying something about that, themselves."

The next flatboat making for shore carried four musicians — a manager, a conductor, a first violinist and a surly harpsichordist — along with the last of the water casks — and Billy watched it go, wondering at the ways of musicians. Why, he wondered, did Alfred Hickman and Tempore DiGaetano keep firm grips on the arms of Joseph Miller? And why did Maestro Galante Pico carry a belaying pin?

As the last lighter set out to deliver frozen casks to *Fury*, Charley Duncan strolled around the village of Morgan's Cove, looking for Jordy Good. The cooper had gone off somewhere, without putting his mark on the bit of paper Billy Caster had drawn up to manifest passenger delivery or something. Good was nowhere in sight, and Duncan was met with hostile glares at the several doors that opened at his rap. People of Morgan's Cove seemed unaccountably sullen, until he realized that to them, he was just another British sailor, no different from those of the cutter, who were quartered in the town by king's order.

Finally he went off to the cabin of Nathan Wyeth, mayor of the village and owner of its fish dock and sheds. Here he rapped again, and when Wyeth opened the door he clicked his tongue. "Not a friendly place to a seafaring man, Mister Mayor."

"What do you want?" The man frowned.

"I've come to settle up for the water and the use of your dock," Duncan said. "But I'd rather discuss it inside. It's cold out here."

"Aye." Wyeth opened the door reluctantly. "Come in, then. Wipe your feet. Not friendly indeed . . . What would the folk here have to make them friendly? Sailors quartered in their houses, foot patrols that come through now and again and steal anything that isn't too heavy to lift, taking meals and never paying for them . . . Aye, and by last count four daughters of God-fearing folk have come into a family way and not a husband among them. And that bedamned cutter, with its guards and its guns . . ."

"Strange they should misplace it so," Duncan said mildly.

"Aye." The mayor cocked a brow at him. "Mightily strange, indeed."

While Duncan rubbed his hands before the hearthfire, Wyeth cyphered casks and docking fees, then paused. "Some of the lads hereabout have even spoken of doing a bit of privateering . . . if only they had the vessel for it."

"Have they, now?"

"Just a notion. They've discussed the point that a nice prize or two — sold where there's discreet buyers — might balance off what's owed the town by the Georgies."

"Just talk, of course," Duncan said.

"Oh, aye, just talk. Where would the lads get an armed vessel to begin with?"

"Even a small one," Duncan agreed.

"Even a small one." Wyeth nodded.

"The value of even — say — a revenue cutter would be considerable," Duncan reflected.

"It certainly would cover the costs of a few casks of water and some dock fees," Wyeth agreed.

"Several times over, I'd think."

Wyeth glanced at his shuttered windows, his closed door, and lowered his voice. "How much over?"

Duncan pulled up a bench and sat. "What do you have?"

On a bright morning the coaster *Christine* came down

246

the blue-water edge off Southampton, following the coastline, and the lookout clinging to her little platform called, "Cap'n Pembroke, there's ships yonder!"

"Whereaway?"

" 'Bout Morgan's Cove, Cap'n. There's one standin' in at the harbor that I'd swear's that same blesset jack-mast brig that took our blankets. Old whaler an' some fishboats in there with it, an' there's the revenue cutter that chased us last month, but it isn't in. It's out."

"What is it doing?"

"Nothing, sir. No sails up at all. It looks battened for winter, except it isn't in harbor. It's resting outside, below the spit."

"Come over to port," Alf Pembroke told his helmsman. "I don't know what the bloody hell they're up to now, but it's no business of ours. Let's just go 'way around."

XXIV

The weather turned as they had predicted, the wind shifting to west of north with sullen gray clouds behind it, and *Fury* departed Morgan's Cove on jib and jigger, then swung her jaunty jib southward and put on traveling sails. South of the spit, men in fishing boats had closed on the lifeless *Purity* and now swarmed over her — releasing lines, raising anchor, putting on sail.

"I can't say I fully approve of the deal we made," Dalton noted, watching them as the snow passed at a distance. "It smacks of partisanship, giving a Crown cutter to rebels."

"Aye, sir." Charley Duncan nodded. "If we had done that . . . but as you directed and we made clear, we never set foot on that cutter, so rightly it never was us that took it. It's the lads from the town, and from what I heard they'd have taken it anyway before the season was out — the hard way. At least this way there was no bloodshed in the town — and we did turn a handy profit, right enough." He raised the steaming teapot between them, gazed at it admiringly, and poured tea into their cups. Teapot, tray, cups, saucers and serving dishes were all of ornate silver, bright in the sunlight. The silver tea service was one of three that Duncan had brought from Morgan's Cove, along with six sides of fresh pork, a cask of allspice, four kegs of rum, a bound volume of the

248

Fighting Instructions for Fleet Engagements, issued three years ago to senior captains and flag officers by the Lords of the Admiralty (where the town of Morgan's Cove had obtained such a volume had not been discussed or disclosed), and the mayor's tricorn hat.

Duncan wore the hat now, and felt it gave him the appearance of a first officer as well as the rank. Billy Caster huddled in his blankets and pored over the puzzling pages of the *Fighting Instructions,* and Dalton sipped his tea and calculated distances and speeds.

"We should round off the Chesapeake within the week," he said, talking mostly to himself. "By that time, God willing, Mister Romart will have delivered Commander Croney safely to the Long Island yards, and Commander Croney will have filed his petition for a search and seizure of *Fury.*"

"I don't understand very much of this," Billy Caster said to no one in particular, frowning at the vague, convoluted language of the master tome of British naval tactics. "Especially the parts that bear Admiral Rodney's name."

"Assuming things are no more chaotic than usual at fleet headquarters," Dalton pursued his thoughts, "it should require no more than four days for Commander Croney's petition to be posted and all fleet officers in port notified. By that time, Captain Selkirk will have received and considered my letter . . ."

"What makes you so sure that scavenger will deliver your letter, sir?" Duncan looked worried. "He has no reason to love any of us."

"I expect he will." Dalton shrugged. "He stands to gain a great deal. Captain Selkirk is in position to give him carte blanche in and about the ways. Alf Pembroke is one who will see quickly how a profit could be had from a senior captain's good wishes."

"The signal system that Admiral Howe worked out seems reasonable," Billy Caster muttered, still buried in his book. "It is like a chess board, sixteen by sixteen, and each row—across and down—has its own bunting. It says here that two hundred and fifty-six different messages can be given, simply by hoisting the correct two flags. Of course, everyone would have to have the same code book."

"It doesn't work well in practice." Dalton glanced around at him. "Far too complex and far too limited. A good signalman can do better with a dozen flags, just by the manner in which they are hoisted. You know yourself how several of our lads can communicate that way."

"Yes, sir." Billy nodded. "But Lord Howe's system makes more sense than anything else I have found so far in this volume."

"The only unpredictable factor"—Dalton returned to his own discourse—"is my assumption that Captain Selkirk will be the senior captain in port at the time. He has passed up flag rank, so I must simply hope that the admiral and the vice-admiral are still in the south. Otherwise they would outrank him."

"Outrank whom, sir?" Duncan was becoming a little confused.

"Captain Peter Selkirk. If either of Their Lordships is present, then he cannot act as Judge Advocate, according to the procedures."

"Oh."

"Listen to this, sir." Billy Caster ran his finger slowly down a page, reading aloud from the *Fighting Instructions*. " 'If the commander-in-chief would have the squadron when on a wind draw into a line on each other's bow and quarter and keep at the distance directed in the first article . . .' ah, that's one or two cables, as signaled . . . 'those ships which shall happen to be to leeward at the time of making the signal, forming the van of the line, and those to windward the rear, and all the ships from the van to the rear bearing on each other on the point of the compass whereon they will be on the other tack— always taking it from the center—he will hoist a red pennant under the flags mentioned in the said article at the

250

mizzen peak and fire a gun, and if he should afterwards tack in order to bring the squadron into a line ahead, the ship that becomes the headmost is to continue leading . . . ' " The boy raised puzzled eyes. "Sir, is that supposed to mean something?"

"It was intended to," Dalton said. "Unfortunately, hardly anyone knows what Lord Rodney was trying to say."

"But, sir, if a commander were to face a line of battle . . . I mean in actual combat on the sea . . . how would he follow these instructions?"

"He wouldn't, Mister Caster. No man in command of a ship or a fleet would seriously try to follow such dither."

"But don't they all study it?"

"Of course. It is important in the training of officers that they be familiar with that material, so they can ignore it. And it is important to the Admiralty to believe that each instruction will be followed to the letter."

"But why, sir?"

Dalton sighed. "Just during your lifetime, Mister Caster, England has built the greatest empire this world has yet seen, and it is based on the might of the British Navy. Would you argue with the logic that has produced such results?"

"No, sir. I don't even understand it."

"Neither does anyone else, Mister Caster."

Before the quarterrail, the companion hatch popped open and Claude Mallory appeared. "Captain, the cooper . . . ah, Mister Good, sir . . . he wants to know if it would be all right if he came onto the quarterdeck to play the harpsichord."

Dalton blinked and looked at Duncan. "The cooper? Didn't we put him ashore at Morgan's Cove?"

"Aye, sir, we did. But the orchestra went and got him and brought him back. They traded Mister Miller for him, sir. Ah . . . I believe the change is noted in the cargo manifest."

Billy Caster glanced up from his book. "Aye, sir. I en-

251

tered the change."

"On deck!"

Dalton stood, looking upward. "Aye, tops?"

"Sail, sir. Hull-down aft, coming out of the storm back there."

"Can you read it, tops?"

"Aye, sir. It's that same brig that we ran past back at Portsmouth. The *Bethune*."

"Is he pursuing, tops?"

"I don't think he will have the opportunity, sir. Those Morgan's Cove lads have sail up on that cutter that they . . . ah . . . found, and it's their wind. They are going out to intercept him, is how it looks."

They gathered at the afterrail, straining their eyes. From the deck, they could barely make out the hard-reefed sails of the brig beating across an ill wind, the full and racing sails of the cutter going out to meet it.

"Courageous lads," Duncan muttered. "For Colonials, that is."

Billy shaded his eyes. "Sir, can a cutter take a brig?"

" 'Nothing is sure in a sea fight,' " Dalton said. " 'When all is done, all else is chance.' That's a thing I remember Captain Selkirk telling us, when I was amidships. I recall it clearly because a classmate of mine — Nelson was his name, I believe — made a great point of quoting it to others . . . and never did quite get it right."

Claude Mallory was still at the coaming. "Sir, may Mister Good come aft and play the harpsichord? The musicians say they want him to practice it, to learn their tunes."

Dalton turned, his mind already going back to his plans and the things he must do to implement them. "Very well, Mister Mallory. Mister Good may come upon the quarterdeck, to play the harpsichord. But only Mister Good. If the rest want to play their fiddles and things, they can stand beyond the bell-mount."

"It might be best if Mister Ferrestrekov were nearer to the harpsichord, sir," Billy Caster suggested. "Bassoons

252

sound best in counterpoint to the long strings."

"Bring up more tea, if you please, Mister Caster. And see if our cargo has any Irish jigs in its repertoire. I don't believe I have ever heard the 'Erin Killee' or 'Dunkerry Doon' rendered by harpsichord and bassoon."

As the chill coastline of upper Long Island veered away to the west, *Fury* headed out to sea, great sails full and by the wind as she drummed southward on a looping course that would come ultimately to the Delaware and Chesapeake waters.

I have accounts to settle, Dalton told himself. Questions to resolve, disputes to end, uncertainties to make certain.

At Chesapeake, Ian McCall still contested whether *Fury* was his or was lost. At Chesapeake, John Singleton Ramsey waited for accountings and Constance Ramsey waited for a commitment. Dalton's eyes glistened as the first strains of "Ode to Molly Muldoon" lifted from the harpsichord, and other instruments beyond joined in, finding the mechanisms of harmony. Constance, he thought. My Constance, can I set straight the accounts I have with you? Can I offer you more than uncertain answers?

Not without honor. A man without honor has nothing to offer—to anyone.

It must be taken in order, he told himself. Like the tactics of naval engagement, like the making of sail to take a fair wind, like the procedure for a trial by court martial, each piece must be in place, and all in proper order.

Fury lifted her nose as her sails were trimmed. She took the rising seas as a racehorse takes the course. She took the spray in her teeth and headed south toward the Chesapeake, and in her wake trailed the haunting music of Ireland, done by orchestra and harpsichord.

The first step in the procedure must be a squaring of accounts.

Part Four
A SQUARING
OF ACCOUNTS

XXV

Felix Croney had never in his life spent a more irritating and frustrating four days than those in which he and Michael Romart traveled the length of Long Island from Montauk's wilds to the shabby streets of New Utrecht, one of several villages clustered about the Long Island yards. First they had walked for most of a day, making wide circuits to avoid settlements that the American identified as Whig hotbeds. Then they had acquired a two-wheeled oxcart and crept along a back road that was hardly more than a footpath while the north wind grew more and more chill and Romart took many a detour to avoid confrontation with people Croney never saw or even heard.

Even when they came to Huntington, where Romart finally decided that the guard officer's person was safe from attack by rebels, there had been a delay in finding transportation because all of the vehicles for miles around — carriages, wagons, carts and riding stock, had been gleaned by General Clinton's quartermasters for the hauling of freight and personnel being ferried across from Flatbush. The final day of the miserable journey, Croney and Romart spent on the swaying back of a draft ox while shifting winds blew fresh snow into their faces.

Croney felt that he could have made the trip in half the time without the assistance of the American, but never once had there been a chance to slip away from him. Every minute of the way, Romart either was with him or some-how had possession of his valise and papers. The man was taking no chance whatever of missing out on payment of his bribe.

And he was so damned *helpful*. Ever attentive to Cro-ney's needs, he had kept the guard officer on the verge of exhaustion attending to them. Ever vigilant for Croney's safety, he had taken them miles out of their way several times to assure that the guard officer faced no threat. Be-tween inclement conditions and sheer exhaustion, Cro-ney had not once in the entire trip had either the opportunity or the inclination to pause and review the sheaf of charges he carried, charges that sooner or later would put an end to the traitor Dalton . . . and give Cro-ney a fair chance at a grant of land and a title.

Had Michael Romart been a man of letters or rank, and had Croney not been so tired and distracted, he might have suspected that the American was deliberately caus-ing his hardships. But Romart was only a simple sailor, and a backwoods Colonial at that.

Finally, though, they arrived at New Utrecht and found food and warmth at a commandeered inn — the very inn, he realized, at which Patrick Dalton had first eluded him, obviously with the aid of the innkeeper. The innkeeper was gone now, and the building had been converted to quarter "non-regulars" — persons of rank or title who dealt with the fleet but were not subject to Admiralty authority. As a senior captain of the provincial guard, equal in rank to a commander of the navy, Croney was entitled to shel-ter, and he did not hesitate to claim his privilege even though it meant the ousting of a pair of junior attachés as-signed to General Clinton's headquarters. Romart tagged along after him, carrying his valise. In the low-ceilinged little room, Romart lit a lamp, held a chair for him, helped him off with his boots, and set a fire in the hearth. Then he left the room, and Croney looked around to make sure his valise was present. It was, and he relaxed, enjoying the warmth of the room. He yawned, and thought about spending an hour getting his papers in order, thought about what to do next. A general order for Dalton, he supposed. It would take a deal of argument to have such an order issued again, after the failed entrapment at Portsmouth. There would be irritation about the wasted time of a seventy-four and other vessels that had gone up there to capture the Irishman at Croney's insistence, only to have him once again slip away. They might even believe that Dalton was dead, his ship sunk by the squall they had endured.

He would have to pull rank, probably — cite his king's commission and Crown warrant — and if necessary, that would be done. All his plans, all his ambitions, rested on bringing Patrick Dalton to justice.

The warmth made him drowsy, and he started to doze, then awakened abruptly when Michael Romart came in carrying a steaming tray.

"Hot rum, sir," the American said. "The very thing for an evening like this." He poured and served, then backed off a respectful distance and squatted on his heels. "Well, sir, we've come to your headquarters, just like I promised you."

"Yes," Croney said sourly, "we have."

"And I've done all that I promised you, haven't I, sir — got you off Dalton's ship, escorted you safely home, kept your belongings intact, watched over you as a very mother hen . . ."

"Agreed." Croney nodded. "You have my thanks, Mister Romart. Now please be quiet. I want to . . ."

"I do cherish your gratitude, sir, but there's the rest of it I have to remind you of now. Let's see — it was citizenship papers, passage to England and a bit of a purse to tide me over. You do recall about that, don't you, sir?"

"We are on Empire grounds now, Mister Romart. I'd have only to lift a finger here to have you arrested and thrown into a prison hulk to die as a rebel and a traitor."

"Aye, sir, I know that." Romart smiled serenely. "But you did give me your word of honor, as a king's officer and

259

a gentleman."

"And what could you do if that should slip my mind?" Croney's fingers brushed the hilt of the short sword he had acquired upon arrival. Romart might be only a dim-witted sailor, but Croney knew from observation that he was quick and very strong.

Yet, Romart seemed not at all offended by the question. He simply shrugged, his smile never wavering, and pointed a thumb toward the door. "Nothing much, sir. Except that while I was out I told a few lads about our agreement . . . good, loyal lads, sir, but civilians, as you might say. It's an odd thing, sir, but I've noticed that military bases of all kinds seem to depend on the civilians around them to keep things goin' smooth. Supplies of things the military doesn't supply, services here and there that go beyond what's provided by the king's regulars . . ."

"What are you getting at, Mister Romart?"

"Just thinkin' aloud, sir. It seems to me that the better an armed force behaves, the more comforts come their way from them that are . . . ah . . . being protected by them, don't you see. And the more faith folks have in the honor of their betters, the less expensive it is for those betters to do business. And I expect English organizations are just like Colonial organizations . . . I mean, when expenses go up, there's going to be somebody that wonders why they did, and then just all sorts of problems come up . . ."

"That is enough, Mister Romart. You've made your point."

"Aye, sir. I knew we'd see eye to eye when it came down to it. I've never doubted a gentleman's honor." Romart squatted on his heels, comfortable and entirely satisfied, while Croney sulked and sipped at his hot rum.

"Never doubted a gentleman's honor either way," the American said, after a while. "That Dalton, now. If I was an officer and a gentleman, like yourself, sir, and it was me that had been knocked on the head and spirited aboard his ship and held prisoner there . . . I mean, and me, a king's officer, being humiliated like that, why, I don't believe I'd tolerate him any more after that."

"I have no intention of tolerating him," Croney snorted, wondering why he was even bothering to explain anything to a bone-headed renegade sailor. "By tomorrow evening, there will be a fleet order out on him."

"Oh. I see. What does that mean?"

Croney sighed, wishing the man would go away or at least be quiet. "It means that ships of the fleet will execute a campaign to bring in your Captain Dalton and put him on trial."

"They tried that before, didn't they, sir? I mean, I took it that was what you were doing at Portsmouth, with that ship of the line standing off out there and that brig darting back and forth."

Croney snorted and reached for the rum kettle. Romart stood easily, came to the table and poured for him, then retreated to his servile distance again. "Was it me, I'd want better assurance than that," he said.

"We shall get him eventually."

"Was it me, I wouldn't wait that long."

Croney cocked a brow, glancing toward the sailor. "Well, then, mister, *was* it you, what would you do?"

"Well, you talk about fleet orders . . . Is it the ship you want, or the man?"

"The man, of course. What do I care about the ship?"

"Then was it me, I'd post a fat reward for Patrick Dalton an' I'd make sure every man-jack in every port on this seaboard — be he British or Whig or whatever — knows about it. Pretty soon, if somebody else doesn't catch him ashore, his own crew will get wind of it and hand him over. That's what I'd do, was it me and was I a gentleman like you."

"That might be easier to argue than a fleet order," Croney said, mostly to himself. He sat in thought for a while, sipping hot rum, then waved a shaky hand at the sailor. "Mister Romart, you shall have what I promised you, tomorrow when I report to the post captain. But right now, I've had all of your company that I can stand. Please either go to sleep by the hearth there or get yourself elsewhere. I

261

am very tired."

Romart stood, concerned and understanding. "Yes, sir. You have had a most trying experience. I believe I'll just leave you to your rest, then. Good night, sir." He went quietly to the door and let himself out.

With luck, Croney thought, some blackguard will knock him in the head in some low tavern and I'll not have to deal with him further—the obsequious lout. The man was almost beyond toleration, and the idea of bestowing citizenship and passage to England on such a one had rankled the guard officer from the beginning.

Outside the inn, Michael Romart pulled up his collar and grinned a frosty grin. He had done all he had been set to do, and he would have wagered a year's wages that it would work. Whether or not, though, his part was done and it remained only for him to get himself away now, and find a place where he could wait for Patrick Dalton to pick him up. He patted the side of his heavy coat and was reassured by the comfortable weight of the purse that hung within. Early on in their travels, he had taken to carrying Felix Croney's purse for him, since—as he had convinced the guard officer—they were in radical rebel territory and it would not be safe for a British officer to show himself, paying lodgings, hiring carts and the like. He expected it would be a day or so before Croney remembered about the purse.

Long association with the likes of Charley Duncan had taught Michael Romart some new skills, and not a few new attitudes about the taking of things that weren't battened down.

At the edge of New Utrecht, Romart headed out across moonlit fields with forest beyond. By break of dawn he would be in the fishing village of Serrey, beyond the roads and ways of Admiral Howe's White Fleet headquarters. There he would haggle with a few boaters, pay out a bit of coin and begin his series of short voyages down the warrent coast toward Chesapeake.

Captain Peter Selkirk had spent the day on Staten Island, reading fleet reports, moderating endless discussions dealing with everything from supply schedules to anchorage placements to disputes among commanding officers over the issuance of blankets, and signing orders. As senior officer in port in the absence of Admiral Lord Richard Howe and the vice-admiral, Sir Walter Jennings, such routine housekeeping fell to him. It was the nature of navy life.

At evening, he had himself rowed across the narrows, had a supper of mutton and Madeira, then was taken by coach to the Navy yards and by launch back to *Cornwall*, which sat at anchor off Bay Point. In the course of a day's duties, he would willingly endure the dull, mind-numbing trivia of attending to fleet business as senior officer present. But when it came time to rest, he preferred his comfortable cabin—aboard his ship—to any breezy stall that the Admiralty might have commandeered for officers ashore.

It was after he had boarded *Cornwall* that he was handed a packet, delivered for him during the day by "one o' th' coasters in port." He took it below.

At his lampstand he opened the packet, rolled back pages and looked at the signature, and his eyes widened in astonishment. Dalton! The astonishment took on a touch of grudging amusement as he noticed the form of the signatory: *Patrick X. Dalton, Lieutenant Commander, HMRN det.* Detached, indeed! A fugitive at large, charged with treason by the Crown and a dozen capital offenses by the Admiral's staff . . . *detached*.

The man called Old Hawser sat down beside his lampstand and began to read. From astonishment and humor, his mood turned to wonder that the young seaman was still alive—Isaac Watson had been sure the snow had sunk in a squall—and wonder touched on irony, that this young man—so many years ago a student of his own, amidships—now turned to him again and asked for wisdom.

He read further, and felt anger. The audacity of the man! The sheer audacity of the young pup, to cite Admiralty law to *him,* and to go so far as to *explain* its workings, in case he might not understand.

Selkirk slapped the message down and barked, "Smollet! Attend me, please!"

In less than a minute his clerk was there, thinning hair tousled, wiping his spectacles with a bit of linen. "Sir?"

"Smollet, bring me the book on procedures for courts martial."

"Yes, sir. Admiralty Board, Common or Extraordinary?"

Selkirk glanced at the letter. "Extraordinary."

"Yes, sir. Moment, sir." He hurried out.

Selkirk read further, frowning as audacity followed audacity. Then he paused. Dalton was not being audacious at all, he realized. Neither was he pleading, nor demanding. He was simply, with care and proper protocol, announcing his right and his intent to submit himself to trial by court martial, and requesting Captain Selkirk . . . as, Hawser suspected, it was proper for an accused to do . . . to serve as judge advocate for the proceedings.

He was even suggesting a frame of time, as one might who seeks an appointment.

Smollet returned with the book. "Procedures for Courts Martial Extraordinary, sir. Can I find something for you?"

"Several things, Smollet. Am I qualified to act as judge advocate for a capital court martial?"

The clerk leafed through pages, then squinted at the print. "Ah . . . yes, sir, you are, I believe . . . by virtue of being the senior captain of a fleet assembly, ah, in the absence of flag rank officers."

"I see. This is a provision only in courts martial of the category *extraordinary?*"

"Yes, sir. It seems so." Smollet leafed pages. "Yes, it appears that in a procedure styled Admiralty Board or Common . . . of which there are certain subcategories, it seems . . . in any case, in absence of a commissioned judge advocate, in those degrees of court martial, then the court martial is delayed until a judge advocate can be present."

"Yes." Selkirk sighed, and a glint of hard humor appeared in his eyes. "Smollet, have you ever ridden to the hounds?"

"Sir?"

"Ridden to the hounds. Fox hunting, for a coarser term. Very popular among the landed gentry in certain circles. A uniquely English sport, I've heard."

"I've never done that, sir. Heard of it, of course, but I haven't seen it done. Why?"

"I didn't think so. You were born and raised in England. Riding to the hounds, in our time, is rarely done on English soil. Our gentry prefer to go elsewhere for their sport — most generally to Ireland. Far less likely to have to answer for the damages they do there."

"Yes, sir. I suppose."

"So, though it's the English who see the chase and taste the sport, it might take an Irishman to consider the viewpoint of the fox. Smollet, that book there . . . That is the collective wisdom of generations of gentlemen who have served as Lords of the Admiralty."

"Yes, sir. It is the book of procedure."

The glint in Selkirk's eyes grew and expressed itself in a chuckle. Smollet blinked. It was rare that the captain expressed amusement.

"The Lords of the Admiralty have been out-foxed, Smollet," Hawser said. "I wager I already know the answer to my next question. What is it that is extraordinary about a Court Martial Extraordinary?"

Smollet turned a page, read for a moment, then looked up. "It is conducted at sea, sir."

"I thought as much. Very well, Smollet. Make a list . . . Here, use my writing desk. Item the first: message to Captain Isaac Watson aboard HMS *Royal Lineage,* my compliments and advise him that the fox he lost is alive and well. Item the second: prepare the memorandum for archive stating that in accordance with orders of the Right Honorable the Lords Commissioners of the Admiralty, request has been received by myself for the convention of a Court Martial Extraordinary to review charges leveled against Patrick X. Dalton, Lieutenant Commander . . . *detached* . . . His Majesty's Royal Navy . . . etcetera — you'll find the proper wording there, of course. There is always proper wording, isn't there? Item the third: prepare a list of captains present in this port, according to seniority, excluding those presently under immediate orders or engaged in port security. Item the fourth: . . . oh, hang it all, Smollet. Just go through those procedures and execute the blasted paperwork for a Court Martial Extraordinary, date of convention pending. It should all be there."

"Yes, sir, it appears to be quite straightforward. There will be summonses to issue . . . certain notices . . . witnesses to secure . . . Do we have a schedule of the charges against this gentleman, sir? We shall require that, as well as any depositions and claims that might be involved . . ."

Selkirk was thumbing through Dalton's message. Now he stopped and looked across at his clerk. "As to that, yes. Make this item the first, Smollet: prepare a summons for . . . ah . . . one Commander Felix Croney, His Majesty's Expeditionary Guard. He is to present himself and all documents in his possession that relate to this matter, to me aboard this ship, immediately."

Smollet blinked. "Sir, Commander Croney went with Captain Watson upcoast, and did not return. It's said he disappeared, sir. At Portsmouth."

"That is as may be." Selkirk sighed. "However, Patrick Dalton says I shall find Commander Croney in or about the Long Island yards . . . though how the devil Dalton would know that is beyond me."

XXVI

On a dark and gloomy sea, the snow *Fury* stood in from beyond the Indies lanes and rounded off Cape Charles to enter the broad reaches of Chesapeake Bay on a fresh southeaster that misted the shores and sent showers of cold rain dancing across the white-capped waves. On half-reefed canvas she strode up the bay, a dark and bristling fighting ship with fresh scars on her hull from a chance encounter with a roving frigate. The exchange of fire had been brief, the frigate stunned by the fury of *Fury* when she turned and attacked after first strike.

The frigate fought its way north now, shy one mast and its upper sternport, and *Fury* came on alone. On shrouded waters off Windmill Point they reduced sail for a time, and Patrick Dalton read from the Book of Holy Evangelists as the bodies of two crewmen were consigned to the deep. Andrew Wilshire would not return to the sound of Bow Bells, and Chilton Sand would not see New York again.

They went on then, up the bay, and in evening they dropped anchor in a hidden cove on the west shore. With his deck secured, Charley Duncan came aft to stand beside Dalton at the rail. Across narrow water—a cable to each side—were the dark forests of tidewater Virginia, muted gray wilderness rising between the green of Norfolk pine and berried yaupon below, the spreading green of live oak above.

The old black mood was upon Dalton again, and Duncan sought ways to dispel it. "It wasn't far from here that Mister Romart and I first saw this snow," he said. "Just up the bay a bit, where they had a hidden yard. They were fitting her out to be a privateer, and I never in my life saw a lovelier sight . . . at least as far as ships go."

"Not far above that," Billy Caster chimed in, "but over on the other side, was where we found the derelict ketch. I wonder if *Mystery* still floats, sir. I hope she does. She was a sound vessel, for a ketch."

"Aye," Duncan said. "Rare's the ketch that has fired a shore battery from its deck and still sailed on . . . and with colored feathers on her sails. Who ever did see such a sight?"

Dalton said nothing, just stared at the darkening forests — or beyond them, it seemed, at things that only he could see.

"Is it the lads who died today, sir?" Duncan tried to draw him out. "Sad that is, indeed, but no one could have avoided it. And we did pay back for them in kind."

"Paid back?" Dalton didn't look around. "How can such be settled in account, then?"

"They died as men, sir. Doing their duty . . ."

"Duty to whom? To me, who took their marks and read them their articles? To a fugitive captain on a ship without a flag? What kind of duty is that, to justify men dying?"

"It's the war, sir. We're all with you because we choose to be."

Dalton glanced around, his eyes brooding. "And you, Mister Caster? Why are you here?"

Billy's eyes widened. "Where else would I be, sir? You are my captain."

Dalton sighed and resumed his moody gazing. "How many have there been? Because I chose to flee from charges, instead of bowing to them, how many men have followed me and died?"

"They're listed in the log, sir. The count is . . ."

"Never mind, Mister Caster. I know how many there have been. I know the name of every one, and I see their faces everywhere I look. Clarence Kilreagh . . . the broth-

268

ers Grimm . . . the brothers Cranston . . . Samuel Coleman . . . John Tidy . . . I see them clearly, and would rather have never known them at all than to have been the cause of their dying. So many of them, and still their ranks swell. There must come an end to it. There simply must come an end."

His voice had gone thin, and as cold as the eddying wind of winter's evening. For a time there was silence, then he straightened and took a deep breath. "An end to it. Well, the end is in the making, if I've judged some people rightly. We shall see soon enough. He gazed again at the darkening forest, then turned away. "The deck is yours, Mister Duncan. I shall be below if you need me."

They watched him down the companionway, and moments later saw lamplight in the little skylight prism in steerage, coming from the cabin below.

"I have moods myself, sometimes." Duncan sighed. "But generally all I need is a rousing fight to set me right again. The captain's different. He's all black Irish, and sometimes I think the stories are true . . . about how they see things others don't see, and hear what others can't hear. He might have been listening to the wail of banshees, for all I could tell."

Billy Caster turned to the rail and gazed at the darkening forest. "Did you notice where he was looking, Mister Duncan?"

"Aye. About there, at the woods yonder."

"I don't think he was looking at the woods. That's near north, or a bit west, I guess. Eagle's Head is up there somewhere. Squire Ramsey's estate. I expect Miss Constance is there, waiting for him."

"Aye," Duncan said, thoughtfully.

"The lady would have him just as he is, you know." The youngster frowned. "All that matters to her would be that he is alive. I heard her say so. She'd make no other demands."

"No, she wouldn't, lad. But he himself does. Our captain's a fierce proud man, Billy. He'll not go to her with a name that's blemished, and offer it to her. He has to make it

269

right first. He's a man of hard rules, and the hardest are his own, for himself."

"Settle his debts, clear his name and choose his flag," Billy muttered.

"What?"

"Oh, it's something I heard him say. He wasn't awake; it was after the storm, when he was still unconscious and Mister Tower was straightening his arm and making the splints. He thrashed about a bit, and we had to hold him down, but he wasn't fighting anyone but himself. Then he quieted, and kept saying Miss Ramsey's name over and over. It seemed to soothe him. I thought he had drifted off to sleep, but then he said, clear as anything, 'I must settle my debts. I must clear my name. I must choose my flag. It is the proper order of things, Constance.'"

"I do declare." Duncan shook his head in wonder. "What do you suppose he meant about the flag, though? We have a flag locker full of flags. We can fly any colors it pleases him to do."

"I believe he means a different thing than that, Mister Duncan. Do you recall when we made into Portsmouth, and raised the privateer stripes? One of the men said something in jest about having enough colors allows us to be anyone we please, anywhere we go."

"Aye. I think it's something Mister Wise said. But I didn't hear the captain reply."

"He didn't reply, but I heard what he said . . . just to himself, like. He said, 'Colors don't make us right, for we have no proper flag.'"

"On deck!"

Duncan raised his eyes. "Aye, Mister Ball?"

"Weather closing, sir. There's a rainshower abeam, moving up the bay. It will be here directly."

"Thank you, Mister Ball. You may clear the tops and go below for supper. There won't be anything to see until it's passed. Tell foretop, as well."

"Aye, sir."

Through the night and into morning it rained—a cold, squally rain that came and went and came again from low dark clouds that were a match for Dalton's mood. By the time it had played itself out, *Fury* was another ninety miles up Chesapeake, being towed into a hidden cove while a messenger rode inland to carry word to Ian McCall and the Ramseys.

Dalton's inspection was brief and distracted; then he called off rowers and set out in the small boat, leaving the ship to Duncan. The sandy-haired sailor watched him go, then went below to talk to the O'Rileys. Soon after, various clatters and reeks grew in *Fury's* little galley where the pair worked over their fire tubs, preparing supper. The noise and the smells carried through the underpinnings, cable tiers and crawlways of the ship, and in the forehold puzzled musicians babbled in several languages. Finally Alfred Hickman and Jordy Good climbed to the deck and confronted Cadman Wise.

"The orchestra wants to know what is going on in the galley," Good explained. "Some of them are pretty upset about it."

"About what?" Wise stared at him.

"About the smell, mostly," Hickman said. "Somebody is burning meat or something."

"Oh, that. It's just the O'Rileys. Mister Duncan told them to make a special mess, and I guess they're workin' on it."

Hickman translated the information to those below, leaning through the hatch to let them know. A spirited discussion ensued below, and Hickman lifted himself. "They say abominations are taking place in the galley. Mister Di-Gaetano wants to know if it is the wish that there be a meal served like the meal he tasted on the little trading ship."

Wise was at a loss. He went for Duncan, and brought him a'fore. It was explained again.

"That's what I had in mind, yes," Duncan agreed. "Captain's in a sad mood. I thought a bit of a feast might cheer

271

him."

Hickman knelt at the hatch and translated. Again there was discussion below. Hickman listened, and stood. "In the opinion of the orchestra, sir, if the captain is fed whatever those people are burning back there, it will not cheer him, but more likely make him very sick."

"We've all been eating what the O'Rileys cook, all this time," Duncan countered. "None of us have took sick yet."

Aside, Cadman Wise noted, "Of course, about all they ever cook is oatmeal porridge, peas and salt-whatzit."

Hickman shrugged. "The orchestra offers the services of Monsieur Cleride in the galley, provided they receive a portion of the special feast . . . and have opportunity to come on deck."

"I don't think a fiddler in the galley is going to improve the O'Rileys' fare," Duncan said.

"Monsieur Cleride is a master chef," Hickman explained. "He has cooked for the Houses of D'Ubreville and Chantogne. It is how he financed his music."

Duncan hesitated. "I think I'd have to ask the captain about that . . . wouldn't I?"

"It's your watch, Charley," the bosun pointed out. "Seems to me like you ought to decide things when it's your watch. What do we have to cook?"

"Leftover goat." Duncan shrugged. "That's what the O'Rileys are burning down there."

Victory Locke had wandered near to listen. Now he asked, "What became of all those ducks and things we brought down with the punt guns while the launch was out earlier? We had some discussion about eating them, didn't we?"

"They're dressed and hung." Duncan shrugged again. "But the O'Rileys don't know anything about preparing duck."

"Ansel Cleride can prepare a duck," Hickman stated.

High in the foremast shrouds, Claude Mallory called, "I'd give a month's wages for a bit of roast duck with lemon and spice."

At the base of the bowsprit Ishmael Bean looked up from splicing line. "Why just the captain, Mister Duncan? Why not just cheer everybody up? We've just ended a hard cruise, and not a notion where we go next."

"I've been a little depressed lately, myself," Purdy Fisk noted.

"Wouldn't take too much to rig a weather pavilion at the quarterrail," the carpenter Joseph Tower suggested. "We could make a banquet of it."

Billy Caster had emerged from the companionway on some errand of his own, and come forward to see what the crowd was doing there. "It might be best to rig a pavilion on the quarterdeck and a separate one forward of steerage," he offered. "That way the musicians could perform while everyone eats."

"They want to eat, too," Hickman pointed out.

"Well, couldn't they take turns? After all, there is a string quartet and a woodwind ensemble, as well as the kettle-drum and the French horn."

"I'd be glad to cut loose on the harpsichord," Jordy Good volunteered.

"It's your watch, Mister Duncan," Cadman Wise repeated. "Your watch, and your deck."

Duncan made up his mind. "Someone go below and tell the brothers O'Riley to belay what they are doing, please. Mister Tower, see to the erecting of pavilions. And Mister Hickman, please tell the orchestra that their offer is accepted. Ah . . . . Mister Caster, I expect we should have a requisition of some kind, for the log."

"For what?"

"Well, we're moving the second fiddler from cargo to the galley, for supper."

"We aren't going to eat *him*, Mister Duncan. Just what he cooks."

"Oh. Well, you and the captain can work that out, then. But what if we get supper ready and he doesn't come back this evening?"

"He said he would return by dark," Billy reminded him.

"He will, therefore, return by dark."

The cove was a small bay, one of thousands of various sizes that flowed together to form the great expanse of Chesapeake. Some of these lesser estuaries had names, usually from the streams that fed them, and some had none. This one, on *Fury's* charts, was shown as Cammack's Cove, and it had been carefully selected. It was too small and remote to handle any shipping, and had no villages nearby. But several miles up its feeder stream a road crossed it, and nearby was a cluster of tobacco sheds and a little inn.

The jollyboat grounded in a brushy nook just below the ford, and Patrick Dalton stepped out and climbed the bank while Pliny Quarterstone and Hannibal Leaf secured mooring lines. Dalton looked around at the bleak forest, and pulled a scrap of foolscap from his coat as the two sailors came up to join him. "The road should be just up there" — he pointed northward. "Then it's just a short way to the inn. Is the boat secure?"

"Aye, sir," Quarterstone frowned, peering about. "But I can't say I like this place, for all that. It looks like the Southampton moors, and wise folks stay away from those lands."

"The Southampton moors are in England, Mister Quarterstone," Dalton reminded him. "This is America."

"Aye, sir, but like places breed like folks, and there's naught but ruffians to be found in the Southampton moors."

Dalton glanced at him, and at Leaf. Both were nearly as tall as he, both whipcord tough, and both carried belaying pins. "I am sure we are quite safe," he said. "Come along; we haven't much time."

For a few minutes they pushed through dense, winter-bare underbrush, then emerged into a narrow clearing with ruts. They had found the road. Dalton turned right, the two sailors following him. Just ahead the road rounded a bend and disappeared. They went along it, walked around the bend, started around another and stopped. The thickets on both sides, just ahead, were sprouting people. One after another, men stepped out into the clear, as soundlessly as ghosts. There were seven of them, all armed with various implements and all grinning with anticipation. Dalton recognized them by their rough dress, and by having encountered their like before. Tidewater hunters . . . backwoodsmen who survived by living off the land when they had to and off travelers when they could.

The one in the lead, a hulking man with untamed whiskers and several missing teeth, nodded. "Told ye somebody's come," he rasped. "Now see wha' we got 'ere. Englishmen."

"By the Lord," Pliny Quarterstone muttered. "Southampton ruffians."

Dalton straightened, holding the leader's eyes with a cold stare. "If you have business with me, state it," he said. "If not, then stand aside."

" 'E wonders if we got business wi' 'im." The lead tough chuckled. "Good 'un, that. We got business, right enough. I'll start wi' yer boots an' that shiny sword ye carry. Now all of ye, just strip down peaceful an' maybe we won't bust yer up too bad."

"That isn't the way to talk to the captain," Hannibal Leaf pointed out. "A bit of respect's in order here."

"They don't understand about that, Hannibal," Pliny Quarterstone told him. He raised his belaying pin. "Mostly, all they'll understand is this. Captain's permission, sir?"

"Granted." Dalton sighed. With a quick, fluid motion he drew his sword. The only one ahead of them who carried a long blade was the leader, so Dalton charged him. The man's curved saber flashed up and down, a stroke from overhead, and Dalton caught the blade on his turnbuckle splints and went in under it. Two quick thrusts, the blade dancing like a serpent's tongue, and the man was on his back, crooning in pain and trying to cradle a midsection that leaked on both sides. A heavy mallet whisked past Dalton's head and he pivoted, driving the sword's hilt against the skull of a raging man who ceased to rage as his eyes went glassy. The man crumpled and Dalton turned, stepping over him. Pliny Quarterstone and Hannibal Leaf were back to back, lashing out with fists and clubs. A woodsman rebounded from Quarterstone's left fist and windmilled backward toward Dalton. Dalton thumped him soundly across one ear with his splint, and crouched to thrust or strike, but as abruptly as it had started it was over. There was no one left to fight. Dalton and his pair of tars stood on the woodland path, the clearing about them littered with fallen men.

In the sudden silence, there were thudding footsteps up the path, and a man rounded the bend, a pikepole swinging before him . . . and skidded to a stop. For a moment he surveyed the litter of war, then he shook his head and grinned. "I just heard about these thumpers going after game," he said. "I came to rescue you, but it doesn't look like any further rescuing will be required. Afternoon, Captain."

"I should have sent Mister Duncan out to fetch you, Mister Romart." Dalton nodded. "He would have thoroughly enjoyed this bit of sport. However, if you are ready, the boat is waiting."

"Aye, sir. I've been ready and waiting for three days." He looked back the way he had come. "It's a drafty and smelly inn yonder, but I'll miss the decent food. They've spoiled me for Mister O'Riley's best efforts."

It was nearly dark under lowering skies when the jollyboat cleared into the wider baylet, and the sound of orchestra music came across the water.

"Are they still at that?" Romart marveled. "I believe that's what they were playing when I jumped ship with your . . . ah . . . friend the accuser, sir."

They rounded a forested spit and *Fury* stood ahead, at anchor. A canvas pavilion hid her quarterdeck, glowing with lamplight, and snugged at her beam with a sleek sailing launch, larger by half than *Something*. Dalton recognized the craft, and the dark mood descended upon him again.

It was John Singleton Ramsey's boat. Company had come.

XXVII

"He'll be here directly, Miss," Charley Duncan told Constance Ramsey for the fifth time, doffing his newfound tricorn again, just as he did each time he addressed the young lady. Done out in velvet and crinoline, with a silver-buttoned traveling coat on her small shoulders and a winter bonnet of lynx pelt that covered her ears and framed her pixie-pretty face, she might have just stepped from a gilded carriage in the chandeliered portico of Boston's Grand Palace of Arts, rather than climbed over the gunwale of a warship deep in the Chesapeake wilderness, and Duncan found the transformation deeply confusing.

This was, without question, the same firebrand girl who had led saboteurs into New York Bay to find her father's stolen schooner, and the very same dainty lass who had tied up her skirts between her legs and stepped to the guns to take the mast off a gunboat — and the bowsprit off an armed vessel at a pirate port in Rhode Island. The same auburn-haired sprite who had set fuse to vent off Cape Cod and sent several pounds of roofing nails screaming across the bloody deck of a frigate. Yet here, bedecked in the finery of a lady of the Colonial gentry, she was every inch the part. And though she had done nothing to promote it, her presence made Duncan acutely aware that he, himself, despite serving as first aboard a man-of-war, was only a simple sailor and entirely out of his element in serving as host to the fine folk he had invited aboard.

277

A pair of squires, a squire's daughter, two import accountants, five armed personal guards and three servants had formed the complement of the sailing launch that came down from the cotton docks at Eagle Head, and the motley crew of *Fury* was more than a little intimidated by such presences. The three gentryfolk, for their part, were amused, amazed and enamored—it seemed—by the welcome they had found aboard the snow. John Singleton Ramsey had wandered from side to side of the quarterdeck, admiring the covered pavilion and its tables and lanterns, until it occurred to someone in the galley to set out a bit of rum. Now Ramsey sat on the quarterrail, one leg athwart the bellbrace, and sipped happily from a cup of two-water grog while Squire Ian McCall—who some said owned about half of Virginia—stood at the aftershrouds listening critically to the orchestra's rendition of something Charley Duncan wouldn't have tried to pronounce.

"I simply can't imagine how Patrick knew we would be here today," Constance told Duncan. "If the messenger had not gone 'round about, and found us at the cotton docks, it might have been two days before we learned that *Fury* had come back."

"I don't try to outguess Captain Dalton, Miss," Duncan said lamely.

Billy Caster came up from below, carrying an ornate silver tea service that made Constance's eyes widen.

"Though the captain had an errand to see to," Duncan added, "he wouldn't have wanted less than the best for yourself and the gentlemen."

Billy set down the silver tray and poured tea, cocking an eyebrow aside at Duncan. "Took this in trade, Miss," the boy said. "Captain has been saving it to serve you when we returned."

"But how could he have known?"

"What, Miss?"

"How could he know that we would arrive this very evening? He must have thought we were at Eagle Head. He instructed his messenger to find us there. And all this!" She turned, her hand indicating the lighted pavilion, the orchestra — the string quartet was performing now *en sotto* except for some lively interruption by the harpsichord, while the woodwinds and horns sampled the rum — and the open companion hatch from which wafted the scents of food quite beyond the capabilities of any O'Riley. "It is . . . well, it is quite lavish. I am very impressed."

"Nothing but the best for Captain Dalton's guests, Miss," Duncan assured her with barely the blink of an eye. "And, of course, particularly for yourself, Miss."

If Constance noted the look that passed between Charley Duncan and Billy Caster, she ignored it. "Yes, Billy, I would love a bit of tea, thank you . . . and if you could slip just a tot of that rum into it, I think it might be even better. Oh, I hope Patrick arrives soon. It has been a very long wait, since he left . . . and I have worried about him, even though he was abrupt in ordering me off his ship . . ."

"My ship, Miss Constance."

"What?" She looked around. Ian McCall had heard her words.

"I said, this is *my* ship, Miss Constance. Though your Irishman has had the use of it to escort merchantmen for me, it *does* remain mine, after all."

"We have been over that several times, Mister McCall," Constance snapped, her eyes glowing. "Patrick feels his claim is just. You did lose your ship, after all. To pirates. And this is a ship he *took* from pirates. In a way, that makes it two different ships."

John Singleton Ramsey glanced down from the bell rail, grinning. "I've warned you about exchanging fire with my daughter, Ian. You haven't the guns for such an exchange . . . any more than I do."

"On deck!"

Duncan looked up, relieved at having something he knew how to deal with. "Aye, tops?"

"Jollyboat returning, Mister Duncan. They've picked up a passenger."

"A passenger? Can you see who it is?"

279

"Can't make him out, but there's four heads in the boat now and only three went out."

"Didn't he tell you where he was going, Mister Duncan?" Constance asked, surprised.

"Well, no, Miss, not really. He just gave me the deck and off he went. Captain's been a bit distracted of late, you might say."

"He should be distracted," McCall muttered, "if he expects to talk me out of my ship."

"You say the cruise was a quiet one, Mister Duncan?" Ramsey asked.

"Oh, aye, sir. Clear sailing all the way to Portsmouth and back, with hardly a thing to break the monotony."

"I suppose that explains the new jibboom," Ramsey sipped at his grog, pursed his lips and nodded. "Just something for your lads to do, to while away the time."

"Aye, sir. Something like that."

"And the splices in the shrouds," McCall rasped. "And the regrommeted sails, and the shoring at both mast-braces, the re-tarred bulwarks, the spanking new gammoning at the stem, rebuilt fairleads as well . . . repaired martingale . . . three reinforced stays that I can see from here . . . By damn, it looks to me as though *Fury* has been virtually rebuilt."

"Well, we did have a bit of weather at one point, sir," Duncan admitted.

Victory Locke, coming down the aftershrouds, apparently had not heard any except Duncan's words, and he grinned at them. "Bit of weather, he says! Not many could have tacked into a black squall under press of sail to outrun a seventy-four and lived to tell about it."

"Mister Locke!" Duncan barked. "Shut up and go about your business!"

"Aye." Locke shrugged amiably. "But there's such a thing as bein' too coy about matters, Mister Duncan." He turned and headed forward, and Constance and the two squires stared after him, their mouths open, their eyes huge.

"A seventy-four?" Ramsey croaked.

"Tacked?" McCall rasped. "Into a squall?"

Duncan crammed his tricorn onto his head and turned to the ladder. "Come with me, Mister Caster. We had best see about supper."

When the jollyboat was alongside, the first one over the rail was Michael Romart. Sailors all along the darkening deck peered at him in surprise, then cheered. Duncan popped up from the coaming to see what the noise was about, and stared at the American. "Michael! Ah . . . I mean, Mister Romart! I'm damned!"

"Probably so, Mister Duncan." Romart grinned. "But it's good to see you again, too." He looked around. "I didn't expect quite such a welcome. I might . . ." His eyes found the Ramseys and McCall, and he stopped, swept off his hat and bowed smartly, then turned again to the rail and reached down to help Patrick Dalton up. "Wish you'd told me, sir. I'd have put on a fresh shirt."

"Told you what, Mister. . . ?" Dalton came over the rail and paused there, astraddle, as he saw the girl at the quarterrail. "Constance," he breathed.

"Hello, Patrick." She smiled, then frowned as she noticed the turnbuckle splints. "What have you done to your arm?"

"What have you done to my ship?" Ian McCall demanded.

Dalton swung his leg over the rail and stood, his dark eyes taking in the girl, noticing each feature in the lanternlight. "It's nothing, Constance," he said. "It is mending nicely." He strode to the ladder and paused at its foot as she came to the top of it. "You look . . . ah, splendid. Just . . . ah, splendid."

"And you look as though you have been fighting," she decided. "Is that blood on your sleeve?"

"It isn't mine. How have you been, Constance? Are you well?"

"I should like your explanation as to why this vessel has a new jibboom," Ian McCall said.

"I'd like to know how you come to have an orchestra aboard your ship," Ramsey said.

281

"*My* ship," McCall snapped. "It isn't his bloody . . ."

"I've been very well, Patrick. Though I have worried about you. With some good cause, I gather, although Mister Duncan hasn't elaborated. How did you know we would be here this evening? I really can't imagine . . ."

"How did I what?"

"We've set everything up just as you said, sir." Billy Caster tugged at Dalton's coattail, urgently. "The dinner, the music . . . and the tea service. *Just as you said . . . sir.*"

"What kind of idiot tacks a square-rigger into a squall?" McCall demanded.

"The orchestra is cargo," Charley Duncan said aside to Ramsey. "At least, most of it is. The harpsichordist is a cooper they traded for at Morgan's Cove, and the harpsichord is a sort of oversight from Portsmouth."

"Cargo." Ramsey looked at the sandy-haired sailor, blankly.

"Yes, sir. We . . . well, *I* had a bit of a misapprehension about the securing of such."

"Did I tell you that you look just . . . ah, splendid, Constance?" Dalton was still gazing at her, as though there were nothing else in the world to be seen.

"Yes, Patrick." She smiled. "I believe you said that several times."

A pair of large, carrot-topped sailors as alike as peas in a pod came up the companionway bearing trays of steaming food. "The fiddler says this stuff is ready," the first said. "Where does it go?"

"What is it?" Ramsey peered and sniffed.

"Roast lemon duck with chives and rice, sir," Billy Caster offered.

"Chives and rice? Where in God's world did you get . . ."

"Actually, the chives are peas and the rice is oatmeal, sir. But Mister Cleride is a wonderful cook."

"Just . . . ah, splendid," Dalton said again, as one in a trance. Then he shook himself and tore his eyes from her. "Forgive me for saying that, Miss Constance. I was seriously mistaken."

"You were *what?*"

"Mistaken. Oh, not about how you . . . Well, of course you are just . . . ah . . . but I should never have said so. Please forget that I did." Instantly, his face went hard, his eyes went cold and he executed a rigid, formal bow. "Welcome aboard, Miss Constance. Oh, and I see your father is here as well. Welcome, sir. And Squire McCall, welcome as well . . . to my ship."

"It is not your ship!"

"Patrick Dalton, what in the world is wrong with you?" Constance demanded.

He looked back at her, controlling with sheer will the warm feelings that threatened to overcome him again. "I have been presumptuous. I apologize. I believe . . . Yes, here is supper. Will you all join me on the quarterdeck?"

Constance tapped a dainty toe and thunder gathered at her eyes. "Patrick Dalton, you are the most totally irritating man I have ever . . ."

Ramsey leaned aside to McCall. "You think you've seen her guns in action, Ian? Not until you've seen them leveled at the Irishman, you haven't."

Ansel Cleride was, in fact, a fine chef. Supper on that cold evening aboard the snow *Fury* was, for most present, the finest meal they had ever tasted. Forward of steerage there wasn't a man-jack who did not thoroughly enjoy the feast. On the pavilioned quarterdeck, though, not everyone did.

Patrick Dalton and Constance Ramsey sat at opposite ends of a hastily assembled trestle table, picking at their food and studiously ignoring each other, while Ian McCall wasted no time in getting to the business at hand.

"First," the trader said around a mouthful of roast lemon duck, "there is the matter of my ship."

"First," Dalton corrected him, "there is the matter of the merchantmen you commissioned my ship to escort up-coast."

"I did not commission your ship," McCall submitted. "I hired your services. You have no ship."

The two locked eyes, and John Singleton Ramsey said, "If you expect to get anywhere, you should first agree upon the things you can agree on. What of the merchant ships?"

"Safely delivered, as agreed," Dalton told McCall. "My clerk, Mister Caster, has the manifests and receipts, as well as delivery documents affirmed by each of your merchant captains and a letter from your proctor in Portsmouth. There also are written complaints from your captains regarding my methods of safeguarding them. How you deal with those is entirely up to you."

"Did they sustain damage?" McCall frowned.

"None except the galley, *Hispania,* and I did that myself, to amuse a passing frigate."

"Yes, I heard about that from Captain Webster. Outrageous bluff, of course, but apparently it succeeded. What of the rest?"

"The barks? Undamaged except for the dispositions of their masters, which was not my concern then or now."

"I shall inspect the records, Captain. What else?"

"My invoice, sir. Mister Caster has calculated what you owe me for the service of my ship, including replacement of stores and provisions. I shall accept payment in good coin, sir. I've no use for Colonial shinplasters or letters of credit . . . though a portion of what you owe me will go to settle my accounts with Squire Ramsey, and the currency of that portion may be whatever is agreeable to him."

"I have no use for shinplasters, either," Ramsey said. "I might consider an open account, though, Ian, if you want to commission Patrick's ship for further escort . . ."

"It is *my* ship!" McCall blurted. "I paid for the damned thing!"

"And lost it to pirates," Dalton pointed out. "Fortunes of the privateer, sir. It happens now and then."

"But it isn't lost. This is it. We are having supper on its deck!"

"No, sir, we are having supper on the deck of a ship I

took from pirates. No prior claims apply to taken vessels. You know that, obviously, since you fitted your snow out as a privateer for exactly that purpose."

"I have letters of marque! My privateering is legitimate!"

"Letters of marque do not apply to dealing with pirates, sir. The ship I took — this ship — was not a lettered man-of-war. It was booty, fair game for anyone. I took it. It is mine."

"You are invoking the law," McCall pointed out. "Yet you are outside the law. You are a fugitive from justice."

"And you are involved in a rebellion against the Crown you swore to uphold."

"I swore no such . . ."

"Yes, you did, Ian." Ramsey grinned. "Back when we fought the French. Just as I did, then."

"Oh, that."

"That." Ramsey helped himself to a measure of grog. "Give it up, Ian. It was settled the day you commissioned *Fury* to escort your sugar barks. You know it as well as I do. You admitted then that the young man's claim was valid."

"I could take this ship from him." McCall bristled.

"I very much doubt that you could. Now I suggest you consider the matter done."

"Why?"

"You do want the contract on my tobacco fields, don't you?"

"Of course I do."

"And I want peace in my house. Done?"

McCall shot another glare at Dalton, then shrugged. "Done, then," he said. He laced a mug of tea with rum and sipped, and a fleeting smile touched his weathered face. "But let it never be said that I didn't argue the point."

The musicians, faces and fingers shiny with roast duck, had launched into a sprightly minuet in double time — an innovation Jordy Good had suggested to the delight of Maestro Pico. With the rippling accompaniment of the harpsichord and the soaring flare of Zoltan Ferrestrekov's bassoon, it had the sound of a Scots band.

"I'd bid a fair bid for the contract to that bunch," Ramsey

said. "What would you consider fair, Patrick?"

"They aren't mine, sir. I've brought them as cargo, on the promise they would pay their fare. They want to earn their keep by their music."

"Then I'll pay their fare if you'll arrange their contract to me."

"The blazes you will," McCall said. "I'll double the offer, Captain. Name the fare."

"You simply want to be the first man to bring an orchestra to Philadelphia when we've cleared the British out," Ramsey snorted. "Where would you have them play in the meantime? Baltimore?"

"There are ballrooms in Baltimore." McCall thumped the table. "Three times the fare, Captain. Take it or leave it."

"I'll match that," Ramsey said. "And I'll buy the bedamned harpsichord."

Charley Duncan sat to one side, his eyes growing wider by the minute. Dalton leaned toward him. "Please go and find Mister Hickman, Mister Duncan. Tell him that his orchestra has reached its destination."

"Aye, sir."

"Partners, then?" McCall asked Ramsey. "Baltimore first, then Philadelphia?"

"You provide the quarters?"

"If you provide the hall."

"I can have a barge here tomorrow."

"But we land at my docks."

"Done."

Dalton sighed, picking at his cold duck. It was settled, then . . . the matter of the ship, and the miscellaneous matters of recompense and cargo. But the hardest thing of all was yet to come. He could not go forth from here, with Constance believing that there was a promise between them. He could make no promises now, could offer nothing except a cordial goodbye. The two traders excused themselves and went to negotiate with the orchestra, Billy Caster tagging after them with the documents for Ian McCall, and abruptly Dalton and Constance were alone. He took a deep

286

breath, raised his head and found himself staring into large, shadowed eyes as enigmatic as the night.

"I know," she said quietly. "Billy told me . . . about your letter to that English captain, and about Michael Romart and the guard officer. Damn your exasperating Irish pride, Patrick Dalton! Damn it . . . but I cannot damn you for it. You must have all of your promises fulfilled, and none left unattended. You must have all of your accounts settled, and I am one of those accounts."

"You understand, then?"

"No, I do not understand!" her eyes flashed, then seemed to mist like dark sails diminishing in distance. "I don't expect I shall ever understand you. But I know. There can be no slightest thought of the future. Not until the present is settled in all accounts."

XXVIII

December was past and a new year in hand when *Fury* came down Chesapeake on cold winds that bore from west of north and shifting. A grim and haughty warship, she strode the miles to seaward, and of those who saw her passing none tried to stay her course. Armies now were in their winter quarters, fleets were on post and for a time the great bay was silent except for the thump of punt guns here and there as men of the tidewaters volleyed migrating flocks of birds.

Off Point Comfort, Patrick Dalton looked to his charts and fared the wind. Soon he must put to sea once more, this time with a white cross flag atop the locker. But there was yet time, and there would be better winds.

"Bring us to windward just past the point," he told bosun and helm. "Mister Duncan, please have the launch swung out. Squire Ramsey has said that's a safe port yonder, and a fair town beyond it. Please take the deck, as well. I shall be ashore for a time, and on my return I'll want an assembly of the entire complement."

"Aye, sir. You'll want an escort at Hampton, though. It is a boisterous place, I'm told, even in winter."

"Especially in winter," Michael Romart corrected. "This time of year, the local lads have little to do except to squabble and drink spirits."

"You have been to Hampton, Mister Romart?"

"Aye, sir, and done my share of hell-raising there,

288

as well."

"Then you may escort me to Hampton, since you know your way around. You, and Misters Unser and Smith, because you are all three Colonials . . . and Mister Hoop in case anyone ashore becomes more boisterous than is warranted in winter. You come, too, Mister Caster, and bring my ledger. I'll have accounts to keep."

"Yes, sir."

With *Fury* secure and under tight watch, the launch put out for Hampton Wharves and Dalton and his escorts went ashore.

"Where would you like to go, sir?" Romart asked when they stood on a rutted street above the ways. "There used to be a theater here, and I know of a dozen decent grog shops and several inns."

"First I want to find a tailor, Mister Romart."

"A tailor?"

"Surely there must be a tailor in a town that has a dozen decent grog shops?"

"I'll ask, sir."

They found a tailor's shop, and Dalton and Billy Caster went in while Mister Hoop presided over the door. The tailor was a stoop-shouldered man with spectacles and a woolen wig. When Dalton told him his requirements, the man went into his storeroom with a lantern, then came back out. "Aye, I have the fabrics, your honor. But I'd not suggest you wear such finery on any streets hereabout. Not in the pattern you describe. There are folk here who'd knock you in the head for dressing so."

"I don't want to wear it here," Dalton told him. "But I want it fitted while I'm here; then I shall return for it this evening."

"I'm afraid day after tomorrow is about the best I can do, sir," the tailor said.

At the door, Mister Hoop cleared his throat. "Captain said he wants it ready this evening," he rumbled.

Billy Caster took out a purse and counted out coin on the tailor's bench, recounted it and added one coin more.

"This evening," he suggested.

The tailor looked at the coins, at Mister Hoop and back to Dalton. "I believe I can work that into my schedule, come to think of it," he said.

Dalton inspected and approved several fabrics, then stripped off his coat and was fitted for new garments, to be precisely to his order. The coat would be of blue, with white facings and cuffs, each faced lapel to have nine brass buttons evenly spaced. The coattails would be pleated and buttoned back, coming just to his knees behind. Completing the uniform would be a shirt of white linen, with white stock and ruffle, a waistcoat and breeches of white, and a blue tricorn hat which the tailor promised to obtain from another merchant and have on hand for delivery.

"Gore, sir," the man said when he had the measurements complete and the fabrics laid out for cutting, "Just add knee breeches, stockings and buckle shoes to all this, and you'd look for all the world like a bloody British lieutenant. That's why I wouldn't want you to be seen so around here."

"I understand," Dalton told him. "Have these things ready for me on my return, please."

"Yes, sir." The tailor watched them go, wondering why a man would want to dress like a British naval officer. He considered it, then grinned and nodded, satisfied with his answer. A privateer, he decided, preparing a new way to amuse the Georgies come spring.

On the street outside, the Americans came across from a lively-sounding place with a sign in front — a picture of a fighting cock. "We stayed warm while you were in there, sir," Romart said. "It isn't just the local lads who miss their sport in winter. There are the wenches, as well. Well, where to now, sir?"

"A cobbler," Dalton said.

"A cobbler. Well . . . I'll ask."

The tailor's door opened and the man peered out, spotted Dalton and waved. "Sir, I forgot to ask . . . that thing on your arm, shall I modify the coat to include it?"

"No, that will not be necessary. Just make the garments."

"Right you are, sir." He went back inside.

They found a cobbler's stall, and Dalton sat on a bench to remove his boots. Billy Caster handed them to the cobbler, who scrutinized them carefully, clicking his tongue. "Nigh done in, aren't they? What are these by design? Grenadier's boots?"

"Lancer," Dalton said, "though they may be the same thing. I need a new pair by this evening."

The man blinked at him. "*This* evening?"

"This evening."

"This evening," Mister Hoop rumbled.

Billy counted out coin.

"This evening," the cobbler agreed.

Outside, the three Americans were not in sight, but a great deal of noise was coming from a place with a carved picture of a lion's head outside its door. They started in that direction, then stopped when the door slammed back and a man somersaulted out to sprawl in the street. Another followed him, then another, and Hob Smith just behind them, brandishing a bung starter. He glanced across, saw his captain and turned to the door. "Captain's aboard!" he shouted, then turned back and came to happy attention.

Another local sailed out the door; then Paul Unser appeared there, stooped to dodge a blow by someone still inside, returned the blow, then stepped out and came to attention beside Smith. Michael Romart peered out, came out, closed the door behind him and grinned.

"There you are," he said.

Dalton shook his head. "Have you gentlemen been staying warm in my absence?"

"Aye, sir," Romart beamed. "That's exactly what we were doing."

"I see."

"Where to now, sir? You name it and we'll find it. I'm remembering my way about this town, now."

291

"An inn," Dalton said. "We've time for a quiet meal while my garments are prepared."

"Aye, sir."

Mister Hoop looked sadly back toward the grog shop as they started on their way. He had missed out on what seemed to have been a bit of fun.

They had an adequate meal at a place near the old armory—a warehouse now, since the removal of militia arms to Williamsburg—then strolled around the waterfront sections of Hampton with Michael Romart pointing out the sights. Not surprisingly, in this season, Dalton saw no shore patrols of any flag, no companies of men in uniform, no recent signs that there was a war going on all up and down the eastern wedge of this land. He was impressed also at the number of roads leading away inland, roads without blockades or sentries. "A man of any persuasion could come ashore here and simply disappear if he was of a mind to," he commented.

"Aye, sir," Romart assured him. "And many have. Not everyone has stomach for life aboard ship . . . or for death at sea."

In late afternoon they returned to the cobbler's stall, and Dalton put on his new boots. They were stiff and restrictive, but they would break in as he wore them. From there they went to the tailor's, and he inspected his new uniform. The man had done a commendable job, except for the folding of the brim on the tricorn hat. The brim was fluted in current Colonial style, and secured with red rosettes. Dalton turned it over in his hands, shook his head, and handed the thing to Billy Caster.

"Hand me those shears there," the boy told the tailor. "And put your teakettle on to boil."

Within a few minutes, Dalton had a proper hat—wide brim flared upward astern and at both bows, mizzen peaks a'beam and a jaunty spinnaker thrust a'fore, and sporting a single blue rosette abaft the port bow.

Dalton sent Mister Hoop to retrieve his three Americans from the Fighting Cock, waited out the inevitable ruckus, then led the men back to the docks and the launch. "A likely town," he said, looking back over his shoulder.

"Aye, sir, it is," Michael Romart agreed. "And you've only seen the least bit of it."

They returned to *Fury*, went aboard, and Dalton sent Billy Caster below to stow his packages, then told Charley Duncan, "I'd like an assembly now, please. The entire crew, just there amidships. Look lively, please, Mister Duncan."

"Aye, sir. Mister Wise, all hands on deck, please. All hands for assembly."

By the time all of the men were assembled before the quarterrail, Billy Caster had come topside again, bringing an account ledger and a chest of coin—the balance from Dalton's settling of accounts below Eagle Head.

Duncan and Wise got the men ranked in proper order, then Dalton came to the quarterrail to look them over. "I shall not waste time in this," he said. "Each of you lads has performed true service to myself and to my ship. Yeoman service. We have completed a difficult cruise, and retained a tidy profit. Each of you, by accepting my articles, has earned the wages agreed to when you read aboard, and a handsome bonus as well. Therefore I have assembled you each and all—with ten exceptions—to receive your pay and be relieved for liberty ashore. Yonder is a likely liberty port, as I myself have seen, and you may have use of the launch to go ashore."

The array of grins that had grown as he spoke erupted now in a bedlam of shouts and stamping, but he waved them down. "First, though, I need ten people to remain on board and stand watch. Mister Caster, please read off the names as I instructed."

Billy Caster opened his book to a list. "Mister Romart," he read. "Misters Donald and Gerald O'Riley. Mister Tower. Mister Unser. Mister Ives. Mister Elmsbee . . ." He squinted at the list, then looked up at his captain. "This is only nine, sir. You said ten."

"You omitted yourself, Mister Caster. You are one of

those who will remain aboard."

"Oh. Ah . . . Mister Caster. And Misters Underwood and Smith."

"Thank you, Mister Caster. You men will remain aboard with me, to stand watch during crew liberty. The rest of you, come forward as your names are called, to receive your pay. But first hear this, and listen closely. Where *Fury* sails from here, will be a hazard unlike any you have seen before. I go to face Crown justice, to clear my name or to seal my fate, as God wills. Many among you have faced Royal Navy discipline, and experienced navy justice. Each of you must decide for himself whether he chooses to return aboard *Fury,* following your liberty ashore. To those who do return, I promise nothing. To those who do not return, I extend my thanks and my blessing. No dishonor will attach to you from your decision. Are there any questions?"

In the ranks, men looked at one another in puzzlement. Then Victory Locke raised his hand. Dalton nodded at him. "Aye, Mister Locke?"

"Not so much a question, sir. It's just . . . Well, sir, there's some of us here has sailed with you since the day we took that schooner *Faith* . . . sailed with you on three different vessels, sir, and under several flags. You say if we sail with you again, you promise nothing. But sir, you never promised anything to begin with, and I can't say as I regret any of what's come about."

Heads nodded in solemn agreement here and there. Claude Mallory, Purdy Fisk, Cadman Wise, Ishmael Bean . . . Dalton sighed, realizing that of the men who had followed him in his flight from a Crown warrant, only eight remained. Six British tars, an American Colonial and a boy. Yet, among the others present, some were agreeing with Locke's words, as well.

"Thank you, Mister Locke," Dalton said. "But where I go from here, no racing sails can save me, no great guns command the day. Only two things can protect me this time—me and any who sail with me—truth and honor.

294

Nothing else will avail. Very well, then. You have your decisions to make. Please come forward as your names are called. Mister Caster has your pay."

There were exclamations as, one after another, the men received their wages. The captain had mentioned a bonus, but most of them had never before owned as much money at one time as they received now. Dalton stood at the stern rail, staring out across the remaining miles of Chesapeake Bay, out toward the open sea beyond.

It took two trips of the launch to carry eighteen rich and eager tars ashore, to be sprung upon an unsuspecting liberty town — a town which might never be quite the same again. Joseph Tower, the carpenter, watched the second load from *Fury's* rail. "Yonder goes the blessing and the bane of any port town," he told himself. "A swarm of erect young men."

On the quarterdeck, Billy Caster also watched the launch depart, then looked around at those who remained on watch aboard the snow. "I expect you have noticed, Captain," he said, "that every Englishman of your crew is now off the ship, and everyone left aboard — except yourself, sir — is American-born."

"I am aware of that, Mister Caster."

"May I ask why, sir?"

"I kept you aboard for two reasons, Mister Caster. First, I do not care to have my clerk taking liberty with fresh-paid sailors in a rough town. You are far too young just yet to deal with that sort of sport. Secondly, I shall need you with me when I encounter Captain Selkirk."

Billy stared at him, his eyes going wide. He looked abruptly stricken. "You mean . . . about what you told the men, sir. About not coming back unless they choose to?"

"Something like that, Mister Caster."

"But sir! Where would I . . . how could you think that I might not come back?"

"I couldn't ask you to, Mister Caster. No more than I could ask them."

"Oh." Billy scuffed his feet, trying to understand.

"Whatever happens to me, Mister Caster, I have made provision for your safety. It will be part of the arrangement with Captain Selkirk, if he agrees at all."

"What . . . what kind of provision, sir? If I may ask?"

"Should the verdict go against me, Billy. Should I be taken away . . . or executed . . . then you will be given the protection of Captain Selkirk. He will admit you as a midshipman aboard his vessel until you reach the age of nineteen. At that time you will stand for examination for a lieutenancy in His Majesty's navy. I have no doubt that you will succeed admirably . . . should it come to that."

"Yes, sir." An awful sadness enveloped the boy, as he realized the inevitability of what his captain had decided to do.

"As to the other Americans," Dalton said quietly, "they will be paid off and put off before I make sail. They are stout lads and have done good service. But I cannot protect them in the custody of Admiralty officers, and what happens to American lads who have sailed against the king is . . . is not pleasant."

XXIX

The liberty at Hampton lasted a full two days, and the fourteen who made it back to *Fury* were a sorry-looking lot when they reassembled on the snow's deck. Pliny Quarterstone had a blackened eye that was swollen almost shut. Victory Locke wore bandages on both hands and had toothmarks on one ear. Purdy Fisk had a fresh knife-cut across the bridge of his nose that gave him a fiendish appearance when he smiled. Ishmael Bean had some gaps among his teeth and Charley Duncan was so bruised that he seemed to have been trampled by a horse race.

By Billy Caster's inventory of returnees, dutifully entered in the log, seven had various injuries, two had converted to the Calvinist faith and four were now married. All fourteen, as best he could tell, were suffering in various degrees from excessive consumption of ale and dark rum. A fine time, apparently, had been had by all.

Of the four who failed to return — Noel Abbott, Oliver Grinnell, Jacob Isaacs and Lloyd Frank — the log would note only, "Dismissed without prejudice." Grinnell, Duncan mentioned, was now the son-in-law of the owner of the Fighting Cock and had been persuaded to stay at Hampton to help organize a constabulary to protect the town against liberty crews. The rest had, simply, gone their own ways.

"What of the returnees, Mister Duncan?" Dalton asked

297

his battered first. "Are they able to hand, reef and steer?"

Duncan cast a baleful look at his charges. "Aye, sir. To a man, I'd judge this lot can do anything they don't have sense enough not to."

"Very well, Mister Duncan. You and the rest, give yourselves a bit of Mister O'Riley's pottage and a few hours at the hammocks, but I shall want every man of them at station to make sail at six bells of the morning watch. Mister Romart!"

"Aye, sir."

"Assemble the watch, please."

"Aye, sir."

As the returned tars cleared for comforts below, Romart and the other Colonials stood to attention before the quarterrail — nine tired young men, awaiting their captain's orders. Dalton looked at them one by one. Americans. The very men — or their ilk — that he had been sent to these shores to fight. Enemies of the king, by right of birthplace . . . yet each one a man equal to any others who had followed him in fugitive flight, and each as undeniably loyal to him as any tar might be.

"It is your turn to be paid now," he told them. "You all heard the instructions I gave to the liberty crew before they went ashore?"

Several nodded.

"My instructions to you lads are different," Dalton said. "Where I go now, you cannot go. Therefore you are one and all released with honor from your obligations, to myself and to this ship. You will be paid, with a good bonus, and put ashore. God bless you all, and may your days be many and bountiful." He felt his voice going ragged, and turned away, then turned back at a voice from the group.

It was Michael Romart. "Moment, please, Captain."

"Yes, Mister Romart?"

"Captain, I don't choose to leave your service. I've found no man I'd rather serve, nor have any of these others here, I warrant."

"It is not your choice, Mister Romart," Dalton said.

"Nor is it mine, that I must go where each of you cannot. So let that be the end of it. Come forth as Mister Caster calls your names, and you will receive your pay, with my thanks. Ah . . . Mister Romart, a word with you in private, please."

By the main pinrail, Dalton took Romart aside. "You'll find an added bonus in your purse, Michael. You have done me a service few could or would have, and I won't forget it."

"Captain, I wish you'd . . ."

"No, Michael. You can't go. The others may not know where I am going, but I suspect you do. You delivered my accuser for me, and I've no doubt you knew why."

"Aye, I know why. But isn't there a way to . . ."

"There is no way, no. But I have a final request."

"Anything, sir."

"Take the launch, Michael. I won't require it further. It is a good boat, and will carry all of you, or as many as want to go. Go back to Eagle Head, with any of these who choose to go with you. Apply to Squire Ramsey. He'll have employment for you, and a new beginning. The squire is a decent man, for all of being a smuggler, and he can use good men about him in these times."

"Sir, do you *have* to go out to meet your justice? I wish you . . ."

"Wouldn't you, Michael Romart? If it were you, wouldn't you go?"

Romart bowed his head. "Yes, sir. I suppose I would."

Dalton laid his good hand on the American's shoulder. "May God bless you, Michael . . . my friend."

Billy Caster's eyes were moist as he doled out their pay, one by one . . . Joseph Tower, the carpenter . . . the brothers Donald and Gerald O'Riley . . . Paul Unser from Maine . . . Hob Smith from Connecticut . . . Phillip Ives from New Jersey . . . Julius Underwood, a Pennsylvanian gone to sea . . . the Rhode Islander Gregory Elmsbee . . . and finally Michael Romart.

"Look after your captain," Romart told the boy. "He's a

299

better man than those who've driven him so."

Charley Duncan came up from below and met Romart at the after shrouds where *Something* waited below. "It's been a run, ye ruddy Colonist," he said, extending his hand.

Romart clasped his hand. "We should do it again some time, Englishman, once you've learned the error of your ways . . . or your bloody idiot king has."

"Where will you go now?"

"Up the bay once more, I suppose. The captain says Squire Ramsey might find use for us there." He swung a leg over the rail. "I don't imagine we'll meet again, Charley."

"I wouldn't wager on it, Michael. Either way."

"You think the captain might come back . . . to Chesapeake?"

"If the Honorable Judge Advocate doesn't hang him first . . . and with Miss Constance Ramsey waitin' here . . . and if he had a way to get back . . . I'll tell you this: I don't know how I'll do it, but I intend to go to France one day and nothing short of death is going to stop me. I guess the captain has equal reason for coming back here."

"Safe journey, Charley Duncan."

"And to you, Michael Romart."

They watched the launch away, a stubby shadow on the darkling waters of evening; then Duncan went to find a hammock and Billy took his ledger below, to light a lamp and enter the day's log "in fine." The 'tween decks of the snow—so long a'bustle with the constant noise of O'Rileys in the galley, of seamen coming and going, testing the depth in the well, bringing up or stowing stores, hurrying back and forth through the crawlways, cable tiers, magazines and holds—now seemed silent and cold, the only sounds the snores of sleeping men here and there, the muted rhythmic creaks and gurgles of the ship riding at anchor in the shelter of Point Comfort to windward. Of more than fifty souls who had so recently boarded the little warship—thirty-six who were ship's company, fourteen who had counted as cargo, the one who had been prisoner, one a working passenger and various who had come aboard as guests — now only sixteen remained, and Billy felt deep down that the little ship was lonely.

Built for the fight, with all guns ablaze, rigged for the chase on endless open seas, there was a melancholy now to *Fury*'s quiet lullaby — as though the ship herself knew that what awaited now was surrender.

Billy closed his book, doused his lamp and went on deck, feeling as lost and sad as *Fury* herself sounded. He closed the companion hatch behind him, pulled his coat collar up around his ears and gazed ahead at the night shadows on the empty working deck.

The voice behind him startled him and he turned. Just above, at the little belfry on the quarterrail, a tall shadow stood against the night sky. "How do you fare the evening, Mister Caster?"

Billy looked aloft at the wind gauge, sniffed to test the air, and said, "Wind is at seven or eight knots, sir. Northwest and coming westward. Skies are clearing just a bit. Tide is near its ebb."

"And how shall it make with the morning, then?"

"We'll have better wind, sir. Twelve to fifteen knots, from the west, tide past high and running seaward."

"At what hour shall we see those conditions, Mister Caster?"

"Six bells, sir. Six bells of the morning watch."

"And how do you know that, so precisely?"

"Because that is the hour when you told Mister Duncan that we shall make sail, sir."

"Aye," Dalton said, quietly. "At six bells we make sail."

In his quarters aboard *Cornwall*, Captain Peter Selkirk looked up as his portal opened and Smollet entered, carrying a stack of foolscap documents.

"Post dispatch is in, sir," the clerk said. "Routine orders from the admiral, except this one that I imagined you'd

301

like to see." He handed across a sealed letter on which the wax had been broken, then resealed with the clerk's stamp.

Selkirk unfolded it and read:

On His Majesty's Service, Richard Lord Howe, Admiral of the White, in camp with the Armies of Expedition — to the Honorable Peter Selkirk, Esq., Captain of His Majesty's Ship *Cornwall*, greetings.

Have read with interest and some amusement your account regarding the schedule of charges sworn by Expeditionary Guard Commander Felix Croney, and the remarkable proposition presented by the fugitive Patrick Dalton. The idea of a man arranging and scheduling his own trial on capital charges — the very audacity of it — gives one pause to consider that there might yet be a touch of backbone remaining in the British character.

In our opinion, sir, justice so cleverly sought is justice deserved. You are therefore confirmed as Officiating Judge Advocate for the purposes heretofore cited, and commanded to proceed according to the articles and requirements of Courts Martial Extraordinary, to secure the accused, Lieutenant Patrick Dalton, as well as his accuser and any and all witnesses, evidences and testimonies pursuant to this cause, and to conduct aboard HMS *Cornwall* a proper trial to find according to evidence on the charges brought by Commander Croney et al.

Further, you are commanded to take HMS *Cornwall* and other vessels in your jurisdiction to sea, to conduct a sweep of the Indies lanes off the central colonies, at such time and by such measure as shall permit of the conduct of this trial at no especial expense to the fleet or to yourself.

Done this 27th day of December, the Year of Our Lord 1777.

Below was a postscript:

Enjoy your entertainment, Hawser. I do envy you this outing, for amusements are in short supply here. Philadelphia as an occupied city has no life nor luster. It seems only to wait in silence, as though waiting for us to leave. It is William's opinion that his position here will become untenable with the advent of spring. Nevertheless, we must press this war as avidly as I wish we could press for peace. I find I grow weary of the conflict now, and await the day when we might return home to England.

Regarding Patrick Dalton, I have nothing to offer in testimony except his service record, which you have in your possession. But I do have an instinct in the matter. Young Dalton may be guilty of a great many things — and from the stories I have heard, he probably is. But he is no traitor, and I believe you know that as certainly as I do. Try him by the evidence, convict him or acquit him as is warranted, but let us not deplore the man. The Empire would be better served if we had more like him at the King's service, and could treat them a bit more fairly.

Selkirk folded the letter and put it away. "Thank you, Smollet. Please ask Misters Thatcher, Holmes, Bliss and Harrington, to assemble here for conference."

"Yes, sir."

"Also, please ask flags to send a 'stand by' to the *Royal Lineage,* and prepare a message from me to Captain Watson. Inquire of him whether he would prefer to attend the niddling mundanities of senior captain in port during my absence at sea, or to join me on a cruise and serve as president of the court that tries the 'ghost' he lost in that squall."

"Yes, sir. Ah . . . Commander Croney keeps asking to speak with you, sir."

"Have you completed the copies of his schedule of charges?"

"Yes, sir. And had Lieutenants Holmes and Harrington certify that the copies are exact, as is required by the procedures. If Captain Watson agrees to serve on the board of inquiry, then one of his lieutenants also will have to certify all copies."

"Very good, Smollet. Let's have every procedure be precisely by the manual. That's what it is for."

"Yes, sir."

"Is the accuser to receive a copy as well?"

"It isn't required until the court is convened, sir. They are, after all, his own schedule of charges. But it is required that the accuser confirm to the officiating judge advocate that the charges are as he has proffered them."

"When?"

"Prior to their being presented to the prisoner, sir."

"We don't have a prisoner."

"No, sir, but by the manual the person being accused is referred to as the prisoner from the moment he receives the charges against him — which must be in advance of the convening of the court, so that he may have opportunity to summon his own evidences and testimonies."

Selkirk glanced at the document from the admiral, confirming him as officiating judge advocate. "I begin to believe that the handling of a vessel in a fleet engagement may be less demanding than the book of procedure for a court martial. One could use a sailing master in such circumstance."

"Yes, sir. Or a studious clerk."

"I count on that, Smollet. I suppose you had best give me a copy of the charges against Dalton, then call Commander Croney in to confirm them."

"With witnesses, sir."

"By all means, with witnesses. Bring whatever lieutenants are nearest to hand."

When Croney arrived at the captain's cabin, Lieutenants Rufus Holmes and Thomas Bliss were waiting there, with Selkirk and the clerk.

"I understand you wanted to speak with me," Selkirk

304

said.

"Yes, sir. Captain, I must insist that you begin a search immediately for the traitor Dalton. I believe, as officiating judge advocate, that is your direct responsibility . . ."

"You knew I had been confirmed, then? How did you know?"

"It is my business to know," Croney said.

"The gentleman has been on deck, sir," Bliss offered. "There have been flag signals from ashore, in codes that our buntingmen do not have."

"Of course, I have agents," Croney snapped.

"Very well." Selkirk nodded. "Yes, I have been confirmed in this matter, and everything will proceed in due course. I have here a copy of the schedule of charges that you submitted, regarding Patrick X. Dalton, Lieutenant, HRMN . . ."

"Captain, unless you intend to try the traitor *in absentia*, then I suggest orders be given to seek him out and arrest him."

"All in good time," Selkirk said coldly. "The copy I have here is an exact copy of your schedule of charges, as certified by two officers of this ship. Now please answer my questions, Commander. Do you state now that this is indeed the schedule of charges against Patrick X. Dalton?"

"If it is a true copy of what I submitted, then it is."

"It is certified true, as prescribed."

"Then yes, I so state."

"Thank you. Commander, are you aware of the nature of these charges?"

"I am."

"Are you aware of the procedures governing Courts Martial Extraordinary?"

"I am. I have studied them."

"Do you here and now wish to change or withdraw any of these charges, or to amend them in any way?"

"I do not."

"Then do you before these witnesses, petition that the accused Patrick X. Dalton be brought to trial, and do you

305

agree to stand as his accuser in such trial, to abide by the procedures cited and to place the matter in evidence before myself and a proper court, for resolution?"

"I do."

"I will require your signature on a document evidencing your responses, and these gentlemen will witness the making of it. Now, please name the person to act as presenting witness, on behalf of the Expeditionary Guard."

"Myself, sir. I shall act both as accuser and presenter."

Selkirk glanced at Smollet, who nodded. The officer could choose to play both roles.

Aside, one of the lieutenants whispered to the other, "He bloody well doesn't want to share his laurels with anybody, does he?"

"It's a Crown case," the other whispered. "He'll be set up for life if he wins it."

"And witnesses for the prosecution?" Selkirk asked. "Have you a list of persons to be summoned?"

"None, sir." Croney's slight smile was chill. "All the testimony I need is in writing, as I believe you have seen."

"And that evidence is in your possession now, aboard this vessel?"

"It is."

"Then I believe we may proceed."

"You have Dalton, then?" Croney gaped at him. "He is here?"

"No, he isn't here, Commander. We are going out to meet him."

XXX

For a time now, the weather over the Atlantic had held clear as brisk, chill winds played counterpoint to the broad currents that swept northward from the Gulf of Mexico before bending away toward European shores. Here, off North America's coast, great rivers wound through the open sea—wide, flowing streams that had made the North Atlantic for two centuries the most profitable merchant sea in the world. Here were the highways of seafaring men, here the winds and currents that carried the cargoes of the western world, thoroughfares for commerce and war.

And here now stood *Fury*, sleek and compact with canvas trimmed to a holding wind as those on her decks watched high sails diminish into the distance at six points of the compass. What only hours ago had been a merchant fleet bound out from New Spain, now was a scattering of separate ships, all fleeing for cover.

"What do you suppose they thought we were, sir?" Billy Caster asked his captain.

"Likely took us for a privateer, in these waters," Dalton said. "Skittish as sheep before a wolf. If I were their escort, I'd nip the tails of every one of them. Breaking out like that, scattering so . . . That frigate will have its hands full, rounding them up again."

"Thought we'd have a bit of sport with that one."

307

Charley Duncan sighed. "But he didn't even challenge."

"We didn't threaten," Dalton pointed out. "He hasn't the time now to fight, even if he wanted to. He might take days regrouping those merchantmen. And as to sport, Mister Duncan, a frigate—even a small one like that twenty-eight yonder—is hardly 'sport' to stand against, when we've barely enough men to handle our sails, much less our guns."

"Aye, sir, you're right. It's just that this bloody waiting has got on my nerves."

"It's early yet, Mister Duncan. We have only been holding here for a few days."

"Do you think Captain Selkirk will come, sir?" Billy gazed northward at the empty sea. "There is so much that could go wrong."

"He will come," Dalton said. "If nothing else, he will come for his own amusement, I think."

"Do you trust him so much, then?"

"Trust him to defend me, or to somehow take my side? No. But I trust him to do his duty, promptly and precisely, and to uphold the letter of Admiralty law. I have no more to ask of him than that."

For a time they stood in silence, then Billy muttered something and Dalton glanced around at him. "What did you say?"

"It was nothing, sir. I only said that one day I should like to learn to play the bassoon."

The last sail out of sight was the frigate; then *Fury* rode an empty sea. Winter's cold sun crept across her forestays to cast the shadows of hard-reefed upper yards on her gundeck. Purdy Fisk came up from the companionway, turned the pinnacle glass and rang the ship's bell twice, then called to Charley Duncan. "Hot food below for anybody whose belly can stand it."

"And what is it today, Mister Fisk?" Duncan asked, sourly. "The ship's staple, I warrant—oat porridge and salt-whatnot?"

"Bit of variety this meal, Mister Duncan," Fisk answered, just as sourly. "The salt meat's the same, but the porridge became thick so I mashed it up in lumps and fried it in hot tallow."

By fives they went below to warm their hands and chew on barely palatable food, and Charley Duncan said, "I would never have thought that I'd miss Mister O'Riley."

"Which Mister O'Riley?" Fisk snapped.

"Either one."

At eight bells Cadman Wise set all hands to take in sail, and Victory Locke brought the snow about on jib and jigger, and lashed the helm, while Dalton put Billy Caster through the drill of reckoning position, course and drift. Through the night, *Fury* would simply ride the flowing current of the stream, retracing the miles northward that her shrouds had taken her southward during the day. It was thus that she waited for *Cornwall*'s arrival—eighty miles or so northward, then the same distance south, riding first the currents and then the winds, tethered on long lead in the Indies Lane, playing its forces one against the other to maintain a daily vigil.

In the portside cabin below, Billy Caster lit a lamp and got out his log, to enter the record in rough:

January twelfth, 1778: Morning clear, wind steady at west of north. Course on the current east of north. Day's first reading at six bells m.w. Reckoned course correction for five leagues to westward. Came about and made sail on the lower yards for course two points west of south at ten knots. Breakfast was oatmeal porridge and salt meat. Deckwatch taking turns acting as cook. Today is Mister Fisk. Several complaints about the food. Maintained course until four bells f.n.w. Sail sighted dead ahead, made to be a merchant convoy escorted by small frigate—28. Near six bells convoy broke up and scattered. Frigate stood off ahead for a time, then made about to find and regroup merchantmen, as we offered no challenge. Slight course change to secure on corrected station, course held until evening. Mister Fisk's attempt at dumplings at midday having been unsuccessful, supper was oatmeal porridge and salt meat, and to each man a lemon. Mister Locke suggested pea and onion dumplings for tomorrow. Course maintained until eight bells d.w., then came about and reefed up for night drift.

No other sightings, no incidents, no sign of *Cornwall*. Captain says she will come, and that none of us are in danger, though we all know that he himself is at extreme hazard when she arrives. Every man aboard has tried to dissuade him from his purpose, but to no avail. He will have it no other way. He will stand trial aboard *Cornwall*.

Counting the captain there are sixteen of us aboard. Without the captain there would be none. God stand at his side, and protect him.

We bear no colors, but the white cross flag of custody is ready to hand.

At six bells of the morning watch they calculated position and course, and lookouts went aloft to spy the day. The call was immediate: "On deck!"

Dalton squinted, peering upward. "Aye, tops?"

"Sail, sir!"

"Whereaway?"

"Port bow, sir! Only a few miles . . . four vessels. Two of the line, two smaller. The lead ship has seen us and flies her colors, sir. It is the Union Jack."

"He has come, then," Dalton said, as though only to himself. Then, "Stand down from make sail, Mister Wise. Helm, restore your lashing. Signals, please. Send, 'Are the conditions accepted?' "

"Aye, sir." Flags rose on *Fury*'s halyards, and were answered directly from the nearer of the great ships bearing down on them.

"He sends, 'Accepted,' sir. He also sends, 'Stand by for close inspection.' "

"Send a 'standing by,' signals. And run up the white cross flag a'fore. We are placing ourselves in his custody."

"We will be prisoners then, sir?" Billy asked.

"We already are prisoners, Mister Caster. Those are a pair of seventy-fours over there, with a brig and an armed schooner to block for them. We couldn't escape if we wanted to."

Within the hour, *Fury* lay adrift on long seas, surrounded by ships of the king. The two seventy-fours loomed huge and deadly at two cables' length off each beam. The brig held back, easing about to windward, and the schooner had slid on past to take up a perimeter patrol, eyes aboard turning in curiosity to look at the rakish lines, the compact structure of the snow, and to wonder at the scuttlebutt they had heard about this smallish warship that — so the stories made it seem — had outsailed and outfought everything that two warring powers could send against it, yet now so meekly placed itself at the mercy of their consorts.

Signals flew, buntings running up and down aboard every vessel, as greetings and orders were exchanged. Aboard the second seventy-four, an ironic salute ran up the halyard. *Royal Lineage* had tipped its cap to the little warship that had outfoxed it in northern waters. Then at the thwarts of *Cornwall* a launch was hove out and lowered, and Dalton turned to Charley Duncan.

"It is your deck, Mister Duncan," he said. "Conduct yourself as an officer in command of a custody vessel — as I have instructed you. And please see to it that the lads in galley don't poison the duty officer who comes aboard. He has done nothing to deserve ill treatment. Mister Caster?"

"Aye, sir?"

"Do you have all the things in readiness, that I had you list?"

"Aye sir."

311

"Very well, then. All hands stand by for launch alongside. Mister Duncan, take the deck, please."

He went below, alone.

When the launch from *Cornwall* was alongside, a ruddy-faced young lieutenant stood in its bow and saluted. "Permission to come aboard?"

Charley Duncan returned the salute, crisply. "Captain's below for a moment, Lieutenant. Can you wait until he's on deck?"

"Of course." The young officer nodded.

Dalton came up then, and his men's eyes went wide. He had removed the turnbuckle splints from his arm, and had changed his clothing. Nine-button coat as blue and bright as any moneyed officer's set off immaculate white waistcoat and breeches. His blue tricorn was perfectly flared, with a blue rosette at the turning of the brim, and he wore his straight sword in a fresh-polished buckler. From the knees up, he was every inch a proper lieutenant of the king's navy, and even the new-blacked boots below seemed proper on him—a touch of individuality that only heightened the impressive propriety of the uniform he wore.

Duncan recovered his composure and saluted him. "Custody officer alongside, Captain. He requests permission to come aboard."

"You have the deck, mister," Dalton reminded him.

"Aye, sir. That I do." Duncan turned to the rail. "Permission to come aboard, Lieutenant."

The young officer climbed over *Fury*'s rail, exchanged salutes with Duncan, then turned to Dalton, his hand pausing as he raised it in salute. "Ah? Oh, it's you," he said. He completed the salute and Dalton returned it, then nodded.

"Lieutenant Harrington, I believe."

"Yes, sir. Oliver Harrington, lieutenant amidships, HMS *Cornwall*. We met before, sir, but I didn't know your name."

"Patrick Dalton," Dalton said. "Your captain is expecting me."

"Yes, I know." Harrington grinned an ironic grin. "The launch will take you across. I am instructed to remain aboard your vessel as custodian." He turned to Duncan and introduced himself again. "Will you be in command, sir?"

"Aye . . . until the captain's return."

"I've brought my kit, if you'll show me where to stow it."

"Portside cabin. Mister Wise will show you the way."

Harrington started to follow the bosun, then paused and looked back at Dalton. "I wish you good fortune, Captain Dalton. I'd be pleased to hear from you one day how so many . . . ah . . . impressive things have come to be accounted in the schedule of charges they have over there."

"Thank you, Lieutenant." Dalton returned the ruddy grin. "I dearly do hope I'll have the chance to tell you about them one day." He turned then. "Mister Caster, do you have my kit and all the other material?"

"Yes, sir."

"Then come along. There are people waiting for us."

The launch was a trim ship's boat with nine banks of oars, all ably manned, and the trip across to *Cornwall* was a matter of only minutes, though to Dalton each minute seemed an hour. He looked back once, running his eyes over the jaunty lines, the sleek high rigging, of *Fury*. She was his . . . by right of capture, by concession of Ian McCall, and more, by his experience of her. He had sailed her, fought her, gone in harm's way with her. He had learned her moods, her touch and her song.

He wondered now if he would ever set foot again on her deck. He looked away, and did not turn back.

The launch was snugged smartly at *Cornwall*'s beam, and the great ship's dark hull curved above—a bulging wall broken by tiers of open gunports and the scars of a hundred patchings. More than once, the seventy-four had stood in line of battle, her huge blunt bow protruding through the smokes, her sides ablaze with the firing of great guns. Stripe-shirted yeomen steadied the launch and the petty officer at the stern cupped his hands and called, "Permission to board prisoner?"

The entry port above the launch was drawn open and the reply given, "Permission to board, aye!"

Had Dalton been an ordinary seaman, or a noncommissioned officer, crewmen would have gone ahead to escort him aboard. But he was senior aboard the launch and not yet under active arrest, so the protocols applied. Seniors last in, first out of boats. Dalton stood, grasped the handline and stepped up to the sill of the entry port where he saluted the waiting escort, then saluted the helm. Billy Caster followed, carrying his valise and kit.

"Thatcher, sir," the lieutenant before him said. "Lieutenant of the watch. Follow me, please."

They followed, up a short ladder to the half-decked upper deck with its catwalks from beam to beam, then aft and up another ladder to the quarterdeck, where Billy stepped aside to wait by the rail. Ten steps after was another ladder, and here Thatcher stepped aside and gestured. "Captain will receive you on the poop, sir." Dalton climbed, feeling the presence of the lieutenant and a pair of marine guards just behind him.

Captain Peter Selkirk waited on the poop deck, accompanied by several other men — another senior captain whom Dalton did not know, a brace of ship's lieutenants, an aging clerk whom he remembered from years gone by — his name was Smollet — and the familiar, triumphant face of Felix Croney.

Dalton stopped before them and saluted, then removed his bucklered sword and held it out, across both hands. "Thank you for coming, sir," he said to Selkirk. "I am your prisoner."

Selkirk took the sword and handed it to his clerk. "We meet once more, Patrick," he said. Then, more formally, "I accept your surrender as officiating judge advocate, and place you and your vessel in the custody of the

314

court, until such time as the charges against you have been heard and decided. You are the court's prisoner from this point forward. I introduce you to the Right Honorable Isaac Watson, Captain and Commander, HMS *Royal Lineage,* who will serve as president of the court, to Commander Felix Croney, His Majesty's Expeditionary Guard, who has brought charges against you and will act as your prosecutor, and to Lieutenants Rufus Holmes and Thomas Bliss, who will sit as members of the court. There will be two other members of the court—Captain Charles Fell of the brig *Saintes* and Commander Sidney Smith of the schooner *Hope.* Do you have any questions or protests regarding the complement of the court?"

"No, sir," Dalton said. "I do not."

"Very well. Then do you request time to compile evidence on your behalf?"

"No, sir."

"Do you require any witnesses who are not presently aboard or available to this ship?"

"No, sir." Dalton was impressed—as he always had been—at the rigorous, methodical precision of his old teacher. He was assembling a court martial with exactly the attention to fine detail he would have devoted to planning a battle . . . or to instructing a midshipman in the arts of sail handling. Hawser would go by the book, always, and never miss a line. Dalton counted on it. The only thing that stood between himself and certain conviction now was the character of Captain Peter Selkirk.

"Then I hereby call for the convention of a court martial tomorrow morning, January the fourteenth, 1778, to be conducted aboard HMS *Cornwall* in accordance with the procedure set out by the Right Honorable the Lords of the Admiralty for the assembling of Courts Martial Extraordinary. Lieutenant Thatcher, please escort the prisoner below to await trial."

"Aye, sir."

As Dalton turned away, he heard the whisper of Felix

Croney, behind him, "What does he have up his sleeve? He doesn't have any witnesses to call?"

And the response of Selkirk, not whispered: "More accurately, Commander, his response was that he has no witnesses not presently aboard this ship."

XXXI

In early evening, guards came for Dalton and Billy, and escorted them to Selkirk's quarters—a spacious cabin with large, ornate galleries, in *Cornwall's* sterncastle. The captain was waiting for them, along with his clerk, Smollet. He offered Dalton a seat at his map table, with Billy perched on a stool at his elbow.

"It is the duty of the officiating judge advocate," he said, "to consult personally with the prisoner prior to convening the court, to inquire what evidence or testimony is to be offered for refuting the charges, or in defense of his conduct. You understand that, I take it."

"Aye, sir, I . . ." Dalton hesitated, then rephrased it. "Yes, Your Honor, I do." He was not addressing the captain of a ship now, but an officer of the court.

Selkirk caught the delicacy, considered it, and decided not to react to it. "In that case, you also are aware that I am not entitled to know the substance of such evidence, but only who will be called to testify."

"Yes, Your Honor. I am aware."

"And are you prepared to advise me of your defense?"

"I am. I believe it also is prescribed that the prisoner is allowed to examine the charges against him

317

and the order in which they will be presented. Is that correct?"

Selkirk glanced at his clerk, who nodded. "Yes, sir. He is so entitled, prior to submitting the schedule of his evidence."

The senior captain sighed, and crossed his arms on the table. "Then show him the bloody thing, Smollet. If you please."

Smollet handed the document across. Dalton glanced at it and handed it to Billy, who took out his own copy and began a meticulous comparison. Selkirk frowned, but said nothing.

"They are still in proper sequence, sir," Billy said, "but there have been charges added. The list is longer now. There were fifteen capital charges on the list I copied for you. Now there are nineteen, as well as a long list of incidental charges labeled as being miscellaneous."

"What are the additional capital charges?"

"Kidnapping an officer of the king," Billy read, "armed attack on a ship of the line—the HMS *Royal Lineage*—interference with a king's convoy, and malicious damage to a crown frigate in exchange of fire."

Dalton turned to Selkirk. "Have any of these charges been stricken in previous examination, Your Honor?"

Selkirk raised a finger. "Smollet?"

"Yes, sir." The clerk adjusted his spectacles and ran a finger down his list. "Ah . . . shall I read them out?"

"Please do," Selkirk said.

"Yes, sir. Item the second has been disallowed. That is the one in which Mister Croney charged sabotage to the Fleet Anchorage in New York Harbor . . ."

"I've seen the reports on that," Selkirk said. "There is no question that you could not have done that,

318

since you were releasing prisoners from the stockade at the time . . . or so the fourth item charges."

"Item the third is stricken," Smollet continued. "Theft of a ship, listed as a civilian schooner. There is no one to bring or prove charges on that because the schooner was never registered as a prize, and its original owner chose not to file a complaint, except against Captain Jonathan Hart, since missing or deceased. And then there are items the sixth, seventh and eighth, dealing with damage and destruction to various Crown vessels, including two cruisers and some gunboats . . ."

"Those charges are in abeyance," Selkirk clarified. "Should they prove to have happened in the commission of a treason, then they shall stand against you. Otherwise, they will be dropped by consent of the court. It would be a bit embarrassing to have to report those damages as being the result of unprovoked attacks by several commanders of king's warships on a poorly armed civilian vessel . . . which escaped unscathed."

Dalton kept his face straight. "I understand, sir."

Smollet continued, "Item the ninth has been stricken, the sinking of a Crown sloop of war. It is noted that subsequent reports prove that Captain Hart did that, rather than the prisoner."

"Item the tenth, failure to report an act of war . . ."

"Abeyance," Selkirk said.

"Then there is item twelfth, sinking of a forty-four-gun warrant frigate, the *Courtesan*."

"That charge is stricken by the court," Selkirk said. "There have been some preposterous stories about a schooner sinking a frigate in a duel at sea, but no real evidence has been submitted. At any rate, if it was the *Courtesan*, Captain Hart had gone outlaw prior to that and no charges are warranted."

"Item the thirteenth is four counts of piracy in and about Chesapeake Bay, committed by the snow *Fury*."

"That was before I . . ." Dalton began.

"We know." Selkirk raised his hand. "You . . . ah . . . didn't have your snow at the time. You were aboard an unlikely-looking ketch, as I myself have testified in preliminary review. The charge is stricken. But not the next two charges—the destruction of two privately owned cutters, and serious damage to a xebec by exchange of fire."

Dalton asked, "Does it specify what vessel destroyed the cutters, sir?"

"It does. The very same ketch that I know you had."

"And the xebec?"

"Your snow."

"Those incidents were simultaneous, sir."

Smollet opened a thick valise and leafed through papers there. "He's right, sir," he told Selkirk. "It all happened at the same time."

"Then you did one or the other?"

"Yes, sir, I did. My vessel was attacked by the xebec and I replied in kind. Exactly as any officer would do . . . in case of an unprovoked attack."

"I shall consult with the president of the court," Selkirk said. "I expect that item fifteen might stand in abeyance, just as the earlier items did, and on the same grounds. As to the business of the cutters, we shall simply have to charge that to whoever had the ketch at that time."

"You told me that you agreed to the terms of my surrender to you, sir," Dalton reminded him.

"And so I did."

"Then the fourteenth item should be stricken, Your Honor. You have agreed that no charges will be made or maintained against any member of my crew."

"It was one of your crew, then? I think I shall not ask which one. Very well, the charge is stricken by prior consent, but I do have one question about that, Patrick. Just my own curiosity. How did one of your men—or all of them, for that matter—destroy two cutters with a slogging ketch?"

Dalton shook his head. "They are really quite resourceful lads, sir."

"Item the seventeenth," Smollet continued reading, "attack on a ship of the line . . ."

"Stricken," Selkirk said. "Commander Croney lodged the complaint, but Captain Watson struck it himself. He says that you did not fire on him, and the less said about your losing him in a squall, the better."

"Yes, Your Honor."

"Item the nineteenth," Smollet said. "Severe damage to a frigate by exchange of fire."

"Abeyance," Selkirk noted. "As with several others."

"Then there are nearly fifty counts of miscellaneous mischief, mayhem and the like," Smollet said, "but all falling short of capital crimes. They are listed collectively as item the twentieth."

"Stricken for the purposes of this court martial," Selkirk grunted. "Those, we feel, are disciplinary matters, and should be addressed other than by this court."

Billy Caster had been counting. "That leaves six charges, sir," he told Dalton. "The first is treason against the king . . ."

Dalton interrupted him. "Will these charges be brought in the order they are listed, sir?"

Selkirk nodded. "They will."

"Thank you, Your Honor."

"Then there is aiding an escape," Billy continued, "and consorting with felons . . ."

"What felons?" Dalton asked quietly.

321

"Those you broke out of stockade," Selkirk said, then hesitated. "Oh, I see. Those are your crew."

"Yes, sir. If there are no charges maintained against any of them, then I have not consorted with felons."

"Do not press me too far, Lieutenant," Selkirk growled. "But very well. Strike that item, Smollet."

"Yes, sir."

"Harboring enemies of the king," Billy read. "Then there are two of the new charges still standing. Kidnapping an officer of the king, and interfering with a king's convoy."

"Interfering with a convoy?" Dalton glanced around. "Who preferred that charge?"

"I don't know what I was thinking at the time," Selkirk sighed. "Strike that item, please, Smollet. And pray I hear no further mention of a concert at sea."

"Four charges, sir," Billy told Dalton.

"In this order," Dalton said again.

"In this order," Selkirk agreed.

"Thank you, Your Honor. I will present evidence regarding two of the four. On the charge of treason against the king, I will present a witness to refute the charge. On the charge of kidnapping an officer of the king, I shall call a witness in defense of my conduct."

"Give their names to Mister Smollet," Selkirk said. "They will be handed summonses and will be made ready to appear."

"One is a member of my crew, aboard *Fury*," Dalton told the clerk. "He is a large lad named Mister Hoop. If he owns a Christian name, I have never heard it."

"Just out of curiosity, Patrick," Selkirk asked, "what charges have we dismissed against this particular man?"

"So far as I know, sir, he has never had charges

against him. He was at one time master at arms aboard a king's vessel, but he was thrown overboard by his mates and somehow never returned to his ship."

"I see." Selkirk shook his head. "Who will be your other witness?"

Dalton turned to Smollet. "The other name is Peter Selkirk, Captain HMRN, commanding His Majesty's Ship *Cornwall*."

Oliver Harrington toured *Fury* with Charley Duncan, asking questions and making lists. Since the vessel was in the custody of the court, the court would require a complete inventory of what it held. And since the men aboard were to be absolved of any crimes charged against them, there must be a roster of who they were and what they were to be forgiven for doing.

All of them were — or had been — sailors of the king, and Harrington required each man of them to swear an oath that he had not conspired with or assisted in any rebel action against England.

Six of them were escapees from the stockade on Long Island, with crimes not unusual among seamen. Duncan himself, whom Harrington now had to address as Commander because he was nominally in command of the snow, had been incarcerated — at least the latest time — for mayhem. Purdy Fisk shared the charge with him. Victory Locke and Ishmael Bean had been jailed for brawling. Claude Mallory and Cadman Wise had been convicted of possession of a gig without authorization. Another half-dozen of the men swore they had no crimes to be forgiven. They had simply been out of work, beached because of a minor mutiny aboard the frigate *Carlson*. None of them, they assured him, had been involved in the infamy, nor any charges proven against them. The captain had simply decided he didn't want them anymore.

Two amused the lieutenant. He pondered what the reaction of Captain Isaac Watson would be when he read the list of forgivees. Ethan Crosby and Floyd Pugh both had been gunners aboard Watson's own *Royal Lineage*. Both had deserted.

The huge, apparently amiable Mister Hoop might have been considered a deserter, Harrington decided, but only because he had not located and returned to his ship after being thrown overboard.

"How many of your mates were involved in putting you off your ship?" Harrington asked him.

Hoop screwed up his face and scratched his head. "About fifteen, I'd reckon it," he said, finally. "Maybe there was more, but I'm not certain of that."

Pliny Quarterstone was an escapee from the Point Barrow stockade, where he had been waiting out a penalty for brawling.

A tough and motley lot, Harrington decided, but obviously capable sailors when well commanded.

"Are there any other crimes that any of you need to be forgiven for?" he asked them at assembly. "Anything that might arise later, that isn't of record now?"

"Nothing I'd care to talk about, sir," Cadman Wise said.

"Little matter of a scrape I got into last year, with some marines," Victory Locke admitted. "But as far as I know, they never knew who it was that thumped them like that, so I don't suppose I've been charged with anything."

"I might have accidentally misappropriated a harpsichord," Charley Duncan said. "But that was from a New Hampshire rebel, so I wouldn't think Crown justice would be very interested in that. Would they?"

"Probably not," Harrington agreed. "A harpsichord," he muttered to himself. "Remarkable."

"They said I took the helm off the vice admiral's flagship," Duncan added. "But I already served out my penalty for that."

"Then that won't need forgiveness," Harrington noted.

"Also, sir, should there ever be question as to what became of the brig *Doughty*'s number two launch, and anybody suggest I might have been involved in its disappearance, then I suppose a bit of forgiveness might be in order."

Harrington gaped at him, decided he was serious, and noted the item. "Anything else, Commander Duncan?"

Charley thought about it for a moment. "Six barrels of salt meat from the frigate *Clemency* . . . some might say I took that. And maybe there could be some misunderstanding about Sir Walter Jennings's hat, and where the *Sotheby*'s flag locker got off to . . . oh, and there used to be a revenue cutter at Morgan's Point that may not be there anymore, but I swear to you, sir, I never set foot aboard that boat. *None* of us ever so much as touched it."

Harrington realized that his mouth was hanging open, and closed it. He looked back at his earlier notes. "It says here, *Commander* Duncan, that your time in stockade was for simple mayhem."

"Aye, sir. That it was, the latest time."

"It appears to me that you are a resourceful man, Commander."

Duncan flushed with pleasure at the compliment. "Thank you, sir. The captain has said the same exact words a time or two."

A boat had come alongside, from *Cornwall*, to collect the lieutenant's lists and to deliver a sealed paper to Mister Hoop. It was handed aboard and Harrington presented it to him. The big man looked at it in perplexity, then asked, "What is it, sir?"

Harrington opened it, read through it and handed it back. "It is a summons, Mister Hoop. It says you are to be transported to the *Cornwall*. You will be called as a witness tomorrow, in court."

"In court? Does it say what I am supposed to witness about, sir?"

"It doesn't say, Mister Hoop. It only says you must be there."

As the big man went to get his duffel, Harrington thumbed through the report he was to send back to *Cornwall*. "Astounding," he muttered. "Quite remarkable."

XXXII

The morning dawned clear and cold upon seas where the great seventy-fours rode with barely a shudder, though the lesser vessels about them rose and fell rhythmically on long gray swells. At six bells of the morning watch Captain Charles Fell, commanding the Crown brig *Saintes,* and Commander Sidney Smith of the Crown schooner *Hope* were piped aboard *Cornwall* and escorted belowdeck where a secure area had been cleared, sealed and equipped with wide trestle tables set end-to-end to make one long table, with chairs along its sides and at each end.

Lieutenant Thatcher was there, setting out the articles prescribed in the book of procedures—at each seat a piece of blotting paper, a sheet of writing paper, a pen, a copy of the act of Parliament commonly known as the Articles of War, and a *Book of the Holy Evangelists*. In the center of the table, a row of filled inkstands waited.

Having done this, with Smollet following along to make certain that everything was exactly as prescribed in the procedures, Thatcher—now duly sworn as deputy judge advocate—formally presented to Lieutenant Holmes—likewise duly sworn as officer of the court—a list of the names of the requested witnesses. With this list in one hand and a handbell in the other, Holmes went to various quarters to summon the members of the court.

At seven bells Captain Isaac Watson, commanding HMS *Royal Lineage,* was piped aboard *Cornwall* and escorted to the courtroom, where Captain Peter Selkirk — as officiating judge advocate — solemnly wrote his name at the head of a list of members of the court, as prescribed in procedures.

With a quick frown at Selkirk — for he had just learned of the pardoning of his two deserted gunners — Watson strode to the head of the table and sat in his chair, being duly sworn as president of the court.

After the president, seating was by seniority. Selkirk, the most senior officer present, sat at Watson's right. Fell, the next, sat at Watson's left. Then Commander Smith at Selkirk's right and Lieutenant Thatcher at Fell's left, and finally Lieutenants Holmes and Bliss to complete the court. Smollet came to lay before Selkirk the items which procedures required the officiating judge advocate to have at hand — the Order for Trial, the judge advocate's warrant, regulations for the ordering of minutes, and the requisite forms, called "skeletons," for the rendering of judgment and the rendering of sentence.

The officiating judge advocate stood, read aloud his own oath, read the oath taken by the rest, then sat, and court was in session.

Hatches opened at both sides of the wardroom and armed marine sentries admitted Felix Croney from one, Patrick Dalton and his clerk from the other. Immediately, Croney stopped and raised his hand. "May it please the honorable members of the court," he said, "I make objection to the prisoner being accompanied."

Watson glanced at Selkirk and Selkirk turned to Smollet, who was hovering at his shoulder. They exchanged whispers, and Selkirk said, "The objection is valid, Mister President. Procedure does not specify that the prisoner may bring his clerk."

"Objection upheld," Watson said.

"Sustained," Smollet whispered.

"Sustained," Watson corrected.

Dalton turned and took the valise of papers from Billy, then shooed him out and the hatches were closed.

Selkirk squinted at the papers before him, then turned to Smollet. "There is one witness not present. Do we have to call him in before we send him out, or can we just leave him out to begin?"

"He doesn't have to be called until the court requires him," Smollet explained.

"Then how about the two witnesses who are already here? I mean myself and Commander Croney. It says here that the Court is to be cleared of witnesses to begin, but since each of us also serves as an instrument of the court . . ."

"The court may rule an exception for cause, sir."

"I move an exception for cause," Selkirk said.

"I sustain the motion," Thatcher echoed.

"Second," Smollet clarified.

"Any objections?" Watson looked around. There were none. "Motion sustained," he said.

"Approved," Smollet said.

"Approved." Watson sighed. "Blast this barrister language, Hawser. Can't we just proceed in honest words and have the minutes cleaned up afterward?"

"I don't see why not, sir," Smollet volunteered.

"Good," Selkirk breathed. He stood then, and read in a teacher's voice the final draft of the charges against Patrick Dalton—treason against the king, aiding an escape, harboring enemies of the king, and kidnapping an officer of the king.

In the moment of silence following, Croney gasped and came to his feet, raising a hand. "Sirs, I must object! I . . ."

"Sit down, Commander," Selkirk growled. "You have already approved the dismissal of some charges and the abeyance of others. We went all through this yesterday."

"Yes, sir, but not the order of the charges. I placed the treason charge last, not first."

"The devil you did. This is an exact copy of what you submitted to me, amended as we discussed yesterday. We didn't change the order of anything."

"But it is changed!" Croney's eyes went hard and he pointed a quivering finger at Dalton. "You changed the order of charges! I know you did!"

Selkirk slapped the table. "Sit down, Commander. Lieutenant Dalton didn't present these charges to me. You did. And some days back you certified before witnesses that these are the true charges you wished to bring, order and all. You can't change it now."

"But I . . . I hadn't really had the opportunity to review the list, not since I was held prisoner aboard this blackguard's ship. First there was the business of getting away from him, then that damned American who guided me kept taking away my valise for safe-keeping . . ."

"Overruled!" Watson thundered.

Smollet checked his book and raised his eyebrows. "By George, that's the right word," he muttered.

Croney subsided, though the glance he shot at Dalton was pure hatred.

"I said sit down, Commander," Selkirk said.

"I can't sit down, sir. The only remaining chair is the witness chair."

"Oh. Well, then, stand in silence until we get this matter begun. Has the prisoner heard the charges against him?"

"Yes, Your Honor," Dalton said, standing at attention.

"Are you and each of you, accuser and accused,

prepared now to swear an oath that all you and each of you present before this court as witnesses shall be the truth as you know it?"

"Yes, sir."

"Yes, Your Honor."

"Well, good. Mister Thatcher, take your *Book of Evangelists* and swear them in."

"The prisoner is Irish," Watson said. "Do we have a crucifix to set in the *Book?* Most Irish are of the Romish faith."

"I brought one, sir." Smollet pulled a small cross from his valise, then bent to whisper to Selkirk, "It doesn't say there can't be other chairs in the room, sir."

"Then get more chairs and stop standing over me."

By the time Croney and Dalton were duly sworn, several more chairs had been delivered by marine guards and set around the room.

"Commander Croney, you may as well take the witness chair," Selkirk said. "It's your turn first."

Croney was obviously flustered when he began his presentation of evidence. He had great stacks of testimony, all properly attested and witnessed *in affidavit.* But now it was in the wrong order. He had counted on offsetting most of the dismissed charges and abeyances on the grounds that the charge of treason still was pending, then to address it last. Now most of his documents were useless, and the rest had to be reassembled. Now he had to address the treason charge first.

Still, he was well prepared. For months, Croney had devoted himself to the capture and arrest of Patrick Dalton. All of the testimonies and points of evidence assembled in London, linking Dalton to the Fitzgerald — that fierce old Irish chieftain who had gone too far in contesting the king and now stood convicted of treason. Only the conviction of Patrick Dalton now stood between him and the grant of lands that he had been promised if this one last detail could be taken care of. Important people in England had promised him—and had given him the means to once and for all convict Dalton.

"Very well," he said finally. "I accuse the prisoner, Patrick X. Dalton, of knowingly and actively participating in a scheme perpetrated by Sean Quinlin O'Day, Lord Fitzgerald, chieftain of clan Fitzgerald of Dunreagh, to circumvent the will of His Majesty the King and the laws of Parliament, by sending an invading force against the Coast of Wales. I present to the court a written detail of the incident and its background, as brought out in trial by the Lords High Magistrates in London during December of 1776, as well as copies of the conviction and sentencing of the Fitzgerald and some seventeen of his followers."

"Let these items be entered in record," Selkirk said, "if it please the court."

"So be it," Watson nodded.

"All of this is in record, Commander," Selkirk said. "And has been reviewed by all members of the court, but I must point out that nowhere in these documents is there mention of Patrick Dalton, the prisoner."

"I am coming to that, sir," Croney said. "Further, I submit nine verified and documented eyewitness accounts attesting that Patrick X. Dalton, the prisoner, was personally acquainted with the Fitzgerald, as well as with many of his retainers and in particular with his daughter, Molly O'Day. These are submitted for record, and I believe also have been reviewed by the members of the court."

"Entered," Watson said.

Dalton sat aside, his eyes hooded. Someone had gone to a great deal of trouble to compile evidence against him, he realized again—someone across an ocean from where he had been all through the

Fitzgerald's decline from power. He wondered if he would ever know why.

"Do you have further evidence regarding the charge of treason, Commander?" Selkirk shifted his bulk, impatiently. "We have seen all of this. Acquaintance does not prove complicity. As far as that goes, I have been acquainted with the Fitzgerald, myself. I hope I am not charged, as well."

"Certainly not, sir." Croney blinked. "I merely wish to establish the nature of the treason and the connection between the prisoner and its perpetrator."

"Then proceed."

"Yes, sir. I now wish to submit, for the first time, one final set of documents which the court has not reviewed because I withheld them . . . as is my right as presenter."

Selkirk turned to Smollet. "Does the accuser have the right to withhold evidence from pre-trial scrutiny by the court?"

"No, sir. The accuser does not. But the presenter of evidence does, and the Commander has been qualified in both capacities."

Dalton fought back a bleak, ironic smile. Clever bastard, aren't you, Croney, he thought. Save your best guns for a broadside, after you've lulled them with small-arms fire.

The court accepted the documents and passed them around to read as Croney announced, victoriously, "These are witness accounts, both from persons within the Fitzgerald's household and from two members of the peerage in London . . . irrefutable testimony, I believe, that the prisoner, Patrick X. Dalton, was present and actively involved when first the plot was hatched at Dunreagh, more than eight years ago. The date is specific, September the ninth, the year 1769. And there, sirs, is your proof that the prisoner before you did actively participate in an act of treason against His Majesty the King."

As the members read the copies, one after another turned to look at Dalton. Watson's gaze was angry, Selkirk's surprised and hurt. Dalton sat still, saying nothing.

Selkirk shrugged. "That seems quite damning. Is that the lot of your evidence, Commander?"

"On this charge, yes, sir. But I have three other charges to address, if I may proceed. I have placed into evidence a number of accounts proving that the prisoner did, on the evening of September the sixteenth last, while in commission of unlawful flight from prosecution, aid in the escape of a number of prisoners from the Naval Detention Stockade at Long Island. I believe they are conclusive, as proof of the charge."

"Entered," Watson said.

"Also, I have submitted prepared evidences and testimony proving that, in making that escape aboard a stolen vessel . . ."

"We have stricken the theft of vessel charge," Selkirk reminded him.

"Yes, sir. While making that escape, then, the prisoner did consort with and harbor enemies of the king, specifically American rebels who may have been involved in . . ."

"We have stricken the sabotage charge as well," Selkirk said. "You showed no evidence linking the prisoner to that incident, beyond purest coincidence."

"Yes, sir." Croney shook his head in irritation. "But they were Americans, and he did harbor them aboard a vessel at his command."

"Entered," Watson said.

"Finally," Croney's voice was almost a sneer, "the court has left me one remaining charge, and on that, the evidence is my testimony as an officer and a gentleman. You have the particulars before you, and I do here and now affirm that Patrick X. Dalton and members of his crew accosted me in the performance of my duties, knocked me unconscious, carried me aboard his vessel and kidnapped me, holding me hostage until I managed to win free."

"Enter the document," Watson said. "And the commander's testimony just given."

Selkirk took a deep breath. "Do you have further evidence, Commander Croney?"

"No, sir. I have presented my case."

Selkirk turned to Dalton. "Does the prisoner care to . . . ah . . ."

"Cross-examine," Smollet whispered loudly.

"Do you?" Selkirk glared.

"Yes, sir." Dalton stood. "I believe that as the accused, I am not bound by the order of charges as the accuser has listed them."

"He's right, sir," Smollet nodded.

"Go ahead, then. Choose your own order."

Dalton approached the still-seated Croney. The man's eyes on him were the eyes of a cat that has caught its mouse.

"Regarding the second and third charges, then," Dalton said, "I have no defense except my word as an officer and a gentleman. May I relate that now as testimony, then proceed with cross-examination?"

"I don't see where he can't, sir," Smollet said. "As long as the accuser gets his chance to cross-examine if he wants to."

"Proceed," Selkirk told Dalton.

"Members of the court, I am accused of aiding in the escape of prisoners from a naval stockade. I did not initiate that escape, nor know about it until it had occurred. I did, however, enlist the aid of the escapees in making my own escape from unwarranted pursuit."

"Whether it was warranted depends upon whether you are as guilty of high treason as these testimonies seem to indicate," Selkirk growled.

"Yes, Your Honor," Dalton nodded. "Forgive me. I

offer in defense only that I was the subject of pursuit by a great many armed men, and had no time or opportunity to disassociate myself from escaped convicts."

Watson looked away, his eyes hard and cold. "Hmph!"

"Commander Croney accuses me of harboring enemies of the king," Dalton said. "To this I can only respond that I had no knowledge of whether the Americans who came aboard my vessel were the king's enemies, nor did I have opportunity to sort it all out, for the reason aforementioned."

"The prisoner pleads ignorance, laxity and being pressed for time," Croney drawled, making a sneer of it.

Dalton ignored the comment and turned to the guard officer. "Commander Croney, will you tell the court why you were in the town of Portsmouth, in the New Hampshire colony, on the day you say I kidnapped you?"

"I will not. I was in the performance of my duties. I need say no more."

"But, Commander, isn't it true that Portsmouth was at that time entirely held and defended by forces of the American revolutionaries? Didn't their flags fly there in harbor?"

"What is your point, Dalton?" Selkirk asked.

"I wonder what duties an officer of His Majesty's Expeditionary Guard has, that might take him to an enemy port, sir. I know of no mission of the Expeditionary Guard that could account for that. Do you?"

"It was a personal matter," Croney snapped.

Watson glared at him. "Do you mean to tell me that you enlisted passage on my ship . . . took me away from my business . . . on a personal matter, Commander?"

"Well, I was in pursuit of a fugitive."

"Which," Dalton pointed out, "is quite beyond the

normal duties of Expeditionary Guardsmen. That is all, Commander, I have no further questions."

"But, by God, I . . ."

"Stand down, Commander!" Selkirk ordered. "We'll have this by the book, by damn. You've had your say."

When Croney was ensconced in one of the extra chairs, away from the court table, Selkirk said, "the prisoner may now present evidence in his own defense."

Dalton remained standing. "I call as witness a member of my crew, known as Mister Hoop."

Hoop was brought in. Even cowed and awed by the august presence before him, he seemed to fill the room. Dalton pointed to the witness chair. "Sit here, Mister Hoop," he said. "Carefully, please."

"Aye, sir."

"Has this witness made his oath?" Selkirk asked.

"Ah . . . yes, sir, he has," Smollet said.

"Then proceed, Mister Dalton."

"Yes, Your Honor. Mister Hoop, do you recall the day when we were in Portsmouth harbor and I asked you to accompany me ashore?"

"Aye, sir. That I do. It was a blustery cold day, wi' gray skies, an' . . ."

"That will do, Mister Hoop. I only wanted to know if you remember."

"Aye, sir. Clear as a bell."

"Do you remember where we went?"

"Aye, sir. Clear as a bell."

"Where?"

"Oh. Well, sir, you remember, we went to the bell-tower so you could talk to the gentleman there."

"And did I talk to the gentleman there, Mister Hoop?"

"Well, not right then, sir. Don't you remember?"

Dalton nodded. "I remember. But we want to hear it from you."

337

"Aye, sir. You didn't talk to him in the belltower."

"Why not?"

"Well, sir, I reckon it was my fault, because I went up first and rapped the gentleman on the head."

"And why did you do that, Mister Hoop?"

"Why, I saw the stairs, so I just went on up . . ."

"No, I mean, why did you rap him on the head?"

"Oh. Well, that was because he tried to hit me with a sword, sir. Didn't I tell you? He didn't even wait to see who was there, he just came at me. So I rapped him on the head."

"Then what happened?"

"Well, sir, you said you still wanted to talk with him, so I brought him along and we went back to the ship. Then they came along with th' harpsichord, you know, an . . ."

"That is all, Mister Hoop. I have no more questions."

"Aye, sir. Any time, sir."

Selkirk turned. "Commander Croney, do you have questions of this witness?"

Croney sneered. "No questions, sir. I believe he has proved my point."

"Well, I have a question," Watson said. "Mister Hoop, did you and the prisoner kidnap the man in the belltower?"

Hoop went pale again, cowed at being addressed directly by a man with epaulettes on both shoulders. "I and who, sir?"

"You and the prisoner. The man questioning you."

"Oh, me and Captain Dalton? No, sir. We didn't kidnap the gentleman. The captain just wanted to talk to him, like I said. But after he was rapped, then we took him to the ship."

"Why?"

"So the captain could talk to him, sir. Besides, the captain said the gentleman . . . that's him right over there, sir, except he has a uniform on, now . . . he said he was a king's officer, so we couldn't very well leave him unattended in that belltower. The whole town was full of Whigs and such like . . ."

Croney snapped to his feet. "I protest!"

"Sit down, Commander," Selkirk growled. "You had your chance. Any other questions by the court?"

There were none, and Mister Hoop was escorted out, to be sent back to *Fury*.

"I have one other witness to call," Dalton told them. "And this is in the matter of the charge of treason against me. I call Captain Peter Selkirk."

Smollet whispered to Selkirk, "You don't have to change chairs, sir. Just be questioned."

The room was very quiet as Dalton turned to Selkirk. "Captain, I direct your attention to the date, September the ninth, 1769 — the date upon which Commander Croney says I was involved in the making of a plan to commit treason against the king. A date on which I was supposedly in Dunreagh, attending clandestine meetings. My first question, Captain, is: where were *you* on that date?"

Selkirk came half out of his chair, his eyes blazing. "See here, young Dalton, if you are trying to implicate *me* in such . . ."

"I have your logs here, sir," the efficient Smollet said. "That was when you commanded the old *Athene*."

"So it was." Selkirk subsided slightly, still scowling at Dalton. "Find the date, Smollet. Where was I?"

Smollet riffed through the old log book. "Ah . . . here it is. You were aboard *Athene*, sir. In the Mediterranean, doing maneuvers off Formentera."

Dalton nodded, smiling openly for the first time. "And that particular morning, sir, between seven and eight bells of the morning watch, what exactly were you doing?"

"Smollet?"

"Yes, sir. I have it. Beginning at seven bells, captain conducted examination of two midshipmen, both having reached the age of nineteen and having applied for examination for lieutenancy."

"And who were they, Captain?" Dalton's voice was very quiet in the still room.

Before Selkirk could shunt the question back, Smollet gasped. "By George," he muttered. "By George! It's here, sir. The midshipmen that day were Misters Nelson and Dalton. Ah, that is Patrick X. Dalton, sir. You qualified him on that day, to stand for his commission."

XXXIII

"Blast that guardsman!" Captain Peter Selkirk turned from *Cornwall*'s gallery, slamming closed a panel with a force that rattled its panes. Below it on the hardwood bench a lamp teetered and Smollet moved to catch it. But Billy Caster was there first, setting it right.

"I suppose we'll never discover whether he knew he was presenting false evidence," Selkirk fumed. "He refuses to comment, and I can't force him. The Expeditionary Guard is answerable to the Ministry of War, not the navy."

"I doubt he knew it was false, sir," Patrick Dalton said. "The man is a zealot, and an opportunist, no doubt, but he hardly seems an intriguer . . . at least not of that class."

Isaac Watson looked up from his tea, raising a brow. "I'd hardly expect you of all people to defend the scoundrel, Dalton. It was your neck he was fitting for the noose."

"Blast necks and nooses, as well!" Selkirk thundered. "I do not appreciate having been used to sort out this mess. I have far better things to do."

"I apologize, sir," Dalton said. "I could think of no other way."

"To do what, Patrick? Save your skin? That is

341

hardly my responsibility, is it?"

"Not my skin, sir. My honor."

"Well . . . that is a . . . No, by damn! That is not the responsibility of myself or His Majesty's Navy, either! And that damnable guardsman! Just look at the havoc that has been done. I may one day decide to accept your apology, Patrick. You were falsely accused, after all. But I shall not forgive or forget Commander Croney. The admiral shall have a full report on this matter, and Lord North as well, if I can manage it." Having vented his frustration on the rattled gallery panel, he stepped to his map table and seated himself. "Well, let us wrap up this matter, gentlemen. We are agreed that Lieutenant Dalton is exonerated regarding the charge of treason."

Around the cabin, the members of the court nodded agreement.

"He is found innocent as well in the matter of kidnapping a king's officer?"

"He is, in fact, as guilty as sin of that," Isaac Watson said. "However, I say innocent. I should like the guard officer at least to have something to answer for . . . to whomsoever he answers to. Why he was in a belltower in a rebel port is a fair question, I think."

The others nodded again.

"Therefore we stand by his acquittal on those two charges?"

Again, the nods. "On those two counts," Captain Charles Fell said.

"Then that leaves the others—ah, aiding an escape, and hobnobbing with rebels . . ."

"Harboring enemies of the king," Smollet amended.

"Yes. Those become disciplinary matters, then, and not subject to the decision of the court."

"It seems so, sir, yes."

"Then is the bedamned court adjourned?"

"Yes, sir. It was adjourned some hours ago. We are working on the minutes, now."

"Very well. Patrick, I believe we can accept no less than your surrender of commission, everything considered. And, of course, that snow out there must remain in custody of the court, since it has no proper registry. Likely it will be sold on the block, to pay for the expenses of this exercise."

Dalton straightened and bristled. "*Fury* is my ship, sir. Registry or not, I took her honorably and she is mine."

Selkirk looked around him, at the others, then sighed and shook his head. "Technically, Patrick, she is not. The vessel is in my custody, and must be accounted for. I could let you sail her back to port, I imagine. You seem to have the feel of her, and of that ragtag baker's dozen you call a crew. You may delay your resignation long enough to do that. But mind you, the snow must fly the custody flag, and it *will* be turned over to the port captain when we arrive at Long Island. Do you agree?"

Dalton simply stared at him, saying nothing.

"It doesn't matter whether you agree or not," Selkirk said. "You may sail her in, but she is the king's from that point on."

Commander Smith had moved to the gallery and leaned to look out at the snow with its white cross pennant. "It *is* always possible that a ship could be blown off course on such a voyage," he suggested.

"Then it would return," Selkirk said. "As long as it flies that custody flag, Mister Dalton is bound by his honor to accompany this squadron at my orders. To do otherwise would indeed be treason."

Fell looked at Dalton, his fighter's eyes a'glitter. "Of course a man can always lower a flag and simply try to escape. For my part, I'd welcome that. The snow would be fair game for taking as a prize then. I'd like a chance at such a prize."

"I'd welcome it, myself," Smith agreed.

"That snow escaped *Royal Lineage* once," Watson

343

rumbled. "It would not do so a second time. Let that custody flag just once be hauled down, and I shall have that vessel under my guns within the hour."

"You see how it stands, Patrick." Selkirk said. "You have your acquittal . . . and your name and honor. But the ship is ours."

"I see how it stands, sir," Dalton said, stiffly. Then he bowed. "If one day you accept my apology, sir, then also accept my thanks for all that you have done."

"All that you manipulated me to do," Selkirk growled.

"If I may take my leave, then, sir, I should like to return to my ship."

"Ship!" Watson snapped. "It is a snow, mister. *This* is a ship."

"Aye, sir."

Selkirk stood, went to a sideboard and got out Dalton's sword. Holding it on the palms of both hands, he presented it to him. "You stand acquitted, Lieutenant Dalton. You are no longer my prisoner. You are free to leave."

As Billy followed his captain along the high deck of *Cornwall*, toward the launch that awaited them at the entry port, Dalton asked, "How do you fare the day, Mister Caster?"

"Winds east of north, sir," the boy said without hesitating. "They'll come east by evening and hold, rising to eighteen or twenty."

"Very good, Mister Caster. That is how I fare it, as well."

"Sir?" the boy glanced around, to make sure no one was listening. "I have been wondering how that twenty-eight-gunner we saw might have gotten along, regathering all those merchantmen it was trying to convoy."

"Slow work, that," Dalton murmured. "Takes time to regroup a flock like that. Possibly two days or so, the way they scattered."

"And those privateers we saw earlier, much farther eastward. I've been wondering about them, as well."

"Hush, Mister Caster. Step lively, now. I am anxious to return to *Fury*, and I am sure the custody officer there is waiting for the launch to bring him back to his own ship."

At the poop of *Cornwall*, Captain Peter Selkirk watched the launches go out, launches returning Isaac Watson to *Royal Lineage*, Charles Fell to his *Saintes*, Sidney Smith to the schooner *Hope*, and Patrick Dalton to the custodied snow. The little fighting ship appeared cowed now, timid under her hated white cross flag.

"Blast your Irish pride, Patrick," Selkirk muttered. "You gave them all a merry chase. A jolly run for the money, eh? Well, you have recovered all that the navy can return to you—the honor of your name. Settle for that . . . if you can."

Beside him, Thatcher also was watching the Irishman in the launch. "Do you think he'll run, sir?"

"Not under that flag, he won't," Selkirk said. "I wager he's flown false colors at times, and who in command has not on occasion, just to amuse the enemy? But the lad will never dishonor the colors he flies. It is not his nature."

"Without that custody flag aloft there, though, he would be under no warrant. The vessel isn't even in registry."

"Aye, he could drop the flag if he chose. But would you, Thatcher?"

The lieutenant considered *Cornwall*, her seventy-four guns a'bristle . . . and just off there, the deadly *Royal Lineage* with as many more . . . and just beyond, the sleek raiding schooner with its high fore-and-afts and its ranging guns at bow and stern . . .

and Charles Fell's gunners aboard *Saintes*, just itching for a fair prize to take. "Not and live to tell of it, sir," he said.

Smollet came up with a valise. "Mister Dalton's young clerk left all his documents aboard, sir," he told Selkirk. "Shall I put them with the other records?"

Selkirk waved him off. "Go through them at your leisure, Smollet. Whatever should go into the records, pray put it there."

"Yes, sir."

Holmes had come to the quarterrail and Selkirk beckoned to him. "How do you fare the day, Mister Holmes?"

"The wind will make easterly, sir. I expect we shall see eighteen to twenty knots by evening."

The launch headed back from *Fury*, bringing Mister Harrington back to his duties. Beyond, Isaac Watson was boarding his ship. At other points, the boats were closing on *Hope* and *Saintes*. "The shunting will be done shortly, Mister Thatcher," Selkirk said. "When all have sent 'secure,' send general signal to make sail by the wind. We'll have a course for Hatteras, I expect. We can make about there and start our sweep northward, toward New York."

Once more he glanced at the custody snow. It was coming alive, hands a'deck and topmen going aloft. At its quarterrail, Patrick Dalton was instructing his first, a sandy-haired seaman who wore a tricorn hat. Like the rest of those in command, Dalton was readying his vessel to make sail.

The white cross flag still flew at the snow's peak, and Selkirk nodded. "You've done the best you can, Patrick," he muttered. "Just leave it alone, now." He turned away. "The deck is yours, Mister Thatcher. I shall be in my quarters if you need me."

Through the rest of the day, the five vessels rode westward. The big seventy-fours held short sail to accommodate the smaller three trying to pace them. At dark, all five put out riding lights and the formation continued toward the coast of the warring colonies.

It was nearly dawn when the *Royal Lineage* maintop first saw the distant lights, hard down off the port bow. A large number of vessels, more than a league distant. He reported the sighting, but could not read identification or course. A convoy of some sort, First Officer Calvin Race decided. And this far out, most likely British.

At five bells of the morning watch, *Cornwall*'s tops saw the approaching sails. Most of them were barks, readily distinguished by their tall stacks of squared sails. A merchant convoy, coming northward, beating across the wind. "They've gotten west of their course," Holmes decided. "They are trying to beat back to the stream lanes."

At six bells, Peter Selkirk was just coming on deck when the call came again from aloft. On the quarter, Holmes raised a speaking horn to reply, "Aye, tops?"

"I read those merchantmen now, sir! It's a fleet, with a single escort—a small frigate drumming at their heels. More sails hard down behind them, sir. The barks are fleeing from privateers. The frigate has seen us, sir. He has run up the Jack, and he asks assistance."

"How many privateers, tops?"

"Eight or nine, sir. It's a whole wolf pack, it looks like."

Selkirk reached the quarter, returned Holmes's salute and nodded. "Yes, I heard. I'll wager those are Dale's raiders yonder, Mister Holmes. We had word that they were massing off the Carolinas, raiding from the cover of shore batteries."

"Orders, sir?"

"The frigate wants our assistance. Very well. Hands a'deck, hands to station, gunners to station.

347

Signals to *Royal Lineage* and the cruisers, course correction, prepare to intercept and engage. Signal to *Fury*, maintain course and visual contact. Do not make about, do not engage."

"Not much he could do, anyway," Thatcher pointed out, coming on deck. "He has barely enough men to handle sail in this wind. He can't use his guns."

"Tops have a read on the privateers, sir," Holmes said. "Two are full frigates, the rest brigs and lesser cruisers. They have several cutters among them, as well. They must truly want those barks, sir. It's an attack in force."

The wolf pack, its sails nearly equalling those of the fleeing merchantmen, was closing on good wind.

"They will attempt to dash in and turn the barks, as many as they can," Selkirk mused. "They've seen us by now, but they'll chance getting a few prizes under cover of shore batteries before we can close on them. Signal *Saintes* and *Hope*, course to intercept raider, engage as able. Signal the escort frigate, disengage and intercept. Signal *Royal Lineage*, come abreast and make all sail. Course to stand block on the merchantmen."

"Aye, sir."

Forty miles off Hatteras that day, on running seas where twenty-knot winds frothed the tops of waves, the largest marine encounter of the winter of 1777-78 took place. Reports would vary as to how many vessels were involved, but would agree on some particulars. A squadron of commissioned privateers and "letters of marque" assembled by the Carolinian Henry Dale, accompanied by the brigantine *Notre Dame* of the navy of South Carolina and the brigs *Raleigh* and *Adventure* flying the colors of Virginia, encountered a British supply convoy making northward from Martinique with a single flag frigate, the *Seques-*

348

tre, as escort. In process of overtaking, the privateers were challenged by a flotilla of English vessels which included two ships of the line, *Cornwall* and *Royal Lineage,* on cruise for the White Fleet. An immediate exchange of fire between *Notre Dame* and a British brig, the *Saintes,* was inconclusive, but allowed the pair of line ships to close on the merchantmen and stand about. The matter would have ended there, had the supply barks held formation, for no commander of any lesser vessel would willingly bring himself under the guns of a pair of seventy-fours. The remaining defenders, *Sequestre, Saintes* and a schooner, *Hope,* had the wind with them, and had signals to withdraw and reform about the line ships. Had this occurred, there would have been nothing left for the Colonial vessels except to break off and seek the safety of a batteried port, to wait for another day.

The supply vessels, though, for reasons known only to merchant mariners, chose that moment to break ranks and flee in all directions. Some would swear later that a separate raider, unseen before, swept down on them from ahead — a vessel some thought was a brig, but that bore twice the sail of any brig they had seen, and that maneuvered like a fox to the kill as it closed on them.

Whatever the reason, the barks' commanders panicked and fled from the security of the Union Jack line, and within the hour there were vessels everywhere, going in every direction the winds allowed — barks with privateers in pursuit, privateers with Royal Navy in pursuit . . . no hearing board would ever be satisfied that it had sorted it all out. And through it all, the widening circle of engagements swept ever closer to the batteried shore of the South Carolina colony.

By evening, little was left to see from any one vantage. The vessels were spread over a half-circle of sea that covered two hundred miles or more.

Three barks were lost, taken by privateers. One privateer, the brig *Endicott*, and three armed cutters were taken under British guns, and the *Adventure* escaped with her sternpost sundered.

By evening light, *Royal Lineage* came from the south, escorting a battered brig with a prize flag, to rejoin *Cornwall* off Manass Point. *Saintes* came limping to them from eastward, an armed cutter in tow and patching on her starboard beam, and by first light of morning the schooner *Hope* had returned with a pair of cutters as prize, and a special dispatch to send across to Captain Peter Selkirk. The dispatch was a wet banner, found afloat some miles away—a white cross flag.

Half a day passed—questioning sailors, prisoners and one another—before they had any word of the custody snow that had flown that device. A second mate from one of the supply barks had clearly seen the threat that came bounding toward them from the north. "It wa' a brig, sir, or almost a brig I'd say. But no brig I seen ever carried so much sail nor moved so fast. Why, time we saw it comin', we could right see the guns at its rails, it moved so."

"This devil you describe," Selkirk asked the man, "what colors did he fly?"

"Why, none at all, sir," the mariner paused, thinking, then affirmed, "That's right, he didn't show colors a'tall. But then, he didn't actually fire on us, either, so I guess there's no dishonor in that, is there?"

"Can you recall anything else about him?" Thatcher asked.

"No, sir, not really. He was just there all suddenlike, right on our nose an' borin' in; then we veered away an' it got so busy I didn' see much more. Oh, did I tell you he had a launch in tow? Right smart ship's launch, just a'bouncin' along behind . . ."

Lieutenant Oliver Harrington's eyes went wide, then his grin. "Duncan," he muttered. "Captain, I'd suggest you have all of our vessels do an inventory. One of us is missing a launch."

Selkirk sat himself at his map table, shaking his head. "The fox," he said to no one in particular. "The damned, wily fox."

He lowered his head to read again the letter lying there, a letter that Smollet had found hours earlier, among the papers left aboard *Cornwall* by Billy Caster.

It was a simple, formal letter, brief and to the point. It was the resignation of Patrick X. Dalton . . . as requested.

351

The Fox & the Fortune

To those who go down to the sea,
whether in jaunty sailing ships
or in the no less lofty vessels
of their imaginations.

Prologue

With coming of spring in the year 1778, came also the turning of tides. The fledgling British Empire, still in its infancy as a world power and spread thin by years of widespread conflicts—first under George II and now under George III and his ruling party—had lost the chance for a quick resolution of the uprising in its American colonies. Now the question in Lord North's administration was how much could be salvaged by negotiation from strength . . . and how much strength was there.

The best efforts of the brothers Howe toward a compromise of interests had failed, and there was war. Clinton and Cornwallis had failed—as British muskets facing American rifles had failed—to either strangle the northern colonies or neutralize the southern ones. Burgoyne's plan for a quick end to the insurgence had failed, and the Howes' occupation of Philadelphia had proven to be less a victory than a hugely unprofitable exercise in defense. Months had become years as the fighting went on, and even the House of Lords now admitted that the situation was rather beyond tidying up.

Where the colonists had fielded little militias, now there was a Continental Army afield, trained under the eye of Von Steuben and directed by Braddock's own protege, General Washington. This army had emerged from a long winter at Valley Forge to wholly disprove the Crown Party's fiction of dealing with a minor annoyance on American shores.

Where there had been privateers pitted against the king's White Fleet, now there was a small but aggressive American

Navy, carrying the battle across the Atlantic to British shores. And now the rebellious colonials had allies. France was enthusiastically involved with the Americans, and Spain—though less enthusiastically, seeing the Anglo colonials as a future threat to Spanish holdings—was yet allowing the supply lines to remain open.

Now also, the rebels in their various colonies had a common identity. The Continental Congress was once again at work in Baltimore, and the Articles of Confederation had been approved for ratification.

Half a hundred colonial battle flags had given way to a new flag—red and white stripes, thirteen in number, with thirteen stars on a field of blue.

In Paris, the Americans Franklin, Deane and Lee worked out final negotiations for a full treaty with Louis XVI. In London, Lord North introduced bills of reconciliation, hoping to avoid further French intrusion into American affairs.

In the great houses of Wilmington and Baltimore, where men gathered to discuss such matters, it was said that Clinton would succeed Howe at Philadelphia and would abandon the city within months. It was said that a king's Commission had been appointed to discuss peace terms. It was said that France—and some mentioned Spain as well—was the salvation of American hopes. It was said also that any man who trusted Spain had stones between his ears, and that France was hardly better, being solely concerned with its own interests and with twisting the lion's tail.

And it was said that never in living memory had there been a time that offered such opportunity for the making of fortunes . . . though the means to do so in such unsettled times were precariously unreliable.

The lines between patriotism and treason, just as between privateer venture and piracy on the high seas, were extremely fine in times when no established authority was at hand to explain and enforce the difference.

One

Where cloud-tattered moonlight touched the crisp tops of waves, silvering the long crests that marched in lock-step measure like so many Prussian grenadiers striding through the sea, two vessels beat landward across the tidal stream. Great shadowy silhouettes, elaborate and sleek, they thrummed and whispered as wooden hulls clove the waves. Their running wakes were bright foam on dark waters. Taut rigging hummed and keened among high sails aslant to take the faltering wind.

Foremost of the two was a solid four-master, a merchant vessel riding low and laden. By her greater size and high-stacked sails, a landsman might have said she was the faster of the two and able to leave her pursuer in her wake. A mariner would have known otherwise at a glance. The merchant vessel was losing her race. Slowly and relentlessly she was being overtaken by the dark shape less than a mile astern.

Any sailor of the time, seeing that pursuit, would have shaken his head at the inevitability of what must follow. For the dark ship in pursuit was a deadly vessel, a ship designed for the chase and for the kill. Larger than a brig, it carried the massive, elaborate sailing gear of a warship — a ship-rigged vessel of frigate class — and the glinting muzzles of great guns, spray-sheened, glistened at its flanks and along its ranked ports.

At his stern rail, Captain John Shelby Butler squinted as he steadied a glass to study the big, dark predator following in his wake. He knew the ship, and he knew the intentions of those aboard. Back there, coming on apace on the moon-scudded water west of Bahama Deeps, was *Valkyrie*. And commanding her was the French Acadian freebooter, Francois Thibaud.

There was no question — no question at all — what Thibaud had in mind. Thibaud was a pirate, *Valkyrie* was a killer ship and the merchantman — alone and laden — was a ready prize.

Beside Butler, Timothy Leech rested big arms on the rail and nodded. "He's comin' on, Cap'n," he growled. "He'll have closed to half a mile by the time we make the cay yonder. He'll have them twin long-twelves aimed right up our stern, an' not a soul about to say him otherwise as he sees it."

For a time, Butler did not respond. As turning winds tugged at his sails aloft, making tackle blocks rattle overhead, he glanced up, deep-set gray eyes thoughtful. With her deep holds full of Ian McCall's goods — ranked cotton bales mostly with a small-hold complement of tobacco, fabrics, wines and spices — *Pride of Falworth* plowed water like a scow . . . or seemed to, dropping her nose listlessly as her high sails began to luff. She lost a knot of way as Butler listened to the rumble of waves against her timbers, then another.

Without looking at his first mate, Butler returned to his glassing of the pirate chasing him. "Hands to those fore and main sheets, Mister Leech," he said. "Let's at least show him that we can keep our canvas trimmed."

"Aye, Cap'n." Leech stepped forward to the quarterrail, past a grim-faced helmsman, and bellowed, "Mister Strode! Hands fore an' foremain to trim to the wind! Stand by aftermain and mizzen."

On the sloping foredeck, men scurried to comply. Leech planted big hands on his hips, watching the shadows of them there. When he was satisfied he returned to the stern rail. "Our . . . ah . . . 'temporaries' are losin' heart, sir," he said. "As they see it, we're dead men already, an' runnin' just delays the obvious." His teeth glinted within his beard, a fierce grin that aimed itself at the dark pirate ship harrying *Pride of Falworth* toward the shoals of an unnamed and uninhabited cay south of the Florida shore.

Butler felt the slight shudder in the decking beneath his buckled shoes as the helmsman turned to look back, breaking his concentration on steering to the sails.

"Mind your helm, Mister Trice," the captain snapped. "You can look at the pirates later."

"Aye, sir." The helm took up rudder, and again *Pride of Falworth* leaned to the weight of slanted sails.

Butler turned to glance forward. The cay loomed dark ahead of them, a low, brushy island rising from moonlit sea. On the charts it had no name, being only one of many little islands that extended in a curving chain from just south of New Spain's barrier peninsula to the curving deeps where the Gulf Stream flowed.

Butler reckoned distances, his ears hearing the whisper of waters along *Pride's* hull and the muted melody of wind in her sails. "Put a sounder in the fore, please, Mister Leech," he said. "One of our regulars, of course."

"Aye." Leech nodded, already striding away. At the quarter-rail he called, "Mister Strode, who can you spare to sound afore?"

There was a pause; then the bosun's voice came back to him. "Mister Summers or Berroth, sir. Or one of the fo'c'sle hands."

"Send Mister Summers to the spreaders to sound," Leech called. "Have Mister Berroth stand by aport with log and line."

"Aye, sir."

Captain Butler's cold voice came from behind the big first mate, "Our pirate is luffing just a bit back there, Mister Leech. He may intend to stand off and let us foul ourselves in the shoals."

"I wouldn't think he'd turn cautious now, Cap'n." Leech squinted, a touch of concern in his voice.

"Nevertheless, he is slowing." Butler pointed. "I wonder if a bit of entertainment might sharpen his attention. Gunners aft, if you please, to man the nines."

"Aye, Cap'n." Leech's grin returned, big teeth glinting among his whiskers in the mottled darkness. He turned and called, "Gunners aft, man the stern chasers! Linstocks an' slow fuse! Look alive!"

Just over half a mile astern, *Valkyrie* had slowed by a knot, lying back, although still overtaking the merchantman. Butler held his glass on the predator. *Thibaud is in no hurry now,* he thought. *He expects that I shall skirt around behind that island and try to*

*buy some time by playing at dodging games. He is wondering whether to
just stand off here and wait for first light to flush me out.* "They say that
Captain Thibaud is a man of temper," he mused, aloud. "They
say he has no patience with those who try him."

"They do say that, Cap'n," Leech agreed. "It's his French ancestry, I shouldn't wonder."

Shadowy forms appeared at both quarterdeck ladders, hurrying aft — men with tubs and pails, with swabs and coiled lines
and muted lanterns. Six men . . . two gunners and four gunners' mates. Butler nodded his approval. Terrence Boyd and
Chad Ames were peerless gunners, as capable with marine ar-
tillery as any man aboard the warships of the great fleets. Nor
were they the only good gunners *Pride of Falworth* carried in her
complement. Though few beyond himself and Leech knew of
it, *Pride*'s crew of regulars was a vastly different mix of men than
might be found aboard the usual merchant vessel of the time.
The ship carried twice as many first-rate gunners, in fact, as the
number of old guns she had. And the captain's private muster
of hands was nearly double the number of men a four-mast
bark required.

Most of them presently were not aboard. The majority on
the ship now — eighteen of the twenty-six men working her
decks — were new hands, temporaries . . . a motley lot of
beached seamen hired on only weeks before at an obscure port
on one of the contested islands.

The gun crews swarmed aft along *Pride*'s quarterdeck and
hauled in her twin nine-pound stern chasers to check loads and
freshen prime.

"Misters Ames and Boyd," Butler said.

Their faces came around, half-lighted by the glow of muted
lanterns. "Aye, Cap'n?"

"What do you make the range of that vessel yonder to be?"

They peered across the intervening water, glanced at each
other, and Chad Ames cleared his throat. "Maybe a thousand
yards, sir. About that. Twice our accurate range with these old
pieces. Even if we had twelves — as the pirate yonder surely
does — we'd still need to close a bit for good effect."

Butler nodded. He knew ranges and limitations as well as
they did. "But a lofted ball might carry that far, might it not?"

"Oh, ayé, sir," Ames agreed. "Might even drop a shot on his deck, with a bit of luck. But a spent ball won't do more than annoy that bloody cruiser, sir."

"Then, by all means," Butler said, "let us see if we can annoy him. You may fire for effect when you are ready."

"Aye, sir." Glancing at each other again, the gunners went to their guns and began lofting the muzzles of them, using pike poles and quoins. By the time they were satisfied with their elevations, the nine-pounders were pointed at the southern sky, standing at rakish angles like a pair of stubby color standards.

The gunners took up their smoldering fuses and aligned on a place above *Valkyrie*, then looked around.

"Proceed," Butler said.

"Aye, sir." With visible shrugs the gunners made final check of notches and lowered their smoking linstocks. Fuse touched primed vents and the nine-pounders bellowed in unison. A cloud of sulphurous smoke rode for a moment astern of *Pride of Falworth*, then drifted across her starboard flank and out to sea.

"Reload and fire again," Butler said.

The guns were run in for swabbing and loading, and Butler raised his glass. He trained it on the dark ship in the distance.

"Something for him to wonder about, at least," Leech said, leaning against the rail. "He's seen our muzzle blasts. I wonder what he thinks we're doing."

"He likely wonders what *we* think we're doing," Butler said, in a cold voice that carried no amusement. He handed the glass to Leech. "Your eyes are younger than mine, Timothy. Tell me what you see."

Leech steadied the glass. "Nothin' yet, Cap'n. That's a long way for a ball to . . . aha! First shot's in the water off his port bow, maybe fifty yards out. Nice plume it made. Where's the other? I don't see . . . by Georgie's broad belly, Cap'n, I believe the lads dropped that ball on his deck! There's a scramble there, an' they've opened some lanterns."

"Well done," Butler husked, nodding toward the gunners. "Would you wager you might do it again?"

"At the right odds, Cap'n." Terrence Boyd grinned. "Now, if we heated the balls first . . ."

"And set him afire?" Butler snapped. "I wish to annoy the

11

gentleman, Mister Boyd. Not burn his ship."

"Oh. Ah, aye, sir. Right. I kind of forgot there for a moment . . ."

"Just do it again, gentlemen, if you can."

"Aye, sir."

Again the twin nines thundered, this time bracketing the distant frigate with tiny-looking plumes of spray. They were doing no real damage, Butler knew. With nines, at such a range. . . .

"He's adding sail," Leech said. "I'd say he has decided to close and deal with us here and now."

"Very good." Butler nodded, turning away. In the fore, a distant voice was calling depths at intervals of a minute or so. And now a second voice, closer, began calling out the readings of log and line. *Pride of Falworth* was making five knots in four fathoms of water, the depth beneath her keel slowly decreasing.

"Trim all yards by the wind, please, Mister Leech," Butler ordered. "Go amidships and direct the helm from there." He peered across dark waters at the looming cay ahead. "The lads know now that we're coming, and bringing company with us. Bring us around the leeward shore, as we discussed, please."

"Aye, Cap'n."

"Send Mister Trahan aft to spell me on deck. I shall be below until we round the cay."

"Aye, sir."

In his little cabin belowdecks, John Shelby Butler closed his gallery shutters and removed the hood from an oil lamp. By its light he spread a chart on the table and traced patterns on it with his finger. The present course line had not been extended since a final daylight reading at eight bells—hours earlier. At that logging, *Pride* had been on course north, not yet in sight of the cays. She had been making six knots on a port reach, and the pirate vessel had been some five miles astern, hull down on clear waters.

Now with the cay dead ahead, he had no need of instruments to locate his course. He knew exactly where he was, and where he was going. Long months of careful planning and preparation were about to pay off.

The cay was inked-in on the chart, a bean-shaped little island with a sheltered cove on its north shore. Two previous courses

12

were marked on the same chart, both dated within the past three months. And both of those also had homed on the same little cay.

"Provisions," he muttered, tracing the first one. Then he moved his finger to the second. "And personnel."

Satisfied, he sat on the bench beneath his shuttered galleries and opened a bound-wood chest. Idly, a cold smile playing at his lips, he withdrew and unrolled a pair of ribboned foolscaps: his commission as a ship's master, issued by the Commonwealth of Virginia, and his charter as master of *Pride of Falworth*, issued by Squire Ian McCall, the vessel's owner. Rolled inside this second document were his standing orders as master, and his latest charge — to carry cargo to the Indies, execute trade on behalf of his sponsor, and then to return to Chesapeake.

A six-month cruise, at most . . . dated nearly a year ago.

One by one, he held the papers over the lamp's wick, then watched them as they burned to ashes. In his mind was the face of Ian McCall, the merchant-patriot. Butler smiled a frosty smile as he addressed the image. "You think me lost at sea, Squire? Have you set bounties yet, to reclaim your properties should they surface at the pirate ports? Have you set your trusted Evan to find me — or word of me — at all cost? I know you have done so, of course. After all, business is business, as I've heard you say so often."

On impulse he opened one of the shutters and looked astern at the dark sea, and the dark ship that rode there. It would do no harm now to show a bit of light to the brute, Thibaud. The pirate knew where he was, and was racing to overtake.

"I served you well, McCall," Butler muttered. "John Shelby Butler served you with honor, and you've turned a nice profit from my labors. Too much, for too long, for too little return. The times, they do change, Squire. Mayhap, if you'd been freer with bonuses now and again . . . mayhap if you'd seen fit to transfer title of my ship to me after six good voyages, as some wise owners have been known to do . . . then again, maybe nothing you could have done would have mattered. You've lost your ship, Squire, and you've lost your faithful captain. John Shelby Butler is no more, only Jack Shelby."

He put the chest away, stamped out the embers among the

13

ashes at his feet, put on a fresh coat, then donned his sword and buckler. Through the soles of his shoes he could feel *Pride* coming aport, swinging through the wind to slide past the little cay's hidden cove. He tensed slightly, enjoying the thrill of imminent action. The coming about would allow the pirate to come within easy gun range. Now everything depended upon *Pride's* playing the role of a surrendering ship—just long enough for *Valkyrie* to come abreast of that cove.

"What I do now is *my* business, Squire," he breathed. "And as you say, 'business is business.'" Hooding his lamp, John Shelby Butler closed the cabin, and Jack Shelby went on deck.

At first bell of the morning watch—half an hour after midnight—the private warship *Valkyrie* overhauled the merchant *Pride of Falworth* in shallows off the north shore of an unnamed cay, and fired across her, bow and stern. The merchant ship immediately lowered its colors and waved lanterns in signals of submission.

Less than eight minutes later, armed sailors aboard four stout launches—put out in secret from the cay—heaved grapples across *Valkyrie's* after rails and swarmed aboard, cutting down the surprised pirates who tried too late to defend their deck.

At second bell of the watch, Jack Shelby and his officers stepped aboard the marauder and took command. Standing on the pirate vessel's blood-slick deck, the man who had been John Shelby Butler had the pirate Thibaud brought before him. "Your career has ended, Thibaud," he announced. "*Valkyrie* is my ship now. I shall waste no time with you or your crew. You are at an end. You will be first, to set the rest an example in valiance if it pleases you to do so. How you take your death is up to you. I am master of *Valkyrie* now, and I warrant I can use her far better than ever you did."

Hard hands lifted Thibaud to his feet and dragged him to the starboard beam where he was doubled over the rail and held motionless. Timothy Leech did the honors, with a belaying pin from *Valkyrie's* fifes. With one well-placed blow he shattered the pirate's skull.

Then three by three, the remaining pirates were hauled to the lee rail and brained with clubs. Splash after splash echoed as their bodies followed that of their captain into the dark, voracious sea. Beyond could be heard the splash of oars where boats plied between ships.

"I can't say I relish the next part, Cap'n," Timothy Leech said as a dozen of their regulars put out in a launch to cross to *Pride of Falworth*.

"Nor do I, Mister Leech." Shelby shrugged. "Neither the men nor the ship. Still, it must be done as we have planned and no less. *Pride* must disappear for good, and we no longer have use for our temporaries, who have already seen far too much. Mister Strode has his orders, though, to make it clean and painless if he can."

Leech looked across at the silhouette of the merchant ship that he and the man beside him had sailed for so long. He felt no real regret, though. It was only a bark. "There's the cargo, as well," he muttered.

"Bales and odds," Shelby said. "Commodities. Too much trouble for what it's worth where we'll be dealing. The ship must be scuttled, and properly. Open a seam or two and let her drift toward the deeps. Nothing need ever be known of this night, Timothy, and best not. But there will be plenty of plunder for us elsewhere. We shall be rich men, Mister Leech . . . every man of us who survives."

"Aye, Cap'n."

"See to the finishing of this business, Mister Leech, then assemble hands for an inventory of *Valkyrie*. This is a fine ship, and we need to know her well."

"Aye, sir." Leech started away, then turned back and raised a big hand in grinning salute. "To piracy, Cap'n."

"Aye, Mister Leech." Jack Shelby nodded. "To piracy."

Aboard the bark, Mister Strode and his mates went about their tasks in businesslike fashion. While sounds of chopping and splintering rang from below decks, the "temporaries" were rounded up, then herded to leeward rails, and the slaughter that had been done aboard *Valkyrie* was repeated . . . this time upon surprised, innocent men. More corpses splashed into the dark sea.

When it was done, Strode looked around. "Was that the last of them, Mister Summers? The count should be eighteen."

Owen Summers shrugged. "I didn't count the buggers. I thought you were counting. But that was all of them."

Dickie Trice came from below. "Her seams are open, an' she's takin' water, Mister Strode. Slow an' steady, like you said."

"Then, let's get back to our new ship." Strode nodded. "We're out of the merchant business, lads. From now on, merchant-men are *our* business."

Two

She was a grim and furtive ship, creeping southward across the flowing gulf stream, avoiding the main shipping lanes and eschewing encounter of any sort. Though fully rigged and well-gunned, a cruiser of the class called snow, she played a hiding game in this season, for she had not the strength to challenge nor the manpower to defend. Her name was *Fury*, and the men aboard her numbered fewer than the guns at her ports — fewer even than the sails that her swift rigging could carry.

Fury was a fugitive ship, escaped from Crown custody and fair game for any vessel that might spot her. And those aboard her, though not a man of them had charges remaining against him — those who once had were now exonerated by proper court-martial conducted at sea — were fugitives as well because they had taken her and flown.

At first light of a clear morning *Fury's* foretopman spotted sails in the distance ahead. Sails odd-set and oddly abank, but sails nonetheless. He steadied himself on the snow's trestletrees and squinted, shading his eyes against the confusing light of the eastern sky to his left, then cupped his hands and called, "On deck!"

Amidships, Charley Duncan — first officer now by act of his captain — raised his eyes. "Yes, Mister Fisk?"

"Sail ahead, sir! Hard down a point on the starboard bow!"

Duncan glanced aft, where Victory Locke manned the helm. There was no one else on the little quarterdeck, and Duncan felt a stab of guilt. It was his watch, and that was where he belonged. But there were other things needing attended to,

17

and little enough time to do them. And now a sighting from the foretop. Duncan strode forward to the rise of the deck, where *Fury's* jaunty bowsprit grew from the planking. He peered into the distance ahead. Low mist obscured the sea from deck level. He turned, looking aloft where the form of Purdy Fisk was silhouetted against dawning sky, ninety feet above.

"What do you make her, Mister Fisk?"

"Hard to tell, sir!" the topman's voice floated down. "Might be a merchantman, but there's something amiss with her settings. She shows sail, but no handling. She looks adrift."

"Very well, Mister Fisk. Keep a good eye on her." Duncan hurried aft, where a half-dozen hammocks were slung along the rails. He tried to remember which of the off-watch might have had the most sleep, then gave up on it and went to the nearest one. The man in the hammock was snoring, and he shook him awake. "On your feet, Mister Quarterstone, if you please. We have sail ahead and need a second lookout."

Pliny Quarterstone sat up, rubbing bleary eyes with hard fists. "Fine thing," he grumbled, "waking a man from a dream like that."

"Like what?"

Quarterstone got to his feet, sighing as he came awake. "Oh, you know. Like that. What other kind is there when a man's been at sea for three months?"

"We haven't been at sea *all* that time," Duncan reminded him. "We did pay call at that island, if you recollect."

"But there wasn't anybody there, Mister Duncan, if *you* recollect. Just a bunch of goats. I'm not the sort of gentleman to dream like that about goats!"

Duncan nodded, understanding, then cocked a thumb toward the mainmast's soaring port stays. "Be that as it may, Mister Quarterstone, we need a second spotter aloft. Mister Fisk is watching a sail yonder, and we need someone to keep a sharp eye for any others."

Quarterstone stepped to the rail, swung up and around the after stay and set his feet on ratlines, nimble as a spider on a web, then hesitated. "We could do with a bit more help on this blessed barge, you know. Forty-five ables is fit complement for a snow. Not fifteen."

Having spoken his mind to the morning, the sailor swarmed aloft, climbing like a monkey to disappear into the intricate silhouettes of the maintops.

There was a chuckle at Duncan's shoulder, and the first officer turned, coming to attention. Patrick Dalton stood there, tall and tired-looking in the gray light. Duncan hadn't heard the captain's approach.

"Morning, sir," Duncan started. "Mister Quarterstone is only a bit out of sorts, is all. He was a'bunk just—"

"I understand," Dalton cut him off, looking aloft. "And he's right, of course. We do need more crew. There is a limit to what the best of men can perform. What is the sighting?"

"Sail, sir. Ahead and a point astarboard. Can't make much of it yet.

"Whereaway?"

"Hard down, Mister Fisk said. Just tops in sight. Maybe twelve miles or so?"

"A fair guess, depending upon the size of the vessel. Can he read it?"

"He isn't sure, sir. May be a merchantman, but he says it looks askew and drifting."

Dalton nodded. "I see Mister Locke is alone at the helm."

"Aye, sir." Duncan scuffed a shoe in embarrassment. "All's been quiet, sir, and I was takin' the time to splice some line. We're down to pickings in the lockers."

"Very well, Mister Duncan. I realize our condition. We'll have to make port soon, no matter who's looking for us. But please take the deck now. I shall relieve you at the bell, and you can have your breakfast."

"Aye, sir. Goat again, sir?"

"Don't think on it, Mister Duncan. Pretend it's partridge. It helps."

"Aye, sir. Although with Mister Wise on galley duty, even partridge might taste like goat."

Duncan headed aft, and Dalton looked around him at the deck of his ship, stifling a sigh. Almost three months had passed since *Fury*'s escape from a Crown escort . . . and from the humiliation of a custody flag atop her lanyard.

Escape had meant freedom. But it also had meant that *Fury*

19

was once again a fugitive ship, fair game for any man-of-war who cared to take her as a prize. The snow had no proper credentials now, no flag to fly and few enough friends to turn to. With a crew of fifteen — barely enough men to handle her sails, much less to work stations in an engagement of any sort — the snow had gone to ground in a manner of speaking. For a time at least, Dalton had no option but to run and hide, to stay far out to sea and scavenge for provisions where they could be found, to avoid contact with anyone. Because anyone — for a small, undermanned warship with scant supplies and no flag — could be the enemy.

Striding the foredeck for a moment, Dalton spied the morning. He would have course reports from Charley Duncan at the turn of watch; but he knew where they were, and he knew — from the feel of the ship, the sounds of its high sails and the song of the sea — their direction and speed. *Fury* was, as mariners in these waters termed it, "in the trough." South of the great Atlantic lanes, north a bit of the slave lanes, and making four or five knots on a steady starboard tack. Somewhere ahead were islands — some part of that great chain of countless land masses that were the Baja Mars . . . or Bahamas . . . the Antilles and the Indies. Somewhere ahead were a thousand opportunities to make landfall.

It would soon be time to make a decision. *Fury* had avoided social contact as long as was practical. Dalton had need of men, provisions, stores, tackle . . . he needed everything, and that meant he needed a place to put in, a place to do business one way or another.

At the stem of the snow's towering foremast, he looked aloft and called, "Report your sighting, Mister Fisk!"

From high above the voice came. "Aye, sir. It's a ship, sir. Still hull down, but I see sails. May be a four-master, sir. Like a bark or such, though it's hard to make out."

"What is it doing, Mister Fisk?"

"It's just . . . there, sir. Not doin' anything as I can see. It's heeled a bit on the wind, but its sails are askew. I think it's just driftin', sir."

Dalton walked the fifteen paces aft to the base of the snow's doubled mainmast — actually two masts rigged in tandem, the

20

big mainmast towering aloft with its three spanning yards, and just aft of it a smaller upright called a trysail standard or jack-mast, which carried the gaff for the ship's big fore-and-aft drive sail, the spanker.

Again Dalton called aloft, "Maintop ahoy!"

Pliny Quarterstone's voice came down. "Maintop aye, sir!"

"Report, maintop."

"Aye, sir. Nothin' in sight on any quarter, except Mister Fisk's bark, sir. A fine clear mornin', an' except for that one we have the ocean all to ourselves . . . sir."

Dalton growled slightly, then shook his head. Now was not the time to berate a man for flippancy. Not a man aboard had managed more than two hours' sleep at a stretch in months, and they were all a bit vague from fatigue. Still, as one who had come up amidships on vessels of the king, it was ingrained in Patrick Dalton that discipline was essential to the handling of a ship. He made a point—had always made a point, when he thought of it—of not tolerating laxity aboard his ship.

Or so he was fond of saying, at any rate.

He shrugged it off. "You're fresh in the tops, Mister Quarterstone. Do you have anything to add to Mister Fisk's report?"

"Ah . . . no, sir. It's just as he said. A square-sailer, looks to be bark-rigged, still hull down, though her courses are in sight. Sails a'shamble an' just driftin' on the tide. I wager she's derelict, sir. Nobody yonder is handlin' sail or rudder."

Dalton turned away, thoughtful. Derelict? Maybe abandoned? A ship of that nature adrift out here with no hand at her helm? It was possible. For three years, the waters of the north Atlantic had been alive with conflict—His Majesty's Royal Navy trying to contain the myriad privateers and letters-of-marque set loose by the rebellious American colonies, colonial against Crown, privateer against whoever got in the way, and more than a few outright pirates feeding off the chaos.

There might be a lost ship adrift in these waters. Or it could be a decoy—bait for someone's trap.

He ran thoughtful fingers along the varnished surface of the jack-mast, admiring its architecture. An American innovation, and one the British had yet to understand. In many respects, the snow resembled an armed brig—a smallish

21

warship, a cruiser and seeker. But the snow was no brig. The Americans had improved upon the brig design — given it a new mast configuration and a deeper, stronger hull to balance increased weight of sail. With long legs and sharp teeth, American-built snows had repeatedly surprised the planners of British strategy.

Though less than a full frigate, *Fury* was far more than a brig — and *Fury* was his. By right of salvage, by right of recovery, by right of prize or right of possession . . . by whatever right it took, *Fury* was Patrick Dalton's ship. His honor and the ship's honor were intact, and she was *his*.

The bane of the Irish, he thought sardonically. The sheer, hardheaded, arrogant Gaelic pride of the black Irish, that when a man won a thing of value it was his. Not the king's, not the Admiralty's, not some colonial claimant's, but his. *I am black Irish, God help me,* he thought. *I acquired this ship fairly and fully, and nothing means more to me than my ship, at my command.*

Well, almost nothing, he corrected himself, thinking — as he always did, it seemed — of Constance Ramsey. *Fury* was not, he admitted, more important to him than John Singleton Ramsey's auburn-haired daughter.

But in the way of the black Irish, he balanced the two devotions and found no need for choices. And with Gaelic honesty he admitted to himself that what he intended — though what the goal might require was yet a mystery — was to have both.

"Keep a sharp eye about us, lads," he called aloft. "For in this time and this place we surely have no friends."

He started aft, hesitating as the companionway hatch banged open and Billy Caster hurled himself up the ladder to the deck, his eyes wide and his hair tousled. Panting, the youth peered at the quarterdeck, then turned. Dalton stifled a grin and said, "At ease, Mister Caster. If it's me you seek, I'm right here."

The youth sighed his relief. "Aye, Captain. Beg pardon, but I thought I'd overslept again, and . . ."

"I'd hardly call two hours of sleep 'oversleeping,' Billy." Dalton shook his head. "Yes, I know you were afoot through the night doing inventory and logs. Have you had your breakfast?"

"No, sir." Billy cleared his throat, trying to control a voice that had an embarrassing tendency to break into adolescent falsetto. "I was in a hurry, sir."

"Obviously. Very well, Mister Caster, I am about to relieve Mister Duncan. You can stand reports with me, then go below and get some of Mister Wise's smoked goat and biscuit. There has been a sighting ahead, but nothing interesting is likely to occur for at least two hours."

"Aye, sir."

At five bells of the morning watch — with only fifteen souls on board, *Fury* had given up all semblance of civilized eight-bell duties, and every man aboard was doing watch and watch — Patrick Dalton assumed the quarterdeck, relieved Charley Duncan and set Claude Mallory to the helm. *Fury* was on course due south, making a sedate four knots on jib, jigger and topsails, and there were no sightings except for the drifting vessel eleven miles out and now dead ahead.

"I believe we must have a look at the stranger," Dalton decided. "Mister Mallory, steer two points to port if you please. The lads coming up from galley can trim sail accordingly. Mister Duncan, your watch can rest, but rest wary. Should this seem a trap or a decoy, we may need to make all sail smartly."

"Aye, sir."

"Mister Caster, have you noted course and intercept orders?"

"Aye, sir."

"How do you read the day, Mister Caster?"

It was an old game that the captain played with his clerk, and Billy had long since grown accustomed to it. Irish or not, navy or not, Patrick Dalton was a British officer to the bone in many ways. And having no complement of midshipmen to instruct, it fell to Billy to be instructed in the ways of navigation and the ways of the sea.

He looked at the sky, and at the few sails braced to the wind. "Wind is westerly and a bit north, sir, at eighteen to twenty knots. A clear day with high clouds on the west quarter, and the sea is running nor'easterly at two knots."

"Very good." Dalton nodded. "And how shall the day make?"

"Rising wind by midday, sir, and clouds overhead. The sea will run more then, because we shall be farther into the stream."

"If the vessel ahead of us is truly adrift on shrift sail, and we steer two degrees east of south, then when will we intercept it?"

Billy hesitated, calculating, then said, "Seven bells of the watch, sir, though we'll be looking at her escutcheons half a glass shy of that."

Dalton nodded again. "Go below and have breakfast, Mister Caster. And try not to think of it as smoked goat. Perhaps roast pork with applesauce would be a helpful fiction."

"Is Mister Wise still in the galley, sir?"

"He is."

"Then, fiction or not, it is still smoked goat."

At just past six bells of the watch *Fury* crept to within a mile of the derelict — for derelict it seemed to be.

A four-master, bark-rigged with a few flapping and luffing sails open upon its yards and no hand at the rudder, the ship drifted askew on the current and leaned astarboard with its wales on that side barely four feet above the cresting waters.

From *Fury*'s little quarterdeck, Patrick Dalton studied the vessel through a telescoping glass, puzzled. Not a hole or a tear showed in hull or sail, not a sign of combat anywhere, but there she drifted. An abandoned ship slowly taking the sea into her holds, she crept sideways across endless ocean, and not a man could be seen anywhere aboard her.

"Odd," he mused. "She has her boats and her tiers, and nothing seems missing from her deck. Her bow anchors hang a-cock-bill, but they are there, at the catheads." He lowered the glass. "Hands a'deck," he ordered. "Tops keep a weather eye about, and let us have the fore portside guns at the ready. We shall approach for boarding."

At three cable lengths the merchantman's escutcheons were clearly visible, and Dalton's memory tugged at him. *Fury* carried no ship's registry, but the vessel there was one he had seen before, somewhere.

Her name was *Pride of Falworth*.

Three

The merchantman had been hull-scuttled, though sloppily in the opinion of Ishmael Bean, who seemed to know more than the average able seaman about such larcenies.

"Had it been me set to scuttle this bucket, sir," Bean assured Patrick Dalton, "she'd have been awash to the scuppers before a man could say 'God save the king,' an' I'd have put her down by the bow or stern, whichever pleased them as gave the orders. From th' looks of things below, though, I'd say what these blokes did was just to prize up a brace of bilge stringers an' drive a splittin' maul between some hull timbers in the keel. Amateur work, sir, as I sees it."

"Still, she would have sunk, eventually, it seems," Dalton pointed out.

"Oh, aye, sir, eventually. As it is, she's shipped water up to her knees, so we can't see very much down there. But Mister Locke, he tripped over a bit of flotsam below deck an' kind of fell in, so we had him feel around a bit down there before we hoisted him out. He says he believes the parting of the timbers has been punched full of cotton, as though someone tried to patch her, sir."

"Patched?"

"Aye, sir. What he said."

"Where is Mister Locke, Mister Bean?"

"Forward, sir. Mister Hoop is danglin' him by the heels to drain bilgewater out of him."

Dismissing the tar, Dalton continued his tour of the merchantman's deck. *Pride of Falworth* was in excellent condition,

25

considering that she had been obviously abandoned, hull-vented and left to sink. Her decks and fixtures were in service-able order, masts and rigging seemed sound and all the accouterments of a working vessel—at least all those visible from the deck, hold hatches and companionway—were present and stowed in orderly fashion. And there was considerable cargo below, bales of cotton visible through the hatches, with no apparent sign of having been vandalized.

The ship obviously had not been looted, and there were no signs of a fight. *Pride* was in every respect a taut and ready sailing vessel, from her varnished sternpost and fresh-painted jib to her suit of sails aloft. Yet here she was, far from the shipping lanes, adrift in mid-ocean, and someone had opened her seams below.

Mutiny? He wondered. Such was not uncommon aboard the long-haul merchantmen of the time. Crewmen driven by too harsh a master or kept for too long on short rations had been known to stage mutiny in retaliation. A crew with a leader and a plan might well overpower the officers of a vessel and take charge. But what then? Why scuttle a good ship with valuable cargo aboard?

To destroy the evidence? Possible, he thought. Possible, but unlikely. Much more likely that the culprits would set sail for a barter port where they might find a buyer for an unregistered vessel and its cargo . . . or for an island somewhere, or at least for a shore where they could land and vanish.

Piracy, then? He looked around him, doubting. The ship had been neither shelled nor boarded in force. There had been no battle here. There were no signs of attack and defense. And *had* a pirate somehow taken the ship without violence, then why was it not now headed for some trading lair? Why scuttle and abandon?

He walked to *Pride*'s starboard bulwark, swung over to her mainstay channel and leapt across to *Fury*'s portside shrouds. With light seas, the ships were lashed alongside, separated only by dangling coils of heavy cable to serve as fenders. Snugged together so, the big four-master towering over the small warship, the two vessels might have appeared almost as a mother and child, but the appearance was deceiving.

Though by far the smaller of the two, the snow was a warship, built and equipped for the chase and the kill, while the bark was only a bark—a vessel with holds for goods and sails to carry them from place to place.

Charley Duncan came to meet him, and Dalton glanced toward the snow's tops. "All clear, Mister Duncan?"

"Not a sight nor a sign, sir. We've this part of the world all to ourselves for a time, it seems."

"Very well." Dalton nodded. "Go across, Mister Duncan. The bark has a hole in its hull, but it can be fothered for a time with sailcloth and tar. I've set Mister Caster to an inventory of stores, beginning with the galley. If we find some decent provisions there, possibly Mister Wise can prepare something tastier than goat for us, to fortify us in our labors. You shall want the bark's pumps rigged, and eight men to man them—four on and four off—until we can inspect the holds. Once we raise the merchantman's main wales above sea level, I believe we can set some of her sails and be under way."

Duncan stared at him, stunned. "Sails? Sir, do you intend to take the bark with us, to . . . to man it and sail it?"

"I do, Mister Duncan. Right of salvage. I believe providence has handed us an answer to some of our problems."

"Aye, sir. Some of them. But who's going to sail the ship, sir? I mean, there are only fifteen of us, and we can barely manage *Fury,* not to mention a second ship . . . and a four-master at that."

"I believe we shall devise a way, Mister Duncan."

"Aye, sir. But . . . well, I don't see how you are going to—"

"Oh, I'm not going to sail the bark, Mister Duncan. You are."

Through the hours of a waning day they labored, pumping seawater from the bark's hull, locating and transferring stores, and perfecting the "fothering" on *Pride's* hull—an awkward but serviceable bandage over her hidden wound, fashioned by lashing a spare topsail to her hull with lines running beneath her keel and secured to the chain plates on each side. Drawn tight with handclamps, these lines secured the sail to the wide hull as though it were a bit of the ship's skin. And when the water level was down to the bilges within, a ring wall of coiled

27

hemp was secured on the inner surfaces around the hole, and the cavity pumped dry so that hot tar could be packed into the broken seams.

The westering sun was low on the horizon by the time this was finished, and Dalton crossed over again to the bark to inspect.

"It isn't a pretty repair," he decided. "But it will hold for a time until we find a place to do it better."

"I still don't see how—" Charley Duncan began, then stopped as a muffled clamor erupted belowdeck, sounds of shouting, scuffling and a pair of screams coming from the bark's forward hold. The men on deck turned to look, and Billy Caster hurried past, his ever-present inventory list clutched in his hand. Victory Locke's head popped from the open hatch, and he waved for attention.

"Hoy!" the tar shouted. "We can use some hands down here, lively-like. Mister Hoop's found somethin' new!"

Billy Caster arrived at the transom just ahead of Dalton and—Duncan, and squinted at his list, then down at Victory Locke. "We've inspected every compartment, Mister Locke. What else did he find?"

"In the chain locker," Locke said as further commotion erupted below. "Mister Hoop was—well, it just occurred to him to have a look there, an' sure enough . . ."

Sounds of a struggle floated up from the cargo hatch, and Locke looked around, then ducked out of sight.

"Mister Locke!" Dalton roared.

The tar appeared again, looking abashed. "Aye, sir?"

"What has Mister Hoop found?"

"Well, sir, so far I believe there's a pot of boiled peas, some biscuit, a keg or two that might be rum, an' two frogs."

"Frogs?"

"Aye, sir, a pair of 'em, an' frisky, too, though . . . ah—" The noise below suddenly stilled, and Locke ducked away, then reappeared. "All under control, sir. Mister Hoop has got the frogs quieted down."

Locke looked around again, then eased aside, and Mister Hoop appeared in his place, head and shoulders almost filling the near end of the forward cargo hatch. If Mister Hoop had a first name, none aboard knew what it was. Mister Hoop was twice the size of most sailors and, though generally docile, was not one that anyone—short of Dalton himself and possibly Duncan—cared to take a chance of riling.

The big man was laden now, by the grin on his homely face and the inert men slung one over each of his massive shoulders. At sight of the captain, he hesitated, then said apologetically, "Hope you don't mind, sir, but I had to rap these gentlemen on their heads. Otherwise it didn't seem like they was willing to come out of the chain locker."

Having spoken his piece, Hoop flipped the unconscious men up and out of the hold, depositing them more or less gently upon the deck.

Locke reappeared then, beside the giant. "I'm certain they're frogs, sir. I don't know what they was hollerin' about, but I know French when I hear it."

Dalton nodded, and squatted beside the two unconscious men, looking them over. Both were dishevelled and rank, dressed in filthy clothing, both unshaven and both obviously sailors by the horny calluses on their hands, the corded muscles of their forearms and the buckle shoes on their feet.

"What were they doing in the chain locker?" Dalton asked.

Hoop shrugged massive shoulders. "From the looks of it, sir, I'd say they've been livin' there, though the good Lord knows a chain locker's no fit place for man nor beast. Why, supposin' you'd decided to drop anchor, sir, these two would have been—"

"I know what occurs in a chain locker, Mister Hoop."

"Aye, sir. I took it on myself to remove them, sir, but I'll be glad to put them back if the cap'n says . . ."

"Never mind, Mister Hoop. You did the right thing."

Hoop blushed with huge pleasure. "Aye, sir. Thank ye, sir." He stepped down into the hold again, then started passing up other items as Victory Locke handed them to him below: a stained pot partially filled with what appeared to be boiled peas, a pair of rum kegs followed by another keg with its bung knocked out—he sniffed at this one, then handed it up. "Rum, sir," he said.

Dalton leaned to smell the breaths of the two unconscious

men, then straightened and shook his head. "It's a wonder these two were conscious when you rapped them, Mister Hoop."

The big man tossed a pile of filthy blankets out of the hold, then a pair of empty kegs and another partially filled one, and finally several tins of sealed biscuit and some empty tins. "Looks like they been there for a while, sir. An' they've had candles, too. Lucky they didn't burn the ship, the shape they're in."

Dalton stood and turned away. "Lay out a bit of bedding amidships and put these men there for now," he said. "We'll sort this out later. Mister Caster, is your inventory complete?"

"Aye, sir. I think it is now."

"You may log the entries 'in fine' at another time, then. For now, simply state in *Fury*'s log that as of this date and this time we have found, secured, inventoried and taken into our possession one four-masted bark and its cargoes and stores, as claimants under Article the Ninth of the Standards for International Commerce."

"Aye, sir. Ah . . . that means salvage, doesn't it, sir?"

"It does. Do you have a question of propriety, Mister Caster?"

The boy frowned, then nodded. "Yes, sir. I believe you instructed me once, sir, that 'salvage' applies to a vessel or contents found sunken or aground and having neither claimants aboard nor a claim flag or keg attached."

"I see no claim flags or floating kegs, Mister Caster."

"No, sir. But the vessel is neither sunken nor aground."

"No, it is neither." Dalton cocked a brow at the youngster. "Therefore, Mister Caster, what would *you* say is our justification for claiming right of salvage?"

Billy thought it over for a moment, then asked, "Because it has been scuttled, sir?"

"Very shaky justification, Mister Caster. Can you elaborate a bit?"

The boy screwed up his face in furious thought, then grinned. "Scuttled and adrift . . . we assume it has been sunken or aground, and was abandoned, then either raised itself or floated off due to natural causes."

30

"Very good," Dalton nodded. "Excellent. List it so, please."

"Aye, sir." Billy wrote one word on his notations: flotsam.

With the clerk padding along behind him, Dalton strode aft to the bark's sterncastle and called for assembly. When the dozen *Furies* aboard were gathered before him, he said, "Gentlemen, we have claimed this vessel as our rightful prize under the standards of salvage. Now we need to take it to a place where we can do something with it. Mister Duncan will be in command of the prize crew."

"Aye, sir," Duncan agreed, looking worried. "Ah, pardon, sir, but how many men can you spare for a prize crew? We're a bit short-handed, it seems to me."

"We are indeed. Therefore your crew will be limited."

"Aye, sir. Who will they be?"

"They will be Mister Hoop. He and yourself will have to manage, by the helm on set sails, and we must hope the wind doesn't change for the next two days."

"Two of us, sir?"

"You have permission to sign those French gentlemen on as crew when they are able. That will make four. We shall cast loose *Fury* on a hawser, long enough for the setting of sails on the bark. I think forward courses and jibs will be sail enough, with the spanker at mizzen to assist the rudder. The rest of us will return to *Fury* then and follow along for a day or two. We should sight land in that time."

"Aye, sir." Duncan continued to look dubious; but he squared his shoulders in readiness, and Dalton nodded. The sandy-haired sailor was a scoundrel, a known thief and a practicing ne'er-do-well; but he was a first-rate seaman for all that, and Dalton was proud of him.

In the assembly, a tenuous hand was raised, and Dalton turned to its owner. "Yes, Mister Mallory?"

"Might I ask where we're bound, sir?"

"Landward, Mister Mallory. Due south or as nearly so as we can manage with two undermanned vessels. Two days of fair sailing with the wind we presently have should bring us within sight of some of the islands. It's a bit hard to say which islands, exactly, but there are quite a number of them."

They all stared at him blankly, astounded to hear such imprecision from the man they had all come to realize seldom made mistakes and almost never left his reckoning to chance. Of the thirteen able seamen and one clerk at Patrick Dalton's command, seven had sailed with him from the moment of that now-legendary escape from New York Harbor aboard a requisitioned trade schooner named *Faith*. . . . now no more than a shattered hulk lying in shipyards at South Point on the Delaware. Of the remaining seven, four had been with him when he turned almost certain defeat at the hands of Spanish pirates into a victory, and captured the jaunty snow, *Fury*. And all of them had seen him tack the snow into a black squall to evade the guns of a seventy-four-gun man-of-war . . . and then escape once again, this time from the very heart of a flotilla of king's vessels. They knew Patrick Dalton as a fighting seaman, a crafty strategist and as a master mariner.

But then, as every man of them realized, precision navigation was unlikely in the circumstances. They would do their best to trim the bark's forecourses for a southward course on a westering wind, but once trimmed the only corrections possible for those left aboard—even if Duncan could get the Frenchies to help—would be by shifting the spanker and by sheer brawn at the helm.

As the final trim was sheeted in on the *Pride*'s forward courses, Charley Duncan and Mister Hoop watched from the bark's sternrail as Dalton and the rest put out by launch to return to *Fury*.

"Bedammed if I don't miss those Americans we had with us before," Duncan muttered. "Bless his colonial heart, even Michael Romart would be a comfort about now—though I've sworn at times that his devilin' tongue would drive me past all tolerance."

"Aye," Hoop rumbled, setting his great shoulders to the tug of the helm. "But Cap'n had to put them off when he did, you know. Otherwise they'd have been took as rebels when we had our court-martial."

"It was *his* court-martial, Mister Hoop. Captain Dalton's. Not ours. He saw we were cleared before ever he went before the magistrates."

"But I testified, I did," Hoop pointed out, proud as a peacock of having stood before senior officers of the Royal Navy, in the great gallery of a ship of the line.

"I just wish we had those Americans back." Duncan sighed.

The helm bucked on a wave, and Hoop's big hands fought the spokes. "I wish we had just about *anybody*, right now, sir."

Four

As fair light of evening colored the great sails of a mismatched pair of ships bound southward beyond the Gulf currents, an entirely different scene was unfolding twelve hundred miles away, above Baltimore at an estate called Eagle's Head. A great coach with four matched bays came to a noisy halt in the curve of the gravel drive, and its right side door swung open. Without waiting for his footman to place a stepping bench, the merchant-patriot Ian McCall sprang to the ground and strode away across tended lawns. At the main house he took the wide porch steps two at a time, brushed past a bowing gardener and pounded at the wide doors, scowling mightily.

After a moment he pounded again, then dropped his arm when the door swung inward and a dark face above a starched collar peered at him. The servant blinked; then his eyes widened. "Why, Mist' Ian! Squire didn' say you was comin' to—"

"Never mind, Colly," McCall growled. He stepped past the old man and went in. "I shall announce myself. Where is he?"

"He . . . uh . . . why, he in the study, Mist'—"

An interior door opened, and a ruddy face appeared, squinting over wire-rimmed spectacles. "Here now! What's all this? Ah! Ian! By heaven, I hadn't expected you, sir, but welcome! Come in and—but you already are in, aren't you? Well, come and sit with me in the study, then. Colly, take Squire McCall's—"

"Where is your daughter, John?" McCall snapped, brush-

34

ing aside the civilities.

John Singleton Ramsey blinked at him, surprised. "Constance?"

"Of course, Constance!" McCall's voice was a growl. "How many daughters have you, sir? Where the devil is she?"

"Only one, mercifully," Ramsey assured his guest, taking the questions in order. "And as to her whereabouts . . ." He shrugged, then glanced past McCall. "Colly, do you know where Miss Constance might have gone?"

"Not exac'ly, sah." Colly shrugged, closing the main door. "Maybe out to visit somebody. She had that Dora send a boy for her carriage; then they gone off."

"Well, I'm certain she won't be gone long, then," Ramsey assured McCall. "Come in and tell me what's—"

"When did they leave?" McCall asked the servant.

Colly frowned, thinking, then raised his eyes. "I b'lieve that was Tuesday, sah."

Ramsey gaped at Colly. "Tuesday? Do you mean to tell me my daughter has been gone for three days?"

"Yes, sah. I b'lieve that's right."

"Aha!" McCall snorted. Hands on hips, he glared at Ramsey. "I suppose it is unlikely, then, that you know where she might have taken my construction crew."

Ramsey stared at him. "Your . . . construction crew?"

"Precisely. Six carpenters, several riggers and a hoist designer. The crew I set to build my new warehouse and loading docks, at South Point. Damn it, man, I have schedules to keep, you know!"

"Schedules . . ."

"Of course, schedules! Within the month, Clinton will withdraw his bedammed redcoats and hessians from Philadelphia, and the last fleet tenders will be off the Delaware. I'm moving all my commodity operations up from Chesapeake— I already told you that—and I count on having facilities to handle my cargoes when they arrive. And now this!"

"This?" Ramsey looked blank. "What?"

"Devil take it, John, I just told you! I came up from Fairleah just this morning, expecting to find my crew putting finishing touches on my warehouse. But what did I find instead? Nothing! Shingles lying about still in their bales and nobody at work. No one even *there* except my watchmen."

Ramsey adjusted his glasses. "And why is that, Ian?"

"Because my construction crew has been taken away," Mc-Call growled. "Because your daughter, Miss Constance Ramsey, came to South Point and . . . and borrowed them."

"Why would she do that?" Ramsey wondered. "For that matter, *how* would she do that?"

"How does your daughter do anything she does? She just does it . . . did it . . . damn it, John, a person doesn't just borrow a man's construction crew . . . I mean, just walk in and *borrow* an entire crew, as casually as one might borrow dried apples from a neighbor! It's . . . well, one just doesn't."

"You're upset, Ian," Ramsey said sympathetically. Taking the taller man's arm, he urged him toward the study door. "Come in and sit down. We'll get to the bottom of this. Colly, bring us rum and well water, unless Squire McCall would prefer brandy to grog. Would you prefer brandy, Ian? Come, let me help you off with your coat. That's the way . . ."

One of the tastes that John Singleton Ramsey had acquired from the young man he sometimes referred to as "Constance's Irish fox," was a partiality to a beverage seldom found in the finer houses of the colonies. Commonly called "grog," the beverage was nothing more than a mix of rum and water. A specialty of low taverns and waterfront dens, it was largely unknown to the gentry . . . unless they had been associating with sailors.

Ramsey, though, had found that he enjoyed the heady drink, and was doing his part to educate his peers on the matter.

"Two-water grog," he said, carefully mixing a second round for himself and McCall. "A bit of this sometimes can cut through the confusions of life and give a man better insight with which to resolve his riddles. Drink this down, Ian. It will clear your head."

"My head is perfectly clear," McCall snorted. "It's my finances I worry about . . . and the nature of my friends. Thank you, I will have another. Do you realize, John, that having you as a friend—and your daughter, of course—has so

36

far cost me in excess of eight thousand pounds sterling, not to—"

"I thought you swore off British standards, Ian."

"I did, except when I become rattled. Your friendship has cost me a good forty thousand dollars, in less than two years. Ever since your daughter took up with that wild Irishman . . ."

"Dalton," Ramsey said mildly. "Patrick X. Dalton. He has a name, and it should be used."

"Many's the time I've heard you call him 'that wild Irishman,' John."

"That's beside the point. You were saying . . . ?"

"Yes. Just the value of that armed snow that he took from me . . ."

"We've been over that before, Ian." Ramsey shrugged, shaking his head. "You did not lose *Fury* to Patrick Dalton. You lost *Fury* to Spanish pirates. Young Dalton acquired the ship that he has by taking it away from Spanish pirates. All perfectly respectable, you know."

"But it's the same ship!" McCall's stubborn jaws clenched. "I owned that ship! I paid to build it and outfit it as a privateer! Now he has it, and he refuses to return it to me."

"Why should he, Ian? It *is* his ship, by rights."

"There's more than one would dispute that, sir. From the talk coming out of New York, there are some Royal Navy folk who'd sail a long way off course for the chance to bring Patrick Dalton under their guns. Nor can I say I blame them, considering what he did."

Ramsey pursed his lips. "The way I hear it, the young man did nothing more than arrange a court-martial for himself to clear his name of that ridiculous charge of treason."

"Oh, aye," McCall agreed. "Reclaimed his honor, he did. Then went sailing off with a ship that wore a custody flag."

"He did no such thing! That custody flag was delivered to Fleet Headquarters along with all the reports. My best spies saw it there with their own eyes."

"But the ship wasn't delivered! Dalton escaped with it!"

"Of course he did." Ramsey smiled. "Quite a piece of doing, that must have been, getting off with an undermanned snow right under the guns of five or six of the Royal Navy's best . . . and at least two of them were seventy-fours, by God! *Cornwall* and *Royal Lineage*—two of the Admiralty's finest! But I am assured he wore no custody flag when he escaped. That would hardly have been the honorable thing to do."

"Honorable!" McCall snorted. "Right this minute your *honorable* Irishman is sailing about somewhere in *my ship!*"

"*His* ship," Ramsey corrected, mixing more grog.

Distantly, they heard the knocker of the main door, but Ramsey ignored it. Colly would attend to it. "And as to your missing constructors, Ian, I'm sure they haven't gone far."

"They are with your daughter," McCall growled. "They could be anywhere. Patrick Henry was right, by God! 'Let us look to our domiciles for the fruits of our actions,' he said. 'Like ourselves who seek self-determination, the ladies, too, have minds of their own.' "

"I never heard him say that."

"Well, he did. *I* heard him."

"Be that as it may, Constance may be a bit of a firebrand, but she isn't likely to lead your men far astray."

"Oh? And how many of *your* men went with her when she sailed off to New York Harbor to bomb British ships?"

"That was a different matter entirely. She went there to bring back my schooner, *Faith,* that some blaggard Georgie stole from the very docks at South Point."

"Oh, of course. And did you get your schooner back, then, sir?"

"You know very well I did not! That bedammed Dalton refurbished it as a bloody warship, and beat it to death sinking a frigate. Now nothing will do for Constance but that I build another one just like it."

"Yes, I've seen your pet project on the ways at South Point. Imagine, fighting tops on a schooner! Quite unusual, I must say."

"It's Constance's doing. She insists that the new *Faith* be identical to the old one. Lot of bother and extra expense, but I expect I can find a way to turn a profit with it."

"Smuggling?" McCall cast a knowing glance at Ramsey.

"Privateering, rather. Smuggling's . . . ah, that is, *free cargo-*

ing is a flat business these days. The war and all, you know. Little enough profit to be had from an enterprise that every man jack with a jolly boat has got into. Far better fortunes to be made in privateering . . . as you of all people have demonstrated, Ian."

The expression on McCall's face changed from skepticism to a sardonic grin. "Privateering. So we may finally see the great—and uncommitted—John Singleton Ramsey . . ."

The study door opened, and Colly came in, carrying a sheaf of papers. Ramsey beckoned him to approach and glanced at the documents. "What's this?"

"Requisitions, sah. Gent'man from South Point say he needs for you to sign them."

"Very well," Ramsey sighed. He uncapped his inkwell, found a fresh quill and scrawled his signature on the requisition lists: John Singleton Ramsey, Esq.

He blotted and dusted the fresh ink, and handed the papers back to Colly, who left the study, closing the door behind him. Ramsey reached for the grog. "Now, Ian. You were saying . . . ?"

"To commission a privateer, John, you must first decide whose side of this blasted war you're on. I have never seen a man so adept at avoiding commitment."

"I'm as committed as any man!" Ramsey snapped.

"You are?" McCall's voice was bland. "One foot on either side of every fence. Do you call that committed?"

"It isn't a question of commitment, Ian, and you very well know it. It isn't always politic to go blithering about shouting 'Down with the king,' you know. I do my bit for the cause, just as you do. It's only that I dislike making a public issue of my private leanings. I—"

Abruptly, Ramsey stopped talking, turned away and stared at his inkwell. "Wait a moment, now," he said.

It was McCall's turn to look blank. "What's the matter?"

"Those documents I just signed. Those were requisitions for marine outfitting and stores. What vessel am I outfitting in this season?"

"You have your schooner, John. The new *Faith*. We were only now discussing it."

"But that schooner isn't ready for outfitting. I don't even have a finishing crew on that job . . ." he paused, then turned to look sheepishly at Ian McCall. "Something tells me," he said, "that I know where my daughter has gone . . . and where your carpenters and riggers are, as well."

Several miles away, at South Point, a brawny young man hopped down from the rear of a trundling wood-cart, tipped his tricorn hat to the driver and said, "Blessings on you for the ride, sir!" The wood-cart went on its way, and the young man replaced his hat atop a brown mane tied back in an unkempt queue, straightened his worn coat and glanced around in the evening light. In the near distance were shipyards, some backed by mould lofts, sheds, cooperages, smithies and all the other appurtenances of a place where stout ships were assembled for the sea. Beyond, the Delaware River flowed wide and dark.

It took only a moment for his eyes to lock on the sight he had come to see. In the largest of the shipyards there, a sleek, deep-keeled hull stood tall on stanchions, two towering masts rising above its silhouette — masts with wide spars cleated into position aloft, seeming to be slim wings above the tapering traceries of shrouds and ratlines, stays and tackle.

He took a deep breath which caught in his throat for a moment, then whispered, *"Faith."*

It wasn't really *Faith*, of course. Not the *Faith* he had known — the *Faith* aboard which he and a handful of other Virginians had joined with a fugitive British officer and a flock of escaped English tars on a wild night in New York Harbor . . . joined forces in a common cause, to escape from the very heart of His Majesty's White Fleet.

He shifted his gaze to the right. No, there was that *Faith* . . . or what was left of her. A shattered, broken hulk lying on the flats, mostly dismantled now and seeming only a montage of wreckage. All that was left of a proud, jaunty lady of a ship that had bested the best that was thrown against her.

And yet . . . he looked again at the proud new schooner alongside, and saw *Faith* again as he had seen her. As though

40

the old hulk in death had given birth to her own likeness. The new schooner was every inch the ship that *Faith* had been, right down to her odd, shingled deckhouse and the startling fighting tops at her mastheads — broad platforms from which men could fire muskets . . . or American rifles.

Most of the yards and ways were still now. Though Admiral Lord Richard Howe had withdrawn his flotillas from the Delaware after General Sir William Howe — his brother — had secured the occupation of Philadelphia, there still were armed vessels that flew the Union Jack on the river, and would be as long as British troops were garrisoned in Philadelphia. And though months had passed since the last shelling of shore installations by Crown warships, there still was the chance that some vessel's captain, suspicious of colonial activity along the river, might lay down a barrage for effect.

More and more now, in this springtime of 1778, the American colonists were pledging themselves to the effort for independence. The scattered flames of uprising that Lord North and the king's ministers had thought to squelch quickly two years ago had not been stopped, but instead had become a full-scale, organized revolution — thirteen embattled colonies waging full-scale war. The embers that "Black Dick" Howe, with his brother and an expeditionary force, had thought to extinguish with a balance of force and diplomacy had become a roaring conflagration.

The colonies now had the Continental Congress, and that congress had an army and a navy. The little navy even now was at sea, carrying the war to the home islands, and the army had wintered and was yet intact at Valley Forge. Few colonists now admitted to Royalist sentiments.

Still, whether Whig or Tory, business was business, and the war was only a war. Most of the commerce of the region had been transferred across to the Chesapeake, and had gone right on being commerce.

The man grinned at the thought, wondering whether that was a sign of how *American* the English colonists had become, or of how English the Americans remained.

American. It still seemed a strange word to him. Yet he accepted it as a second definition of his own status, though he

41

still thought of himself mostly as a Virginian.

There were people aboard the new schooner, and around it. Lanterns glowed in the dusk, and the sounds of men working came clear across the vacated yards between. He headed that way.

At his approach, a lantern was raised to show him clearly, and a small, great-coated figure appeared at the railing overhead. He waved, recognizing the auburn hair which escaped around her bonnet.

"Mr. Romart?" she called down. "Is that you?"

"Aye, Miss Constance," he hailed her. "You sent word you'd need of me, so here I am. How can I be of service, miss?"

"Come aboard," she said. "There's a ladder amidships somewhere. Not a one of these men ever saw how *Faith* was rigged after Patrick modified her, and I don't know enough of ship talk to explain it to them."

Five

The winds held true for the time, and through a day and a night *Fury* herded her prize southward on a vacant sea while Dalton kept a reckoning of their course as best he could on charts that could tell him little until there were landmarks. Even for a master mariner, the reckoning of longitude required certain knowledge of where one had been the day before, and the day before that. He could judge his latitude with some certainty, and did. Twenty-three degrees north latitude, he reckoned. Very near to the Tropic of Cancer. But what lay ahead — two or three days' sail — could be most anything from Hispaniola to the Leeward Islands of the Lesser Antilles.

Holding *Fury* close by to *Pride of Falworth*, he fared the winds and reckoned currents and drift while Billy Caster stayed near at hand to note positions. Twice during the daylight hours, when the seas allowed it, *Fury* hove alongside the bark at a cable's length, and the snow's launch raised mast and sail to carry cooked food across to those manning *Pride*.

With the bark standing pace on fore courses and jibs, and making little more than three knots against a flowing current, the launch with its stubby lateen sail had no difficulty keeping pace and shuttling between the ships. Dalton watched the first transfers and a smile tugged at his cheeks. *Enjoy your dinner, Mister Duncan,* he thought. *It is being delivered by your own means.*

Just a few short weeks before, the big launch had rested

in its davits on the boat deck of His Majesty's Capital Ship *Royal Lineage*. How Charley Duncan had managed to spirit away something the size of a whaleboat, from the busy and ordered midships of a seventy-four-gun Royal Navy battler, was one of those mysteries that would endure. But then, when it came to appropriating things, Charley Duncan was indeed a resourceful young man.

On the second ferrying, Dalton turned the deck over to Cadman Wise and went across with the launch. The cargo was a feast of far-better stuff than they had been eating in recent weeks, thanks to the stores they had found in *Pride's* larders—boiled beef with onions, oat pudding with a bit of honey and a flask of sweetened lemon juice from *Pride's* stores—though with Mister Wise's ministrations in the snow's little galley, it *did* still resemble goat-and-porridge.

Snugging the launch to *Pride's* shroud stays, Dalton climbed to the gunwale of the big bark and leaned over to receive the packets as Pliny Quarterstone handed them up. When he had them all, he called, "Stay with the launch, Mister Quarterstone. We shall be returning shortly." Then he carried the feast aft to where Mister Hoop was lashing the helm.

"Something to tide you lads over until breakfast," he told the big man, setting the packets on the sterncastle coaming. He looked around. "Where is Mister Duncan?"

"Below, sir." Hoop nodded. "He's got the frogs to give him a tour, lookin' for hidey-holes an' such. Shall I fetch him?"

"Not necessary, Mister Hoop. I'll have a look, myself." He let himself down through the open hatch and into the spacious cockpit of the merchantman. The area was well-lit from skylights set in the quarterdeck, and he noticed two more kegs of rum sitting beside the ladder. Hidey-holes, he thought. Every ship had them and every sailor learned soon enough where they were . . . and what they were for.

Down another ladder, and he was in the sterncastle with its cabins and its lockers, flanking a commodious galley. Little details here and there—the bright trim on cabin hatches, polished gleam of the bulkheads, the neat logic of

44

the galley's arrangement — told him this was a ship that had been well-mastered and tightly run . . . until it was abandoned and left to sink. It was a puzzle.

Voices ahead led him forward, and he found them amidships in the low, crowded space between pump wells and holds. The two Frenchmen were prying back paneling from a short inner bulkhead while Duncan kept up a running chatter.

"Two more here, you say?" the sandy-haired tar was asking. "Uh . . . oughtry duh, uh, ay tee-see?

"Oui. M'sieur le Capitain." one of the Frenchmen muttered. *"Autre deux. C'est le dernier."* They peeled away planking, and one of the Frenchmen reached in and lifted out a keg, panting and sweating as he worked. *"Voila, monsieur,"* he said. The other was hauling out a second keg.

"Exploring the ship, Mister Duncan?" Dalton asked casually.

Duncan turned, surprised, then grinned. "Aye, sir. These lads has got their wits about them after a nice sleep, so I had them show me around a bit."

"So I see. Have you learned anything from them?"

"Aye, sir. So far we've discovered four fresh kegs of good contraband and—"

"I mean about this ship, Mister Duncan. How it comes to be adrift in these waters, or what became of its crew?"

"Ah, no, sir, nothing like that. I don't speak French, you see, and these good lads haven't but a word or two of English. Good hands they are, though, in spite of being French. Able seamen, the both of them. They can hand, reef or steer. I had them splicing line this morning while their heads deflated, and I expect I can set them to the sheets shortly so that Mister Hoop can have a rest while I'm at helm." He motioned with a hand, and the two Frenchmen set down their burdens. "This is Francois, sir, and the one with the pigtail is Rene. They're both from Calais, originally, though they've spent time with the French navy. They signed aboard this ship at Martinique, after they were beached there by, ah, unfortunate circumstances. Rene has

45

two sisters at home, and Francois can play a dulcimer . . . except he doesn't have one right now. Lads,"—he waved a hand in presentation—"this is Captain Dalton, master of *Fury*."

The Frenchmen bowed formally. *"Bonjour, M'sieur le Capitain."* Rene said. *"Comment allez-vous?"*

"Tres bien, merci." Dalton nodded. To Duncan he said, "You never cease to amaze me, Mister Duncan. You speak no French, yet you have the life history of these two, it seems."

"Sailors understand sailors, sir." Duncan shrugged.

"But nothing about this ship."

"Well, no, sir. I didn't really try to ask."

"Then ask, Mister Duncan, if you please."

"Aye, sir." He rounded on the two sailors and raised his voice. *"Attendez-vous, s'il vous plait, q'uel . . . ah . . .* ship is this?" He rapped his knuckles against a handy upright and waved his arms, indicating the entire ship. The sailors looked at each other in puzzlement, then muttered together, and Rene shrugged. *"Quel bon bateau, M'sieur le Capitain. C'est bon."*

Francois frowned, then corrected, *"Quel bateau,* Rene. *Quel bateau!"* To Duncan he said, *"Pri'e of Falwort', m'sieur. Il c'est un grand bateau du commerce."*

Duncan glanced around. "Nothing yet that we don't already know, sir, but we're working on it."

Dalton shrugged. "Carry on, Mister Duncan. In the meantime, please see if you can have these gentlemen carry all the rum you have found topside and hand it down to Mister Quarterstone in the launch. We'll put it with the rest, aboard *Fury*."

"Aye, sir." Duncan looked disappointed. "Exactly what I had intended, sir."

Dalton climbed to the deck and nodded at Hoop, then strolled forward, his eyes and ears testing the rigging and trim of the bark. The color of the sky on the horizon said there would be a change in the weather, but until it came, *Pride* would cruise steadily southward at three knots, with no need for sail handling. He hoped they would not need more time than that to reach a shelter of some sort.

When the four kegs were aboard the launch, Dalton clapped Duncan on the shoulder. "Keep your heading, Mister Duncan. God willing, we'll find the time and place to test those casks. We are in weird waters here, and need our wits about us. But we shall find a way."

"Aye, sir. I'll count on it."

As Dalton swung over the rail, one of the Frenchmen waved. *"Au revoir, M'sieur Capitain. A bientot."*

With its stubby spar holding to the wind and Quarterstone at the tiller, the launch scudded off toward *Fury* hovering astarboard. Dalton glanced back. "Do you speak any French, Mister Quarterstone?"

"No, sir . . . well, a few words, maybe, but they wouldn't do in polite company."

"Do any of the other lads, do you think?"

"Speak French, sir? I wouldn't think so. We was mostly all raised good Englishmen, I expect, and a man's judged by the company he keeps, y'know. Myself, I wouldn't want to have anyone back home think I'd hobnobbed with frogs. It's notions like that can get a man's head busted in any decent pub."

As the launch pulled alongside *Fury* and Dalton swung up to the boarding port, Cadman Wise raised his bosun's whistle, hesitated, then let it drop on its thong, looking disappointed. Since reducing the snow's crew to the impossible few she now carried, Dalton had attempted to lighten the work load on all hands by eliminating as many of the frivolous practices as he could—including the traditional ceremony of piping the captain aboard when he had been off ship. Along with a half-hundred other niceties of maritime tradition, this was in abeyance. But the captain wondered at times whether his judgment had been sound. Rather than being relieved of nonessential duties, and appreciating it, the tars seemed almost to mourn the loss of such practices.

I need to find more seamen, he told himself for the hundredth time as Quarterstone eased the launch astern and cast a line for tow. *A few good, able seamen the like of these I have . . . and of*

47

those I have lost.

He went aft and took command of his deck, set Hannibal Leaf at the helm and sent Billy Caster to ask about as to whether anyone aboard spoke any French.

Stifling a sigh, Dalton set a night watch schedule and settled in to the dreary task of playing shepherd to a creeping bark across trackless open sea. There had been no sightings, no sign that anyone other than their own company even existed in the far, lonely reaches of water and wind that had been *Fury's* world since her escape from Admiralty custody.

Leaning against the snow's after rail as stars came out overhead, he sighed audibly, and started as a voice at his elbow said, "Sir?" He hadn't realized that Billy Caster was there beside him.

"Nothing, Mister Caster," he said. "Just thinking."

There was a pause; then the boy asked, "About Miss Constance, sir?"

In a thin voice, not looking around, Dalton said, "Yes, blast it, about Miss Constance! And about a great many other things as well."

The boy's response was apologetic. "Beg pardon, sir."

"Oh, I wasn't criticizing your inquiry, Mister Caster. Just giving vent to . . . never mind. I fear I have been moody of late, and that won't do. Make note of this, Mister Caster, for the day when you are master of your own vessel. The captain of a ship can neither afford nor tolerate distraction of any sort, and must forever guard against profitless revery. It is laxity, sir. Laxity of the worst kind, because it rests in the seat of command. It is not to be condoned or tolerated."

"Yes, sir."

"Did you find anyone who understands the French language?"

"No, sir. Not really. Mister Fisk can say a few words like 'parlie-voo grog' and 'conbienes say la june filly,' but he isn't sure what they mean. And Mister Bean can recite a verse in French, but he cautioned me never to repeat it in the presence of armed Frenchmen. A few others have heard a word or two, but that's all."

Dalton sighed again. "Go and get your rest, Mister Caster. I shall just have to leave it to Mister Duncan to interrogate our Frenchmen."

"Does Mister Duncan speak French, sir?"

"Hardly a word of it. A few pleasantries, no more than I speak, myself. Good night now, Billy."

"Aye, sir."

It was in the dark of morning that Claude Mallory, in *Fury*'s foretops, sighted light low on the horizon, off the starboard bow. And with first light, those high in the tops could see land—in two places. Hard astarboard, windward and abeam, a low green line stood clear in the westward distance. And dead ahead, hard down, a fainter line on the horizon stretched beyond sight off both bows. Puzzled, Dalton scanned the coastlines and decided it was time to refer to the charts. Assuming where he thought he was, what he was seeing shouldn't be here. Frowning, he stepped to *Fury*'s gunwale, swung outboard on the main shrouds and swarmed aloft, his booted feet as sure on the ratlines as any tar's buckle shoes or bare toes. At the head of the lower mainmast he nodded to Ishmael Bean squatting on the trestles, and looked where the man pointed. Then he swung outward again and climbed higher, agile as a monkey on the narrow maintop stays that dwindled to nothing more than a pair of wrapped cables at the topsail spar blocks. Clinging there, more than a hundred feet above dark water rolling away from the snow's portside wales, he peered into the distance and had a suspicion of where they were. As first officer aboard His Majesty's Brig of War *Herret*—such a long time ago now, that seemed—he had seen similar coastlines before. Clinging to the spar's bullblock, his boots planted on ratlines, he scanned the horizons and the nearer waters. The waters were not as dark as they had been, and seemed clearer. A half mile away, ahead and a bit to starboard, the bark *Pride of Falworth* eased along, with no eyes in her tops. Dalton cupped his hand to shout, leaning down, "Mister Bean!"

Twenty feet below, the maintop lookout peered upward. "Aye, sir?"

"We have come upon shallows, Mister Bean. From the look of those islands we may be in the Bahamas. That could be the Caicos Banks ahead, or something very like it. Please hail the deck and have them signal Mister Duncan to ease sail and stand where he is, before he runs afoul of a reef."

"Aye, sir." As Bean hailed the deck to relay his orders, Dalton scanned the horizons once more, alert for any sign of sails. He found nothing, but paused for a moment, gazing at the low line of the nearer island, to the west. Something there had caught his eye for an instant, it seemed, but now there was nothing to see except the bright thread of beaches capped by greenery. Low haze above the land mass was just catching its first morning sunlight.

What island? A fair-sized one, it seemed, but there were hundreds of such in this part of the world. Was the place inhabited? He didn't know, but he had the impression that it was not. What he could see of the east portion of it seemed a wilderness. This had not the look of the northwest islands, but more like those to the east, fronting the Windward Passage. If so, this was far from the main islands of the group once named Baja Mar by the Spanish but now commonly called Bahama by the British subjects who had colonized them. Yet something had caught his eye off there, and there had been a light sighted hours earlier.

He shook his head, feeling the steady wind in his face, knowing that there was no way to go and explore. The island was directly to windward, miles away, and it would be a day's task to tack across the intervening distance — even if he had all of his men aboard and no second vessel to worry about.

With a final look around, he eased down from his perch and began the descent to *Fury*'s deck. Far below, a man was at the snow's cathead, waving a pair of attention banners, while nearer at hand buntings climbed their halyards. He paused to gaze across at the creeping bark and saw no sign of response. Voices rose from below, and Ishmael Bean was waiting for him at the maintop.

"Deck says they don't answer our signal, sir," the tar said. "Mister Locke wonders if it would be all right if we saluted them with the bow chasers."

Dalton squinted, trying to make out figures on the bark's deck. Were they asleep over there? Duncan should have shown a response by now.

"Tell Mister Locke to salute them," he said. "Then lower and repeat the stand-to signal."

"Aye, sir." As Dalton started down the mainshrouds, Bean's voice directly above him was almost deafening. "Captain says salute them, deck! Bow chasers, then lower and repeat th' stand-to! Captain's on his way down!"

"Aye, tops!" the answer drifted up from below, and men scurried forward along *Fury's* fighting deck to man the pair of long cannons in her nose. Ethan Crosby and Floyd Pugh were followed by others to lend a hand with the run-in and run-out of the guns.

Crosby arrived at his gun first and knelt to the quoins.

"Don't become overly enthusiastic and try to hole him, Mister Crosby," Dalton muttered to himself. "We simply want to get his attention."

Almost as though he had heard the thought, Crosby stood away from the chaser's elevating mechanism and bent to the lines.

As Dalton swung to the gunwale and stepped down to the deck, the first of the nose guns thundered, and a cloud of white smoke drifted off eastward, hanging above the water like a small thunderhead. A moment later the second gun fired, and Dalton paused to watch as a pair of iron balls threw geysers of water a few cable lengths out from the snow's climbing bowsprit.

Rings rattled above as the signal buntings dropped, then rose again on their halyards.

From aloft came a call, "On deck!"

Dalton cupped his hands. "Aye, tops?"

"We have his attention now, sir. He's showing color at his sternpost."

Dalton headed for the quarterdeck. "Mister Locke, add to our signal, please. Tell him to drop anchor and stand where he is. We'll hull that bark on a reef if we try to take it through these passes without top lookouts."

Six

"My apologies again, sir." Charley Duncan scuffed his foot on *Fury*'s decking as the snow got under way with all hands at station. He glanced beyond the stern features of his captain, at the big bark resting at anchor, receding now behind the rejuvenated snow. No longer burdened — for the moment — with playing shepherd for an under-sailed prize, *Fury* had put on more sail and was lifting her jaunty nose now as she cut spray, heading for the thread of coastline to the south.

"I was having a chat with the Frenchies," Duncan explained, "tryin' to find out about their ship and all, as you asked. But it turned out that Mister Hoop had got himself a'dangle between the helm's kingpin and the footrope on the spanker boom, and didn't have the time to keep an eye out astern. I take full responsibility, sir."

A'dangle between the helm and the spanker boom? Dalton considered it and decided he would like to have seen that. Of all the seamen he had known, only Mister Hoop might have had the brute strength to steer a bark by manhandling both the spanker and the wheel . . . but even for him, keeping his feet on the deck would have been difficult should a gust of wind take the spanker while its sheet lines were loose. "Consider it forgotten, Mister Duncan," he said now, his eyes roving the workings of his ship where a dozen men were doing the work of twenty. "Did you learn anything?"

"Aye, sir. I learned to keep a better eye on my escort when I—"

"I mean about the bark, Mister Duncan. Did you learn anything from the Frenchmen?"

"Oh. Aye, sir, I think so, though it seems a bit garbled. I take it they were crew on the bark, sir. Them and a baker's dozen-odd others — I can't get at whether there was eighteen or sixteen all together — was beached at Martinique and this ship come along and signed them on. The mate as took their marks was a M'sieur . . . ah, a *Mister* Leech. I haven't found out who the captain was, but it seems like he was a cold, gray man. Y'know, sir, I believe that Francois has the soul of a poet, the way he can describe things so you don't even have to know what he's sayin' to kind of understand. Did I tell you that he can play the dulcimer . . . ?"

"Mister Duncan!"

"Aye, sir?"

"About the ship, please. What happened?"

"Oh. Well, that's an odd thing, sir. They were chased by pirates, and run to ground at a little island somewhere; then the pirates attacked, and a lot of men in boats put out from the little island — *petite ile,* they called it, but they sort of like drew me a picture, y'see — and boarded the ship . . ."

"I saw no signs of a struggle aboard that bark."

"It wasn't the bark that was boarded, sir. It was the pirates' ship that was boarded. There was a lot of fighting; then they started knocking people in the head and throwing them over . . ."

"On the pirate ship?"

"Aye, sir, I think so. At first, it seems like that's what was going on. But then everybody came back to the bark and rounded up all the new marks and started braining them, just the way they had done on the pirate ship."

"Who was doing that?" Dalton scowled, trying to make sense of it. "The pirates?"

"Doesn't seem that way, sir. Seems like it was the bark's crew — the regular crew, and some others that the French gentlemen hadn't had the honor of meeting — that was doing the head knocking. It all gets a little confusing in French, don't you see."

54

"I can certainly see how it might." Dalton nodded. "What happened then?"

"Well, sir, our two—Francois and Rene—they managed to slip off and hide in the chain locker; and when they finally came out there wasn't anybody on board except them, and no island or other vessel in sight, and the bark was beginning to list from being scuttled. They cut open a cotton bale and plugged the leak the best way they could; then they went and found some rum and got drunk."

"And how long was the ship adrift before we came across it?"

"They don't seem to have any idea, sir. From the amount of rum they put away, my guess would be at least a week . . . though that's assuming they were God-fearing Englishmen, sir. I don't rightly know the capacities of Frenchmen, where rum's concerned."

Dalton turned to look back at the bark growing distant now astern. He had left it manned by Mister Hoop, Abel Ball in the tops, and the cheerful Frenchmen—who now, it seemed, considered themselves to be part of his crew. Every empty water cask from both ships now rested on the snow's decks, and it was Dalton's intention to have a look at the coastline southward. If he could manage a close look at it, he might find it on his charts and verify where they were. In any event, he wanted to try to get his bearings, take on water if there was water to be had, then return to the bark's anchorage to consider his next course. He estimated twelve miles to the shore ahead. If the weather held, he could be there and back before sundown, and the anchored bark would never be entirely out of sight.

In waters that ran to shoals and shallows, and sported reefs that could tear the guts from an unwary ship, Dalton was navigating by what Senior Captain Peter Selkirk of His Majesty's Royal Navy—the man who was Patrick Dalton's teacher in his days as midshipman—called "thump and pray passage." It meant make good sail, put spotters in the tops and at the spreaders where the jib boom thrust forward of the bowsprit, "thump" constantly for depth changes and pray that the ship did not run into anything in the process of passage.

Selkirk had made it very clear to all of his charges that he did not approve—not in the slightest—of such use of a vessel.

In essence, Dalton agreed. If a man must put a ship at jeopardy, there were far more honorable ways of doing it. But at times, such as now in strange waters with a defenseless prize vessel waiting *Fury*'s return and barely enough hours of daylight remaining for the task at hand, there wasn't much choice.

"Keep a sharp eye on Mister Wise yonder, Mister Locke," he reminded his helmsman. "Steer by his signal."

Cadman Wise, relieved again from galley duty for need of a bosun, stood amidships forward of *Fury*'s mainmast, his arms spread like soaring wings, ready to relay steering orders to the quarterdeck as he listened to the chant of Purdy Fisk sounding depths, and to the calls of Ishmael Bean on the crosstrees and Claude Mallory in the foretop, both of them peering into the waters ahead for signs of shoaling. All the rest aboard except Dalton and his clerk stood by sheet lines ready to handle sail at the captain's command.

They had sailed in this manner before—at least some of them had—and Dalton had learned to trust their competence just as they trusted his judgment in choosing to navigate so in such waters. Still, there were worried looks each time they saw—or the foretop lookout saw—wreckage of some unfortunate vessel broken on the shallow reefs that bounded the narrow fairway of their course. By the time the shoreline ahead was in clear view, they had passed three such wrecks, and Dalton wondered how many more such there were that they didn't see.

Billy Caster voiced the same thought. "So many," the boy breathed, peering over the portside rail at the broken hulk of an old ship, clearly visible a hundred yards away, bits of its hull protruding from the water like black fangs.

"Rocks and reefs, Mister Caster." Dalton glanced at the wreckage and turned back toward the land ahead. "And more than bad luck, I'd warrant. These were trade lanes before the recent hostilities, and in waters like these I'm certain there were wreckers at work. Wreckers and who knows what else. These are weird waters. Weird waters indeed."

"Wreckers, sir?"

"The oldest form of piracy at sea." Dalton nodded. "Find a treacherous sea like this, then set fires or signal flares to lure passing ships onto the rocks. Many a good ship has fallen to wreckers."

The boy looked at him, wide-eyed. "Do they still do that, sir?"

Dalton shrugged. "Given the opportunity for a fast profit, there are always some willing to act on it. Trade lanes may shift from time to time, but not human nature."

From the foretop, Claude Mallory's voice called, "On deck!" Amidships, Cadman Wise responded, "Aye, tops!"

"Shoaling, deck! Dead ahead! The reefs close in there!"

"Whereaway?"

"Six cables or about!"

At the port bow, Purdy Fisk's soundings increased their cadence as he flung and read his sounding line. "An' a quarter, four! . . . An' a quarter, four! . . . By the mark, four! . . . By the mark, four! . . . An' three quarters, three! . . ."

"Shoaling," Dalton muttered, striding to the quarterrail. He stood spread-legged beside the bell-arch, his hands clasped behind him.

Far ahead, out on the spreader stays, Ishmael Bean raised his right arm. He had the reefs in sight. Immediately Cadman Wise relayed the signal, turning his right arm up at the elbow as though pointing to the sky. Behind Dalton, Victory Locke eased the wheel to port . . . a point, and then another when Wise held the signal position.

Out on the spreaders, Bean raised his left arm and touched his hands above his head. Instantly Cadman Wise lowered his arms and turned. "Sir," he shouted, "no clear passage!"

At the bow, the sounding chant went on. "An' a half, three! . . . An' a half, three! . . . An' a quarter . . ."

Dalton cupped his hands. "Luff the sheets, please, Mister Wise!"

"Aye, sir! Hands a'sheet, loose your lines!"

"Ease the spanker!" Dalton said, realizing even as he shouted that the only one available on the quarterdeck to cast loose and ease off big boom's sheet lines was Charley Duncan. As Duncan reached the starboard blocks, Dalton hurried to those aport. Two pairs of strong hands working in unison hove the big drive sail aport, easing it slowly alee. *Fury* settled into the swells and stood, dead in the water except for drift.

Duncan secured his sheet line and glanced across. "Chancy, that," he noted.

Dalton cupped his hands and raised his head. "Foretop ahoy!"

From more than two hundred feet ahead and above, Claude Mallory's voice drifted down. "Aye, sir?"

"Read our drift, Mister Mallory, if you please! What's aport?"

There was a pause, then, "Clear for a bit, sir, then we'll hit shoals!"

"Can you see a break in the reef ahead?"

"No, sir! From here it looks as though we're in a pocket!"

Dalton swore under his breath. So much for running along the shoreline yonder and having a look at it from the ship. The island—if such it was—was still nearly three miles away. He turned. "Mister Duncan, take four hands and man the launch, please. Take as many casks as you can, and go have a look at that land yonder. Observe what you can of it, quickly, and bring back water if you can find some. I shall drop a kedge and hold here as long as I can."

"Aye, sir." Duncan hurried to the quarterrail. "Misters Fisk, Quarterstone, Nelson and . . . ah . . . Leaf! Aft for shore patrol! Haul the launch alongside!"

Dalton turned to Billy Caster. "Break out five of the American rifles, if you please, Mister Caster. With powder and ball."

"Aye, sir." The clerk headed below.

"On deck!"

Amidships, Cadman Wise took the call. "Aye, tops?"

"We seem to be in a current, deck! We're drifting at a good clip, an' those shoals are comin' up!"

Dalton turned to the port rail and peered over. The water beneath *Fury*'s keel, though still some twenty feet deep, was as clear as morning sky, and each detail of the bottom stood clear. Schools of bright fish played here and there above a bottom that looked like craggy peaks and valleys, with great stands of coral spread among them. Eerie fans and feathers waved in the current. The school of fish just below exploded off in all directions as something large and dark disturbed them.

"I may not be able to stand here, Mister Duncan," he said. "Yon is no bottom for a kedge. I'll need way."

"Aye, sir." Duncan squared his shoulders and tried a grin that failed to show much cheer. "You'll be somewhere about, though, I warrant."

"We shall do our best, Mister Duncan. Good luck to you."

"Aye, sir."

At the starboard gunwales, casks were being lowered overside to the launch. Duncan headed that way, pausing to relieve Billy Caster of an armload of rifles as the boy struggled through the companion hatch with them.

British sailors, Dalton thought. *And American rifles. We are what we are and we use what we have.* He cupped his hands. "Mister Wise, stand by to make sail. Jib and jigger, and keep your lookouts in place. When the launch casts off, bring us through the wind for a port tack, please."

"Aye, sir. Are we going back to deep water?"

"We are looking for a place where we can wait without the seabed rising up to scuttle us, Mister Wise."

"Aye, sir. Hands a'deck, stand by th' sheets, jib an' jigger! Spotters look alive!"

Dalton removed his coat, rolled up his sleeves and headed for the waist pinrails where the spencer sail's sheets were secured. He saw Billy Caster rolling up his own sleeves and nodded. "Mister Caster!"

"Aye, sir?"

"Can you ride a jibtop, Mister Caster?"

"Aye, sir," the boy called. "I can try."

"Then, go forward please, Mister Caster, and relieve Mister Bean for sail handling."

"Aye, sir!" Tense with excitement, the boy hurried off toward *Fury*'s jutting stem. Never before had he ridden the spars thirty feet ahead of a ship's bow, but he had watched others read the waters from there and was sure he could manage it.

"Pray don't fall, Mister Caster," Dalton muttered under his breath. "I'm not sure I could ever forgive myself."

Fury's entire complement now was eight. With one at the helm, one out on spreaders and one in the foretop, that left five to handle the sails and the working deck. *Fury* now could not afford the luxury of captains and clerks. It would be all that all of them could do just to keep the ship in the narrows between shoals.

"On deck!"

Dalton peered upward. "Aye, tops?"

"That island, sir . . . the one to the west, that we saw . . . there is something going on over there, sir."

"What do you see, Mister Mallory?"

"Can't rightly say, sir! Too far away! But I think I see boats in the water there. Some of them have sails!"

"Very well, Mister Mallory. Keep a sharp eye out."

Dalton shook his head, setting his shoulders to the controlling of sheet lines. Whatever was occurring at the island to windward would just have to occur. There was absolutely nothing that *Fury* could do about it now, whatever it was.

Looking like a little barge from the ranked water casks lining its length, moving cautiously on four sweeps while Charley Duncan hung over the bow and peered into the teeth of reefs just below, the launch made its way south and then west, seeking an opening for its five feet of keel. *More than a clear fathom,* Duncan kept telling himself, *for when we come back we shall be carrying water . . . I hope.* They had skirted three hundred yards of reefline before he found the opening he wanted, and he marked it with a float—a rope with a twelve-pound cannon ball at one end and an empty rum keg at the other.

Carefully, then, he guided the launch through surging breakers and into clear water beyond. Satisfied, he had his shore party rest the sweeps and raise the boat's lateen sail. With Purdy Fisk at the tiller, the launch took fair wind and headed for shore.

Duncan wiped sweat from his forehead. "Break out the rifles, lads," he said. "Let's have proper loads and dry pans when we set foot on that beach, for we have no idea who might be there to welcome us."

He glanced back the way they had come. In the sunny distance, *Fury* crept northward, away from them, unsheeted sails dangling from her high yards and only her jibs, spencer and spanker taking wind.

Purdy Fisk was looking back, too. "By my count," he said, "there's not but eight souls on the snow's deck now. I wonder that they can handle her at all."

Duncan didn't respond, but he was thinking the same thing. Off there, creeping on minimal canvas, was a proud, fighting warship . . . or a ship that should have been such. Eighteen guns she carried. Eighteen guns, and all the sail a ship of her size might want. Thirteen standard sails — four square sails on each of her two great masts, plus three staysails at her stem, the fore-and-aft spencer in her waist and the big spanker on its own jack-mast. And sails beyond that, should she need them. With a proper crew, and the need to fly, the snow could increase her sails by fifteen and her total canvas by two-thirds . . . studding sails, a gafftop amidships and a ring-tail on the driver, and *Fury* could baffle most pursuit.

But only with proper crew. Seven men and a boy could do no more than make her creep.

Duncan turned away. There was something very melancholy in the sight of the proud, jaunty ship reduced to a scow by lack of manpower.

With clear water under her keel, the launch cut a nice vee of wake as it headed for the land that they could now see was a tight-packed group of islands presenting a long, sand-beach coastline from east to west with only narrow breaks where channels separated the lands.

Closer at hand, the shoreline was a vision of white beaches backed by lush, green forest rising slightly into the distance. As they neared the beach, Duncan had Fisk steer aport. Before making landfall, he wanted to see at least a mile or so of the place. For a time the launch sailed eastward, running parallel to the sandy beach a hundred yards away. A haze lying on the wind beyond the low rise of the forest puzzled Duncan. Smoke? Or simply a mist rising into the wind to be swept away?

"I believe we can go ashore now, Mister Fisk," he decided.

"Observe as much as you can," he told those with him, turning. "Captain Dalton will want a thorough report."

Finian Nelson was shading his eyes, peering almost directly ahead as the launch veered toward the beach. "What I'm observing right now, Mister Duncan," he said, "is those people who are observing us. I wouldn't say they look too friendly, would you?"

"What people?" Duncan jerked around, squinting. Directly ahead, a dozen or so men had appeared among the nearer trees. They were working at something, and as they turned, Duncan could see what it was. A brass cannon stood there, mounted on carriage wheels.

Duncan raised his arm, started to wave a cheery greeting, and one of the men ashore lowered a smoking fuse to the old weapon's vent. A thick cloud of white smoke billowed outward, and the gun's roar was accompanied by a resounding splash as an iron ball sheeted water across the launch, dousing everyone aboard.

"What th' bloody 'ell!" Duncan sputtered, his cheeks going livid. "Out sweeps!" he roared. "Rifles and cutlasses at the ready . . . row!"

Above the beach, the men were working furiously to reload the old cannon. They were a ragged and motley bunch, some wearing no more than stained shreds here and there. The launch arrowed toward them, driven by its lateen sail and four sets of powerful shoulders. In its bow, Charley Duncan stood upright, rifle in one hand and cutlass in the other. Dripping wet, outraged and ready for a fight, he stood poised, waiting for the scrape of sand on the launch's keel.

Seven

More than two miles away, aboard *Fury*, Claude Mallory glanced aft in time to see the smoke on the shore behind them. "On deck!" he shouted.

"Aye, tops?"

"Sir, there's been a cannon fired yonder where the launch went. I see the smoke!"

"Can you see who fired it?"

"Not rightly, sir. Maybe there are people ashore there."

Fury slid past a wreck, Victory Locke spinning the helm grimly as he read channel signals from amidships. He reversed the spin, and the snow slithered to the starboard, edging within a cable's length of a submerged reef that rippled the waves above it. "Like tryin' to thread a needle in th' blinkin' dark," he muttered.

"How far to blue water, tops?" Dalton called from the port sheets.

"Channel widens a bit just ahead, sir! Maybe another mile to the clear!"

"Let's get some decent water around us," Dalton called to Cadman Wise, "then we'll lay to and have a look."

"Aye, sir."

Fury crept past another wrecked hulk, and Billy Caster, perched forward on the jib cap, his knees gripping the spreader yards, turned to shout over his shoulder, "The channel is widening, sir! Clear water both sides and ahead."

"Tops?" Dalton called.

63

Mallory scanned, then shouted, "Th' lad is right, sir. We're comin' up clear in just a bit."

With a sigh, Dalton tightened the trim on the sheeting line, securing it to a belaying pin at the fife rail. "Trim and secure, please, Mister Wise," he said. "When we have open water, stand to the wind for reckoning. I'm going aloft."

"Aye, sir."

Going aft, Dalton ducked through the companion hatch and reappeared a moment later with his telescoping spyglass. He pulled on his coat and dropped the glass into a tail pocket. He strode to the gunwales, swung into the shrouds, then hesitated, turning toward the helm. "Did you hear the order, Mister Locke?"

"Aye, sir, that I did."

"At Mister Wise's signal, then."

"Aye, sir. Stand down at the signal."

Dalton headed aloft. At the mainmast's head he swung over the balustrade onto the snow's wide trestletrees. Capping both the lower mainmast and the spanker's jack-mast, the trestletrees here were a substantial platform of heavy timbers secured with iron collars and framing. Nearly thirty feet ahead of him, and a trifle below, Claude Mallory grinned and waved in the foretop. "Come up for a look aft, sir? There was *something* goin' on back there, but I can't see much now."

"I brought up a glass," Dalton said. He pulled the telescope from his tail pocket, extended it and leaned against the base of the main topmast to brace himself. Even with the glass, the shoreline aft was a long way off. He scanned along it slowly, then found the launch in its view. The boat stood empty, drawn partway up a sand beach. He searched around it, and saw no one. Just above the launch, though, at the edge of the forest, something bright glinted in the sun.

A cannon? He couldn't be sure, but if Mallory said he had seen gunsmoke, then that was what he saw.

He turned. "Did you see the people who fired the cannon, Mister Mallory?"

"I might have, sir. Too far to be sure, but there was movement yonder, like people just where th' green starts. Then

Mister Duncan put the launch ashore, and everybody just sort of disappeared into the woods."

Dalton started to lower the glass, then squinted through it. Just atop the distant beach, where brass glinted in the sunlight, he saw something else. A tiny figure separated itself from the dark forest and stepped into sun . . . and waved.

It was Duncan. Even at this distance, he knew the sandy-haired sailor. The figure continued to wave, now with both arms, as though signalling. But what? Dalton squinted, peered through the glass, and gave up. Duncan was trying to tell him something, but he had no idea what it was.

The maintop seemed to shiver and lean, and Dalton clung to a line as the mast below him pitched to starboard . . . not a severe lean, but enough so that the deck far below seemed to slide aside and what was directly beneath him was water. Sedately, *Fury* eased her prow to port, coming into the wind, and he heard the slap of slacking canvas as the ship came dead in the water. He looked down and cupped a hand to his mouth. "Ahoy the helm!"

Victory Locke straightened from lashing the helm and looked up. "Aye, sir?"

"Are you secured now, Mister Locke?"

"Aye, sir. Rudder's amidships."

"Then, break out the buntings, please, and run up a signal. Say, 'Message not understood.' "

"Aye, sir. Comin' up."

Moments passed; then the signal lanyard rattled in its blocks, and buntings rose from the deck, fluttering in the wind. Dalton raised his glass again. Duncan was still visible on the beach, not waving now. For a moment he stood; then he disappeared into the brush. Several minutes crept by before he reappeared, with others trailing behind him. Dalton counted them idly. Three . . . four . . . five . . . six. He caught his breath and squinted. A dozen tiny figures were there now, and more coming behind them . . . carrying things, pulling things. . . . Dalton swore under his breath. What was going on over there?

"Captain . . ."

Dalton steadied himself and tried to see details.

"Ah, Captain, sir . . ."

He waved his free hand in dismissal, trying to make sense of the view in his glass.

"Captain Dalton! Sir!"

He lowered the glass and turned. "Mister Mallory, I am trying to—"

"Aye, sir, but you'd best have a look the other direction, as well."

Frowning, Dalton shaded his eyes and looked northward. In the distance stood the bark *Pride of Falworth*, resting at anchor as he had left it. Then something else caught his eye, and he looked to the left, then raised his glass to peer through it. Coming out from the windward island, the one to the west, were boats. Boats of all sorts, it seemed, and all making for *Pride*.

Dalton's roar of exasperation brought the foretopman to abrupt and vertical attention on his crosstrees. "Sir?"

"Never mind, Mister Mallory. I was just—Mister Mallory, please don't stand unsupported at the foretop. You could fall."

"Aye, sir." Mallory grabbed a tops'l shroud and swung there for a moment, regaining the balance he had just lost. "I'm sorry, sir, but I didn't catch exactly what you said."

"I swore an oath, Mister Mallory. It was a very profound oath, one of the best I know. I swore it because I have left that prize vessel helpless out there, assuming the island yonder to be uninhabited; and now it seems it is not, and I am as helpless to defend those lads at the moment as they are to defend themselves."

Mallory gazed across at him, real admiration on his homely face. "You swore all that, sir?"

"In a word, yes." He hitched himself around the maintop couplings and raised his glass again, staring southward. There seemed a truly remarkable number of people over there now. Thirty—forty—perhaps even more. They were too far away to count, but what they were doing was even more amazing. Charley Duncan stood apart from the rest, again waving his arms enthusiastically. A few others—those would be the launch crew—were bunched to one side, and beyond them stretched a long, single-file line of men, all—he could think of no other explanation — all *dancing.*

Dalton stared through his glass, entranced. Like players on a stage, the figures on the beach moved this way and that in perfect synchronization. They stepped to the right, then bent and backed leftward, their arms out in exaggerated pantomime. Like clockwork figures performing on a music box, he thought. Or like — his brow lifted — like a pantomime of deck hands playing anchor line to the pawls of a capstan. Blinking, he shifted the glass, and saw what he had expected to see. To one side of the miming line, a smaller group walked around and around in a tight circle, their arms held stiffly out ahead of them.

There on the distant beach, under a tropical sun, men gestured in pantomime as though on a theater stage. And what they mimed was the raising of an anchor.

They were sailors!

Dalton almost dropped his glass getting it closed and into his tail pocket. He swung down from the trestletrees, planted his boots in ratlines and shouted, "Mister Wise!"

"Aye, sir?"

"Back to the sheets, Mister Wise! Mister Locke to the helm, please! Let's have some way for the rudder, then smart about for starboard tack by spanker, jigger and jib. Spotters in place, and look alive. We are going back for Mister Duncan."

Fury made better time now, with experience of the shoals at helm and lookout, and the lateened launch drove out to meet her well outside the reef pocket.

Without waiting for the boat to be snugged alongside, Charley Duncan scrambled over the gunwales and snapped a grinning salute at his captain. "Sir, I've complemented the crew, by your leave," he said.

Dalton returned the salute, hardly realizing that he had done so. "Complemented, Mister Duncan? Do you mean you have signed on additional hands?"

"Not exactly 'signed on,' sir. I told the lads you'd have to approve, but I did sort of promise as many berths as we could ship. They're a fine, raw bunch of lads, sir. Full of spirit. They tried to sink us at first sight, then set up fortification abaft the beach and held us off for the better part of an hour before we managed to thump a number of them into havin' better sense. We do need sailors, sir, and these lads can hand, reef and steer to a man, all except Mister Claremore who hasn't but one arm . . . and he can cook."

Dalton raised a speculative brow, peering at the beach beyond the reef-ringed shallows. There were quite a few people over there, loading casks and packets aboard several makeshift rafts.

Duncan pressed on, excitedly. "Those are our water casks, sir. Once the hostilities were ended, the lads on the island were happy to haul and fill them for us, just on the chance of a berth and passage to civilization."

"I see," Dalton said. "Well, it may be our good fortune at that. We could use a few more hands, of course. Ah, how many did you recruit, Mister Duncan?"

"Sixty-seven, sir."

"Sixty-seven?"

"Aye, sir. It might have been more, but the rest decided to stay on where they are. They've taken a liking to the place, you might say. One way or another."

"Mister Duncan, who are those people and how do they come to be here?"

"Crew of the trader *Tyber*, sir. British registry, general cargo. They were wrecked on rocks, then marooned when their officers took all the boats and set out for Hispaniola. They never came back. That was more than a year ago, as best these lads can tell. Since then, they've been livin' off the land and standin' off pirates and Whigs and Frenchmen. At least, that's who they expect the people on the island northwest probably are."

"Remarkable." Dalton shook his head.

"Aye, sir. We all had a nice chat after we'd finished fighting one another. Can we sign them on, sir?"

"I'll approve the cook if he can cook," Dalton decided. "I shall inspect the rest after they have delivered our water casks."

"Aye, sir." Duncan grinned, snapped another salute and headed for the launch to lead the rafts through the reefwall.

"Sixty-seven?" Dalton muttered. "Mister Caster!"

"Aye, sir?" the boy responded, almost at his elbow.

"Oh, there you are, Mister Caster. You heard all that, I presume?"

"Aye, sir. Sixty-seven recruits, sir. Shall I bring up the roster and log for swearing them aboard?"

"In a bit, Mister Caster. Have you identified these islands on the chart?"

"I think so, sir. There is a grouping like this north of Hispaniola, though I'm confused at the names. In one reference they're called the Caicos Islands, but elsewhere they seem to be called Providenciales. I imagine that's Spanish."

"I'll have a look when there's time." Dalton nodded. "Have you identified the island northwest, that we passed coming in?"

"I think so, sir. There is such an island on the charts. It's called Mayaguana. It is listed as uninhabited, the same as these."

"Listings can be confusing, Mister Caster. Especially in troubled times."

"Aye, sir."

"Sixty-seven," Dalton muttered. "And fifteen is eighty-two. Famine to feast, it seems. Bring up the company roster and logs, Mister Caster. We likely will be expanding our company presently."

"Aye, sir. Ah, what articles will you read them, sir? We have no flag, do we?"

Dalton thought it over. A ship's company was bound by the vessel's articles to the law of a land, but at present *Fury* had no allegiance. He shrugged. "The Articles of War, Mister Caster, the one same discipline as remains to all the rest of us, from our own various swearings-in. I have no doubt of the men who have sailed with me heretofore. The loyalty of our *Furies* is beyond question. But our new hands will have had no such experience. A code of behavior must be required, and the Articles of War require no nationality."

It was a strange-looking complement that came aboard *Fury,* following the water casks and such other stores as Charley Duncan's shore party had liberated. By fives and tens as they boarded, Dalton questioned them and noted the motley,

69

threadbare attire, the unkempt hair and beards, the sun-dark features of men long marooned in the tropics. They were a mix of seafarers of their time, though a fair number looked to have sailed at one time or another on king's ships.

Some among them admitted readily to past sins, crimes and breaches of conduct, and Dalton could find little fault with their admissions. Few indeed were the sailors of the time who had not committed such, and worse — mayhem, thievery, fornication and cheerful disrespect for authority were more the rule than the exception. Yet he noticed an absence of guilt — or at least admitted guilt — of a number of more serious breaches of conduct. Not a man of them, it seemed, had ever so much as carried a lighted candle into a ship's hold, much less assaulted an officer, been party to a mutiny or participated in sabotage or the keeping of secrets.

After several group interviews, he took Duncan aside and mentioned this phenomenon.

Duncan shrugged and grinned. "Well, sir, we did a bit of inquiring when we were ashore. You might say we sort of shook out the chaff, as it were."

"I see. Then, those who decided to remain here and not join us . . . ?"

"Aye, sir. Rummy lot, mostly. Several had done mutiny, or simple murder. And then, there were a few that may have been stranded a bit too long. They had some funny habits, sir."

"How did you ascertain such guilts, Mister Duncan?"

"How did we what, sir?"

"How did you persuade them to tell you what their crimes were?"

"Oh. Well, sir, since we had the honor of *Fury* to consider, and yourself not available to guide us, we just made do."

"Obviously," Dalton said. "But how?"

"We picked out a dozen of 'em and had them kneel down. Then one by one we stuck a rifle barrel in their mouths and offered them a choice between swearing allegiance to us or sampling the grace of God. Naturally, they all decided to be on our side. After that, it was just a matter of them telling us all there was to know about each of the rest. There aren't

70

many secrets when men have been marooned for a year in hostile waters."

"Selection by sworn jury," Dalton said. "Mister Duncan, sometimes I wonder if the Admiralty itself might not benefit by seeking out your wisdoms."

"I don't know, sir," Duncan admitted. "They never asked me for any of those."

Dalton continued his interviews. When he had finished he assembled the entire enlistment on *Fury*'s gundeck and read them the Articles of War as the Articles of Service aboard *Fury*. Some of them—those with Royal Navy service—had heard the articles before. Most of them, he guessed, had not, judging by the frightened eyes and creeping pallor of many among them as he recited the dread document with its ominous words, its strict and thorough listing of acceptable and unacceptable behaviors, and its blunt and dreadful descriptions of the dire punishments that were sure to befall any transgressor.

He recited the articles in full, made certain that every man understood them, then accepted their solemn oaths to abide by them and by his orders as captain. With the entire group duly sworn, he set Billy Caster to enter their names into ship's records and get their marks.

A dozen or so that he judged to be capable sailors he took aside from the line and set to deck and top duties. Among these were two or three that he made mental note to watch closely, as possible troublemakers. The rest he gave over to the charge of his first officer.

"Drill them to this deck and these riggings," he ordered Charley Duncan. "Before we recontact our prize bark, I shall require an assessment of each man, as able seaman or ordinary seaman, and a brief of any certain skills each might have. As an example, see whether any of them speak French."

"Aye, sir," Duncan said happily. He turned to his charges and bellowed, " 'Oy now, you beggars! Form up in companies amidships fore an' main! Count off by sixes for going aloft, manning the capstan, stowing the casks, sheeting and trimming, cable-tiers drill and batten-down drill! To places by the count! Look lively and keep yourselves out of the way of the sailing crew, for the captain's got a ship to handle while you lubbers learn the ropes!"

Like a marine drill sergeant with recruits, he marched them off amidships while the others on deck gazed after them.

"Mister Duncan might have made an officer had he mended his ways," Cadman Wise muttered to Victory Locke. "He has the very soul of a tyrant."

"Brings to mind a bosun's mate aboard the old *Clemency* that I sailed on my first up." Abel Ball nodded. "Sad case, that. Some of the fo'c'sle lads knocked the bastard in the head and fed him to the fishes."

Dalton strode to the quarterdeck and turned at the rail. "Stand by helm," he ordered. "Mister Wise, hands a'deck to stations, stand by to make sail. Tops aloft, please. Mister Fisk, do the honors at the jibcap. Stand by to make sail and trim for port tack. At my order, please, Mister Wise."

He looked around him, satisfaction in his dark eyes. Where before had been a scant handful to do the work of many, now *Fury* was crowded with men. The decks that had seemed so forlorn now teemed with bustling humanity.

"Have you learned the channel, Mister Locke?"

"Aye, sir. By signal, sir, I can steer it."

"Very well, then. Steer it we shall. Make sail, please, Mister Wise. Jibs alee. Courses and tops. Sheet home!"

The bosun's pipe wailed, and *Fury* seemed to sprout sails even as her nose came across the wind. More sails than she had worn since her escape from custody in the north Atlantic. Powerfully, gracefully she turned and leaned, trimming to the wind while rippling waters along her hull rose in pitch to the thrum of a rigged vessel taking the wind.

"By the signal and by the mark, helm," Dalton said. "Take us to where there's good water, and we'll see how it feels to have wings again."

Fury gained way and headed for the open sea while aromas of cooking drifted up the companionway from the galley and larders where one-armed Nathan Claremore, once second-watch cook for the merchantman *Tyber,* banged and rattled about, converting stores from the bark *Pride of Falworth* into a meal for ninety or so aboard the snow *Fury.*

Eight

Pride of Falworth had old, nine-pound stem and stern guns, and a brace of small carronades at each beam. The bark had not been designed or intended to fight, but no vessel of her time put to sea without at least a bit of a sting for the occasional social encounter. From a masthead, Pliny Quarterstone watched the flotilla of boats put out from the large island to windward, and when it became clear that the boats were heading for *Pride*, he called down, "Mister Hoop, we will have callers! Do you think we should load some guns?"

Hoop considered this, his big face writhing at his efforts of thought, then shouted, "I expect that's what Captain would want done if he was here."

"Can you manage that, Mister Hoop, or do you want me to come down?"

"You'd best stay aloft and keep an eye on those people," Hoop decided. "I've got these frogs here; maybe they can help." He strode forward to where the two Frenchmen sat cross-legged, patching canvas. "I'll need you lads to help me run in some guns for loading," he said.

They looked up blankly. *"Excuses-moi, nous ne parlez pas bien anglais, M'sieur 'Oop."* one of them explained. *"Parlez-vous francais? Peut-etre un petit?"*

Hoop scowled at them, raised his voice and said, slowly, "You pair is to lend a hand at loadin' the guns!"

Still they only stared at him.

With a rumbling curse, he strode to the nearest beam gun and pointed at it. "Gun!" he explained.

73

"Gun," they repeated in unison.

"Aye, now we're makin' progress," Hoop beamed. "Gun . . . you see?"

They got to their feet and came closer, listening intently. "Gun . . . hew see?" they repeated.

"Gun!" he shouted.

"Gun!" they shouted in unison.

Quarterstone's jeering voice came from above. "You lads sound like true repentance at a Calvinist town meeting!"

"Shut your bleedin' mouth, Mister Quarterstone!" Hoop roared.

"Shu' 'er bleetin' mout', Mees'ehr Cortehrstone!" the Frenchmen echoed.

"Load th' friggin' cannon, ye blighters!" Hoop thundered at them.

"Loa' th' frickin' cannon, 'e blotters!" they sang, getting into the spirit of it.

"Blast!" Hoop roared, turning away and ignoring the chorus of "Blest!" and the cackle of Quarterstone laughing aloft. With a heave, he rolled the gun inboard on its carriage and grabbed a swab. "I'll charge th' blinkin' things myself," he grumbled.

Behind him, the Frenchmen chatted together for a moment; then one of them tapped him on the shoulder. He turned, scowling, and the man said something incomprehensible to him.

"I don't know what the bleedin' 'ell you're talkin' about, frog," he snapped.

From aloft came Quarterstone's suggestion. "I expect they're saying that if you want the cannon loaded, Mister Hoop, they'd be glad to help out."

"*Oui, M'sieur,*" a Frenchman said, reaching for the loading swab. "*Mais c'est un plaisir.*"

"Mother of God," Hoop muttered as they bent to the loading of the gun.

Francois grinned up at him. "*N'est-ce pas, m'sieur.*"

With charges and balls in both of the starboard beam pieces, Hoop led his Frenchmen to the fore and set them to the chasers. They were willing but awkward with the longer weapons, and Hoop decided that whatever they had been before, they were not gunners.

"Some of those boats are getting close, Mister Hoop!" Quarterstone shouted from aloft. "Maybe you'd better hail them!"

"And say what?" Hoop shouted back.

"I don't know! What would Captain Dalton say if he were here?"

"How would I know that? I'm no blinkin' ship's master!"

"Well, you ought to do something!"

The Frenchmen rammed a ball home, primed the vent and straightened, gazing over the bark's lofting bowsprit at the approaching flotilla. Rene pointed. *"Alons, M'sieur 'Oop! Les bateaus!"*

"Boats," he corrected them. "Those are boats."

"Boats," they said in unison. " 'Ose ehr boats."

"Right. Boats."

"Rot. Boats." Rene glanced at Francois. *"Ou'est-ce que c'est 'boats'?"*

Francois shrugged. *"Les bateaus."* He gazed at them, counting. *". . . dix-huit, dix-neuf, vingt, vingt et un . . . formidable!"*

With a grunt, Hoop hauled them aside and started them aft. "Stop yer chatterin' now and go get me a linstock with fuse."

"M'sieur?"

"Oh, blast!" He gritted his teeth and mimed the firing of a cannon, leaning down as though touching fuse to vent.

Francois brightened. *"Ah, mais oui! Le few! Oui, M'sieur 'Oop!"* With a grin he grabbed Rene and both of them hurried away amidships.

From aloft came Quarterstone's shout. "Mister Hoop, are you going to have a talk with those people or not?"

Hoop strode to the rail. There seemed to be nearly thirty boats bearing down on the bark, boats of all descriptions from masted launches to gigs and jolly boats. And in the distance, rafts. All full of people. The nearest ones were barely a hundred yards out now.

At the gunwale he cupped his hands. "Ahoy the boats! Stand off and identify yourselves!"

75

In the bow of a whaleboat, one of the nearest, a man stood and cupped his hands to shout, "Ahoy yourself! What ship is this?"

It seemed a reasonable question, and one that Dalton might answer. "Prize bark *Pride of Falworth!*" he shouted.

For a moment there was silence; then the man called, "Prize, you say? Whose prize is it?"

"Prize of the snow *Fury,* Captain Patrick Dalton commanding! What do you people want?"

The boats continued to approach. "We don't see any snow, nor any sort of prize escort!" the man shouted. "Are you Captain Dalton?"

"Of course not," Hoop shouted, aghast. "I'm nobody but Hoop! Stand off, now, blast you! I'm warning you!"

"Warning?" The man's voice took on a jeering tone. "I see you well, sir, and I think that's a drift ship. Not a soul on quarterdeck or at helm. We are refugees, in desperate need of a ship, you see, and maybe yours is for us."

"Be damned if it is!" Hoop roared. "We're tendin' this ship for Captain Dalton. Now stand off!"

"Three or four men. So few of you aboard and you warn' us away, sir? I think not . . ."

Hoop's temper had reached its limit. "Few!" he bellowed. "Why . . ."

Six feet to Hoop's right a cannon roared, almost deafening him and blinding him with thick, sour smoke that rolled back over the gunwales. He choked, turned and gaped. There in the haze were his Frenchmen, grinning like idiots as a gun recoiled in its lashings.

Francois raised a smoking linstock, showing him. *"Le feu."* he said proudly.

Pliny Quarterstone scrambled down the shrouds and thumped to the deck, breathless. "I hope your intentions were to make those people angry, Mister Hoop, because I believe you just did."

Hoop spun to the rail. On the sea to starboard and fore, boats were pulling in all directions, but mostly toward *Pride.* "Did we hit anything?"

76

"Not unless it was a fish," Quarterstone said. "Why did you commence firing?"

"I didn't! The frogs did that. With *le feu.*"

"Le what?"

"Feu!"

The second cannon roared, and this time there were answering sounds beyond the smoke—a crash, shouts and the hard reports of several muskets. A ball sang past Hoop's ear, and he ducked, pulling Quarterstone down with him. The Frenchmen pounded past them, heading for the bow.

Cautiously, the two *Furies* peered over the rail. Beyond was a boat slowly capsizing while men dived from it in all directions. As the boat rolled, it exposed a gaping hole in its bilges, cutting across its keel.

Ignoring musket balls and shouted curses, Hoop came upright and sprinted after the Frenchmen. "No!" he shouted. "Stop that! Cease fire!"

Pliny Quarterstone peered wide-eyed at what Hoop had just seen. In many of the approaching boats, those farther out, were women and children.

And even as the sight registered with him, boats thumped alongside *Pride* and angry men came over the rails.

Ringed around by cocked muskets and angry faces, Hoop and Quarterstone stood sweating amidships while the pair of French sailors with them gawked about, trying to understand. The leader of the boarding party was a stocky, brown-faced man with the high boots and fringed hat of a planter. His name was Aaron Fairfield, Esquire, and he had made it clear—at least to the two who spoke English—that he was within a whit of braining the lot of them and throwing them into the sea.

"It's God's pure mercy that no one was killed," he snapped at Hoop. "What manner of man opens fire on helpless refugees without at least hearing them out?"

"It was accident, sir," Pliny Quarterstone intervened. "You see, these frogs here don't speak barely a word of English, and we don't speak frog; and I believe they misapprehended something. Mister Hoop may have said in passing, was why they touched off the guns."

"Accident or not," Fairfield said, "Mister Hoop is responsible for the conduct of his men, and I hold him accountable . . ."

"But they aren't his men, sir, beggin' your pardon. Mister Hoop is a simple sailor, like my own self. We can't be held responsible for what we've no authority to control, you see."

Fairfield pinned the topman with a glare. "If he wasn't in charge on the gundeck, then why would these French blighters have taken orders from him, if as you say that's what they thought they were doing?"

"It might be that they may have thought I was in charge, sir," Hoop suggested.

"And why would they think you are if you are not?"

"I expect they haven't got the vaguest idea of who's in charge here." Hoop shrugged. "They aren't rightly ours."

"Then, whose are they?"

"We don't know, sir. They just sort of come with the vessel when Captain Dalton claimed it for salvage. We found them in the chain locker, which is no fit place for even a Frenchman to be."

Some of Fairfield's men came from below. "Nobody else aboard, Squire," one of them said. "These four is it."

At both rails now, boats were snugged in, and more and more people were coming aboard. Landsmen, by the looks of them. Planters and merchants, craftsmen with their kits, clerks and potters and smiths . . . and a large number of women and children, being helped aboard over the wide gunwales.

"I don't know what Captain is going to have to say about this," Quarterstone muttered to Hoop. "He said we should—"

"Quiet!" Fairfield snapped. "I'm trying to decide what to do with you four. Salvage ship, I believe you said? A prize?"

"Yes, sir," Hoop assured him. "Claimed all proper by Captain Dalton. It's his vessel, an' we're his crew."

Fairfield turned, looking around. "I see no sign of this being a prize vessel, mister. For all I know it could be a mutiny ship and the four of you mutineers and murderers."

Hoop's big face went dark, and his muscles bulged. "I don't take to bein' called things like that," he started, then subsided slightly as several musket-muzzles prodded him. "What I mean is, sir, we're no such a thing as that, an' we'll swear by it. All we are is honest sailors."

"What's your flag, then?"

"Our flag?" Hoop blinked at him, then nudged his companion. "What's our flag, Mister Quarterstone?"

"I don't know," Quarterstone admitted. "I guess you'd best ask Captain about that."

"I see no captain here, though."

"He'll be along directly," Hoop assured the man. "Maybe if you'd all like to get back in your boats and wait a bit . . ."

"Get back in our . . ." Fairfield stared at him. "Why would we do that? We have this ship, mister! We are in control here, and if you aren't daft, you can bloody well see that."

"Yes, sir," Hoop admitted readily. "But what I mean is, well, Captain Dalton is one for the proprieties, sir, an' he hasn't given you permission to come aboard."

At Fairfield's shoulder a man with a musket snorted. "Why listen to any more of this, Squire? Let's throw them overboard and be on our way. Governor Dobbs could have ships on the way right now to—"

"Do you know how to sail a ship like this, Claude?" Fairfield asked.

"Well, no, but . . ."

"Do any of us, do you think?"

"No, but how hard can it be to sail a ship? You simply unfurl those canvases up there so they hang from those timbers, and let the wind do the rest."

Some among them nodded their agreement, but others shook their heads.

"You've been on ships, Claude," one said. "Did you watch the sailors, to see what they did . . . or how they did it?"

"Of course not," the man snorted. "I'm a tailor, not a sailor."

"And how about navigation?" another put in. "Do we have anybody who can guide a ship to where we're going?"

"Where is it you gentlemen want to go?" Hoop asked, curious despite himself.

"Virginia," someone said.

"The Carolinas," another chimed in.

"Grand Bahama," another suggested. "My wife has kin there."

"It's our business where we go, mister," Fairfield said, glaring around at the rest, silencing them. "But the lads may be right about one thing. We've little enough of the nautical skills among us. Now you four, though—"

"We're swore to *Fury*," Hoop cut him off. "At least two of us are. We don't know how to swear frogs. Might be you could work out something with Captain Dalton, though. For fee passage, he might . . ." he paused and glanced upward. High aloft, on *Pride*'s foremast, spars rattled and creaked in their mounts. Hoop spun around, staring over the heads of the landsmen ringing him, and roared, "Here! You there, stop that! God's name, do you mean to dismast us?"

Shoving aside men and muskets, he plunged forward through a scattering crowd of people. The decks seemed packed with people everywhere. In the fore, a dozen or more men had discovered the bark's forward capstan and were trying to use it, hauling a heavy line that shivered from capstan to the portside deadeyes, then downward out of sight.

Hoop reached them and pointed a large, shaking finger. "Back that off, you blighters! Now! Steady and easy . . . just back it down to slack!"

Wide-eyed and surprised, the men complied. The capstan creaked in reverse, the spars overhead complained, and then the line went slack.

Hoop breathed a great sigh of relief, then rounded on the culprits, seeming to tower over them. "Are you all daft? That's no kind of use for a capstan. Worse yet, you nearly cost us our shrouds!"

"Sh-shrouds?" one of them stammered.

The big man pointed. "Those! Like big cables that goes aloft? That's shrouds! It's them that keeps the mast from fallin' down an' takin' the ship with it most likely."

At his side, Pliny Quarterstone looked on in amazement. "Would you look at that?" He pointed. "What kind of way is that to clew a capstan? Like windin' wool on a spindle . . . you

80

can't use even a windlass that way, ye bedammed fools, much less a capstan."

Aaron Fairfield was with them then, pushing through the crowds on the deck. "What's wrong here?"

"You tell your people to unhand the workin' decks!" Hoop demanded. "Or there won't be a ship here to talk to Captain Dalton about. Jesus have mercy!"

Quarterstone went to the rail and looked over. Below were several large rafts with railed sides. "Mister Hoop, come here," he called.

Hoop hurried to join him, and Quarterstone pointed overside. "Cows," he said. "They was trying to hoist cows aboard, by God."

"I concede a point, gentlemen," Fairfield said. "We don't know how to operate a sailing ship. Therefore, I believe I must talk with your captain Dalton."

"Well, you'll have your chance to do that, right enough." Hoop pointed southward.

Just out there, closing on a thousand yards of distance, stacked sails taking the wind like a falcon to the kill, came *Fury*. The people crowding *Pride*'s deck stared for a long moment at the lithe, compact, predatory grace of the warship; then one after another, without a word, the armed men aboard laid down their muskets and backed away from them to await the return of the prize ship's master.

Nine

With seven men in its close confines, the little starboard cabin in *Fury*'s sterncastle was as packed as biscuits in a tin. Patrick Dalton sat at the ward table, gazing across at the three landsmen who stood before him, flanked by Charley Duncan on one side and Cadman Wise on the other. Billy Caster crouched in the shuttered gallery behind his captain, quill and ink at hand, ready to write any orders or comments Dalton might require.

"Refugees, Mister Fairfield?" Dalton raised a brow. "Refugees from what?"

"Squire," Fairfield said. "It is *Squire* Fairfield, Captain."

"Squire, then. You are all from that island yonder, I take it?"

"We are. The island is called Mayaguana, one of four under the governorship of Sir Edward Dobbs. And it's Dobbs who's the cause of our evacuation. The blaggard has brought in troops against us because we—those of us here, at least—refused to pay taxes on our taxes. He's declared us rebels, is what he's done. So we—those of us here—we all moved across to the east end of the island hoping we might find a ship, and here we are."

"I see. And are you indeed rebels, Squire Fairfield?"

"Who is asking, Captain Dalton?"

"I claim no flag, sir. Circumstances have dictated that *Fury* and her company are—for the moment at least—ah, independent."

Fairfield arched a brow. "Does that mean that you are rebels, Captain?"

"We have joined no cause, Squire."

"Nor have we, Captain. We simply desire passage to some decent place beyond the jurisdiction of Edward Dobbs, where we might seek justice by whatever means presents itself. We are willing to pay for passage, in some reasonable amount."

"Misters Hoop and Quarterstone report that you boarded my prize vessel without permission, and at gunpoint."

"We had little choice in the matter. Your men were firing cannons at us."

"Yes." Dalton made a steeple of his fingers and frowned. "It may be that an apology is due on that account. It was a misunderstanding, I'm told, having to do with the oddities of the French language." He looked up. "Do any of your people happen to speak French?"

Fairfield looked at the two with him. They shrugged. "Not that I know of, sir," he said. "Possibly we could ask about . . . in the course of our journey."

Dalton sighed. The care of a band of refugee colonials was not something he coveted, but he knew already that he was not going to send them back to their island. There were innocents among them, and it was wartime. "How many of you are there?"

Fairfield glanced at Claude Dunstan, beside him.

"Two hundred and twelve, sir," the man said. "Forty-nine men, thirty-one married women and twenty-six children . . . and the servants, of course. About forty indentures and the rest black Africans."

"And you propose to take your slaves along, as well?"

"Well, of course we do! They're most of what Dobbs is after us for. To take them for himself. He plans to build a fort and needs the manpower."

Dalton glanced around. "Mister Caster, what would you expect a trade vessel to charge for passengers?"

"In Provincial coin, sir? Ah, fourteen dollars a head . . . I believe that's what Mister Romart said Squire Ramsey's ships charge for Indies passage. And a fourth that for servants, he said, if their masters provision them." He had been noting the count as Claude Dunstan recited. Now he tallied it and showed the page to Dalton. It was a fair amount of money.

"Can you pay this amount, Squire?" Dalton asked.

Fairfield turned to the second man with him, a wiry, gray-whiskered gentleman named Prosper McPherson.

"We might pay half that," McPherson admitted. "The rest would have to be in barter or in kind—or paid when we have arrived where we want to go and had a chance to sell some wares."

"Half now, half when we land you," Dalton decided. "You have your funds with you?"

"On the other ship, sir," McPherson said. "All our money is in a chest that we set on the deck. Mister Keith Darling is sitting on it."

"Keith Darling?"

"One of our group," Fairfield said. "A trustworthy and sturdy lad, nigh a match for your Mister Hoop in size."

"It should be safe enough, then," Dalton observed. "Very well, gentlemen, I might accommodate you, depending upon where you want to go."

"Virginia," Fairfield said.

"The Carolinas," Dunstan said.

"Grand Bahama," McPherson said, then added, "although there's several as believe we should make for Rhode Island."

"We are not going to Rhode Island," Fairfield stated.

"If you do, it will not be aboard my ship," Dalton agreed. "Nor do I intend to sail for Grand Bahama, for reasons of my own."

"The Carolinas, then?" Dunstan suggested.

"Virginia," Fairfield insisted.

Dalton shook his head and stood, careful not to crack his head on the low timbers of the little cabin. "I am willing to set a course generally west by north, and hold to it for as long as seems prudent, and to do my best to put you and your party ashore at some Christian port away from the immediacies of the war," he said. "But whether that will be on the Chesapeake, the Delaware or somewhere farther south will depend upon what we encounter along the way. If that satisfies you . . ."

Fairfield squinted at the tall young man. "I took you for British," he said. "Those are not likely British ports, are they?"

"If any are, then we will not land there," Dalton assured

him. "I have reasons for avoiding the exchange of pleasantries with His Majesty's navy right now."

"You are American, then? Colonial?"

"As I said, Squire, *Fury* is an independent party at the moment. Do we have a bargain?"

Fairfield shrugged. "I suppose we have no other choice. When do we make sail?"

"Immediately." Dalton addressed his first officer. "Mister Duncan, have you drilled our recruits?"

"Aye, sir. They know the workings of a snow now, sir."

"Then, take thirty of them and teach them the workings of a bark, if you please. I give you command of the prize vessel and its stores and passengers. You may have Misters Hoop, Nelson and Quarterstone with you, and you'll need a bosun . . ."

"One of the marooned lads is a bosun, sir," Duncan said. "His name's Jim Porter. He was bosun aboard *Tyber.*"

"Then, take Mister Porter, and select your crew. But leave me any with experience aboard a warship. Mister Caster, go along and keep the rosters, if you please."

Fairfield raised his hand, interrupting. "Captain, we have a bit of livestock as well, and several rafts of hay and grain, but we shall need some help in getting them aboard the ship."

"Livestock," Dalton breathed. "Yes, so I heard. Mister Duncan, when you are assembled aboard *Pride,* have someone show the squire's men how to rig a hoist and the proper use of a capstan." He turned to Fairfield again. "Squire Fairfield, when Commander Duncan is ready to sail, we sail. Pray have your cattle, your hay and anything else of importance to you aboard ship at that time."

"And our boats, Captain? What of our boats?"

"Abandon them, Squire. My men will have a look at them. Any that might be of use, we shall keep and credit to you. The rest can go where God and the currents take them."

As Charley Duncan hustled the landsmen through the companionway to the ladder that led to *Fury's* main deck, Fairfield glanced back and asked, "How can a man be uncertain of his nationality?"

"Who, sir?"

"Your captain. He doesn't seem at all sure what he is."

"Oh," Duncan grinned. "There's no question there, sir. Patrick Dalton is Irish. As true a black Irishman as ever was. But since an Irishman has to be something else as well, and since *Fury*'s not on the best of terms with His Majesty's Admiralty right now, it *is* just a bit uncertain what else we might be besides Irish."

It was six bells of the dogwatch when *Pride of Falworth* edged northward into deep water, with *Fury* flanking her as a herd dog flanks its sheep. The wind had come to south of west at a good eighteen knots that scudded wisps of pink cloud across the evening sky, and more than one soul aboard each ship breathed a happy sigh as hands in the tops unfurled great sails while hands a'deck heaved sheeting lines to the pinrails to trim for course.

It seemed like an age — to those who had come to these waters — since they had truly had the manpower to rig and run a jaunty ship so that she could sail the winds and sing the songs of passage.

Pride would set the course for now. With her massed stacks of square-rigged canvas, the big bark was designed for tail or quarter winds and was limited in tacking. She could angle no closer than sixty degrees to the wind, without losing way. So the snow, which could trim to fore-and-afts for a tighter tack, would follow her lead northward until they found more favorable winds for a westerly course.

On *Fury*'s quarterdeck, Patrick Dalton set himself to feel the little warship's song through her planking, and gazed westward. The last flush of evening played on dark eyes in a ruddy face, and the wind from that quarter tousled the dark hair that seemed always to be escaping from its bound queue.

"She sails again as she should," he said, addressing no one. "A sweet snow with canvas aloft and the hands to play her as she deserves." He turned to the helm. "Give us two points to port, please, Mister . . . ah . . ."

"Popkin, sir," the helmsman said. "Peter Popkin. Aye, sir. Two points it is."

"Strongly but gently on the helm, please, Mister Popkin. Have you steered a snow before?"

"No, sir, but I've helmed a brig, and this seems very like it to —" The wheel went over, and *Fury* seemed to surge, leaping gracefully and powerfully into the course correction. "Bleedin' 'ell!" Popkin gasped.

"This is not a brig, Mister Popkin," Dalton said. "This is a snow. Learn her helm, Mister Popkin, and make no mistake about what manner of vessel she is."

"Aye, sir."

Dalton turned. "Mister Caster, please note. When breakfast is finished in the morning, I shall want assembly. All hands on deck for maneuvers. I think it is time to put *Fury* through some paces for the benefit of our new gentlemen on board. We wouldn't want any of our lads to misapprehend the nature of their ship. There might be others who haven't learned the difference between a brig and a snow."

Below the quarterrail, Cadman Wise grinned a devilish grin. Nearly fifty men were aboard *Fury* now, thirty-seven of them new hands. A dozen or so had sailed warships, and all had sailed something. But not one of them, he warranted, had ever seen a snow shaken out — and certainly not by Patrick Dalton.

They had an experience in store. By the time Dalton completed his "maneuvers," they would all be men to match their ship — all, except those who might have fallen overboard or something.

Lucas Peady was a pirate.

Through sixteen years of early life in Essex — first as a drayman's son and later as a fugitive from press-gangs — he had dreamed of becoming a pirate, of roving the trade lanes with a fast ship and great guns, taking what it pleased him to take. Three miserable years as a seaman aboard His Majesty's Escort Cutter *Sprite*, doing wartime patrol in the British Indies, had evolved for him first a plan and then actual opportunity to become what he had dreamed. Lucas Peady had bided his time, schemed his schemes and recruited his accomplices carefully and with fine craft. Then he had acted.

In the shoaling waters off San Salvador, following an abrupt and bloody mutiny, five Crown officers and eight loyal sailors had gone over *Sprite*'s leeward rail to feed the fishes. By a simple replacing of escutcheons and a quick layover at the Island of San Rafael to recruit a few practiced cutthroats and a makeshift black flag, His Majesty's Cutter of War *Sprite* had ceased to exist. In her stead now sailed the venture cutter *Mako,* and she stood at sea in the trade lanes awaiting her prey.

Nearly thirty men were aboard her, men enough to man the wide sails and the eight ranging guns of the little predator. Though hardly longer than a large launch in her hull, *Mako* was deep-keeled and swift, with massive sails and trim lines. A proud cutter of her time, she was all legs and teeth, a killer boat rigged to rake and take much larger vessels — provided they were merchant vessels.

At six bells of a fine tropic morning, the spotter aloft on *Mako*'s high mast made sails — a bare three miles away and slogging northward on a westerly wind. Lucas Peady himself climbed the shrouds for a look, and his grin glinted in the morning light. A bark she was. A four-master, riding heavy.

"Charge all guns," he ordered his mates. "There's easy prey yonder, and we've the advantage of the wind. Make all sail, lads. At this range we'll be on them before they can even come about."

Eyes a'glitter at sight of a prize that could make wealthy men of them all no matter what it carried, they spread *Mako*'s wings, and the cutter sliced bright water as it shot forth to head off the bark. It had closed to a distance of two miles before the merchantman turned hard astarboard, getting the wind on its tail for a run.

Lucas Peady laughed aloud and slapped the nearest man on the back. "Outrun a cutter, would he? See how that ship slogs; there's cargo yonder an' plenty. Passengers as well, by the looks of it. Bless us, lads, I'd wager there's women aboard that ship. Rig for wing and wing, there! Look alive, now, for today we take our first ship!"

Within a bell, *Mako* had closed to less than a mile of distance, and the gunners stood by her cannons with smoking fuse. Through his glass, Peady could read the bark's escutcheon. *"Pride of Falworth,"* he gloated. "Bring us to range of the bow guns, Mister Skinner, and let's pierce her sterncastle with a pair of loads!"

At half a mile the bow gunners aligned their notches . . . and aligned them again as the big bark rounded into a change of course, coming sharply to port, losing way as its square sails took the quartering wind.

"He's giving us his broadside." Peady grinned. "Gunners, fire!"

Mako's bow chasers thundered, and smoke drifted on the wind. Peady squinted, then frowned. The first ball spumed just aft the bark's rudder. The second fell short.

"Blast!" Peady swore. "You there, reload an'—"

He didn't finish his order. Just beyond the turning bark, hidden until now by its larger silhouette, was a second ship— smaller by far than the four-master, but rigged as no merchantman was rigged.

"What th' devil is that?" a man nearby shouted. "A brig?"

Peady brought his tiller over sharply, then shaded his eyes, squinting into the sun-haze. A brig? Possibly . . . but within moments he knew it was not, for no brig ever could have moved the way that vessel moved. Like a fox after a chicken, the warship made way on tight tack, standing into the gap between *Mako* and the fleeing bark. Then it brought its stem directly into the wind, and even as it came about for the chase, its bow chasers thundered.

The two shots *Mako* had fired were all that she ever would. An iron ball threw spray thirty feet into the air ahead of her, then skipped like a thrown stone and crashed into her bow alongside the jutting sprit. Men screamed and wreckage flew as the ball travelled half the cutter's length, shearing away decking and timbers.

The second ball took out her portside shrouds and three guns—and their crews.

Again there was smoke and thunder, this time a drumroll that belched and rippled along the warship's gunwales, and seemed to go on and on. The last thing Lucas Peady saw in this world was a bow escutcheon, breasting through the smokes of hell as the warship turned to close.

The name on the escutcheon was *Fury*.

All along the portside rails of *Pride*'s main deck, wide-eyed faces stared at the drifting smoke astern, the shower of blasted wreckage still pelting the waves . . . and at the small, jaunty warship just breasting through its own smokes several hundred yards beyond.

"He blasted the blighters to kingdom come," someone breathed.

Near the quarterrail, Charley Duncan leaned on a stanchion and grinned. "Bonny lads, those," he declared. "But they were in error not looking beyond their prize to see what else awaited."

"You led them right into a trap," Aaron Fairfield accused. "What sort of people are you, to do that? It was only a small boat."

"Boat?" Duncan blinked. "That was a cutter, Squire. An armed cutter that intended to sink or take this ship—and would have."

"Phaw! Bit extreme, if you want my opinion . . . blowing the little thing right out of the water like that."

Duncan shook his head. *Landsmen!* "Captain Dalton has no liking for pirates, Squire," he said. "No liking whatsoever." He glanced forward, then gawked and roared, "Mister Hoop! What are those cattle doing on the main deck?"

"Some of the ladies led them up for milking, sir!" Hoop shouted from ahead.

"Have them milked somewhere else! Not on my working deck!"

Pliny Quarterstone came hurrying aft. "We're having something of a problem with that, Commander," he explained. "Most of the passengers have taken up residence in the forward hold, you see, and that's where the cows are, too; but there's no room there for milking them, and the main hold is up to its timbers with cotton bales, so . . ."

Duncan gritted his teeth. "Sort it out, Mister Quarterstone. Just get those cattle off the handling deck."

"Aye, sir. We'll see what we can do."

Ten

Four hundred miles to the west, on the same day that Dalton exercised *Fury*'s gunners and Lucas Peady's fledgling pirates went the way of Davy Jones, another encounter was taking place. The cruiser *Valkyrie* was no darting cutter playing at piracy games, but a full-rigged and heavily armed vessel of frigate class, and her master was no ambitious deckhand, but a calculating and experienced mariner who knew the ways of sail and the habits of merchantmen as well as any captain of his time.

On this day *Valkyrie* stood to leeward of Hawksbill Cay, a stalker at rest and almost invisible against the background jumble of hundreds of little islands flanking the west expanse of Exuma Sound. For nearly a week the predator had lain in wait here while eyes in her tops scanned the northward horizon. There was no happenstance in her being just here, for the man who now called himself Jack Shelby left little to luck. He was here because he knew what he would find, and on this day his information proved correct.

"On deck!" the foretopman called.

Amidships the bosun, Caleb Strode, responded. "Deck aye, Mister Summers!"

"Sail off the starboard bow!" The shout drifted down through abruptly silent rigging. "Three ships hard down an' comin' on!"

Strode turned toward the stern of the ship, to carry the message, but Timothy Leech was there.

"I heard, Mister Strode," the big first said. "Let's have fresh eyes aloft to watch their progress. Stand by to weigh anchors and make sail, at the captain's order."

"Aye." Strode nodded. "Are they the ones, do you think?"

"We'll know that when Captain Jack tells us," Leech said. "Just stand ready."

Leech didn't bother going to the gunwales. If the sightings were hard down from the tops, there would be nothing to see from the deck for a while. Instead he strolled aft, pausing here and there to cast a critical eye on the positioning of gun carriages, the lashings of clewing lines, the general readiness of the vessel. The men who made up *Valkyrie*'s company were of a type, and it was a thing well to keep in mind. Ruthless and bloodthirsty, fighters without mercy when there was a fight to be had, they shared the tendency to become surly and lax if they weren't kept busy.

It was Leech's task — and his pleasure — to keep them busy and alert. His authority came from the captain. His right he had established himself, by personally beating to death the first among them to test him and by flogging into submission those few who had offered to interfere. The exercise had cost *Valkyrie* six crewmen — three of those he had flogged were dead now, and two others had gone overside in the night — but it was well worth the small loss. *Valkyrie* was a tight and well-disciplined vessel and would remain so.

Jack Shelby demanded no more, and would settle for no less. As a merchant captain he had learned the ways of pirates. He knew the strengths of the breed and the weaknesses, and Leech shared with him the belief that what befell most pirate ventures in the end — barring bad luck or an encounter with a ship of the line — was sloth. Sheer laxity and sloth.

They had vowed that such would not be the fate of *Valkyrie*.

When Jack Shelby came on deck, Leech gave him the sighting report and an evaluation of *Valkyrie*'s readiness for assault. Within the hour, top lookouts had descriptions of the three vessels coming down on the wind. Two merchantmen and an escort.

Shelby nodded. "It's them," he told Leech. "My man in Vir-

ginia has earned his commission. Two fine prizes. The Spaniard will pay well for what they carry."

With select hands reading winds and currents, Shelby studied his charts. "Here," he noted, pointing. "They sail southward as though to skirt Eleuthera to the east. As though they
were making for Hispaniola. But they will turn into the northeast channel, out of sight of Hatchet Bay, and set new bearings
on Hawksbill. Their destination is the Camaguey trade
ports."

"Cunning," Leech said. "The merchant becomes elusive."

"Not so cunning, Mister Leech." Shelby gazed northward
with cold gray eyes, pulling his coat about him. "Predictable,
in fact. It's a trick I myself taught McCall's mariners . . .
when I sailed for him."

"And the escort ship, Cap'n? Will it come, too?"

"Oh, aye. It will come, with a weather eye eastward, expecting a challenge from Crown ships at Governor's Harbour."

"But there are no Crown vessels in Governor's Harbour,
Cap'n. They're all out looking for us, thanks to that evening's
amusement we gave them."

"Aye, but McCall's agents don't know that, and neither do
his captains."

"Then, we attack from the west . . ." Leech grinned.

"Aye, from the west." Shelby looked at his charts again and
then at the sky. "With the wind at our stern to give us the advantage and the sun behind us to blind them until we are on
them. I trust the men are prepared?"

"Blood in their eyes an' fire in their bellies, sir."

"I'll want to make short work of the escort, Mister Leech.
Once we engage, you may direct fire from the gundecks. No
flag, no dancing about, and no quarter. Sink the escort as you
please, but quickly."

"Aye, Cap'n. With pleasure."

As the three ships came in sight off Dunmore Point, skirting the shoals above Exuma Sound, Leech made the rounds of
his gundecks to personally order his strategy. Bow chasers and
the heavy guns in the fore would be charged with ball, and the
gunners would sight for close-range waterline strikes. The

portside batteries would be charged with chain and barbel to devastate rigging and clear the decks. Stern guns would fire heated balls.

Silent as a panther, *Valkyrie* waited, anchors up and sail ready, still hidden by the camouflage of the cays and by the glare of the lowering sun beyond her. By seven bells of the dog watch, just as Shelby had predicted, the little flotilla was abreast and sailing southward, bound for Cuba's coastal ports. The escort ship, a refurbished brig that had been some privateer's prize, had edged toward the east flank of the two square-riggers, alert for challenge from British sail.

Jack Shelby went to his quarterdeck. "To helm, Mister Trice," he ordered. "Mister Strode, hands a'deck to make sail. Gunnery to stations. Misters Boyd and Ames, you'll take your firing orders from Mister Leech. Mister Trahan, command the tops. Stations, if you please."

Men scurried to stations, and Caleb Strode's pipe shrilled amidships. "Hands to make sail! Hands a'sheet! Tops aloft! Make sail! Sheet home . . . sheet home . . . sheet home!"

"Trim for port reach," Shelby ordered. "Full and by." Sails drummed taut, and *Valkyrie* lifted her stem and took spray in her teeth, a predator beginning its charge.

"Steer to intercept that brig, Mister Trice," Shelby said. "Cut the wake of the two square-riggers if you can. A bit of panic there will do us no harm."

The helm came over, and *Valkyrie* threw sheets of bright spray into the wind as she homed on her kill.

"A fine, bloodthirsty ship," Leech noted. "She growls and keens for the fight."

"A ship for our purpose." Shelby nodded. "Thibaud was a fool to lose her so." He crossed his arms and judged the closing distance ahead. "To station now, Mister Leech. You know the maneuver. Fire as you will, and sink that brig."

"Aye, Cap'n." His eyes aglow, Timothy Leech headed amidships.

Shelby's tactic was sound. *Valkyrie* was within a thousand yards of the nearest merchantman when abrupt activity aboard that vessel said she had been seen. Buntings ran aloft,

94

and the merchantman's yards hove about for a dodge, then rattled and leaned when her helm fought rudder to avoid colliding with the second vessel just beyond. A cannon belched smoke at the first vessel's stern as *Valkyrie* rammed across its wake barely two chains aft, but Shelby and his crew ignored it. Their first target was the private brig beyond the pair, the armed escort just now fighting its sails to come about, leaning as its captain tried to bring his nose — and his ranging guns — to windward. With perfect wind on her quarter, *Valkyrie* closed relentlessly.

Leech counted the seconds as the range between the two diminished to a thousand yards, to seven hundred, to five hundred and smoke billowed at the waist of the brig. Aloft, a ball ripped through the foretop, and screams sounded there. Bits of wreckage clattered down. Two flailing men, both screaming, plummeted from above, one to the foredeck, the other overside. Leech raised his arm, still counting, then lowered it. "Forward batteries, fire!"

Flares of hell spat from *Valkyrie*'s stem and bows, and in the rolling smoke ahead there were the sounds of chaos.

As though dancing to a silent tune, *Valkyrie* came smartly to starboard, riding it seemed on the echoes of her cannons. Leech raised his arm again. "Portside batteries, rake their decks! Ready . . ." He lowered his arm. "Fire!"

. This time he could see clearly the devastation of his guns — clearly and near, for the brig was a scant hundred yards away. Well within point-blank range. Chain shot and barbel, devilish whirling engines of death, smashed into the shrouds at deck level, taking with them everything in their way. Howling their banshee wails, the lengths of chain tore apart rigging, rails and the flesh beyond them while the whirling barbels gouged out great gaps in masts and uprights. For a moment it seemed that the entire midsection of the brig had exploded, leaving only its stem and its little quarterdeck intact. Then a delayed volley raked its stern and the quarterdeck, and those on it were carried away.

The effects of the first volley were there as well — gaping holes in the brig's hull just at waterline.

95

He had only a moment to admire his gunners' work. *Valkyrie* was continuing her turn, hard hands shifting spars and recleating sheets at orders from the command aft.

He has no doubt of our effect here, Leech thought, grinning. *He said to make short work of the brig, and that is what he expects. He has dismissed the brig entirely now, and is aligning to run down the merchantmen. Captain Jack Shelby has no thought of failure or delay, because neither is a thing that he will tolerate.*

There was no answering fire now from the brig. It sat asunder upon the waves, beginning even now to list as its bilges filled, and the only sounds that carried across were the shrill screaming of maimed men and the staccato rattle of falling rigging.

Leech hurried to the after command and raised his arm. "After batteries and chasers ready," he ordered. Along both quarters and below in the stern, sweating men used great double forks of heavy iron to lift heated balls from their flaming beds in sand tubs and set them into the muzzles of cannons. Gouts of steam erupted as loaders seated them in the breaches, with wet rams. The guns were trundled out and secured, and linstocks hovered over their vents.

Leech brought down his arm. "Fire!"

Cherry-red and trailing ropes of smoke darker than the clouds that billowed outward at their release, the heated balls smashed into the hull of the brig, and more screams echoed back.

"That should do it nicely," Timothy Leech said, speaking to no one in particular. *Valkyrie* was already gaining speed on a new course, away from the shattered brig, her feral stem pointing like death's finger at the pair of fleeing merchantmen amassing sail for a run down Exuma Sound. Leech gazed aft for a moment more, admiring his work, then raised a hand in casual salute. "Misters Boyd and Ames," he called. "Have all batteries reload with shot and stand by stations. You may give your gunners a 'well done,' but please admonish them that their next volleys will be at prize vessels and it's our loss, one and all, should anyone cause them to sink."

The brig in their wake was wreathed in smoke as Leech

joined Captain Shelby on the quarterdeck. Shelby didn't even look around as he asked, "I assume the escort is sunk, Mister Leech."

"Very soon she will sit on the bottom, Cap'n. She's —"

A roar like the thunders of hell echoed across widening waters. Leech looked back and grinned. The brig had exploded. From the looks of it, fire had reached her main magazines. The explosion seemed to go on and on, fire and thunder mounting ever higher where the ship had been. Myriad tiny things that might have been bits of wreckage, kegs of stores or human bodies — or some of each — tumbled and flew in all directions.

"Like to amend the report, Cap'n," Leech said. "There isn't any brig anymore."

Still, Shelby did not look back. Hard-eyed and intent, he focused on the prizes fleeing ahead. "I thought not," he said coldly. Then to his helmsman, "Port a point, Mister Trice. Bring us onto the flank of those two as they run — close enough to discourage them from making for land yonder, but hold back a bit. We'll let them have their run."

"It will be dark in an hour, Cap'n," Leech pointed out. "Shouldn't we . . ."

"There are people on that island over there, Mister Leech. A capture this close might tempt them to come out with boats or something and interfere. No, we shall let the prizes run for a time. There is no place for them to go once the light fails, except the way they are going, and we shall be right here behind them to hurry them on their way. By morning we should have open sea about us. We can take them then, one at a time, at our leisure."

In the brief dusk of a spring evening, boats were sent out from Governor's Harbour to search and salvage among the bits of flotsam that were all that remained of a private brig that had been escorting trade vessels. From floating wreckage the searchers identified the brig *Pliny*. Admiralty records would reveal that *Pliny* had been a Crown vessel, taken by colonial privateers off Hatteras the year before and sold to persons unknown in the Carolinas. Witnesses ashore, who had watched the Exuma Sound encounter through glasses, would confirm that the attack had been an act of piracy and not of war . . . the dark frigate had shown no colors and issued no challenge. It had simply appeared and attacked.

As long as there was light enough to see, and for an hour afterward with lanterns, the searchers gleaned the flotsam for survivors. They found none.

Long after the bronze bell in the little fort's tower had sounded midnight, a piece of shattered decking washed ashore a mile to the south, and something moved there in the misty starlight. For a time the man lay silent, struggling to get his wits about him. Finally he got to unsteady feet and looked around, remembering.

He would not forget that dark frigate. Its every line was engraved in his memory, as was the name his glass had picked out on its port bow just before the deck beneath his feet had erupted and flung him over the side.

Valkyrie.

And as he trudged northward along a starlit beach, a resolution grew in him. First, he must find a way back to Virginia, where his voyage had begun. He must personally report to Ian McCall on the loss of the cargo ships that it had been the brig's duty — and his own duty — to escort safely. Secondly, he must find employment. Another ship, perhaps? Another command? Would anyone again trust a former Royal Navy officer who now had had two ships shot out from beneath his feet?

Unlikely, that seemed. But he could only ask.

And finally, somehow, some day, he must go in search of that pirate.

Whatever it took, whatever the means, Lewis Farrington resolved that night to find *Valkyrie* and end her career.

Nearing Governor's Harbour, he paused. He could seek help in the little Crown settlement. It would not be difficult to seem a subject of the king. Until recent years he had in fact been a subject of the king. But much had happened since then . . . too much.

He skirted around the settlement and continued northward. Somewhere ahead was Gregory Town, and there—where the riots had occurred—he would find rebel sympathizers. *Once a man has changed coats,* he told himself, *the honorable thing is to abide by his own commitment.* Lewis Farrington had little interest in the rebellion in America, and less in the politics and causes of it. He had never been one for causes. British by birth, he was American now by circumstance and—he admitted—by choice. It was as simple as that, no matter of causes. Relieved of his commission by misfortune and Admiralty politics, stranded thus in the colonies with nowhere to go, he had become Colonial.

But he had a cause now. Rogues with frigates had pushed him just too far. He clenched his jaws, remembering. That rogue commanding *Courtesan* had shelled his own flag and cost Lewis Farrington his sloop and his career. *Courtesan* was gone now, he had heard—sent to the bottom, unlikely as it seemed, by the very schooner her captain had been so bent upon recapturing. But the pirate *Valkyrie* still sailed, and Lewis Farrington made a resolve—to find and sink the *Valkyrie*.

Eleven

Morning sun and spring breezes kissed the ways at South Point. Warm zephyrs soft with the combined scents of salt water and new-plowed fields drifted across the shipyards there and became raucous airs heady with the smells of hot tar and new rope, loud with the sounds of enterprise. Clatter of tackle hoisted aloft for fitting, song of shrouds and stays being drawn to pitch like great strings on giant violins, the chants of teams of burly young men working windlass and capstan, whine of stressed spars coming about in their fittings to the cadence of fitters and riggers at their lofty tasks — all of these were the music of the ways, where vessels lay for careening and refitting, where new hulls sprouted the trappings of sailing ships to suit the needs of those whose fortunes required them.

Along the Delaware it seemed almost a time of peace. Few Crown vessels remained on the river, and those kept themselves well up the river — support for the impending evacuation of Philadelphia, official reports to the White Fleet's headquarters said, although it was surmised by many a Colonial that the captains of His Majesty's ships on the Delaware were either exceedingly nervous or secretly mortified after a winter of fighting what Squadron Commander Carlson had termed "UFO's." Unidentified Floating Objects. To many, the saga of David Bushnell's exploding kegs was a subject of glee. But not to the British Navy. How many thousands of cannon rounds, grapeshot charges and volleys of musketry had been expended on logs, bits of driftwood and — some said — even a pair of unfortunate muskrats, would never be known. But the "Battle of the Kegs" had made history. The only certain casualties of Bushnell's floating mines with their spring-lock detonators were a small dinghy and a barge, but for a time the Delaware had been a very noisy river.

The entire episode — British men-of-war doing battle against anything seen floating on the water — had lasted for weeks and had provided high entertainment for the residents of the area, few enough of whom now harbored any Royalist or Tory sentiments after three years of war.

But now the kegs were gone, and to all intents and purposes, so were the king's ships. Now it was back to business as usual. There were crops to be planted, barns to be mended, crafts to be practiced, trade goods to be traded and ships to be repaired . . . and built.

One such was the sleek, and oddly feral-looking, schooner nearing completion at the yard of John Singleton Ramsey below Wilmington. The schooner was a subject of local curiosity for a number of reasons. It was crafted as a cargo vessel might be; but it had the deckhouse and fighting tops of a warrior, and rumor had it that it would mount at least seven cannons. It was, some said, a near-exact duplicate of an earlier schooner, the wreckage of which lay alongside the ways where the new one was now being outfitted. Strange tales were told about the hulk, and about those who had sailed it. Some even whispered that it had bested a forty-four-gun frigate in head-to-head combat.

And, oddest of all, the work proceeding at those ways seemed not to be directed by Ramsey, nor by any of his usual overseers, but by a small, striking, auburn-haired young woman whom some said they recognized . . . Squire Ramsey's pretty daughter, Constance, they said.

In each tavern and grogshop from South Point to Wilmington there had been lively debates about what the schooner's use would be, who would command it and why an attractive and headstrong young woman seemed to be in charge of its equippage. Most of those actually working on the project were not locals at South Point, and close-mouthed about the matter. All the local gossips could glean was that the men rigging the schooner for sea either didn't know what use it would be put to or chose not to say.

101

Locals had singled out nine among them who seemed to be confidants of Mistress Ramsey — all sailors, it seemed. But only three of the nine even hailed from the southern colonies — one Michael Romart, who was obviously a Virginian, and a pair of red-haired brothers named O'Riley, who spoke as Carolinians did. The ship's master carpenter, some felt, might be a Maryland man, but the remaining five were from other parts entirely.

In all, the schooner and its readiers remained a mystery to most who were curious. Yet each day they were there, the lady, her maidservant and her motley assemblage, directing a swarm of workmen and purveyors, riggers and sailmakers, fitters and chandlers, none of whom learned much of substance beyond such facts as "The young lady, why, she trimmed the notches and fined the carriage of each great gun aboard yon ship. Aye, herself, personal. Skirt tied up an' sleeves rolled like a man's, and orderin' quoinin' same as any gunnery officer. Mates, ye've never seen th' like!"

The jaunty schooner would soon be ready for sea, and she wore proud escutcheons salvaged from her wrecked companion alongside.

Her name was *Faith*.

On a bright morning a polished carriage rolled into South Point and up to the head of the ways there. The footman swung down and set a step stool, then swung the lacquered door open, and a portly gentleman of middle years stepped out. Wide-shouldered and sturdy, he evidenced in his arms; his stout hands and the lines of his ruddy face, the signs of a man who has known hard work; and in his alert eyes and fine dress, the evidences of one who has profited from his ventures.

"Take the carriage around to Master Jack's, Colly," he instructed the immaculately garbed black servant who was with him. "Wait there and take your ease for a time. I shall send for you when I need you."

"Yes, sah." Colly sat back in the cushioned seat and rapped his stick on the carriage top. "Master Jack's livery, Wilson," he said.

The carriage made a smart turn and rolled away. The man watched it go, then strolled through the gate and into the ship-yard, nodding at a sentry. "Morning, Albert."

"Morning to you, Squire Ramsey," the sentry said. "Inspection this morning, sir?"

"No inspection, Albert. I've come to visit with my daughter. I assume she is aboard that schooner?"

"Expect so, sir. She usually is. Do you want escort for boarding, sir?"

"Why would I want escort?"

Albert swallowed, lowering his eyes. "Well, sir, since they started shipping stores aboard, them folks has been right choosy about who comes around."

Ramsey turned, his mouth dropping open. "Choosy? By God, I own this yard! I'll go where I please within it."

"I meant about folks comin' around th' schooner, Squire." Albert sounded as though he were forcing the words out. "They, ah . . . well, they mean for folks to stand off."

"I own that schooner, too! At least, I seem to be paying for it. *Choosy?* By the great . . ."

"Maybe you'd best talk to them that's aboard, sir. If that's what you've a mind to do. I was just sayin' how it seems that it is. To me, I mean . . . it seems so."

Ramsey squinted at the young man, wondering if he had come down with the vapors or something. Albert seemed to be making less and less sense.

"Let us hear no more about it, Albert," the great man said. "In my yards I go where I please." With that he turned away and headed for the schooner standing tall upon its slipways.

On the angling dray path, he stepped aside to allow an ox cart to pass. The ox driver glanced at him, scowling. "Mind w'at ye're about wi' them folk, guv'ner. They be touchy as ear fleas."

Approaching the bright new schooner, Ramsey heard a shout overhead and looked up. High above him, balancing on the ship's spreaders, a young man frowned down at him.

"I said, stand off!" the challenger repeated. "What's your business here, anyway?"

"My business is my own business!" Ramsey snapped. "Who are you?"

"Ives is the name," the man above said. "Phillip Ives. State your business and go away." He squinted, cocking his head. "Don't I recognize you from somewhere? I've seen you, I know."

"I am John Singleton Ramsey!" Ramsey announced.

The man peered down at him. "No, that doesn't seem right."

"What do you mean, 'that doesn't seem right'? You think I don't know who I am?"

"No, but I've seen you somewhere, for certain. I remember your hat." The young man grinned suddenly and snapped his fingers. "Aye, that's it. When I sailed for Cap'n Dalton, aboard *Fury*, you an' some others had dinner aboard with th' lady . . . blazes, I think you're right! You're Squire Ramsey!" He turned, as agile as a cat on the soaring structure of the schooner's stem, and trotted toward the high bow, his arms spread for balance. "Mister Romart! Gentleman below says he's Squire Ramsey! I believe he's right!"

Ramsey planted his fists on his hips, grunting in disbelief. After a moment a head appeared above the vessel's trim gunwale, peering downward.

Ramsey blinked. "Romart? Is that you? Where have you been?"

"Why it *is* you!" Michael Romart declared. "Morning to you, Squire. Where have I what?"

"Been!"

"Lately, sir? Right here, sir, giving the lady a hand with her schooner. Lovely sight, isn't she, sir? Spitting image of her mother."

"Mister Romart, what do you know of my daughter's mother?"

"Not a thing, sir. I meant the schooner. Just as the lady ordered, we've made her the very image of *Faith*. Right down to the rooftree bolsters at her knees and the barn shingles on her deckhouse. Have you noticed the tops? Mister Tower is special proud of those tops, sir. Why are you standing down there, sir? Wouldn't you like to come aboard?"

"I have every intention of it! Where is the gangway?"

"We don't have a gangway, sir. We've been shipping by hoist. Keeps the curious from sneaking aboard, you see."

"Then, where is a ladder?"

"No ladders, either, sir. Same reason. Would you like a hoist?"

Cursing under his breath, clinging to tar-dark cables and trying to balance his dignity in a swaying, turning mesh of rope net, John Singleton Ramsey was hoisted aboard the new *Faith* like so much kegged salt pork destined for the galley.

Finally on deck, he gazed around, remembering. The spanking-new vessel was, indeed, very much as the old one had been — not as she had been when first he'd had her, but as she had been when Constance and her wild Irishman brought her back from that improbable adventure in the northern colonies. Not a harmless, pretty cargo schooner, but something quite else — something that fugitives by dint of luck, skill and desperation had wrought upon the semblance of that.

"It's like before," he muttered, almost expecting to see the bloodstain on the deck that the other schooner had worn. "It is a jolly-be-damned warship, and no less."

Michael Romart hovered beside him, so pleased with the vessel that the sparkle of his grin was matched by proud moisture in his eyes. "Aye," he said. "She's Cap'n Dalton's *Faith* as ever was."

"The devil she is," Ramsey snapped. "I've paid through the very teeth for this folly, though no one has yet explained to me just why I should. Where is my daughter?"

"Miss Constance? Why, she's gone to the chandler's to order out some special stores, sir. She'll be back in a bit. Would you care for tea, sir?"

"I would indeed, Mister Romart, thank you."

Romart turned. "Mister O'Riley!"

Aloft at the mainmast's binding and below at the fife rail, similar carrot-topped heads turned. "Aye, Mister Romart?" they asked in unison. Then the lower one added, "Which Mister O'Riley did you have in mind, then?"

"It doesn't matter." Romart shrugged. "You'll do, Gerald. Go below and get Squire Ramsey some tea, please."

"I'm not Gerald," the indicated one said. "I'm Donald. That's Gerald aloft." But he went, hurrying aft to disappear below the companionway's coaming.

"They're our cook," Romart explained.

"Which one?"

"Whichever one is handy." The Virginian shrugged. "Hardly anybody can tell them apart. They're from the Carolinas."

Ramsey gazed around, noticing faces. "All these men look familiar," he said.

"Aye, sir, I expect they do. They all sailed with us — with Cap'n Dalton an' the rest of us — aboard *Fury*. Of course, I'm the only one here who sailed with him aboard *Faith*. That's why Miss Constance needed me here, sir. These are all good lads, but none of them ever saw *Faith* . . . I mean the first *Faith*, of course, as she was when we went to kill the frigate. She was like this. And some of her . . . as much as could be salvaged . . . is in this *Faith*."

Ramsey studied him, trying to understand what he was getting at. There was just no understanding sailors, he thought.

"What I mean is, sir" — Romart wiped his eyes — "is . . . well, this schooner here may not be quite exactly that schooner yonder, but she's the blessed same schooner for all that, seems to me, for in her beats the same true heart."

"Poppycock!" Ramsey snorted. "A ship is a ship, man. That's all it is. A ship."

"Aye." Romart dropped his gaze and shrugged. "Aye, there was a time — I suppose — when every one of us thought the same."

A man came from below, carrying tools in a wooden kit, and Ramsey recognized him both from Dalton's escapades and, more recently, as an employee of Ian McCall. Joseph Tower, a carpenter. Without glancing around, Tower set his kit on the coaming and said grumpily, "She's sealed to the bilges, Mister Romart, though why a decent ship should have such a thing is beyond—" He turned then, saw Ramsey and clamped his mouth shut.

"This is Mister Tower, Squire." Romart waved a casual hand. "He was ship's carpenter of *Fury* before Cap'n Dalton beached all of us colonials. Mister Tower, do you recollect . . . ?"

"Aye," Tower said sheepishly. "Th' lady's father. How do, Squire Ramsey?"

"What sort of thing?" Ramsey's eyes narrowed, pinning him. "Sir?"

106

"What sort of thing is it that you don't know why a decent ship should have, that this one does?"

"Nothing whatever, sir. I tend to talk to myself at times."

"Mister Tower is from Maryland," Romart observed.

"That should have no bearing on anything," Ramsey declared. "Please answer my question, Mister Tower."

"It's really nothing of note, sir. I . . ."

From the masthead a voice rang down. "On deck!"

Seeming generally relieved, Michael Romart lifted his eyes. "Aye, Mister O'Riley?"

"Th' lady's approachin', Mister Romart. Two points on the port bow."

"Thank you, Mister O'Riley." Romart favored Ramsey with a reassuring smile. "Here comes your daughter now, Squire. I'm sure you can ask her anything you want to know about *Faith*." He turned to call, "Mister Ives! Hands to the scaffold, please. Miss Constance is back."

"Aye! You men, lend a hand on this scaffold now!"

Ramsey watched open-mouthed as a neat scaffold was lifted over the bow rail and lowered on block and tackle. He strode to the fore, saw Constance, Dora and a pair of cutlass-wielding sailors step out of a coach, and glared at Phillip Ives. "Why didn't you tell me you had a boarding scaffold?"

"You didn't ask, sir. You asked about a gangway or a ladder, but not a scaffold."

When Constance arrived on *Faith*'s deck, she hugged her father, fended off his questions and took his hand. "Come with me," she ordered. "I have a surprise for you."

Down the companionway she led him, to a tiny sterncastle that seemed an exact duplicate of that in the original *Faith*. But when he paused to look around, she urged him on, into a tight little galley where one of the O'Riley's offered tea, then stepped aside so that they could pass. At the galley's fore bulkhead Constance smiled, raised her hand and slapped the sheer surface sharply.

"Well," she asked, "what do you think?"

Ramsey blinked. "About what?"

"About this! Honestly, Father. You yourself specified how the first *Faith* should be. Don't you remember?"

He looked again, and remembered. "Ah," he said. "Aha!"

Constance nodded. "Exactly. A false hold, just as before. It was the rum in it that paid you a handsome profit on *Faith,* even though you lost her. So what do you think?"

"Think?" he asked blankly.

"Of course. If I am to take this schooner to sea, I shall require—"

"You? You . . . take this to sea?"

"Certainly. Why did you think I was having it outfitted? But there are yet some items I'll need. First, a reliable captain . . ."

"You shall do no such thing! Constance, you are a woman. Women of my acquaintance do not put out to sea with—"

"Oh, poo! We've been over all that before. I have been to sea. And as to going again, I certainly can and I certainly shall. All you need worry about is . . ."

"I absolutely forbid it!"

". . . is a cargo worthy of *Faith II.* You know the kind of cargo I mean, Father."

"I take it you are referring to contraband of some sort . . ."

"Of course. Last time, it was rum. I suppose rum would do nicely again, but I leave that to you, as you certainly know far more about such things than I do."

"I forbid it! I absolutely forbid it! My daughter is . . . well, my daughter is no smuggler!"

"Nonsense!" She stood straight and determined, her eyes ablaze. "I expect I am a very good smuggler. After all, I learned the business from you, didn't I?"

Ramsey lowered his head, gritting his teeth. "So that's what all this has been about? This schooner and all? You want to smuggle contraband?"

"Poo! That's simply a means to make a venture profitable. It isn't the venture itself. My intention is to go and find Patrick Dalton. Now, do you find me a captain and a cargo, or must I find them myself?"

Twelve

As Dalton had fully expected, the wind had come southerly. Now *Pride of Falworth* rode strong on easy seas, her stacked squares driving on the sort of wind that commodity vessels cherish — a steady twenty-five knots abaft her port quarter. For three days no sail or land had been seen, and the two ships drove steadily onward, holding a northwestward course that required no sail handling beyond an occasional trim.

At least for *Pride,* there was no such fuss. Charley Duncan's mission as commander aboard the prize vessel was simply to take her where Dalton — whenever he saw fit to decide upon a destination — ordered, in as efficient and timely a manner as possible.

Aboard *Fury* it was another matter.

For the first time since he acquired the snow, Patrick Dalton had a full complement of hands to man her, and he wasted no time in — as he put it — "taking the measure of her limits."

It was a puzzle to some of those who had sailed with him before. A ship that had fought xebecs, had escaped a pursuing seventy-four, had played hopscotch through the very heart of a Royal Navy troop convoy and had weathered a black squall under tack sail, they supposed, had already had her limits fairly well measured. But it was the captain's way. Given a ship at his command, and a chance to truly sail it, he would play it to its limit as delightedly as a child putting a stick horse through its paces. Those who had sailed with him knew this, and while they might see fit to comment, still they shrugged and bore with him.

It fell, then, to the new hands aboard to stagger about in wide-eyed awe as *Fury* cavorted on the winds, trying first this and then that sail configuration, ranging far out from her larger charge, darting here and there in rushes and passes that most of them would never have believed a vessel of her size could accomplish and — simply as a matter of crew and sail drill — now and then sailing tight circles around the straight-running bark.

"Captain's got the bit in his teeth and the spray in his face," Cadman Wise remarked to Billy Caster as *Fury*, hands aloft and all stations fully manned, did a smart come-about through the wind a half mile ahead of *Pride*, then sheeted home on a starboard tack and shot off on a new course that made her timbers groan and her stays whine. "Puts me in mind of when we first boarded that schooner, up at Long Island, and managed to shake loose from the gunboats. Mercy, how he did shake the sleep out of that *Faith*. Like he had decided a ship can fly and was out to prove it."

Purdy Fisk had wandered near, carrying an armload of chain for repairs on the foremast stays. "Aye," he muttered. "As I recollect, we wound up makin' hull patches while half the world was lookin' to shoot the devil out of us, too."

Aloft a shout rang out. "On deck!"

Wise cupped his hands. "Aye, Mister . . . ah — !" he turned to Fisk — "who is that in the maintop?"

"I believe that's Mister Livingston." Fisk squinted. "He's a good lad aloft, the cap'n said."

Wise cupped his hands again. "Aye, Mister Livingston?"

"Signals from the bark, Mister Wise. They want to know whether the captain's decided yet where we might be going."

Billy Caster frowned, perplexed. "They can't say that, can they, Mister Wise? With buntings, I mean . . . there is no such message in the manual of codes."

Wise grinned at the clerk. "Liberal translations, Mister Caster. Far more can be said with buntings than's in any Admiralty manual. I expect what they signal is 'request destination,' or some such thing." He turned aft. "Quarter ahoy!"

On the snow's little quarterdeck, Patrick Dalton waved. "I heard the report, thank you, Mister Wise."

Billy Caster deposited his load — two buckets of tar — at the fore starboard pinrail, and headed aft in time to see banners rising on *Fury*'s stern lanyards. The message was simple, as he read it. "Maintain course," it said.

110

As he passed the bosun he tilted his head. "What would be the 'liberal translation' of that, then, Mister Wise?"

Wise glanced around. "That? Why, lad, that says, 'Attend to your business, Mister Duncan, and I shall attend to mine.' "

"Oh."

Dalton called new sailing orders from astern and Wise shrilled his pipe. All along *Fury's* rails and aloft, men scrambled to trim sails as the snow's rudder bit water and the ship slewed about in a hard turn, throwing sheets of spray alee.

"Is that madman out to capsize us and drown us all?" one of the new hands complained.

Billy called over his shoulder, "Mind your tongue, I'd advise, Mister Pleasant. The captain knows what he's doing."

"Then, what is it that he knows he's doing?" another sailor chided.

From behind him, Billy heard still another voice — one of the ex-Royal Navy sailors among the recruits — respond. "He's makin' a sailor of you, Henry. Of us all."

"By damn, I already *am* a sailor!"

"Well, when he's done, you'll be *his* kind of sailor. Now shut your mouth and lend a hand on this sheet."

On the quarterdeck, Billy Caster stalked toward the stern rail, then stopped when Dalton wagged a finger at him. "Sir?"

"Don't involve yourself in forecastle chatter, Mister Caster. As clerk, you rank amidships, and it might be taken amiss."

"Aye, sir," Billy fumed. "But, sir, some of them say —"

"I have a fair idea of what they say, Mister Caster. Pay it no mind."

"But, sir . . ."

"Mister Caster, at the moment fully two-thirds of *Fury's* crew are new recruits. And half of those have not sailed aboard a fighting ship. There are drills and reactions that they must learn, and the sooner the better. They will complain, but they will learn, and be glad they did should we have need of fancy sailing against an enemy."

"Aye, sir." Still fuming, Billy turned away.

Dalton said, "Speak your mind, Mister Caster."

He turned back. "Aye, sir. Well, I realize the new men may not be accustomed to our . . . ah, to your standards, but can't they realize it may save their lives to drill? You said, 'sailing against an enemy,' sir. Isn't that all we have of late? Enemies, I mean?"

For an instant, Patrick Dalton looked as though he would smile. But he held his face in check. "Feeling lost and alone, Mister Caster?"

"It does seem that everyone's hand is against us, sir."

"Oh, I expect we have few enough seeking to do us harm. There likely was a search for us, after we parted company with the king's custodians. I expect Captains Selkirk and Watson may have been a bit miffed at our departure, and I'm certain those cruiser commanders, Fell and Smith, would give their pensions for a crack at us. It was necessary that we go to ground for a time. But I imagine those gentlemen have by now found other ways to amuse themselves, so I expect we can go about our business now. And fortune has attended to our other problem. We are no longer short-handed."

"No, we aren't short-handed, sir," Billy agreed, glancing at the teeming deck and yards.

"All that being the case, we no longer need to rest in seclusion. You have noted, I'm sure, that at present we are pursuing a course."

"I apologize, sir. I was only thinking . . ."

"It has been a long, tiresome time since any of us saw a snug harbor, eh? Well, you are right in that, Mister Caster. Long enough, I'd say."

"Do you know where we are going yet, sir? Where we will take the bark, and all those people from the islands?"

"We should know soon enough." Dalton gazed critically forward, along *Fury*'s working deck, then cupped his hands. "Mister Wise! I should enjoy seeing another downwind come-about, if you please! Hands to sheets for trim!" He turned to the helm. "Come a quarter to starboard, please, Mister Locke. Smartly now."

"Aye, sir." The wheel spun, and *Fury* shook herself like a fox in the rain, then skidded into a hard turn as sails aloft were brought about to respond to the rudder.

"Ah," Dalton said. "I believe we are getting the hang of it. At the next drill, Mister Caster, I'd like all gunnery stations equipped for tutelage. Also please advise Misters Pugh

112

and Crosby that I shall need them to instruct."

"Gun and sail, sir?"

"By all means. Directly after breakfast tomorrow."

"Aye, sir . . . sir?"

"Something else, Mister Caster?"

"Yes, sir. You said you will know shortly where we are going. Beg pardon, sir, but how will you know?"

"A fair enough question. We are coming into sea lanes now, and can expect traffic. At the first opportunity, I intend to make inquiries." He raised his head, listening to the sounds of *Fury's* rigging as the snow came trim on her new course. "She sings, Mister Caster. With practice she will sing better, but doesn't she have a lovely voice?"

Billy listened and kept his peace. He knew his captain well enough not to speculate on how much of the thought was admiration for a trim vessel and how much of it was loneliness . . . how much of the distance in Dalton's voice was the distance of open sea to that shore where Constance Ramsey waited for him.

Aboard *Pride of Falworth,* Aaron Fairfield leaned burly arms on the bark's quarterrail and frowned, gazing at the cavorting warship in the distance. "Where the blazes is he going now?" he grumped. "If he's to escort us to safety, then why isn't he here now, escorting?"

"Captain Dalton?" Charley Duncan looked where Fairfield was looking, and grinned. "He's shaking out his ship, sir. Putting it through its numbers, and breaking in new crew as well. Don't worry your head about it. He'll be here should we have need of him."

"Well, I wish he would stay closer at hand. And I wish to blazes he'd tell us where he intends to take us. I've had near rebellion on my hands for the past two days. My people want to know where we're going, and they aren't pleased that the matter is entirely up to a man who seems bent on sinking his own ship before we get there."

"Get where, sir?"

"To our destination, confound it . . . wherever that proves to be. Why won't he tell us?"

113

"Beggin' your pardon, Squire, but you folks haven't been very specific yourselves about where you want to go. I believe I've heard every port in the Americas mentioned at one time or another since we allowed you aboard — Mister Quarterstone! Look yonder, at the portside topyard . . . who is that up there running along the footropes?"

Quarterstone squinted. "One of the children, I fancy. Do you want him got down?"

"I certainly do! What lunatic let a child go aloft like that?" Duncan rounded on Fairfield. "Squire, I must insist that you keep a tight check on your people. This is a sailing ship, not a bloody nursery!"

Forward on the passenger deck a woman looked up, screamed and vaulted to the rail, trying to climb the shrouds. Sailors there caught her and set her back on the deck, then several of them started up the ratlines. High above them a small figure clambered about happily, oblivious to height and danger.

"That was Mistress Cabot," Fairfield said. "It must be her boy up there."

"Does Mistress Cabot have a whaling rod, I wonder?"

"The widow Cabot is a devout woman, Mister Duncan, and not one to lay on with the rod where her children are concerned."

"Possibly she doesn't know the correct procedure," Duncan decided. "Mister Nelson, take deck watch, please. I'll be back in a bit."

Forward, sailors had closed on the child overhead and made their capture. Now they were handing the lad down, hand to hand, toward the deck. Duncan strode from the quarterdeck to the promenade and headed forward, pausing for a moment at the mizzen skirts to select a bit of stiff, wiry clew rope, cut a two-foot length of it and swat it against the open palm of his hand. Satisfied then, he went forward to demonstrate ship's discipline in the best traditions of East London Town, where he himself had learned it not so many years before, as a sandy-haired tyke in the warrens of Picadilly.

The arrival of the vessel's commanding officer amidst the crowd on *Pride*'s forecastle deck caused a stir even beyond the stir already in progress there. Passengers and sailors stood back to let him pass, then closed behind him, curious. "Some of you men."

114

He scowled. "I have noticed the cattle are tending to drift aft. I'll have the working decks clear of livestock." He stepped forward then, separated the salvaged child from its frantic mother and stood over the lad, glaring downward. "Your name, boy?"

The offender looked up at him with wide eyes and swallowed noisily, then managed, "Henry, sir. Henry Cabot."

"And how old are you, Henry Cabot?"

"Ah . . . nine years, sir. Almost."

"Were you told not to climb into the rigging, Henry?"

"Sir, I only wanted to—"

"Answer my question! Were you told not to go up there?"

"Well, they said don't, but I just wanted to—"

"Hush!" Duncan turned to Henry's mother. "Mistress Cabot, do you intend to discipline Henry for disobedience?"

"I most certainly do," she said. "I'll give him such a talking to that—"

"Nonsense!" He held out the length of stiff rope. "This is fit discipline, mistress. Will you apply it?"

"Oh, no, sir!" She seemed shocked. "I don't hold with violence. Children should be raised in the—"

"Then, I will," he said. He turned, knelt and hoisted the struggling boy across his leg, pinioned him there and delivered five sharp whacks to his behind. Then he set him on his feet, stood over him and roared, "Silence!"

Henry Cabot's wail of outrage cut off instantly.

"That's better," Duncan said. "Now, Henry Cabot, what is it that you are not to do?"

"C-climb up where th' s-sails are, sir."

"Bright lad." Duncan grinned. He turned again to the miscreant's aghast mother. "I've not had children of my own, Mistress Cabot; but I was one once, and I know that a child is most impressionable in early years. This—" he indicated the rope—"is a fine impressor." He handed it to her, turned with all the dignity he could muster and stalked off aft, scattering passengers and several chickens as he went. At the taffrail, Mister Hoop and his Frenchmen—the big man seemed to have taken personal charge of the pair—were watching with interest.

"Nicely done, Mister Duncan," Hoop said.

115

"Tres formidable, M'sieur le Commandant," one of the Frenchmen agreed.

"Little something I learned from Patrick Dalton," he admitted, stepping aside to allow passage of a pair of goats. "On a well-run ship, laxity cannot be tolerated." He gazed at the Frenchmen. "Have you learned anything more from this pair, Mister Hoop?"

"Aye, I believe so. Francois there . . . ah, Mister Leblanc, that is, he once kept company with three sisters all at the same time, and not a one of them knowin' about the other two, least 'til they found out some way, and that's why he became a sailor."

"I mean about what the captain wants to know, Mister Hoop. Anything about this vessel and why somebody tried to scuttle her?"

"Oh, that. Well, it seems likely it was her own officers done it, sure enough, so they could become pirates and nobody know who they'd been before. The captain's name was Boodelair, though it seems odd he'd have a French name and him bein' colonial English."

"Bood-lair?"

"Oui. m'sieur." Francois nodded. *"Le Pri'e d' Falwort', M'sieur le Capitain Bootlair. Jean Chelvie Bootlair. Oui."*

"Odd indeed," Duncan agreed. "But I'll report it, and maybe Captain Dalton can make sense of it."

"On deck!"

Duncan glanced up. "Mister Hoop, there are chickens in the main shrouds. Please have them cleared. Who is that at top lookout?"

Hoop shaded his eyes. "Aye, sir. That would be Mister Singleterry, I think."

Duncan cupped his hands. "Aye, Mister Singleterry?"

A man passing beside him stopped and turned. "Aye, sir?"

"I was calling to Mister Singleterry," Duncan said.

"Aye, sir. That's who I am. John Singleterry."

"Then, who is that in the tops, at lookout?"

"That's Raymond Mudd, sir. It's his turn."

Duncan tried again. "Aye, Mister Mudd?"

"Sail ahead, deck! One ship, tops in view!"

All around him, passengers and deckmen turned to squint to

116

the rails, although there was nothing to be seen yet from the deck. Hoop and his Frenchmen collared a few landsmen and began collecting chickens.

Astern again, Duncan retrieved his deck from Finian Nelson. "Run up the buntings, please, Mister Quarterstone," he said. "Sail sighted, dead ahead."

"And might I ask who you're signalling to?" Aaron Fairfield sneered.

"To *Fury*, of course. We are an escorted vessel, Squire. When there's a sighting, it's up to our escort to deal with it."

"What escort? I haven't seen that gunship since you left the deck to insult Mistress Cabot. Where is he?"

"I imagine you've been looking the wrong direction, Squire." Duncan grinned and pointed aport. *Fury* was there, just a few hundred yards away, bearing down from astern as though the bark were standing still. As they watched, the snow — big guns abristle and sails full of wind — dashed past and shot out ahead, going to intercept.

"Belay the buntings, Mister Quarterstone." Duncan grinned. "Captain's seen it himself and is off to have a better look. Aye, and isn't she a bonny sight!" He glanced down, then turned. "Mister Nelson, why is there a cat on the quarterdeck?"

"I don't know, Commander. I expect it belongs to some of the passengers."

"Animals do not belong on the quarterdeck, Mister Nelson. Even on a bedammed bark. Take it below and give it to the cook."

Nelson was a newcomer, but he was ex-Royal Navy and only paled slightly at the command. "Aye, sir. Ah, how would you like it prepared, sir?"

"I don't want it cooked, Mister Nelson. A cat's place is the galley, where there may be rats to catch."

Odd, he thought as Finian Nelson headed below with the new ship's cat, only a moment before he had watched the trim snow bound past, and had mentioned what a thing of beauty she was. But he wasn't at all sure whether he had been thinking of *Fury* at that moment, or of the golden hair of the widow Cabot.

Thirteen

At three miles' distance the stranger was fully visible — a single vessel sailing a slow, methodical easterly course and making no attempt to elude interception by *Fury*, though the snow obviously had been seen. Dalton laid his glass on the stranger, then climbed aloft on the port shrouds for a better look.

The ship was not of a design usually seen in these lanes, but he knew its class. Some might call it a barkentine, from the set of its sails, but the vessel was more than a barkentine. Stubby and square-nosed, with the sloped deck of a cargo cruiser and a wide belly that somehow avoided the ambling-cow look of many freighters — rather it had the appearance of that breed of man who might seem fat at first impression but was in fact as broad and solid as a keg of drawn nails — the vessel was of the type called corrida.

Dalton had seen such ships before, in his service amidships in the Mediterranean, and now this one lofted its pennants in greeting.

Thirty feet above him, in the main trestletrees, Purdy Fisk also was watching the stranger. "He flies a trade crest, sir," he called. "Is it one you know?"

"I've seen it, Mister Fisk. The gull and shield of the Calderas."

"The Portuguese company? What would their ship be doing here?"

"Trading, I imagine. That is what Caldera ships do."

"But alone, sir? In these waters? He's just asking to be taken."

118

Despite himself, Dalton grinned. "I wouldn't want to be the pirate who tried it, Mister Fisk. More than one hound has burrowed for the hare and found the badger. And bled for his efforts. That ship may look like a stodgy cargo vessel, but it has skin six inches thick and most certainly as many guns as we do."

"Well, sir, he sees us now for what we are, though he hasn't a notion *who* we are, yet he hasn't so much as hove a spar to avoid us. So it stands to reason he's confident, right enough."

"Keep him well in view, Mister Fisk. And you and Mister — who is that forward? Mister Hemingway?"

"Aye, it's him, sir."

"You may both keep a wary eye for other sails as well, if you please."

"Aye, sir."

Dalton swung down to the deck and strode aft. "Mister Caster!"

"Aye, sir?"

"I believe we have an East India Company ensign in the flag locker, do we not?"

"Aye, sir. We have just about any flag you might want, sir."

"Bring it up, then. Mister Locke, stand by the lanyards please. We shall favor the gentleman ahead with colors."

"Aye, sir."

As the two ships closed to within a mile, *Fury* raised her colors with salute pennants at fore and main, and buntings aft requesting an interview. For long minutes there was no response, though Dalton knew the Caldera captain was glassing both him and the distant bark in the background, making up his mind whether this was, in fact, a friendly cruiser on peaceful escort, or possibly a trap.

"Badger he may be, as you said to Mister Fisk," Victory Locke allowed. "But he is cautious."

"Well he might be, Mister Locke." Dalton stood casually at *Fury*'s rail, waiting out the inspection. "These are weird waters in these parts, and many a ship that's sailed here was never seen again."

"Pirates, sir?"

"Pirates, aye. And war, and storms . . . and some say other things as well."

119

"On deck!" the call came from aloft. "He's running up signals."

"I see him, Mister Fisk." He raised his glass. The two ships now were close enough that he could read the name on the trader's bow escutcheons. She was the *Sao Molino*. At least a dozen guns he could count at fore and bows, and they were more than the popguns usually found on cargo vessels. These were ranging guns and fighting guns, and he had no doubt the men behind them knew the use of them. Above her port wales, buntings flew. "Approach and be recognized" was the signal.

"He says to come over and have a chat, but mind how we behave ourselves," Victory Locke read, helpfully.

"I read him, Mister Locke. Please respond that we will come about for him."

"Aye, sir."

"Two points astarboard, helm. Hands a'deck, stand by to come about and rig for starboard tack. Stand by to furl mains and tops."

"Aye, sir."

Amidships pipes shrilled as *Fury* lay over to her right, swept cleanly out away from the trader's path, then turned her jaunty nose through the wind to stride alongside at three chain lengths' distance, giving *Sao Molino* courtesy of the wind.

Across the intervening water, at the trader's poop, her captain grinned and raised his hat, then said something to a man beside him, and more buntings went aloft.

"He makes us for a brig, sir," Victory Locke said. "He wonders what sort of repairs we have made, that there is an extra mast aft our mainmast."

"Run up our request for interview again, please," Dalton ordered.

This time the request was granted, and the corrida lost way as her mains were reefed. *Fury* followed suit, edging closer in the process until the two vessels crept along-side by side, not fifty yards apart.

Billy Caster was standing by with a speaking horn, and Dalton raised it. "Ahoy *Sao Molino!* Do you speak English?"

The trader captain's dark beard parted to reveal white teeth. He raised his own horn. "I speak English most good," he called.

"Pasco Santua at your service, senor! Who are you?"

"Patrick Dalton, captain of *Fury*, on civil escort. What can you tell me of lanes and conditions westward?"

"I can tell you more over a little Madeira in my cabin than I can with this idiotic cone, senor. Will you come across for a visit?"

"Delighted," Dalton called. "Myself and my clerk, by launch."

Billy Caster stared wide-eyed at the strange ship so close alongside. "Are you sure, sir? Do you see the guns he has pointed at us?"

"Aye, and he sees what we have aimed at him. At this range, we would both likely go to the bottom if anyone fired. Therefore, I believe we will behave ourselves as gentlemen. Mister Wise! Hands to davits to lower the jolly boat, please. And four rowers."

"Aye, sir."

"Mister Locke, please signal Mister Duncan to maintain course and keep his distance."

"Aye, sir."

Pasco Santua's private cabin in *Sao Molino*'s wide sterncastle was as richly appointed as Dalton's own cabin aboard *Fury* was Spartan. And the Portuguese trader was totally at home in his surroundings. A short, burly man with a wide belly, thick arms and a pair of mischievous eyes above his full, dark beard, Santua was every inch the merchant trader as he offered ornate, cushioned chairs to Dalton and Billy, and poured scarlet wine into silver mugs from a crystal decanter.

"Saludes, senores!" He raised his goblet and tossed back a long sip, then perched on an elaborate tapestried divan with ornate silver scrollwork. "Now we can exchange information, eh? Where are you bound with your cargo vessel?"

"That depends a bit on conditions in the colonies," Dalton said. "I have passengers who are somewhat choosy about who they encounter."

"Ah." Santua grinned. "The Whigs and the Tories, eh? Things are most upset in the English colonies now. Royalists, loyalists, patriots, privateers, pirates. Here am I, simple Pasco Santua, a man of peace trying only to deliver a bit more than

121

my respected factors—the Family Caldera—require so that I, too, might share a bit of profit, and see! Two months at the American ports and still I sail with half a cargo." For a moment, it seemed the mischievous eyes above the dark beard might fill with tears. Then he shrugged. *"Hors d'combat,* as the French might say, *senores.* Victim of the misfortune of other peoples' wars. Tell me, which sort of colonial would your people prefer to encounter . . . those who presently favor the English king or those who do not?"

"You've seen my colors, Captain," Dalton said, watching him closely.

"The British Indies flag? Of course. It is what I myself would have chosen had I met me here and wanted to talk about the west. Tell me, Captain, why does a British brig such as your *Fury* have such odd masts . . . and such rigging as though for a great many more sails than it has shown?"

"Because it isn't a brig," Dalton said. "It is a snow. A design originated in the American British colonies. You used a French term, Captain. Do you also speak French?"

"A bit," Santua admitted. "In order for a Portuguese trader to trade, it is useful to have a number of languages. That is because hardly anyone outside of Portugal—and of course some of the South American colonies—ever seems to speak Portuguese."

"And you sail with short cargo? What cargo were you hoping to acquire, Captain?"

"Ah, any number of things make trade. Indigo, some spices, smelted copper, a little American rum, perhaps. What I most expected was a cargo of cotton to be transshipped. A neutral transporter is useful to people whose vessels are subject to seizure. But the ship from Virginia never arrived at the traders' port, so I go home half-empty. It is very sad."

"Many things can happen to a merchant ship these days." Dalton nodded.

"More than usual, lately." The Portuguese spread his hands. "The pirates, they multiply like rats it seems. At Governor's Harbour they tell of one who destroyed a warship almost in the fairway, then took two merchantmen the following day. Those ashore could even see the villain's name. It was *Valkyrie.* That was Thibaud's ship, but they say it has a new master now. Jack Shelby, he calls himself."

Dalton shook his head in revulsion, then changed the subject. "Cotton, you said?" He glanced at Billy Caster, who was already assembling inventories atop his ledger case. "Captain Santua, we are well-met, I think. Perhaps we can do a bit of business."

Charley Duncan held *Pride* on a wide course and was abreast of *Fury* and the trader at a distance of two miles when his top lookouts read signals at the snow's high arms. Even at this distance there was no mistaking the message or its source. Patrick Dalton requested his presence.

"How do you know that is a true signal?" Aaron Fairfield protested as *Pride* came hard aport and hands went aloft to reef her mains and topsails while sheets were hauled a'deck to trim for the difficult sixty-degree tack.

"I know it's true because it is from Patrick Dalton." Duncan sighed, holding his patience between his teeth.

"You don't know what is going on over there," Fairfield argued. "That could be a bloody pirate ship. Likely the blaggard has gulled your captain into surrender and now waits to take us as a prize."

"Hard over, Mister Hoop," Duncan called. "You men! Let's haul about those yards in unison! This may be naught but a slogging square-rigger, but let's look alive and see if we can't make it go in the proper direction!" Turning, he almost collided with a goat that had cleared the portside ladder at a bound and now was nibbling at the stern sheets wound about their pins. With a curse he shooed it away and wagged an irritated finger under Fairfield's nose. "I have asked you politely, Squire, to have your people keep their bloody livestock forward of the stem, and preferably below. And while you're about it, if you don't care for the way I direct this vessel, you may leave the quarterdeck and good riddance."

Fairfield herded the errant creature down to the deck and wagged a finger at a large young landsman, who hurried aft to collect it.

"You have no call to address me in such manner, sir," Fairfield growled up at Duncan. "We are paying passengers aboard this ship."

"Then, act like it!" Duncan turned his back on the man, exasperated, and strode to the helm. Almost at his heels, young Henry Cabot trailed after him, copying his every move.

"If you deliver us into the hands of pirates, it's on your head!" Fairfield called.

Duncan didn't look back, but clenched his right fist and swatted it upward, slapping his arm with his left hand in a gesture he had learned in the Mediterranean. Behind him, Henry Cabot copied the motion.

At the helm, Mister Hoop's eyes widened. "Beg pardon, Mister Duncan, but I didn't know that ship's officers knew about things like that."

"I'm in command because Patrick Dalton put me here," Duncan seethed. "But you mind your tongue, Mister Hoop. I'm no more a bleedin' officer than you are, and well you know it."

"Oh, aye." Hoop lowered his eyes in apology. "I know that, Mister Duncan. But, well, *somebody* has to be an officer here. Otherwise how will any of us know what to do? You see?"

"You'll do what I say to do. Captain Dalton said so."

"Aye, that's what I mean. Folks is as folks does, I say, an' I never saw any officer make gestures like that."

Duncan took a deep breath, knowing the man was right. He had to set the example, or risk laxity aboard his ship. "What do you suppose a proper officer would do about a bloody nuisance like that squire, Mister Hoop?"

The big man scratched his head, thinking. "Hard to say for certain. Knock the bugger in the head, maybe, or throw him overboard. But he'd doubtless be polite about it."

Pride could manage no more than three knots on a hard tack, but she hadn't far to go. *Fury* and the trader came to meet her, sailing side by side on an easy reach, *Fury* with her greater press of sail holding the lee position as was customary between ships met at sea.

At three cables the pair went about and reefed their sails, and *Pride* crept between them at Dalton's order.

Nearly rail-to-rail, Duncan looked down at his captain on

124

the snow, and Dalton hailed him. "Snug your vessel to the trading ship, please, Mister Duncan, and rig your yards for cargo handling. Captain Santua has agreed to buy all of the cotton you have on board."

"Aye, sir. That's good news. We can well use the extra space below."

"I daresay you can. When you are snugged, Mister Duncan, please send your Frenchmen across to the *Sao Molino*. They speak French there, and have agreed to interrogate them."

"Aye, sir. May I send Mister Hoop to look after them, sir? They seem to trust him."

"As you please, Mister Duncan. Look alive, now."

"Aye, sir."

"Mister Duncan?"

"Aye, Captain?"

Dalton pointed. "What is that, standing beside you?"

Duncan glanced aside and down, then shrugged. "It's a child, sir. His name is Henry Cabot, and I whaled him for climbing aloft. Now he keeps following me about, sir."

"I see. And what are those, along your taffrail?"

"Those are chickens, sir. I've had them forward a dozen times, but . . . well, sir, chickens do seem to just go where they please when they wander."

While the sheered yardarms of *Pride*'s fore-and-aft mainmast courses were reinforced with cable from the topsail cleats and pressed into service as gantries for the transfer of heavy cotton bales, Dalton invited Pasco Santua to supper.

It was a fine occasion, around a hastily erected trestle table on the neutral ground of the bark's quarterdeck. Warm tropic breezes wafted from astern, muting the clatter amidships where winches whined and strong men sweated in transfer of cargo, carrying off the stench of livestock assembled at the forecastle taffrails and the chatter of passengers there trying to keep their families and their goods safely distant from the working arena.

Nathan Claremore proved himself a worthy cook by sending up from *Fury*'s little galley a four-course meal. Pea soup with

125

onions was followed by a heaping platter of what might once have been smoked goat, though the one-armed cook had so laced it with salt and lemon juice that it might have been anything. And the main course brought applause from those at table — all except Aaron Fairfield, who frowned when he recognized it.

Baked chicken.

Dessert was oat cakes with honey, and Santua capped the meal with a bit of fine brandy, tobacco and pipes from his personal stores aboard *Sao Molino*.

As they settled back, as relaxed as men might be aboard a thin-skinned bark flanked by fighting ships with crews at their guns to keep things honest, the trader raised his goblet. "To war and fortune, senores," he said.

"At least to fortune," Dalton responded.

Fairfield, Duncan and Santua's first officer raised goblets in response.

"My sailing master has brought to date your charts," Santua said. "And your clerk has note of all the latest intelligences that I have heard. You will note that the English fleet seems to have withdrawn itself from the Chesapeake and the Delaware. They say the American general, Senor Washington, is on the move with his army now, and the English generals have gone to meet him in the north; so that is where King George's ships must be."

"I rely upon your assessment and your ears, sir," Dalton assured him. "And by the way, have we learned anything new from my Frenchmen?"

"The name of their captain, the one who scuttled his own ship."

"We already knew that, sir," Duncan reminded Dalton. "A Frenchy name. Boodelair or some such."

Santua grinned. "Not Boo'dlair, Mister Duncan. Butler. A good English name, I believe."

"Butler?" Dalton frowned in thought. Somewhere he had encountered the name. A Captain Butler.

"One other thing that might interest you," Santua said. "Not from the French sailors, but from the guild codes."

"Guild codes?"

"On the cotton I have just bought from you. Guild codes.

126

The cotton was consigned by a Virginia gentleman, Senor Ian McCall. Maybe this was his ship that I was waiting for at the islands."

Only one who knew him very well might have known that just at that moment, a puzzle came together in Patrick Dalton's mind.

Fourteen

Tropic dusk was on the sea when *Pride*'s crew secured from cargo-handling and swung the bark's yardarms back to sailing position. In the forecastle and forward holds, Aaron Fairfield's fugitives were hard at work fitting themselves into expanded accommodations. At the stern, Dalton and Santua stood at ease, watching the sun's last haloes recede beyond westward waters. The sunset had been spectacular, a brilliance of crimsons and golds that flared and danced aloft before muting down to a whisper of brilliant red just at horizon . . . red, then deep rose, then abruptly, just for an instant, a flash of bright green as final day bowed out.

"We take our amusements where we find them, eh, senor?" Santua puffed his pipe contentedly. "It is the way of the sea."

Dalton nodded, but a tracery of concern played at his brow. He tasted the breeze, read its messages in the whisper of rigging aloft and in the unruly dark hair teasing about his ears. "Weird waters," he muttered.

Santua glanced around at him. "Senor?"

"It was nothing, Captain Santua. Just an odd fancy."

"Ah? What means this word, 'weird'?"

"It is a Saxon word, I suppose. Or possibly Nordic. It means a thing is unusual, or seems unsettling somehow. Possibly it is just a change in the weather, as those cloud colors might indicate."

"You have sailed these latitudes before, Captain Dalton?"

"Only a very little, some years ago."

"Maybe it is the little ones . . . the little people . . . telling you their secrets." Santua grinned. "Yes, I know of the stories of the Irish. Some of them are very like the tales of the mountain folk in the north of my own land. Very odd."

"Children's tales." Dalton shrugged.

"You think so? Once I had a sailor on my ship—my first ship—who was from Toska. More than once he warned me of dangers that had not yet occurred. I learned to listen when he spoke. He was often right."

"Valuable man to have in your service. Is he still with you?"

"Alas, no. One evening off Pascobal he came to me and asked that I write for him a letter, to his family. He said he would not see them again. The very next morning he was in the forward hold, securing netting, and a wave caused some cargo to shift. He died instantly."

"Secured from off-loading, Captain," Charley Duncan called. "We are ready to make sail."

"Then, we shall leave you your deck, Commander." Dalton turned. "Mister Caster, are the accounts settled?"

"Aye, sir. Cargo shipped aboard *Sao Molino* and payment received, as agreed. I've fixed your seal to the lading for Mister . . . ah, Senor Letitho, Captain Santua's cargo officer, and he has given us receipt."

"Very well. Captain Santua, it has been a pleasant meeting. Possibly we shall meet again."

"My pleasure, senor." The trader's mischievous eyes twinkled in lantern light. "Possibly ashore next time, though? Even the best of meals is better enjoyed when one is not sitting between the muzzles of loaded cannons. Such nervous situations give rise to . . . ah . . . weird notions."

"I agree," Dalton said.

With great ceremony, two captains shook hands, descended to the bark's main deck and parted there, each bridging an opposite rail to return to his own command. *Sao Molino* cast off first, taking on way from her sails even as she cleared the bark's bow and signalled a goodbye with her stern buntings. When she was clear and away, Dalton looked at the sky, gauged the wind and said, "Mister Locke to helm, please. Mister Wise, hands a'deck to make sail. Stand by to cast off and come to the wind. Course north by west."

129

He paused when a commotion broke out yards away and above, on *Pride*'s higher deck. After a moment, Charley Duncan appeared there with a lamp. "Moment, Captain," he called. He turned away, listening to someone out of sight, then reappeared. "Captain, I'm sorry to report, sir, but there are some aboard that Portugee vessel who are less than honorable people."

"What is the problem, Mister Duncan?"

"Our best cargo windlass seems to be missing, sir. It was secured at the port stanchions, but now it's gone. It looks as though the Portugues stole it." At Duncan's side a small head appeared at the rail, gazing eastward at the vanishing corrida. As though punctuating what Duncan had said, little Henry Cabot slapped his fisted arm upward in a gesture of derision.

Dalton sighed. It was far too late now to do anything about it, even if he had been tempted to confront an armed corrida over the loss of a windlass. "Never mind, Mister Duncan," he said. "When I am clear, you may make sail by the wind on course north by west."

"Aye, sir. Do we know where we're going yet, sir?"

"We are bound for Virginia, Mister Duncan."

"Aye, sir. I've some aboard who'll sleep better for knowin' where we're bound. I'll tell her straight away."

"Her?"

"I mean them, sir. The passengers. Ah, sir?"

"Yes, Mister Duncan?"

"Bit of a surprise for you below, sir. In your cabin. Something you might see fit to enjoy, and I couldn't very well keep it here aboard *Pride*, what with all them thievin' Portugees about."

"What is it, Mister Duncan?"

"Oh, just a bit of a comfort, sir. We're standin' by to loose lines whenever you want to cast off."

"Very well, Mister Duncan. Mister Wise, stand by lines fore and aft, please. Cast off and make sail to come about to course."

"Aye, sir." Pipes shrilled, and *Fury* shivered as pike poles thrust the two vessels apart and her jib sails rose to take the wind. In evening's last light the jaunty snow veered out from the bark, making a long, languid half circle while the larger vessel got the wind in its sails and picked up way. Only when *Pride*

130

was rigged and running on a course that aimed her at the distant American shore did *Fury* make her final trim, move in on the bark's windward flank and secure for the dark-hours watches.

When all was well, Dalton turned his deck over to Claude Mallory and went below.

And found Charley Duncan's "bit of a surprise" in his cabin. An elaborate, tapestried divan with ornate silver scrollwork. The very settee that had been in Pasco Santua's sumptuous cabin on *Sao Molino*.

As Billy Caster, on his way to his own quarters, paused to gawk past his captain, Dalton sighed and shook his head. "Mister Duncan, you are incorrigible," he muttered. "And you so righteously indignant over the loss of a windlass, too."

Distantly, through the open companion hatch overhead, he heard, "On deck!" and the reply, "Aye tops?"

He couldn't hear the report, but he heard rapid footsteps above the skylights and swung to the ladder just as a silhouette appeared at the hatch.

"I'm here, Mister Mallory," he said. "What is it?"

"Fog risin' ahead, sir. Tops says it looks deep."

"I am coming up, Mister Mallory. Please have a'standby lamps fore and aft."

"Aye, sir."

He buttoned his coat and hurried to the deck, turning to peer ahead. There rode *Pride*, three cables off the starboard bow, and beyond was the dark sea with starlight overhead. But there was another thing, as well. In the distance, the horizon had become thicker . . . an indistinct dark band between the bowl of sky and the distant star-glittered sea.

Behind him, Dalton heard Billy Caster arrive on deck. Without turning, he asked, "How do you fare the night, Mister Caster?"

"Wind at twenty and steady," the youth said. "Holding on the port quarter. Clear sky."

"Do you see what lies ahead, Mister Caster?"

"Aye, sir. I see the fog."

"And is this fog weather, would you say?"

"No, sir. I wouldn't have said so."

131

"Nor would I," Dalton admitted. "These are indeed weird waters." He went up the short quarterdeck ladder in two steps. "Have you a standby on bow lamps, Mister Mallory?"

"Aye, sir. Both bow and stern."

"Have you signalled the *Pride* yet?"

"No, sir. But he has seen the fog, sir. He signalled it."

"Very well, Mister Mallory. Signal *Pride* to display lanterns astern, port and starboard, and to tell spotters to keep a good eye on our lanterns. Visibility may be limited ahead."

"Aye, sir."

Dalton went to the quarterrail. "Mister Wise, open our bow lamps if you please. Spotters afore to keep the bark's stern lamps in sight, and we'll hold course and lay close back until the weather passes."

"Aye, sir."

Billy Caster was gazing ahead, where the fog bank seemed to grow like a rising wall, doubling its height minute by minute. "Pardon, Captain, but how can we approach so quickly? Is it coming toward us? Against the wind?"

"Not moving against the wind, Mister Caster. Rather, I'd say it is growing rapidly. Widening toward us."

Billy watched in fascination as the tenuous dark wall ahead began to tower into the night sky. Then his attention was caught by peculiar lights at the base of it — little shapeless glows of greenish hue that moved about here and there like the glow of lanterns carried by men obscured by heavy mist.

The foretop had seen it, too. "On deck! Lights ahead, in the fog!"

Everyone on deck was peering forward now, straining to make out what could be there.

Dalton studied the pattern of the lights — a random, running movement of glows within the fog, this way and that, with no obvious reason or order. The lights glowed and muted, moving from left to right to left again, low in the fog. They seemed to be floating about on the sea. And they were all of a color. A pale, pulsating green.

"Foxfire," he muttered.

"Sir?"

"Foxfire, Mister Caster. Or something like it. Vapors in the seaweed, possibly. Mister Wise, sounder afore please. Sound at intervals, report shoaling at mark eight."

"Aye, sir." The whistle shrilled. "Sound for depth at the bow! Hail at mark eight!"

"Weird waters," Dalton muttered. "Very well, we shall simply keep each other in sight and hold course."

"Sir?" Claude Mallory was at the compass stand, holding a hooded lantern high, tapping the glass face of the compass case.

"Mister Mallory?"

"You'd better have a look, sir. The compass has gone amok. It's spinning this way and that as though we were going in circles."

"On deck!"

"Aye, tops?"

"The bark has entered fog, sir!"

"Spotters afore! Keep an eye on those lamps!"

For a minute there was no answer; then Cadman Wise came scurrying aft. "Pardon, sir, but we can't find *Pride*'s lights. She must be dead ahead, sir. She was a bit ago. But there's nothing to be seen there now."

"Was he changing course?"

"Not that anybody could see, sir. True an' steady on he was . . . then he just wasn't there."

At the helm, Victory Locke held a steady trim to winds that sang aloft with no sound of change in them. Yet there was no sign of *Pride of Falworth,* which had been barely a hundred yards away off the starboard bow.

Then, abruptly, *Fury*'s stem penetrated fogs, and the warship slid into inky darkness. Dalton could not even see Cadman Wise, a few yards away on the working deck, almost under the cockpit. He turned. Claude Mallory's raised lamp was a fuzzy glow in darkness, and neither Victory Locke at the helm nor even Billy Caster, who had been just beside him, was visible.

"What is this?" he swore. "What the blazes is going on?"

Trawlers had been at work off Grand Bahama in recent days, whole fleets of stubby little boats with lateen sails and catwalk decks around teeming holds as capacious as their hulls would allow. The weather had been fine for trawling. Clear skies held above seas that rolled in a steady twenty-knot offshore wind, and the fishing had been better than any in months.

The waters were shallow here and teemed with fish, and the season was right for the netting. Flotillas of boats spread across the waters with each dawning, casting and hauling their nets. Some ranged as far out as Little Abaco, where onshore winds, if they came, could swell the sea into mighty rolling waves crashing shoreward from the nearby deeps—waves that could swamp a small craft. But when the winds were seaward, it was time for the taking of fish, and for many days the boats had ranged the banks, doing their work, returning home by moonlight to sort their catches.

On this evening, though, there was a feeling to the winds that raised the bristles on men's arms and sent the prudent among them homeward while there was yet a little light in the sky.

"El Malo de Mar," some called it. Or *"La Obscuridad."* The dark time. It was not wise to be on the sea at such times, the fishermen knew. Strange things occurred, and sometimes boats—even big ships—disappeared in the dark mists never to return. At first sign of a compass acting strangely, or the crackling of sparks along spray-soaked masts, or the ominous rising of fogs in the distance like great mushroom caps growing, swelling from the sea, the fisher-boats made for home or for the nearest shelter.

Too many stories were told of the *Malo de Mar* for anyone not to take heed.

On this evening there were the sparks, and to the east the domes of fog where green lights danced on the sea, and those who had magnetic compasses saw them gyrate wildly. A hundred boats put about in the fisheries above Little Abaco. A hundred lateens took the quartering wind and made for shore, and each man in each boat prayed for the feel of solid ground beneath his feet.

In a tiny pool of hazy light surrounded by blind darkness, Charley Duncan and Pliny Quarterstone huddled over *Pride's* useless compass, moisture beginning to drip from their chins.

"Blimey, I've not seen the like of this," Duncan admitted. "This stuff is as thick as storm rain, but it didn't come from clouds. It just rose right up out of the water, like."

"Well, we're not likely to be through it soon," Quarterstone frowned. "It's closed in behind, but it's ridin' with us, on the wind. Would you look at that, now? By this box, we're heading due south, not west by north as before."

Duncan turned. Behind him was only darkness. "Mister Nelson, have you . . . Mister Nelson? Are you still at helm?"

"Aye, I'm here," the darkness said.

"Have you altered course at all, then?"

"Not so much as a nudge, sir. Rudder's amidships just as it's been, steering by the wind."

"It's the blinkin' compass that's afoul, then," Duncan decided. "If there was a wind shift, we'd have heard it aloft right enough."

"I can't see hide nor hair of *Fury*." Quarterstone squinted into darkness. "She should be just there, a'flank on our port quarter."

A flicker of greenish light appeared suddenly, alongside the bark, and seemed to sweep across the ship's deck before vanishing beyond. Duncan felt the hair at his nape bristle and tug, as though trying to follow where the light had gone. "What th' bloody 'ell!" he snapped.

From the region of his belt, a small voice echoed him, "What th' bloody 'ell?"

He swung the lantern aside and downward. Henry Cabot stood close beside him, straining to see the erratic compass in its case. Duncan's jaw dropped for an instant; then he caught the boy by the arm. "Here now! What are you doin' aft? Didn't I tell you stop tagging me about, then?"

"Y-yes, sir."

"Then, why aren't you forward, boy? Your mother will be sore fretful."

"I just came aft to fetch the milk goat, sir; then it got to be awful dark, so I came here. Is it rainin', sir? It seems wet enough to be."

"It's only a mist, boy. Now, you get yourself forward where you . . ." He looked into the inky murk beyond the quarterrail.

"No, belay that. You'd likely get lost or fall overside. Just stay here for now, but keep out of the way."

"Yes, sir."

Pliny Quarterstone frowned at the youth. "Not *yes,* sir'," he scolded. "On the quarterdeck it's *'aye,* sir.' "

"Y-yes, sir. Aye, sir, sir."

Again there was an abrupt greenish glow that seemed to wash across the ship, and trailed eerie little balls of swirling light in its wake. Duncan felt the ship slew to the left, heeling slightly as its rudder went slack, and turned. "Mister Nelson . . . !"

Where there had been darkness, now there was light, and Finian Nelson crouched wide-eyed beyond the spinning helm, his arms spread at his sides. Just above the hub of the wheel floated a glowing orb, a sphere of light in the mist, and the spokes of the helm glistened as they danced through it. A faint hissing, crackling sound came each time a spoke touched the light.

"Mister Nelson, mind the helm!" Duncan roared, bounding toward the helm box. "It's only foxfire! Control the helm!"

Nelson hesitated for a second, then gritted his teeth and caught the spinning wheel. Dim radiances seemed to run up his arms, and the glowing ball of light diminished and shrunk, then disappeared with an audible pop.

In the darkness Duncan heard the helm being righted, and felt the rudder taking its bit below, but now the set of sails aloft had an unhappy sound. Canvas luffed and fluttered at high yards. *Pride* had lost her trim.

"Put to port a bit, Mister Nelson," he started, then raised an invisible hand and shook his head. "Belay that. Hold as she goes. Captain Dalton will expect us to hold fast to course, and if we come aport, we may collide with him."

"But we've altered course, Commander," Pliny Quarterstone said. "We're astarboard of where we ought to be."

"I know that, Mister Quarterstone!" Duncan snapped. "I just don't know how much or how far. Does the compass tell us anything yet?"

"Accordin' to this bloody thing, we might be going in a circle."

"Well, there's little enough we can do about it, except to try not to fall behind. Mister Hoop!"

"Aye, sir?" Hoop's voice came from just below the quarter-rail.

"Mister Hoop, hands to sheets, please, to trim to present course."

"Aye, sir." Feet scuffled below, and Mister Hoop's bellow echoed in the darkness: "Hands to sheets! Hands to sheets!"

Somewhere near, a voice complained, "I can't even find the blinkin' buttons on me bleedin' trousers, an' he wants me to find the blarsted pinrail?"

Somewhere else there was a thud, followed by cursing and scuffling sounds, and an angry voice. "Watch w'at ye're about there, mate!"

"You watch out, yourself, bloater! I'm tryin' to see what I — by God, it's a goat! Sails to make an' no bloody light to see by an' I've stumbled over a bedammed goat!"

Hoop's roar overrode the chaos on deck. "Look alive, there, blast your blind eyes! Get hands on those sheet lines and let's get the blinkin' sails to trim!"

Fifteen

"Steady ahead, Mister Locke," Patrick Dalton said, peering into a darkness that was complete except for the murky glow of nearby lanterns and the erratic, occasional rippling of what he had decided was either foxfire or some strange sort of lightning.

"On deck!" The hail came from the maintop, high above.

"Aye, tops?"

"It's closed in aloft, sir. No visibility at all."

"Have you had sight of *Pride of Falworth?*"

"No sight now, sir. But before we closed th' fogs, she was where she'd been, three cables off the starboard bow."

"Trust Mister Duncan to hold course until this passes, then," Dalton mused. "Steady on, please, Mister Locke. Mister Wise!"

"Aye, sir?" The voice was disembodied, somewhere afore.

"Mister Wise, do you think we could manage to ease sail just a bit on the courses? I should like to lose a knot of way."

"Aye, sir, we'll try. You lads! Whoever can, find your way to the brails! Captain wants a bit of sail taken in!"

Just astern, a faint glow of greenish light drifted across *Fury's* unseen wake, like a sad ghost searching for its grave. Near at hand, Billy Caster muttered, "Weird waters. It's as though we suddenly were somewhere else entirely."

"Weird, indeed, Mister Caster," Dalton agreed. "But yet sailing waters, and the same water. If we can't see it beneath our hull, we can hear it there, and the world remains as it was even in darkness."

"Sir?"

138

"It isn't a thing to worry about unduly," Dalton explained, letting his voice carry to any who might be listening. "We are in some sort of storm, nothing more. Beyond it you will see the same ocean we sailed before, and we shall be holding the same course. The seas shift and flow, Mister Caster, but they do not change their locations any more than the land does. All that moves here is ourselves, and we move by the winds, on the waters, just as we always did."

"Aye, sir. I'd feel better, though, if we could see the other ship over there."

"Precisely the reason we are standing back a bit. Without visibility, we need adequate distance so that there is no chance of an accidental collision. Mister Duncan will do his best to hold his course and speed, I imagine. We shall hold course and slack our speed by a knot."

Deck lanterns appeared forward of the quarterrail, a few muted glows increasingly dim with distance, and those astern knew that there were more there than they could see. The mist lay about them like a thick rain that didn't fall but just hung suspended in the air. Sound carried, though — the rattle of tackle blocks aloft as the snow's courses were loosed and reefed, the busy sounds of a deck at work. And *Fury* slacked her speed as the blocks rattled, the croon of waters along her hull diminishing in tone.

Several times during the next hour they tried to hail *Pride*, but with no response. Dalton realized that Charley Duncan might have added sail when visibility was lost, for the same reason that he himself had slacked his speed — to put a safe distance between the two until they again had eyes to see. He decided that likely was what he had done.

For a time the eerie lights in the mist seemed to subside; then abruptly they returned — eerie, dancing glows that moved about the ship and beyond, like things alive, glows that sometimes passed directly across the vessel, turning the inky mist to bright, silver-green cloud that still kept them blind but for moments seemed as bright as day. And each time a light touched the ship there were sounds — muted sizzling, crackling noises that seemed to run up and down the masts and along the yards, limning the structures aloft in hisses of sound. One such whis-

139

pering light drifted across amidships, seemed to pause there, then turned and moved forward.

Excited shouts from the foredeck were relayed back. The weird light had found the portside cathead and clung there for moments, then had coalesced and "wrapped its blinkin' self about the anchor, hove there in its fish tackle." For a moment, they said, the anchor and all of its tackle had glowed like blue fire. Then it had popped, sizzled and extinguished itself.

With each light the errant compass swung wildly.

Long hours passed that seemed like days, and at each bell Billy Caster recorded the readings and soundings, writing on a tablet of stretched wet linen, with a sharpened bit of lead.

At eight bells Ishmael Bean and Purdy Fisk came from below to relieve Claude Mallory and Victory Locke. Dalton remained on deck, pacing and listening, noting every sound and feel of *Fury's* course. What his eyes could not tell him of how the ship fared, his ears and the soles of his boots could—except for what lay beyond in the darkness.

At three bells of the midwatch there was a freshening of the wind, and the sound of sails aloft said it was shifting, coming more to the south.

"Accommodate the wind, please, Mister Fisk," he told the helmsman. "Bring us over to full and by. Mister Bean, whose stand is it amidships?"

"Mister Ball is there, sir. He relieved Mister Wise at change of watch."

Dalton stepped to the bell posts. "Mister Ball! Quarter please!"

A moment passed; then Abel Ball appeared in the murk below the rail. "Aye, sir?"

"The wind is veering a bit, Mister Ball. For the time, we shall adjust to it. But have your lads at station on the sheets, please. If we need sail handling, I'll want it done smartly."

"Aye, sir. Ah, sir, some of the new lads are being a bit grumbly. I expect this odd weather has got on their nerves."

"I see. Is it anything that you can't handle?"

"Not so far, sir. I've told them that I'm in something of a mood myself, and if they can't behave themselves as gentlemen, I might take it in mind to crack a few skulls. An' I've got Misters

140

Leaf and Ransom standin' by with belaying pins."

"Very good, Mister Ball. Carry on."

"Aye, sir."

"On deck!"

Dalton turned away, letting Ishmael Bean respond. The tar cupped hard hands and shouted, "Aye, tops?"

"I think it's raining up here, deck. The mist is moving."

"Moving? Moving where?"

"With the wind."

Bean stepped close enough to Dalton to see his features in the lamplight. "Would you say it is raining, sir? I can't really tell."

Dalton was staring at the glow of the nearest lamp. After a moment he nodded. "I believe it is, Mister Bean."

"Well, sir, at least that's something different."

"More than that is changing," Dalton said, raising his head to listen. "The wind is freshening, and seems cooler. Mister Fisk, how much have you corrected to accommodate the wind?"

"Four turns, sir. A point or so each, I'd make it. To starboard each time."

"Ah. Mister Caster, are you here?"

"Aye, sir. Right here, sir."

"Please make note of the hour, Mister Caster, and enter an estimation of northwest by north, fifteen knots on reefed courses and gaining way, wind freshening to . . . ah — Ahoy, tops! Can you read the gauge?"

"Sorry, sir." The voice drifted down from aloft. "I can't even see the blessed thing."

"Estimated wind near thirty and freshening," Dalton said. Striding to the bell rail, he called, "Mister Ball, do you have hands at station?"

"Aye, sir. I think so."

"Then, let's reef a third in the tops'ls, please. Lively now."

"Aye, sir."

The rain increased steadily, a drenching, soaking downpour that hammered at *Fury*'s flanks and sluiced along her decks, driven by a wind that rose and whined, changing the weird darkness of earlier hours to a whining, singing darkness. And now there was real lightning — brilliant flashes in the murk all around them, with

141

thunderclaps that rolled and echoed like cannonfire.

A brilliant bolt exploded just off *Fury*'s portside, the crack of its thunder deafening, and as eyes turned to where it had been, a second bolt struck, farther away but still near enough to flare the murk like silver sunlight. And there, a black silhouette against the glare, was a ship. Three masts with high spars were ebon tapestry illuminated among glare-lighted sails, and in the echo of the thunder they could hear the booming of a great hull slamming through wave crests with the wind at its back.

The two vessels, *Fury* and the stranger, were barely a cable's length apart and angling toward each other on collision course.

"Helm astarboard!" Dalton shouted. "Hard over, Mister Fisk!" Billy Caster grabbed a rail and clung as the keening snow answered its rudder, rearing on a running wave and heeling hard aslant. Aloft, cables sang and whined, sails snapped in the wind and stressed timbers shrilled. Deep within her hull, *Fury* growled as massive knees and footings took the stresses transmitted from masts to keel. Darkness had followed the lightning's flare, and in the darkness was chaos on the snow's driving decks: shouts and scufflings, creak of cannons shifting in their slings, clatter of deadeyes and great blocks dancing at their cables. Forward somewhere, there was a shrilling of taut line and the loud report of something breaking apart. Someone screamed somewhere.

Then just beyond, surging alongside in the darkness, were other sounds that were undertone and counterpoint to *Fury*'s song—the thrumming, slapping roar of a heavy ship under sail and driving through tossed seas.

For a moment, the thunder alongside drowned out all other sounds, and a lightning flash glared on the towering flank of a big ship. A warship, larger than *Fury*, directly alongside the turning snow and crowding in . . . then passing.

As abruptly as it had come, the phantom was gone—vanished into the darkness and the sheeting rain.

"Rudder amidships, Mister Fisk," Dalton ordered. Shaking herself like a warhorse denied battle, *Fury* held footing on the churning sea for a moment, then slowly righted herself. In the diminishing whine of her rigging, there was a sound almost of regret.

Wide eyes staring into the darkness, Billy Caster got his feet under him and gasped, "What was that?"

"Mister Ball, report, please," Dalton called.

Ishmael Bean stooped to retrieve a fallen lantern. "Far too close a thing for my liking," he muttered.

At the helm, Purdy Fisk was considering Billy's question. "A warship, right enough," he said. "And big, too. Maybe a frigate, though its silhouette seemed a bit odd."

Beyond the quarterrail, Abel Ball called, "Something broke in the fore, Cap'n. We don't know yet what it was, but the shrouds seem secure and the sheets are responding."

"Anyone injured or swept over?"

"Don't know that, either, sir. Not just yet."

"Can we handle sail, Mister Ball?"

"Aye, sir. That we can."

"Stand by to trim to the rudder, then. Mister Fisk, bear off a point aport and steady us there. Mister Bean, can you see the compass?"

"Aye, but it's not — belay that, Cap'n. It seems to be working again. At least it stands steady and shifts with the helm."

"What is our heading by the compass?"

"Nearly due north now, sir, so it says."

"Direct the helm by the compass, please, Mister Bean. Bring us back to west by north, then have Mister Ball's crew trim to course and sheet home. And stand by to make or reef. God only knows what this weather is going to do."

"Aye, sir."

In the rain-drenched darkness behind the snow, something whined through the air and splashed somewhere astern. Distantly to the north, there was a report that was unlike a thunderclap, then another.

"Those were cannon shots," Ishmael Bean blurted. "That ship, sir? The one that skimmed us . . . do you think . . . ?"

"It could hardly be anyone else, Mister Bean. He fired blind, but at where we might have been had we held true."

"But why would he shoot, sir? We've passed and gone. We've no encounter. Blazes, we don't even know each other . . . do we?"

"I think not," Dalton said slowly, staring into the blind north.

"I can think of a few reasons why a vessel might shoot without acquaintance, but none of the reasons are honorable."

"Are we going after him, sir? Teach the blighter some manners, as they say?"

"Just steady on course, Mister Bean. We've more pressing business at the moment. Possibly we'll encounter that gentleman at another time. Then maybe we shall have cause to amuse him."

"I hope that vessel doesn't happen upon Mister Duncan," Billy Caster said. "All those people he's carrying . . ."

"I'm thinking the same thing, Mister Caster," Dalton admitted. "If Mister Duncan has held his course, though, he should be ahead of us somewhere and well out of range of that wing-top."

"That what, sir?"

"Wing-top, Mister Caster. Did you notice his silhouette in that moment when we had him in sight?"

"Well, yes, sir, I suppose I did. It was a ship-rigged vessel, big but less than a ship of the line. I took it for a frigate, or something."

"Very good, Mister Caster. Basically a frigate, yes. But modified a bit. That vessel's tops'l yards and royals were blocked for studding sails. That's done on occasion in the Mediterranean. Leeward shores, surface calms with winds aloft, that sort of thing. But it isn't a popular modification. It's unusual."

"On deck!"

"Aye, tops?"

"We have some visibility, sir. Clearing ahead a bit."

"Sightings, tops?"

"Nothing, sir, but I can see the sky."

As abruptly as they had entered the fogs, they left them. Now *Fury* sailed in clear airs, an eerie, contained clear with starry sky above and good visibility about — but for no more than a mile in any direction.

"Now we sail in a bottle," Dalton muttered, gazing around at the high cloudbanks that hid every horizon. "Weird waters, these. Very weird."

"Weird," Billy Caster agreed.

It *was* as though the snow sailed in a bottle, alone in a strange,

144

starlit arena where the winds rose and fell in fitful gusts, a place where nothing existed except the ship, the dark sea and high, encircling walls of fog where lightnings flickered here and there. There was no sign of *Pride of Falworth* as far as they could see, nor of any other vessel or thing.

Abel Ball came aft, long-faced and pale in the lamplight of the deck. "Damage report, sir," he said.

"Report, Mister Ball."

"What broke yonder in the fore was our portside fish tackle," the sailor said. "The anchor is still there, a'dangle at the cat block, but the fish cable is broken at the channel. And we've . . . uh . . . we've lost a man, sir."

"What man?"

"Mister Finch, sir. Tommy Finch, one of the new lads. I guess he went overside when the line broke. It's where he likely would have been."

Dalton sighed, looking back the way they had come. A man lost. And no chance now of even finding him, much less rescuing him. If Tommy Finch had gone into that stormy sea, then Tommy Finch was dead.

"Spread and search, Mister Ball," he said. "We should —"

"Pardon, sir, but we've done that. His mates from old *Tyber* have gone stem to stern. He's gone, sir. Sorry."

"Aye. Well, then, there's nothing more to be done." Dalton turned to Ishmael Bean. "We'll want crew assembly in the morning, Mister Bean. Time of opportunity. All hands, for memorial."

"Aye, sir."

"On deck!"

"Aye, tops?"

"Eyes aft, sir! Weather coming!"

Behind *Fury*, the ring of cloud had bulged inward. Now it drove toward them, a wall of storm a'seethe, driven by sudden gale-force winds.

"Hands to sheets, Mister Ball," Dalton shouted. "Shrift sail and batten down. This bedammed weather hasn't finished with us yet."

To Billy Caster, it was obvious that his captain was worried. He wondered if it was the strange weather and "weird waters" that vexed him so, or the loss of a man overboard — or possibly the absence of any sign of Mister Duncan's prize bark.

In the darkness and the murk, Charley Duncan had no real notion of which way he was going, but he held *Pride* with the wind and hoped it had not changed.

Just once through the hours he left the quarterdeck, leaving Pliny Quarterstone in charge there while he felt his way forward to inspect the holds and the forecastle deck — glimpses by lamplight and lightning flash.

The transshipping of the cotton had relieved most of the hold space in the bark and — for the first time — all of the passengers and all of their livestock were below, secure from the drenching mist and the whipping rains that now came through it.

Making his way back, the length of the long deck, he went from rail to rail at each mast, identifying and encouraging the men stationed at pinrail and fife. "We'll be clear of this soon enough," he told them at each station. "We're on course and holding speed. It'll clear, and *Fury* will be close by to take up escort."

He saw no reason to mention that *Pride's* course had most likely changed. There was, after all, the off chance that what he said to them was true.

Part of it proved to be so. In the first gray light of dawn, *Pride of Falworth* broke free of the storms that had pummeled her through a long night. Fogs clung all about, drifting skirts of hazy mist taking on the first colors of morning, but there was a bit of visibility . . . a little piece of ocean where mists confused the eye, but better by far than the blindness that had engulfed them for so long.

All along the bark's dripping deck, sailors grinned at one another in sheer relief at being able once again to see.

"Far better," Charley Duncan breathed, looking around. "Very well, I think we should do a bit of inspection before those landspeople come up from below again. Mister Hoop, rouse two watches, please. We'll stand inspection on deck and rigging, and I'll want topmen aloft to have a look at clews and bindings."

"Aye, sir." The big man turned to go forward.

"And have a look at the fothering on our hull, if you please. If it's taken a bulge in the night, we'd best correct it."

"Aye, sir. I'll tend to that myself."

Pliny Quarterstone came from below, carrying a mug of tea. "By gor," he said. "We can see."

"That we can, Mister Quarterstone. And I've set a quick inspection stem to stern while we've a chance to move about without tripping over passengers and their livestock. Have you had your breakfast?"

"Aye, I just did."

"Then, maybe you'd take a watch while I go below and get a bit for myself?"

"Aye, I will."

Pride's deck and yards came alive as sailors scattered about the vessel, inspecting lines, ties, lashings and stowage. After a long, blind night of storm, they were a jolly, grinning lot on this misty morning.

The grins froze on stunned faces when a dark warship, as big as a frigate and heavily armed, nosed through the mists a half mile away, altered course and headed for *Pride* like dark destiny.

Sixteen

The instant *Valkyrie* cleared the cloudbank, her lookouts spotted the bark a half mile away. In the drifting tatters of fog and mist, painted brilliant by dawnlight, the merchantman might have been a phantom ship—elusive and indistinct, sailing on a cloud of surface mist among the gauzy hazes. It required only a moment's decision for Timothy Leech to give the orders to come to starboard and close with the vessel. "Target of opportunity," he told his helmsman. Then, "Misters Ames and Boyd! Crews to guns, please! Mister McNair . . . you, there! McNair! Look alive! Go below and tell the captain we've a merchantman at hand!"

The bark had seen *Valkyrie*. Across the distance, the ship now flew colors—what appeared to be the banner of one of the noncombatant trading companies—and was putting on sail. Leech grinned. "Look at him, Mister Trice. Claimin' disinvolvement while he makes to run." He squinted. "Is that a ship we've seen before? It seems familiar."

Dickie Trice studied the silhouette across the waters. "It's rigged much like old *Pride of Falworth*. If I didn't know she was at the bottom of the sea, I'd almost say it was her. But then, a bark's a bark. With better light an' a closer look . . ."

"Aye, I expect that's what struck me. It does look a bit like old *Pride*. No matter, though. Whatever ship it is, it's a poor, lost lamb for the takin' of the wolves, eh? And not an escort in sight."

"That little cruiser we passed in the rains—a brig or the like—maybe that was its escort, do you think?"

"Like enough." Leech nodded. "Separated in the storm. Well, our gain, then. Mister Strode! Increase sail for chase! The lost sheep is making to run for it."

Handling *Valkyrie's* big wheel, Trice peered ahead. "What do you make of that bit of color on the vessel's portside hull, Mister Leech. Could that be fothering? Is she patched?"

"If so, then all the better." Leech leaned big, contented hands on the bell rail and watched the distant bark putting on sail, trimming to the wind. "If he's wounded, he won't take so long to catch . . . aye! See there, Mister Trice! Whoever commands that deck has his wits about him, for all that. He hasn't come to starboard for distance. He knows where that bark's best wind is, and he's taking it — dead astern."

Jack Shelby came on deck then, and Leech pointed. "A prize of chance, Cap'n. We cleared th' murk and there she lay. What's your pleasure?"

Shelby studied the fleeing bark, and as the light of morning gained, his cold gray eyes grew puzzled. "I know that ship, Mister Leech."

"We had a chat about that, Cap'n. It does bear a likeness to old *Pride of Falworth,* for a fact. Course we know it isn't."

Shelby stood silent, staring after the bark now full-sailed and running, trailed by the billowing mists that lay upon the sea. The light continued to improve, though the tantalizing curtains of the fogs still hung all about. Shelby squinted, and the cold frown on his face deepened. Finally he stepped to the bell rail. "Mister Strode!"

The bosun hurried aft. "Aye, Cap'n?"

"Mister Strode, when we took *Valkyrie,* did you scuttle *Pride of Falworth?*"

"We did, sir. Just as you said. A slow rip in her wales so she'd drift into deeps before she went under."

"Did you inspect the hulling yourself?"

"Aye, sir. Mister Trahan ordered the work, and I looked on as it was done."

"Where were the wales breached, then?"

"Portside bilges, sir. Just forward of the larders. Easy to get to, there. Beg pardon, but why do you ask?"

149

"Because that scuttled ship still floats, Mister Strode, and there are people aboard it who've fothered the hulling." He pointed, scowling. "That is *Pride of Falworth* yonder. I know the ship I sailed."

Timothy Leech frowned, but he kept his thoughts to himself. He remembered clearly how *Pride* had been dealt with. No one left aboard, and scuttled to sink, and no one about who might have made repairs. And he knew that if Misters Trahan and Strode said a ship was scuttled, it was scuttled. Jack Shelby was not a man to make mistakes, but Leech was sure he had made one now. That was a bark that resembled *Pride,* but it could not be *Pride*.

But then, it didn't really matter. Within an hour—two at the most—they would have the merchantman under their guns, whoever it was. And if Shelby wanted it sunk, they would sink it . . . after taking from it anything that it might carry, that they might want.

To have a close look at the hull's canvas patch, Mister Hoop—tagged after by his Frenchmen—had a small boat lowered alongside *Pride,* with a long tether from the fore portside channel of the bark. With this as a platform, and the Frenchmen and two others aboard to do his hauling, he could inspect the fothering closely, even though a heavy mist still clung to the sea, rising almost to *Pride's* gunwales. In the boat were all the tools he might need to inspect the ship's tied-on bandage and—if necessary—to make repairs.

They boarded the boat below *Pride's* channel hatch, with a man standing by to work the tether, but by the time Hoop had everyone in place, the boat was thirty feet astern of the still-moving bark, swinging on its line.

"Shoulders to the line, lads," Hoop instructed. "Heave away now, smartly."

With all of them playing in the tether, coiling it in the boat's bilges as they took slack, the boat caught up with *Pride* and came alongside her misted stern, heading forward. Then an odd sound caught Hoop's attention, and he held up a hand.

"Have we got something afoul there?" he pointed toward the bark's big sternpost with its iron-bound rudder.

They all listened, peering in the mist.

"Don't know as I can tell, Mister Hoop." Matthew Cobley admitted. "Can't see past arm's length down here in th' fogs."

"Might be seaweed," John Singleterry suggested. "Little enough harm in that, though. Just cut it away if it builds about the rudder."

"Well, let's see to the patch; then we can have another look," Hoop decided. "They went back to the tether, and the boat drew alongside *Pride*, riding the smooth waters of the ship's sidewake as it headed forward.

At the sailcloth patch, Hoop leaned outboard to peer at the repair, running a big hand along its surface. "We've took in some water," he decided. "The cloth is soft here, like a blister. One of you frogs hand me the pry bar there, will you?"

He held out his hand, waited a moment, then turned, scowling into puzzled faces. "Blast," he said.

"Blest," they agreed in unison.

"Pry bar!" He pointed.

"P'y ba'," the Frenchmen agreed.

"Well, hand it to me!"

"Ah!" Francois took his meaning. *"La torque! Oui. Tout de suite, m'sieur. Rene, la torque pour M'sieur 'Oop."*

"Oui." Rene picked up the pry bar and passed it across. *"Voila, m'sieur."*

"Thank you," Hoop breathed.

"De rien."

Using the pry bar against the thick wales of *Pride's* hull, Hoop forced a narrow breach in the cable cinching the sailcloth. Accumulated water flowed out, and gradually the stretched sail flattened itself against the hull, like a canvas skin.

"That should do it for now," Hoop decided. "Now, since we're here, let's swing back and have a look at that rudder." He raised his eyes and his voice. "Mister Reeves?"

Above, at *Pride's* gunwale, a tar-hatted head appeared. "Right here, Mister Hoop. Have you finished?"

151

"All done here, Mister Reeves. Now I wish you'd loose our tether there and walk it astern. I want to look at the rudder."

"Aye, I'll loose it, but don't go adrift now."

"We're not going adrift. Just give us a sternpost cleat, Mister Reeves."

Above, the rope was released, and the boat began to drift back along *Pride*'s towering hull.

Above and ahead, Reeves' voice said, "Hand here, Jaimie. Let's feed this line past the channels. There's a good . . . Jaimie! Blast it, don't . . . !"

Something splashed into the water ahead of the boat. Francois blinked, leaned forward and lifted the tether rope. It hung slack in his hand. *"Le corde,"* he said. *"C'est n'est pas attache!"*

"Mister Reeves!" Hoop shouted. "You've dropped the bleedin' tether!"

High above, a voice sang out, "On deck! Ship off the port quarter!"

Other voices followed, a chaos of them, and men appeared overhead, lining the rail, peering outward.

Pipes shrilled, and a voice said, "Hands to make sail! Stand by!"

Reeves' voice was nearly lost in the tumult. "Beg pardon, Mister Quarterstone, but Mister Hoop an' them are . . . Mister Quarterstone? Mister Quarterstone, sir, I . . ."

The boat neared *Pride*'s stern, and just overhead Charley Duncan's voice roared, "Up colors! Hands to sheets! Mister Quarterstone, let's have some order there! Helm, hold amidships! Ready all masts to make sail!"

"Mister Duncan!" Hoop called.

"Mister Reeves, did Mister Hoop complete his inspection of the patch?"

"Aye, sir, he did, but he's—"

"Never mind, Mister Reeves. Mister Nelson, quarter please! Misters Toddy and Sharp, see to the guns! Make sail, Mister Quarterstone! Trim full and by!"

Hoop stood upright in the rocking boat and cupped his hands. "Mister Duncan!" he roared.

"Moment, Mister Hoop. Let's get some way under us; then

we can talk. Mister Mudd! Mister Mudd, get tops aloft, please. Smartly now . . ."

"Mister Duncan!"

The bark's stern swept past, tall, dark and indifferent to the little boat bouncing now in its rolling wake.

"Mister Duncan! We're not aboard yet!"

"He's seen us, sir," a diminishing voice above the closing mist said. "He's making about to give chase."

"Sheet home! Sheet home there! Full and by the wind!"

"That's a warship, Mister Duncan! That's a blasted frigate! Where's his colors?"

"His colors may be entirely his own, Mister Nelson. I think that yonder is a pirate ship."

"Mister Quarterstone, I—"

"Not now, Mister Reeves! Get your back into that line!"

For a moment the voices hung in the air, receding with distance, overlying the thrum of the bark's big hull taking the sea in stride as it picked up speed, going away.

Then there was nothing. Only the lonely gurgle of water against the boat's planks.

Francois stared into the mist, then raised a forlorn hand in salute. *"Au revoir, vaesseau,"* he muttered sadly.

"C'est la vie." Rene shrugged.

"Rot!" Hoop rumbled.

Matthew Cobley and John Singleterry exchanged worried glances. The five of them were alone, fog-bound and adrift in a small boat without a mast, far at sea and hopelessly lost.

"I wish we at least had a bigger boat," Cobley said.

"Unship those oars, you," Hoop said. "There's no sense in just sitting here."

"Aye," Singleterry began unlashing the boat's two pairs of sweeps. "And where do you think we might make for, Mister Hoop? Back to that bedammed island, perchance?"

"Shut up and row."

With nothing else to do, they rowed, hoping that they were going in the general direction *Pride* had gone. Minutes passed, then tens of minutes; then Francois, in the bow, lifted his head and cupped a hand to his ear. *"Alons!"*

153

he said. *"Ecoutez avec moi! Autre vaesseau."*

Hoop glanced around. "What?"

"Ecoutez, s'il vous plait! Le bruit!"

"Brute?"

"Le bruit . . . le son! Ecutez!"

"I don't know what you're goin' on about —"

Rene put a finger to his lips and hissed, "Sh-h-h!"

"You hear something?" Hoop listened, too, then raised a big hand in command. "Belay that rowing, there. The frogs hear something."

They all heard it, then, somewhere aft and approaching — the unmistakable sounds of a ship under sail.

"Maybe they've come back for us," John Singleterry said. Shipping his oars, he cupped his hands to shout. Hoop's massive hands clamped his palms to his face.

"Quiet!" the big man hissed. "It isn't them. It's some other vessel. Now be still!" He stood, bracing himself on Singleterry's head, and stretched as tall as he could, trying to see above the mists. There was something there, vaguely. He stared, squinting, then dropped to a crouch. "Man those oars, you two. Pull with a will or we'll be run down. There's a warship bearing on us."

They pulled, while Hoop wrestled the tiller. The little boat swerved right, bobbed for a moment and scooted up the slope of a wave and down the other side. The growing sounds of the approaching ship had become a very thunder, seeming to be directly over them.

"Pull!" Hoop ordered.

Suddenly a tall, dark stem pierced the mists, thrusting like a thrown harpoon directly over them. The mists rang with the sounds of driving sails, straining lines and the thunder of waters keening past a rushing hull. The great, dark jib speared past above, and a wide prow with curling waters breaking from it bore down on them.

"Pull," Hoop rumbled.

They pulled.

For a moment it seemed the massive hull would grind them under. Then the little boat crested another wave and skittered aside like flotsam as the ship's bow wake slapped at it. A dark hull with ranked gunports streamed past, thundering through the waves, and the little boat spun full circle atop its wake. A moment, then it was past, a tall sternpost huge and shadowy spraying them with salt.

"Whoo," Hoop muttered. "Close, that."

The following wake of the big vessel spun the boat again, bouncing it like a cork a'bob on a rippled pond, and taut cables slapped it as another shadow bore down at it.

"Gor!" Matthew Cobley hissed. "Pull, mate!"

"Un autre bateau," Francois pointed out. *"Au compagnie le vaesseau travers le brouillard."*

"They got a launch in tow," Hoop told himself as a boat far larger than their own sliced past them. On purest impulse, he grabbed the coiled tether line and threw it. Its cleat hook bounced into the towed boat's bilges, caught on something there, and the line payed out as Hoop tried to bring the little boat's nose about. "Pull!" he bellowed.

The line came taut, sang with strain, and abruptly they were all clinging for dear life as their boat sliced through the waves, in the tow of the ship's tow.

"What the bejaysus did you do that for?" John Singleterry gasped, ducking the flailing shanks of his oars.

"I don't know," Hoop admitted. "I just did. Here, let's get those oars shipped before they brain us all . . . ah, that's better. Now, man that tether yonder and let's haul ourselves ahead."

Long minutes passed while they hove in tether, inching their way toward the stern of the towed launch. Then they were there, and Hoop tied off their line and clambered across into the larger boat. He looked around him in the flowing mist and grinned. "A sailing launch," he muttered. "A thirty-footer at the very least."

The others scrambled past him, crouching and crawling in the bounding launch. Amidships stood a sturdy mast with lateen rigging and a furled sail. Great sweeps four a'bank were lashed at the rails, and in the bow stood a swivel gun, ranked by stacked shot, a pair of powder kegs and all the

155

loading and firing paraphernalia of a mounted cannon.

Francois and Rene hurried to the fore and hovered there, gaping at the great sterncastle barely visible above the mists ahead. After a moment, Rene burrowed into the sheltered supplies beneath the swivel gun and came out with a chest. Inside were strikers, fuse and the fittings of a linstock. *"E voila!"* he announced. *"Le feu!"*

"This here is no sniggin' punt gun," Cobley decided, admiring the mounted cannon. "This is a full four-pounder. An' it's charged."

"Keep your voice down," Hoop warned. "Whoever's ship that is, they're not friendly. This is why Mister Duncan made sail and got us lost, is because this ship was chasing him."

"Your frogs have become excited about something, Mister Hoop." Singleterry pointed. In the bow, Rene and Francois were chattering about something while Rene squatted abaft the swivel gun, working at something under cover of the fore decking.

Francois gestured at Hoop and pointed upward, through the mists. *"C'est la* Valkyrie," he said emphatically. *Le criminel . . . les . . . les* pirates!"

"Pirates?" Hoop gawked at the escutcheon dimly visible on the tall stern ahead. "What pirates?"

"Oui, m'sieur. Malsaiteures. Brigands. Pirates. *N'importe lequel* pirates . . . *ceux la!* Pirates!"

"Keep your voice down, then," Hoop tried to hush him. "Best we not . . ."

Just behind him, Rene came up with a glowing fuse on a linstock, smoke trailing from fresh-sparked punk in the firebox, and said, determinedly, *"Pour mons potes . . . Le feu!"* Before Hoop or anyone else could react, the Frenchman cranked around the swivel-mounted four-pounder, raised its notches toward the stern ahead of them, and set off its vent.

Smoke blossomed in the mist ahead, obscuring all sight of the ship at the other end of the towing cable, and the four-pounder's roar was echoed by a crash just ahead.

". . . let them know we're here," Hoop finished lamely, his eyes growing wide, then "Jesus have mercy!"

"My God in Heaven," Cobley muttered as shrilling voices clamored in the mist just ahead. "That's capped it off nicely." He almost collided with Singleterry as the two of them raced for the mast with its furled sail. "For mercy's sake, Mister Hoop, cut us loose!"

While Hoop wrestled with the towing line, Rene and Francois were reloading. The stench of smoke in the flowing mist receded, and just ahead and above they heard shouted commands, and the unmistakable sound of big deck guns being run out.

As the launch swung free, grasping at the wind with its squat sail, Francois LeBlanc squinted at the stern rails of the tall ship just ahead. Suddenly his eyes went wide. *"C'est* m'sieur Leech," he pointed.

"M'sieur Leech?" Rene glanced up and saw the familiar face at the rail. *Ah . . . mais oui! C'est le malsaiteur! Le brigand . . . le ma'chant . . . le . . ."*

"Fils de pute?" Francois suggested.

"Oui! Le fils de pute!" He aligned the swivel gun again and brought the smoking fuse down. *"C'est pour vous,* m'sieur Leech! *Le feu!"* Again the four-pounder roared, and again there was a crash echoing back through the blinding smoke.

"Touche, M'sieur Leech," Rene muttered.

The launch swerved on tossing wakes as far greater thunders crashed and bellowed in the mist ahead, and tall spumes of water erupted on either side to rain down on them. Hoop half-ran, half-stumbled the length of the launch to throw himself onto the bucking tiller. "Get that sail up all the way!" he roared. "We are in serious trouble here!"

157

Seventeen

On an eerie sea where morning light slanted through trailing skirts of fog, swept aloft from the blanket mists by topsail winds, *Pride of Falworth* fled northward while eyes aboard looked back — back at the tall, stacked sails of the dark ship in pursuit, back across an emptiness that gave no sign of *Fury* . . . back at the drifting fogs where five crewmen had been left behind, adrift in a little boat.

Her hatches were battened, her decks alive with sailors who knew that the bark was no match for the stalking frigate slowly closing on their wake, and in the holds below frightened passengers huddled. Of the passengers only three — Squire Aaron Fairfield, Caleb Smith and a burly young farmer named Darling — had gone a'deck before the battening, and those remained there.

"What kind of seaman loses his escort?" Fairfield had demanded at first sight of the warship bearing down upon them. Then, "And what kind of escort loses his charge?"

"Mind your tongue or go below," Charley Duncan had snapped in response. "I've no time for chatting."

Now the landsmen huddled beside hammock nettings at the foot of the quarterdeck ladder and watched in horror as the dark ship grew astern. Dimly across the waters had come the sounds of cannon fire, just moments before. Several distinct thumps they had heard, though the range was yet far too great for shooting.

And looking up at Duncan on the quarterdeck, they knew that he was as puzzled as anyone as to why guns had

158

been fired. There was no doubt, though, that they would hear the sounds again once the pursuing ship was in range. For the dark ship had shown colors as the chase began — arrogant colors intended to create panic aboard the bark. A black flag.

At *Pride*'s stern rail and along her beams, hands were at work quoining up the merchantman's inadequate cannons. Commander Duncan, it seemed, was not a man to meekly strike colors in the face of overwhelming force. If all else failed, he intended to fight and had made that clear to one and all.

But first, he would run, and with the wind at his back and sails stacked high on the bark's four masts, he would make it as difficult as possible for the sleeker frigate to overtake them.

"I wonder what Patrick Dalton would do now," he muttered as he watched the errant winds aloft. "I know he would find some way to amuse those people back there . . . but how?"

"Sir?"

Duncan turned and shrugged. "Nothing, Mister Nelson. I was talking to myself."

"Aye, sir."

"How do we read, Mister Nelson?"

"Twelve knots steady by log and line, sir. We are full and by the wind."

"Twelve knots." He frowned, glanced aloft at the gauges at their spars, then looked astern, scowling at the big cruiser back there. It was closer than it had been, and coming into line with their course. He watched its great sails align and trim, and frowned again. There was something about it . . . he shook his head, puzzled. "Twelve knots on a wind that's making eighteen to twenty. He'll do better than that, Mister Nelson. A ship-rigged vessel of that size, he'll make fifteen easily, when he's trimmed . . ."

Again he squinted, studying the ship a half mile away. By his own estimates, it would be within range of big guns

159

within the hour. And it carried big guns. He had no question on that score. Though not quite a proper frigate by Royal Navy standards, the pursuer was the size of a frigate and designed for the same thing—to seek and destroy. And it had the legs and the teeth for its purpose.

He stood silent for long minutes, watching the ship astern, then pointed. "Mister Nelson, what would you say he is doing now?"

"He's chasing us, Commander."

"I mean his maneuver. What is he doing, exactly?"

Nelson hesitated, gazing aft, then shrugged. "He angled to dead astern of us, and now he's coming over a bit—a point I'd say—to follow up our wake until his bow chasers can reach us. And that won't be long, either . . . sir."

"Shouldn't a frigate make about more smartly than that, Mister Nelson? Should it balk at the turn, as he seems to?"

"I don't know, Commander. I sailed under the Union Jack for a time, but I was posted to a brig. I never sailed on a frigate." He squinted, trying to see what Duncan was getting at. "Maybe it's because of his rigging. He has run-outs on his tops. Could it be that gives him a balky rudder? I don't know."

"Possibly." Duncan nodded.

"Mister Quarterstone, he sailed aboard a frigate, he said, his last tour before going aboard old *Tyber*."

"That's right, I heard him say that." Duncan turned and strode to the bell rail. "Mister Porter!"

"Aye, sir?"

"Please find Mister Quarterstone and ask him to come aft if he will."

"Aye, sir."

Quarterstone arrived within moments, and Duncan met him at the ladder. "Come astern, please, Mister Quarterstone. I'd like your opinion of how that vessel back there handles its course corrections."

"Aye, sir."

Side by side they headed for the stern rail. In the nettings, Aaron Fairfield growled, "Blast all sailors! Here we are, running for our very lives, likely to be blown out of the water at any moment, and they discuss the sailing habits of the enemy."

"Maybe Mister Duncan is making a plan," Keith Darling suggested. He was silenced by the scowls of the two older men.

Astern, Pliny Quarterstone planted himself at the rail and squinted aft. Even in morning light, the sea had an eerie, otherworldly appearance with its low cover of heavy mist from which curtains seemed to rise and swirl as the topsail winds drew skirts of fog upward. The phenomenon played puzzles with the eyes. But the dark prowler was clearly visible, even so. Less than half a mile astern, it had come onto *Pride*'s track and was pursuing under full sail—even the odd-looking studding sails at its tops were full of wind.

"Not just exactly a frigate," Quarterstone judged, "but close kin for certain. What did you want me to look at, Mister Duncan?"

"How he makes his turns," Duncan said, realizing as he said it that the pursuer was no longer turning. It had come to course. "Stand and watch for a bit." He turned to the helmsman. "Bring us a point to starboard, please, Mister Mudd."

"Aye, sir." The helm spun, and the bark shivered as its rudder fought the trim of its sails, then took control.

Duncan went to the bell rail and called, "Hands to trim, please, Mister Porter. We are exercising the ship."

"Aye, sir. Hands a'sheet! Trim to course!"

"Now the fool is conducting sailing practice," Aaron Fairfield muttered darkly in the nettings.

Pride lost a bit of way, trimming to a new course, but she took the wind again and made it back. Astern, the dark ship had gained a bit, but now was off course, and still beyond good range of even heavy guns. As they watched, it altered to match course, and Pliny Quarterstone frowned

161

and shook his head. "Sloppy, that," he muttered.

Duncan was beside him. "What do you see?"

"Poor helmsmanship. I'd expect better."

"Be more specific, can't you?" Duncan demanded. "What are they doing wrong?"

"I'd call it a lazy rudder, myself." Quarterstone shrugged. "He is slewing on his helm. Very sloppy."

"What could cause that, do you think?"

"Some bumbling landsman at the helm would." Quarterstone glanced pointedly around at the three passengers in the nettings.

Duncan ignored the jibe. "Not too bloody likely, that," he said. "What else?"

"Any number of things, I suppose. Do you think we might have another look at it?"

"Mister Mudd, bring us a point to port, please." Duncan again went to the bell rail. "Mister Porter, we are turning again. Hands to—"

"I know very well what we're doing!" Porter sounded a bit testy. "Run your quarterdeck, Commander. My lads know what to do with the sheets."

"Sorry." Duncan scowled. "Just get on with it, then."

"Aye, sir. Hands a'sheet! Retrim!"

At the stern rail, Quarterstone watched carefully as the pursuer again corrected, coming onto their course again.

Duncan said, "Well?"

"That's a right trim warship yonder," Quarterstone opined. "Beats me why he'd sail it with such a handicap."

"What handicap, Mister Quarterstone," Duncan asked through clenched teeth.

"Why, with the couplings askew on the rudder, of course. That's his problem. His rudder's fouled, in its bandings. Hard as the devil to sail a ship that way. Any captain worth his salt, with a problem like that, why he'd lay over and fix it, he would."

"Will it keep him from catching us?"

"If he lays over to fix it, it probably will."

162

"And if not?"

"Oh, if he keeps coming, he'll catch us, right enough. In an hour or so, is my guess. But he's having a devil of a time with course changes. He really should repair that rudder."

"Thank you, Mister Quarterstone." Duncan looked aloft at the gauges, judging the wind. "Two points to starboard, helm," he ordered. He started toward the bell rail, then changed his mind. Mister Porter was surly about being told to trim, so he wouldn't bother him with such things. But trim they would, and trim again. "If that villain yonder is suffering his turns," he told Finian Nelson, "then let's give him as much suffering as we can."

"Sir?"

"We zig," Duncan said. "And when he zigs to follow we zag. Then when he corrects we zig again."

Sweating at the helm, Raymond Mudd muttered, "I never thought I'd miss Mister Hoop, but I do now."

"If it's muscle you want, just show me what to do."

They all turned at the unfamiliar voice. It was the burly young passenger, Keith Darling. He had come to the helm box and stood there, glaring at Pliny Quarterstone. "Landsman at the helm, eh? I be no sailor, swabby, but I can turn a bloody wheel as well as any man."

"You don't belong—" Duncan started.

"Take these spokes here," Mudd cut in. "Just hold them firm . . . like this, you see. Nothing much to steering. Just turn the wheel when I turn, and stop when I stop."

Leaning and shivering, hands at eight pinrails racing to trim and retrim sails, *Pride of Falworth* began a random zigzag course northward, pursued by a dark and bitter frigate with a sore tail.

Though Charley Duncan had no way to know that two four-pound iron balls, fired point-blank from a launch in tow, had fouled *Valkyrie*'s rudder, he did know that the pursuer was lamed in some manner. He knew also that—even lame—the stud-sail frigate coursing behind him still had the power to run down and kill his ship.

Hands clasped behind his back in the way he had seen ship's masters do, Duncan paced *Pride*'s quarterdeck deep in worried thought. *What would you do now, if you were me, Patrick Dalton,* he wondered. *And for that matter, where the devil are you? We sorely need you now.*

"Frenchmen!" Timothy Leech hissed, peering into the baffling mists that ebbed in to hide *Valkyrie*'s wake. "I swear they were Frenchmen, Captain, though how they managed to get aboard our whaleboat is beyond me."

"Beyond you, Mister Leech?" Jack Shelby turned cold eyes on his big second. "Then, you should ponder upon it. They obviously came from that merchantman there ahead, to attempt sabotage upon us. Purest luck that they were able to do so, but that is what they did."

"Then, you think that's who has *Pride* now—if that *is Pride?* Frenchmen?"

"That would be the obvious deduction, Mister Leech." Shelby turned toward his helm, where four men were struggling with the double wheel. "Confound it, helm! Must we slew about that way? I don't care to devote the entire day to the taking of that bedammed bark!"

"Sorry, Cap'n," a crewman puffed. "We're doin' the best we can."

"Like I told you, Cap'n," Leech put in, "they've maimed our latches. The rudder binds at every turn."

"And that captain is taking every advantage of it," Shelby spat. "He alters course every time we correct. He knows what he's done, right enough. Likely it was what his boat party was set to do."

"I don't see what Frenchmen would be doing in these waters."

"Harassing the British, obviously. It's well known that they've taken an interest in the Colonial cause. As to how they came into possession of *Pride of Falworth*, we'll know more about that when we have them under our guns—or

164

sunk. I shall need a few prisoners to chat with, Mister Leech . . . though I shan't need many. Keep that in mind when we catch them."

"Aye, Cap'n." Leech turned away, shaking his head. There was much about the loss of the towed launch that just didn't make sense in any way that he could see. Still, there was no question what had happened. Someone had boarded their whaleboat and fired its swivel gun — twice — into *Valkyrie*'s stern. And the shouts he himself had heard were in the French tongue.

With a good sail set on a stubby mast, the big launch coursed to its best pace — a broad tack that held such wind as could be had three points abaft the port beam. The little work boat followed on a tether.

"I'd say we're makin' two-three knots at best, Mister Hoop," John Singleterry announced bitterly. "What is it about these waters, that the winds can sing aloft so and yet not come down to where our sail is?"

"Weird waters." Hoop shook his head. "Myself, I like the trade lanes better. A man generally knows what God has on his mind there."

"How far do you suppose it is to America, then?"

"I haven't got the slightest idea. But I think we're going the right direction."

"How come your Frenchies opened fire like that on that ship that had us in tow?" Matthew Cobley wondered.

"They're not *my* Frenchies." Hoop glared at him. "Anyway, how does a body know why Frenchies do anything they do? Some way or another, they decided that was a pirate ship, so they just naturally opened fire, that's all."

"Seems to me the prudent thing might have been just to quietly cut loose and go away."

"That was what I was about to suggest when the shooting started. Have you finished looking at the stores aboard?"

"Not much to look at." Cobley shrugged. "Two casks of

165

water, a bit of biscuit and a stack of netting that's all fouled with bits of wood and twigs. I'd say this launch had spent some time bein' hid someplace, by the looks of it."

"I'd feel better if you'd get those two away from that cannon," Singleterry suggested. "The way they act, they might take a notion to turn it around and open fire on us."

Hoop frowned, turned to glance at the smug-seeming Frenchmen in the bow, then turned back. "Why would they do a thing like that? We're all in the same boat."

"They *are* French," Singleterry pointed out.

Hoop thought it over and turned toward the Frenchmen again. "You frogs! You keep that gun stowed unless I say otherwise!"

Francois and Rene looked at each other, puzzled, then shrugged in unison. *"Oui, M'sieur 'Oop,"* Francois agreed. Stepping carefully aft, squeezing under the sail's lower edge, he made his way astern and began hauling in the little boat's tether. When it was snugged against the launch he lashed the line, leapt across into the boat, then returned to the launch. *"Voila!"* he said, handing Hoop the pry bar. *"Le torque."*

"We'll stand shifts of two," Hoop said tiredly. "Tiller and watch. That way we can take turns getting some sleep."

North of Bahamas Passage, under cloudy skies, the packet *Cricket* was making its own way northward by a bit west, bound from Cape Jane to Wilmington with news of ship losses . . . and with a passenger.

Lewis Farrington, once commander of His Majesty's Sloop *Wolf*, more lately in command of escort for a pair of lost merchantmen on the Indies run, leaned forlornly on *Cricket's* gunwale. "Its name was *Valkyrie*, all right," he repeated. "I saw it clearly, just as my ship was destroyed."

Beside him, Captain Nat Simms frowned. "But *Valkyrie* was Thibaud's ship. The pirate. And he's gone. I heard fishermen found his corpse washed up on one of the cays . . .

him and several others. Not a lot left of any of them, but it was Thibaud, fair enough. They knew him by his beard and by the locket he always wore. Everybody figures the *Valkyrie* for sunk."

"Thibaud or not," Farrington said, "that pirate was *Valkyrie,* and the man commanding her was as black a villain as I've heard of. No signal, no call nor quarter . . . he just opened fire on us and kept shooting until there was nothing left."

"Lor'." Simms shivered. "I hate to hear about a thing like that. And I'd hate to be the one to tell Squire of it. What do you plan to do then?"

"Plan?" Farrington blinked, glancing around. "I don't know," he said vaguely. "Except I need a ship."

"You'd go out again . . . after that?"

"I *have* to go out. If I don't get back under sail now, I'll never sail again. I need a ship," he said it slowly. "A fighting ship, if there's one to be found."

"On deck! Sail ho!"

Simms straightened, peering aloft at *Cricket's* single masthead. "Whereaway, Toby?"

"Off the starboard beam, Cap'n. Hard down."

"Can you read it?"

"No, sir, but I'll keep an eye on it."

It was later in the day when Toby advised that the sail abeam looked like a boat. "Maybe a whaleboat or sailing launch, sir!" he called.

Simms shook his head. What was a boat doing way out here? He thought it over, then called aft, "Bring us hard to starboard, helm. Whoever that is yonder may need some help."

Eighteen

With fair light, *Fury* had eyes aloft in both tops, searching for sign of *Pride of Falworth*, but nowhere on the obscured horizons was there any sail at all. Patrick Dalton read a memoriam for young Tommy Finch, able seaman once of His Majesty's Royal Navy, now lost to the sea; then splicers and pulley teams went to work to repair the snow's broken port fish tackle while Dalton looked at his charts and read the morning's fairing.

"We haven't overrun them in the darkness," he decided. "Mister Duncan would keep his sail aloft in those winds. Nor have we altered course by more than a mile or two. Therefore, he has changed course for some reason."

"But where?" Billy Caster traced the markings on the makeshift chart. "And in which direction?"

Dalton was thoughtful for a time, his eyes scanning down the list of watch reports and conditions. "North, I believe," he said, finally.

"That warship that passed us . . . it was going north, wasn't it?"

"Yes, it was. Mister Wise, how are the repairs forward?"

"We haven't fished the anchor yet, sir," Cadman Wise said, "but the tackle is in place. All the work's a'deck now."

"Very well, Mister Wise. Have hands to station please, to trim to course. We are going to look for Mister Duncan."

"Aye, sir."

"Mister Locke, two points to starboard if you please. Bring us a point east of north. Mister Mallory, I shall want all possible sail very shortly. At my call, please."

"Aye, sir."

With topsails and topgallants spread to take the wind, *Fury* shook off the slumbers of the night and leaned into a new course, lifting a jaunty jib above the mists of morning as the rising keen of her sleek hull echoed in the spray at her bow.

"How do you fare the morning, Mister Caster?" Dalton asked offhandedly as topmen swarmed aloft to stand by the studding wings and others made ready the run-out gaff and boom of the snow's great ringtail astern.

"Odd weather, sir," the boy said. "The gauges aloft read a wind of twenty knots or more and rising, though here on deck it's hardly ten."

"Weird waters," Dalton muttered. "What else?"

"The mist seems to be shredding, sir. The winds are drawing it aloft. It's . . . it's pretty, sir. Like ladies' skirts sweeping across a ballroom."

Dalton glanced at his clerk. The boy did have a way with words sometimes. "I have eyes, Mister Caster. I can see all that. What will it do?"

Billy hesitated, looking again at the blowing gauges in the tops, the swirling, dancing motions of curtains of mist rising from the fog-covered sea, then spread his hands. "If it keeps doing what it's doing now, sir, I'd warrant the winds will rise to thirty knots or near it, and once the mists have cleared we'll have low overcast and a good general wind that's as fresh down here as it is up there."

"Interesting," Dalton said. "How do you come to that prediction?"

"I don't know, sir. It just seems as if that's what it's trying to do. Am I correct?"

"I don't know, Mister Caster. Your guess this time is as good as mine. But I find no fault with it."

He stepped to the quarterrail. "Double your hands at the sheets, please, Mister Wise. We are putting on more sail."

"Aye, sir. How much?"

"All of it, Mister Wise. Studding sails top and topgallant

169

yards, royals aloft, top main staysail and the ringtail. By the numbers, Mister Wise."

"Aye, sir."

"You lads is in for a show now," Purdy Fisk announced to some of the new hands at the main fife rails. "What would you wager this vessel's hull speed to be?"

"Fourteen, maybe fifteen," Virgil Hemingway judged. "A king's brig of this size might do that or near."

Fisk grinned. "Aye, that would be proper—if *Fury* was a brig. But a snow is somethin' else again. I'll wager a week's pay that Captain Dalton gets eighteen knots out of her . . . no, by heaven, I'll wager he gets twenty."

"Why would you wager such a thing?" Noel Ransom frowned at Fisk. "That isn't even . . ."

Ishmael Bean, hurrying past, paused. "Don't jeopardize your wages on that, lads. Remember, some of us have sailed with Dalton longer than any of you." He cocked a brow at Fisk. "And there's some who don't hesitate to take advantage of others' ignorance."

High aloft, the tall royals billowed on *Fury's* fore and main skymasts, then snapped taut as brawny men at the pinrails below trimmed them to the wind. *Fury* seemed to shudder, like a racehorse quickening its gate, then leapt forward as rollers of bright water cut through the mists riding along her hull. She surged again when the upper staysail unfurled from its gaff above the spencer, and as the big ringtail ran out astern, increasing the size of her driving spanker by a third. She twitched her behind like a stalking cat and pranced upon the waters. Above her jutting prow great batwings of jibsail and fore topmast staysail arched aloft, taking the wind's angle a'fore just as the spanker took it astern.

Twelve great sails she spread now, only her main course furled up to give the spencer advantage of the tacking wind.

Like a dancer at center stage she took spray in her teeth and rose on a throbbing keel to race across blanketed waters.

Then at Dalton's command, the studding sails ran out, at

port and starboard, six on the foreyards and four on the mains — big, bright extensions of the tops and topgallants, great wings spread from the forecourse. Here aside and aloft was the best wind, and the ship's rigging sang like harp strings as the structure of masts, shrouds, yardarms and stays adjusted to take the massive press of sail. Aloft, topmen clung to pitching, surging footropes, while all along the deck men grabbed supports to keep from falling.

"Sweet Jesus," Noel Ransom gasped, then turned to stare at the beaming face of Purdy Fisk.

"Told you." Fisk grinned. *"Fury* isn't a brig."

Just forward of them, Ishmael Bean had taken his first cast with log and line, and turned to relay his report. "Seventeen knots by log, Mister Wise! Seventeen and climbing!"

The whine of singing waters along the hull rose in pitch, and rose yet more as surging gusts settled from aloft to thrum and snap in the ringtail and spanker. The curling spray off both bows had become tall, bright cockscombs of clear water, rising as high as the deadeyes where the shrouds were cleated before curling out and down to fall back into the misted sea.

From the quarterrail, Dalton gazed at the quivering, driving spanker with its ringtail extension aft, and nodded. "You've faired it well, Mister Caster," he said. "The lofty winds are lowering to give us their advantage."

"By log eighteen and climbing!" Ishmael Bean called from ahead.

Bell by bell, the weather changed. Sea mist was swept aloft and settled there to canopy a gray sky. The high winds came down to replace the mists, and increased to a steady twenty-eight knots on *Fury*'s port quarter, and the visible world became steadily wider as the air was swept clean between sea and sullen sky.

Fury thrummed northward, booming deep in her hull as she overran and clove the rolling waves, her wake a long sheen of foam where she had been. A gust sent the gauges flying to thirty-plus knots, and the snow growled like thunder deep in her knees as rigging aloft shrilled at the press of sail on the delicate counterbalances of mast, yard and stay. On the working decks men glanced around, wide-eyed at each new sound and rumble.

"By the log . . . and a half, twenty!" Ishmael Bean called from the fore.

"The captain's a madman," new hands muttered. "He'll destroy us all if he keeps this up."

"I'm for taking in a bit of sail," one suggested. "No ship can—"

"I'd mind my tongue if I were you, swabby," Cadman Wise growled. "Captain Dalton says what sail we press, not the likes of you."

"But he'll kill us!" another said. "Listen to the footings, man. He'll break us apart pressing the ship so."

"I think I agree," another said.

Wise turned, surprised. "You, Mister Tucker? You, a first-rate seaman with line duty behind you?"

"I've sailed a fine ship or two." Euclid Tucker nodded. Heavy muscles corded and rippled in his bare shoulders. "And with fine commands. But no man can press a ship so and not come to ill. Are they right, Mister Wise? Is Captain Dalton mad?"

"Not mad." Wise shook his head. "Sanest man I've met, for an officer."

"Then, what drives him so?"

Wise shrugged. "Maybe it comes of bein' black Irish. They sometimes aren't like other folk, you know. Moody, that's the way of 'em. And it's my notion that the captain's in a black mood right now. But if Captain Dalton says this vessel shall take wing and fly, then I for one intend to find myself a good spot at the midships rail."

Credence Tapp squinted at him. "A spot at the rail? Why?"

Wise grinned. "Because I've never seen what the earth looks like from above the clouds."

"Somebody needs to talk to him," Tucker persisted. "If

172

you won't do it, Mister Wise, then I will."

"Suit yourself." Wise shrugged. "Though I'd advise against it."

"Who's with me?" Tucker raised his voice. "Who'll demand caution with me?"

Several raised their hands, and Wise shrugged again, glancing at the knowing faces of Claude Mallory and Purdy Fisk. "And if Captain doesn't agree?"

"Then, by the Lord we'll press our point."

Dalton was, as Wise had guessed, "in a mood." Long weeks on lonely seas, the frustration of the fugitive—the grounded fox waiting for the hounds to abate their chase—the uncertainty of what to do next, to keep both the ship and the honor that he had fought to win, and now the anxiety of the lost *Pride,* somewhere on an unfriendly sea where predators lurked, all weighed heavily upon him as he pushed *Fury* to new limits and scanned the seas ahead.

Cloud cover still limited the view. Low and jumbled the clouds lay, narrowing the span between sea and sky. Murky distances playing tricks with the eyes. Bell succeeded bell, and no sighting came from the mastheads, nor even from the agile topmen who braved the topgallant shrouds for a bit now and again, clinging more than a hundred feet above the deck on a racing snow that skimmed and pitched as she ran.

Far below, on the quarterdeck, Patrick Dalton worried and paced. "I've an ill feeling about that frigate, Mister Locke," he said, not so much to his helmsman as to himself. "Neither trader nor escort that, nor yet a proper instrument of belligerents." He glanced around. "Is the helm behaving as it should? At this press of sail, it could become skittish."

"Docile as a lamb, sir." Locke nodded, then braced himself as a surge of wind belled in the taut ringtail and the ship tried to turn of its own accord. "Best I should say a weaned colt, I expect, sir. She does have a friskiness to her at this speed."

"Manageable?"

173

"Oh, yes, sir. Manageable, aye."

"Keep a good grip, then, Mister Locke. If we've no sign of *Pride* in the next hour, I shall add more sail."

Behind him a querulous voice gasped, "More sail?"

Dalton turned. Several sailors were massed at the quarterdeck ladder, some on the steps and one or two already on the command deck.

"You men!" Abel Ball snapped, from the bell rail. "Avast there. You've no business on the quarterdeck!"

"Business with the captain." The lead among them frowned, then straightened and faced Dalton. "Sir!"

"Well?"

"Sir, we've come to petition you to ease sail a bit. It seems to us that we are likely to break up at this press."

Dalton gazed at them, one by one. "We?" he asked. "You six?"

"Aye," the leader hesitated; then his face grew pugnacious. "Aye, we bring a fo'c'sle mandate, Captain. Slow down this ship, or we will."

"You will," Dalton breathed. Near at hand, Billy Caster was edging toward a rack of belaying pins. Dalton halted him with a raised hand. "You men, do you recall the articles you agreed to when I gave you berths on *Fury?*"

"Aye, sir," the leader said. "And we mean no breach of articles, sir, but by God we aim to save our skins if you won't."

"By mutiny?"

"No, sir. By persuasion, sir."

"And who here would like to do the persuading, then?"

"I might attend to that, sir, by your leave. Euclid Tucker, sir. Able seaman, at your service."

"I know you, Mister Tucker." Dalton sighed, then removed his sword and buckler and handed them to Billy. "Very well, Mister Tucker. You have leave. Feel free to persuade me."

Tucker blinked in surprise, then shrugged and grinned. "No hard feelin's, Captain?"

"Not in the slightest. Begin."

174

Like a pouncing cat, Tucker launched himself at Dalton, knotted arms swinging, hard fists clenched. The sailor was shorter by inches than Dalton, but widely built and equipped with broad, powerful shoulders and burly arms as hard as shroud cable. And he was quick . . . though not quick enough. His first rush carried him directly through where the Irishman had been an instant before, and he sprawled on the deck, tripped by a booted foot.

Dalton called over his shoulder, "Mister Caster, pass the word. I am not yet persuaded. Ask Mister Mallory to break out the flying jib, please. That should give this bumbling tub a bit more speed."

"Aye, sir."

Tucker scrambled to his feet, wild-eyed. "You are a madman!" he shouted, then lowered his voice. "Beg pardon, sir, but the calling of names is part of leave, isn't it?"

"Right you are." Dalton nodded. "Call away."

"Madman!" Tucker repeated, then came in low, rushing the captain with arms spread wide to grapple. He didn't see the hard fist that took him at the cheekbone and looped him around, but he felt the booted foot that connected with his posterior and sent him sprawling exactly where he had been before.

Dalton straightened. "Mister Caster, ask Mister Mallory to break out that spritsail we carry, and sling it below the spreaders."

"Aye, sir." Even as he responded, *Fury* seemed to leap into a new stride, answering to the pull of the high-flying jibsail at her nose. "Mister Mallory, Captain would like the spritsail, if you please."

Tucker got to his feet more slowly this time, dizzy and shaking his head. "You're still adding more sail?" he coughed.

"I have not been persuaded otherwise, Mister Tucker."

Like a bull fighting flies, Tucker shook his head from side to side, muttering, and braced himself to charge again. The charge never began. Dalton stepped in front of him, ducked

175

a roundhouse swing and bent the man double with a fist to his midriff, then straightened him up again with a blow to the chin. Tucker wobbled, almost fell, then crouched, hands on knees, trying to catch his breath.

"Mister Mallory," Dalton called. "Sheet and trim the main course, please."

"The main . . . ah, aye, sir."

Like fiddles in torment, *Fury*'s singing shrouds howled as the big sail dropped home and took the wind. Deep within her hull the snow crackled and boomed, mast footings straining and grating against their keelson stays. Timbers rumbled and chattered as her knees took the strain. She leapt forward as though she would take flight, and the thunders of her torment were deafening for a moment, then eased.

From forward, the amazed voice of Ishmael Bean shouted, "By log, twenty-two . . . no, twenty-three! Ye Gods, twenty-three?"

Dalton listened to the sounds of his ship, his dark eyes alight with interest, a brow cocked in judgment.

"Marvelous," he breathed. He looked at the groaning Tucker. "You still have leave to continue, Mister Tucker, though I've run out of sails, I'm afraid. We've pressed on every stitch of canvas that we've anything to hang it from, unless we invent something new. What is your pleasure?"

Tucker looked up, dizzy and battered. "Twenty-three?" he croaked. "Twenty-three knots?"

"It seems so," Dalton said happily. "To be honest, I wouldn't have thought it could be done. I owe you a debt of thanks, Mister Tucker. Without your . . . ah . . . persuasion, I might never have had the nerve to really try all sail in such a wind. Good to know what we can do if we set our minds to it, though, isn't it?"

"Twenty . . . three?"

"On deck!" The hail from aloft was distant, but clear.

"Aye, tops?"

"Sail, sir! Ahead and a point aport, a mile at most! Two

176

ships, sir, and cannon fire! One is *Pride of Falworth!* The other wears a black flag!"

"Ah," Dalton said. "It's time we earn our keep, then." He straightened himself, retrieved his sword and slapped Euclid Tucker on the back, urging him forward. The man's companions backed away before him. Dalton waved them forward. "To stations, lads. We've work to do. And by the way, Mister Tucker, well done! I was in something of a mood, but I feel much better now."

Nineteen

Despite the best of Charley Duncan's evasions, as the hours passed the dark warship bore down relentlessly—closing, ever closing on the fleeing bark. Though awkward in its corrections because of its binding rudder, still the frigate was fast and lean. Its three masts carried as much sail—and in greater variety—as *Pride*'s four, and its timbered hull was sleek and trim.

Though strongly manned now, despite the loss of Hoop and his companions aboard the little boat, *Pride* with all the weight of sail that could be pressed onto her stacked spars was yet only a bark—a merchant sailing vessel designed and rigged for the transport of cargoes—and no match in speed or agility for the ship-rigged cruiser on her tail. Nor were her guns—a mere handful of antiquated cannons, the largest of which were the brace of old nines at her stern—any match for the banked guns of the frigate, as Charley Duncan saw clearly when the first smoke-roses bloomed at the pirate's nose.

"Ranging guns," he muttered as a pair of balls whined overhead, tearing gaping holes in the courses there. "Long twelves. He'll tear us to pieces with those if we don't heave to."

"Aye," Pliny Quarterstone said darkly. "Then bring his broadsides to bear and blast us out of the water when we do. That ship is not inviting surrender, Mister Duncan, nor offering quarter. I believe he intends to kill us, no matter what we do."

178

Duncan squinted through a glass, then lowered it with a sigh and handed it to Quarterstone. "You likely are right," he said. "Read her name."

Quarterstone glassed the pursuer. "*Valkyrie*," he read. "Isn't that the ship that . . . ?"

"Aye. The one the Frenchmen told us about. The same people who had *Pride* once, then tried to scuttle her."

Again the frigate's bow chasers blazed. A ball skipped across the waters thirty feet off *Pride*'s portside beam, to sink in a geyser of spray ahead. A second whined across stern timbers astarboard, gouging out a half-moon of bright wood.

"He's aiming to hull us at waterline!" Finian Nelson shouted.

Duncan counted the seconds, clicking his tongue in slow rhythm to keep the count. Then he turned. "Point aport, helm. Bosun, trim to—"

"I know, I know!" Porter's growl carried astern.

Pride came over into a graceful turn as the smoke-roses blossomed again behind them. This time both shots were wide to starboard, but Duncan shook his head. "That likely won't work but once," he admitted. "Mister Reeves? Where's Mister Reeves?"

Reeves came racing aft, skidding to a halt at the netting ladder. "Sir?"

"Mister Reeves, when Mister Hoop inspected the fothering, what did he find?"

"A blister, sir. The patch cloth had taken in water. He let it out."

"Then, likely it has taken more, and it's dragging on us. Was there water below decks from the patch?"

"I don't know, sir, I . . ."

"It's dry below," Keith Darling said. "Nothing's leaking that we could see down there."

Duncan made a decision. "Mister Reeves, break out axes and cut away that fothering."

"Aye, sir. Shall we hoist it . . ."

"Cut it away and let it go," Duncan said. "Now!" He turned to the helm. "Point to starboard, helm . . . no, belay that! Just a bit more to port, then lay over two to starboard."

"Aye, sir." Again *Pride* veered to the left, and this time the fire from the pursuer's bow chasers was farther off to the right.

Duncan let out a deep breath, then sighed and shook his head. "That's another move that won't work again," he muttered. "Stern guns, do you have his range yet?"

"Not bloody likely," a hand at the nearest of the ancient nines growled. "Not with these popguns."

"Well, damn it, shoot anyway!"

"Aye, sir."

As the nines bellowed in ragged volley of two, *Pride* answered to her helm and swung gracefully to the right. Smoke rode across her tail, but its shredding mist could not obscure the twin clouds that grew at the nose of *Valkyrie*. Too late to reverse, Duncan knew that this time the pursuer had outguessed him. He braced himself for the impact of iron ball, then staggered as *Pride* seemed to shoot forward, gaining speed as though kicked from astern. Aport, a sprawl of sailcloth drifted past her beam.

Twin iron balls threw spray from her wake, missing by scant yards.

"That fotherin' was full of water!" someone called forward. "Like we was draggin' a lake around."

"Trim to course!" Duncan shouted.

"We're trimmin', blast it!" James Porter snapped. "Stop tellin' us our bedammed job!"

In the nettings, Squire Aaron Fairfield's caustic voice was raised, "What sort of officer takes that kind of backtalk from his crew?"

Duncan looked around, fuming, then stalked to the quarterrail hatch. "I am not a damned officer!" he roared at the startled passengers just below. "And if you call me that again, I'll have you thrown overboard. Now will you be silent?"

Fairfield blinked at him. "I was only just . . ."

"Will you be silent?"

"Well . . . yes."

"What?"

"Yes, I said!"

"Yes . . . what?"

"Yes, *sir.*"

"That's better." Duncan nodded, turning away. "Laxity aboard ship is not to be tolerated," he muttered.

Between *Pride's* sudden release from the bondage of her hull patch, and the pirate's binding rudder, the bark had gained a bit of space. But *Valkyrie* had compensated now and was coming on, hard in pursuit.

"Well, Mister Duncan, do you have any more tricks?" Pliny Quarterstone asked bleakly.

"On deck!"

Duncan peered aloft, then turned to look astern. The grim set of his freckled face softened, then became a vicious grin. "Aye," he said. "One more. Mister Porter!"

"I know!" the grumpy voice bellowed. "Trim to—!"

"Mister Porter, shut your bleedin' mouth and listen! I want you to stand by to come about."

"Come about?"

"Come about?" Quarterstone echoed.

"Into the wind?" Nelson gaped.

"You're daft!" Aaron Fairfield yelped, then clapped a hand over his mouth.

Duncan ignored them all, gazing out at the killer in his wake, his grin feral. "At my call, helm," he said evenly.

At the helm, two pairs of wide eyes stared at him, but without argument.

"Squire Fairfield," Duncan said, "you can make yourself useful now. Go below and get all of your people into the after holds. No person is to be forward of the foremain footings."

"Now see here . . ." Fairfield blustered.

"Do it now!"

Fairfield and his shadow scurried away, muttering.

"Mister Nelson, hands to all guns, please. I want every gun we have hauled to the bow, three each side of the sprit. Secured, loaded, primed and aimed straight ahead level."

"Are you sure you know what you're doing, Mister Duncan?" Pliny Quarterstone scowled at him. "Sure, an' we come about for a fast bow volley, we'll do a bit of damage . . . but then that blaggard will blast us out of the water."

"I know what I'm doing," Duncan gritted.

"Well, what *are* you doing?"

"I am amusing the enemy. Keeping him entertained, just as Captain Dalton might do. I hope . . . ," he added under his breath. Then, "Lend a hand with those guns there."

"Aye . . . sir."

Valkyrie was closing again, and again her long twelves thundered. A ball smashed into the bark's sterncastle, taking out bulkheads below deck, and emerged howling through the steerageway to demolish a yard of starboard rail. Its companion gouged splinters from the mizzen mast.

"Whatever you're about to do, you'd best do it now!" someone shouted.

"Aye," Duncan breathed, still grinning. "Hands to all guns in the fore! Fire as your target bears! Ready? Now, strike our colors!"

The trade pennant crawled down its lanyard. Duncan watched it until it was taken in. Behind, very close now, he could see the faces of men at *Valkyrie's* rails, the smoke of burning fuse at linstocks poised above cannon vents. "Do I have your full attention now, ye bleedin' cutthroats?" he muttered. "Well, watch closely, for there's more yet to see." He turned. "Helm hard astarboard! Come full about, smartly!"

Pride reeled like a drunken thing as her rudder bit the current and her tail sidled out of line. Her sails fluttered uselessly, and for a moment it seemed she would come dead in the water. But her momentum carried her into the scudding turn, and abruptly she came about, her nose swinging into and through the wind.

Only a few hundred yards away, now suddenly dead ahead on a collision course, *Valkyrie* fought her stubborn rudder, edging to port. Two more shots blossomed at her nose, but both went wide. Then *Pride*'s bow guns began to speak, a ragged rhythm of thunders that washed great clouds of acrid smoke back along her decks. Six roars sounded, and ahead there was the sound of balls striking. Six shots, then silence except for the shouts of men and the growing thunder of the big warship closing on its treacherous prey.

Quarterstone was at Duncan's side. "Well, that was a bit of sport, right enough, though I can't see that it has done us much good."

"Can't you?" Duncan pointed. "Look yonder, then, beyond him. See what has closed in while we kept the blighter amused."

Quarterstone raised his eyes, and they went wide. Beyond the pirate ship were other sails — massive, stacked sails above a lethal hull that seemed to fly across the waters. Like an angel of mercy, or an angel of death, *Fury* bore down on the frigate at near twenty knots — a sharp-toothed, dashing fox on the wolf's blind side, roaring in to bite and rend, to tear and maim. At twenty knots, she closed on a collision course.

Aboard *Valkyrie* they saw the bark veer and hesitate, then saw the trade flag descend its lanyard.

"He's done, Cap'n Shelby." Timothy Leech grinned. "He strikes his colors. What signal shall we make?"

The man who had been John Shelby Butler scratched idly at his whiskered chin, cold eyes gazing out at the four-master under his guns. Then he clasped his hands behind him. "No signal, Mister Leech," he said. "We shall speak with our guns. When we've closed to three cables, have the bow guns take down his mizzen mast, then recharge and break down his stern post. Starboard batteries stand by to hull him at the water when he's crippled."

"That'll sink him, right enough." Leech nodded. "But don't you want to see who's aboard?"

"We'll pluck a few survivors from the sea to question," Shelby said. "That will be enough. I want that bark sent to the bottom, so get on with it."

"Aye, Cap'n." Leech wondered at the man's determination to destroy what yet might be a prize, but he didn't press it. He had learned long since that John Shelby Butler—now Jack Shelby—made his own plans for his own reasons, and that those reasons were valid, whether expressed or not.

At his relayed command, the gun crews in the bow bent to their long twelves, waiting for the order to fire. The bark was dead ahead now, the range nearly point-blank for the ranging guns. At three cable lengths the slaughter would begin, and they would not miss.

The bark had not veered again, but now—abruptly—it did. It responded to hard rudder, shook itself like a tormented bear, and came hard over to the right.

"Bear on him, helm!" Leech roared. *Valkyrie* slid into the turn, trying to keep her nose in line with the vessel ahead, then suddenly was charging down upon it. The bark had continued its turn, had come right about into the wind, and now sat motionless, head-on to its charging pursuer.

"Rudder aport!" Leech shouted. "Veer off! Veer off!"

"He's insane," Shelby muttered. "He wants us to collide with him."

Valkyrie had barely begun to answer her helm when smokes erupted at the nose of the bark, now less than two cables away. Ragged thunders rolled across the water, and iron balls screamed into the nose of the frigate, ripping and tearing.

In an instant there was chaos in the bow as *Valkyrie* struggled to bear aside, to avoid collision. The binding rudder balked and struggled stubbornly. In the fore, stunned gunners got their feet under them and fired the twin ranging guns, realizing as they did that they were no longer on point. The shots went wide, uselessly, thrown off their mark by their own ship's turn.

In the same instant, a panicked cry rang down from aloft, "On deck! Attacker on our port quarter, bearing in . . . lor', but he's dead on us!"

The echoes of the shout were massed thunders riding on the wind. Those on the quarterdeck turned as screaming shot ripped into their structures and whined across their decks. The ship there was under full sail—twice the sail that it seemed so small a vessel could press—and it bore down on the larger frigate at an impossible speed. Again guns volleyed, their smokes riding ahead of them to mist the specter of imminent, grinding collision.

"Port batteries!" Shelby shouted. "Align and fire. Stern guns hard over! Fire!"

Somewhere within *Valkyrie* big guns thundered, rocking the ship, but they were not those aport. The starboard batteries, ready to fire, *had* fired—wildly—not at the attacker but in the direction of the wind-locked, motionless bark just now sliding past to starboard.

Timothy Leech gripped the rail and stared at the ship thundering down on *Valkyrie*. A brig, his mind registered, then corrected itself in an instant. No brig could put on such sail. No brig could move so fast—and the speed was headlong, directly toward the larger ship. "He's making to ram," he muttered, gaping. Nearer and nearer, faster than seemed possible, the attacker swept in, a deadly, blasting phantom shrouded in the smokes of its cannons—smoke that rolled with the thunders of its guns, that billowed and spread, that rode on the wind and seemed a part of the ship.

In *Fury*'s bow and abaft both her catheads, Ethan Crosby and Floyd Pugh worked furiously, directing four gun

185

crews—quoining, aiming and firing as fast as searing-hot guns could be run in, charged and run out. Steam from scorched swabs rose in clouds as dense as the acrid smoke of the volleys.

Amidships, Cadman Wise danced from rail to rail, setting his sail-handlers to their tasks, his eyes turning at each breath toward the quarterdeck where Patrick Dalton directed the attack. Through the smoke, the figures there— Dalton and others—looked vague and far away, but Wise knew that when Dalton called or raised his arm to signal, he must respond instantly . . . as must the entire working deck. "Maybe now you swabbies will learn why the captain ran you through all those drills," he barked, for any who might hear. "Now is when it counts!"

Aft, Dalton ceased his pacing and stood, squinting, peering ahead through the smokes. *Fury* was closing rapidly on the larger ship now, her speed unabated, all of her sails set aloft and all of them full of wind. Dead ahead, the pirate seemed to falter uncertainly. And beyond was the bark, wind-locked and helpless now but in the position it had taken to decoy the attacker. *Well done, Mister Duncan*, Dalton thought. *A nice ploy, indeed*.

He had heard the muted roar of a broadside fired by the frigate, but not at himself, and his eyes went flat and cold. If not at *Fury*, then it was at the helpless, wind-locked bark standing "in irons" just beyond the pirate. Round after round flew from *Fury*'s guns, and he could only guess at their effect. The smoke rode on the wind, shrouding everything.

He knew almost to the second the point at which the pirate had spotted *Fury*, and he estimated the reaction time aboard. Counting seconds by counting the beats of his heart, he squinted, judging distance, then turned to the helm. "Hard astarboard now, if you please, Mister Locke. Smartly!" In the same instant he raised his arm and brought it slicing downward, trusting to Cadman Wise to see his signal.

186

Fury shook like a warhorse, crested a wave and bit water with a wide rudder. For a moment she seemed to hang suspended; then she leaned hard over and skidded into a tight turn, sheeting bright spray from her portside hull. Rumbling growls of torment erupted below as timbers and bracing took a sudden new strain, then eased as the yards above swung into new positions, hauled about by those on the sail deck.

"Gunners aport!" Dalton shouted, signalling with his arm. "Fire as she bears!"

Shrouds screaming, sails drumming and timbers grinding, men clinging to whatever was at hand to avoid being thrown over, *Fury* braced her keel against deep waters and turned, skidding and sheeting spray. Through the smokes an abrupt darkness grew off her port bow, then amidships— the great, dark silhouette of the frigate, so close it seemed they might reach out and touch it. Faces along the rails came clear, faces gaping, faces shouting, faces cursing . . . and disappeared in smoke, fire and thunder as beam guns on both vessels roared. Crashing, rending sounds echoed and re-echoed through the turmoil.

Aloft, above the smokes, big yardarms crashed against shrouds as the high structures collided, spar against cable, spar against spar, a confusion of timbers and stays in swift opposition. Somewhere a man . . . or more than one, Dalton could not tell . . . screamed, plummeting from high above.

The chaos dinned, peaked and suddenly stopped. Dalton's breath hissed through clenched teeth. "Rudder amidships, Mister Locke! Gunners aft, to the stern chasers!"

"We've been hit, sir." Billy Caster's adolescent voice broke in pitch as he turned from the rail, his face pale against a curtain of smoke that almost hid the frigate, now off their port quarter and receding. "I heard a hit . . . or maybe two or three."

In the waist, sailors hauled at sheet lines, trying to cor-

187

rect the battered set of spars aloft. Crosby and Pugh raced past, others following, to train and fire the twin stern chasers while yet they had a target. The guns thundered, and a ball came in response, singing overhead. Guns quoined high for the decks of a tall bark were too lofted for the much smaller snow.

"Run in studding sails!" Dalton called. "Run in the ringtail! Loose courses fore and main!" He turned. "Point to port, please, Mister Locke. Hands a'deck, ease topgallants and royals! Down the flying jib!"

As abruptly as the engagement had begun, it was over. Smoke drifted down the wind, and revealed a sea where ships stood at odds—the bark still nose to the wind, in irons, the snow just coming about off its flank, and the frigate still moving, under sail, retreating northward with a quartering wind.

"Do we go after him, sir?" Victory Locke strained at the helm, his eyes glittering with excitement.

Dalton shook his head. "Not this time, I'm afraid, Mister Locke. We've reclaimed our prize, and drawn first blood, but our duty is to *Pride*. I'm afraid *Valkyrie* shall have to wait for another time, to join us in a sport."

Billy Caster gazed out at the retreating frigate. It was still going, making no effort to turn. "Mightn't he come back, sir? He outguns us. He might . . ."

"I think not," Dalton said. "We've damaged him, and we have the weather gauge. He knows that I won't give him the upwind position. Bring us over, helm. Let's have a look at Mister Duncan and his command."

Twenty

Aboard a ragged and crippled *Valkyrie*, Jack Shelby paced his deck, staring darkly back at the pair of vessels diminishing behind. The armed snow had made no attempt to pursue. Having completed its surprise attack, it stood now, alee of the far larger bark, letting the merchantman drift down to it.

He was not surprised that the snow did not continue the engagement. Its attack had been sudden and ferocious, conducted with either extraordinary skill or extraordinary luck, but it was still only a small cruiser. Hardly a match for a frigate-class vessel in head-to-head combat. And the captain had his escort to worry about. He would hardly jeopardize the merchantman by heading off into a lopsided engagement.

Neither could he, himself, go back now. *Valkyrie* had extensive damage. Nothing that couldn't be repaired, but enough to cripple her for now. Almost overhead, on the mizzen, a broken spar dangled from its tackle, swaying afoul of the stays. Torn sailcloth whipped and fluttered in the wind. Belowdecks, the entire sterncastle was a chaos of debris thrown by iron balls smashing through the frigate's timbers. He had lost six men — four dead and two so wounded as to be of no use to him. The ship's galley was out of service, the after pumps heavily damaged and the cable tiers awash in the muck of shattered kegs from ship's stores.

All of that, and the crippled rudder.

Valkyrie would lay by for repairs. And his chance of destroying *Pride of Falworth,* that floating evidence of his treachery, was gone.

Sooner or later, now, Ian McCall would have an answer to the riddle of what became of his merchantman.

But would McCall deduce that it was his own trusted captain who now sailed *Valkyrie?*

Shelby pondered on that. No, he thought, that might remain a mystery, even now. For who alive could tell the squire that Jack Shelby was John Shelby Butler?

And as long as that was secret, Jack Shelby's career could continue. As long as no one knew who he was, he would know what cargoes were shipped and where they might be intercepted.

Timothy Leech appeared beside him, big and dour. "Beg pardon, Cap'n," he said. "We've listed th' damages. Mister Strode expects we'll need a week to get her shipshape again."

"A week," Shelby muttered.

"Aye, and we'll need to make land first, to do it right. That blighter has bled us. Luck was on his side this day."

"Luck?" Shelby spoke the word as though holding it suspended, studying it. "How much luck can one renegade Irishman have?"

Leech turned to gaze at him, puzzled. "You know who that is?"

"I know the vessel," Shelby said. *"Fury.* A snow that Ian McCall commissioned as a privateer, then lost. And I've heard of the man they say has it now. I expect you've heard the name as well. Patrick Dalton."

"Dalton?" Leech's eyes widened. "The Britisher that brought so much grief to the king's ships back . . . ?"

"That one." Shelby nodded.

"But he's dead, isn't he? Seems like I heard that."

"Not dead. Escaped and missing, along with that snow. Bring us over to westerly, Mister Leech. We'll make for the cays, and Mister Strode can have his week while you and I go to visit the Spaniard. There are messages to be sent and things to be done."

"Aye, Cap'n. What of the dead and wounded? What do you want done?"

"Drop them overboard," Shelby grunted impatiently.

"Wounded too, sir? Some of the others might . . ."

"Every man aboard this ship knows our articles, Mister Leech. And every man has agreed to them. We carry no dead weight aboard *Valkyrie*. Drop them overboard."

Pride's prow was a shambles, as were her forward holds. Though most of the pirate's broadside, fired wildly and without aim, had gone astray, the bark had taken several solid hits. Six crewmen were gone, including the prize ship's only veteran bosun. A ball had smashed into one of *Pride's* nine-pounders, throwing the old gun entirely off its carriage. It flipped and fell, and when it hit the deck, James Porter was under it. George Reeves was dead, as were William Anglen, Clifton Foote, Terry Harp and a joking, laughing young topman named Romeo Martell.

In the forward hold there were dead animals. At least a third of the island refugees' livestock had fallen to cannon fire coming through the ship's nose. Blood was everywhere.

Surprisingly, there was only one casualty among the passengers. A farmer named Whitworth was dead. A panicked milk cow had broken through a plank bulkhead and gored him.

As *Pride* drifted down on the wind toward the waiting *Fury*, Charley Duncan turned the deck over to Finian Nelson and sent Pliny Quarterstone forward to begin a damage assessment. He directed hands to assemble the remains of the dead and cover them with sailcloth, and to carry the injured, of whom there were several, below to the galley for treatment. These things done, he went amidships and let himself down the midden ladder to inspect the passengers.

In the murky belly of the bark, nightmarish chaos ensued. Forward, still mostly contained by the plank "fences" the landsmen had hammered together, animals of all sorts stood among the bloody remains of their fallen mates.

191

The stench of blood and manure was eased by the fact that *Pride*, drifting without set sails except her fore-and-afts, had turned her tail to the stiff wind. Open hatches became breezeways, carrying the stink away.

One of the low plankings had been broken, and men were working to repair it while others labored in a sweating line. Some were tearing up decking in the after holds, some carrying the planks forward and others beginning the erection of chutes for hauling the dead beasts up to the foredeck where grapples could reach them. Duncan gazed around, shaking his head in disbelief. It was hard to tell who had done the most damage here—the pirates or the passengers.

Farther back, in the rearmost spaces just short of the stores and galley, were huddles of women and children. Aaron Fairfield was flitting here and there, trying to direct all the activities, and generally was being ignored.

As Duncan approached, a small figure broke loose from one of the huddles and hurried toward him, skirting perilously close to one of the gaping holes where decking had been lifted away.

"Here! Be careful!" Duncan barked, and rushed to catch the child before it could trip or fall. He grabbed the boy up, and shuddered as he looked beyond, down into the deep bilges of the bark—a maze of timbers, treenailed structures and dark holes filled with the great heaps of metallic rubble that were *Pride's* ballast.

"You should stay with your mother," he told the boy. "It isn't safe to run about like that."

"I was looking for you, sir," Henry Cabot said as Duncan set him on his feet. The boy's eyes were bright with excitement. "I heard all the cannons shooting. There was a lot of noise."

"Yes, there was," Duncan agreed. "Where's the lady your mother, lad?"

"She's back there, in the shed."

"Shed?"

The boy pointed.

Duncan shook his head. "Ships don't have sheds, lad.

192

Yonder is the capstan track. On a cargo vessel like this it's housed so men can work there without fear of shifting loads. Come along, then." He took the boy's hand.

"But I have something to show you," Henry balked. "Something I found."

From the "shed" came the sound of a woman's voice, raised above the clamor. "Henry? Henry, where are you?"

"Women!" the boy muttered, then tugged at Duncan's sleeve. "What I found is—"

"Later, lad," Duncan said. "Come along. Your mother is worried about you."

"But there's a whole lot of—"

"Whatever it is will keep. Come on now. Let's return you to Mistress Cabot."

With the youth firmly in tow, Duncan approached the capstan housing, peered inside, then removed his hat. Somehow the passengers had converted the little space into a sleeping accommodation for women and children. Hammocks lined the entire enclosure, and the stubby capstan in the center had become a hold-high pillar, extended by stub-nailing braces of hardwood that could only have been ladder rails. All around it were slung small hammocks and trundles for children.

"Bleedin' hell," Duncan swore, then blushed as several women turned to gape at him. "Pardon, ladies," he said. "I just never realized how much damage a bunch of refugees could do to a perfectly good sailin' vessel." He gazed around at other modifications the people belowdecks had made to accommodate themselves. "Worse'n bore-worms," he breathed.

Priscilla Cabot pushed through the crowd, a vision of large, frightened eyes in a pale face. She glanced at Duncan, then turned her attention to the boy. "Henry? What have you done now?"

Duncan released the boy and gazed at the woman. "He did nothing, Mistress Cabot. I only came below to inspect the damages, and Henry came to bid me hello."

"No, I wanted to show you the—" the boy started.

Priscilla's color returned somewhat. "Thank you, Captain. Is the . . . the cannon-firing over for now?"

"It's over, mistress. The bedam—the foul pirate has been chased away by our escort. Are you . . . ah . . . is everyone here well?"

"Very well, thank you . . . thanks to Squire Fairfield, who had the foresight to move everyone to the back of the ship . . ."

"Stern," Duncan corrected.

"Yes, he can be that at times, though he's mostly bluster. But he said for everyone to stay in the cellar and . . ."

"Below deck," Duncan put in.

"Pardon?"

"It's *below deck*. Ships don't have cellars."

"Oh. Well, downstairs anyway. Oh, it was awful, though. So much noise, and those poor beasts . . . and then I couldn't find Henry. Would you care for tea, sir?"

"I think not, right now," he said, backing away. He noticed again how large her eyes seemed. Abruptly he felt confused and disoriented. "I have inspections to make . . . and repairs. Ah . . . good day to you, mistress." He backed away, put his hat on his head and turned, nearly bumping into Aaron Fairfield.

"We could use some help building the chutes," the squire said, "since you seem to have impounded our only carpenter to help you turn your wheel."

"Helm." Duncan glared at him.

"Call it what you like." Fairfield shrugged. "And we could use some more lumber, as well."

"You people are doing more damage here than that pirate did," Duncan hissed. "Look at that. And that! I warn you, sir, the first man to take a pry to my hull timbers will be stretched over the bore of a cannon." He spun away. Nearby, men were wrapping a body in quilts. It was Whitworth, the man gored by the cow. Duncan turned back. "My sympathies for your loss. Have the man brought on deck and we'll bury him with honor, along with the others."

A small hand tugged at his sleeve. "Here, sir," Henry Cabot chirped. "This is what I wanted to show you."

Duncan glanced down. The boy held a canvas sack, which he lifted with difficulty. Absently, Duncan took it and glanced inside, then stared. "Where did you get this, boy?"

"I found it in the basement when they took up the floor, sir."

"Bilges," Duncan said.

"Oh, no, sir, I really did. And there are a lot more of them, too. I . . ."

Shoving the sack into his coat, Duncan shouted, "Squire Fairfield!"

Nearby, the squire turned, frowning.

"You said your party has money," Duncan said. "Is it secure?"

"It is." Fairfield nodded. "I checked it myself."

"None of it is missing?"

"Not a penny." Fairfield scowled at him suspiciously. "Why?"

"Never mind, Squire. Go about your business." Taking Henry Cabot by the hand, Duncan strode forward to the midden ladder, raised his head and shouted, "On deck!"

A sailor appeared at the hatch. "Sir?"

"Find Mister Quarterstone, please. And Misters McGinnis and Mudd. Tell them report to me immediately, below deck at the shed."

The man looked blank. "At the what, sir?"

"The sh—I mean, the aft capstan housing. Look alive!"

"Aye, sir."

"Now, boy"—Duncan looked down at Henry Cabot—"show me where you found this."

Though the wind had shifted through the day, coming now from east-southeast, its force held steady at close to thirty knots—a stiff wind that fought the surface currents and put rolling waves upon the ocean's face.

On such a sea, there would be no snugging together of the two vessels, though Dalton could see clearly as the bark

195

drifted down toward him that a lay-by for repairs would be needed. *Pride*'s prow had taken some shot, including one that had cut the spreader stays on the starboard side. With her jib weakened, she would not be able to mount staysails in the fore, and without the staysails the big vessel would be impossible to control on a long run.

Fury also had damage, though of lesser consequence. Two twelve-pound balls had punched through the snow's portside hull just below the after channel. One of the wounds was a gaping hole between the channel and the chain plate that would have to be reinforced or jeopardize the mainmast shrouds.

As *Pride* neared, Dalton maneuvered *Fury* around the larger ship on jib and jigger, assessing need, planning approach. Finally he edged the snow as close as he dared, staying to windward of the bark, and had Billy Caster bring up a speaking horn. With this at his mouth he hailed the bark. On *Pride*'s high quarterdeck a man stepped to the rail and responded.

"Who are you?" Dalton called.

"Nelson, sir," the other answered. "Finian Nelson. Commander Duncan's second. He's below with Mister Quarterstone."

"Report your condition, Mister Nelson."

"Damage in the fore, Captain. Above waterline. A bit astern, too, though that's minor. Six men dead, sir. Seven, counting a passenger. Five missing. Mister Hoop had the dinghy out, with Misters Singleterry and Cobley and those two frogs. They're gone. Several injuries, being tended in the galley. Bleedin' merchantman's got no orlop deck . . . but I guess you know that, sir."

"What is the activity in your fore, Mister Nelson?" Dalton responded. "Have you begun repairs?"

Nelson turned to gaze forward, then called, "That's the passengers, sir. They're building ramps or something, to fetch up dead livestock. The animals took the brunt of the pirate's volley."

In the strong wind, the two ships had begun to drift

196

apart, *Pride* on the downwind side taking more wind on her high stern than the smaller snow. Dalton studied the westward sky, the lowering sun, the angle of drift, and called, "I'll want tethers fore and aft, Mister Nelson, with fenders. A pair of yardarms should do nicely. Splice them into the hawser and drift them out when they are secured. We will fish them out at this end and lash the ships together for assessment and repair."

"Aye, sir."

Dalton turned away, looking for Billy Caster, and found the young clerk at his elbow. "Mister Caster, I'll need the rosters of recruits, both vessels."

"Aye, sir. I have them right here. Seven of the men from the island have done at least a bit of carpentry, and of course all of us who were originally aboard have done a bit, but I can't find any real carpenters. We'll have to—"

"Ahoy *Fury!*"

Dalton turned. The voice that hailed them was a different voice than before. The man who stood at *Pride's* rail was a large, broad-shouldered young man holding Finian Nelson's speaking horn. Vaguely, Dalton recalled seeing him among the Mayaguana refugees. "I hear you!" he responded. "Who are you?"

"Keith Darling," the man shouted. "You'll be needing a carpenter here, sir. That's what I am. A carpenter."

The sun was afloat on the west horizon when they got the two ships tethered in the only manner that the wind and running sea would allow—snugged by hawsers at bow and stern, with yardarm timbers between them to keep them apart.

When it was done, *Fury's* launch was brought around and lashed between the vessels, below the fending yards. The boat made an adequate bridge between the two ships.

As Dalton turned his deck over to Purdy Fisk and started across, he saw others coming from the other deck, and stepped back to await them. The one in the lead was Charley Duncan. He and the three following him were bent under heavy, wrapped parcels resting across their shoulders. Long moments passed, and Duncan hailed *Fury's* deck from below. Hands went to lift aboard the thing he carried . . . a canvas sack that seemed far too small for the heavy thump it made when it was deposited on the deck.

Duncan scrambled aboard, saluted Dalton bleakly, then turned to help lift aboard the burdens carried by the other three men. When their loads were aboard *Fury*, he sent them back to *Pride*.

That done, he turned to Dalton, gesturing at the canvas-wrapped packs at his feet. "Thought this would be safer here than yonder, sir," he said. "A boy found all this hid in the aftermain well."

"What is it?" Dalton prodded a sack with the toe of his boot.

Duncan glanced around and lowered his voice. "What it is, sir, is a bloody fortune. A treasure. Jewels and goblets, crucifixes, everything under the sun. And coin, sir. Silver and gold. More flamin' money than I ever even imagined there was."

Twenty-one

For days, the turning winds of spring had held traffic on the Delaware to a minimum. Square-rigged vessels tended to avoid the precarious closeness of river channels in seasons of chancy wind, and those fore-and-afts in merchant service in the middle colonies — states, they called themselves now — plied mostly out of Chesapeake because that was where the big carriers were.

As for warships, few were to be seen now. General Washington had come forth from Valley Forge, and the king's ground forces were aligning in the north. Where armies campaigned, there were the navies to support them, and His Majesty's White Fleet was deployed off New York to give aid and transit to Clinton's forces . . . and off the New England shores to guard against French troops being imported by adventurers such as the marquis de Lafayette.

Along the Delaware it was a time of quiet . . . almost a time of tranquility. And the seasonal winds that often swung about to blow strong and steady upstream, adding their force to the incoming tides, made it a good season in which to launch ships.

Despite business losses which seemed insurmountable and unexplainable reverses — ships and cargoes that sailed away and never returned — which had him to the point of distraction, Ian McCall had come across from Chesapeake at John Singleton Ramsey's grudging invitation, to witness the christening of the schooner *Faith II*.

Accompanied by his most trusted commercial factor and a

pair of clerks, McCall went first to Eagle's Head, where Ramsey waited. Colly met them at the great door, showed McCall and his associate into Ramsey's study, then led the clerks away to show them where they would sleep the night.

As the two men waited in the plush study, McCall paced the floor moodily, still thinking of the latest reports his factor had brought him. "Two more," he muttered. "Just disappeared somewhere. No word, no sign, no report even on their escort?"

"Nothing, sir." The man shrugged. "I am sorry."

"First *Pride of Falworth*, then the *Kerry*, and now three more—both *Christopher* and the *Lady Chance* . . . and even the brig, *Pliny!* Disappeared without a trace. I am being bankrupted, Evan. And we don't know what is happening!"

"No, sir," the man said quietly. "I have inquiries out in every quarter I can reach, sir . . . especially regarding the first one, of course, but for all. But there is nothing. Just . . . nothing."

He sounded so distraught that McCall turned to him. "Of course you do, Evan. I have no doubt you're doing your very best. My God, I realize it's your own brother you're searching for, as well. But . . . just nothing? No word at all?"

"Nothing, sir."

"Pirates," McCall muttered. "It must be pirates, but blast it all, what kind of pirate can operate without anybody knowing about him? I've never encountered the like."

"Nor have I, sir."

McCall paced a bit more, then shook his head. "Well, to the matter at hand. You have secured the . . . ah . . . special cargo we discussed?"

"Of course, sir. It is under guard on Chesapeake. Your own guards, as you instructed. Do you know what ship is to carry it, sir?"

"I know," McCall said. "Though I doubt you'll believe it when you see it, Evan. It's the schooner we came to see launched. The *Faith*."

"Ramsey's daughter's own schooner? He'd chance that ship with such cargo?"

"So he says." McCall shrugged.

Evan tugged at his lip. "I'd have taken Squire Ramsey for a

200

more . . . ah . . . conservative gentleman than to risk such . . ."

"I expect he had little enough to do with the decision. You haven't met Constance Ramsey, have you, Evan?"

"I've not had the privilege."

"You probably shall, shortly. And I caution you, good Evan, should you ever find yourself in disagreement with that young lady, it's best to simply concede defeat and retreat as gracefully as circumstances allow. It's my studied opinion that there's only one man alive who's a match for Constance Ramsey."

"And who is that, then?"

McCall's brow lowered. "Patrick Dalton," he snapped. "Ramsey's damned Irishman."

A door had opened across the study, and a voice heavy with protest said, "How many times must I tell you, Ian? Dalton isn't *my* Irishman!"

McCall turned, still scowling. "If he isn't yours, John, then why didn't the scoundrel make off with one of your ships, instead of one of mine?"

"Oh," Evan muttered. *"That* Dalton."

"He *did* make off with one of mine," John Singleton Ramsey huffed, glaring at his friend and guest. "In case you have forgotten, it was him that wound up with the first *Faith* . . . through no doing of mine."

"As I recall," McCall gritted, "you had already lost *Faith* to that black-hearted devil's spawn Jonathan Hart, and it was *that* gentleman from whom Dalton took it."

"And you lost *Fury* to a bitch-whelped Spanish pirate, not to Dalton. He simply took it from *that* gentleman."

Behind Ramsey, a lovely young woman appeared at the door, and Evan straightened his shoulders admiringly.

"Don't you two *ever* get tired of this argument?" the girl snapped. "Mercy!" Then her frown became a dazzling soft smile, and she curtsied. "Good day to you, Squire McCall. So nice of you to come for *Faith's* christening."

"I wouldn't have missed it." McCall bowed. Then he turned. "Mistress Ramsey, I don't believe you have met my personal factor. Evan, may I present Constance Ramsey.

201

Constance, this is Evan Butler. He accompanied me from Fairleah because of press of business."

Evan bowed smartly. "Mistress Ramsey. A right honor."

Constance curtsied again. "Mister Butler." Then, "Please, gentlemen, do be comfortable. I've asked Colly to fetch tea."

"And grog?" Ramsey glanced around. "You did order a tot of grog, didn't you?"

"And grog." She nodded. "Though if either of the gentlemen would prefer brandy . . ."

"In my house we'll drink grog," Ramsey stated. He indicated chairs, and they sat, the three men in a semicircle facing the hearth, Constance demurely to one side. "Well, then, Ian," Ramsey opened. "I take it you have a cargo for me?"

"I do." McCall frowned. "Evan has secured it at my docks on Chesapeake . . ."

"The Wilderness Dock," Evan added. "Below Selden Road. It can be shipped aboard your vessel there, sir. Might I ask where it is bound?"

"For Savannah," Ramsey said after a pause. "You'll understand, I'm sure, that all of this requires the utmost secrecy."

"Certainly." Evan nodded.

"You may rely on Evan's discretion, John," McCall assured. "I trust him completely."

"Of course." Ramsey waved it off. "I simply—"

"You simply can't abide the idea of anyone realizing how active a patriot you are," McCall said. "You've postured as a damned—pardon, Constance—fence-straddler for so long that it galls you to have it known that you've taken sides. You're an American Patriot, John. Admit it."

"I'll admit no such thing!" Ramsey growled. "This is strictly business, and I am simply a businessman. I disdain politics."

"Of course you do," McCall drawled, winking. "A shipload of the best Austrian small arms for the colonials in Georgia certainly has nothing to do with politics . . . even if they *are* delivered on credit."

"Who said they are consigned on credit?" Ramsey demanded.

"Don't beat about the bush with me, old friend. I've done a bit of business with Andrews and his lot myself. On credit."

"Hmph!" Ramsey snorted.

The servants' door opened, and Colly entered, bearing a silver tray with a jug of rum, a pitcher of water and three pewter mugs. Behind him was a maid with a tea service. Constance took charge and busied herself serving the three men. As she poured tea for Evan she said, "I'm so glad you came, sir. I hope you can come to South Point tomorrow for the launching of *Faith*."

"*Faith the Second*," her father corrected.

"Of course. Whatever. You will come, won't you, sir?"

"We shall both be there," McCall said. "I've already mentioned to—"

"I'm sorry," Evan said. "I must make my apologies, but I shall have to start for Chesapeake at first light. There are things I must attend to."

McCall turned sharply to stare at him. "Return? But I thought . . ."

"I'm sorry, sir. I've just this moment recalled some things that must be attended to, immediately. Somehow I had forgotten them. Forgive me."

McCall shrugged. "Very well, then. If you must, you must." As Constance chatted with Evan, McCall turned to Ramsey, speaking in a muted whisper. "An excellent employee," he said. "But he hasn't been quite himself of late. Not since his brother failed to return from a voyage to the Bahamas."

"His brother?"

"Aye. One of my best merchant captains. John Shelby Butler. Evan is his younger brother."

Dinner that evening was to have been a sumptuous affair, replete with roast partridge, greens from Ramsey's kitchen garden where the great man enjoyed experimenting with such notions as stepped irrigation, crop variety rotation and dustings of wheat flour to confuse the insects—all to the exasperation of his servants—and a cobbler made from fresh-gathered dewberries. Dinner was to have been all of that. It was, in fact, a disaster.

Midway through the roast partridge, Dora appeared at Constance Ramsey's side, bending to whisper in the young lady's ear. Constance listened for a moment, then scowled and said, "Bedamme!" As the gentlemen looked up in astonishment, she gathered her skirts about her, rose to her feet and turned to Ramsey. "I'm sorry, Father, but you'll have to excuse me. I must return to South Point immediately. Dora has my coach waiting."

"Return? Now?"

"Now. My apologies, gentlemen."

"But what is it? Has something happened?"

"Has something . . . oh, no. Nothing much. It's just that one of your yardmen got a hauling winch afoul of *Faith*'s way-blocks and decided to break it loose by main force. Now *Faith* is atilt on half a running rail, and my men are standing off your drydock crewmen at gunpoint to keep them from doing any more blasted damage! Dearest father of mine, I've asked you ever so nicely to keep your dolts away from my ship. Now I must go and see if it is necessary for me to shoot the bleedin' arses off a brace or two of them." Amidst stunned silence she straightened her sleeves, brushed her auburn hair into her bonnet and put on a pretty smile. "Gentlemen, do have a nice evening."

She was gone then, Dora trailing after her, and the three men looked at one another.

"You see now what I meant about her," McCall whispered to Evan.

"Afoul of the way-blocks?" Ramsey muttered to himself. "How on earth would anyone get a hauling winch afoul of way-blocks, unless . . . unless he was using draft animals and they strayed . . ."

"Remarkable," Evan breathed.

Colly had just served the cobbler when there was a caller at the door. Colly disappeared into the front hall and returned a moment later. "Gent'man to see Mist' Evan Butler," he announced. "Urgent, he say."

Butler frowned, surprised, then wiped his lips and stood. "By your leave, gentlemen. I was not expecting anyone, but whatever it is, it shouldn't take a moment."

He hurried out as Colly leaned over John Singleton Ramsey's shoulder to serve his cobbler. "Gent'man outside's got a horse that's rid near to death," the servant whispered.

Ian McCall squinted at the lamp-lustered oak of the door that had closed behind his employee. "Must be important," he said. "I wonder if it's news of his brother . . . and of my ship."

In silence the two businessmen tasted their cobbler, both of them noticing how abruptly the dining hall had become spacious.

Evan Butler was back within minutes, his expression oddly reserved, as though he were holding a fear hidden behind his hooded eyes. "Squire, I must apologize," he said, bowing slightly toward McCall. "Something unforseen has come up. I must return to Chesapeake immediately."

"Is it about your brother?"

"Ah, no, sir, though I wish it were. It's just a . . . ah, there's been a minor disturbance at the Wilderness Docks. It's something I must attend to, so that we may be sure that nothing goes amiss with your . . . ah . . . the special cargo consigned to Squire Ramsey's new schooner. Don't trouble yourself about it, sir. It really is only a minor thing."

"Then, you'll certainly miss the christening!" Ramsey put in, then reconsidered. "If there is a christening." He shook his head. "How could a hauling winch become afoul of wayblocks? I've never heard of such a thing."

Another odd thing occurred to him as Evan Butler put on his greatcoat, retrieved his tricorn hat and headed out to begin his trip overland to Chesapeake. Why would a man ride a horse almost to death, all the way from below Fairleah to Eagle's Head—from the Chesapeake to the Delaware—just to report a disturbance so minor that one man could attend to it? And why had Evan Butler seemed frightened?

Ramsey glanced at his remaining guest, wondering just how well McCall *did* know his trusted employee.

By evening sunlight filtering through the upright poles that were the wall of a sturdy cargo shed, Mister Hoop paced among bales and kegs, his face a study in huge worry. Since the packet *Cricket* had stood off the east bank of Chesapeake to disgorge its passengers into the towed launch with its towed dinghy, since they had bid their benefactors goodbye—or, in

205

two cases, *adieu* — and pointed the launch's bow toward Squire Ian McCall's lower docks, much had happened, but nothing that made sense.

The packet's passengers were six — three ex-British tars and a pair of Frenchmen picked up at sea, and a young ex-British officer named Farrington who, the others gathered, had been in command of a civilian trading convoy but had lost his command to pirates.

He was on his way to report to his employer, Squire Mc-Call. Having nothing better to do, the others — Misters Hoop, Singleterry and Cobley and the two Frenchmen — tagged along behind him.

With the launch and the dinghy secured at a rough pier, they went ashore. The Wilderness Docks were at the rear of a small, dredged harbor, a busy and businesslike place recently reopened after removal of activities from the Delaware. Dairy roads and barns, sheds and low warehouses clustered above empty docks now. The only sailing ship in sight was a corvette at anchor just off the upper quay. Its escutcheons proclaimed it the *Resolute*.

"All this is Squire McCall's," Lewis Farrington told the others. "His main operations are up the bay at Fairleah, but a lot of cargo is assembled down here at the wilderness docks."

"Some bein' done now." Hoop pointed. In the distance, men worked at a group of barns or sheds, preparing stacks of tarp-covered goods for skidding down to the docks to be shipped aboard a vessel, though there were no ships there.

Farrington led the way up the slope toward the buildings, and was confronted by armed men patrolling the area. "Lewis Farrington," he told them. "I've come to report to Squire Mc-Call."

A beady-eyed man with a full beard pushed through the guards. "Squire ain't here," he said. "What is it you want to report?"

"It's for McCall's ears," Farrington said. "Or for his personal factor. Where is he?"

"Not here either," the man said. "So you can just tell me about it. I'm Budge. Mister Evan left me in charge here."

"I'll wait for the Squire," Farrington decided.

"Suit yourself." Budge frowned. "But stay away from the sheds." He glanced at the others behind Farrington, his eyes lingering on the giant form of Mister Hoop. "Who be these? Yours?"

"Not mine." Farrington shrugged. "We found them at sea. They're off a ship that was taken by pirates, then reclaimed as salvage."

Budge's eyes narrowed. "Reclaimed, ye say." He looked at the others, one by one. "An' what ship might that be, now, mates?"

Hoop decided he didn't like the man, but he held his temper. "*Pride of Falworth,*" he rumbled. "That's her name, if it's any of your business, *mate.*"

For an instant, Budge looked as though he had been swatted across the face. "*Pride of . . .?*"

"*Falworth.*"

What happened then was abrupt and startling. Budge made a signal with his hand, and suddenly the newcomers were surrounded by levelled muskets.

"Take them to the stowage barn," Budge growled. "All of 'em. Lock them in and guard 'em. Somebody bring me a horse. Evan needs to know of this."

Now they were locked in the barn, all six of them, trying to make sense of it all.

It was Farrington who expressed a course of action. "If we could get out of here," he suggested, "I'd go and find Squire McCall. He can sort out whatever misunderstanding there is here."

"Do you know where to find him, then?" Hoop stopped his pacing and turned.

"No, I don't. Not that it matters. We're barred in here until somebody decides to—"

"Oh, that's nothin'." Hoop shrugged it off. "But if you don't know where he is . . ."

"I really don't."

Hoop ran big fingers through his untidy hair. "It's a notion, though," he said. "We don't know where that squire is, but I know where there's another squire. Squire Ramsey. Cap'n Dalton thinks fair of him, so maybe he'd help us."

"But we're locked in!"

Hoop shrugged. "Misters Singleterry and Cobley, do you have a calculation on the guards out there?"

"Aye," Singleterry said. "There's two of them, one on each side of that barred double door."

"Do they have muskets?"

"Aye, they both do."

"Good. We might want some muskets with us, for we've a night's hard travel ahead."

"Where we goin', then?" Cobley blinked.

"I just told you. Across to the Delaware to see Squire Ramsey. Stand clear now." As the others scurried aside, Hoop looked around at the stacks and provisions in the stowage barn. In one corner an anvil stood, stud-mounted on the sawn top of an oak log two feet across and four tall. "This should do nicely," he said, inspecting it.

"You intend to do a bit of smithin', Mister Hoop?" Singleterry drawled.

"Thinkin' of a ram," Hoop said, squatting beside the anvil and butt.

"That?" Cobley frowned. "Lord's mercy, man, that thing must weigh three-four hundred pounds."

"Likely," Hoop agreed. Sucking in a great breath, the big man wrapped his arms around the log and stood, balancing on spread legs as he shifted it, holding it horizontally under one arm, bracing with the other. Veins stood out on his bull neck. He steadied the massive thing, anvil to the fore, then turned, sighted on the crack where the two doors met, and charged.

Hoop and his ram hit the door dead center, and beyond it a drawbar shrilled and cracked. The twin doors flew open, smashing back against the outer wall on each side of the portal. Hoop set down his ram and stepped through, catching the echoing doors as they rebounded. Sodden thuds sounded beyond them, where battered men fell to the ground, unconscious.

"My Lord in Heaven!" Lewis Farrington breathed.

"Bring along the muskets," Hoop said. "Lively now, lads. We've some ground to cover."

208

"C'est magnifique!" a wide-eyed Frenchman chirped as they all followed Hoop out of the barn and toward the nearby forest, making northeastward.

Twenty-two

Askew on her way-blocks, her nimble stern standing dry above the dredged cut on the Delaware's right bank, *Faith II* stood aslant in the midday sun, her tall masts casting shadows below, where nearly a hundred men labored to right her for launching.

Virtually every man in South Point was involved in the enterprise. Most of them were in the employ of John Singleton Ramsey and had found their services abruptly requisitioned by the great man's daughter. Others working shoulder to shoulder among them were innocents who had happened to be in or about South Point's three inns and five taverns when a squad of Colonial sailors led by the Virginian, Michael Romart, made a sweep of the village for "volunteers." They worked now with a will, intensely aware of the armed sailors standing watch at the schooner's rails overhead.

At first they had tried to careen the vessel to port, to lift its hull away from the damaged slideway under its starboard timbers so that the slideway could be repaired. But the schooner had only settled more securely into its gap, and the plans were revised.

Great hawsers now led from the tops of both mainmast and foremast, firmly cleated there, out to a row of buried "dead man" stanchions fifty yards away, and with the schooner held in check against further shifting, work was progressing on the lowering of the portside way so that it would match the fallen one at starboard. Meanwhile, beneath the jutting stern, almost at the heel of the great rudder, men with teams of mules were dredging a deep trench for the hull to settle into when it was released.

Beyond the works there were spectators—there had been spectators since the initial crash when the dry-docked new ship had lurched off its starboard way—and among them were grizzled veterans of the yards who, in many years at South Point, had seen almost everything. These scratched their heads now and stared in awe at the work in progress. They had seen nothing quite like this before.

Yet the man in charge, a ship's carpenter named Joseph Tower, went stolidly about his business with the assurance of a man who knew exactly what he was doing. "It will work," he assured Constance Ramsey as she prowled the yards, fretting. "It may be a unique launching, but launch her we will."

"In a ditch?" the girl asked, frowning. "Wouldn't it be as easy just to set winches and drag her to the water's edge?"

"We'd likely mar the coppering if we did that." He shrugged. "Then she'd have to be careened for repairs. Seems to me it bodes bad luck to have to repair a vessel from its own christening."

"There is that," she admitted. "But Mister Tower, how did you decide on such a . . . well, unusual procedure as this?"

"Oh, that was nothing. I just asked myself, 'What might Captain Dalton do in such a situation?' And the answer came to me, just like that."

"On deck!"

They looked upward, squinting against the sun. High aloft, clinging to the slant of *Faith's* foremast fighting top, Phillip Ives cupped his hands and repeated the call, "On deck!"

On the schooner's foredeck, Michael Romart responded, "Aye, Mister Ives?"

"People coming, Mister Romart. Crossing the cartage road. One of them seems to be Mister Hoop."

"It can't be Mister Hoop," Romart said. He turned, shaded his eyes and peered westward. "Mister Hoop is with Captain Dalton and *Fury.*" Then he grunted and his eyes widened. "By all that's proper, I believe that *is* Mister Hoop! On de—I mean, on the ground!" He looked down, waved at Constance and Tower and pointed. "There's Mister Hoop yonder, com-

211

ing this way with some other men! What do you suppose he's doing here?"

"Mister Hoop?" Constance looked around.

"One of Dalton's Britishers, miss," Tower said. "You might recall him from when we all had supper that time, over on Chesapeake. When we had th' orchestra. Hoop was the big one. Twice the size of any other man I ever saw."

"The man with the flat nose," she recalled.

"That's the one. I've always wondered who managed that."

The party coming down from the road was in sight for them now, Mister Hoop hulking huge, followed by five other men. Beyond them, up on the road, Squire Ramsey's carriage had just come into sight, heading an entourage coming down from Eagle's Head.

When the walkers approached, Michael Romart called from the rail, "Ahoy, Mister Hoop! Is that you?"

"As ever was," the bull voice bellowed back. "Who's that, then? Mister Romart?"

"Aye! Where did you come from, Mister Hoop? Has *Fury* landed?"

"I don't know! We haven't seen *Fury* since just after the storm!"

"What storm?"

"That weird one, off—oh, you weren't there, were you. Anyway, we got set off in the bark's dinghy and—!"

"What bark?"

"One we found. But Mister Duncan had to run from pirates, so when we got on their launch and the frogs opened fire, we . . . !" They pushed through a scattering of spectators, and Hoop spotted Constance. In sudden confusion he stopped in his tracks, oblivious to those who bumped into him from behind. "Miss Ramsey? Ah . . . Miss Constance, is that you?"

"How do you do, Mister Hoop." Constance curtsied. "Where is Patrick?"

"Who, miss?" Hoop shouted, then realized that he was still bellowing. His face went scarlet, and he lowered his voice. "Who, miss?"

"Patrick. Captain Dalton. Weren't you with him?"

"No, miss. Not just lately. Commander Duncan took us as prize crew on *Pride*. An' now we don't rightly know where anybody is because we got lost." He glanced at the carpenter. "How do, Mister Tower."

"Mister Hoop. Who are these with you?"

"These? Oh." He pointed. "That's Mister Singleterry there, and that's Mister Cobley. They're first-rates. An' those two yonder, grinnin' at the lady, they're frogs, the both of 'em."

Realizing that introductions were being made, the Frenchmen executed elegant bows toward Constance. *"Bon soir, mademoiselle,"* Francois said.

"Mon dieux," Rene muttered. *"C'est magnifique, la jeune fille."*

Hoop rounded on him with a roar. "You mind your mouth! There's a lady present!"

"It's quite all right, Mister Hoop," Constance said. Then she curtsied again. *"Bon soir, m'sieurs. Comment allez-vous?"*

Francois beamed. *"Ah! Tres bien, merci, mademoiselle. Enchante. Je m'appell Francois LeBlanc. Presente mon ami, Rene Escobier, vient de Marseilles."*

"Enchante," she said. "Mister Hoop, I don't recall Patrick having any French people in his crew. Where did these gentlemen come from?"

"France, I expect, miss," Hoop managed, confused by the sudden torrent of foreign language. "But where I got them was out of the chain locker of the bark. They was drunk as lords, they was."

Above them, Michael Romart repeated his earlier question, "What bark, Mister Hoop?"

"Pride of Falworth's its name. We found it an'—"

"Pride of Falworth?" Constance cut in. "But I think that was the name of Ian McCall's ship that . . ." She looked around, suddenly aware of the sixth newcomer, a tall, ruddy young man with deep blue eyes. "Oh, I'm sorry. You, sir? I didn't get your name. I'm Constance Ramsey."

He bowed slightly, smiling. "Lewis Farrington, miss. At your service."

"He ain't exactly with us," Hoop explained. "It was just that, well, we went with him to see Squire McCall; then when they locked us in the barn, he come with us to find Squire Ramsey."

"Locked you in the barn?" Tower frowned. "Why?"

"We don't any of us exactly know. That's why we come to find Squire . . ." he broke off, just noticing the odd angle of the schooner looming over them. "Do you realize this ship is tilted? What be ye doing with it?"

"We're trying to launch it. I don't understand . . ."

"I can see that. Generally, ships are launched straight up."

"Upright," Singleterry corrected. "Not straight up."

"Haven't we met before?" Constance asked Farrington. "You look familiar to me."

"And you to me, miss. And this odd schooner even more so. When I commanded His Majesty's sloop *Wolf*, there was a schooner with fighting tops . . ."

"Ah! Was that you who ran aground there in that bay?"

"And you were aboard the schooner! Yes, I saw you there, later, firing a cannon. Quite remarkable."

"It was an ordinary enough cannon," she said.

"What about the bark?" Michael Romart stormed above them. "And where the blazes is Patrick Dalton? And Charley Duncan?"

"M' sieur le commandante Duncan," Rene brightened. *"C'est bon!"*

Hoop's face registered immense confusion. "Miss, can you tell what these two is chatterin' about? None of us has been able to make head nor tail of it."

"I believe we must all compare notes," Constance decided. "Mister Romart, send down a scaffold, please. We can talk better aboard." She turned and waved at the men stepping down from the carriage which had just arrived. "Father! Bring Ian with you and come aboard *Faith!* We have mysteries to unravel."

Farrington turned and spotted Ian McCall. He raised his hand and called, "Ah, there you are, Squire! I tried to report to you at the Wilderness Dock but . . ."

McCall's eyes widened. "Farrington? What are you doing here? Why aren't you on . . . ?"

"We can talk aboard," Constance said. "Come along, everyone." To the Frenchmen she said, *"Par ici, s'il vous plait."*

"C'est un plaisir, mademoiselle." Rene grinned.

"Mercy," Tower muttered, shaking his head in confusion.
"De rien, m'sieur," Francois assured him.

It was a somber and uncomfortable conference that was
held that day on the bright-planked afterdeck of *Faith II.*
Some of the discomfort came from the acute cant of the
schooner's deck. Chairs, benches and stools were hoisted
aboard for the visitors, but the furniture tended to slide to
starboard at every opportunity, and the discussion kept winding up athwart the after rail or in the racks. Mostly, though, it
was the story that began to piece itself together as Constance
questioned the Frenchmen, and Hoop and his mates added
their information to the weave.

Ian McCall sat stunned, shaking his head in disbelief as the
betrayal aboard *Pride of Falworth* unfolded.

"I can't believe it," he muttered, again and again. "I simply
cannot. Not of John Shelby Butler."

"There is a lesson in this," Ramsey noted. "Revolution or
not, this piracy situation has gotten completely out of hand.
We fight the British and the British fight us, and the field is so
open to freebootery that even the most trusted of men can be
seduced. I believe it is time to press our case with the Continental Congress, Ian. We need a coastal patrol, whether or
not there is a war."

"The Continental Congress turns a deaf ear to such pleas."
McCall frowned. "They see coastal patrol as a provincial matter, to be dealt with by the individual colonies."

"Then, let's call on Governor Henry, by God!"

Through it, Lewis Farrington sat pale and silent. He had
reported, briefly, on the loss of his brig and his charges, then
sat in dismal resignation, wondering what would come next.

Now, though, Constance was talking to the Frenchmen
again, and suddenly Farrington's head came up. *"Valkyrie?* Did
they say the name *Valkyrie?"*

"That was the name of the pirate ship that was lured and
taken," she said.

"The same ship!" Color flushed his cheeks and his eyes went
steely. "It was *Valkyrie* that sank me, and took my escort.
Squire, I swear that devil knew exactly where I would be and

215

when. Do I understand now that it was one of your own captains who did that?"

"So it would seem," McCall rasped. "It seems I've had a very conspiracy amidst my most trusted people. I think there can be little doubt that Butler did know precisely where and when to find you."

Ramsey turned to him. "His brother?"

"Evan." McCall nodded, looking bleak and gray. "My own true Evan."

There were sudden crashing sounds, and *Faith* lurched violently, then resumed her sedate slant. In the fore, a voice shouted, "Let's be a bit easier with those hawsers, you men! There's gentlefolk aboard, here!"

John Singleton Ramsey picked his dignity up off the deck and retrieved his chair. "I don't suppose we could hold off on the construction long enough to lay our plans?" he suggested. But the only answer he received was the ring of hammers and the creak of winches as those around *Faith* resumed their activities with renewed enthusiasm.

As the meeting came to order again, the Frenchmen were a few steps aside, chattering and gesturing. Constance listened for a moment, then said something in French.

"What are they arguing about?" McCall wanted to know.

"Something about a treasure," she said. "They are trying to decide whether to tell us about it."

"Treasure?" Ramsey's brows went up. "By all means, tell them to tell us about it."

She spoke with them for a moment, then said, "They are worried. It seems Mister Duncan signed them aboard as crew when they were found, and read them their articles, but they don't know what restrictions those include, because they were in English."

"Confound it!" McCall stamped a buckle-shoed foot. "*Pride of Falworth* is my ship and I'll say what articles—"

"Not if Patrick has claimed it as salvage," she pointed out. "In that case, I imagine it's his ship."

"Not bloody likely! That confounded Irishman has already done me out of one ship, and he'll not do it again. Tell them they answer to me!"

216

Constance's chin went up in determination. "If Patrick claimed a ship you had already lost, Squire McCall, then he has 'done you out' of nothing."

"Don't look at me, Ian." Ramsey shrugged. "I can't argue that."

Again *Faith* lurched and thrummed, and they clung to stays to keep their balance. In the distance Mister Tower's voice called, "That's getting it, mates. Now let's pull back those dredges and . . ."

"Hell's humping haggards," McCall swore. Then, "Pardon, Miss Constance."

Francois was beside Constance, trying to get her attention. *"M'selle . . . l'argent?"*

"What about it?" she snapped, then said, "Oh, I believe they have decided to tell us about the treasure. *N'est-ce pas, m'sieur?"*

"Oui. L'argent." He nodded vigorously, took a breath, and said, *"Quand ils monterent abord du bateau, deux d'entre eux trouverent de l'argent. Certaines pieces etaient en or. Ils le ranamerent dans dis petite sacs —"*

"What the blazes is he saying?" McCall glared.

"Hush!" Constance raised a small, imperious hand. *"Oui, Francois?"*

"Les sacs," he continued. *"Petites sacs. Encachette du Capitaine."*

"The captain? Captain Butler?"

"Oui. Bood'lair."

"Boodelair!" Hoop said. "That's the Frenchy pirate they was goin' on about when we found 'em."

Constance ignored him. *"Por qua encachette de* Butler?" she asked.

"Ils voualient le garder pour euxmemes." Francois shrugged.

She waved him to a stop and turned to the squires. "He says that when they went aboard the other ship, they —"

"Other ship? The *Valkyrie?"* McCall prodded.

"Q'uell bateau, Francois? Valkyrie?"

"Oui. Valkyrie."

"Yes. When they went aboard, some of them found money. A lot of money and other things, including gold. They brought it back . . . back to *Pride of Falworth,* apparently, in

217

little sacks, so that the captain wouldn't see it. They hid it."

"From their captain?" McCall sounded outraged.

"Easy, Ian," Ramsey said. "It's pirates we're talking about here."

"Oh. Right. Go on, Constance. What about the treasure?"

"If you'll let me, I'll find out. Francois?"

"Oui, m'selle. Ji les ai vous avec l'argent avant quils le cachent, mais j'ni sais pas du ils l'ont mis. Mais abord du l'Pri'e o' Falwort'." He turned to Rene. *"N'est-ce pas,* Rene?"

"Oui."

"He saw them . . . the other men . . . with the treasure before they hid it, but they don't know where they put it."

"What about the men who hid it?"

Constance translated the question. Francois sighed. *"Ils sont morts maintenant. Ils faisarent partie de ceux qui le capitaine avait mis a'mort."*

"They are dead," she translated. "They were among those the captain had put to death."

"Incredible," Ramsey muttered.

"Oui," Rene agreed. *"C'est incredable."*

"I don't wonder these two was hidin' in th' chain locker," Mister Hoop allowed. "Bloody business, that."

"Shocking." McCall shook his head. "John, there's no question about it. That villain must be run down and punished. And others like him, as well. I am ready to petition Patrick Henry for a coast patrol and hang the cost."

Faith shuddered, then shuddered again, and a clamor of voices erupted below, on the surrounding ground. Rising above them was Joseph Tower's strident shout, "She's righting herself! You there! Cut away those hobbles!"

The schooner seemed to convulse itself, its deck wobbling as ominous rumblings erupted below. Then, suddenly, its slated masts rose tall overhead, and the entire ship seemed to fall, as though into a hole. The crash was horrendous, and muddy water shot upward in great sheets along both rails. On deck, people rolled and flipped in all directions. In the pitching foretop, Phillip Ives clung to shrouds, swinging like a monkey in a tree.

Constance rolled over, untangling herself from a pair of

Frenchmen. Even sprawled on the deck, she noticed, they seemed determined to give her far more of a hand—or of their hands—than she required. She got to her feet and planted her little fists on her hips. "Mister Romart! What was that?"

In the fore, Michael Romart was unwrapping himself from the stem rail. He peered over, then turned. "Looks to me like *Faith* has just launched herself, miss. We're afloat . . . and so is most of the yard crew."

Lewis Farrington had gotten his feet under him. Now he ran from rail to rail, looking over, then shouted, "Hands aloft! Make sail! Make sail! Forecourse, jib and jigger! Let's get this vessel out of this ditch before we ground ourselves!"

An instant's surprised silence answered him, then a chorus of "Aye, sir!" and the crew aboard swarmed into action. Farrington planted himself at the tiller and shouted, "Two men aft to raise the gaff! Lively now! You . . . whoever you are, loose those sheets and trim to the wind. Ready? Haul away! Ah, that's it. She's coming free. Hands aloft, trim until we're clear of the bank, then let them luff. I'll bring her around on her spanker."

"Aye, sir."

Amidships someone asked, "Who the blazes is that givin' the orders?"

"I don't know," someone else said, "but he's doin' it right, so don't argue."

Constance gazed at Farrington with calculating eyes. She *did* still require a captain for *Faith* if she was going to use the schooner as she planned.

Jaunty as ever a proud topsail schooner could be, *Faith II* eased out of her ditch and into the swelling lap of the Delaware. With Lewis Farrington at her tiller, she slid about in a graceful arc, dropped sail and nudged gently against the pier.

"She's a sweet lady," Farrington said, his eyes alight with the love of a seaman for a fine ship. "I'd warrant she has fine legs, and I can see she has teeth."

For an instant, Constance Ramsey felt disoriented. The young man was certainly not Patrick Dalton, but just in that moment he had sounded like him.

Twenty-three

The White Fleet's blockade of the central shores was stretched thin now as more and more of the Admiralty's hardware cruised northward to support General Clinton's sortie against the winter-hardened forces of General Washington. Thus, though the blockade continued, those ships that might have sighted the battered bark nearing Colonial waters were small cruisers widely spread, and none inclined to test the temper of the fierce-looking little snow that rode herd upon it. By its maneuvers and its general aspect, the snow conveyed clearly that it would like nothing so much as a reason to blow somebody out of the water.

Therefore the cruise from asea to sight of land was uneventful for *Fury* and *Pride*. When their tops raised the light at Cape Henry, they adjusted course and steered for Chesapeake, *Fury* in the lead.

The bark still limped from its wounds, and Charley Duncan held a sedate seven knots on a quartering southerly wind while the agile snow seemed to surge and fret at its bonds at such a pace; but Patrick Dalton was content. The luck of the Irish had shone upon him once more. He had now what he had lacked before — a fully crewed ship, the wherewithal to dictate his own destinies for a time, and tasks to complete. The refugees from the islands could be put ashore at Ian McCall's wilderness yards, and would be safe enough from there. The bark in his custody was a questionable salvage claim at best, but it would serve as a trading point with McCall. And there was the treasure, now safe aboard *Fury*.

Every man involved in the adventure would receive a share, of course. He wondered whether any of them realized that they stood to be wealthy men very soon. But even after the sharing, there would be a staggering fortune left over. And Dalton had some ideas about that.

"It would be folly for me to ever return to England," he had told Billy Caster. "There are no charges against me now; but there is nothing there for me, and I have come to terms with that knowledge. So, I will stake my destiny in this land. It has much to offer, it seems to me."

Including Constance Ramsey, the clerk thought. But what he said was, "There is still a war, sir."

"Aye, there is a war." Dalton's moody eyes roved the morning sea and the approaching land. "And that's a problem."

Billy said nothing. He knew exactly what his captain's quandary was. Despite having resigned with honor from His Majesty's service, Dalton still felt an allegiance—or at least a respect—for the Union Jack and the nation it represented.

Not once in all the time since his escape from false charges at Long Island had Patrick Dalton dishonored that respect. Oh, they had fought against vessels that flew the Empire's colors. When they had to. But never once had a ship under Dalton's command, whether the captured schooner *Faith*, the poor, slogging ketch *Mystery* or the little warship that now was his by right of recovery, the *Fury*, ever initiated such an encounter. And not once had he ever fired the first shot.

"There's honest work for a fighting ship," Dalton said finally. "There's work that has nothing to do with politics or war."

If he had a plan in mind, Billy had not yet heard it. But the boy had come to know that when Patrick Dalton mapped a course, however devious it might seem, there would be a proper destination at the end of it.

Past Cape Henry they sighted only one vessel—an armed corvette coming downbay toward them. The ship had sails laid on and was tacking for best advantage of the wind, but still was moving slowly, fighting the spring tides. As they closed to scanning range, Dalton glassed it. It was a ship he had seen before. Taken as a prize by a Royal Navy frigate two or three years ago, it had stood for a time at anchor in New York Harbor, waiting to go on the auction block.

He read the escutcheons at a half mile. The corvette *Resolute*. The same vessel. He recalled seeing it again, since, either on the Delaware or off one of the Chesapeake ports. Probably some Colonial merchant had bought it for escort service. Well-armed on its single deck, the corvette could be formidable in an encounter, though the axe-blade shape of its hull would allow barely room for stores and none for cargo.

"Show him our colors," Dalton said.

"The East India flag, sir?"

"No. Our true colors. We're past the cordons. We have as much right as any to be in these waters."

It took a few minutes for Billy Caster and Purdy Fisk to find and bring up the tattered flag. It was a long time since *Fury* had worn the blue and white of what some called the "freeman's flag," the pennant of the private armed vessel on private business, aloof from any conflicts around it.

By the time *Fury*'s colors were aloft, Charley Duncan had already run up colors on *Pride*'s lanyard—the prize flag of a claimed vessel under armed escort.

They had introduced themselves. Now they waited for the corvette to respond to the civility. But no colors showed on the stranger.

Ill-mannered, then? Or hostile? Dalton's eyes went dark. "Stand to guns afore and aport," he said.

"Aye, sir." The snow's deck came alive as men scurried to battle stations.

"If he doesn't respond to colors, we'll try a salute presently," Dalton said. "Steady on, Mister Locke."

"Aye, sir."

The corvette came on, still showing no colors, then broke off just beyond gun range. Hauling about its yards, the stranger hesitated, angled to the left and took a new wind, skimming ahead on a starboard reach to cross the incoming ships' path and make for the east shore. Within minutes it was again a half mile away and gaining distance. At a mile or more—almost within the shallows of Cape Charles—it corrected again. Beating southward now, it headed for the open sea.

"Standoffish sort of person, that," Billy Caster suggested. "He didn't care to show us any colors at all."

Dalton gazed astern at the fleeing corvette. "Odd," he muttered. Then he shrugged and faced forward. "Bring us a point to starboard, please, Mister Locke. If the fairway is clear at Squire McCall's harbor, we'll have Mister Duncan anchor there and see about debarking his passengers."

Fury answered her rudder with an easy grace, coming a point to the right. A few cable lengths back, *Pride of Falworth* adjusted to follow. Dalton looked back once more, past the bark with its crowded decks—at this distance he could even see a few of the ubiquitous chickens that seemed to roam everywhere—and frowned as his eyes caught the distant sail that was the corvette. The slender vessel now was making for the point of Cape Henry, beating its course with a press of sail aloft. Someone there was in a great hurry, to push the vessel so. No one was pursuing it, no one threatening it, yet the corvette called *Resolute* had bent on enough canvas to swamp her should she catch fair gusts past the point.

"On deck!"

Dalton peered upward. "Aye, Mister Livingston?"

"Smoke ashore, sir! Dead ahead!"

With his glass, Dalton found it. Tendrils of smoke drifting above the treetops beyond the screened mouth of an inlet. He turned, glanced at the chart that Billy Caster had unfolded, and frowned. The inlet was Ian McCall's lower yards, what the trader called his Wilderness Dock.

"Buntings, please, Mister Leaf. To *Pride*. Say to stand off and wait. We shall have a closer look."

"Aye, sir."

"Give us topsails and gallants, Mister Ball. Trim to course. Mister Locke, bring us off that inlet yonder and stand by to come about smartly."

"Aye, sir."

"Man guns afore and both bows. Mister Fisk, take a squad into the tops with rifles, please."

223

At the bell, *Fury* stood off the inlet, and Dalton glassed the clearings beyond. The smoke arose from what might once have been a barn or shed, but was now just a shattered hulk of a structure, still burning.

"Powder magazine?" Billy Caster supposed.

"Or stores." Dalton nodded. There were men in the compound, some of them waving at sight of the snow. The only vessels in sight were a launch and a dinghy, lying at the stub dock. He raised his eyes. "Tops?"

"Something exploded yonder, sir. I see men, but they mostly aren't armed. Some of them are waving at us. And I see a few on the ground, sir. Dead or injured."

Dalton put away his glass. "Take us in, please, Mister Locke. We'll see what has happened there."

As *Fury* came to a standstill in the little bay, her guns covering the whole area, men put out from shore in the launch and came alongside. Dalton recognized several of them — workers employed by Ian McCall.

The story they had to tell was simple. Squire McCall was away, but his personal factor, Evan Butler, had come galloping into the yards on a spent horse, ordered everyone off work, and — backed by the compound's guards and foragers — begun looting the stores. Some of the yard crews had objected, and several had been shot before they organized themselves and found muskets with which to fight back.

Faced with opposition, the Butler band had blown the powder magazine for diversion, then boarded the corvette *Resolute* and made their escape.

Which explained the odd actions of the corvette that had passed *Fury* in the outer channels.

With *Fury* riding at anchor, her guns at the ready, Dalton signalled Charley Duncan to bring *Pride of Falworth* in. The mystery of the Wilderness Docks would wait. First, there were things to do.

As the hours passed into evening, *Pride of Falworth* disgorged passengers, livestock and gear, oddments of cargo and stores, until the yards above Wilderness Docks had the look of a bustling town. The four-master was no proper fighter; but her decks and holds were capacious, and when they were empty, Ian McCall's clearing was full. People were everywhere, it seemed— penning cattle, chasing down errant sheep, devising shelters, building cookfires, chattering, exploring and, in the case of Aaron Fairfield, Esq., complaining bitterly.

"This is no destination!" the good man shouted at Charley Duncan for the seventh or eighth time. "This is a wilderness! If we had to come to the Virginias, you might at least put us off at Baltimore or Williamsburg, or Philadelphia . . ."

Duncan had developed the knack of simply not hearing Fairfield's voice, consigning its mouthings to the category of meaningless sound much as the keening of wind in shrouds or the lowing of cattle on the foredeck. He saw no reason to change this happy decision now that he was rid of the man and his motley followers. Brushing past the man, Duncan gave his arm to Priscilla Cabot to walk the lady down the gangway to the dock.

"You'll be in good hands here, mistress," he assured her. "All of this belongs to Squire McCall, and as Captain Dalton says, the squire is a fair man. You'll not have to worry about that island governor following you here . . . or any other for that matter."

"I'm sure of it, Commander." She smiled up at him. "You've really been most kind through all of this. I can't understand why Mister Fairfield considers you uncivil."

"Why he what?"

"Oh, it's just something he says. I'd pay it no mind if I were you. For myself, I find you quite civil." She reached into the bag she was carrying, brought out a length of stiff rope and showed it to him. "And instructive, as well. Ah, if you'd care to join us, I expect I can find something to cook this evening."

"I should like that, mistress, I . . ."

A man hurried past them, carrying an armload of folded canvas, and Duncan stared after him, then looked beyond, where the clearing rose away from the docks. There seemed to be tents springing up everywhere. Tents, hammocks, trestle tables, livestock pens. . . .

225

"I . . . ," Duncan started to continue, then frowned. "Excuse me, mistress." He turned and headed back up the gangway.

Keith Darling was coming down, carrying a large trunk on his shoulder. As Duncan approached, the big landsman said, "I think that's all of us, Commander. If you'll find Mister McPherson, he can settle accounts with—"

"That's between him and Captain Dalton." Duncan brushed past him, cleared *Pride's* rail and headed for the hold coamings. "Mister Quarterstone, bring a lantern! We're going below."

Three of them descended into the holds—Quarterstone with a lantern, Charley Duncan and little Henry Cabot, trailing after Duncan as though he were his shadow. By the lantern's light, Duncan stared around in amazement. The entire enclosure forward of the aft capstan had been gutted—planking pulled up for the building of pens and trestles, every scrap of loose cable, every keg and barrel, everything that wasn't nailed down and much that should have been, had been pressed into service by the busy refugees. And what they had used—as though theirs by right of service—had gone ashore with them. In the bowels of *Pride of Falworth* there was nothing except a cat stalking a pair of stray chickens.

"May God have mercy," Quarterstone muttered.

"Sweet Jesus." Duncan shook his head.

"Watch where you step," Henry Cabot warned. "Most of the floors and walls got used for pens."

"Deck and bulkhead," Duncan breathed.

"What?"

"It's deck and bulkhead. Ships don't have floors and—what are you doing down here?"

"Nothing," the boy assured him.

Quarterstone handed the lantern over, moved away, then returned. "They emptied the sail locker," he said. "And cleaned out the larder and stores."

"Worse than bore-worms," Duncan muttered, shaking his head in disbelief.

Distantly, from *Pride's* tops, came the call, "On deck!" Finian Nelson's response followed, then a pause, and Nelson appeared at the hatch. "Mister Duncan, you'd best come on deck. The snow has signalled that there's sail off the quay."

Still stunned by the stripping of the bark's interior, Duncan hurried to the main deck, strode astern and peered toward the open bay beyond the inlet, where *Fury* stood at guard. A ship was just coming into sight beyond. Past the forest screen a jaunty jib slid into view, batwing sails billowing above a sleek bowsprit . . . then a graceful bow, a jutted foremast with spencer sail on its gaff and topsail above, partly obscuring a sturdy fighting top.

Charley Duncan's mouth hung open, and he stared, a man seeing a ghost. Two years ago—more than two years—he had seen the shattered carcass of a lovely schooner hauled to final rest on the banks of the Delaware. A proud, fighting schooner that had done heads-on combat with a frigate, then had limped home to die.

He had sailed on that schooner. He had seen its destruction. Yet now, just standing in the mouth of the inlet, was—so far as he could tell—that same schooner, as fresh and bright as new.

"It's *Faith*," he said, to no one but himself. "Sweet Mary, holy mother, that's *Faith*."

As empty as Ian McCall's "Wilderness Docks" had been just a day before, now they were as full. The compounds and clearings were full of people, and the inlet was full of ships.

The big four-master, tied off, dwarfed the stub dock while the snow and the schooner stood at anchor in the moonlight beyond, and although the hour was late, fires still burned brightly here and there, lamplight was everywhere and boats of all descriptions plied back and forth. There was so much to report, so much to sort out, so many questions to be answered, so many decisions to be talked through, that it would be morning or beyond before most of them took time to rest.

The story of the brothers Butler had been related, Dalton

227

and Duncan adding their accounts of their encounter with *Valkyrie* at sea, and of the escape of Evan Butler and his men aboard the corvette *Resolute*.

The finding of *Pride of Falworth* adrift in the Indies Lanes had been hashed and rehashed, though each time the mention of treasure came up, Dalton and Duncan either changed the subject or went silent. Ian McCall was almost beside himself, about almost everything, until John Singleton Ramsey breached a keg of rum and began the quelling of his friend with repeated tots of grog.

Mister Hoop had become caught up in the general reunion of ex-British fugitives who had arrived aboard *Fury* and ex-Colonial fugitives who were part of the crew of *Faith,* and had wound up being carried to a hammock by two Frenchmen and six Americans as a result of too much rum.

Charley Duncan and Michael Romart had exchanged grins, back-slaps and mutual insults, and Patrick Dalton and Lewis Farrington had exchanged remembrances of a time that now seemed long ago when their two vessels had stood each other off in a foggy little bay on upper Long Island. Another thing the two young captains exchanged was veiled, cautious glances each time one or the other set eyes on Constance Ramsey — which was at every opportunity.

By the time the encampment had quieted itself somewhat — well past midnight — the courteous demeanor that had been between the two of them had become something else. Something that bordered upon hostility.

And it came to a head when — a dozen of them sitting around a blazing fire in the wilderness — Constance Ramsey mentioned her own plans.

"I have decided to go ahead with my shipment," she told Ian McCall. "I understand your special cargo is intact in the barns there, so you can have your men begin the loading of *Faith* at first light."

"Right you are," McCall slurred, staring at the fire.

"I can fill out a complete crew from among the extra sailors Patrick found," she said.

"Right you are," McCall mumbled, as one mesmerized.

"Of course, we shall replan the route to Savannah," she said. "And I'm sure you won't mind that I have offered the command to one of your captains, will you, Ian?"

"Right you are," he said.

John Singleton Ramsey leaned over and waved a hand in front of his friend's eyes. McCall didn't even blink. "Ah, the efficacy of two-water grog," Ramsey beamed. "You'll have to tell him all of that tomorrow, Constance. I doubt he's heard a word that's been said the past hour."

Across the fire, though, Patrick Dalton had looked up from his own contemplations of grog and philosophy. "You are making a shipment, Constance? Aboard the new *Faith*?"

"I am." She nodded. "Ian has gathered a load of Austrian musketry, which will find a market in Savannah. Father is sponsoring it, and *Faith* can serve a noble purpose on her maiden voyage."

"I see." Dalton nodded gravely, glancing beyond at the moonlit waters where the ships stood. "It tugs at my heart to see the new schooner, Constance. She looks so very like . . . like *Faith*. You, ah . . . mentioned a captain for her?"

"Why, yes. I have asked Captain Farrington to undertake the voyage. He has experience of fore-and-afts."

"Oh."

His voice sounded so distant that she looked up, startled by a sudden intuition. "Well, I couldn't very well ask you, Patrick. I mean, you have *Fury* now, your own ship . . ."

"Ill-gotten gains," the glaze-eyed McCall muttered.

"Of course," Dalton said. "I understand."

"I was sure you would," she said. "Of course, once we return and I square accounts with my father, then perhaps you and I might —"

"We?"

"What?"

"You said, 'when *we* return.' We, who?"

"Well, of course I am going along on my *Faith*'s maiden voyage. I mean, after all . . ."

The bench on which Dalton had been sitting crashed over backward, his booted feet hitting the ground with a thud as he came upright. "The devil you are!"

She blinked. "What?"

"I forbid it! I absolutely forbid you to go sailing off on some wild adventure with . . . well, with anybody!"

John Singleton Ramsey also came to his feet, somewhat unsteadily. "Patrick, I advise you, this is not the way to—"

"You . . . *forbid* me?" Constance's eyes narrowed.

"I most certainly do. I won't have it!"

Now she was on her feet, too, small and resolute, her eyes blazing, hands on her hips in battle stance. "You . . ."

"You've made a serious tactical error, Patrick," Ramsey pointed out. "I can tell you from long experience that . . ."

Lewis Farrington appeared at Constance's side, quick eyes assessing the situation, glaring across the fire at Dalton. "See here, Dalton, if you have offended this lady . . ."

"Stay out of it," Dalton growled, a hand on his sword.

"Stay out, yourself," Farrington snapped, his own sword at the ready.

"Oh, shut up, the both of you!" Constance commanded. "Captain Farrington, I'll want *Faith* loaded and ready for sail at the earliest opportunity tomorrow. You shall be in command, and I intend to go along."

"See here, miss," Farrington hesitated. "Yourself? I don't know if that is such a good—"

"Do you want the command, or not?"

"Yes, miss, I believe I do."

"Then, don't argue!"

"No, miss."

"God's name, Patrick," Ramsey said sadly. "I thought you were wiser than to set her off. I've told Ian the same, a hundred times, haven't I, Ian? I've said . . . Ian? Where . . .? Oh."

Ian McCall had fallen off his perch and now lay curled in sleep on the grassy ground.

With nothing else to do, Patrick Dalton glared for a moment longer at Constance Ramsey, then turned and strode away, tall and stiff-backed. Charley Duncan, Billy Caster and a few others followed, silently.

At water's edge, Dalton stopped and looked out at the moonlit schooner riding a cable's length from his own proud snow. "Jaunty," he murmured. "Proud and steady and ready for the winds and what they'll bring."

"Aye, sir," Charley Duncan said, for lack of anything else to say.

As though he had not heard him, Dalton sighed. "As beautiful as ever I'd remembered," he muttered. "Aye, even more so. Graceful and proud. Spirited. Give her a course and she'll leap to it. Aye, with a vengeance she will. But it'll take more than a strong hand on her tiller to hold her to tack. A wise hand is what's needed. Wise, indeed."

Duncan and Billy Caster glanced at each other, confused, each suddenly uncertain whether their captain was commenting about the schooner at all, or whether he had some other subject in mind.

Dalton turned, noticed them standing there, and sighed again. "Mister Duncan, round up our crew, please. There'll be tide at first light. *Fury* sails on it."

"Aye, sir. Ah, where are we going, Captain?"

"We are going to find ourselves a fight, Mister Duncan. You've no objection to that, I trust?"

The glint of Charley Duncan's grin in the moonlight matched the feral gleam of his eyes. "Not in the slightest, sir. Not in the least."

Twenty-four

There had been traitors in Ian McCall's company—traitors in positions of trust who knew the sailing schedules, cargoes, itineraries and course charts of merchant vessels, traitors who somehow passed that intelligence to a bloody pirate lurking in the Indies Lanes. The pirate had waylaid McCall's ships—and maybe others sailing from his ports—and taken what he wanted from them. Cargoes, valuables, even the ships themselves, sailed by prize crews to some freebooter haven where they could be sold.

A bloody pirate. A deadly pirate with a deadly, killing ship.

The traitors were Evan Butler and his men. The pirate was John Shelby Butler, who now—from what the Frenchmen had overheard—called himself Jack Shelby. The killing ship was *Valkyrie,* and Patrick Dalton had seen that ship and would not forget: a dark, heavily armed vessel of frigate class, with the distinctive silhouette of yards blocked for studding sails. A ship designed for battle and modified for piracy by men whose business was piracy—commanded now by a ruthless master seaman.

A murderous vessel, sailed by murderous men.

The errant weather of coastal spring was changing again now and *Fury* sailed under low, sullen skies as she crooned down lower Chesapeake toward Cape Henry and the sea. The shifting of weather in the night had given her a solid wind on her starboard beam, and runnels of spray curled from her bows as she knifed along on a beam reach, great sails thrumming aloft.

The foreboding clouds seemed a reflection of the moody set of Patrick Dalton's face, a gloom that seemed to deepen as the snow came to course east of the cape light, trimming sails to a tighter tack in the steady offshore winds.

He would not have been surprised to see the wreckage of the corvette that had come this way. Those aboard had been pressing the sleek vessel hard for speed, hard enough for the narrow hull with its press of sail to be in jeopardy of capsizing when it reached the open sea. But the corvette apparently had made it to sea, and he knew it had turned south.

"How do you fare the day, Mister Caster?" Dalton asked, not looking around.

Billy Caster hesitated, studying the sky and the run of the waves, then said, "Wind westerly, sir, at about twenty and a bit, heavy sky and a running chop. The tide is with the wind."

"And what will it do?"

"It will hold steady through the morning, sir, and there'll be squalls now and then. Limited visibility, generally a few miles at best."

"Very good, Mister Caster. You saw the corvette that gave us wide berth yesterday. Where would you think it is now?"

"I . . . ah . . . that would depend upon where it was going, sir."

At the bell rail, Charley Duncan glanced around. "I'd wager I know where it was going, sir. From what we heard, it's heading right down to the islands to make rendezvous with that pirate ship. They're in league."

"A fair assumption, Mister Duncan. But suppose you were Evan Butler, and your brother were the pirate, and you had to make regular contact to report on ship movements without any one suspecting you. How would you do it?"

"I don't rightly know," Duncan said. "It's a long way from Chesapeake to the Indies Lanes for the like of a trader's coastal packets."

233

"Precisely." Dalton nodded. "So maybe Evan Butler's little packets don't go all that far. I've a hunch there is a contact base much closer . . . somewhere nearby, where messages can be relayed to swift sails, for relay to *Valkyrie*. To operate from Chesapeake, there would have to be a base closer than the lanes."

"Closer? But where? This is all Colonial coastline, most of it either patrolled or blockaded . . . ah! Wait a bit! There's the Carolina barrens, and the Hatteras shores. Where we played tag with that Spaniard, when we had the ketch."

"Right," Dalton said. "Albemarle Sound, Pamlico, the Currituck and the Croatan . . . desolate waters, those, and all fronted by Hatteras. The only shores north of Florida where the Spaniard still plies his trade. I've a hunch that corvette hasn't gone very far. I've a hunch we'll see him soon enough."

"Him . . . and maybe his relays as well," Duncan pointed out.

"They said Butler knew of the plan to ship small arms aboard the schooner," Billy Caster said, troubled eyes watching the distant shore. "Is that what you're thinking, sir? That the pirate might lay in wait somewhere . . . that *Faith* and . . . and Miss Constance might . . ."

Dalton's eyes were as dark as the clouds overhead. "A proud and jaunty lady," he murmured. "A proud and headstrong woman. She's made it clear that she does not appreciate interference with what she sets out to do."

Duncan looked at him, quizzically. "Then, you don't mean to attend to the safety of Miss Constance, sir?"

"Miss Constance? Of course not," Dalton growled. "I would not presume to take such liberties. Not unless she asked me to, which she has not done." A shadow of humor lurked behind his eyes. "Not that she and the schooner will require assistance in these waters, any time soon."

"Well, beggin' your pardon, sir, in that case just what *are* we doing here?"

234

"I propose to exercise my ship," Dalton said. "Sail handling and gunnery drill. We've been too long in escort duty, gentlemen. Escort duty can lead to laxity, and I'll have no laxity aboard my ship."

"Oh." Billy Caster looked confused for a moment, then grinned. "Aye, sir. Sail handling and gunnery."

Duncan also had begun to grin, the fierce, hard-eyed grin of the natural fighter. "Might be we should give *Fury* a real shaking down, sir. I mean, cutting capers on an empty sea is no proper test for a warship, is it? A cotillion is far better if there's someone to dance with."

"And gunnery," Billy Caster added. "Cannons do sing better when they have a target. And a pirate's corvette might render a pleasant tune."

"My thoughts exactly," Dalton agreed. "So, let us keep a sharp eye out and see if we can find someone willing to play."

Through the last hours of day while the found bark had been unloaded, the provisioning of *Fury* had been under way. What Dalton needed he took, from Ian McCall's barns, while Billy Caster had kept meticulous accounting. There had been much to resolve—the claim against the bark, its cotton sold at sea to the Portuguese trader, the fate of the island refugees from Mayaguana, the recovered shipwrecked mariners, damages to the bark in transit, sums owed for ships' stores and provisions, wages and shares to those who had become crew . . . and the strongbox in Dalton's quarters aboard *Fury*. Counting claims, contracts and fees, there was a wonderful lot of sums owed by various people to various people, all of which accounts must be settled.

Dalton had shrugged it off earlier. "I have made certain arrangements, Mister Caster. Just keep the tallies and accounts, please."

For the moment, then, it was Billy's job simply to keep records of everything so that all the accounts could be made good when the time came.

235

Dalton's abrupt decision to put to sea had added to the recordkeeping. *Fury*'s crew now was a select forty-seven, most of whom had arrived on the snow, but some of whom had been with Mister Duncan aboard *Pride*.

Billy Caster had added one requisition lot to Dalton's bill. The rosters, musters, tallies and logs the clerk was keeping had become sizeable. He drew fresh supplies of foolscap, ink and nibs from the squire's stores.

Now as *Fury* cruised southward on a somber wind, Billy completed his muster and day notes and took them below to put away . . . and made a discovery. Pale and frightened, he hurried a'deck and tugged at Dalton's sleeve. "Sir," he whispered, "did you move the strongbox? It isn't there."

Dalton glanced around, seeming distracted. "I had Mister Hoop carry it ashore last night," he said. "Don't fret yourself, lad. It is in good hands. I told you I had made certain arrangements. Have you completed the crew muster?"

"Aye, sir." Billy breathed a sigh of relief, though he remained puzzled. Of all those who had remained at the Wilderness Docks, who might Captain Dalton have so trusted as to leave with him a recovered pirate treasure that amounted to a fortune?

Fury now was manned as a warship should be. At stanchions, rails and tops, at sheets, trims and helm, at gunnery and greves, from stem to stern, from captain to clerk to the one-armed cook Nathan Claremore, every man was an experienced first-rate. Fourteen of them had sailed with Dalton since the day he acquired the snow, and of those, seven were from the fugitive crew of the original *Faith*.

All the rest were hand-picked from the sailors brought from the shipwreck island, and most of those had Royal Navy experience gained aboard HMS *Tyber*.

The men Dalton had wanted for *Fury*, he got, and to a man they came willingly. Only nine might he have wanted who were not aboard. Michael Romart and the other eight Colonials who had once sailed aboard *Fury* now were committed to berths aboard *Faith II*. Dalton and Duncan did not even approach them. They had sworn their service to the lady.

Off the Back Bay cut where the shoreline became that string of bays and estuaries that opened toward Albemarle Sound, Dalton had the snow trimmed to a new course, closer in, and put fresh eyes in the tops. "Ready all guns, Mister Ball," he said. It was a task of only a moment. *Fury's* guns were trimmed and ready, with each its complement of tub and pail, ram and swab, ball and deck loads, quoins, grapples and linstock. All that lacked was ready fuse and fire, and these now joined the stations that were *Fury's* fighting teeth.

The snow strode southward, leaning to a beam wind from the misted shore astarboard, Victory Locke at the helm holding her in check against the pressure of her sails. The land they scanned was barrier island, with bays and inlets beyond where incipient squalls rolled and tumbled. Tricky waters, inshore and at sea. Behind the fronting island were shallows, with only here and there a channel deep enough for the draft of a sailing vessel, and much that was there was hidden by thickets and forests of seashore pine. And offshore were shoals and sandbars where the unwary could run aground.

A proper hidey-hole for pirates, Dalton thought. A lair where one who knew the channels could go to ground, and from which a killer could sail forth to strike his prey.

Instinct told him the corvette had not gone far. Hunch told him the larger pirate ship was nearby, waiting for word of prey. And his seaman's senses told him that neither, in these circumstances, would be easy to flush out.

As though reading his mind, Charley Duncan said, "If the scoundrels are in there, sir, they'll have the advantage of us. If we go in after them, they have a hole to defend, and if they come out in this wind, they'll have the weather gauge."

"We shall see." Dalton nodded. "Mister Caster, do we still have the charts from *Mystery?*"

237

"Right here, sir. I thought you might have use for them."

"Thank you, Mister Caster. I recall that there is a cut just ahead that showed on no charts."

"It does now, sir. On these. I drew it in."

"I remember that cut, sir," Duncan said. "But it was barely deep enough to allow a ketch draft, an' that with good tide. *Fury* would ground there."

"The launch wouldn't," Dalton pointed out. "I'm thinking of a scouting party if we—"

"On deck!"

"Aye, tops?"

"Sail, sir. Dead ahead and hard down."

"Can you read it, tops?"

"Not rightly, sir, though it is something less than a frigate."

"The corvette, do you think?" Duncan squinted, trying to see what the tops saw.

"That would prove my hunch, wouldn't it?"

Ian McCall, still red-eyed and shaky from the night's bout with John Singleton Ramsey's rum concoction, watched in irritated disapproval as the loading of cargo aboard the bright new schooner continued. Bale after bale of canvas-wrapped merchandise was hoisted on the schooner's spencer gaff, swung inboard and lowered to stowage in the holds.

"Contraband," McCall said for the dozenth time as he held back velvet curtains to peer from the loft window of his main warehouse. "Contraband aboard a ship owned by a fool and ordered by the daughter of a fool." He turned, scowling at the servants and clerks busy around him, and caught the eye of one of them. "Claremore," he beckoned.

The clerk blinked at him. "Me, sir?"

"Of course you," the merchant snorted. "Would I have called out your name if I wanted someone else?"

"No, sir. But you said, 'Claremore,' sir. My name is

Clarendon, just like it's always been."

"Clarendon." McCall rubbed his aching temple and closed his eyes tightly, then sighed. "Right you are, Clarendon. What is keeping Squire Ramsey, do you know?"

"Not exactly, sir. He said he had matters to attend this morning, but he's somewhere about. Do you want me to go and find him, sir?"

"Never mind, Clarem . . . Clarendon. I shall go myself. The fresh air might do me good."

"Yes, sir."

McCall went downstairs and out the main door, pausing again to stare at the schooner being loaded at the stub dock. Down there, in the midst of the feverish activity, was Constance Ramsey, stalking about, issuing orders as though she owned the place. On the schooner's deck, he could see the men who would sail her. Lewis Farrington was there, directing the preparations aboard.

A hundred yards away, tied and silent, stood the four-master *Pride of Falworth,* and McCall gritted his teeth. Once again he had lost a ship only to have it turn up in the hands of that wild Irishman Dalton, claimed as prize or derelict. He had meant to have it out with Dalton today, to stand toe to toe with the rascal if necessary and explain to him the civilized way of doing things. But Dalton was gone. He had boarded *Fury* in the predawn hours and sailed away somewhere, and none seemed to know where he had gone.

With a growl that echoed in his aching head, McCall turned away, then growled again at sight of the sprawling tent city that occupied most of his clearing. Refugees, they had said. People fled from some island, and dumped on his doorstep like so many waifs in the wilderness . . . by Patrick Dalton.

"Ye gods," he hissed, shaking his head.

Near the north tower he found John Singleton Ramsey, in cheerful conversation with several men McCall did not know.

As he approached, Ramsey raised a hand in greeting.

239

"Ah, Ian! Up and about, I see. Top of the day to you, sir. While you rested, I have been taking care of some of your business for you."

"What business? Who are these people?"

"Ah. You haven't met your guests? Let me present Aaron Fairfield, Esq., recently of the island of Mayaguana, and some of his associates, Claude Dunstan, Prosper McPherson, Caleb Smith and Manning Renfrow . . . and the sturdy young man just over there is Keith Darling, an excellent carpenter. Gentlemen, I present your host, Ian McCall, Esq., the owner of these properties."

The men bowed curtly, and McCall returned the gesture, then squared about at Ramsey. "I don't know what I am expected to do with all these people . . ."

"Why, lease them space, of course, and give them employment. Didn't Patrick tell you?"

"I haven't had the opportunity for private conversation with your damned Irish fox," McCall growled. "Though I certainly intend to. What kind of idiotic claim is that that he has against my bark? 'Salvage of flotsam'? What idiocy . . ."

Ramsey raised a hand. "Calm down, Ian. Patrick asked me to attend to some things for him, and I am doing so. One of them is to help you get these people settled. In return, he has warranted their full passage fee—which they will pay in good coin—to you."

McCall squinted. "Why would he do that?"

"The only provision of the agreement," Ramsey continued, "is that you employ such of the men as want to work, long enough for them to build cabins and plant crops. You will, of course, receive rents when the crops are in."

McCall started to sputter, then hesitated. It was, in fact, a godsend to him—an opportunity to turn the Wilderness Docks into a year-round, profit-making investment. A settlement.

"Then there's the bark, *Pride of*—"

"Which is, by God, mine and not Patrick Dalton's! I shall

240

fight that claim, John, I swear I will . . ."

"No need for that, Ian. Patrick has empowered me to issue a quit-claim to you. You can have the bark back."

McCall raised a suspicious eyebrow. "In return for what?"

"In return for your quit-claim against the snow, *Fury*. In Patrick's own words, Ian, 'Let's put an end to this rubbish about what ship is whose.' *Fury* is his, fair and square, and he wants to hear no more about it. And the bark is yours if you accept it . . ."

"Done," McCall said.

". . . as is."

"What?"

"Nothing. You said, 'done.' The deal stands."

Walking back toward the warehouses, McCall felt confused and a bit light-headed. Still, he scowled as he pointed toward *Faith*. "I may be a fool, John, but you're a bigger one. Don't you realize your daughter will be in critical danger, sailing southward with a cargo of muskets?"

"She isn't sailing southward," Ramsey said happily. "She thinks she is, but she isn't."

"Then, where in blazes is she going?"

"To Philadelphia. The British have pulled out of there, you know. They're off chasing General Washington. So the muskets are going to Philadelphia as legitimate cargo."

"How did you arrange that?"

"Oh, I'm only following instructions from the owner of the vessel . . . and of its cargo. When *Faith II* sails, its ladings and orders will read, Philadelphia."

"The owner . . . but *you* are the owner."

"Not anymore." Ramsey grinned. "Patrick Dalton bought the ship from me, cargo and all. It's his now, and must go where he says. I must say, I got a good price, as well. It seems the lad has come into a good bit of money in his travels. In his absence, he has entrusted me to handle his affairs."

"Oh, Lord." McCall let the enormity of it sink in. "Your daughter is going to . . ."

"Yes, I know." Ramsey's grin widened. "She is going to pitch a royal fit. And, when it's done, if she still wants to take passage aboard 'her' schooner—and if Captain Farrington still wants to command the vessel—then we shall have a pleasant journey up the Delaware. To Philadelphia. You're invited to come along, if you care to."

Twenty-five

A white squall swept down from the North Carolina coast, and for a time there was nothing to be seen to the south, even for those in *Fury's* tops. The gusting storm was no more than two miles wide as it tracked out to sea, but it spread wings of chilly rain as it passed, and the sea and sky were joined by a curtain of weather.

One tantalizing glimpse of distant sail, and then nothing. Dalton held his course on shrift sail and waited, grim and impatient. Hunch as strong as the Celtic blood in his veins said the vessel ahead—eight to ten miles, he guessed—was the corvette *Resolute*. But the weather—his clerk had fared the day properly—had betrayed him. The weather, and his position. This close to a bay coastline, offshore winds became squalls abruptly, offering no chance to plan around them. As *Fury* had sighted the corvette, it was likely that the corvette's spotters also had sighted *Fury*. Eyes worked both ways at sea. And if the corvette knew of its pursuer, the squall creeping along between them would give it plenty of time to design an escape.

"If he's seen us, he'll put the wind on his starboard quarter and run for sea," Charley Duncan allowed, thinking the same thoughts. "That knife-keeled weasel can be hard to catch if it has a start."

"Aye . . . he can run to sea, or he might make for the bays. He could hide from us there, at least for a time."

"Maybe he didn't see us," Billy Caster suggested. "It was

243

only a moment, and not everyone has the eyes of Mister Mallory."

"It could be, lad." Dalton shrugged. "We'll know soon enough."

Driving rain swept in sheets across the snow's deck as *Fury* nosed into the trailing edge of the squall, blind at eight knots, not even the barrier islands of upper Hatteras visible now. In the rains were gusting winds which pushed and tugged at the half-press of sail aloft, making the decks roll. From the partially open companionway forward of the bell rail came a clattering of pans and kettles, and a string of sulphurous curses. Nathan Claremore was below, in the galley, trying to prepare a meal from newly stowed stores.

Dalton wagged a thumb at Billy Caster. "Please tell cook to batten down, Mister Caster. We shall be through this weather presently, but then we may have a corvette to fight."

"Or chase," Charley Duncan added. "Or find."

Billy went below. In the gloom of the tight little galley, lit by swinging lanterns, the one-armed veteran was cursing through clenched teeth, kicking fallen copperware about as he tried to wield a mop with his only hand. Billy took the mop from him and began collecting pots. "Captain says to please batten down, Mister Claremore," he said. "We've come into a squall, and beyond it is a ship that will run, fight or hide if it can."

Claremore subsided, accepting a handful of pot-bales from the clerk. "Ah? The pirate's in sight?"

"We had a sighting. Captain believes it is the corvette that fled Chesapeake. I don't know whether those people are pirates, but they're in league with pirates."

"Pirates be pirates." Claremore nodded. "Them as does an' them as gives comfort to 'em, they be all alike, an' all deservin' of the same."

"The same?" Billy looked up from his mopping.

"Aye. Hang them from a leeward yard or send them to the bottom with grapeshot and hot ball."

The grizzled man sounded so fierce that Billy paused.

"That is much like Captain Dalton's opinion of pirates," he observed.

"Aye, I thought so. The captain wasted neither time nor concern on that black-flag cutter yonder in the islands. Man after me own heart, he is."

"You've dealt with pirates, then, Mister Claremore?"

"You might say that, lad. It's how I lost my arm. I made a miscalculation. We had a pirate in custody, an' I was with the prize crew. I took the word of a cutthroat that he'd mind his manners. I took it for an honest vow, and turned my back on the blaggard. It cost me an arm, and cost two of my mates their lives."

Billy shivered, his eyes on the stump of the cook's lost arm. "I'm sorry, Mister Claremore," he said.

Claremore shook his head. "No need of it, lad. Twas a long time ago. But mark my word well, never put your trust in pirates, not even for the blink of an eye. There's no honor in men who'd sail under the black flag, lad. Not even among themselves."

"Captain Dalton says much the same. He says pirates are to be despised."

"Aye, an' right he is, too." Claremore chuckled, righting a stack of parcels on the galley table. He used his good arm and his stump as one who had long since learned such arts. "I believe it's a thing even enemies can agree on. I've seen the time a pair of warships locked in fray raised flags of truce long enough to sail together after a pirate. They were enemies, ye see, but civilized men all the same, an' no civilized man tolerates pirates."

Distantly, beyond the companionway, they heard the hail from the tops. "On deck!"

"I'll be needed on deck," Billy said. He set the mop aside and headed for the ladder, then paused to glance back. "Thank you, Mister Claremore."

"Aye, lad." The cook was stowing bundles in his pantry.

On the snow's little quarterdeck, Patrick Dalton had his glass to his eye, looking ahead. "It is the corvette, Mister

Duncan," he said. "The same one. It stands where we saw it before, just off that misted cut where the dunes are."

"He didn't see us, then." Duncan grinned.

"It's hard to say, Mister Duncan. Odd, though. He has come full about. He is facing us now." He lowered his glass. "Make sail fore and main, Mister Wise. We've waited long enough. Trim for courses and tops, a beam reach. Stand by topgallants, please."

"Aye, sir."

As sails were spread and sheeted home, *Fury* shook herself and surged, throwing off the sedate pace of shrift canvas, taking spray in her teeth. Almost as though she were a thing alive, the snow seemed to drum a war chant as she crested the sidling waves and raised her proud nose to taste the wind.

Billy Caster squinted, peering ahead. The corvette was fully visible now, hull up and adding sail, but not to run or hide. Its narrow hull slender under stacked sail, it leaned from the wind, gained way and headed toward them.

"He's coming to meet us," Charley Duncan said, confused.

"Aye, an' raising his colors," Victory Locke noted. "The audacious blaggard intends to fight!"

Dalton rubbed his chin thoughtfully. The corvette had guns, right enough. It was well-armed and well-manned, a vessel capable of putting up a fight and inflicting damage. Yet, in final analysis, a corvette was hardly a match for a snow. Odd, that it should challenge so readily. "Stand by chasers," he said. "Stand by starboard batteries. Mister Locke, when we close I'll give him the courtesy of a demand and a warning. If he does not strike colors, we shall engage. Bow chasers and starboard broadside, then stand ready to come through the wind, full about. Bow guns, quoin to rake his deck. Starboard and port batteries, level for waterline at four cables."

"Aye, sir."

Charley Duncan stood, grasping the bell rail in hard

hands, a grin of sheer anticipation on his freckled face. A born combatant, Dalton thought, just spoiling for a fight. Keeping his voice level, Dalton said, "Mister Duncan, you did well, bringing that bark in."

"Aye, sir." Duncan didn't look around. "Thank you, sir."

"Burden of command is not easy for any officer, Mister Duncan."

Duncan's grin slipped as he looked around. "Aye, sir, but . . . please the captain, I never felt right. I mean, tryin' to be an officer an' all. It doesn't come natural."

"I see. Mister Duncan, would it amuse you to command the batteries when we engage the corvette?"

The grin returned, bigger than ever. "Aye, sir. It would."

"Then, by all means, go forward and command the guns."

"Aye, sir!"

At half a mile, closing on opposite beam reaches, Dalton glassed the corvette again. Like a knife through water it came, its slim hull bladelike below massed wings of slanting sail. He could see the guns at its bows, the figures of men a'deck making ready for battle. *"Resolute,"* he read its escutcheons. "Resolute indeed, but overmatched. Odd that they didn't run." He lowered the glass. "Signals, please. Tell him to strike his colors and stand to."

The signals ran high on their lanyard. There was no response from the corvette.

"Fore battery, lay a shot ahead of his bow, please."

"Aye, sir." Echoing the words, one of *Fury's* bow chasers thundered. Moments passed, then a plume of spray rose just ahead of the approaching vessel. In answer, twin clouds of smoke billowed at the corvette's nose, and a ball cut water alongside *Fury's* driving hull while a second one skipped across the waves farther out.

"We have his answer." Dalton nodded. "Helm dead on, Mister Locke. Forward guns, fire at will."

The ships closed to five hundred yards, then four hundred, and the corvette's bow guns blossomed again. A ball sang through *Fury's* rigging, punching holes in two sails.

247

Duncan had held off, judging range, but now he let fly. Both bow chasers roared, dense smoke drifting seaward on the wind. The corvette's starboard bow seemed to explode, a shower of shards and bright splintered wood erupting there.

"Point aport, helm," Dalton ordered.

Victory Locke spun the big wheel. Responsive as a coursing hound, *Fury* edged to the left, swinging her thrusting jib off line with the corvette. At a distance of four cables the ships passed, beam to beam, and thunders rolled and roared. Dalton heard several hits on *Fury,* and the sounds of chaos astarboard where drifting smoke hid the corvette.

"Bring us about, helm," Dalton ordered. "Hard astarboard, through the wind. Hands a'deck, to sheets for a full about!" Answering her rudder, the snow shouldered starboard seas and began a graceful turn toward the wind. Sails aloft went luff, yards making about to resheet for a port reach, as momentum carried her into her turn. In the near distance, the corvette also was turning, but not through the wind. Instead, the lean vessel had turned downwind, seaward, and the wind in its sails pushed it into a long arc away from shore.

"He has made an error, there," Dalton said judiciously. "Tell me, Mister Caster, what is his mistake?"

Billy glanced around. He was at the stern rail, where he had been trying to count the adversary's wounds. There were several. "He turned the wrong way, sir," he said.

"How so?"

"Well, by coming through the wind, sir, we have held our ground. When we complete, we will be where we were, only faced about. But he is turning with the wind. By the time he is about, he will be seaward of us . . . and downwind. He has given us the weather gauge, sir."

"And can you think why he has done that?"

"No, sir. Poor seamanship, I suppose."

"One might assume that." Dalton nodded, frowning as he considered it. Poor seamanship? Possibly. Certainly in mak-

248

ing such a come-about the corvette had lost any chance it might have had for an equal battle. It had given *Fury* a huge advantage. But then, *Fury* had held the advantage from the outset. The corvette was not the warship that a snow was. Even if the master of *Resolute* were not familiar with snows— even if he thought *Fury* to be a brig—still he would have been better advised to run than to fight.

Fury completed her turn, and a bit more. With her stem aligned on the corvette—now a quarter-mile away and taking the wind on its starboard beam—the snow's wind was aft, on the port quarter. No better wind could an attacker ask.

"Sheet home," Dalton ordered. "Hold on him, helm, and a bit ahead. Fore and portside batteries, at the ready."

Big sails booming, *Fury* raised her prow above twin sheets of spray and picked up speed, seeming almost gleeful as she raced toward the corvette.

In the forecastle, Charley Duncan was directing gun crews. The long bow chasers would have first fire, quoined to deck level and aimed at the corvette's masts. Then the port beam guns would broadside as they closed, aiming at waterline to hole the hull and break down the timbers within.

The corvette's guns thundered at them as they closed, but the shots were wild, the rhythm ragged as though no one were directing their fire. At nearly eighteen knots, *Fury* closed, content to wait for shots that would not miss.

"On deck! On deck!"

The shouts aloft were almost a scream. Dalton glanced up, then turned. Behind *Fury* another vessel had shouldered through the rolling mists—a big, dark ship with stacked sails full of wind and curling combs of spray angling back from its driving hull. He knew the ship the instant he saw it. *Valkyrie!*

"It's a trap!" Victory Locke rasped. "The corvette was only bait."

"A trap, aye, and we've fallen into it." Dalton's eyes were

249

as cold as winter storm. Impelled by great weight of sail, the frigate was already within range of ranging guns, and now it began to speak. Smokes billowed at its nose, obscuring everything below its courses, and a ball screamed through *Fury*'s rigging. Lines aloft sang and snapped. Something crashed astern, and the snow lurched crazily, fighting its rudder. "Steady on, helm!" Dalton shouted. "Steady ahead. Mister Duncan, finish the corvette!"

Fury's forward guns thundered and roared.

"Point to starboard now, helm!"

Fury eased to the right, and great balls from astern threw spray where her tail had been. Dalton did not look back. "Broadside now, Mister Duncan," he muttered.

As though he had heard the command, Charley Duncan barked at his beam crews, and guns all along the snow's port side crashed, the ship rolling from their recoil. Just off the port beam, the corvette seemed to come apart. Ball after ball tore through its hull, some of them going entirely through to open gaping wounds on the far side.

People ran through the smoke, coming aft, and Billy Caster dodged aside as a lurching figure nearly bowled him over. Abruptly, *Fury*'s twin stern chasers were manned, stooped figures at the starboard gun working to align it while two men at the port gun seemed to be wrestling with it. Billy gaped, his eyes stinging from the smoke. No quoining or aligning there. Only two men, but now he saw them. One was a huge bull of a man, great arms wrapped around the cannon's midsection. The second man held a smoking fuse aloft with the only arm he had.

"A bit more, Mister Hoop," Nathan Claremore shouted. "Up a tad . . . just . . . there!" The linstock came down upon the vent and the gun roared. Just aft, invisible in the rolling smoke, wood and metal disintegrated. A second later the second stern chaser thundered, and again there was chaos astern . . . chaos and the clear roar of a single large gun. Something exploded directly in front of Billy. In a roaring, stinking darkness full of shouting voices and crashing things, he felt himself lifted and thrown. For an instant that went on and on, he hung suspended it seemed, floating like a gull on wind currents . . . or like a proud and beautiful sailing ship cresting a wave that had no end.

Then there was nothing.

Twenty-six

Where there had sailed three ships, dancing to the deadly song of great guns a'thunder, now there was only one. Bloodied and torn, it limped and faltered as it took the seaward wind on its beam, and the sound of it whining across shattered railings was a low chorus of regret.

As men labored a'deck to mend what could be mended and clear away what could not, they looked often astern, their eyes bleak with the mourning of lost mates . . . and with an outrage that all of them shared. Far astern now was the drifting wreckage of what had been a handsome corvette. *Resolute* had been bait for a trap. As bait, she had been expendable. She had gone down by the bow within minutes of *Fury*'s final sweep.

But beyond the grave of *Resolute*, somewhere in the murking distance, was the target of their outrage.

The pirate frigate, *Valkyrie*, had made one run at *Fury*. Like a hunting cat the big ship had hidden in the mist while the corvette played out its role — luring *Fury* into position to be killed. *Valkyrie* had made her move then. In a single pass she had raked and hammered at the snow. But then, taking two fair hits in the bow, the pirate had changed his mind. Faced with a ship that yet had teeth to bite him, he had simply turned away. Turned, and gone south without so much as a salute for those sacrificed to his purposes.

Expendable. The corvette . . . and his own brother aboard the corvette. Expendable.

Valkyrie had attacked, then simply sailed away, and *Fury* stood alone on the sea. Battered and crippled, her decks red with the blood of good men, she stood, then turned away in disgust.

Silent and somber, the snow turned northward. Repairs would be needed, the mending of what could be mended.

They had tried to carry Charley Duncan below; but he fought them off, and finally they had brought splints and wraps and set his broken leg there on the midships deck where he fell. Through it he clenched his teeth and went pale, but not once did he utter a sound. When it was done, he lay against the bell rail and stared back the way they had come.

Patrick Dalton was everywhere for a time, seeing to the tending of his injured and the wrapping of his dead, the clearing of his decks and the splicing of his rigging. Only when there was nothing more to be done did he return to the quarterdeck. Purdy Fisk came from below then, and beckoned him. "The lad's awake, sir," the sailor said. "He took a good knock, but he's sturdy and will be sound again soon enough. He's asking after you, sir."

Dalton took a slow look along the decks of Fury, assessing everything. His eyes paused at the midships rail where four shrouded forms lay, wrapped in canvas; then he turned away for one more look back, this time not at where the frigate had gone, but at where two more *Furies* had gone to the deep. Then he nodded. "Thank you, Mister Fisk. Please relieve Mister Locke at helm, and hold us at this course. I shall be below for a bit."

"Aye, sir."

Billy Caster lay in a bunk in Dalton's own cabin, his pale face lit by lanterns and by the gray evening light from an open transom. His head was wrapped in swathing, and he had plasters on one cheek and a forearm. As Dalton stooped to enter the little cabin, the boy's eyes brightened. "I didn't lose any of the musters and ladings, sir," he said. "I was afraid I had, but Mister Fisk found them."

"Well done, Mister Caster." Dalton looked at his head wrappings, then sat on a bench beside him. "We shall be in

Chesapeake again soon, and it will be well to have our accounts in order."

"Mister Fisk said we lost some of the men, sir. Who . . . ?"

"Aye." Dalton sighed and lowered his head. "Misters Nelson, Leaf and Popkin in the fore, and Mister Waverly in the tops, all to be buried at sea at first light of morning. There'll be memorials, as well."

"Memorials, sir?"

"Mister Hoop." Dalton sighed again, his voice thin. "And Mister Claremore. It was the shot that scored you, lad. It took out our port stern chaser . . . and them with it. The pair of them, and the cannon. They went over the side. We searched for them. We found two men from the corvette, but Mister Hoop and the cook are gone."

Billy's eyes grew moist, and he looked away, then back. "Still, we won, sir."

"Aye, we won the day. *Valkyrie* is run off, and the corvette is sunk."

"And *Fury*, sir?"

"In need of carpentry and smithing, a rigger and a sailmaker. But she's sound enough. We'll put her together again."

For a time the boy lay still, thinking about it. Then he asked, "Sir, did we . . . did we do what we came to do?"

Dalton stood, crouching slightly to avoid the low beams, and stepped to the transom. He leaned there, looking out, his eyes bleak and hooded. "Maybe we began it," he said finally. "But far more needs to be done."

"*Valkyrie*, sir?"

"Aye, *Valkyrie*. That pirate, and other pirates." He seemed to be speaking more to himself than to Billy. "War breeds confusion, Mister Caster. Where there are fields of honor, the plunderers abound. They are the pestilence that war brings, breeding on chaos. War may always be with us, just as kings and councils are, but piracy must be addressed somehow, even in wartime." He turned from the transom, though his eyes still seemed to gaze at distances. "I've wondered whether kings and councils, even at war, can't agree to address such matters."

"I've heard of it being done, sir."

Dalton blinked. "Ah? And have you, now?"

"Mister Claremore told me of enemies joining forces to fight pirates."

"A very civilized notion." Dalton nodded. "I wonder if our kings and councils are as civilized as was *Fury*'s cook."

Long after his captain had returned to the upper decks, Billy Caster puzzled over the nature of things . . . and remembered the words of a one-armed cook who later joined a giant to smash an iron ball into the bow of a pirate ship.

Epilogue

In the late spring of the year 1778, Governor Patrick Henry of Virginia received a petition calling for the establishment of a coastal patrol, declared noncombatant in matters involving the disagreement between the English crown and the Confederated Colonies, to serve as a deterent against acts of piracy on the high seas.

More or less simultaneously, similar petitions were received by members of the Continental Congress at Philadelphia, and by ministers of His Majesty George III of England.

It became a matter of some debate, the idea that opposing forces in wartime might under certain circumstances agree to, and act jointly upon, the reduction of criminal elements that plagued them both.